THE CHRISTIAN FICTION COLLECTION FOR MEN

TED DEKKER

TIM DOWNS

DAVIS BUNN

THOMAS NELSON
Since 1798

NASHVILLE DALLAS MEXICO CITY RIO DE JANEIRO BEIJING

Thomas Nelson, Inc. titles may be purchased in bulk for educational, business, fundraising, or sales promotional use. For information, please email SpecialMarkets@ThomasNelson.com.

ISBN 1-59554-426-7

Printed in the United States of America
07 08 09 10 11 QW 5 4 3 2 1

THR3E

TED DEKKER

THOMAS NELSON
Since 1798

NASHVILLE DALLAS MEXICO CITY RIO DE JANEIRO BEIJING

THREE

Published in Nashville, Tennessee by Thomas Nelson. Thomas Nelson is a trademark of Thomas Nelson, Inc.

Thomas Nelson, Inc. titles may be purchased in bulk for educational, business, fundraising, or sales promotional use. For information, please email SpecialMarkets@ThomasNelson.com.

Library of Congress Cataloging-in-Publication Data

Dekker, Ted, 1962–
Three / by Ted Dekker.
p. cm.
ISBN 0-8499-4372-8 (HC)
ISBN 0-8499-4449-X (IE)
ISBN 1-5955-4137-3 (mass edition)
ISBN 1-5955-4192-6 (SE)
ISBN 0-8499-4512-7 (TP)
I. Title.
PS3554.E43T48 2003
813'.6—dc21

2003003818

Printed in the United States of America

07 08 09 10 QW 5 4 3 2 1

1

Friday
Noon

THE OFFICE HAD NO WINDOWS, only electric lanterns to light the hundreds of spines standing in their cherry wood bookcases. A single lawyer's lamp spread its yellow hue over the leather-topped desk. The room smelled of linseed oil and musty pages, but to Dr. John Francis it was the scent of knowledge.

"Evil is beyond the reach of no man."

"But can a man remove himself beyond the reach of evil?" Kevin asked.

The dean of academic affairs, Dr. John Francis, gazed over bifocals at the man who sat opposite him and allowed a small smile to nudge his lips. Those blue eyes hid a deep mystery, one that had eluded him since their first meeting three months earlier when Kevin Parson approached him after a philosophy lecture. They'd struck up a unique friendship that included numerous discussions such as this one.

Kevin sat with his feet flat, hands on knees, eyes piercing and unmoving, hair ruffled despite a compulsive habit of running his fingers through his loose brown curls. Or because of it. The hair was an anomaly; in every other way the man groomed himself perfectly. Clean shaven, fashionably current, pleasantly scented—Old Spice, if the professor guessed right. Kevin's ragged hair begged to differ in a bohemian sort of way. Others fiddled with pencils or twirled their fingers or shifted in their seats; Kevin ran his fingers through his hair and tapped his right foot. Not now and then or at appropriate breaks in the conversation, but regularly, to the beat of a hidden drum behind his blue eyes. Some might consider the idiosyncrasies annoying, but Dr. Francis saw them as nothing more than enigmatic clues to Kevin's nature. The truth—rarely obvious and almost always found in subtleies. In the tapping of feet and the fiddling of fingers and the movement of eyes.

Dr. Francis pushed his black leather chair back from the desk, stood slowly to his feet, and walked to a bookcase filled with the works of the ancient scholars. In many ways he identified with these men as much as he did with the modern man. Put a robe on him and he would look rather like a bearded Socrates, Kevin had once told him. He ran a finger over a bound copy of the Dead Sea Scrolls.

"Indeed," Dr. Francis said. "Can man step beyond evil's reach? I think not. Not in this lifetime."

"Then all men are condemned to a life of evil," Kevin said.

Dr. Francis faced him. Kevin watched, unmoving except for his right foot, tapping away. His round blue eyes held steady, stared with the innocence of a child's, probing, magnetic, unabashed. These eyes attracted long stares from the secure and forced the less secure to avert their gaze. Kevin was twenty-eight, but he possessed a strange blend of brilliance and naiveté that Dr. Francis could not understand. The full-grown man thirsted for knowledge like a five-year-old. Something to do with a unique rearing in a bizarre home, but Kevin had never been forthcoming.

"A lifetime *struggle* with evil, not a life of evil," Dr. Francis clarified.

"And does man simply choose evil, or does he create it?" Kevin asked, already many thoughts beyond his initial question. "Is evil a force that swims in human blood, struggling to find its way into the heart, or is it an external possibility wanting to be formed?"

"I would say man chooses evil rather than creates it. Human nature's saturated with evil as a result of the Fall. We are all evil."

"And we are all good," Kevin said, tapping his foot. "The good, the bad, and the beautiful."

Dr. Francis nodded at the use of the phrase he'd coined, which referred to the man created in God's nature, the beautiful man, struggling between the good and the bad. "The good, the bad, and the beautiful. Indeed." He stepped for the door. "Walk with me, Kevin."

Kevin ran both hands past his temples and stood. Dr. Francis led him from the office and up a flight of steps to the world above, as Kevin liked to call it.

"How is your paper on the natures progressing?" Dr. Francis asked.

"Guaranteed to raise your eyebrows." They stepped into the empty main hall. "I'm using a story to illustrate my conclusion. Not conventional, I know, but since Christ preferred to use fiction to communicate truth, I figured you wouldn't mind if I borrowed from him."

"As long as it makes the point. I look forward to reading it."

III

Kevin walked with Dr. John Francis down the hall, thinking that he liked this man beside him. The sound of their shoes striking the hardwood floor echoed through the chamber steeped in tradition. The older man strolled casually, his ready smile hinting at wisdom far beyond his words. Kevin glanced up at the paintings of the divinity school's founders along the wall to his right. Bold, gentle giants, Dr. Francis called them.

"Speaking of evil, all men are capable of gossip, don't you think?" Kevin asked.

"Undoubtedly."

"Even the bishop is capable of gossip."

"Of course."

"Do you think the bishop does gossip? Sometimes?"

The dean's answer waited three steps. "We are all human."

They came to the large door that opened to the central campus and Dr. Francis pushed it open. Despite the ocean breezes, Long Beach could not escape periodic stretches of oppressive heat. Kevin stepped out into the bright midday sunlight, and for a moment their philosophical bantering felt trivial in light of the world before him. A dozen seminary students walked across the manicured park, heads bent in thought or tilted back with smiles. Two dozen poplars formed an avenue through the expansive lawn. The chapel's steeple towered over the trees beyond the park. To his right, the Augustine Memorial Library glistened in the sun. The Divinity School of the Pacific, South, was at a glance statelier and more modern than its parent, the Episcopal seminary in Berkeley.

Here was the real world, made up of normal people with sensible histories and ordinary families pursuing an admirable profession. He, on the other hand, was a twenty-eight-year-old convert who really had no business attending seminary at all, much less leading a flock one day. Not because he didn't have honorable intent, but because of who he *was.* Because he was Kevin Parson, who had really only discovered his spiritual side for the first time three years ago. In spite of his wholehearted embrace of the church, he still felt no holier—and maybe less—than any drunk on the street might. Not even the dean knew his whole story, and Kevin wasn't sure the man would be so supportive if he did.

"You have a brilliant mind, Kevin," the dean said, gazing out at the grounds. "I've seen a lot of people come and go, and few of them have your same tenacity for the truth. But believe me, the deepest questions can drive a man mad. The problem of evil is one of those questions. You'd be wise to court it slowly."

Kevin looked into the graying man's eyes, and for a moment neither spoke. The dean winked and Kevin offered a slight smile. Kevin liked this man as much as he might like a father.

"You're a wise man, Dr. Francis. Thanks. I'll see you in class next week."

"Don't forget your paper."

"Never."

The dean dipped his head.

Kevin took one step down to the concrete landing and turned back. "Just one last thought. In absolute terms, gossip isn't so different from murder, right?"

"Ultimately, no."

"Then the bishop is ultimately capable of murder, isn't he?"

The dean lifted his right eyebrow. "That's a bit of a stretch."

Kevin smiled. "Not really. Neither is more evil."

"You've made your point, Kevin. I'll be sure to warn the bishop against any sudden urges to kill his fellowman."

Kevin chuckled. He turned and walked down the steps. Behind him the door closed with a soft thump. He turned back. The steps were empty.

He was alone. A stranger in a strange world. How many grown men would stare at a flight of steps just vacated by a professor of philosophy and feel utterly alone? He scratched his head and ruffled his hair.

Kevin headed for the parking lot. The sense of solitude left him before he reached his car, which was good. He was changing, wasn't he? The hope of change was why he'd chosen to become a priest in the first place. He'd escaped the demons of his past and begun a new life as a new creature. He had put his old self in the grave and, despite the lingering memories, he was coming to life, like an aspen in the spring.

So much change in so little time. God willing, the past would remain buried.

He swung his beige Sable out of the lot and merged with the steady flow of traffic on Long Beach Boulevard. Evil. The problem of evil. Like traffic—never ending.

On the other hand, grace and love weren't exactly running scared, were they? He had more to be thankful for than he ever imagined possible. Grace, for starters. A fine school with fine teachers. His own home. He might not have a rack of friends to call on at his every whim, but he did have a few. One at least. Dr. John Francis liked him.

He humphed. Okay, so he had a ways to go on the social front. Samantha had called him, though. They'd talked twice in the last two weeks. And Sam was no slouch. Now there was a friend. Maybe more than a—

His cell phone chirped loudly from the cup holder. He'd gotten the thing a week ago and had used it once, placed a call to his home phone to see if it worked. It had, but only after he'd activated the voice mail, which had required a call to the salesman.

The cell rang again and he picked it up. The thing was small enough to swallow if you got hungry enough. He pushed the red button and immediately knew it was the wrong one. Ignore "Send" above the green button. Green is go and red is stop, the salesman had said.

Kevin lifted the phone to his ear, heard silence, and tossed it on the passenger seat, feeling foolish. It was probably the salesman, calling to see if he was enjoying his new phone. Then again, why would a salesman bother to check on a nineteen-dollar purchase?

The phone chirped again. Behind him, a horn honked. A blue Mercedes crowded his bumper. Kevin punched the accelerator and picked up the phone. Red brake lights cut across all three lanes ahead. He slowed down—the Mercedes would have to chill. He pressed the green button.

"Hello?"

"Hello, Kevin."

NEVER FORGET

Male voice. Low and breathy. Drawn out to accentuate each syllable.

"Hello?"

"How are you doing, my old friend? Quite well from what I can gather. How nice."

The world around Kevin faded. He brought the car to a halt behind the sea of red taillights, felt the pressure of the brakes as a distant abstraction. His mind focused on this voice on the phone.

"I . . . I'm sorry. I don't think—"

"It doesn't matter if you know me." Pause. "I know you. In fact, if you really think you're cut out for this seminary foolishness, I must say I know you better than you know yourself."

"I don't know who you think you are, but I don't have a clue what you're talking—"

"Don't be stupid!" the voice yelled into his ear. The man took a deep, scratchy breath. He spoke calmly again. "Forgive me, I really don't mean to yell, but you're not listening to me. It's time to quit pretending, Kevin. You think you have the whole world fooled, but you don't have me fooled. It's time to let the cat out of the bag. And I'm going to help you do it."

Kevin could hardly comprehend what he was hearing. Was this for real? It had to be a practical joke. Peter? Did Peter from Intro to Psych know him well enough to pull a stunt like this?

"Who . . . who is this?"

"You like games, don't you, Kevin?"

There was no way Peter could sound so condescending.

"Okay," Kevin said. "Enough. I don't know what—"

"Enough? Enough? No, I don't think so. The game is just starting. Only this one is not like the games you play with everyone else, Kevin. This one's for real. Will the real Kevin Parson please stand up? I thought about killing you, but I've decided this will be much better." The man paused, made a soft sound that sounded like a moan. "This . . . this will destroy you."

Kevin stared ahead, dumbfounded.

"You may call me Richard Slater. Ring any bells? Actually, I prefer Slater. And here's the game Slater would like to play. I will give you exactly three minutes to call the newspaper and confess your sin, or I will blow that silly Sable you call a car sky-high."

"Sin? What are you talking about?"

"That's the question, isn't it? I knew you'd forget, you stupid brick." Another pause. "Do you like riddles? Here's a riddle to jog your mind: *What falls but never breaks? What breaks but never falls?*"

"What? What's—"

"Three minutes, Kevin. Starting . . . now. Let the games begin."

The phone went dead.

For a moment, Kevin stared ahead, phone still plastered to his ear.

A horn blared.

The cars ahead were moving. The Mercedes was impatient again. Kevin pressed the accelerator, and the Sable surged forward. He set the phone down on the passenger seat and swallowed, throat dry. He glanced at the clock. 12:03.

Okay, process. Stay calm and process. Did this really just happen? Of course it just happened! Some madman who called himself Slater just called my cell phone and threatened to blow up my car. Kevin grabbed the cell phone and stared at its face: "Unavailable, 00:39."

But was the threat real? Who would really blow up a car in the middle of a busy street over a riddle? Someone was trying to scare the snot out of him for some maniacal reason. Or some sicko had randomly chosen him as his next victim, someone who hated seminary students instead of prostitutes and really intended to kill him.

His thoughts spun crazily. What sin? He had committed his

sins, of course, but none that stood out immediately. *What falls but never breaks? What breaks but never falls?*

His pulse pounded in his ears. Maybe he should get off the road. Of course he should get off the road! If there was even a remote chance that Slater meant to carry out his threat . . .

For the first time, Kevin imagined the car actually filling with a blast of fire. A shaft of panic ripped down his spine. He had to get out! He had to call the police!

Not now. Now he had to get out. Out!

Kevin jerked his foot off the accelerator and slammed it down on the brake. The Sable's tires squealed. A horn shrieked. The Mercedes.

Kevin twisted his head and glanced through the rear window. Too many cars. He had to find a vacant spot, where flying shrapnel would do the least damage. He gunned the motor and shot forward. 12:05. But how many seconds? He had to assume three minutes would end at 12:06.

A dozen thoughts crowded his mind: thoughts of a sudden explosion, thoughts of the voice on the phone, thoughts of how the cars around him were reacting to the Sable jerking along the road. *What falls but never breaks? What breaks but never falls?*

Kevin looked around, frantic. He had to dump the car without blowing up the neighborhood. *It's not even going to blow, Kevin. Slow down and think.* He ran his fingers through his hair several times in quick succession.

He swung into the right lane, ignoring another horn. A Texaco station loomed on his right—not a good choice. Beyond the gas station, Dr. Won's Chinese Cuisine—hardly better. There were no parks along this section of road; residences packed the side streets. Ahead, lunch crowds bustled at McDonald's and Taco Bell. The clock still read 12:05. It had been 12:05 for too long.

Now true panic muddled his thinking. *What if it really does go off? It's going to, isn't it? God, help me! I've got to get out of this thing!* He grabbed at his seat belt buckle with a trembling hand. Released the shoulder strap. Both hands back on the wheel.

A Wal-Mart sat back from the street a hundred yards to his left. The huge parking lot was only half-filled. A wide greenway that dipped at its center, like a natural ditch, surrounded the entire lot. He made a critical decision: Wal-Mart or nothing.

Kevin leaned on his horn and cut back into the center lane with a cursory glance in his mirror. A metallic screech made him duck—he'd clipped a car. Now he was committed.

"Get out of my way! Get out!"

He motioned frantically with his left hand, succeeding only in smashing his knuckles into the window. He grunted and swerved into the far left lane. With a tremendous *thump* he crashed over a six-inch-high median and then into oncoming traffic. It occurred to him that being rammed head-on might be no better than blowing up, but he was already in the path of a dozen oncoming cars.

Tires squealed and horns blared. The Sable took only one hit in its right rear fender before shooting out the other side of the gauntlet. Something from his car was dragging on the asphalt. He cut off a pickup that was trying to exit the lot.

"Watch out! Get out of my way!"

Kevin roared into the Wal-Mart lot and glanced down at the clock. Somewhere back there it had turned. 12:06.

To his right, traffic on Long Beach Boulevard had come to a screeching halt. It wasn't every day that a car blasted through oncoming traffic like a bowling ball.

Kevin sped past several gaping customers and zeroed in on the greenway. Not until he was on top of it did he see the curb. The Sable blew a tire when it connected; this time Kevin's head struck the ceiling. A dull pain spread down his neck.

Out, out, out!

The car flew into the ditch and Kevin crammed the brake pedal to the floor. For a fleeting moment he thought he might roll. But the car slid to a jolting halt, its nose planted firmly in the opposite slope.

He grabbed at the door latch, shoved the door open, and dove to the turf, rolling on impact. He scrambled to his feet and raced up the slope toward the lot. At least a dozen onlookers headed his way from the sea of parked cars.

"Back! Get back!" Kevin waved his arms at them. "There's a bomb in the car. Get back!"

They stared at him for one moment of fixed horror. Then all but three turned and fled, screaming his warning.

Kevin swung his arms furiously at the others. "Get back, you idiots! There's a bomb!"

They ran. A siren wailed through the air. Someone had already called the cops.

Kevin had run a good fifty paces from the greenway before it occurred to him that the bomb hadn't gone off. What if there wasn't a bomb after all? He pulled up and whipped around, panting and trembling. Surely three minutes had come and gone.

Nothing.

Was it a practical joke after all? Whoever this caller was, he'd done almost as much damage through the threat alone as he would have by detonating an actual bomb.

Kevin glanced around. A gawking crowd had gathered on the street at a safe distance. The traffic had stalled and was backing up as far as he could see. Steam hissed from a blue Honda—presumably the one that had hit his right rear fender. There had to be a few hundred people staring at the nut who'd driven his car into the ditch. Except for the growing wail of sirens, the scene had grown eerily silent. He took a step back toward the car.

At least there was no bomb. A few angry motorists and some bent fenders, so what? He'd done the only thing he could do. And really, there still could be a bomb. He'd leave that for the police once he explained his story. Surely they would believe him. Kevin stopped. The car tipped into the dirt with its left rear tire off the ground. From here it all looked kind of stupid.

"You said bomb?" someone yelled.

Kevin looked back at a middle-aged man with white hair and a Cardinals baseball cap. The man stared at him. "Did you say there was a bomb?"

Kevin looked back at the car, feeling suddenly foolish. "I thought there—"

A deafening explosion shook the ground. Kevin instinctively crouched and threw his hands up to protect his face.

The bright fireball hung over the car; boiling black smoke rose into the sky. The red flame collapsed on itself with a soft *whomp.* Smoke billowed from the charred skeleton of what was only a moment ago his Sable.

Kevin dropped to one knee and stared, dumbstruck, wide-eyed.

2

WITHIN THIRTY MINUTES the crime scene was isolated and a full investigation launched, all in the purview of one Detective Paul Milton. The man was well built and walked like a gunslinger—a Schwarzenegger wannabe with a perpetual frown and blond bangs that covered his forehead. Kevin rarely found others intimidating, but Milton did nothing to calm his already shattered nerves.

Someone had just tried to kill him. Someone named Slater, who seemed to know quite a lot about him. A madman who had the forethought and malice to plant a bomb and then remotely detonate the device when his demands weren't met. The scene stood before Kevin like an abstract painting come to life.

Yellow tape marked a forty-yard perimeter, and within it several uniformed police officers gathered pieces of wreckage, labeled them with evidence tags, and stacked them in neat piles on a flatbed truck to be transported downtown. The crowd had grown to well over a hundred. Bewilderment was fixed on some faces; other spectators wildly gestured their version of the events. The only injury reported was a small cut on a teenage boy's right arm. As it turned out, one of the cars Kevin had clipped in his mad dash across the street was none other than the impatient Mercedes. Once the driver learned he'd been following a car bomb, however, his attitude improved significantly.

Traffic on Long Beach Boulevard still suffered from curiosity, but the debris had been cleared.

Three news vans were in the lot. If Kevin understood the situation correctly, his face and what was left of his car were being televised live throughout the Los Angeles Basin. A news helicopter hovered overhead.

A forensic scientist worked carefully over the twisted remains of the trunk, where the bomb had clearly resided. Another detective dusted for prints on what was left of the doors.

Kevin had spilled his story to Milton and now waited to be taken down to the station. By the way Milton glared at him, Kevin was sure the detective considered him a suspect. A simple examination of the evidence would clear his name, but one minor fact haunted him. His account of events omitted Slater's demand that he confess some sin.

What sin? The last thing he needed was for the police to begin digging into his past for some sin. Sin wasn't the point. The point was that Slater had given him a riddle and told him that phoning the newspaper with the riddle's answer would prevent Kevin from being blown sky-high. That's what he'd told them.

On the other hand, willfully withholding information in an investigation was a crime itself, wasn't it?

Dear God, someone just blew up my car! The fact sat like an absurd little lump on the edge of Kevin's mind. The front edge. He smoothed his hair nervously.

Kevin sat on a chair provided by one of the cops, tapping his right foot on the grass. Milton kept glancing at him as he debriefed the other investigators and took statements from witnesses. Kevin looked back at the car where the forensic team worked. What they could possibly learn from that wreckage escaped him. He stood unsteadily, took a deep breath, and walked down the slope toward the car.

The forensic scientist at the trunk was a woman. Black, petite, maybe Jamaican. She looked up and lifted an eyebrow. Pretty smile. But the smile didn't alter the scene behind her.

It was hard to believe that the twisted pile of smoldering metal and plastic had been his car.

"Whoever did this had one heck of a chip on his shoulder," she said. A badge on her shirt said she was Nancy Sterling. She looked back into what was left of the trunk and dusted the inside lip.

Kevin cleared his throat. "Can you tell me what kind of bomb it was?"

"Do you know bombs?" she asked.

"No. I know there's dynamite and C-4. That's about it."

"We'll know for sure back at the lab, but it looks like dynamite. Leaves no chemical signature that ties it to a specific batch once it's been detonated."

"Do you know how he set it off?"

"Not yet. Remote detonation, a timer, or both, but there's not too much left to go on. We'll eventually get it. We always do. Just be glad you got out."

"Boy, no kidding."

He watched her place tape over a dusted fingerprint, lift it, and seal the faint print on a card. She made a few notations on the card and went back to work with her flashlight.

"The only prints we've found so far are in places where we would expect to find yours." She shrugged. "Guy like this isn't stupid enough not to wear gloves, but you never know. Even the smartest make mistakes eventually."

"Well, I hope he made one. This whole thing's crazy."

"They usually are." She gave him a friendly smile. "You okay?"

"I'm alive. Hopefully I don't hear from him again." His voice shook as he spoke.

Nancy straightened and looked him in the eye. "If it's any consolation, if this was me, I'd be in a pool of tears on the sidewalk. We'll get this one, like I said; we always do. If he really wanted to kill you, you'd be dead. This guy's meticulous and calculating. He wants you alive. That's my take, for what it's worth."

She glanced up to where Detective Milton was talking to a reporter. "And don't let Milton get to you. He's a good cop. Full of himself, maybe. Case like this will send him through the roof."

"Why's that?"

"Publicity. Let's just say he has his aspirations." She smiled. "Don't worry. Like I said, he's a good detective."

As if on cue, Milton turned from the camera and walked straight for them.

"Let's go, cowboy. How long you here for, Nancy?"

"I have what I need."

"Preliminary findings?"

"I'll have them for you in half an hour."

"I need them now. I'm taking Mr. Parson in for a few questions."

"I'm not ready now. Half an hour, on your desk."

They held stares.

Milton snapped his fingers at Kevin. "Let's go." He headed for a late-model Buick on the street.

|||

The station's air conditioner was under repair. After two hours in a stuffy conference room, Kevin's nerves finally began to lose the tremble brought on by the bomb.

An officer had fingerprinted him for comparisons with the prints lifted from the Sable, then Milton spent half an hour reviewing his story before abruptly leaving him alone. The ensuing twenty minutes of solitude gave Kevin plenty of time to rehash Slater's call while staring at a large brown smudge on the wall. But in the end he could make no more sense of the call than when it had initially come, which only made the whole mess more disturbing.

He shifted in his seat and tapped the floor with his foot. He'd spent his whole life not knowing, but this vulnerability was somehow different. A man named Slater had mistaken him for someone else and very nearly killed him. Hadn't he suffered enough in his life? Now he'd fallen into this, whatever *this* was. He was under the authorities' microscope. They would try to dig into his past. Try to understand it. But even Kevin didn't understand his past. He wasn't about to let them try.

The door banged open and Milton walked in.

Kevin cleared his throat. "Anything?"

Milton straddled a backward chair, slapped a folder down on the table, and drilled Kevin with his dark eyes. "You tell me."

"What do you mean?"

Milton blinked twice and ignored the question. "The FBI's bringing someone in on this. ATF wants a look, CBI, state police—the lot of them. But as far as I'm concerned, this is still my jurisdiction. Just because terrorists favor bombs doesn't mean every bomb that goes off is the work of terrorists."

"They think this is a terrorist?"

"I didn't say that. But Washington sees terrorists behind every tree these days, so they will definitely go on the hunt. It wouldn't surprise me to see the CIA picking through the files." Milton eyed him, unblinking, for a few long seconds, and then blinked three times in rapid succession. "What we have here is one sick puppy. What confuses me is why he picked you. Doesn't make sense."

"None of this makes sense."

Milton opened the file. "It'll take a couple days for the lab to complete their work on what little we found, but we have some preliminary findings, the most significant of which is nothing."

"What do you mean, nothing? A bomb about blew me to pieces!"

"No evidence of real investigative value. Let me summarize for you—maybe it'll shake something loose in that mind of yours." He eyed Kevin again.

"We have a man with a low, raspy voice who calls himself Richard Slater and who knows you well enough to target you. You, on the other hand, have no idea who he could possibly be." Milton paused for effect. "He constructs a bomb using common electronics available at any Radio Shack and dynamite, rendering the bomb virtually untraceable. Smart. He then plants that bomb in the trunk of your car. He calls you, knowing that you're in the car, and threatens to blow the car in three minutes if you can't solve a riddle. *What falls but never breaks? What breaks but never falls?* Right so far?"

"Sounds right."

"Due to some fast thinking and some fancy driving, you manage to drive the car to a relatively safe location and escape. As promised, the car blows up when you fail to solve the riddle and phone it in to the newspaper."

"That's right."

"Preliminary forensics tell us that whoever planted that bomb left no fingerprints. No surprises there—this guy's obviously not the village idiot. The explosion could have caused significant collateral damage. If you'd been on the street when it blew, we'd have some bodies at the morgue. That's enough to assume this guy's either pretty teed off or a raving lunatic, probably both. So we have smart and we have teed off. Follow?"

"Makes sense."

"What we're missing is the most obvious link in any case like this. Motivation. Without motivation, we've got squat. You have no idea whatsoever why anyone would want to harm you in any way? You have no enemies from the past, no recent threats against your well-being, no reason whatsoever to suspect why anyone on this earth might want to hurt you in any way?"

"He didn't try to hurt me. If he wanted to kill me, he could've just blown up the bomb."

"Exactly. So we're not only clueless as to why someone named Slater might *want* to blow up your car, we don't even know why he *did*. What did he accomplish?"

"He scared me."

"You don't scare someone by nuking their neighborhood. But okay, say he just wanted to scare you—we still don't have motivation. Who might want to scare you? Why? But you don't have a clue, right? Nothing you've ever done would give anyone any reason to hold anything against you."

"I—not that I know of. You want me to just make something up? I told you, I really don't know."

"You're leaving us high and dry, Kevin. High and dry."

"What about the phone call?" Kevin asked. "Isn't there a way to track it?"

"No. We can only track a call while it's being made. What's left of your cell is nothing more than a lump of plastic in an evidence bag anyway. If we're lucky, we'll have a shot next time." He closed the file folder. "You do know there'll be a next time, don't you?"

"Not necessarily." Actually, the thought had plagued him, but he refused to give it any serious consideration. Freak occurrences like this happened to people now and then; he could accept that. But a deliberate, drawn-out plot against him was unfathomable.

"There will be," Milton said. "This guy went to great lengths to pull this trick. He's after something, and we have to assume he didn't get it. Unless this was random or some kind of hellacious mistake, he'll try again."

"Maybe he mistook me for someone else."

"Not a chance. He's too methodical. He staked you out, wired the car, knew your moves, and blew it with careful deliberation."

True enough. Slater knew more than even the police knew. "He scared me. Maybe that's all he wanted."

"Maybe. I'm open to anything at this point." Milton paused. "You're sure there's nothing else you want to tell me? We don't have much on you. Never been married, no record, college grad, currently enrolled in seminary. Not the kind of person you'd expect to be involved in a crime of this nature."

Slater's demand crossed his mind.

"If I think of anything else, trust me, you'll be the first to know," Kevin said.

"Then you're free to go. I've put in an order to tap your phones as soon as we can clear the red tape—the boys should be out first thing tomorrow morning. I may also place a black and white outside your house in Signal Hill, but I doubt we're dealing with anyone who would approach your house."

"Tap my phones?" They were going to dig, weren't they? But what was he afraid of, as long as they didn't start prying about his past?

"With your permission, of course. You have any other cell phones?"

"No."

"If this guy makes contact in any other way, I want to hear about it immediately, you understand?"

"Of course."

"And pardon my insensitivity, but this isn't just about you anymore." His eyes twinkled. "We have reporters all over the place and they want an explanation. You might have some media attention. Don't talk to them. Don't even look at them. Stay focused, *capice?*"

"I'm the victim here, right? Why do I get the feeling I'm the one under investigation?"

Milton placed both of his palms on the table. The air conditioning kicked in above them. "Because you are. We have a monster out there and that monster has chosen you. We need to know why. That means we need to know more about you. We have to establish motivation. That's the way it works."

Kevin nodded. Actually, it made perfect sense.

"You're free to go." The detective handed him a card. "Call me. Use the cell number on the back."

"Thanks."

"Don't thank me yet. Do you always stare people down while you're talking to them, or are you hiding something?"

Kevin hesitated. "Has it ever occurred to you that you have a tendency to terrify your witnesses, Detective?"

The man did one of his flash-blink routines—four this time. Paul Milton might have political aspirations, but unless the people decided to turn the country over to vampires, Kevin didn't think the detective had a chance.

Milton stood and walked out.

3

Friday
Afternoon

A FRIENDLY COP NAMED STEVE ushered Kevin out the back and took him to the Hertz rental-car agency. Twenty minutes later Kevin held the keys to a Ford Taurus, nearly identical to the Sable that was no more.

"You're sure you're okay to drive?" Steve asked.

"I can drive."

"Okay. I'll follow you home."

"Thanks."

The home was an old two-story that Kevin had purchased five years earlier, when he was twenty-three, using some of the money from a trust fund established by his parents before the car accident. A drunk driver had slammed into Ruth and Mark Little's car when Kevin was only one—their deaths had reportedly been immediate. Their only son, Kevin, had been with a baby-sitter. The insurance settlement went to Ruth's sister, Balinda Parson, who received full custody of Kevin and subsequently adopted him. With a few strokes of a judge's pen, Kevin ceased being a Little and became instead a Parson. He had no memories of his real parents, no brothers or sisters, no possessions that he knew of. Only a trust account beyond anyone's reach until he turned eighteen, much to Aunt Balinda's chagrin.

As it turned out, he had no need to touch the money until he turned twenty-three, and by that time it had grown into a sum in excess of three hundred thousand dollars—a small gift to help him build a new life once he got around to discovering he needed one. He'd called Balinda "Mother" until then. Now he called her his aunt. That's all she was, thank God. Aunt Balinda.

Kevin pulled into the garage and stepped out of the Taurus. He waved as the cop drove by, then closed the garage door. The timed light slowly faded. He stepped into the laundry room, glanced at a full hamper, and made a mental note to finish his laundry before he went to bed. If there was one thing he hated, it was disorder. Disorder was the enemy of understanding, and he'd lived long enough without understanding. How meticulous and organized did a chemist have to be in order to understand DNA? How organized had NASA been in reaching out to understand the moon? One mistake and *boom.*

Mounds of dirty clothes reeked of disorder.

Kevin walked into the kitchen and set the keys on the counter. *Someone just blew up your car and you're thinking about doing laundry.* Well, what was he supposed to do? Crawl into the corner and hide? He'd just escaped death—he should be throwing a party. Let's toast life, comrades. We have faced the enemy and we have survived the bomb blast down by the Wal-Mart.

Please, get a grip. You're babbling like a fool here. Still, in light of the past several hours, it was a blessing to be alive, and gratefulness was warranted. *Great is thy faithfulness. Yes indeed, what a blessing we have received. Long live Kevin.*

He stared past the breakfast nook with its round oak dinette, through the picture window that overlooked the front yard. An oil pump sat dormant on a dirt hill beyond the street. This was his view. It's what two hundred thousand dollars bought you these days.

On the other hand, there was that hill. Kevin blinked. With a pair of binoculars, anyone with a mind to could park himself at the base of that oil pump and watch Kevin Parson organize his laundry in complete anonymity.

The trembles were suddenly back. Kevin rushed over to the window and quickly lowered the miniblinds. He spun around and scanned the main floor. Besides the kitchen and laundry room, there was the living room, the bathroom, and sliding glass doors, which led to a small lawn encircled by a white picket fence. The bedrooms were upstairs. From this angle he could see right through the living room into the backyard. For all he knew, Slater could have been watching him for months!

No. That was stupid. Slater knew of him, maybe something from his past—a demented motorist he'd hacked off on the highway. Maybe even—

No, it couldn't be that. He was just a kid then.

Kevin wiped his forehead with his arm and stepped into the living room. A large leather sofa and a recliner faced a forty-two-inch flat-screen television. What if Slater had actually been *in* here?

He scanned the room. Everything was in its place, the coffee table dusted, the carpet vacuumed, the magazines in their rack beside the recliner. Order. His *Introduction to Philosophy* text sat on the dinette beside him. Large two-by-three-foot travel posters covered the walls in a hopscotch arrangement. Sixteen in all, counting the ones upstairs. Istanbul, Paris, Rio, the Caribbean, a dozen others. An unknowing person might think he ran a travel agency, but to Kevin the images were simply gateways to the real world, places he would one day visit to broaden his horizon.

To expand his understanding.

Even if Slater had been here, there would be no way to tell, short of dusting for prints. Maybe Milton should send out a team.

Easy, boy. This is an isolated incident, not a full-scale invasion. No need to tear the house down yet.

Kevin paced to the couch and then back. He picked up the remote control and turned on the television. He preferred to spin through the channels on the huge Sony picture tube rather than settle on any particular channel for long. The TV was yet another window into life—a wonderful montage of the world in all of its beauty and ugliness. Didn't matter; it was real.

He flipped the channels, one every other second or so. Football, a cooking show, a woman in a brown dress showing how to plant geraniums, a Vidal Sassoon commercial, Bugs Bunny. He paused on Bugs. *I say, what's up, doc?* Bugs Bunny had more truth to speak about life than the humans on the tube. "If you stay in the hole too long, it becomes your tomb." Wasn't that the truth. That was Balinda's problem—she was still in the hole. He flipped the station. The news . . .

The news. He stared at the aerial images, fascinated by the surreal shots of the smoldering car. His car. "Wow," he mumbled. "That's me." He shook his head in disbelief and ruffled his hair. "That's really me. I survived that."

What falls but never breaks? What breaks but never falls? He will call again. You do know that, don't you?

Kevin clicked the tube off. A psychobabblist once told him that his mind was unusual. He'd tested with an IQ in the top one percentile—no problems there. In fact, if there was a problem—and Dr. Swanlist the psychobabblist certainly didn't think there was a problem at all—it was that his mind still processed information at a rate normally found in others during their formative years. Age normally slowed down the synapses, which explained why old folks could be downright scary behind the wheel. Kevin tended to view the world through the eyes of an adult with the innocence of a child. Which was really psychobabble for nothing of any practical value, regardless of how excited Dr. Swanlist got.

He looked at the stairs. What if Slater had gone up there?

He walked to the stairs and took them two at a time. One master bedroom on the left, one guest bedroom that he used as an office to his right, and one bathroom between the two. He headed for the guest bedroom, flipped on the light switch, and poked his head in. A desk with a computer, a chair, and several bookcases, one with a dozen textbooks and the rest heavy with over two hundred novels. He'd discovered the miracles of stories in his early teens, and ultimately they had set him free. There was no better way to understand life than to live it—if not through your own life, then through another's. There was once a man who owned a field. Brilliant, brilliant, brilliant. Not to read was to turn your back on the wisest minds.

Kevin scanned the fiction titles. Koontz, King, Shakespeare, Card, Stevenson, Powers—an eclectic collection. He'd read the books eagerly in his recent renaissance. To say Aunt Balinda didn't approve of novels was like saying the ocean is wet. She would feel no better about his philosophy and theology textbooks.

The travel posters in this room boasted of Ethiopia, Egypt, South Africa, and Morocco. Brown, brown, green, brown. That was it.

He closed the door and walked into the bathroom. Nothing. The man in the mirror had brown hair and blue eyes. Gray in bad light. Somewhat attractive if he was any judge, but generally average looking. *Not the kind of person stalked by a psychopath.* He grunted and hurried to his room.

The bed was made, the dresser drawers closed, the shade open. All in order. *You see, you've been hearing ghosts.*

Kevin sighed and peeled off his dress shirt and slacks. Thirty seconds later he'd changed into a pale blue T-shirt and jeans. He had to get back to a semblance of normalcy here. He tossed the dress shirt into the laundry bin, hung up his trousers, and headed for the door.

A flash of color on the nightstand caught his eye. Pink. A pink ribbon peeked out from behind the lamp.

Kevin's heart responded before his mind did, pounding into overdrive. He walked forward and stared at the thin pink hair ribbon. He'd seen it before. He could swear he'd seen this ribbon. A long time ago. Samantha had given him one exactly like it once, and it had gone missing years ago.

He spun around. Had Sam heard about the incident and driven down from Sacramento? She'd phoned recently but hadn't mentioned coming to visit him. The last time he'd seen his childhood friend was when she'd left for college at age eighteen, ten years earlier. She'd spent the last few years in New York working in law enforcement and had recently moved to Sacramento for employment with the California Bureau of Investigation.

But this ribbon was hers!

"Samantha?" His voice echoed softly in the room.

Silence. Of course—he'd already checked the place. Unless . . .

He snatched up the ribbon, ran for the stairs, and descended them in three long strides. "Samantha!"

It took Kevin exactly twenty seconds to search the house and rule out the possibility that his long-lost friend had paid him a visit and was hiding like they had as children. Unless she had come, left the ribbon, and then departed, intending to call him later. Would she do that? Under any other circumstance it would be a wonderful surprise.

Kevin stood in the kitchen, perplexed. If she'd left the ribbon, she would have left a message, a note, a phone call, something.

But there was no note. His black VTech phone sat on the kitchen counter. Number of messages: a big red "0."

What if Slater had left the ribbon? He should call Milton. Kevin ran a hand through his hair. Milton would want to know about the ribbon, which meant telling him about Samantha, which meant opening up the past. He couldn't open up the past, not after running from it for so long.

The silence felt thick.

Kevin looked at the pink ribbon trembling slightly in his hand and sat slowly at the dinette. The past. So long ago. He closed his eyes.

III

Kevin was ten years old when he first saw the pretty girl from down the street. That was a year before they met the boy who wanted to kill them.

Meeting Sam two days after his birthday was his best present. Ever. His brother, Bob, who was really his cousin, had given him a yo-yo, which he really did like, but not as much as meeting Samantha. He would never tell Bob that, of course. In fact, he wasn't sure he'd tell Bob about Samantha at all. It was his secret. Bob might be eight years older than Kevin, but he was a bit slow—he'd never catch on.

The moon was full that night, and Kevin was in bed by seven o'clock. He always went to bed early. Sometimes before supper. But tonight he'd been under the covers for what seemed like an hour, and he couldn't sleep. He thought maybe it was too bright with the moonlight coming through the white shade. He liked it dark when he slept. Pitch-dark, so he couldn't even see his hand when he put it an inch from his nose.

Maybe if he put some newspapers or his blanket over the window, it would be dark enough.

He climbed out of bed, pulled off the gray wool blanket, and hefted it up to hook over the rod. Wow, it was really bright out there. He glanced back at his bedroom door. Mother was in bed.

The shade hung from a spring-loaded roll at the top, a smudged sheet of canvas that covered the small window most of the time. There was nothing to look out at but the backyard anyway. Kevin lowered the blanket and lifted the bottom edge of the shade.

A dull glow shone over the ashes in the backyard. He could see the doghouse on the left, like it was day. He could even see each board in the old fence that ran around the house. Kevin lifted his eyes to the sky. A bright moon that glowed like a light bulb smiled down at him and he smiled back. Wow!

He started to lower the shade when something else caught his eye. A bump on one of the fence boards. He blinked and looked at it. No, not a bump! A—

Kevin dropped the shade. Someone was out there, staring back at him!

He scrambled off his bed and backed to the wall. Who would be staring at him in the middle of the night? Who would be staring at him period? It was a kid, wasn't it? One of the neighborhood boys or girls.

Maybe he just thought he saw someone. He waited a few minutes, lots of time for whoever it was to move on, and then he worked up the courage for just one more peek.

This time he barely lifted the shade so that he could just see over the sill. She was still there! Kevin thought his chest might explode from the fright, but he kept looking. She couldn't see him now; the shade was too low. It was a girl; he could see that much. A young girl, maybe his age, with long blonde hair and a face that would have to be pretty, he thought, although he couldn't really see any details of her face.

And then she dropped from sight and disappeared.

Kevin could hardly sleep. The next night, Kevin couldn't resist peeking out, but the girl was gone. Gone for good.

He thought.

Three days later he was in bed again, and this time he knew he had been lying awake for at least an hour without being able to sleep. Mother had made him take a very, very long nap that afternoon and he just wasn't tired. The moon wasn't as bright tonight but he had covered up the window to make it darker anyway. After a long time he decided that he might be better off with more light. Maybe if he could trick his mind into thinking it was the next morning already, it would be tired after not sleeping all night.

He stood, tore off the wool blanket, and sent the shade flying up with a flip of his wrist.

A small, round face had its nose against the window. Kevin jumped back and rolled off the bed, terrified. He scrambled to his feet. She was there! Here! At his window! The girl from the other night was right here, spying on him.

Kevin almost screamed. The girl was smiling. She lifted a hand and waved as if she recognized him and had just stopped by to say hi.

He glanced at the door. Hopefully Mother hadn't heard. He turned back to the girl in the window. She was mouthing something to him now, motioning for him to do something.

He could only stand there and stare, frozen.

She was motioning for him to lift the window! No way! And he couldn't anyway; it was screwed shut.

She didn't look frightening, really. In fact, she was actually very nice looking. Her face was pretty and her hair was long. Why was he so scared of her? Maybe he shouldn't be. Her face was so . . . kind.

Kevin glanced again at the door and then slid back onto the end of his bed. She waved again, and this time he waved back. She was pointing at the window sill, motioning again. He followed her hands and suddenly understood. She was telling him to unscrew the window! He looked at the single screw that fastened the sash in place and for the first time realized that he could take it out. All he had to do was find something to turn the screw with. Something like a penny. He had some of those.

Suddenly energized by the idea, Kevin grabbed one of the pennies from an old tin can on his floor and placed it in the screw. It came loose. He unwound it until it was out.

The girl jumped up and down and motioned for him to lift the window. Kevin gave his bedroom door one last look and then yanked on the window. It flew up silently. He knelt on his bed, face to face with the girl.

"Hi," she whispered, smiling from ear to ear.

"H . . . hi," he said.

"Do you want to come out and play?"

Play? Fear replaced excitement. Behind him the house was quiet. "I can't come out."

"Sure you can. Just crawl out the window. It's easy."

"I don't think I'm supposed to. I . . ."

"Don't worry, your mother won't even know. You can just climb back in later and screw the window shut again. They're all sleeping anyway, right?"

"You know my mother?"

"Everyone has a mother."

So she didn't know Mother. She was just saying that she knew mothers didn't like their kids sneaking out. As if all mothers were like his mother.

"Right?" she asked.

"Right."

What if he did go out? What harm would it do? Mother had never actually told him not to climb out of the window at night, at least not in those words.

"I don't know. No, I really can't."

"Sure you can. I'm a girl and you're a boy. Girls and boys play together. Don't you know that?"

He didn't know what to say. He'd never played with a girl before, that was for sure.

"Just hop down."

"Are . . . are you sure it's safe?"

She reached out a hand. "Here, I'll help you."

He wasn't sure what made him do it; his hand just seemed to reach out for hers on its own. His fingers touched hers and they were warm. He had never touched a girl's hand before. The strange sensation filled him with a good feeling he'd never felt before. Butterflies.

Ten seconds later, Kevin was out of the window trembling under a bright moon next to a girl about his own height.

"Follow me," the girl said. She walked for the fence, lifted a loose board, stepped out, and motioned him on. With one last anxious look back at his window, he followed.

Kevin stood beyond the fence shivering in the night, but not from fear so much as from excitement again.

"My name's Samantha, but you can call me Sam. What's yours?"

"Kevin."

Sam stuck out her hand. "Glad to meet you, Kevin." He took her hand and shook it. But she didn't let go. Instead she led him away from his house.

"We moved here from San Francisco about a month ago. I didn't know any children lived in this house, but a week ago I heard my parents talking. Your parents are pretty private people, huh?"

"Yeah, I guess."

"My parents let me walk down to the park at the end of the street where a lot of kids hang out. It's lighted, you know. You want to go down there?"

"Now?"

"Sure, why not? It's safe. My dad's a policeman—if it wasn't safe, believe me, he would know."

"No. I . . . I can't. I really don't want to."

She shrugged. "Suit yourself. I was on my way down the other night when I looked over your fence and saw you. I guess I was spying. Do you mind?"

"No."

"Good, because I think you're cute."

Kevin didn't know what to say.

"Do you think I'm pretty?" She spun away from him and twirled around like a ballerina. She wore a pink dress and pink ribbons in her hair.

"Yes, I think you're pretty," he said.

She stopped her twirling, looked at him for a moment, and then giggled. "I can already tell that we're going to be wonderful friends. Would you like that?"

"Yes."

She skipped back, grabbed his hand, and dragged him into a run. Kevin laughed. He did like her. He liked her very much. More, in fact, than anyone he could ever remember liking.

"Where are we going?"

"Don't worry, no one will know. No one will even see us. I promise."

For the next hour Sam talked to him about her family and their house, which was three down from his. She went to something she called a private school and didn't get home until six every night, she said. Her dad couldn't afford it on his income, but her grandmother had left a trust fund for her and the only way they could use any of the money was if she went to a private school. The kids there weren't really her type. Neither were most of the neighborhood kids. When she grew up, she was going to be a cop like her dad. That's probably why she liked to sneak around, because cops do that to catch the bad guys. She asked Kevin some questions but then backed off when she saw that he was shy.

Sam liked him—he could tell. It was the first time Kevin had felt that kind of friendship from anyone.

At about eight o'clock Samantha told him that she had to get home or her parents would worry. They squeezed back through the fence and she helped him climb back through his window.

"This will be our secret, okay? No one will know. If you hear me tapping on your window at about seven o'clock, you'll know that I can play if you want to. Deal?"

"You mean we can do this again?"

"Why not? As long as you don't get caught, right?"

"Get caught?" Kevin looked at his window, suddenly fighting an urge to throw up. He wasn't sure why he felt sick; he only knew that if Mother found out she wouldn't be happy. Things went funny when Mother wasn't happy. How could he have done this? He never did things without asking. Never.

Sam put her hand on his shoulder. "Don't be afraid, Kevin. No one will know. I like you and I want to be your friend. Would you like that?"

"Yes."

Sam giggled and flashed her bright blue eyes. "I want to give you something." She pulled one of the pink ribbons from her hair and handed it to him. "Don't let your mom find it."

"This is for me?"

"So you don't forget me."

There was no chance of that. No way.

Sam held out her hand. "Until next time, partner. Slip me some skin."

He looked at her, confused.

"My dad says that. It's a street thing. Here, like this." She took his hand and slid her palm on his. "See ya. Don't forget to screw your window down."

Then Sam was gone.

Two nights later she was back. With more butterflies in his stomach and shrill warning bells ringing in his mind, Kevin slipped out his window.

Mother would find out. Sam took his hand and that made him feel warm, but Mother would find out. The ringing in his head wouldn't stop.

III

Kevin snapped out of the memories. A shrill bell screamed. He jerked to the sound. It took him a moment to make the transition from the past.

The black phone on the counter rang. It was a modern contraption with an old-style bell that sounded like an old desk phone. Kevin stared at it, suddenly unsure whether he wanted to pick it up. He rarely received phone calls; few people had reason to call him. Mostly telemarketers.

He'd set the answering machine for six rings. What if it was Samantha? Or Detective Milton?

The phone rang again. *Answer it, Kevin. Of course. Answer it.*

He stepped over to the counter and snatched the receiver from its cradle. "Hello?"

"Hello, Kevin. Did you find my little gift?"

Kevin went numb. Slater.

"I'll take that as a yes. We've had an eventful day, haven't we? First a little phone call and then a little boom and now a little gift. And all within four hours. Makes all the waiting worth it, don't you think?"

"Who are you?" Kevin demanded. "How do you know me?"

"Who am I? I am your worst nightmare. I promise you, you'll agree soon enough. How do I know you? Tsk, tsk, tsk. The fact that you even have to ask justifies everything I have in mind."

It had to be the boy! *God in heaven, save me!* Kevin slumped slowly to the floor. This couldn't be happening. "Oh God—"

"Not God, Kevin. Definitely not God. Now, I want you to listen carefully, because I'm going to give you a lot of information in a short time. Every single bit is critical if you want to survive this little game of ours. Do you understand?"

Kevin's mind raced through the years, searching for someone who might have sounded like this man, anyone who might have any reason at all to speak to him this way. Anyone but the boy.

"Answer me, you creep!" Slater said.

"Yes."

"Yes, what?"

"Yes, I understand."

"Yes, you understand what?"

"That I have to listen carefully," Kevin said.

"Good. From now on you answer me when I ask you a question, and you speak only when I say you speak. Do you understand?"

"Yes."

"Fine. There are only three rules to our game. Remember all of them. One, you say nothing to the cops about my riddles or my phone calls until after the time has passed. Then you may tell them all you want. This is personal—having the whole city coming unglued over a little bomb that might go off wouldn't be useful. Are we clear?"

"Yes."

"Two, you do exactly what I say, or I promise you will pay. Abundantly clear?"

"Why are you doing—"

"Answer me!"

"Yes!"

"Three, the riddles keep coming until you confess. As soon as you do, I go away. It's that simple. One, two, three. Get it through your thick skull and we'll do fine. Understand?"

"Please, if you'll just tell me what to confess, I'll confess. Why are you using riddles? Can I confess without solving riddles?"

Slater remained silent for a moment. "The answer to the riddles and the confession are the same. That's the first clue and that's the last clue. The next time you try to squeeze something out of me, I'll walk in there and cut off one of your ears, or something as interesting. What's the matter, Kevin? You're the brilliant seminary student. You're the smart little philosopher. A little riddle scares you?"

The riddles and the confession are the same. So then maybe it wasn't the boy.

"This isn't fair—"

"Did I ask you to speak?"

"You asked me a question."

"Which requires an answer, not a lecture. For that you will pay an extra little price. I've decided to kill to help you along with your understanding."

Kevin was aghast. "You . . . you just decided—"

"Maybe two killings."

"No, I'm sorry. I won't speak."

"Better. And just so we're clear, you of all people are in no position to talk about being fair. You may have that old fool at the seminary fooled, you may have all the old ladies at that church thinking you're a sweet, young fellow, but I know you, boy. I know how your mind works and I know what you're capable of. Guess what? I'm about to let the snake out of his dungeon. Before we're done here, the world is going to know the whole ugly truth, boy. Open the drawer in front of you."

The drawer? Kevin stood and looked at the utility drawer beneath the counter. "The drawer?"

"Open it and pull out the cell phone."

Kevin eased the drawer out. A small silver cell phone sat in the pencil tray. He picked it up.

"From now on you keep this phone with you at all times. It's set to vibrate—no need to wake up the neighbors every time I call.

Unfortunately, I won't be able to call you on your home phone once the cops bug it. Understand?"

"Yes."

That Slater had been in Kevin's house was no longer open to question. What else did Slater know?

"There's one other little matter that needs our attention before we continue. I have good news for you, Kevin." Slater's voice thickened and his breathing grew heavier. "You're not alone in this. I intend to bring someone else down with you. Her name is Samantha." Pause. "You do remember Samantha, don't you? You should; she called you recently."

"Yes."

"You like her, don't you, Kevin?"

"She's a friend."

"You don't have a lot of friends."

"No."

"Consider Samantha as my insurance. If you fail me, she dies."

"You can't do that!"

"Shut up! Shut up, you foul-mouthed lying punk! Listen carefully. *In life he's your friend, but death is the end.* That's your little bonus riddle for being so dense. You have exactly thirty minutes to solve it or your best friend will indeed go boom."

"What friend? I thought this was about me! How will you even know if I've solved the riddle?"

"Call Samantha. Ask for her help. The two of you can put your stinking heads together and figure it out."

"I'm not even sure I can reach Samantha. How will you know what I tell her?"

Slater's deep chuckle filled the phone. "You don't do what I'm doing without learning the tools of the trade, boy. I have ears and eyes everywhere. Did you know that with the right toys you can understand a man inside a house from over a thousand yards away? Seeing is even easier. The clock is ticking. You're down to twenty-nine minutes and thirty-two seconds. I suggest you hustle."

The line clicked.

"Slater?"

Nothing. Kevin shoved the phone into its cradle and looked at his watch. 4:15. There was going to be another explosion in thirty minutes, this time involving his best friend, which made no sense because he had no best friends. *In life he's your friend, but death is the end.* No cops.

4

FBI SPECIAL AGENT JENNIFER PETERS hurried down the hall, her pulse hammering with an urgency she hadn't felt for three months. The Long Beach bomb report had come in several hours ago, but she hadn't been told. Why? She rounded the corner and shoved the Los Angeles bureau chief's door open.

Frank Longmont sat at his desk, phone pressed to his ear. He didn't bother looking up at her. He knew, didn't he? The weasel had purposefully stalled.

"Sir?"

Frank held up his hand. Jennifer crossed her arms while the chief talked on. Only then did she notice two other agents, whom she didn't recognize, seated at the small conference table to her left. Looked like East Coast stiffs. Their eyes lingered. She turned from them and steadied her breathing.

Her blue business suit had only the smallest of slits up her left leg, but she couldn't shake the certainty that what was decent, even conservative in her mind, still drew frequent glances from men. Her hair was dark, to her shoulders, and her eyes a soft hazel. She had the kind of face others might spend their lives trying to imitate—symmetrical with soft skin and rich color. There was no disguising her physical beauty. *Beauty is a gift,* her father used to say. *Just don't flaunt it.* A gift. Jennifer had found beauty just as often a handicap. Many people of both genders had difficulty accepting both beauty and excellence from the same person.

To compensate, she tried her best to ignore her appearance and instead focus on excellence. *Brains are also a gift,* her father used to say. And God had not been stingy. At age thirty, Jennifer Peters was regarded as one of the best forensic psychologists on the West Coast.

But in the end it hadn't mattered. Her excellence hadn't saved her brother. Which left her as what? A beautiful woman who was much more interested in being smart than beautiful, but who wasn't so smart after all. A nothing. A nothing whose failure had killed her brother. And now a nothing who was being ignored by the bureau chief.

Frank set down his phone and turned to the two men at the table. "Excuse us for a moment, gentlemen."

The two agents exchanged glances, rose, and left. Jennifer waited for the click of the door latch before speaking.

"Why wasn't I told?"

Frank spread his hands. "You obviously were."

She glared at him. "It's been five hours! I should already be in Long Beach."

"I've been on the phone with the Long Beach police chief. We'll be there first thing in the morning."

We'll? He was being cagey. She walked to his desk, hands on hips. "Okay, cut the innuendos. What's going on?"

Frank smiled. "Please, Jennifer, take a seat. Take a breath."

She didn't like the tone of his voice. *Easy, girl. Your life's in this man's hands.*

"It's him, isn't it?"

"We don't have enough yet. Sit." They locked stares. She sat in one of the large chairs facing the desk and crossed her legs.

Frank tapped his finger on the desk absently. "I was thinking of letting Craig take over the on-site investigation. Let you work here in a coordination role."

Jennifer felt her face flush. "This is my case! You can't just remove me!"

"Did I say remove? I don't remember using that word. And if you haven't noticed in your six years with the bureau, we juggle agents quite frequently for a host of reasons."

"No one knows this case like I do," she said. The chief wouldn't actually do this. She was way too valuable on the case!

"One of those reasons is the relationship between agent and critical parties, including victims."

"I've spent a year breathing down this guy's neck," Jennifer said. She let the desperation creep into her voice. "For heaven's sake, Frank. You can't do this to me."

"He killed your brother, Jennifer."

She stared at him. "This suddenly becomes germane? The way I see it, the fact that he killed Roy gives me a right to hunt him down."

"Please, I know this is hard, but you have to try to look at the situation objectively. Roy was the killer's last victim. We haven't heard a peep in the three months since. You ever ask yourself why he chose Roy?"

"It happened," she said. She had, of course. The answer was patently obvious but unspoken.

"He kills four other people in the Sacramento area before you start to close in. You come within five minutes of apprehending him. He takes offense and chooses someone close to you. Roy. He plays his little game of riddles and then kills Roy when you come up short."

Jennifer just stared at him.

The chief held up one hand. "No, that didn't come out like I—"

"You're saying the Riddle Killer killed my brother because of me? You have the audacity to sit there and accuse me of playing a part in my own brother's execution?"

"I said that's not what I meant. But he likely chose Roy because of your involvement."

"And did that fact affect my performance?"

He hesitated.

Jennifer closed her eyes and drew a careful breath.

"You're putting words in my mouth," Frank said. "Look, I'm sorry, really I am. I can only imagine how it was for you. And I can't think of anyone who is more qualified to go after this nut, but the equation changed when he killed your brother. He has it out for you. You're a critical party, and frankly your life's in danger."

She opened her eyes. "Don't patronize me with the danger nonsense, Frank. We signed on for danger. This is precisely what the Riddle Killer wants, you realize. He knows I'm his biggest threat. He also knows that you'll likely pull me for the very reasons you're citing. He *wants* me off the case."

She said it with a strong voice, but only because she'd long ago learned to stuff emotion. For the most part. The bureau did that. The better part of her wanted to scream at Frank and tell him where he could put his objectiveness.

He sighed. "We don't even know this is the same killer. Could be a copy cat; could be unrelated. We need someone here to piece this together carefully."

The Riddle Killer had started playing his little games nearly a year ago. He picked his victims for a variety of reasons and then stalked them until he knew their routines intimately. The riddle usually came out of thin air. He gave the victims a specified amount of time to solve the riddle under the threat of death. Inventive and cold-blooded.

Her brother, Roy Peters, had been a thirty-three-year-old attorney newly employed in Sacramento by Bradsworth and Bixx. A brilliant man with a wonderful wife, Sandy, who worked for the Red Cross. More importantly, Roy and Jennifer had been inseparable right up to college when they'd both pursued law. Roy had bought Jennifer her first bicycle, not because her father couldn't, but because he wanted to. Roy had taught her to drive. Roy had checked out every boy she'd ever dated, often to her feigned chagrin. Her brother had been her soul mate, the standard no other man could measure up to.

Jennifer had replayed the events leading up to his death a thousand times, knowing each time that she could have prevented it. If only she'd pieced the riddle together twenty minutes earlier. If only she'd gotten to him sooner. If only she hadn't been assigned to the case.

Until this moment, no one had even hinted at blame—to do so would be beneath the Bureau. But her own blame had beaten her raw over the last three months. The fact was, if she had not been on the case, Roy would be alive. Nothing would ever change that. In some way she *was* personally responsible for the death of her brother.

Her mission in life was now painfully simple. She would stop at nothing to remove the Riddle Killer from the face of the earth.

If Frank knew the depth of her obsession, he might have pulled her from the case long ago. Her survival depended on her ability to remain calm and reasonable.

"Sir, I'm begging you. You have to let me lead the investigation. He hasn't killed yet. He's growing bold, but if we let him think he can play the FBI, he'll grow bolder. Pulling me from the case would send the wrong message."

The thought dawned on her only as she spoke it. By the look on Frank's face, he hadn't considered that angle yet.

She pressed. "I've had three months to grieve, Frank. Last time I took inventory I was lucid. You owe it to the public to let me go. No one stands a better chance of stopping him before he kills again."

Frank looked at her in silence.

"You know I'm right."

"You've got tenacity; I'll give you that. Tell me that you have no leanings to any kind of personal vendetta."

"I want him out of circulation. If that's personally motivated, so be it."

"That's not what I mean."

"You think I would compromise justice with a quick trigger?" she said with a bite of sarcasm. "Or withhold information from other agencies to get the collar myself? Do you think so little of me?"

"None of us are exempt from strong emotional pulls. If my brother had been killed, I'm not sure I wouldn't turn in my badge and go after him outside the law."

She wasn't sure what to say. She'd considered the same a dozen times. Nothing would give her more satisfaction than pulling the trigger herself when it came right down to it.

"I'm not you," she finally said, but she wasn't so sure.

He nodded. "You don't see the kind of love you shared with your brother much these days, you know. I've always respected you for that."

"Thank you. Roy was an incredible person. No one will ever replace him."

"No, I guess not. Okay, Jennifer. You win. You'll have a half-dozen agencies climbing around; I want you to work with them. I'm not saying you have to spend all day playing footsie with them, but at least give them the respect of keeping them up to date."

Jennifer stood. "Of course."

"Detective Paul Milton will be expecting you first thing. He's not the gun-shy type if you know what I mean. Be nice."

"I'm incapable of anything less."

5

KEVIN CLEARED THE FIRST FOUR STAIRS in his first step. He tripped on the last and sprawled on the landing. "Come on!" He grunted and jumped to his feet. Samantha's phone number was on his desk—please say it was still on his desk. He crashed through the door. His best friend. Who could that possibly be?

He shuffled through papers and knocked a hermeneutics textbook off the desk. He'd left it right here on top; he could swear it! Maybe he should just call Milton. Where was that number!

Slow down, Kevin. Gather yourself. This is a thinking game, not a race. No, a race too. A thinking race.

He took a deep breath and put his hand to his face. *I can't call the cops. Slater will hear the call. He's got the house bugged or something. Okay. He wants me to call Samantha. This is about her too. I need Samantha. Only two minutes have passed. Twenty-eight left. Plenty of time. First thing, find Sam's number. Think. You wrote it down on a white piece of paper. You used it to call her last week and you put the paper somewhere safe because it was important to you.*

Under the phone.

He lifted the desk phone and saw the white slip. Thank God! He grabbed the receiver and punched in the number with an unsteady hand. It rang. It rang again.

"Please, please pick up—"

"Hello?"

"Hello, Sam?"

"Who's calling?"

"It's me."

"Kevin? What's wrong? You sound—"

"I have a problem, Sam. Oh dear God, I've got a problem! Did you hear about the bomb that went off down here today?"

"A bomb? You're kidding, right? No, I didn't hear of a bomb; I have this week off, unpacking from the move. What happened?"

"Some guy who calls himself Slater blew up my car."

Silence.

"Sam?" Kevin's voice trembled. He suddenly thought he might start to cry. His vision swam. "Sam, please, I need your help."

"Someone named Slater blew up your car," she repeated slowly. "Tell me more."

"He called me on my cell phone and gave me three minutes to confess a sin, which he said I would know by a riddle. *What falls but never breaks? What breaks but never falls?* I managed to get the car into a ditch by a Wal-Mart and it blew up."

"Holy . . . You're serious? Was anyone hurt?"

"No. I just—"

"Is the FBI investigating? Good night, you're right—I just turned on the television. It's all over the news up here."

"Samantha, listen! I just got another call from this guy. He says I have thirty minutes to solve another riddle or he's going to blow up another bomb."

Sam seemed to switch into another mode immediately. "Riddles. You've got to be kidding. How long ago?"

He glanced at his watch. "Five minutes."

"You've already reported it?"

"No. He said I can't tell the cops."

"Nonsense! Call the detective in charge right now. Get off the phone with me and call them, you hear me, Kevin? You can't let this guy play his game. Take his game away from him."

"He said that this bomb will kill my best friend, Sam. And I know he can hear me. This guy seems to know everything. For all I know he's watching me right now!"

"Okay, calm down. Slow down." She paused, reconsidering. "Okay, don't call the cops. Who's Slater talking about? Who are your friends down there?"

"I . . . That's the problem. I really don't have any."

"Sure you do. Just give me three people you would consider friends and I'll get the local authorities on them. Come on, let's go."

"Well, there's the dean at the school, Dr. John Francis. The priest at my parish—Bill Strong." He searched his mind for another, but nothing came. He had plenty of acquaintances, but really no one he'd call a true friend, much less a best friend.

"Okay. Good enough. Hold on a second."

She put the phone down.

Kevin lifted his T-shirt and wiped the sweat from his face. 4:24. He had until 4:45. *Come on, Samantha!* He stood and paced. *In life he's your friend, but death is the end. What—*

"Kevin?"

"Here."

"Okay, I put in an anonymous call to the Long Beach police warning that Francis and Strong could be in immediate danger. Enough to get them moved from wherever they are, which is all we can do."

"You talked to Milton?"

"He's the lead? No, but I'm sure he'll get the message. How sure are you that this guy will come unglued if you talk to the authorities?"

"He's already unglued! He said I could only speak when spoken to and he's doing this because I said something."

"Okay. You'll probably get a call any minute from the police, checking on this threat I've just reported. You have call waiting?"

"Yes."

"Ignore the beep. If you talk to the police when they call, Slater will know. What's the riddle?"

"There's something else, Sam. Slater knows you. In fact, he suggested I call you. I . . . I think he might be someone we both know."

The phone sounded hollow for a few breaths.

"He knows me. What's the sin he wants you to confess?"

"I don't know!"

"Okay, we can cover this later. We're running out of time. What's the riddle?"

"In life he's your friend, but death is the end."

"Opposites."

"Opposites?"

"*What falls but never breaks? What breaks but never falls?* Answer: Night and day. What in life is your friend, but death is the end, I don't know. But they're both opposites. Any ideas?"

"No. I don't have a clue." Night falls, day breaks. Clever. "This is *crazy!*" He ground the last word out between his teeth.

She was quiet for a moment. "If we knew the sin, we could infer the riddle. What sin are you hiding, Kevin?"

He stopped pacing. "None. Lots! What do you want me to do, spill my whole life of sins to the world? That seems to be what he wants."

"But there must be something you did that sent this guy to the moon. Think of that and think of this riddle. Anything connect?"

Kevin thought about the boy. But there was no connection between the riddles and the boy. Couldn't be him. Nothing else came to mind.

"No."

"Then let's go back to your best friend."

"You're my best friend, Sam."

"Sweet. But this guy wanted you to call me, right? He knows I would be warned, and if he knows me, he also knows that I have the capability of escaping his threat. I think I'm safe for now. There's another best friend you're missing. Something more obvious—"

"Wait! What if it's not a person?" *That's it!* He glanced at his watch. Fifteen minutes to go. Barely enough time to get there. Call waiting sounded in his ear. That would be the police.

"Ignore it," Sam said. "Such as—"

"I'll call you back, Sam. I don't have time to explain."

"I'm coming down. I'll be there in five hours."

"You . . . you are?"

"I'm on leave, remember?"

Kevin felt a surge of gratitude. "I have to go."

He hung up, nerves buzzing, stomach in knots. If he was right, it meant going back to the house. He hated going back to his aunt's house. He stood in the office, fists clenched by his sides. But he had to go back. Slater had blown up the car, and now he was going to do worse unless Kevin stopped him.

Slater was forcing him back to the house. Back to the past. Back to the house and back to the boy.

III

Kevin's watch read 4:39 when he passed the park at the end of Baker Street and pointed the car toward the white house. The faint sound of children playing on the swing sets faded. Then silence except for the purr of the Taurus. He blinked.

A row of twenty elms lined the left side of the dead-end avenue, one in the front yard of each house, casting a dark shadow over the entire length. Behind the homes, a narrow greenway fed into the park he'd just passed. To his right, warehouses backed up to train tracks. The street had been freshly paved, the lawns were all neatly manicured, the houses modest but clean. By all appearances it was the perfect little street on the edge of town.

He had not visited in over a year, and even then he'd refused to go inside. He needed Balinda's signature for the seminary application. After four failed attempts to secure it through the mail, he finally dragged himself to the front porch and rang the doorbell. She appeared after several minutes, and he addressed her without making eye contact and told her that he had some evidence in his old bedroom that would interest the authorities and would make the police station his next stop if she refused to sign. It was a lie, of course. She turned up her nose and scribbled her signature.

The last time he'd seen the inside of the house was five years ago, the day he'd finally worked up the courage to leave.

Rolling down the blacktop under the canopy of elms wasn't so different from driving through a tunnel. One that led to a past he had no desire to visit.

He passed the houses slowly—the green one, the yellow one, another green one, a beige one—all old, all unique in their own way despite the obvious similarities that came from having a common builder. Same gutters, same windows, same shingle roofs. Kevin locked his eyes on the white house, the fifteenth of the twenty on Baker Street.

Here resides Balinda and Eugene Parson with their thirty-six-year-old retarded son, Bob. Here is the childhood home of one Kevin Parson, adopted son, formerly known as Kevin Little until his mommy and daddy went to heaven.

Five minutes. *Okay, Kevin, time's running out.*

He parked the car across the street. A two-foot picket fence ran around the front yard and then rose to six feet for its run around the back. Here the fence was painted brilliant white, but once you stepped past that gate to the right, it wasn't painted at all, except by years of black ash. A flower bed ran the length of the front porch. Fake flowers, pretty and maintenance-free. Balinda replaced them every year—her idea of gardening.

A gray stone statue of some Greek goddess stood on a pedestal to the right of the Parsons' elm. The front yard was immaculate, the neatest on the street, always had been. Even the beige '59 Plymouth in the driveway had been recently polished so that you could actually see a reflection of the elm in its rear quarter panel. It hadn't been moved in years. When the Parsons had reason to leave the house, they favored the ancient blue Datsun parked in the garage.

The shades were drawn and the door had no windows, making it impossible to see inside, but Kevin knew the inside better than he knew his own house. Three doors down stood the smaller brown house that had once belonged to a cop named Rick Sheer, who had a daughter named Samantha. Her family had moved back to San Francisco when Sam went off to college.

Kevin wiped his palms on his jeans and climbed out. The sound of his door slamming sounded obscenely loud on the quiet street. The shade on the front window separated momentarily, and then closed. *Good. Come on out, Auntie.*

Suddenly the whole notion of coming felt absurd. Slater obviously knew his facts, but how would he have knowledge of Bob's dog? Or that the dog had indeed been Kevin's best friend until Samantha had come along? Maybe Slater was after Dr. Francis or the priest. Sam had made the call. Smart.

Kevin paused on the sidewalk and stared at the house. What now? Walk up and tell Balinda that someone was about to blow up the dog? He closed his eyes. *God, give me strength. You know how I hate this.* Maybe he should just leave. If Balinda had a phone, he would have called instead. Maybe he could call the neighbors and—

The door opened and Bob stepped out, grinning from ear to ear. "Hello, Kevin."

Bob wore a lopsided crew cut, undoubtedly Balinda's doing. His beige slacks hung a full six inches above a pair of shiny black leather wing tips. His shirt was a dirty white and sported large lapels reminiscent of the seventies.

Kevin grinned. "Hello, Bob. Can I see Damon?"

Bob lit up. "Damon wants to see you, Kevin. He's been waiting to see you."

"Is that so? Good, then. Let's—"

"Bobby, baby!" Balinda's shrill voice cut through the front door. "You get back in here!" She appeared out of the shadows wearing red high heels and white pantyhose patched up with streaks of clear fingernail polish. Her white dress was lined with age-stained lace embedded haphazardly with a couple dozen fake pearls, the surviving remnant of what had once been hundreds. A large sun hat perched on jet-black hair that looked freshly dyed. A string of gaudy jewels hung around her neck. But it was the white makeup she applied to her sagging face and her bright ruby red lipstick that planted Balinda firmly in the category of the walking dead.

She glared past heavily shadowed lids, studied Kevin for a moment, and then turned up her nose.

"Did I say you could go out? Get in. In, in, in!"

"It's Kevin, Mama."

"I don't care if it's Jesus Christ, pumpkin." She reached forward and straightened his collar. "You know how easily you catch cold, baby."

She ushered Bob toward the door.

"He wants to see—"

"Be nice for Princess." She gave him a little shove. "In."

God bless her soul, Balinda really did intend good for that boy. She was misguided and foolish, certainly, but she loved Bob.

Kevin swallowed and glanced at his watch. Two minutes. He cut for the gate while her back was still turned.

"And just where does the stranger think he's going?"

"I just want to check on the dog. I'll be gone before you know it."

He reached the gate and yanked it open.

"Gone! You've turned running away into a new art form, haven't you, college boy?"

"Not now, Balinda," he said calmly. His breathing came faster. She marched up behind him. He strode down the side of the house.

"At least show a little respect when you're on my grounds," she said.

He checked himself. Closed his eyes. Opened them. "Please, not now, Princess."

"That's better. The dog's fine. You, on the other hand, are not."

Kevin rounded the house and stopped. The familiar yard sat unchanged. Black. Balinda called it a garden, but the backyard was nothing more than one huge ash heap, albeit a fairly tidy ash heap, three feet deep at its center, tapering off to two feet along the fence. A fifty-five-gallon drum smoldered at the center of the yard—they were still burning. Burning, burning, every day burning. How many newspapers and books had been burned back here over the years? Enough for many tons of ash.

The doghouse stood as it always had, in the back left corner. A toolshed sat unused and in terrible need of paint in the other corner. The ash had piled up against its door.

Kevin stepped onto the hardened ash and then ran across the yard for the doghouse. Less than a minute. He dropped to one knee, peered into the doghouse, and was rewarded with a growl.

"Easy, Damon. It's me, Kevin." The old black lab had grown senile and testy, but he immediately recognized Kevin's voice. He whimpered and limped out. A chain was latched to his collar.

"What do you think you're doing?" Balinda demanded.

"Good boy." Kevin stuck his head into the old doghouse and squinted in the darkness. No bomb that he could see. He stood and walked around the small house.

Nothing.

"What is he doing, Princess?"

Kevin turned back to the house at the sound of his uncle's voice. Eugene stood on the back porch, staring out at him. He wore his customary English-style boots and riding pants complete with suspenders and a beret. The skinny man looked more like a jockey to Kevin, but in Balinda's eyes, he was a prince. He'd worn the same outfit for at least ten years. Before that it was a Henry V outfit, awkward and clumsy on such a petite man.

Balinda stood at the edge of the house, watching Kevin with wary eyes. The shade lifted in the window to her left—Kevin's old room. Bob peered out. The past stared at him through those three sets of eyes.

He looked down at his watch. Thirty minutes had come and gone. He reached down and patted the dog. "Good boy." He unleashed him, tossed the chain to the side, and headed back for the gate.

"What do you think you are doing with my property?" Balinda asked.

"I thought he could use some exercise."

"You came all the way out here to let that old bat off his chain? What do you take me for? An idiot?" She turned to the dog, who was following Kevin. "Damon! Back in your house. Back!"

The dog stopped.

"Don't just stand there, Eugene! Control that animal!"

Eugene immediately perked up. He took two steps toward the dog and flung out a flimsy arm. "Damon! Bad dog! Get back. Get back immediately."

The dog just stared at them.

"Try it with your horse training accent," Balinda said. "Put some authority in your voice."

Kevin stared at them. It had been a long time since he'd seen them like this. They'd slipped into their role-playing on the fly. For the moment he didn't even exist. It was hard to imagine he grew up with these two.

Eugene stood as tall as his short frame would allow and expanded his chest. "I say, dog! To the kennel or the whip it'll be. Be gone! Be thou gone *immeeediately!*"

"Don't just stand there; go after him like you mean it!" Balinda snapped. "And I really don't think *thou* is appropriate with an animal. Growl or something!"

Eugene crouched and took several long steps toward the dog, growling like a bear.

"Not like an animal, you idiot!" Balinda said. "You look foolish! He's the animal; you're the master. Act like one. Growl like a man! Like a ruler."

Eugene pulled himself up again and thrust out an arm, snarling like a villain. "Back in the cage, you foul-mouthed vermin!" he cried hoarsely.

Damon whimpered and ran back into his house.

"Ha!" Eugene stood up, triumphant.

Balinda clapped and giggled, delighted. "You see, didn't I tell you? Princess knows—"

A muffled explosion suddenly lifted the doghouse a foot into the air and dropped it back to the ground.

They stood, Balinda at the corner, Bob in the window, Eugene by the porch, and Kevin in the middle of the yard, staring with incredulity at the smoldering doghouse.

Kevin could not move. Damon?

Balinda took a step forward and stopped. "Wha . . . what was that?"

"Damon?" Kevin ran for the doghouse. "Damon!"

He knew before he arrived that the dog was dead. Blood quickly darkened the ash at the door. He looked in and immediately recoiled. Bile crept up his throat. How was it possible? Tears sprang into his eyes.

A screech filled the air. He looked back to see Balinda flying for the doghouse, face stricken, arms outstretched. He jumped back to avoid her rush. On the porch, Eugene was pacing and mumbling incoherently. Bob had his face planted on the window, wide-eyed.

Balinda took one look into Damon's smoking house and then staggered back. Eugene stopped and watched her. Kevin's mind spun. But it wasn't Damon that now made him dizzy. It was Princess. Not Princess—Mother!

No! No, not Princess, not Mother, not even Auntie! *Balinda.* The poor sick hag who'd sucked the life out of him.

She turned to Kevin, eyes black with hate. "You!" she screamed. "You did this!"

"No, Mother!" *She's not your Mother! Not Mother.*

"I—"

"Shut your lying mouth! We hate you!" She flung her arm toward the gate. "Get out!"

"You don't mean that . . ." *Stop it, Kevin! What do you care if she hates you? Get out.*

Balinda balled both hands to fists, dropped them to her sides, and tilted her head back. "Leave! Leave, leave, leave!" she screamed, eyes clenched.

Eugene joined in, chanting with her in a falsetto voice, mimicking her stance. "Leave, leave, leave, leave!"

Kevin left. Without daring to look at what Bob might be doing, he whirled around and fled for his car.

6

THE AIR IS STUFFY. Too hot for such a cool day. Richard Slater, as he has decided to call himself this time, strips out of his clothes and hangs them in the one closet beside the desk. He crosses the dark basement in his bare feet, pulls open the old chest freezer, and takes out two ice cubes. Not really cubes—they are frozen into small balls instead of squares. He found the unusual ice trays in a stranger's refrigerator once and decided to take them. They are wonderful.

Slater walks into the center of the room and sits down on the concrete. A large white clock on the wall ticks quietly. It's 4:47. He will call Kevin in three minutes, unless Kevin himself makes a phone call, in which case he'll remotely terminate the connection and then call Kevin back. Short of that, he wants to give Kevin a little time to digest things. That is the plan.

He lies back, flat on the cool cement, and places one ice ball in each eye socket. He's done a lot of things over the years—some of them horrible, some of them quite splendid. What do you call tipping a waitress a buck more than she deserves? What do you call tossing a baseball back to the kid who mistakenly throws it over the fence? Splendid, splendid.

The horrible things are too obvious to dwell on.

But really his whole life has been practice for this particular game.

Of course, he always says that. There's something about being in a contest of high stakes that makes the blood flow. Nothing quite compares. Killing is just killing unless there's a game to the killing. Unless there is an end game that results in some kind of ultimate victory. Extracting punishment involves making someone suffer, and death ends that suffering, cheating the true pain of suffering. At least this side of hell. Slater shivers with the excitement of it all. A small whimper of pleasure. The ice hurts now. Like fire in his eyes. Interesting how opposites can be so similar. Ice and fire.

He counts off the seconds, not in his conscious mind, but in the background, where it doesn't distract him from thought. They have some pretty good minds on their side, but none quite like his. Kevin is no idiot. He will have to see which FBI agent they send. And of course the real prize exudes brilliance: Samantha.

Slater opens his mouth and says the name slowly. "Samantha."

He's been planning this particular game for three years now, not because he needed the time, but because he's been waiting for the right timing. Then again, the wait has given him more than enough opportunity to learn far more than he needs to know. Kevin's every waking move. His motivations and his desires. His strengths and his weaknesses. The truth behind that delightful little family of his.

Electronic surveillance—it's amazing how technology has advanced even in the last three years. He can put a laser beam on a window at a great distance and pick up any voices inside the room. They will find his bugs, but only because he wants them to. He can talk to Kevin any moment of the day on his own phone without being detected by a third party. When the police get around to finding the transmitter he affixed to the telephone line down from Kevin's house, he will resort to alternatives. There are limits, of course, but they won't be reached before the game expires. Pun intended.

Two minutes have passed and his eyes are numb from the ice.

Water leaks down his cheeks and he reaches his tongue up to touch it. Can't. One more minute.

The fact is, he's thought of everything. Not in a criminal kind of let's-do-a-bank-robbery-and-think-of-everything-so-they-won't-catch-us way. But in a more fundamental way. Precise motivations and countermoves. Like a chess match that will be played in response to another's moves. This method is far more exhilarating than taking a club to someone else's pieces and declaring yourself the victor.

In a few days, Kevin will be a shell of himself, and Samantha . . .

He chuckles.

There is no way they can possibly win.

Time's up.

Slater sits up, catches what's left of the ice balls as they fall from his eyes, tosses them into his mouth, and stands. The clock reads 4:50. He walks across the room to an old metal desk lit by a single shadeless lamp. Thirty watts. A policeman's hat sits on the desk. He reminds himself to put it in the closet.

The black phone is connected to a box, which will prevent tracing. Another remote box hides at the hub that services this house. The cops can trace all they like. He is invisible.

"Are we ready, Kevin?"

Slater picks up the phone, flips a switch on the scrambler, and dials the cell phone he's instructed Kevin to keep with him.

|||

Kevin ran to his car and started it before it occurred to him that he had nowhere to go. If he had Samantha's cell number, he would have called her. He almost called Milton but couldn't get past the thought of the cops turning this house into a crime scene. It was inevitable, though—he had to report the bomb. Not telling Milton about Slater's true demand had been one thing; covering up a second bomb was in a whole different league. He considered returning to explain the dog's death to Balinda, but he didn't have the stomach to face her, much less form an explanation that would make any sense.

The explosion had been muffled by the doghouse—none of the neighbors seemed to have heard. If they had, they weren't running around saying so.

Kevin sat in his car, running his fingers through his hair. A sudden fury spread through his bones. The phone in his pocket buzzed loudly against his leg and he jumped.

Slater!

It buzzed again. He fumbled for the cell phone, pulled it out, flipped it open.

"Hello?"

"Hello."

"You . . . you didn't have to do that," Kevin said, voice wavering. He hesitated and then continued quickly. "Are you the boy? You're the boy, aren't you? Look, I'm here. Just tell me what—"

"Shut up! What boy? Did I tell you to lecture me? Did I say, 'I feel badly in need of a lecture at this time, college Kevin?' Don't ever do that again. You've broken the don't-speak-to-me-unless-engaged rule several times now, college boy. The next time, I kill something that walks on two legs. Consider it negative reinforcement. Understand?"

"Yes."

"That's better. And I think it's best not to tell the cops about this one. I know I said you could after the fact, but this little bonus was just something I planned in the event you weren't a good listener, which you were so quick to confirm. Mum's the word on this one. Okay?"

Don't tell the cops? How could he—

"Answer me!"

"O . . . okay."

"Tell Balinda to keep her trap shut too. I'm sure she'll agree. She won't want the cops searching through the house, now, will she?"

"No." So Slater knew about Balinda.

"The games are on. I'm the bat; you're the ball. I keep slugging until you confess. Lock and load."

Kevin desperately wanted to ask him what he meant by that word: *confess.* But he couldn't. He could hear Slater breathing on the other end.

"Samantha's coming down," Slater said in a soft voice. "That's good. I can't decide whom I despise more, you or her." The line clicked and Slater was gone. Kevin sat in silent shock. Whoever Slater was, he seemed to know everything. Balinda, the dog, the house. Samantha. He exhaled and closed his fingers to a fist to steady their trembling.

This is really happening, Kevin. Someone who knows is going to blow the lid off. *What falls but never breaks? What breaks but never falls?* Night and day. *In life he's your friend, but death is the end.* In life the dog was a friend, but death was the end of him. But there was more. Something Slater wanted him to confess was night and day, and life and death. What?

Kevin slammed the steering wheel with his fist. What, *what?*

"What boy?" Slater had said. What boy? So then he wasn't the boy?

Dear God . . . Dear God . . . Dear God what? He couldn't even think straight to pray. He put his head back and took several long, calming breaths. "Samantha. Samantha." She would know what to do. Kevin closed his eyes.

III

Kevin was eleven years old when he first saw the boy who wanted to kill him.

He and Samantha had become the very best of friends. What

made their friendship most special was that their trips into the night remained a secret. He saw other kids now and then, but he never talked to them. Mother didn't like that. But as far as he knew, she never did discover his little secret about the window. Every few nights, whenever they'd planned, or sometimes when Sam would tap on his window, or even sometimes when he went out and tapped on Sam's window, he would sneak out and meet her.

He didn't tell Sam what was happening inside the house. He wanted to, of course, but he couldn't tell her the worst of it, although he wondered whether she might have guessed anyway. His time with Sam was special because it was the only part of his life that *wasn't* about the house. He wanted to keep it that way.

The private school Sam attended held classes year-round, so she was always busy during the day, but Kevin knew he could never sneak out during the day anyway. Mother would find out.

"Why don't you ever want to play at the park?" Sam asked him one night as they walked through the greenway. "You'd get along great with Tommy and Linda."

He shrugged. "I just don't want to. They might tell."

"We could make them swear not to. They like me; they'd promise not to tell. They could be part of our club."

"We have fun together without them, don't we? Why do we need them?"

"Well, you have to start meeting some other people, Kevin. You're growing up, you know. I can't understand why your mom won't let you out to play in the first place. That's kinda mean—"

"Don't talk about her that way!"

"Well, it is!"

Kevin lowered his head, suddenly feeling suffocated. They stood in the quiet for a moment.

Sam put her hand on his shoulder. "I'm sorry."

The way she said it made tears come to his eyes. She was so special.

"I'm sorry," she said again. "I guess just because she's different doesn't mean she's mean. Different strokes for different folks, right?"

He looked up at her, unsure.

"It's a saying." She wiped a tear that had leaked from his right eye. "At least your mom isn't one of those parents who abuse their kids. I've heard my dad talk about some things." She shuddered. "Some people are horrible."

"My mom is a princess," Kevin said softly.

Sam grinned politely and nodded. "She's never hit you, has she, Kevin?"

"Hit me? Why would she hit me?"

"Has she?"

"Never! She sends me to my room and makes me read my books. That's all. Why would anyone hit someone else?"

"Not everyone's as sweet as you, Kevin." Sam took his hand and they started to walk. "I think my dad might know about us."

Kevin pulled up. "What?"

"He's asked a few questions. Mom and Dad talk about your family every once in a while. He is a cop, after all."

"Did . . . did you tell him anything?"

"Of course not. Don't worry. Your secret's safe with me."

They walked for a few minutes, hand in hand.

"Do you like Tommy?" Kevin asked.

"Tommy? Sure."

"I mean, is he your . . . you know . . ."

"Boyfriend? Don't gross me out!"

Kevin flushed and giggled. They came to a large tree behind her house and Sam stopped. She faced him and took both of his hands in hers. "I don't have any boyfriends except you, Kevin. I like you."

He looked into her bright blue eyes. A gentle breeze lifted her blonde hair so that it swam around her, highlighted by the moon. She was the most beautiful thing Kevin had ever seen. He was so taken with her that he had trouble even speaking.

"I . . . I like you too, Sam."

"We're like secret lovers," she said softly, and suddenly her face softened. "I've never kissed a boy before. Could I kiss you?"

"Kiss me?" He swallowed.

"Yes."

Kevin's throat was suddenly dryer than baking powder. "Yes."

She leaned forward and touched her lips to his for a moment.

She pulled back and they stared at each other, wide-eyed. Kevin's heart throbbed in his ears. He should do something! Before he lost his nerve, he bent and returned the kiss.

The night seemed to disappear around him. He floated on a cloud. They looked at each other, suddenly awkward.

"I should go now," she said.

"Okay."

She turned and ran toward her house. Kevin spun around and tore home, and honestly he wasn't sure if his feet really were on the ground. He did like Samantha. He liked her very, very much. Maybe even more than his mother, which was pretty impossible.

The next few days floated by like a dream. He met Sam two nights later and they made no mention of the kiss. They didn't need to. They resumed their playing as if nothing at all had changed between them. They didn't kiss again, and Kevin wasn't sure he wanted to. It might somehow spoil the magic of that first kiss.

Sam didn't come to his window for three straight nights, and Kevin decided to sneak out and go to her house. He took the greenway past the two houses between his and Sam's on light feet, careful not to make the slightest sound. You could never know who might be out at night.

They had hidden from the sound of coming voices and approaching footsteps a hundred times before.

A half-moon sat in the black sky, peeking around slowly drifting clouds. Crickets chirped. Sam's house came into view and his heart thumped a little louder. He eased up to the picket fence and peered over it. Her room was on the bottom floor; he could see the faint glow of light past the tree in front of the window. *Please be there, Sam. Please.*

Kevin glanced around, saw no one, and pushed aside the board Sam had loosened long ago. Her dad might be a cop, but he'd never found this, had he? That's because Sam was smart too. He climbed through and brushed his hands. *Please be there, Sam.*

Kevin took a step. The tree in front of Sam's window moved. He froze. Sam? Slowly a dark head and then shoulders came into view. Someone was peeking into Sam's room!

Kevin jerked back, panicked. The form stood taller, angling for a better view. It was a boy! A tall boy with a sharp nose. Staring in on Sam!

A dozen thoughts screamed through Kevin's head. Who? What was the boy doing? He should run! No, he should yell. Was that Tommy? No, Tommy had longer hair.

The boy spun around, stared directly at Kevin, and then pushed his way past the tree. He stood tall in the moonlight, and a terrible smile twisted his face. He took a step toward Kevin.

Kevin didn't bother with the loose plank—he went over the fence faster than he could have ever imagined possible and ran for a large tree on the edge of the greenway. He pulled up behind it, panting.

Nothing happened. There was no sound of running or of heavy breathing other than his own. He would have run for home but was afraid the boy was waiting by the fence for the first sign of movement. It took him a full five minutes to work up the courage to peek ever so slowly around the tree.

Nothing.

Another five minutes and he was peering over the fence again. Nothing. Whoever the boy was, he'd gone.

Kevin finally worked up the courage to tap on Sam's window. She climbed out, all smiles. She was waiting for him, she said. Waiting for the dashing young man to come to the window of the maiden. That's how it was done in the movies.

He told her about the boy, but she found it funny. One of the neighborhood guys had a crush on her, and her prince charming had sent him packing! Hearing himself tell it, the story did sound funny. They had a good hoot that night. But Kevin had a hard time shaking the image of the boy's horrible smile.

Three nights went by before Kevin saw the boy again—this time in the greenway on his way home. At first he thought it was a dog or some animal running behind the trees, but after he'd climbed into bed, he began to wonder if it was the boy. What if he was going to spy on Sam again? He tossed and turned for half an hour before working up the resolve to go back and check on Sam. He would never go to sleep until he had.

For the first time in a year, he went out for a second time in the same night—prince charming to check on his damsel in distress. He didn't really expect to see anything.

Kevin poked his head over the fence in Sam's backyard and went rigid. The boy! He was there, peering into Sam's window again! He'd waited until Kevin went home and then snuck up to her window to spy on her!

Kevin ducked and tried to calm his breathing. He had to do something! But what? If he yelled and then took off running, the boy wouldn't catch him. At least then he might scare off the boy. He could throw a rock. No. What if he broke Sam's window?

He went up slowly for another peek. The boy was doing something. He had his face planted against the window and was . . . he was moving his face around in circles. What was he doing? Kevin blinked. Was he . . . ? A chill snaked down Kevin's spine. The boy was licking Sam's window in slow circles.

Something ballooned in Kevin's head. Whether it was rage or just plain terror, he couldn't be sure, but he spoke while courage strengthened him.

"Hey!"

The boy spun around. For one long, still moment, they stared at each other. The boy stepped forward and Kevin fled. He bolted through the greenway, pumping his skinny arms and legs as fast as they would go without tearing loose. He dove through his fence, flew into his bedroom, and shut the window, surely making enough racket to wake the house.

Ten minutes later the night slept in silence. But Kevin couldn't. He felt trapped in the small room. What was the boy doing? Had he been stalking Sam every night? He had, hadn't he? Kevin had only stumbled on him twice, but there was no telling how long the boy had been stalking Sam.

An hour passed, and Kevin could hardly shut his eyes, much less sleep. That's when he heard the tap on his window. He bolted up in bed. Sam! He scrambled to his knees and lifted the shade.

The boy stood at the back fence, head and shoulders in plain view. He stared directly at Kevin, twirling something in his hand. It was a knife.

Kevin dropped the shade and flung the covers over his head. He lay trembling for two hours before peeking again, ever so carefully, just barely lifting the shade. The boy was gone.

The next three days dragged by like a slow nightmare. Each night he peeked out his window a hundred times. Each night the backyard remained vacant except for the doghouse and the toolshed. Each night he prayed desperately for Sam to come for a visit. She'd talked about going to a camp, but he couldn't remember exactly when she was supposed to go. Was it this week?

On the fourth night, Kevin couldn't wait any longer. He paced in his room for an hour, peering out of his window every few minutes, before deciding that he had to check on Sam before the anxiety killed him.

It took him half an hour to work his way up to her house, using the trees in the greenway as cover. The night was quiet. When he finally inched his head over Sam's fence, her light was out. He scanned the yard. No boy. Sam was gone and so was the boy.

He collapsed at the base of the fence with relief. She must be at that camp. Maybe the boy had followed her there. No. That was stupid. How could a boy follow a girl all the way to camp?

Kevin eased his way back to the cover of the greenway and headed home, feeling at ease for the first time in nearly a week. Maybe the boy had moved. Maybe he had found something else to occupy his sick little mind.

Maybe he had snuck into Sam's room and killed her.

He pulled up. No. Kevin would have heard about that. Her father was a cop and—

A blunt object slammed into the side of Kevin's head and he staggered. A groan broke from his throat. Something wrapped around his neck and jerked him upright.

"Listen, you little punk, I know who you are and I don't like you!" a voice snarled in his ear. The arm jerked him around and shoved him against a tree. Kevin wobbled at arm's length from his attacker. The boy.

If his head wasn't throbbing so badly, he might have panicked. Instead he just stared and tried to keep his legs from collapsing.

The boy sneered. Close up, his face reminded Kevin of a boar. He was older than Kevin and a foot taller, but still young, with pimples all over his nose and chin and a tattoo of a knife high on his forehead. He smelled like dirty socks.

The boy brought his face within a few inches of Kevin's. "I'm going to give you one warning and one warning only, squat. That girl is mine, not yours. If I ever see you so much as looking at her again, I'll kill her. If I catch you sneaking out to see her again, I may just kill the both of you. You hear me?"

Kevin just stood dumb.

The boy slapped him across the cheek. "You hear me?"

Kevin nodded.

The boy stepped back and glared at him. A slow lopsided grin split his face at a cruel angle. "You think you're in love with this little tramp? Huh? You're too stupid and too young to know what love is. And so is she. I'm going to teach her love, baby, and I don't need a squat like you messing with our little romance." He stepped back.

Kevin saw the knife in the boy's hand for the first time. His mind cleared. The boy saw his eyes on the knife and he lifted it slowly.

"You have any idea what a nine-inch bowie can do to a squat like you?" The boy twirled the blade in his hand. "Do you know how persuasive a bright shiny blade can be to a young girl?"

Kevin suddenly felt like he was going to vomit.

"Get back to your little room, squat, before I decide to cut you just for looking so stupid."

Kevin fled.

7

Friday
Night

KEVIN SAT IN HIS RECLINER, waiting impatiently for Samantha, flipping through the channels to hear the various versions of the "car bomb," as they were calling it. He nursed a warm 7UP in his left hand and glanced up at the wall clock. Nine o'clock—nearly five hours had passed since she'd left Sacramento.

"Come on, Samantha," he muttered softly. "Where are you?" She'd called him halfway down. He told her about the dog and begged her to hurry. She was already doing eighty, she said.

Back to the television. They knew Kevin's identity, and a dozen reporters had tracked down his number. He'd ignored the calls per Milton's suggestion. Not that he had anything to add anyway—their theories were as good as his. Channel nine's suggestion that the bombing might be the work of a well-known fugitive dubbed the Riddle Killer interested him most. The killer had taken the lives of five people up in Sacramento and had vanished three months ago. No more details, but the speculation was enough to plant a knot in Kevin's throat. The pictures of the charred wreckage, taken from the sky, were stunning. Or terrifying, depending on how he thought of them. If he'd been anywhere near the thing when it blew, he'd be dead. Like the dog.

After Slater's call, he'd forced himself to return to the backyard and explain the situation to Balinda, but she wouldn't even acknowledge him. She'd already put the matter behind them by executive order. Poor Bob would somehow be convinced that Damon was alive and well, just gone. Balinda would have to explain her initial screaming flight across the ash after the explosion, of course, but she was an expert at explaining the unexplainable. The only time she even responded to Kevin was when he suggested they not call the police.

"Of course not. We've got nothing to report. The dog's fine. Do you see a dead dog?"

No, he didn't. Eugene had already dumped it in the burn barrel and set it on fire. Gone. What were a few more ashes?

His mind drifted to the call with Slater. *What boy?* Slater didn't seem to know of any boy. *What boy?* The key to his sin was found in the riddles. As far as he could see, the riddles had nothing to do with the boy. So then Slater *couldn't* be the boy. Thank God, thank God, thank God. Some secrets were best left buried forever.

The doorbell chimed. Kevin set down his 7UP and clambered out of his chair. He stopped at the hall mirror for a quick look. Haggard face. Smudged T-shirt. He scratched the top of his head. The bell chimed again.

"Coming."

He hurried to the peephole, peered out, saw that it was Samantha, and unlocked the door. It had been ten years since he'd kissed her on the cheek and wished her well in conquering the big bad world. Her hair had been blonde and long; her blue eyes sparkling like stars. She'd had one of those faces that looked airbrushed all the time, even without a speck of makeup. Smooth rounded cheeks and soft upturned lips, high arching eyebrows and a soft pointed nose. The most beautiful girl he'd ever seen. Of course, he wasn't seeing a lot of girls in those days.

Kevin fumbled with the knob and opened the door. Samantha stood under the porch light, dressed in jeans and smiling warmly. He'd thought of her a thousand times since she'd left, but his mind's eye could never have prepared him for seeing her now, in the flesh. He *had* seen a lot of girls in the last five years, and Sam was still the most beautiful girl he'd ever laid eyes on. Bar none.

"Are you going to invite me in, stranger?"

"Yes. Sorry, of course! Come in, come in."

She walked past him, set down her bag, and faced him. He shut the door.

"My, you've grown up," she said. "Put on a bit of muscle."

He grinned and ran his hand over his head. "I guess."

He was having difficulty not staring at her eyes. They were the kind of blue that seemed to swallow whatever they gazed upon—brilliant and deep and haunting. They didn't reflect the light so much as shine, as if illuminated by their own source. No man nor woman could look into Samantha's eyes and not think that there was indeed a God in heaven. She stood just up to his chin, slender and graceful. This was Samantha, his best friend. His only real friend. Looking at her now, he wondered how he'd survived the last ten years.

She stepped forward. "Give me a hug, my knight."

He chuckled at her childhood reference and hugged her tight. "It's so good to see you, Samantha."

She stood up on her toes and kissed his cheek. Beyond that one blissful kiss when they were eleven, their relationship had remained platonic. Neither of them wanted romance from the other. They were bosom buddies, best friends, almost brother and sister. Not that the thought hadn't crossed Kevin's mind; a friendship had just always been more appealing. She had always been the damsel in distress, and he the knight in shining armor, even though they both knew she had rescued him in the first place. Now, despite the fact that it was she who'd again come to his rescue, their childhood personas came naturally.

Sam turned to the living room, hands on her hips. "I see you like travel posters."

He walked with her and grinned self-consciously. *Quit rubbing your head; she'll think you're a dog.* He lowered his hands and tapped his right foot.

"I'd like to go to all those places someday. It's kinda like looking at the world. Reminds me there's more. Never did like being shut in."

"I like it! Well, you've come far. And I knew you would, didn't I? You just had to get away from that mother of yours."

"Aunt," he corrected. "She never was my mother."

"Aunt. Let's face it, dear Aunt Balinda did you more harm than good. When did you finally leave?"

He walked past her to the kitchen. "Twenty-three. Drink?"

She followed him. "Thanks. You stayed in that house five years after I left?"

"Afraid so. You should've taken me with you."

"You did it on your own—that's better. Now look at you, you have a college degree and you're in seminary. Impressive."

"And you graduated valedictorian. Very impressive." He pulled a soda from the fridge, popped the tab, and handed it to her.

"Thank you," she said. "For the compliment." She winked at him and took a sip. "The drink's nice too. How often do you go back?"

"Where? To the house? As little as possible. I'd rather not talk about that."

"I think that *that* might be tied to this, don't you?"

"Maybe."

Samantha set the can down on the counter and looked at him, suddenly dead serious. "Someone's stalking you. And by the sound of it, me. A killer who uses riddles who's selected us for his own reasons. Revenge. Hate. The baser motivations. We can't shut out the past."

"Right to the point."

"Tell me everything."

"Starting—"

"Starting with the phone call in your car." She walked to the front door.

Kevin followed. "Where are you going?"

"We. Come on, let's take a drive. He's obviously listening to everything we say in here—let's make his life a little more interesting. We'll take my car. Hopefully he hasn't gotten to it yet."

They climbed into a beige sedan and Samantha drove into the night. "That's better. He's probably using lasers."

"Actually, I think you're right," Kevin said.

"He told you that?"

"Something like that."

"Every detail, Kevin. I don't care how insignificant, I don't care what you told the cops, I don't care how embarrassing or stupid or crazy it sounds, I want everything."

Kevin did as she requested, eagerly, with passion, as if it were his first real confession. Sam drove haphazardly and stopped him frequently to ask questions.

When was the last time you left your car unlocked?

Never that I can remember.

Do you lock your car when it's in the garage?

No.

A nod. *Did the police find a timing device?*

Not that he knew about.

You found the ribbon behind the lamp?

Yes.

Did Slater call me Sam or Samantha?

Samantha.

An hour passed and they covered every conceivable detail of the day's events, including the information he'd hidden from Milton.

Everything except his speculation that Slater could be the boy. He'd never told Sam the whole truth about the boy, and he wasn't eager to do so now. If Slater wasn't the boy, which he claimed not to be, there was no need to dig up that matter. He'd never told Sam the whole truth and he wasn't eager to do so now.

"How long can you stay?" Kevin asked after a lull.

Sam glanced at him with a coy smile. "The big boy needs a girl in his court?"

Kevin grinned sheepishly. She hadn't changed a bit. "Turns out girls make or break me."

She arched her brow. "I technically have a week off to finish my move. I have boxes overflowing in my kitchen still. The case I was assigned to when I first arrived a couple months ago has been pretty quiet, but it just heated up. I wouldn't be surprised if they called me in."

"California Bureau of Investigation, huh? Big change from New York."

"Not really, other than being new. I've managed to do a couple things right and have my department head appropriately impressed at the moment, but I still have to earn my stripes with them, if you understand how law enforcement works. Same thing with the CIA before I switched to this job."

"CBI, CIA—gets a bit confusing," Kevin said. "You glad you made the move?"

She looked at him and grinned. "I'm closer to you, aren't I?"

He nodded and turned sheepishly. "You have no idea how much I appreciate this. Really."

"I wouldn't miss it for the world."

"Can't you pull some strings?" He faced her. "Convince them to let you stay down here?"

"Because I know you?"

"Because you're involved now. He *knows* you, for heaven's sake!"

"It doesn't work that way. If anything, that's reason for them to remove me from the case." She stared ahead, lost in thought. "Don't worry, I'm not going anywhere. The CBI is made of a dozen units, roughly a hundred agents in all. My unit is unique—hardly known to most agents. We work outside the system, technically part of the Bureau, but it's directed as much by the attorney general. Troubleshooting the harder cases. We have some latitude and discretion." She looked at him. "You, my dear, are definitely within the scope of the discretion. More than you know."

Kevin stared out his window. Black. Slater was out there somewhere. Maybe watching them now. A shiver ran down his spine.

"So. What do you think?"

Sam pulled the car to the curb a block from Kevin's house and shoved the stick into park. "I think that we have no choice but to follow Slater's demands. So far the demands involve no one but you. This isn't like a threat of terror, where either we release a hostage or they blow a building. This is either you confess or he blows up your car. Confession doesn't exactly pose a threat to society." She nodded to herself. "For now we don't involve the police like he wants. But we also take him at his word. He said *cops*—we avoid the cops. That excludes the FBI. We tell the FBI everything."

She cracked her window and stared at the sky. "I also think that Richard Slater is someone one or both of us knew or know. I think his motivation is revenge and I think he means to extract it in a way that will never be forgotten." She looked at him. "There has to be someone, Kevin."

He hesitated and then fed her part of the truth. "No one. The only enemy I can even remember having is that boy."

"What boy?"

"You know. Remember that boy who was spying on you when we were kids? The one who beat me up?"

She grinned. "The one you saved me from?"

"I asked Slater if he was the boy," Kevin said.

"Did you, now? You omitted that little detail."

"It was nothing."

"I said *every* detail, Kevin. I don't care if you think it's nothing or not. Okay?"

"Okay."

"What did he say?"

"He said, 'What boy?' It's not him."

She didn't respond.

A car drove by. SUV with bright taillights.

"Ever hear of the Riddle Killer?" Sam asked.

Kevin sat up. "On the news tonight."

"The Riddle Killer was given that name for a series of murders up in Sacramento over the last twelve months. It's been three months since his last victim—the brother of an FBI agent who was on his tail. I can guarantee that the FBI will be all over this. Same MO. Guy calls on the phone with a riddle and then executes his punishment if the riddle goes unsolved. Low, gravelly voice. Sophisticated surveillance. Sounds like the same guy."

"Except . . ."

"Except why would he choose you? And why me?" Sam asked. "Could be a copy cat."

"Maybe he's trying to confuse us. Guy like that's obviously into games, right? So maybe this just ups the thrill for him." Kevin lowered his head into his hands and massaged his temples. "Just this morning I had a discussion with Dr. Francis about mankind's capacity for evil. What's the average person capable of? Makes me wonder what I'd do if I met up with this guy." He took a deep breath. "It's hard to believe that people like this actually exist."

"He'll get his due. They always do." She reached over and rubbed his shoulder. "Don't worry, my dear knight. There's a reason I advanced as quickly as I did in the company. I haven't been handed a case so far I couldn't crack." She smirked playfully. "I told you I was gonna be a cop. And I didn't mean street beat either."

Kevin sighed and smiled. "Well, you have no idea how glad I am that it's you." He caught himself. "Not that I'm glad he's after—"

"I understand." She fired the car. "We'll beat this, Kevin. I'm not about to let some ghost from the past or some serial killer push either one of us around. We're smarter than this psycho. You'll see."

"What now?"

"Now we go find some bugs."

Twenty minutes later Sam held six eavesdropping devices in a gloved hand. One from the living room, one from each bathroom, one from each bedroom, and the infinity transmitter from the phone.

Her eyes twinkled like a competitive athlete who'd just scored a goal. Sam had always seemed beyond any kind of discouragement; her optimism was one of her most admirable traits. She carried it around her like a fragrance. As far as Kevin was concerned, Sam had what it took to one day run the CBI or CIA or whatever she so desired.

"Won't slow him down much, but at least it'll let him know that we're engaged. These types tend to get trigger-happy if they think the other side is slacking off."

She filled up the sink, dropped the devices into the water, and peeled off the surgical gloves. "Under normal circumstances I'd take these in, but if I'm right, the FBI has jurisdiction. They would scream bloody murder. First thing in the morning, I'll call my office, explain the situation, and then let Milton's office know of my involvement. Not that they will care—I guarantee that the town will be crawling with agencies by morning. I'd have a better shot working on my own than through them anyway." She was talking to herself as much as to him. "You said they'd be out first thing to sweep for bugs?"

"Yes."

"Tell them you found these lying around. I'll make sure they dust for prints. At this point you have nothing else to tell Milton, so let him do his job, and try to stay out of his way. When the FBI makes contact, cooperate. I've got a few other things I want to run down first thing. We tracking?"

"And if he calls?"

"If I'm not here, you call my cell immediately. We'll go from there." She started for the door and then turned back. "Slater will call. You do know that, don't you?"

He nodded slowly.

"Get some sleep. We'll get him. He's already made his first mistake."

"He has?"

"He pulled *me* into the game." She grinned. "I was born for cases like this."

Kevin walked over, took her hand, and kissed it. "Thank you."

"I think it would be better if I crashed down at the Howard Johnson. No offense, but you don't have a second bed and leather couches remind me of eels. I don't sleep with eels."

"Sure." He was disappointed only because he felt so alive around her. Secure. In his mind, she was absolutely perfect in every way. Of course, he wasn't exactly a Casanova, groomed to judge these things.

"I'll call you."

Then she was gone.

|||

Slater sits in a red pickup one block from Kevin's house and watches Sam back out of the driveway then drive south. "There you go; there you go." He clucks his tongue three times slowly, so that he can hear the full range of its sound. There are two sounds, actually—a deep popping as the tongue pulls free from the roof of the mouth, and a click as it strikes the gathered spittle in the base of the mouth. Details. The kind of details most people die without considering because most people are slobs who have no clue what living is really all about.

Living is about clucking your tongue and enjoying the sound.

They had found the bugs. Slater smiles. She has come and he is so very glad she has come quickly, flaunting her skinny little body all through the man's house, seducing him with her wicked tongue.

"Samantha," he whispers. "It is so good to see you again. Give me a kiss, baby."

The interior of the old Chevy is immaculate. He'd replaced the black plastic instrument panel with custom-fitted mahogany that shines now in the moonlight. A black case beside him carries the electronics he requires for his surveillance—mostly extras. Samantha found the six bugs he'd expected the cops to find, but there are still three, and not even the FBI will detect those.

"It's dark down here, Kevin. So very dark."

Slater waits an hour. Two. Three. The night is dead when he eases himself out of the cab and heads for Kevin's house.

8

Saturday
Morning

JENNIFER CROSSED HER LEGS and stared at Paul Milton across the conference table. She'd made the trip down to Long Beach the previous evening, visited the crime scene where Kevin Parson's Mercury Sable had blown up, made a dozen phone calls, and then checked into a hotel on Long Beach Boulevard.

She spent the night tossing and turning, reliving that day three months earlier when Roy had been killed by the Riddle Killer. The killer didn't use a name, never had. Only a riddle. He'd asphyxiated his first four victims, striking once every six weeks or so. With Roy he used a bomb. She found his body in pieces five minutes after the explosion ripped it apart. Nothing could wash away the image.

After a couple final hours of sleep she'd headed for the station where she waited an hour for the rest to arrive.

With Roy's death the fundamentals of life became stunningly vivid, while virtually all of her aspirations had died with him. She'd taken her relationship with him for granted, and when he was snatched away, she became desperate for every other thing she took for granted. The sweet smell of air. A burning hot shower on a cold morning. Sleep. The touch of another human. The simple things in life sustained her. Life wasn't what it seemed, she'd learned that much, but she still wasn't sure what life really *was*. The parties and the promotions felt plastic now. People rushing around, climbing imaginary ladders of success, fighting to be noticed.

Like Milton. Milton was a walking media package, right down to the bone, complete with a beige trench coat, which now hung in the corner. He was holding a news conference, of all things, just past sunup when she'd first entered the station.

There was no new news; they all knew that. His insistence that the media had a right to know at least that much was no more than smoke blowing. He wanted the camera eye, end of case. Not exactly her kind of man.

Her thinking wasn't exactly professional; she knew that. He was a law enforcement officer with the same ultimate objective as hers. They were in this together, regardless of any personal differences. But Jennifer didn't find the process of putting all the nonsense aside as easy as she had before Roy's death. That was why the Bureau tended to distance agents in her situation from the front line, as Frank had attempted.

Never mind, she would rise above it all.

To her left sat Nancy Sterling, Long Beach's most experienced forensic scientist. Next to her, Gary Swanson from the state police and Mike Bowen from the ATF. Cliff Bransford, CBI, rounded out the gathering. She'd worked with Cliff and found him exceptionally tedious, but smart enough. For him, everything was by the book. Best to stay clear of him unless he approached her.

"I know you all have varying interests in this case, but the FBI has clear jurisdiction—this guy's rap includes kidnapping," Jennifer said.

Milton didn't bat an eye. "You may have jurisdiction, but I've got a city—"

"Don't worry, I'm here to work with you. I'm recommending that we use your offices as a clearinghouse. That puts all the information at your fingertips. We'll coordinate everything from here. I don't know what the CBI or the ATF will want to do about personnel placement, but I would like to work out of this office. Fair enough?"

Milton didn't respond.

"Sounds good to me," Bransford said. "We're fine out of our own offices. As far as I'm concerned, this is your case."

Bransford knew about Roy and was giving her his support. She gave him a slight nod.

"We'll stand off for the meantime," the ATF agent said. "But if explosives show up again, we'll want a larger role."

"Granted," Jennifer said. She faced Milton. "Sir?"

He stared her down and she knew then that her opinion of him wouldn't change. Even if he'd linked this case to the Riddle Killer, which was likely given the profile of the killings in Sacramento, Jennifer doubted he knew of her personal stake in the case. Roy's identity had not been circulated. Even so, she didn't care for his arrogance.

"What's your specialty, agent?" Milton asked.

"Forensic psychology, Detective."

"Profiler."

"Psychological profiles based on forensics," she corrected. She almost spoke the rest of the thought: *That's why they put the word* forensics *in there, for those who grew up in Backwater, Louisiana.*

"Fair enough. But I don't want you talking to the media."

"I wouldn't think of robbing you of all that airtime, sir."

"I think we have an understanding."

"Good. I reviewed your file as of an hour ago." She looked at Nancy. "You do quick work."

"We try," Nancy said. "You might want to take a look at it again. We found a timer."

"Preset?"

"No. A receiver set the timer off, but from what I can gather, there was no way to terminate the timer once it was engaged."

Jennifer glanced at Milton. "So whoever did this had no intention of terminating the detonation, regardless of his threat."

"So it seems."

"Anything else?"

Milton stood and turned to the blinds behind his chair. He parted them and looked down at the street. "So what does your crystal ball tell you on this one, Agent Peters?"

"It's early."

"Humor me."

They were undoubtedly thinking Riddle Killer, but she went with a conservative analysis.

"Best guess, we have a white male who is extremely angry, but not angry enough to compromise his precision or method. He's smart. And he knows it. He knew what kind of bomb to build, how to place it, how to detonate without detection. In fact, he knew that Mr. Parson would escape unharmed, and he knew that his riddle would go unsolved. That's why he didn't bother wasting resources on a termination switch."

"Random victim?" Nancy asked.

"Nothing with this guy is random. If the victim isn't a past acquaintance, then he was selected for specific reasons. His profession, his habits, the way he combs his hair."

"Which is why Parson's insistence that he doesn't know anyone who might hold a grudge doesn't add up," Milton said.

"Not necessarily. You're a cop who can list a hundred people who would take your head off, given the opportunity. The average citizen doesn't have those kinds of enemies. We're dealing with someone who's probably insane—a sideways look on a train could mark you as his next target." She paused. "That's what I would say based solely on what you've given me. But as it turns out, I have more."

"Riddle Killer," Nancy said.

Jennifer looked at her and wondered if she knew about Roy. "Yes. Same MO. The last killing we've attributed to this guy was three months ago in Sacramento, but from every indication, we're dealing with the same man."

"He used riddles, but did he ever *not* kill a victim?" Milton asked.

"You're right; this one's different. All five of his victims were given one riddle and then killed when they failed to solve it. Which means he's not finished with Kevin Parson. He didn't just blow up a car without hurting anyone for the fun of it. He's stretching himself. He's bored. He wants a new challenge. Stringing together multiple riddles is the logical progression, but it also takes more time. He would have to study his mark well enough to sustain continued threats. That means lots of surveillance over many days. It's one thing to pull off one stunt. This guy's planning on doing this again. That kind of planning takes time. Could explain why the Riddle Killer has been so quiet over the last three months."

"This guy gave a name," Bransford said. "Slater. The Riddle Killer remained nameless."

"Again. A progression, in my opinion." Jennifer pulled a thick file from her briefcase and set it on the desk. The tab had two capital letters on it: R. K.

"Don't let the size fool you; we don't know as much as you might think. There's a lot of psychological profile data in here. When it comes to evidence, this guy's as clean as they come. None of the bodies was abused in any way. The first four were asphyxiated; the last was killed with a bomb. All four asphyxiated bodies were reported to the police by the killer himself and left on park benches. For all practical purposes they were evidence-free. This killer finds satisfaction in the game more than the actual killing. The killing is only a prop, something that provides stakes high enough to make the game interesting."

She put her hand on the file. The green edges were worn white from use, mostly her own. She could practically recite the contents, all 234 pages. A full half of the writing was hers.

"A copy of the file is being reproduced for each of you as we speak. I'll be happy to answer any questions once you've had a chance to review it. Has there been any additional contact with the victim?"

"Not today," Milton said. "We have a team on the way to sweep his house. He found some bugs. More accurately, a friend of his found six of them throughout the house. A Samantha Sheer called us this morning. She's connected with the attorney general's office. Just happened to be with him last night and did us a favor. Do you know what falls but never breaks? What breaks but never falls?"

"No."

He grinned disingenuously. "Night and day."

"She gave you that?"

He nodded. "Pretty smart. On the other hand, there are too many fingers in this pot already, and the case is less than a day old."

"The case is a year old," Jennifer said. "She met with him without your knowing? You're not watching the house?"

He hesitated. "Not yet. Like I said—"

"You left him alone overnight?" Jennifer felt her face flush with anger. *Easy, girl.*

Milton's eyes narrowed slightly.

"Who do you think we're dealing with here, a cub scout? Do you even know if Parson's still alive?"

"We are under no standing threat," Milton said. "There is no direct evidence that this is the Riddle Killer. Kevin insisted he was—"

"The victim's in no position to know what's best for himself." Jennifer unfolded her legs and stood. "As soon as I get back, I'd like to get a firsthand look at the evidence, if you don't mind, Nancy."

"Of course."

"Where are you going?" Milton asked.

"To see Parson. As far as we know, he's the only living victim of the Riddle Killer. Our first job is to keep him that way. I'd like to spend a few minutes with him before your people start tearing up his house. An associate of mine, Bill Galager, will be here shortly. Please treat him with the same graciousness you've extended to me."

|||

Jennifer left the station and sped for Kevin Parson's house, knowing that she had walked a thin line back in the conference room. Or maybe she was being too self-conscious about her cooperation because of the bureau chief's concerns. All things considered, except for the mistake of leaving the victim unguarded, Milton had handled the case well enough thus far. But one mistake and they would have another dead body on their hands. She wasn't in a position to accept that. Not this time.

Not after she'd led the Riddle Killer to Roy.

Why is that, Jenn? Kevin Parson is a victim, deserving life, liberty, and the pursuit of happiness like every other potential victim, but no more. That was the objective view of her situation.

But, no matter what face she tried to put on the matter, the bureau chief had pegged her. She *had* lost just a bit of objectivity, hadn't she? Regardless of Kevin Parson's makeup, he was now special. Perhaps more special to Jennifer than any other person in any other case, save her brother. He could be a total fool with a habit of running down the 405 freeway naked, and that much wouldn't change.

Fact was, in some small way, Kevin Parson offered her a glimpse of redemption. If Roy had died because of her, maybe Kevin would live because of her.

Because of her. She had to *personally* save him, didn't she? An eye for an eye. A life for a life.

"God, let him be a decent man," she muttered.

Jennifer dismissed the thoughts with a sigh and pulled onto his street shortly after eight. Old track houses, mostly two-story, modest, decent starter homes. She glanced at the file Milton had given her. Kevin Parson lived in the blue house two doors up. She pulled to the curb, shut off the engine, and glanced around. Quiet neighborhood.

"Okay, Kevin, let's see what kind of man he's chosen this time."

She left the file and walked to the front door. A morning newspaper featuring a front-page spread of the car bombing sat on the porch. She picked it up and rang the doorbell.

The man who answered was tall with messy brown hair and deep blue eyes that held hers without wavering. A white T-shirt with a "Jamaica" logo over the pocket. Faded blue jeans. He smelled of aftershave, although he obviously hadn't shaved today. The rugged look worked on him. Didn't look like the kind of man who'd run down the freeway naked. More like a man she'd expect to find featured in *Cosmopolitan.* Especially with those eyes. Ouch.

"Kevin Parson?" She flipped open her wallet to show her badge. "I'm Agent Peters with the FBI. Could I have a few words with you?"

"Sure. Sure, come in." He ran his fingers through his hair. "Sam said you'd probably be coming this morning."

She handed him the paper and walked in. "Looks like you made the news. Sam? That's your friend from the attorney general's office?"

Travel posters covered the walls. Odd.

"Actually, I think she's with the California Bureau of Investigation. But she just started. You know her?" He dropped the paper out on the porch and closed the door.

"She called the police this morning and reported the bugs. Could I see them?"

"Sure. Right over here." He led her to the kitchen. Two soda cans sat on the counter—he'd had a drink last night, presumably with Sam. Otherwise the kitchen was spotless.

"Here." He indicated the sink and placed the two cans in a small recycling bin. Four small eavesdropping devices that resembled watch batteries, one infinity transmitter she'd obviously pulled off the phone, and a device that resembled a common electrical splitter all sat in the water.

"Did Sam wear gloves when she removed these?"

"Yes."

"Good girl. Not that we'll find anything. I doubt our friend's stupid enough to leave prints on his toys." She faced him. "Anything unusual happen in the last twelve hours? Any phone calls, anything out of place?"

His eyes twitched, barely. *You're going too fast, Jennifer. The poor guy's still in shock and you're giving him the nth degree. You need him as much as he needs you.*

She held up her hand and smiled. "Sorry. Listen to me, barging in here and interrogating you. Let's start over. You can call me Jennifer." She reached out her hand.

He searched her eyes, took her hand. Like a child trying to decide whether to trust a stranger. For a moment she felt drawn into his gaze, exposed. They held their grip long enough to make Jennifer feel awkward. There was an innocence about him, she thought. Maybe more. Naiveté.

"Actually, there *is* more."

She dropped his hand. "There is? More than you told the police?"

"He called me again."

"But you didn't call the police?"

"I couldn't. He told me that if I called the police, he'd do something. Carry out his next threat prematurely." He looked around nervously, breaking eye contact for the first time. "I'm sorry, I'm a bit on edge. I didn't sleep that well. Do you want to sit down?"

"That would be nice."

Kevin pulled out a chair and seated her. Naive and chivalrous. A first-year seminary student who graduated from college with honors. Not exactly the kind of guy who wakes up in the morning thinking of ways to make enemies. He sat across from her and ran a hand haphazardly through his hair.

"When did he call you?"

"After I got home last night. He knows when I'm here; he knows when I'm gone. He can hear everything I say. He's probably listening to us right now."

"He may very well be. There'll be a team here in less than an hour. Until then there's not much we can do about surveillance. What we can do is try to get into this man's head. That's what I do, Kevin; I figure people out for a living. But to do that I need you to tell me everything he said to you. You're my link to him. Until we put this guy away, you and I are going to have to work very closely. No secrets. I don't care what he says you can or can't do—I need to hear it all."

"He said I couldn't tell the police anything. He also told me the FBI would be involved, but he didn't seem bothered by that. He doesn't want the city to come unglued every time he calls me."

She nearly broke her professional facade then. The killer expected the FBI. Did he expect Jennifer? It really had started again, hadn't it? He knew that she would come after him again—even welcomed it! The faint taste of copper washed through her mouth. She swallowed.

Kevin tapped his foot and stared at her without breaking eye contact. His gaze was neither piercing nor intimidating. Disarming perhaps, but not in a way that made her uncomfortable—his eyes held a quality she couldn't quite put a finger on. Maybe innocence. Wide, blue, tired innocence.

Not so different from Roy, really. Was there a connection?

You're staring back, Jennifer. Suddenly she was uncomfortable. She felt a strange empathy for him. How could any sane man threaten someone as innocent as this? Answer: *No* sane man.

I'm going to keep you alive, Kevin Parson. I won't let him hurt you.

"One step at a time," Jennifer said. "I want you to start from the phone call after you got home and tell me exactly what he said."

He relayed the phone call in meticulous detail while she asked questions and took notes. She covered every conceivable angle—the choice of words, the sequencing of events, the tone Slater used, the nearly unlimited ways in which Slater might have had access to his life.

"So you think he's been in here on more than one occasion. On one of those occasions he found Samantha's number. He thinks you and Samantha are romantically involved, but you're not."

"That's right."

"Have you ever been?"

"No, not really." Kevin shifted in his seat. "Although I'm not sure that wasn't a mistake on my part."

Obviously Slater had decided that Kevin and Samantha were more than friends. Who was mistaken, Slater or Kevin? She eyed the man before her. How naive was he?

"You should talk to her," Kevin said. "Maybe she could help somehow. She's not a cop."

"Sure." Jennifer dismissed the suggestion even as she spoke. She had no interest in consulting some rookie at this stage. All she needed was one more gunslinger on the case. "How long have you known her?"

"We grew up together here in Long Beach."

She made a note and changed the subject. "So actually Slater called you three times yesterday. Once on your cell phone, once at home here, and once on a cell phone he left for you? The third call just to make sure the phone worked."

"I guess. Yes, three times."

"We have three minutes, three calls, three rules, a riddle with three parts, three months. You think our guy likes threes?"

"Three months?"

She had to tell him. "You ever hear about the Riddle Killer?"

"The guy from Sacramento."

"Yes. We have reason to believe this is him. He killed his last victim three months ago."

"I heard that on the news." Kevin closed his eyes. "You really think it's him?"

"Yes, I do. But he's never let anyone live that we know of. I'm not trying to be crass—there's just no other way to deal with this. We have a chance, an excellent chance, of stopping him before he goes further."

He opened his eyes. "How?"

"He wants to play. It's not the killing that drives him; it's the game. We play."

"Play?" He stared at her desperately and then lowered his head. She wanted to put an arm around him, to comfort him, to hold this poor soul and tell him that everything was going to be okay. But that would be both untrue and unprofessional.

"You ever play chess?"

"A game or two."

"Think of this as a chess match. He's black and you're white. He's made his first move and you've made yours. You lost a pawn. As long as he's interested in the game, he'll play. Your job is to keep him playing long enough for us to find him. It's the only way to beat him."

Kevin ran both hands through his hair. "And what if he's listening right now?"

"We always assume he's listening. He's undoubtedly got the technology to hear what he wants to hear. But for him to hear what I just told you is music to his ears. He's back in some hole right now, rubbing his hands in anticipation of the game. The longer the better. He might not be sane, but he's brilliant. Probably a genius. He'll never toss a match and run scared just because some two-bit FBI agent's on to him."

I hope you are listening, you snake. She clenched her jaw.

Kevin offered an anemic smile. Apparently he understood, but he wasn't in a place to like anything about Slater's game. "The threes could be coincidental," he said. "Maybe."

"Nothing is coincidental with this guy. His mind works on a whole different plane than most. Can I see the cell phone he gave you?"

He pulled it out of his pocket and handed it to her. She flipped it open and scrolled through the activity log. One call at 4:50 yesterday afternoon, as reported.

"Okay, keep this with you. Don't give it to the police, and don't tell them I told you not to give it to them."

That earned her a soft grin, and she couldn't resist returning it. They'd take a crack at tracking Slater's number and triangulating his position, but she wasn't optimistic. There were too many ways to beat the system.

"We'll bug the phone—"

"He said no cops."

"I mean we, the FBI. We'll use a local device that will attach to the cell. I doubt a conventional listening device will do us any good—too easy to scramble and limited on range. The recording device will be noticeable, a small box we'll fix to the back here." She drew her finger through an inch square on the back of the silver phone. "It'll contain a small chip we can remove for analysis later. Not exactly real-time surveillance, but it may be all that we get next time."

He took the phone back. "So I do what he says? Play his game?"

She nodded. "I don't think we have a choice. We'll take him at his word. He calls you; the second you hang up, you call me. He'll probably know about it, and then I guess we'll know what he means by no cops."

Kevin stood and paced to the kitchen counter and back. "Detective Milton grilled me on motivation. Without motivation you have nothing. I can understand that. I think I have an idea."

"Go ahead."

"Hate."

"Hate. That's pretty broad."

"Slater hates me. I can hear it in his voice. Raw contempt. There are few things left in this world that are pure, from my observation. The hate in this man's voice is one of them."

She looked up at him. "You're observant. The question is why. Why does Slater hate you?"

"Maybe not me, but my type," Kevin said. "People tend to react to other people in wholesale rather than detail, right? He's a minister, so I hate him. She's beautiful, so I like her. One month later you wake up and realize you have nothing in common with the woman."

"Do you have firsthand experience on the subject or are you just spinning this from a sociology text?"

Kevin blinked, caught off guard. Unless her intuition was misfiring, he had very little experience with women.

"Well . . ." He ran his hand over his head. "Both, sorta."

"This may qualify as new knowledge, Kevin, but there are men who judge a woman by more than her appearance." She wasn't sure why she felt obligated to say as much; she'd found no offense in his remark.

He didn't bat an eye. "Of course. I see you and you're beautiful, but my attraction to you is based on your caring. I can tell that you really do care about me." He broke eye contact again. "I mean, not in the way it sounds. As your case is what I mean. Not as a man—"

"I understand. Thank you. That was a nice thing to say."

The short exchange felt absurd. Kevin sat back down and for a moment neither spoke.

"But your point is valid," Jennifer said. "Most serial offenders choose victims based on what they represent, not on personal offenses. It's the meticulous thought that Slater has put into this case that makes me wonder if we aren't dealing with personal motivation here. Obsession comes to mind. He's taken a very personal interest in you."

Kevin looked away. "Could be that he's just a very meticulous person." He seemed particularly interested in depersonalizing the motive.

"You're a profiler—what is my profile?" Kevin asked. "Based on what you know, what is there about me that might set off someone?"

"I don't have enough to offer—"

"No, but based on what you do know?"

"My first blush? Okay. You're a seminary student. You take life seriously and have a higher intelligence than most. You're caring and kind and gentle. You live alone and have very few friends. You're attractive and carry yourself with confidence, notwithstanding a couple nervous habits." It occurred to Jennifer as she ran down the list that Kevin was an unusually good person, not merely innocent. "But it's your genuine innocence that stands out. If Slater has no personal stake in you, he hates you for your innocence."

There was more to Kevin than she could see at first glance, much more. How could anyone dislike, much less hate, Kevin Parson?

"You remind me of my brother," she said. Then she wished she hadn't.

What if the Riddle Killer wanted Jennifer to see the similarities between Roy and Kevin? What if he'd chosen Kevin because he intended to make Jennifer live through the hell once again?

Pure speculation.

Jennifer rose. "I have to get back to the lab. The police will be here shortly. If there's anything you need, or if you think of anything else, call. I'll have one of our men watch the house. Promise me you will never leave alone. This guy likes to drop his little bombs when they're least expected."

"Sure."

He looked lost. "Don't worry, Kevin. We'll make it through this."

"In one piece, hopefully." He grinned nervously.

She put her hand on top of his. "We will. Trust me." She once said those same words to Roy to calm him down. Jennifer removed her hand.

They stared at each other for a moment. *Say something, Jennifer.* "Remember, he wants a game. We're going to give him a game."

"Right."

Jennifer left him standing in his doorway looking anything but confident. *Trust me.* She considered staying until the techs arrived, but she had to get back to the evidence. She'd cornered the Riddle Killer once, before he'd gone after Roy, and she'd done it through careful analysis of the evidence. She did her best work when climbing around in criminals' minds, not holding their victims' hands.

On the other hand, Kevin was no ordinary victim.

Who are you, Kevin? Whoever he was, she decided that she liked him.

9

KEVIN HAD NEVER FELT entirely comfortable around women—because of his mother, Sam insisted—but Jennifer seemed different. As a professional it was her job to engender trust, he knew, but he'd seen more than the expected professional facade in her eyes. He'd seen a real woman who'd warmed to him beyond the demands of her job. He wasn't sure how that translated to her capability as an investigator, but he felt certain he could trust her sincerity.

Unfortunately, it did nothing for his confidence.

Kevin walked to the telephone and dialed Samantha's number. She answered on the fifth ring.

"Sam."

"Hi, Sam. The FBI was just here."

"And?"

"Nothing new, really. She thinks it's the Riddle Killer."

"She?"

"The agent. Jennifer Peters."

"I've heard of her. Listen, there's a chance I may need to fly back to Sacramento today. Actually, I have my office on the other line. Can I call you right back?"

"Everything okay?"

"Give me a few minutes and I'll explain, okay?"

He hung up and glanced at the clock. 8:47. Where were the

police? He checked the dishwasher. Half full. He dumped in some detergent and turned it on. It would take him a week to fill the thing up, and by that time it would begin to smell sour.

Slater would have his hands full; that much was good. Surely between Sam, Jennifer, and the Long Beach police he would be safe. Kevin crossed to the refrigerator.

Jennifer thinks I'm nice. I don't care if I'm nice—I want to be alive. And I wouldn't mind if Slater were dead. How nice is that? If a man gossips, is he not nice? The bishop gossips, so he's not nice. Kevin sighed. *Here I am rambling again while the world's blowing up around me.* What would the psychobabblist say about that?

I don't know why I do it, Doctor, but I think the strangest things at the oddest times.

So do all men, Kevin. So do all men. Women don't, of course. The female tends to be the more intelligent or at least the more stable of the sexes. Turn the country over to them and you'll wake up to find the potholes down your street filled in like they should have been a year ago. You're just a man finding his way in a mad world gone madder, madder hatter. We'll break that down next session if you drop another check in the pay box over there. Two hundred this time. My kids need . . .

Kevin twitched. He didn't remember opening the fridge, but now, standing in front of the open door, the milk jug filled his vision. Someone had scrawled a large 3 on the Albertsons jug with a black magic marker, and above it three words:

It's so dark

Slater!

Kevin released the door and stepped back.

When? What's so dark? The *fridge* is so dark? Was this another riddle? He had to tell Jennifer! No, Samantha. He had to tell Sam!

Dread crept into his bones. Where is it so dark? In the cellar. The boy! He stood still, unable to breathe. The world began to spin. *It's so dark.*

Dear God, it *was* the boy!

The door closed on its own. He backed to the wall. But Slater had said he wasn't the boy! *What boy?* he'd said.

The events of that night so long ago swept over him.

|||

For a whole week after young Kevin's encounter with the bully, he waited in agony. Dark circles gathered under his eyes and he caught a cold. He made up a story about falling out of bed to explain the bruises on his face. His mother had put him to bed early in the afternoon to fight the cold. He just lay there, sweating on the sheets. His fear wasn't for himself, but for Samantha. The boy had promised to hurt her, and Kevin was sick with worry.

Six days later a tap had finally sounded on his window. He'd eased the blind up, holding his breath. Sam's smiling face stared at him from the backyard. Kevin nearly hit the ceiling in his excitement. As it turned out, Sam had been away at camp. She was horrified by his haggard features, and only after much urging did she convince him to come out to talk. No one would see them; she swore it. He made her search for the boy all around the yard, just to make sure. When he did sneak out, he went only just beyond his own fence, keeping a watchful eye on the greenway. They sat there, hidden in the shadows, and he told Sam everything.

"I'll tell my dad," she said. "You think if he licked my window we'll still be able to see it?"

Kevin shuddered. "Probably. You have to tell your dad. You should go tell him right now. But don't tell him about me sneaking out to see you. Just tell him I was walking by and saw the boy at your window and he chased me. Don't even tell him that he . . . did anything to me. Your dad might tell my mom."

"Okay."

"Then come back and tell me what he says."

"You mean tonight?"

"Right now. Go home by the street and watch out for the boy. He's going to kill us."

By now Sam was scared, despite her typical optimism. "Okay." She stood and brushed off her shorts. "My dad might not let me back out. In fact, he might even make me stay home for a while if I tell him."

Kevin thought about that. "That's okay. At least you'll be safe; that's the main thing. But please, come back as soon as you can."

"Okay." She held out her hand and pulled him up. "Friends for life?"

"Friends for life," he said. He gave her a hug and she ran off toward the street.

Sam didn't come back to his window that night. Or the next. Or for three weeks. They were the loneliest weeks of Kevin's life. He tried to convince his mom to let him out, but she wouldn't hear of it. He tried to sneak out during the day twice, not through the window, of course—he could never risk Mother discovering the screw or the loose board. He went over the back fence, but only got as far as the first tree on the greenway before Bob began to wail. He barely made it back onto the ash heap before Mother hurried out in a tizzy. The other time he went through the front door and made it all the way to Sam's house only to find, as he had known he would, that she was gone to school. His mom was waiting for him when he tried to sneak back in, and he spent the next two days in his room.

Then, on the twenty-second day, the tap came at his window. He peeked very carefully, terrified that it might be the boy. He would never be able to describe the warmth that flooded his heart when he saw Sam's face in the moonlight. He fumbled with the screw and yanked the window open. They threw their arms around each other before he tumbled out and ran with her through the fence.

"What happened?" he asked, breathless.

"My dad found him! He's a thirteen-year-old who lives on the other side of the warehouses. I guess the boy has caused trouble before; Dad knew him when I described him. Oh, you should have seen my dad, Kevin! I've never seen him so angry. He told the boy's parents that they had two weeks to move, or he was going to haul their boy off to jail. Guess what? They moved!"

"He's . . . he's gone?"

"Gone." She raised a palm and he absently high-fived it.

"You sure?"

"My dad let me out, didn't he? Yes, I'm sure. Come on!"

It took Kevin only two outings with Sam to lose his fear of the night again. The boy was indeed gone.

Two weeks later Kevin decided that it was about time he take the initiative to visit Sam. You could only play white knight so many times without actually flexing your muscle some.

Kevin snuck along the treelined greenway toward Sam's house, picking his way carefully. This was his first time out alone in over a month. He made it to her fence easily enough. The light from her window was a welcome sight. He bent down and pulled the loose picket aside.

"Pssst."

Kevin froze.

"Hello, squat."

The horrible sound of the boy's voice filled Kevin with images of a sick twisted smile. He suddenly felt nauseated.

"Stand up," the boy said.

Kevin stood slowly and pivoted. His muscles had turned to water, all except for his heart, which was slamming into his throat. There, ten feet away, stood the boy, grinning wickedly, turning the knife in his right hand. He wore a bandanna that covered his tattoo.

"I've decided something," the boy said. "There are three of us on this little totem pole here. But I'm at the bottom and I don't like that. I'm going to take out the top two. What do you think about that?"

Kevin couldn't think clearly about anything.

"I'll tell you what I'm going to do," the boy said. "First I'm going to cut you in a few places you'll never forget. I want you to use your imagination for me. Then I'm going to come back here and tap on Samantha's window like you do. When she opens the shade, I'm going to stick my knife right through the glass."

The boy chewed on his tongue; his eyes flashed with excitement. He lifted the knife and touched the blade with his left hand. He glanced down and fixated on the sharp edge. "I'll be through the glass and in her throat before she can . . ."

Kevin ran then, while the boy's eyes were still diverted.

"Hey!"

The boy took after him. Kevin had a twenty-foot head start—a fifth of what he needed to outrun the larger boy. At first sheer adrenaline pushed Kevin forward. But behind him the boy began to chuckle and his voice grew closer. Now terror pounded Kevin in unrelenting waves. He screamed, but nothing came out because his throat had frozen shut. The ground seemed to slope upward and then sideways and Kevin lost his sense of direction.

A hand touched his collar. If the boy caught him, he would use the knife. And then he would go after Sam. He might not kill her, but he would at least cut her face. Probably worse.

He wasn't sure where his house was, but it wasn't where he desperately needed it to be. So Kevin did the only thing he knew to do. He turned to his left and tore across the street.

The chuckling stopped for a moment. The boy grunted and doubled his efforts—Kevin could hear his feet pounding with a new determination.

The chuckling started again.

Kevin's chest ached and his breath came in huge gasps now. For a terrible moment he considered just falling down and letting the boy cut him up.

A hand swatted him on the head. "Keep running, squat. I hate it when they just lie there."

Kevin had lost his sense of direction completely. They were coming up to one of the old warehouses in the district across the street. He saw a door in the building directly ahead. Maybe . . . maybe if he could get through that door.

He veered to his right, and then broke for the building. He slammed into the old door, yanked it open, and plunged into the darkness beyond.

The stairwell five feet inside the door saved his life, or at the very least some of his body parts. He tumbled down the stairs, crying out in pain. When he came to rest at the bottom landing, his head felt as though it had come off. He struggled to his feet and turned back to the stairs.

The boy stood at the top, backlit by the moonlight, chuckling. "The end," he said and started down the steps.

Kevin spun and ran. Right into another door. A steel door. He grasped the handle and twisted, but the bulk refused to budge. He saw the deadbolt, threw it open, and plunged headlong into a pitch-black room. He stumbled forward and smacked into a concrete wall.

The boy grabbed Kevin's hair.

Kevin screamed. His voice echoed crazily about him. He screamed louder. No one would hear them; they were underground.

"Shut up! Shut up!" The boy hit him in the mouth.

Kevin summoned all of his fear and struck out blindly into the darkness. His fist connected with something that cracked. The boy hollered and let go of Kevin's hair. Kevin's legs gave way and he collapsed.

It occurred to him in that moment that whatever the boy had initially planned for him could no longer compare to what he would do now.

Kevin rolled and staggered to his feet. The door was to his right, dull gray in the faint light. The boy faced him, one hand on his nose, the other tight around the knife.

"You just lost your eyes, boy."

Kevin bolted without thought. He sprang through the open door, spun around, and slammed it shut. He threw his left hand up and rammed the deadbolt home.

Then it was just him, in the concrete staircase, breathing hard. Silence swallowed him.

A very soft yell reached beyond the steel door. Kevin held his breath and backed up slowly. He lunged up the steps, got halfway up before the sound of the boy reached him again, just barely. He was yelling and cursing and threatening him with words Kevin could barely understand because they were so quiet.

There was no way out, was there? If he left, the boy might die in there! No one would hear his screams. He couldn't leave.

Kevin turned back and slowly descended the stairs. What if he slipped the bolt open and made a break for it? He could make it, maybe.

"I swear I'm gonna kill you . . ."

Kevin knew then that he had only two options. Open the door and get cut, maybe die. Run away and let the boy die, maybe live.

"I hate you! I hate you!" The scream was eerily distant, but raspy and bitter.

Kevin whirled around and flew up the steps. He had no choice. He had no choice. For Samantha, that's what the boy got. It was his own fault anyway.

Kevin shut the outer door behind him and ran into the night. He didn't know quite how or exactly when, but sometime while it was still dark, he made it back into his bed.

|||

Something rattled violently. Kevin jerked up. The tabletop reflected the morning sun at eye level. The cell phone vibrated slowly toward the edge.

Kevin scrambled to his feet. *Dear God, give me strength.* He glanced at the clock. 9:00 A.M. Where were the police?

He reached his hand for the phone, hesitated, and then snatched it off the table. Play the game, Jennifer had said. *Play the game.*

"Hello?"

"How is our chess player doing this morning?" Slater asked.

So he *had* been listening! Kevin closed his eyes and focused his mind. His life depended on what he said. Be smart. Outthink him.

"Ready to play," he said, but his voice didn't sound ready.

"You'll have to do better than that. Kevin, Kevin, Kevin. Two little challenges, two little failures, two little booms. You're beginning to bore me. Did you see my little gift?"

"Yes."

"What's three times three?"

Three times three. "Nine," he said.

"Smart boy. Nine o'clock, time to rock. Time for the third. *What takes you there but takes you nowhere?* You have sixty minutes. It'll be worse this time, Kevin."

The phone on the counter rang shrilly. He had to keep Slater on the phone.

"Can I ask a question?" he asked.

"No. But you may answer the room phone. Maybe it will be Sam. Wouldn't that be cozy? Answer the phone."

Kevin slowly lifted the room phone off the hook.

"Kevin?" Sam's familiar voice filled his ear, and despite the impossible situation, he felt a bucket of relief wash over him. He wasn't sure what to say. He held the cell phone against his right ear and the room phone against his other ear.

"Tell her hello from Slater," Slater said.

Kevin hesitated. "Slater says hello," he said.

"He called?" she asked.

"He's on the other line."

"Too bad Jennifer left so early," Slater said. "The four of us could throw a little party. Time's running out. Fifty-nine minutes and fifty-one seconds. Your move." The cell phone clicked.

Sam spoke again. "Kevin, listen to me! Is he still on—"

"He's gone."

"Don't move. I'm turning up your street now. I'll be there in ten seconds." She disconnected.

Kevin stood, immobile, a phone in each hand. Play the game. Play the game. It was the boy; it had to be the boy.

The door flew open. "Kevin?" Sam ran in.

He spun. "I have sixty minutes."

"Or what?"

"Another bomb?"

She stepped up to him and cradled her hands under his wrists. "Okay. Listen to me, we have to think this through clearly." She eased the phones out of his hands and then took him by the shoulders. "Listen to me—"

"We have to call the FBI."

"We will. But I want you to tell me first. Tell me exactly what he said."

"I know who the Riddle Killer is."

She stared, stunned. "Who?"

Kevin sat heavily in a chair. "The boy."

"I thought he told you he *wasn't* the boy."

Kevin's mind began to work faster. "He said, 'What boy?' He didn't say he *wasn't* the boy." He ran to the refrigerator, opened the door, pulled out the milk jug, and slammed it on the counter.

She stared at the thick-stroked letters. Her eyes shifted to him and then back. "When was—"

"He was in here last night."

"*It's so dark.* What's so dark?"

Kevin paced and rubbed his head.

"Tell me, Kevin. Just tell me. We're running out of time here."

"Your dad made the boy leave, but he came back."

"What do you mean? We never saw him again!"

"I did! He caught me on my way to your house two weeks later. He said he was going to hurt you. And me. I ran and somehow . . ." Emotions clogged his head. He glanced at the clock. 9:02. "Somehow we ended up in a storage basement in one of the warehouses. I don't even remember which one anymore. I locked him in and ran away."

She blinked. "What happened?"

"I had to do it, Sam!" He spoke desperately now. "He was going to kill you! And me!"

"It's okay. It's okay, Kevin. We can talk about it later, okay? Right now—"

"That's the sin he wants me to confess. I left him to die in the dark."

"But he *didn't* die, did he? Obviously he's alive. You didn't kill anyone."

He paused. Of course! The dark night flashed through his mind. Unless Slater wasn't the boy, but someone who knew about the incident, a psychopath who'd discovered the truth somehow and had decided that Kevin should pay.

"Either way, I locked a boy in a basement and left him to die. That's intent. That's as good as murder."

"You don't know that this has anything to do with the boy. We have to think this through, Kevin."

"We don't have time to think this through! It's the only thing that makes any sense. If I confess, this crazy game stops." He paced and rubbed his head, suppressing a sudden urge to cry over the thought of actually confessing after all that he'd done to rid himself of his past. "Oh God, what have I done? This can't be happening. Not after everything else."

She stared at him, digesting the new information, her eyes wrinkled with empathy. "So then confess, Kevin. That was almost twenty years ago."

"Come on, Sam!" He whirled to her, angry. "This will blow sky-high. Every American who watches the news will know about the seminary student who buried another kid alive and left him to die. This will ruin me!"

"Better ruined than dead. Besides, you had reason to lock up the boy. I'll come to your defense."

"None of that matters. If I am capable of attempted murder, I am capable of anything. That's the reputation that will follow me." He gritted his teeth. "This is nuts. We're running out of time. I have to call the newspaper and tell them. It's the only way to stop that maniac before he kills me."

"Maybe, but he's also demanding that you solve the riddle. We may be dealing with the same killer from Sacramento—"

"I know. Jennifer told me. Still, the only way to stop him is to confess. The riddle is supposed to tell me what to confess." Kevin headed for the phone. He had to call the newspaper. Slater was listening—he'd know. This was insane.

"What was the riddle?"

He stopped. "*What takes you there but takes you nowhere?* He said it would be worse this time."

"How does *that* tie in to the boy?" she asked.

The question hadn't occurred to him. *What takes you there but takes you nowhere?* "I don't know." What if Sam was right? What if his confession about the boy wasn't what Slater was looking for?

"What connection is there between the boy and the three riddles he's given?" She grabbed a piece of paper. "Sixty minutes. Yesterday it was three minutes and then thirty minutes. Today it's sixty minutes. What time did he call?"

"Nine o'clock. Three times three. That's what he said."

Her eyes studied the riddles she'd jotted down.

"Call Agent Peters. Tell her about Slater's call and the confession. Ask her to call the newspaper and tell her to get over here as fast as she can. We have to crack these riddles."

Kevin punched in the number Jennifer had left him. The clock read 9:07. They still had fifty-three minutes. Jennifer picked up.

"He called," Kevin said.

Silence.

"He called—"

"Another riddle?"

"Yes. But I think I might know who he is and what he wants."

"Tell me!"

Kevin told her the rest in a halting run-on that ate up several minutes. An urgency he hadn't expected crowded her voice. She was impatient and demanding. But her intensity reassured him.

"So you think you know who he is, and you neglect to tell me about his demand that you confess. What are you trying to do to me? This is a killer we're dealing with!"

"I'm sorry, I was scared. I'm telling you now."

"Any other secrets?"

"No. Please, I'm sorry."

"Samantha's there?"

"Yes. You have to get this confession out," Kevin said. "That's what this is about."

"We don't know that. I don't see the relationship between the riddles and the boy."

"He was here, last night, and he wrote on my milk jug," Kevin said. "It has to be him! You wanted motivation; now you have it. I tried to kill someone. He's mad. How's that? You have to get this confession on the air."

Silence stretched on the line.

"Jennifer?"

"We need more time!" she said and then took a breath. "Okay, I'll put the confession on the wire. Stay put. Do not set foot outside that house, you hear me? Work the riddles."

"Sam—"

But Jennifer had hung up. Now there was a no-nonsense girl. He found comfort in the fact.

Kevin hung up. 9:13. "She'll call the paper."

"Three," Samantha said. "Our guy's tripping over his threes. Progressions. Three, thirty, sixty. And opposites. Night and day, life and death. *What takes you there but takes you nowhere?*" She stared at her page of notes and numbers.

"She wasn't exactly thrilled about you being here," Kevin said.

Sam looked up. "What takes you there? The obvious answer is transportation. Like a car. But he did a car. He won't do a car again. He's into progressions. More."

Kevin's mind spun. "A bus. Train. Plane. But they take you somewhere, don't they?"

"Depends on where somewhere is. I don't think it matters—*there* and *nowhere* are opposites. I think he's going to blow up some kind of public transport!"

"Unless the confession—"

"We can't assume that'll stop him." She jumped to her feet, grabbed the phone from its cradle, and punched the redial.

"Agent Peters? Sam Sheer here. Listen, I think—" She paused and listened. "Yes, I do understand jurisdiction, and as far as I'm concerned, Kevin has always been *my* jurisdiction. If you want to press the matter, I'll get authorization from the attorney gen—" Another pause, and Sam was smiling now. "My thoughts exactly. But how long will it take to evacuate all public transportation in Long Beach?" She glanced at her watch. "By my watch we have forty-two minutes." Sam listened for a while. "Thank you."

She hung up. "Sharp gal. Feisty. The news already has your story. It's going out live on television as we speak."

Kevin ran to his television and flipped it on.

"The next edition of the paper won't hit the street until tomorrow morning," Sam said. "Slater didn't mention the paper this time, did he?"

"No. I'm sure television will work. God help me."

Empathy lit Sam's gentle eyes. "Jennifer doesn't think this will satisfy him. The real game's the riddle. I think she's right." She paced and put both palms on her head. "Think, Sam, think!"

"They're evacuating the public—"

"There's no way they can get them all out in time," Sam said. "It'll take them half an hour just to get the clearances! There's more here. Slater's precise. He's given us more."

The program on the television suddenly changed. The familiar face of Tom Schilling, news anchor for the ABC affiliate, filled the screen. A red "Breaking News" banner scrolled across the picture tube.

The graphic behind Tom Schilling was a shot of Kevin's charred car with the words "Riddle Killer?" superimposed in a choppy font. The anchor glanced off-camera to his right and then faced the audience.

Kevin stared, spellbound. Tom Schilling was about to drop the hammer on his life. Goose bumps rippled up his neck. Maybe confessing *had* been a mistake.

"We have a shocking new development in the case of the car explosion on Long Beach Boulevard yesterday. Kevin Parson, the driver of the car, has come forward with new information that may shed light on the investigation."

When Kevin heard his name, the room faded, the picture blurred, and the words grew garbled, as if spoken underwater. His life was over. Tom Schilling droned on.

"Kevin Parson is a seminary student at . . ."

You're dead.

" . . . the hopeful clergyman has confessed . . ."

This is it.

" . . . locked the boy in an underground . . ."

Your life is over.

He thought it odd that this exposure brought on a sense of impending death even more acutely than Slater's threats had. He'd spent five years pulling himself out of Baker Street's sea of despondency, and now, in the space of less than twenty-four hours, he found himself overboard, drowning again. Someone would start digging into the rest of his childhood. Into the truth behind Balinda and the house.

Here am I. Kevin Parson, a shell of a man who is capable of the most wicked sin conceived of by man. Here am I, a wretched pretender. I am nothing more than a slug, role-playing its way through life in human form. When you learn everything, you will know that and more.

Thank you. Thank you, Aunt Balinda, for sharing this with me. I am nothing. Thank you, you lousy, sick, twisted auntie for slamming this nugget of truth down my throat. I am nothing, nothing, nothing. Thank you, you demon from hell for gouging out my eyes and pounding me into the ground and . . .

"—vin? Kevin!"

Kevin turned. Sam sat at the table, remote in hand, staring at him. The television was off. It occurred to him that he was trembling. He exhaled and relaxed his balled hands, ran them through his hair. *Get a grip, Kevin. Hold yourself together.*

But he didn't want to hold himself together. He wanted to cry.

"What?"

"I'm sorry, Kevin. It's not as bad as it sounds. I'll get you through this, I promise."

It's not as bad as it sounds because you don't know the whole story, Sam. You don't know what really happened in that house on Baker Street. He turned away from her. *God, help me. Please help me.*

"I'll be okay," he said and cleared his throat. "We have to focus on the riddle."

A stray thought whispered to Kevin.

"It's the numbers," Sam said. "Public transportation is numbered. Slater's going to blow a bus or a train identified with the number three."

The thought raised its voice. "He said no cops!"

"What—"

"No cops!" Kevin shouted. "They're using cops to evacuate?"

The fear he felt spread through her eyes. "Dear God!"

III

"I don't care if they have to delay every flight in the country!" Jennifer said. "We have a credible bomb threat here, sir! Get the governor on the line if you have to. Terrorist or not, this guy's going to blow something."

"Thirty-five minutes—"

"Is enough time to start."

The bureau chief hesitated.

"Look, Frank," Jennifer said, "you have to put your neck on the line with me here. The local police don't have the muscle to push this through fast enough. Milton's working on the buses, but the bureaucracy's thicker than molasses down here. I need this from the top."

"You're sure about this?"

"Meaning what? That I'm jumping the gun? We can't afford to risk—"

"Okay. But if this turns out to be a hoax . . ."

"It won't be the first."

She hung up and took a deep breath. It had already occurred to her that they'd violated one of Slater's rules. No cops. But she saw no alternatives. She needed the local police.

A junior detective, Randal Crenshaw, burst through the door. "Milton says they're tracking down the director of local transport now. He should have an answer in ten minutes."

"How long will it take them to clear the buses once they have the word?"

"Dispatch can move pretty quick." He shrugged. "Maybe ten minutes."

She stood and paced the length of the conference table. They now had the first significant lead in the case. The boy. If indeed it was this boy. He'd be how old now? Early thirties? More importantly, someone other than Kevin knew the killer: Samantha Sheer's father, a policeman named Rick Sheer, who'd caught the boy spying.

"I want you to track down a cop who worked Long Beach about twenty years ago," she told Crenshaw. "Name's Rick Sheer. Find him. I need to talk to him. Run a search on any of his logs that mention a boy who was threatening the children in his neighborhood."

The detective scribbled the name across a piece of paper and left.

She was missing something. Somewhere in the notes she'd taken this morning was the identity of the bus or the train or whatever Slater planned on blowing, if indeed they were right about the riddle referring to public transportation.

The target wasn't Kevin, and Jennifer found relief in the realization. For the moment it wasn't *his* life at risk. For now Slater was more interested in playing. Play the game, Kevin. Lead him on. She snatched up the phone and dialed his number.

He picked up on the fifth ring.

"Any thoughts?"

"Just going to call you. It could be a bus or something identified with a three," Kevin said.

That was it! Had to be. "Three. I'll have them put a priority on anything with a three in the identifier."

"How are they doing?"

"Looks good. We should know something in ten minutes."

"That's cutting it pretty close, isn't it?"

"It's the best they can do."

III

Sam snapped her cell phone closed and grabbed her purse. "That's it, let's go!" She ran for the door. "I'll drive."

Kevin ran after her. "How many?"

"Long Beach proper has twenty-five buses, each identified with several letters and a number. We want number twenty-three. It runs down Alamitos and then back up Atlantic. That's not far. With any luck we'll run into it."

"What about three or thirteen?"

"They started the numbering at five and skipped thirteen."

The tires on Sam's car squealed. She was certain Slater had a bus in mind. The planes were less likely targets for the simple reason that security was far tighter than it once had been. She had checked the trams—no threes. Trains were a possibility, but again, high security. It had to be a bus. The fact that there was only one with three in its designator offered at least a sliver of hope.

Twenty-nine minutes.

They flew across Willow toward Alamitos but were stopped by a red light at Walnut. Sam glanced both directions and sped through.

"Now is one time I wouldn't mind a cop on my tail," she said. "We could use their help."

"No cops," Kevin said.

She looked at him. Two more minutes passed before they hit Alamitos.

"You see a bus, it's probably number twenty-three. You yell."

But they passed no buses. They crossed Third Street through a red. Still no bus.

Ocean Boulevard, right; Atlantic, north. No bus. Horns honked at them on several occasions.

"Time?" she asked.

"Nine thirty-seven."

"Come on! Come on!"

Sam backtracked. When they hit Third again, the light was red and cars blocked the intersection. A bus numbered "6453–17" rumbled by, headed west on Third Street. Wrong bus. The car was stuffy. Sweat beaded their foreheads. The intersection cleared and Sam shoved the accelerator down. "Come on, baby. Where are you?"

She'd cleared the intersection by fifty feet when she slammed on the brakes.

"What?"

She jerked her head around and stared back toward Third Street. She frantically grabbed her cell phone, hit the redial button.

"Yes, could you tell me which bus runs down Third Street?"

Kevin heard the deep male voice from his seat. "The Third Street bus. You need—"

Sam slammed the phone shut, yanked the wheel around, and pulled directly into traffic. She pulled through a screaming U-turn, cutting off a white Volvo and a blue sedan. Horns blared.

"They call the buses by their street names, not their numbers!" Sam said.

"But you don't know if Slater—"

"We know where the Third Street bus is. Let's clear it first and then go for twenty-three." She squealed onto Third Street and honed in on the bus, not a hundred yards ahead. Obviously dispatch hadn't reached the driver yet.

Nineteen minutes.

Sam pulled directly in front of the bus and braked. The bus blasted its horn and ground to a halt behind them.

"Tell the driver to evacuate and stay clear for at least half an hour. Tell them to spread the word to the other cars on the street. Tell them there's a bomb—it works every time. I'm calling Agent Peters."

Kevin ran to the bus. He hammered on the door, but the driver, an older man who must have been three times his recommended weight, refused to open.

"There's a bomb on board!" he yelled, flinging his hands out like an explosion. "A bomb!" He wondered if any of them recognized him from the television. *The kid-killer is now downtown pulling old women off of buses.*

A young man who looked like Tom Hanks stuck his head out an open window. "A what?"

"A bomb! Get out! Clear the bus. Clear the street."

For a moment, nothing happened. Then the door hissed open, and the same young man stumbled out. He yelled back into the bus.

"Get them out, you idiot! He said there's a bomb on this bus!"

A dozen passengers—half by what Kevin could see—bolted from their seats. The driver seemed to catch the fever. "Okay, everyone out! Watch your step. Just a precaution, ladies and gentlemen. Don't shove!"

Kevin grabbed the Tom Hanks look-alike. "Clear this street and stay clear for at least thirty minutes, you hear? Get them all out of here!"

"What is it? How do you know?"

Kevin ran for Sam's car. "Trust me. Just get them clear. The police are on their way." The passengers didn't need any encouragement. Cars stopped and then sped past the bus or backed away.

He slid into the car.

"Hold on," Sam said. She sped off, took an immediate right on the next street, and headed back toward Atlantic.

"One down. Fifteen minutes left."

"This is nuts," Kevin said. "We don't even know if Slater's—"

The cell phone went berserk in his pocket. Kevin froze and stared at his right thigh.

"What?" Sam asked.

"He . . . he's calling."

The phone vibrated again and this time he grabbed it. Samantha slowed.

"Hello?"

"I said no cops, Kevin," Slater's soft voice said. "No cops means no cops."

Kevin's fingers began to shake. "You mean the FBI?"

"Policemen. From now on it's you and Sam and Jennifer and me and no one else."

End call.

Sam had slowed way down. She looked at him with wide eyes.

"What did he say?"

"He said no cops."

The ground suddenly shook. An explosion thundered. They both ducked.

"Turn around! Turn around!"

"That was the bus," Sam whispered. She spun the car around and sped back the way they'd come.

Kevin stared as they rolled onto Third. Boiling flames and thick black smoke engulfed the surreal scene. Three blackened cars parked next to the bus smoldered. God only knew if anyone was hurt, but the immediate area looked vacant. Books lay scattered among the shattered glass of a used bookstore's windows. Its "Read It Again" sign dangled over the sidewalk dangerously. The shop owner stumbled out, stunned.

Sam shoved the gearshift into park and stared at the unearthly scene.

Her cell phone screeched and Kevin started. She lifted it slowly. "Sheer."

She blinked and immediately refocused. "How long ago?" She looked at Kevin and then the bus. A siren wailed. A car Kevin immediately recognized as Jennifer's squealed around the corner and headed toward them.

"Can Rodriguez question him?" Sam asked into her phone. "I'm in a bit of a pinch here." She turned away and lowered her voice. "He just blew up a bus. I'm parked in a car, fifty feet away from it. Yes, I am pretty sure." She listened.

Jennifer roared up and stuck her head out of her car's window. "You okay?"

"Yeah," Kevin said. His fingers were numb and his mind dazed, but he was okay.

Samantha acknowledged Jennifer with a nod, turned to the side, and covered her exposed ear. "Yes, sir. Right away. I understand . . ." She glanced at her watch. "The ten-thirty flight?"

Kevin shoved his door open.

Jennifer stopped him. "No, stay put. Don't move, I'll be right back." She drove toward the bus.

Sam finished her conversation and closed the phone.

"Do you think anyone was hurt?" Kevin asked.

She looked at the bus and shook her head. "I don't know, but we were lucky to find it when we did."

Kevin groaned and ran both hands through his hair.

"I have to go," Sam said. "That was the call I thought I might get. They want me to question a witness. His attorney will have him out by midafternoon. Unfortunately, I can't miss this. I'll explain it when I get—"

"I can't believe Slater did this," Kevin said, staring around again. "He would have killed over twenty people if we hadn't stumbled onto this bus."

She shook her head. "This changes the game. Look, I'll be back on the first flight this evening, okay? I promise. But I have to leave now if I'm going to make the flight." She rubbed his shoulder and looked in Jennifer's direction. "Tell her I'll call and give her my take; she'll take care of you." Three marked police cars had arrived and surrounded the charred bus. "We'll make it, my dear knight. I swear we'll make it."

Kevin nodded. "This is insane."

10

WITHIN FIVE MINUTES OF THE EXPLOSION, a couple dozen law enforcement officials—mostly local police but including some from her own office and several from state agencies—isolated the crime scene and began the forensic investigation. They had quickly located the bomb. By all initial appearances it was the same as the bomb in Kevin's car, only larger.

Jennifer situated Kevin in a coffee shop four doors down from the bus with strict instructions not to move—she'd be back in twenty minutes.

The parameters of the investigation had just changed. Bill Galager from the Los Angeles office arrived, as well as two junior investigators, John Mathews and Brett Mickales. They would work the case from an evidence angle, freeing her to focus on the psychology of it. One conclusion required no degree in criminal psychology—when Slater said no cops, he meant absolutely no cops. And he had the means to know if cops were involved.

According to Kevin, Slater had mentioned her by name. Jennifer. The maniac was drawing her into another trap, wasn't he? By the looks of the bus, he'd graduated into a new class.

No cops. No CBI, except Samantha, who happened to be connected to Kevin by his childhood and the boy. No ATF. No sheriff or state police. Just FBI and, specifically, just Jennifer.

"Still eager to take him on?"

Jennifer turned to Milton, who'd walked up behind her. "Eager?"

A touch of defiance glimmered in his eyes, but he didn't elaborate.

"Why did he blow it early?"

"He said no cops. He obviously learned that your department had been informed—"

"They always say no cops. You're not a cop?"

"According to Kevin, he said FBI only."

Milton scoffed.

Jennifer frowned. "No cops. Evidently the history he has with us figures into his game. Bottom line is, he laid down a rule; we broke it; he blew the bus early."

"And what if he said no FBI? Would you back out? I don't think so. This is my city. You don't have the right to cut me out."

"I'm not cutting you out, Milton. Your men are all over the place."

"I'm not referring to mopping up. He's going to call again and the city knows that. They have a right to know."

"The city? You mean the press. No, Milton. The press has a right to know anything that might lend to the city's safety. You're looking at a bus this time; the next time it could be a building. You willing to risk that for the sake of protocol? If you'll excuse me, I have a case to attend to."

Milton's stare grew hot. "This is my city, not yours. I have a personal stake; you don't. Unfortunately, it seems that I'm powerless to do anything about your jurisdiction, but I was assured by your bureau chief that you would cooperate. Slater so much as coughs and you withhold it, I'll have your replacement here in five minutes."

Jennifer was tempted to slap his smug mug. She'd have to call Frank and explain. In the meantime, Milton was a thorn she would have to deal with.

"I don't like you either, Detective. You're too interested in your own good for my tastes, but I suppose that's personal. I'll keep you updated through Galager and I'll expect *your* cooperation in assisting us in any way you can. We're not stupid enough to refuse all the help we can get. But you will do nothing without my authorization. If Slater suspects your involvement, he may do 'your' city more harm than you're willing to take the heat for. Agreed?"

He eyed her carefully and then relaxed. *Didn't expect that, did you, Colombo?* She had no intention of keeping him materially involved, she realized, and the thought surprised her. In fact, in more ways than one, she welcomed Slater's restrictions. This was between her and Slater and Kevin, regardless of how personal Slater wanted to get.

"I want to put a full-court press on his house," Milton said. "Complete electronic surveillance, including wiretaps. You haven't ordered them?"

"Not wiretaps. Slater's not using the landline. The cell wizards have been monitoring the frequency on the cell phone he gave Kevin for the past forty minutes—I put in the request as soon as I left his house this morning. Slater called Kevin thirty minutes ago, just before he blew the bomb. Nothing even registered with our wizards. He's not dumb enough to talk without scrambling. This isn't your typical hack. I have an order in to fix a recording device, an AP301, to his phone ASAP, but we didn't have it on this call."

Milton glared. "I'll put someone on the house."

"No. No cops, or didn't you get that part?"

"For crying out loud, woman! You just chewed me out less than three hours ago for not having someone on him last night!"

"I'll put my own agents on the house. Keep your men clear. If you want to go head-to-head, I'll leak this to the press." She hesitated. "You get anything on the officer I asked about?"

Milton looked away and answered with some reluctance. "Officer Rick Sheer. He moved back to the San Francisco area ten years ago.

Died of cancer five years ago. There's no record that we can find of any incident involving the boy you mentioned. But that doesn't surprise me. Cops routinely deal with neighbors off the record. You say he threatened the boy's father—the incident obviously blew over. No official complaint, no arrest."

Jennifer's heart sank. That left Kevin. And Samantha. Hopefully one of them would recall something that might give them a clue to the boy's identity. All they currently had was Kevin's description, which was practically useless.

"Can you have them look again? What about a personal notebook or—"

"We wouldn't have anything like that."

"Cooperation, remember? Have them look again."

He nodded slowly. "I'll see what I can do."

"Thank you. I assume you've met Agent Galager. You'll be dealing primarily with him from here out."

"And you?"

"I'm going to do what I was trained to do, try to figure out who Slater is. Excuse me, Detective."

She walked past the bus, found Galager. "What do you have?"

"Same guy who did the car." Bill Galager was a redhead with too many freckles to count. He glanced at Nancy, who knelt over fragments of twisted metal at the flash point.

"She's good."

Jennifer nodded. "Work over the evidence in her lab with her and then send it on to Quantico for more testing. Bring this to Milton's attention, and please do your best to keep him off my back."

"Will do. What about any evidence they find at his house?"

A team had arrived at Kevin's house twenty minutes earlier and was scouring the place for anything Slater might have left. She doubted they would find anything. The victims' houses in Sacramento had yielded nothing. Slater might have no scruples, but he had plenty of discipline.

"Same. Let's do our own sweep as well. If you find anything, let me know. I'll be by your office in a couple hours."

He nodded. "You think it's him?"

"Until I find evidence that contradicts it."

"There are some differences. Could be a copy cat."

"Could be. But I don't think so."

"And I'm assuming Kevin matches the victim profile?"

Jennifer searched Galager's eyes. Bill was one of the only agents who'd known Roy well enough to call him a friend.

"He could be Roy in another life," she said. Then she turned toward the coffee shop.

At least five hundred onlookers had gathered behind the police lines now. The news crews were set up, sending live feed across the country. Both Fox News and CNN were undoubtedly running alerts. How many times had the American public seen pictures from Israel of twisted bus wreckage? But this was California. Here, you could count the incidents over the past ten years on one hand.

Milton was giving the vultures an update. Good for him.

11

JENNIFER'S VOICE JARRED KEVIN from his thoughts. "Hey, cowboy, you want a ride out of here?"

He looked up from the corner table and blinked. "Sure."

"Let's go."

She didn't take him home. Detectives were still searching the place for anything Slater might have left. It would take them a few hours.

"They're not going to dump my underwear drawers, are they?"

Jennifer laughed. "Not unless Slater left his shorts."

"Probably just as well I'm gone."

"You like things neat, don't you?"

"Clean, sure."

"That's good. A man should know how to do laundry."

"Where're we going?"

"You have the phone with you?"

He instinctively felt his pocket. Amazing how small phones could be. He pulled it out and flipped it open. It fit in his palm, open.

"Just checking," she said, turning onto Willow.

"You think he'll call again?" he asked.

"Yes, the confession wasn't what he was looking for."

"I guess not."

"But he does want a confession. You're sure about that, right?"

"That's what he said. When I confess, he goes away. But confess what?"

"That's the million-dollar question, isn't it? What does Slater want you to confess? You have no inkling whatsoever?"

"I just ruined my career and only God knows what else by telling the world that I tried to kill a boy—believe me, if I'd thought of any alternative to that confession, I'd have spilled my guts."

She nodded and frowned. "The demand for a confession's the only part of this puzzle that doesn't fit the Riddle Killer profile. Somehow he dug something up on you that he thinks is significant."

"Like what? How many sins have you committed, Agent Peters? Can you remember them all?"

"Please, call me Jennifer. No, I guess I can't."

"So what does Slater consider significant? You want me to go on television and list every sin I can ever remember committing?"

"No."

"The only thing that makes sense is the boy," Kevin said. "But then the confession should have gotten a response, right?"

"With Slater, yes. I think so. Unless, of course, he *is* the boy, but he wants you to confess something besides your attempt to kill him."

"It wasn't an attempt to kill him. It was more like self-defense. The kid was about to kill *me!*"

"I can accept that. Why did he want to kill you?"

The question took Kevin off guard. "He . . . he was after Samantha."

"Samantha. She just keeps cropping up, doesn't she?"

Jennifer looked out her window and for a few minutes the car remained silent.

|||

Kevin was only eleven when he trapped the boy in the cellar and nearly died of fear. He'd left the boy to die—no matter how badly he tried to tell himself otherwise, he knew he had locked the boy in a tomb.

He couldn't tell Sam, of course. If she knew, she would surely tell her father, who would set the boy free and maybe send him to jail, and then he would get out, probably within a couple months, and come back and kill Sam. He couldn't ever tell her.

But he couldn't *not* tell her either. She was his bosom buddy. She was his best, best friend, whom he loved more than he loved his mother. Maybe.

On the third night he meant to go in search of the warehouse, just to take a peek; just to see if it had really, really happened. But after an hour pacing outside his window, he climbed back into his house.

"You're different," Sam told him the next night. "You're not looking me in the eyes like you used to. You keep looking off at the trees. What's wrong?"

"I am not looking off. I'm just enjoying the night."

"Don't try to fool me. You think I don't have a woman's intuition? I'm almost a teenager, you know. I can tell if a boy's bothered."

"Well, I'm not bothered by anything except your insistence that I'm bothered," he said.

"So then you *are* bothered. See? But you were bothered before I said you were bothered, so I think you're not telling me something."

He felt suddenly angry. "I am not!" he said.

She looked at him for a few seconds and then gazed up into the trees herself. "You are bothered by something, but I can see that you're not telling me because you think it might hurt me. That's sweet, so I'm going to pretend you're not bothered." She took his arm.

She was giving him a way out. What kind of friend would ever do that? Sam would do that because she was the sweetest girl in the whole world, no exceptions.

It took Kevin four months of agony to finally work up the courage to go in search of the boy's fate.

Part of him wanted to find the boy's bones in a rotting pile. But most of him didn't want to find the boy at all, didn't want to confirm that the whole thing had really happened.

The first challenge was to find the right warehouse. Guarding a flashlight as closely as he could, he looked through the warehouses for an hour, sneaking from door to door. He began to wonder if he'd ever find it again. But then he opened an old wooden door and there, five feet away, was the dark stairway.

Kevin jerked back and very nearly ran for his life.

But it was only a stairway. What if the boy wasn't there anymore? He could see the latch on the steel door in the shadows below. Seemed safe enough. *You have to do this, Kevin. If you're anything like a knight or a man or even a boy who's already eleven, you have to at least find out if he's in there.*

Kevin played his light down the stairwell and forced his feet down the stairs, one step at a time.

No sound. Of course not—it had been four months. The steel door latch was still closed as if he'd thrown it closed yesterday. He stopped in front of the door and stared, unwilling to actually open it. Visions of pirates and dungeons full of skeletons clattered through his mind.

Behind him the moonlight glowed pale gray. He could always run up the stairs if a skeleton took after him, which was incredibly stupid anyway. What would Sam think of him now?

"Hello?" he called.

Nothing.

The sound of his voice helped. He walked forward and knocked. "Hello?" Still nothing.

Slowly, heart thumping in his ears, palms wet with sweat, Kevin eased the latch open. He pushed the door. It creaked open.

Black. Musty. Kevin held his breath and gave the door a shove.

He saw the splotches of blood immediately. But no body.

His bones shook from head to toe. It was real. That was blood all over the floor. Dried and darkened, but exactly where he remembered it should be. He pushed the door again, to make sure no one was behind it. He was alone.

Kevin stepped into the room. A bandanna lay in the corner. The boy's bandanna. He had definitely locked the boy in this cellar, and there was no way out that he could see. That meant one of two things had happened. Either the boy had died in here and someone had found him, or someone had found him before he'd died.

His mind ran through the possibilities. If he'd been found alive, it would have been in the first couple weeks. Which meant he'd been free for over three months and said nothing to the police. If he'd been found dead, of course, he couldn't say anything. Either way, he was probably gone for good. Maybe even alive and gone for good.

Kevin hurried out, slammed the door closed, latched it, and ran into the night, determined never, ever to even think about the boy again. He'd saved Sam, hadn't he? Yes, he had! And he hadn't been arrested or sent to the gas chamber or even accused of doing anything wrong. Because he had done what was right!

Elated and overcome with relief, he ran straight to Sam's house, even though it was past her bedtime. It took him fifteen minutes to wake her and convince her to climb out.

"What is it? My father will kill us if he finds us, you know."

He grabbed her hand and ran for the fence.

"Kevin Parson, I am in my pajamas! What is this all about?"

Yes, what's this about, Kevin? You're acting like a maniac!

But he couldn't help himself. He'd never felt so wonderful in all his life. He loved Sam so much!

He stepped past the fence and she followed him. "Kevin, this is . . ."

He threw his arms around her and hugged her tight, squeezing off her words. "I love you, Sam! I love you so much!"

She stood still in his arms, unmoving. It didn't matter; he was so overwhelmed with joy. "You are the best friend a boy could ever, ever have," he said.

She finally put her arms around him and patted his shoulder. It felt a bit polite, but Kevin didn't care. He pulled back and brushed blonde strands of hair from her face. "I won't ever let anyone hurt you. Ever. Not if I have to die first. You know that, don't you?"

She laughed, caught up in his show of affection. "What's gotten into you? Of course I do."

He looked away, wishing for a response as enthusiastic as he felt. It didn't matter; he was a man now.

Her hand touched his chin and turned his face toward her. "Listen to me," Sam said. "I love you more than anything I can imagine. You really are my knight in shining armor." She smiled. "And I think that it's incredibly sweet of you to drag me out here in my pajamas to make sure I know how much you love me."

Kevin smiled wide, stupidly, but it didn't matter. He didn't have to pretend with Sam.

They hugged tight then, tighter than they had ever hugged before.

"Promise to never leave me," Kevin said.

"I promise," Sam said. "And if you ever need me, all you have to do is knock on my window and I'll come flying out in my pajamas."

Kevin laughed. Then Sam laughed, and Kevin laughed at Sam's laughing. It might have been the best night of Kevin's life.

III

"—Samantha?"

Kevin faced Jennifer. "Pardon?"

She looked at him. "Why was the boy after Samantha?"

"Because he was a demented wacko who found pleasure in cutting up animals and terrorizing the neighborhood. I didn't exactly have the time or the presence of mind to sit him down and run a psychological profile on him. I was scared to death."

Jennifer chuckled. "Touché. Too bad, though. Now we're sitting twenty years beyond that night, and I have the formidable task of trying to do it myself. Whether you like it or not, you may be my best hope of understanding him. Assuming the boy and Slater are one and the same, you're the only person we know who's had any meaningful contact with him, then or now."

As much as the thought of going back to the past made Kevin nauseated, he knew that she was right. He sighed. "I'll do whatever I can." He looked out the side window. "I should have made sure he was dead then."

"You would have done society a favor. In self-defense, of course."

"And what if Slater does show up on my doorstep one of these days? Do I have the right to kill him?"

"We have law enforcement for a reason." She paused. "On the other hand, I might."

"You might what?"

"Take him out. If I knew for sure it was Slater."

"What evil is man capable of?" Kevin said absently.

"What?"

"Nothing." But it was something. It struck Kevin for the first time that he had not only had the capacity to kill Slater, but also the *desire* to do so, self-defense or not. What would Dr. John Francis say to that?

"So. The boy was taller than you, about thirteen, blond and ugly," Jennifer said. "Nothing else?"

The sensation that there was something else nagged at Kevin, but he couldn't remember. "I can't think of anything."

They passed a store that Kevin recognized. "Where are we going?"

Suddenly he knew. His foot began to tap. They drove around a deserted park filled with elm trees.

"I thought I'd take you to your aunt's home. See if we can jog loose a few memories. Visual association can do wonders . . ."

He didn't hear the rest. A buzz lit through his mind and he felt claustrophobic in her car.

Jennifer looked at him but said nothing. He was sweating; she could surely see that. She turned onto Baker Street and drove under the elms toward his childhood house. Could she hear his thumping heart too?

"So this is where it all happened," she said absently.

"I . . . I don't want to go to the house," he said.

She looked at him again. "We're not going to the house. Just down the street. Is that okay?"

He couldn't say no—might as well wave a red flag in front of her. "Sure. I'm sorry. I'm not on the best terms with my aunt. My mother died when I was young and my aunt raised me. We've had our differences. Mostly over college."

"Okay. That's not uncommon."

But she saw more in him, didn't she? And so what if she did? Why did he feel so compelled to hide his upbringing? It was weird but not demented. Samantha said otherwise, but she was biased. It wasn't like he was a victim of physical abuse or anything so horrifying.

He took a slow breath and tried to relax.

"You think the boy chased you into one of those old warehouses across the tracks, that's what you said?"

He looked to his right. The memory of that night came back fresh and raw. "Yes, but I was scared out of my mind, and it was dark. I can't remember which one."

"Have you ever checked any of them? To see if there even is one with a basement?"

Kevin fought a wave of panic. He couldn't let her into the past. He shook his head. "No."

"Why not?"

"It was a long time ago."

She nodded. "There are only a few possibilities. Hopefully nothing's changed. You know we'll have to search."

He nodded. "And what if you find him?"

"Then we know he's obviously not Slater."

"And what about me?"

"We'll know that you killed him. In self-defense."

They drove past the white house. "This is where your aunt lives?"

"Yes."

"And that's the old Sheer residence?"

"Yes."

"None of this jogs your memory of any details?"

"No."

She remained silent to the end of the street, where she turned around and headed back.

Kevin's world felt like it was crumbling around him. Coming here alone was hard enough, but doing it with Jennifer somehow seemed profane. He wanted to tell her what Balinda had really done. He wanted her to comfort him, the little boy who had grown old in this world of madness. Waves of sorrow swept through his mind. His eyes went misty.

"I'm sorry, Kevin," Jennifer said softly. "I don't know what happened here, but I can see it left its mark on you. Believe me, if we weren't up against a clock, I wouldn't have brought you back here in your present state."

She cared for him, didn't she? She really did. A tear slipped from his eye and ran down his cheek. The emotion was suddenly beyond him. He began to cry, and then immediately tried to swallow it, which only made the condition worse. He hid his face in his left hand and started to sob, horribly aware of the foolishness of it all.

She drove out of the neighborhood and then stopped. He looked up through blurred eyes and saw that they were by the park. Jennifer sat still, looking at him with soft eyes.

"I'm . . . sorry," he managed past a tight throat. "It's just . . . my life's falling apart . . ."

"Shh, shh, shh. It's okay." Her hand touched his shoulder. "It's okay, really. You've been through hell these last two days. I had no right."

Kevin put his hands over his face and took a deep breath. "Man. This is crazy. Nothing like making a fool of yourself."

Her hand rubbed his arm again. "Don't be silly. You don't think I've seen a grown man cry before? I could tell you some stories. There's nothing quite like watching a three-hundred-pound, heavily tattooed gorilla sob uncontrollably for an hour. I don't know any decent man who could go through what you've gone through without a good cry."

He smiled, embarrassed. "Is that so?"

"That's so."

Jennifer's smile softened and she looked away. "The Riddle Killer's last victim was my brother. His name was Roy. That was three months ago. He was chosen because I was closing in on the killer."

Kevin wasn't sure what to say. "Your brother?"

"You remind me of him, you know." She faced him. "I won't let this maniac kill you, Kevin. I'm not sure I could survive that."

"I'm so sorry. I had no idea."

"Now you do. Want to go for a walk? I think we could both use some fresh air."

"Okay."

They walked side by side over an emerald green lawn, past a pond with ducks and two large geese. She was laughing and telling him about a goose that had once chased her for the sandwich she held. Next to the horror that had swept over him not five minutes earlier, Kevin felt unusually peaceful, as if he were walking with his guardian angel. He wondered about Jennifer's true intentions. She was a professional, doing her job. All FBI agents talked and laughed like this—it was their way of making someone in his shoes feel comfortable enough to work with them.

The thought made him feel suddenly awkward. Clumsy. Like a three-hundred-pound gorilla. On the other hand, she'd lost her brother.

He stopped.

She touched his arm. "Kevin? What is it?"

"Like a three-hundred-pound, heavily tattooed gorilla."

"That's what he—"

"The boy had a tattoo," Kevin blurted.

"The boy you locked in the cellar? Where?"

"On his forehead! A tattoo of a knife."

"You're sure?"

"Yes! He had it covered with a bandanna that last night, but I saw it the first night."

They exchanged stares. "How many men have a tattoo on their foreheads? Not many." A smile nudged her lips. "That's good," she said. "That's very good."

12

Saturday
Afternoon

SAMANTHA WAS THE LAST PASSENGER to board the flight to Sacramento. An hour and a half later she entered a little-known conference room at the attorney general's headquarters, the office of the California Bureau of Investigation's "Alpha Division," as it was known by some. A bulldog of a man named Chris Barston, who was up on suspicion of aiding terrorists by promulgating bomb-construction methods on the Internet, sat across the table. They'd hauled him in last night. His Internet dealings were not her concern, but the information he had to share evidently was, or Roland, her boss, wouldn't have insisted she come. Roland sat at the head of the table, leaning back in his chair. She'd liked the chief from the moment they were introduced, and when she came to him two days after her orientation and asked to be assigned to the Riddle Killer case, he'd agreed. The FBI and the CBI were both active in the case, but Samantha suggested that the killer had inside connections, and the possibility had intrigued Roland.

The call from Kevin had blindsided her. She hadn't expected the Riddle Killer to surface in Southern California at all. She wasn't necessarily convinced that the Riddle Killer and Slater were the same. If Slater was the Riddle Killer and he was also the boy, it would explain his ties to her, Kevin, and Jennifer. But certain details about Slater's calls to Kevin nagged at her.

"Thanks for coming, Sam. Enjoy your holiday?"

"I wasn't aware I *was* on a holiday."

"You're not. Your witness." Roland looked at Chris, who stared past him.

Sam pulled up her chair and opened a blue file Rodriguez had brought to her at the airport. She'd read the contents on the way in.

"Hello, Mr. Barston. My name's Samantha Sheer."

He ignored her and kept his eyes in Roland's direction.

"You may look this way, Chris. I'm going to be asking the questions. Have you ever been questioned by a woman before?"

The man stared at her. Roland grinned. "Answer the woman, Chris."

"I agreed to tell you what I know about Salman. That'll take thirty seconds."

"Great," Sam said. "Then we can limit our exposure to each other so we don't . . . you know, rub off on each other. I think we can stomach thirty seconds, don't you?"

The man's face darkened.

"Tell us about Salman."

He cleared his throat. "I met him in Houston about a month ago. Pakistani. You know, India and all. Speaks with an accent."

"Pakistanis live in Pakistan, not India. That's why they call it Pakistan. Go on."

"You going to mock me for the full thirty seconds here?"

"I'll try to control myself."

He shifted. "Anyway, Salman and I had a mutual interest in . . . you know, bombs. He's clean; I can swear that. He had this tattoo of a bomb on his shoulder. I got one here of a knife." He showed them a small blue knife on his right forearm. "Then he showed me one on his back, a huge dagger. Said he wanted to have it removed because the chicks didn't dig it back in wherever."

"Pakistan."

"Pakistan. He told me he knew a guy who had a tattoo of a knife on his forehead. He didn't tell me nothing about this guy except that his name was Slater and he was into explosive devices. That's it. That's all I know."

"And you think the name Slater interests us why?"

"The news of Long Beach. They said it could be a man named Slater."

"When did your friend know this Slater?"

"I said that's it. That's all I know. That's the deal. If I knew more, I would tell you more. I already wrote down where this Salman guy works last I knew. He's straight up. Talk to him."

Sam looked at Roland. He nodded.

"Okay, Chris. I guess your thirty seconds are up. You're free to go."

Chris stood, glared at her one last time, and left.

"What do you think?" Roland asked.

"I'm not sure what our man would be doing all the way down in Houston, but I think I'm going to Texas. I want to make contact first. For all we know, Salman doesn't even exist. It may take a day or two to track him down. Until then I want to go back to Long Beach."

"Fine. Just keep a low profile down there. If the Riddle Killer's working with someone inside, we don't want him suddenly running scared."

"I'm limiting direct contact to the FBI agent in charge. Jennifer Peters."

"Just watch what you say. For all we know, Agent Peters is Slater."

"Unlikely."

"Just tread lightly."

|||

The prior twenty-four hours had produced more evidence than the entire year combined, but the leads weren't pointing to any quick answers. Meticulous lab work took time, a commodity Jennifer wasn't sure they had enough of. Slater would strike again, and sooner or later they would have bodies to contend with. A car, a bus—what was next?

The city was reeling from news of the bus. Milton had spent half the day preparing and issuing statements to hungry reporters. At least it kept him out of her hair.

She sat at the corner desk Milton had graciously given her and stared at the loose sheets of paper spread before her. It was 4:30, and for the moment she was stuck. A Subway veggie sandwich she'd ordered two hours ago sat on the edge of the desk, and she considered unwrapping it.

Her eyes dropped to the pad under her fingertips. She'd split the page horizontally and then vertically, creating four quadrants, an old technique she used to visually compartmentalize data. Kevin's house, the warehouse search, the knife tattoo, and forensics from the bus.

"Who are you, Slater?" she mumbled. "You're here, aren't you, staring up at me, chuckling behind these words somewhere?"

First quadrant. They'd swept and dusted Kevin's house and turned up exactly nothing. Hundreds of prints, of course—it would take time to work through all of them. But in the high-probability contact points—the phone, the doorknobs, the window latches, the desk, the wood dinette chairs—they had found only Jennifer's and Kevin's prints, and some partials that were unidentifiable. Probably Sam's. She'd been in the house, but according to Kevin she hadn't stayed long or handled anything except for the phone, where they'd found the partials. Either way, the chances that Slater had walked around the place pressing uncovered fingers against dense surfaces had been absurd from the beginning.

No eavesdropping devices turned up either, again not surprising. Slater had used the six bugs they'd uncovered because they were convenient at the time. He had other means of listening in—remote laser transmitters, relayed audio scopes—all of which they would eventually track down, but not likely soon enough. They'd found disturbed ground at the oil rig's base, two hundred yards from Kevin's house, and taken casts of four different shoe prints. Again, the evidence might help them incriminate Slater, but it wasn't identifying him—at least not quickly enough.

The writing on the milk jug was in for analysis at Quantico. Same story. Comparisons could and one day would be made, but not before they actually had Slater in their sights.

They'd affixed the AP301 recording device to Slater's cell phone and were monitoring the house using an IR laser.

Let the games begin.

Jennifer had left Kevin in his house at noon, pleading that he get some sleep. She watched him wander around his living room like a zombie. He'd been pushed beyond himself.

You like him, don't you, Jenn?

Don't be stupid! I hardly know him! I feel empathy for him. I'm attributing Roy's goodness to him.

But you like him. He's handsome, caring, and as innocent as a butterfly. He has magical eyes and a smile that swallows the room. He's . . .

Naive and damaged. His reaction to driving through his old neighborhood had been in part precipitated by the stress of Slater's threats, granted. But there had to be more.

He was similar to Roy in many ways, but the more she thought about it, the more she saw the dissimilarities between this case and the ones in Sacramento. Slater seemed to have a specific, personally motivated agenda with Kevin. He wasn't a random victim. Neither was Jennifer nor Samantha. What if Kevin had been the Riddle Killer's prime mark all along? What if the others were just a kind of practice? Warmup?

Jennifer closed her eyes and stretched her neck. She'd made an appointment to see the dean at Kevin's seminary, Dr. John Francis, first thing tomorrow morning. He attended one of those huge churches that held a service on Saturday evening. Jennifer picked up the sandwich and peeled back the wax paper.

Second quadrant. The warehouse. Milton had somehow convinced the bureau chief to speak to her about his involvement. The man was starting to become a major irritant. She'd reluctantly agreed to give him the warehouse search. The fact was, she could use the manpower and they knew the territory. She made it clear that if he breathed one word of his involvement to the media, she'd personally see to it that he took full responsibility for whatever negative consequences resulted. He'd taken four uniformed officers and a search warrant to the warehouse district. The likelihood that Slater was watching the neighborhood was minimal. He might be a surveillance crackerjack, but he couldn't have eyes everywhere.

Based on Kevin's story, he might have stumbled into any of a couple dozen warehouses that night. Milton's team was searching each one now, looking for any that might have a subterranean storage room, an oil pit, a garbage dump—anything similar. Most warehouses today were built on slabs, but some of the older buildings featured underground units that were cheaper to cool.

She could understand Kevin's subconscious erasure of such a traumatic location. It would either be stamped indelibly on his brain or gone, and there was no reason for him to hide any knowledge at this point. Discovery of the basement would be a windfall. If indeed the boy was Slater.

Third quadrant. The knife tattoo. Jennifer took a bite out of the sandwich. Hunger swarmed her with the first taste of tomato. She'd missed breakfast, hadn't she? Seemed like a week ago.

She stared at the third quadrant. Again, assuming the boy was Slater, and assuming he hadn't removed the tattoo, they now had their first bona fide identifier. A tattoo of a knife on the forehead—not exactly something you see on every corner. Twenty-three agents and policemen were quietly working the search. Tattoo parlors that had existed twenty years earlier in the immediate vicinity were first to be scrutinized, but finding one that had any records was near impossible. They were working in concentric circles. More likely was finding a tattoo parlor that remembered a man with a knife tattoo on his forehead. Not all tattoo bearers frequented parlors, but ones with Slater's profile might. For all they knew, he was now covered in tattoos. All he needed was one—a knife in the center of his forehead.

Fourth quadrant. The bus. Another bite. The sandwich was like a slice of heaven.

Same guy, no doubt. Same device: a suitcase bolted behind the gas tank, loaded with enough dynamite to shred a bus, detonated using tungsten leads stripped from an incandescent bulb on a simple five-dollar, battery-operated alarm clock. A mechanical servo could override the clock and either terminate or trigger the detonation. The bomb had been planted days, even weeks ago, based on the dust they'd lifted off one of its bolts. If they could ID what was left of the servo, they might have a shot of tracing its origins. Unlikely.

How long had Slater been planning this?

The phone chirped. Jennifer wiped her mouth, took a quick swallow from a bottle of Evian, and picked up the phone. "Jennifer."

"We think we found it."

Milton. She sat up. "The warehouse."

"We have some blood here."

She tossed the rest of the sandwich in the waste bin and grabbed her keys. "I'm on my way."

|||

Kevin looked out between the blinds for the fourth time in two hours. They'd decided to place one unmarked car a block up the street—FBI. Slater seemed ambiguous about the FBI. Either way, the agent behind the wheel would watch only. He would not follow if or when Kevin left at Slater's next beckoning. Static surveillance only.

Kevin released the slats and paced back into the kitchen. In the park, Jennifer had reached out to him and he'd let her. He found her fierce nature compelling. It reminded him of Samantha.

Where was Samantha? He'd called her twice and gotten only her voice mail. He desperately wanted to talk to her about the visit to Baker Street with Jennifer. She would understand. Not that Jennifer didn't, but Sam might be able to help him sort out these new feelings.

He walked to the refrigerator, opened it, and pulled out a liter of 7UP. Feelings. Extremes. The hatred toward Slater that had begun to swell in his gut wasn't so strange. How was he supposed to feel toward someone who had come within a few seconds of taking not only his life, but countless others for undisclosed reasons? If Slater would just quit being so idiotic and tell him what the deal was, Kevin could handle the man. As it was, the imbecile was hiding behind these stupid games, and Kevin was losing patience. Yesterday he'd been too shocked to process his anger. A common form of denial, Jennifer had said. Shock breeds denial, which in turn tempers anger. But now the denial was giving way to this bitterness toward an enemy who refused to show his hand.

Kevin poured half a glass, swallowed the 7UP in several long drafts, and slammed the empty glass on the counter.

He ran his hand through his hair, grunted, and walked to the living room. How could one man wreak so much havoc in the space of one day? Slater was nothing less than a terrorist. If Kevin owned a gun and Slater worked up the stomach to confront him face to face, he was pretty sure he'd have no compunction about putting a slug or two in the man's face. Especially if he was the boy. Kevin shivered involuntarily. Shoulda gone back and made sure the stinking rat was dead. He would have been within his rights, if not according to the law, then in the eyes of God. Turn the other cheek shouldn't apply to sick sewer rats with knives in their hands who licked neighborhood girls' windows.

Slater was listening now, right? Kevin looked around the room and settled on the window.

"Slater?" His voice bounced back at him.

"You hear me, Slater? Listen, you sick scab, I don't know why you're stalking me or why you're too terrified to show your face, but you're only proving one thing. You're toilet water. You're a punk without the guts to face your adversary. Come on, baby! Come and get me!"

"Kevin?"

He whirled around. Sam stood in the rear sliding-glass doorway, staring at him. He hadn't heard the door slide open.

"You okay?" she whispered.

"Sure. Sorry, I was just having a word with our friend, in case he was listening."

Sam shut the door and lifted a finger to her lips. She walked to the front window and pulled the drapes.

"What . . ."

She motioned him quiet again and led him to the garage. "If we talk quietly here, we won't be heard."

"Slater? The car up the street's FBI."

"I know. Which is why I parked two blocks up and came in the back. You don't think Slater's going to see them?"

"He didn't say no FBI."

"Maybe because he is FBI," she said.

"What?"

"We haven't ruled it out."

"We? Who's we?"

She held his gaze for a moment. "Just an expression. They find anything else here?"

"No. Some footprints by the oil rig up the hill. They took a bunch of fingerprints, the milk jug. Jennifer didn't think any of it would help them much."

Sam nodded. "She told me about the tattoo. You never told me about the tattoo."

"I didn't tell you anything about him after that night, remember? He was gone. End of story."

"Not anymore. They'll find the warehouse, and when they do, they'll find more—who knows, maybe the boy."

"Actually, I went back four months later."

"What?"

"He was gone. There was blood on the floor and his bandanna, but he was gone. They won't find him."

Sam looked at him for a few moments. He wasn't sure what she was thinking, but something wasn't quite right.

"You said, *we* haven't ruled it out," he said. "You've always been straight with me, Sam. Who is we?"

She looked into his eyes and put a hand on his cheek. "I'm sorry, Kevin, I can't tell you everything—not now, not yet. Soon. You're right, I have always been straight with you. I've been more than a friend. I've loved you like a brother. A day hasn't gone by these past ten years that I haven't thought about you at least once. You're part of me. And now I need you to trust me. Can you do that?"

The revelation made his head spin. She was somehow involved, wasn't she? She'd been onto Slater before yesterday. It was why Slater knew her!

"What . . . what's going on?"

Her hand slid down his arm and took his fingers. "Nothing's changed. Slater's the same person he was yesterday, and I'm going to do my best to get to him before he hurts anyone. I'm just not at liberty to tell you what we know. Not yet. It wouldn't make any difference to you anyway. Trust me. For old time's sake."

He nodded. Actually, this was better, wasn't it? The fact that she had some inside track and wasn't just blindly feeling her way around this case—that was good.

"But you think the FBI is involved?"

She put her finger on his lips to seal them. "I can't talk about it. Forget I said it. Nothing's changed." She reached up, kissed him on the cheek, and released his hand.

"Can I trust Jennifer?"

She turned. "Sure—trust Jennifer. But trust me first."

"What do you mean, first?"

"I mean if you have to choose between me and Jennifer, choose me."

He felt his pulse thicken. What was she saying? *Choose me.* Did she think he would ever choose Jennifer over her? He wasn't even sure what he felt for Jennifer. She had offered to ease his pain and confusion in a time of vulnerability and he had let her. That was all.

"I would always choose you. I owe my life to you."

She smiled and for a moment he imagined that they were kids again, sitting under an elm with a full moon on their faces, laughing at a squirrel's inquisitive head poking through the branches.

"Actually, I think it's the other way around. I owe you *my* life," she said. "Literally. You saved me from Slater once, didn't you? Now it's my turn to return the favor."

In a strange way, it all made perfect sense.

"Okay," she said. "I have a plan. I mean to flush the snake from his hole." She winked at him and glanced at her watch. "The sooner we get out of here the better. Grab your toothbrush, a change of clothes, and some deodorant if you want. We're taking a trip."

"We are? Where? We can't just leave. Jennifer told me to stay here."

"Until what? Did Slater tell you not to leave?"

"No."

"Let me see the phone."

He fished out the cell phone Slater had left him and handed it to her.

"Did Slater tell you to keep this on?"

Kevin considered the question. "He said to keep it with me at all times."

Sam pushed the power off button. "Then we'll take it."

"Jennifer will have a cow. This wasn't the plan."

"Change of plans, my dear knight. It's time for a little cat and mouse of our own."

13

THE WAREHOUSE was less than a hundred yards from Kevin's old house, two rows back from the road, an old wooden storage facility that had been white before flaking paint revealed its gray underbelly. From the side entrance, none of the houses on Baker Street was visible.

"This it?"

"It's abandoned. Looks like it has been for a while," Milton said.

"Show me."

Two uniforms stood by the door, watching her. One of them handed her a flashlight. "You'll need this."

She took it and turned it on.

The warehouse smelled of a decade's worth of undisturbed dust. Beyond the side door was a single stairwell descending into blackness. The rest of the three-thousand-or-so square feet of concrete sat vacant in dim light filtered by a dozen cracks in the walls.

"Don't they tear these things down?" she asked.

"They used to hold all kinds of goods in these warehouses before the navy moved in just south of here. The government bought this land and hasn't seen fit to rebuild yet. I'm sure they'll get around to it."

A lone cop stood at the bottom of the stairs, shining his flashlight on the threshold. "The door was locked from the outside—took some jarring to get it loose."

Jennifer descended. A steel door led into a ten-by-ten room, concrete, empty. She played her torch over the pitted walls. Exposed floor joists held the ceiling. Most of it. One small section had rotted through.

"The blood's over here," Milton said.

Jennifer directed her light to where he stood looking down at two large dark stains on the concrete. She squatted and studied each.

"The splatter's consistent with blood." The basic position of the stains also matched Kevin's story—both he and the boy had bled. "At this age we probably won't get any reliable DNA evidence, but we can at least verify species. I knew Kevin was hiding something the first time I talked to him."

She glanced at Milton, surprised by his tone.

"And this isn't the last of it. I guarantee he's hiding more," he said.

Milton was a first-class pig. She stood and walked over to a small, almost unnoticeable hole in the ceiling. "The boy's way out?"

"Could be."

So, assuming this read as fact, what would it mean? That Kevin hadn't killed the boy? That they had fought and that Kevin had locked the door from the outside, but then the boy had managed to crawl out through the rotting ceiling? Who knew why he hadn't come back to terrorize Kevin until now?

Or it could mean that the boy actually had died in here, only to be discovered by some passerby years later, body disposed of. Unlikely. Unless a drifter or anyone else had reason to hide the body, it would have been investigated. She'd already run a search for reports and found none.

"Okay, we need to do a bloodstain distribution analysis. I want to know what happened down here. Assuming it is blood, did anyone lie in it? Any blood on the walls or up through the ceiling? I want species identification and, if possible, blood type. Send a sample to the FBI lab immediately. And this stays out of the press."

Milton said nothing. He looked up at the corner and frowned. A shadow passed over his face. It occurred to her that she might actually hate the man.

"Don't get any ideas, Detective. Everything goes through me."

He looked at her for a moment and then walked for the door. "Sure."

III

Kevin drove them along Palos Verdes Drive, west toward Palos Verdes. Slater's bugged phone sat on the dash, turned off.

Sam stared ahead, eyes sparkling. "If Slater can't make contact, how can he play the game? He's driven by the riddles, but if we neutralize his ability to communicate a riddle, then there *is* no riddle, is there? At the least he has to rethink his strategy."

"Or blow up another bomb," Kevin said.

"We're not technically breaking one of his rules. He detonates a bomb and *he's* breaking the rules of engagement. I don't think Slater will do that."

Kevin thought about Sam's plan. On one hand, it felt good to be doing something—anything—besides waiting. The idea made sense on its surface. On the other hand, he didn't trust Slater to follow his own rules. Sam knew him better, maybe, but it was his life they were messing with.

"Why not just turn off the phone and stick around?"

"He'd find a way to communicate."

"He still might."

"Possible. But this way we also get you out of there. The one thing we need now is time. A dozen new leads have surfaced in the last twenty-four hours, but we need time."

There was the *we* word again.

"We should at least tell Jennifer, don't you think?"

"Think of this as a test. We cut off all contact and then we gradually resume contact. Unless Slater's following us now, he'll be lost. His opponent will have disappeared. He may rant and rave, but he won't play the game without you. We add some people to the loop and see if Slater suddenly knows more than he should. Follow?"

"What if he has the car bugged?"

"Then he did it today under the noses of the FBI. They swept it this morning, remember?"

Kevin nodded. The idea was growing on him. "Just like that we're gone, huh?"

She grinned. "Just like that."

"Like sneaking out at night."

It took them half an hour to reach the quaint hotel—an old Victorian mansion that had been converted and expanded to accommodate forty rooms. They pulled into its parking lot at ten after six. A cool, salty breeze drifted off the Pacific, half a mile down green sloping hills. Sam grinned and pulled out her overnight bag.

"Do they have rooms available?" Kevin asked.

"We have reservations. A suite with two bedrooms."

He looked up at the hotel and then back toward the sea. A Conoco station with a Taco Bell stood a hundred yards to the north. Outback Steakhouse, fifty yards south. Cars drifted by, a Lexus, a Mercedes. The madness in Long Beach seemed distant.

"Come on," Sam said. "Let's settle in and get something to eat."

Half an hour later they sat across from each other in a cozy café on the hotel's ground floor, overlooking a dimming horizon. They'd left their cell phones, turned off, in the room. She still wore her office pager, but Slater had no way to reach either of them. It seemed that Sam's simple plan wasn't such a bad idea.

"What would happen if I just disappeared?" Kevin asked, cutting into a thick New York strip.

She forked a small bite of cheese-smothered chicken into her mouth and dabbed her lips with her napkin. "Just up and leave until we find him?"

"Why not?"

"Why not. Leave him high and dry." She took a drink of iced tea and cut another piece. "You could move up to San Francisco."

"He's ruined my life down here anyway. I don't see how I can continue in seminary."

"I doubt you're the first seminary student to have his sins exposed."

"Murder isn't exactly your typical confession."

"Self-defense. And as far as we know, he lived."

"The confession sounded pretty ominous. I think I'm finished."

"And how's murder so different from gossip? Wasn't that your point to the dean? You're no more capable of evil than the bishop, remember? Murder, gossip—what's the difference? Evil is evil."

"Evil is evil as long as you keep it in the classroom. Out here in the real world, gossip doesn't even feel evil."

"Which is why any good detective learns to trust the facts over feelings." She went back to her food. "Either way, I don't think you can run. He'll track you down. That's how his kind works. You raise the stakes and he's likely to come back with higher stakes."

Kevin looked out the window. Darkness had all but swallowed the horizon. Jennifer's words came back to him. Take him out, she'd said.

"Like a hunted animal," he said.

"Except that you're not an animal. You have the same capacities he does."

"Jennifer told me that if I had the opportunity I should blow him away." Anger boiled through his chest. He'd come so far, worked so hard, pulled himself out of the deepest despair, only to be hijacked by some ghost from the past.

He slammed the table with his fist, rattling the dishes.

He met the stares from an older couple two tables down. "I'm sorry, Kevin," Samantha said. "I know this is hard."

"What's to prevent *me* from being the hunter?" he asked. "He wants a game; I'll give him a game! Why don't I throw out a challenge and force *him* to respond to me? Would you do anything different?"

"Fight terror with terror."

"Exactly!"

"No," she said.

"What do you mean, no? Maybe the only way to corner him is to play the game his way."

"You don't fight evil with evil; it just leads to anarchy. We have rules and we have scruples, unlike Slater. What are you going to do, threaten to blow up the convention center unless he gives himself up? Somehow I don't think he'd do anything but laugh. Besides, we have no way of contacting him."

The maître d' approached from Kevin's right. "Excuse me, sir, is everything all right?"

Someone had complained. "Yes. I'm sorry, I'll try to control myself." Kevin flashed him an embarrassed smile. The man dipped his head and left.

Kevin took a deep breath and picked up his fork, but his appetite was suddenly gone. The fact was, when he thought about what Slater was doing to him, he could hardly think of anything but killing him. Destroy the destroyer.

"I know it sounds a bit pretentious right now, but Slater doesn't scare me," Sam said, staring off into the darkness outside, wearing a coy smile. "You'll see, Kevin. His days are numbered."

"And mine might be as well."

"Not a chance. I won't let that happen."

He wasn't brimming with her confidence, but he couldn't resist her infectious smile. This was his Samantha. G.I. Jane.

"Jennifer said that, huh?" Sam asked. "Blow him away."

"Actually, I think she said 'take him out.' Makes sense to me."

"Maybe." She stared at him across the candle flame. "You like her, don't you?"

"Who, Jennifer?" He shrugged. "She seems like a good person."

"I don't mean in a 'good person' kind of way."

"Come on, Sam. I hardly know her. I haven't dated anyone for years." He smiled sheepishly. "Good night, the last girl I kissed was you."

"Is that so? When we were eleven?"

"How could you forget?"

"I haven't. But you do like her. I can see it in your eyes when you say her name."

Kevin felt his face flush. "She's an FBI agent who's trying to save my neck. What's there not to like?" He looked to his right and caught the continuing stare of the older couple. They looked away. "She reminds me of you."

"Really? How so?"

"Kind. No-nonsense. Pretty . . ."

"Like I said, you like her."

"Please—"

"It's okay, Kevin," she said softly. "I want you to like her."

"You do?"

"Yes. I approve." She grinned and placed the last small bite of chicken in her mouth. Even the way she chewed her food was nothing less than spectacular, he thought. Her chin and cheeks were so smooth in motion.

"What about . . ." He trailed off, suddenly self-conscious.

"What about us? That's very sweet, my knight, but I'm not sure we could ever be romantically involved. Don't get me wrong, I love you dearly. I'm just not sure we want to risk what we have for romance."

"Great things always come at great risk," he said.

She stared at him with those intoxicating eyes, caught off guard by his forward statement.

"Isn't that right?" he asked.

"Yes."

"So then don't say we could never be romantically involved. I kissed you once and you sent me to heaven. Didn't you feel something?"

"When you kissed me?"

"Yes."

"I was floating for a week."

"You never told me that."

She grinned, and if he wasn't mistaken, now she was embarrassed. "Maybe I wanted you to make the next move. Isn't that what a knight does for his damsel in distress?"

"I guess I never was a very good knight."

"You've turned into quite a dashing one," Sam said with a twinkle in her eye. "I think she likes you."

"Jennifer? She told you that?"

"Woman's intuition. Remember?"

Sam set down her napkin and stood. "Would you like to dance?"

He glanced around. No one else was dancing, but several colored lights turned slowly on the tiny dance floor. Michael Bolton crooned over the speakers.

"I . . . I'm not sure I know how to—"

"Sure you do. Just like when we were kids. Under the moonlight. Don't tell me you've never danced since then."

"No, not really."

She looked at him gently. "Then we definitely should. Will you?"

He smiled and dipped his head. "It would be my pleasure."

They held each other gently and danced for several long minutes. It wasn't a sensual dance or even romantic. It was just the right thing to do after ten years of separation.

Slater did not call that night.

14

Sunday
Morning

THE WALL IS DARK BROWN, almost black, and pitted. Slightly damp in spots, leaking an odor of mold and mildew and something else he never has been able to place. A single incandescent bulb glows in the bathroom, casting just enough light into the main basement for Slater to see the darkness of the wall.

These are the things he likes: cold, dark, wetness, mildew, and chocolate sundaes with equal portions of ice cream and fudge. Oh, yes, and he likes fascination. In fact, he likes to be fascinating above everything else, and really, in order to be properly fascinating, he has to dispense with the expected and deliver only what they don't expect. This is why confused teenage boys pierce their eyelids and tattoo their foreheads, and why girls out to impress them shave their heads. It is all a pathetic, hopeless attempt to be fascinating.

The problem with doing something so senseless as piercing an eyelid is that it reveals your intentions. *Here am I, a poor teenage slug who requires your attention. Look at me, see how I resemble a puddle of dog vomit? Won't you please throw your fingers to your teeth and be wildly fascinated by me?*

The pitiful first gropings of the dark man.

But Slater knows what they do not. He knows that the dark man is most fascinating when he moves in complete obscurity. Hidden. Unknown. That's why he is called the *dark* man. That's why he has started in the dark. That's why he does all of his best work at night. That's why he loves this basement. Because for all practical purposes, Slater *is* the Dark Man.

Someone famous should write a comic book based on him.

Slater stands from his stool. He's been looking at the pitted wall for over an hour without moving. He finds it fascinating. Darkness is always fascinating. He's never quite sure what he's looking at, unlike a piece of white paper, which only grows fascinating if he puts a black pen to it.

It's light outside—he knows this because of the single crack in the corner. Samantha has taken Kevin and gone into hiding. Which means that after all these months, she's learned something new.

Slater hums softly and walks toward a small vanity. The secret of being the Dark Man is not looking like a dark man at all. That is why the world looks at stupid little teenagers with rings in their noses as idiots. It's like walking around school, stripped to the waist in a Charles Atlas pose all day. Please. Too obvious. Too stupid. Too boring.

Now the angel of light routine—those who pile on the white to obscure the Dark Man, like Sunday school teachers and clergy, like priests—not a bad instinct really. But these days, a white collar is no longer the best disguise.

The best disguise is simply obscurity.

Slater sits and tilts the mirror so that it catches enough light from the bathroom to cast his reflection. You see, now there is a Nobody. A strongly built man with blond hair and grayish eyes. A wedding band on his left hand, a closet full of pressed shirts and Dockers and a silver Honda Accord out on the street.

He could walk up to any Betty in the mall and say, "Excuse me, do I look like the Dark Man to you?"

"What on earth are you talking about?" she would say. Because she wouldn't associate him with a name like Dark Man. She, along with ten thousand other mall flies, would be fooled. Blind. Shrouded by darkness.

That is his secret. He can walk under their noses without the slightest hint of guilt. He is virtually transparent, for the very reason that he is so much like them. They see him every day and don't know who he is.

Slater frowns at himself and wags his head in mockery. "I like you, Kevin. I love you, Kevin." Sam can be such a cockroach. He should have killed her when he had the chance, long ago.

Now she's in the thick of things again, which is good because he can finish the job, once and for all. But her audacity makes him nauseated.

"Let's run away and play hide-and-seek," he mocks again. "What do you take me for?"

The fact is, Sam knows more about him than any of the others. True, her little disappearing act will gain them nothing, but at least she's made a move, which is more than he can say for the rest. She's trying to flush him out. She might even know that he's been under their noses all along.

But the Dark Man isn't that stupid. They can't hide forever. Kevin will eventually stick his slimy head out of his hole, and when he does, Slater will be there to bite it off.

He leans the mirror against the wall and crosses to the room he's prepared for his guest. It is slightly larger than a closet, encased in concrete. A steel door. Leather restraints lay on the floor, but he doubts he'll need them. The game will end here, where it's been designed to end. The rest of this cat-and-mouse foolishness is only a smoke screen to keep them in the dark, where all good games are played. If the newspapers think they have a hot story now, they are about to be reeducated. The occasional destruction of a car or bus by way of explosion a story hardly makes. What he plans will be worthy of a book.

"I despise you," he says softly. "I loathe the way you walk and the way you speak. Your heart is vile. I will kill you."

III

The anger had worked its way up to a seething through the night. Kevin tossed and turned in a fitful attempt at sleep. Sam's optimism sat like a light on the horizon of his mind, but as the night wore on, the light grew dim until it faded altogether, obscured by bitterness toward the man who had stomped into his life uninvited.

Fury was a good word for it. Rage. Indignation. They all worked. He relived that night twenty years ago a hundred times. The boy sneering at him as he turned the knife in his hands, threatening to shove the blade through Sam's chest. The boy's name was Slater—had to be. How he'd escaped was beyond Kevin. Why he'd waited so long to come after him made no sense either. He should have killed Slater then.

His pillow felt like a wet sponge. His sheets clung to his legs like mildewed leaves. He couldn't remember a time when he was so upset, so distraught, since the boy had first threatened him so many years ago.

Sam's plan was brilliant, except for the obvious fact that it only delayed the inevitable. Slater wasn't going away—he would wait out there in the dark, biding his time while Kevin slowly dehydrated beneath the sheets. He couldn't do this. He couldn't just wait and waste away while Slater chuckled under his rock.

The idea ignited in his mind with the sky's first graying. *Buy a gun.* His eyes sprang open. Of course! Why not? Become the hunter.

Don't be absurd. He closed his eyes. *You aren't a killer.* The discussion with Dr. Francis was one thing—all that talk about gossip and killing being the same thing. But when it came right down to it, he could never kill another human. He couldn't line up a man in the gun's sights and send a slug through his head. *POW!* Surprise, creep.

Kevin slowly opened his eyes. Where would he get a gun anyway? A pawnshop? Not with today's laws. Not legally, anyway. On the other hand, for the right price . . .

Forget it. What was he going to do, shoot the phone if Slater called again? The man was too good to walk into danger. How could he lure Slater into a confrontation?

Kevin rolled over and tried to put the idea from his mind. But now the notion began to grow, fed by his own loathing. In the end Slater would kill him—nothing else made any sense. So why not take the fight to him first? Why not demand a meeting? Face me, you slime bucket. Come out of the shadows and look me in the eyes. You want a game?

Suddenly the thought of anything less seemed weak. He had to at least try.

He wrestled off the sheets and slid to the floor. Sam wouldn't agree. He would do this without her, now, before she awakened and stopped him. He quickly pulled on his jeans and a T-shirt. The details didn't seem so critical at the moment—where he'd find a gun, how he'd hide it, how he'd use it. With enough money . . .

Kevin grabbed his wallet off the nightstand and fumbled through it. It would have to be cash. He'd stuffed his emergency cash, the four hundred dollars from under his mattress, into his wallet before leaving the house. Still there. Surely with that much he could buy a gun on the black market.

Kevin eased out of his room, saw that Sam's door was still closed, and walked for the door before pulling up. He should at least leave a note. *Couldn't sleep, went to put a slug in Slater's head, be back soon.*

He found a pad of paper with the hotel's insignia stenciled across the top and scribbled a note. *Couldn't sleep, went for a drive, be back soon.*

The morning air felt cool on his clammy skin. Six o'clock. The underworld was undoubtedly still stirring. He had to get out before Sam awoke or he wouldn't be going anywhere. She would worry if he didn't return quickly. As soon as the night crawlers made their appearance, he would pull over and ask one of them the dreaded question: Where can I buy a gun to blow away the man who's after me?

He started the car and headed south.

And what if the night crawler recognized him? His face had been plastered on the news. The jarring thought made Kevin flinch. He swerved. A white sedan on his tail flashed its lights. He quickly pulled over, as if it had been his intention all along. The car sped by.

Maybe he should have brought a sock to pull over his head. Kmart special over here—one bad man with a stocking over his head, holding up a night crawler with a wallet. Give me your gun, buster.

Twenty minutes later he emerged from a 7-Eleven with a pair of dark glasses and an orange Broncos baseball cap. With a day's stubble, he looked nothing like the man he'd seen on television the previous day. But he decided to take the drive up to Inglewood just to be sure. Probably more guns to be had up there anyway.

An accident on 405 stretched the hour trip into two hours. It was eight-thirty before he'd pulled onto Western Avenue in Inglewood. He had no idea where to begin looking. Sam would be up now.

He drove aimlessly, palms sweaty on the steering wheel, telling himself he had no business asking anyone where to buy a gun, much less buying one. If he headed back over to Hawthorn and headed south, he could be back in Palos Verdes in under an hour.

But Palos Verdes was within spitting distance of Long Beach. And Slater was waiting in Long Beach. He had to find himself a gun. Maybe a knife would be better. Definitely easier to find. Then again, killing with a knife somehow felt more evil than killing with a gun, and harder, assuming he could do either.

What would Jennifer say to this sudden madness that had overtaken him? Take him out. No, that was figurative, Kevin. He swallowed, suddenly swamped with the foolishness of what he was doing. He didn't even have a plan! *God, help me.*

For someone studying to be a priest, he sure hadn't prayed much in the past two days. He'd been too busy confessing his sin to the world. He wasn't sure he even believed that God *could* save him. Could God really reach in and save his people? He imagined a huge finger flicking the head off Slater's shoulders. For that matter, what did it take to become one of God's people? How was the soul truly regenerated? Through the sinner's prayer? *Take my heart, take my soul; wash my mind as white as snow. And if anyone comes after me with a gun, please put him in a place where there is no sun—preferably six feet under in a concrete tomb.*

He'd never really prayed like that. Oh, he'd prayed plenty in church. He'd committed himself to vocation and to ministry. He'd said what he needed to say to become who he was trying to become, and he was doing what he needed to do to help others become like him. But he was no longer sure what he'd become. He'd broken with his past and started fresh.

Or had he?

Sure he had. Out with the old, in with the new, yippee-kie-ay, yabba dabba doo. *Are you regenerated, Kevin? Are you saved? Are you worthy of feeding at the trough with the others in the flock? Are you fit to shepherd the sheep grazing in God's green pastures?*

I was three days ago. At least I thought I was. At least I was successfully pretending to think I was.

Praying to a heavenly Father filled his mind with images of Eugene, dressed in his riding boots, issuing commands in a phony

English accent. Fathers were silly men who went about pretending they were important.

Kevin cleared his throat. "God, if anyone ever needed your help, I do. However you do it, you have to save me. I may not be a priest, but I do want to be your . . . your child."

Tears filled his eyes. *Why the sudden emotion?*

It's coming because you never were anyone's child. Just like Father Strong used to say. God's waiting with outstretched hands. You never really took that seriously, but that's what becoming a child is all about. Trust him at his Word, as the good reverend would say.

Kevin pulled into a Burger King. Three young men walked out in baggy jeans with chains that hung from their belt loops to their knees.

A gun. Right now he didn't need God's Word. Right now he needed a gun.

|||

Jennifer picked up her phone, dialed Kevin's number, and let it ring a dozen times. Still no answer. He'd been gone since five o'clock last evening, and she had hardly slept.

They had set up audio surveillance with a single laser beam, which when placed on any one of Kevin's windows could turn the glass into an effective diaphragm for sounds beyond. Slater had probably used a similar device. The problem with the laser technology was that it picked up sounds indiscriminately. A digital-signal processor decoded the sounds and filtered voice, but the settings had to be adjusted whenever the operator changed windows, or when conditions—such as the closing of drapes—changed sufficiently to interfere with the acoustics of the room. For some reason Kevin had decided to close the drapes just before his departure.

A young agent named McConnel was resetting the laser receiver when Kevin had come out. McConnel said he heard a barrage of static in his earphone and looked up to see the garage door open and the rented Ford Taurus pull out. He'd reported the incident immediately, but his hands were tied. No following.

The fact that McConnel had heard nothing resembling a phone call before Kevin's departure was somewhat comforting, but the call could have come while the agent was adjusting the receiver.

Jennifer had tried to reach Sam at the Howard Johnson hotel, on the whim that she might know Kevin's whereabouts. No luck. The agent wasn't picking up her cell and the hotel clerk said that she'd checked out yesterday morning. She remembered Sam because she'd been tipped twenty dollars. Any agent who'd leave a tip for a desk clerk was unusual at the least.

Jennifer only hoped that Slater would have as much difficulty reaching Kevin as she did. If so, the disappearing act might actually offer some benefits. No bombs. So far. Hopefully the statewide bulletin on the Taurus wouldn't trigger one. She wasn't sure why Kevin had left—most probably a reaction to the stress—but in doing so he may have inadvertently stalled Slater.

Jennifer called the agent on duty by the house and learned, as expected, nothing new. She decided to try the dean a few minutes early.

Dr. John Francis lived in an old brick house on the edge of Long Beach, two blocks west of Los Alamitos. She knew that he was a widower with doctorates in both psychology and philosophy who'd lived in the same house for twenty-three years. Other than that all she knew was that he had taken Kevin under his wing at the seminary. And that he liked to drive fast, judging by the black Porsche 911 in his driveway.

Five minutes after pulling up to his house, Jennifer sat in a cozy living room, listening to quiet strains of Bach, nursing a hot cup of green tea. Dr. Francis sat opposite her in an armchair, legs crossed, smiling without trying to. He was quite distressed over all the news he'd heard about his student, but she would never guess it with a glance. The professor had one of those faces that couldn't help but reflect God's goodness, regardless of what might be happening.

"How well do you know Kevin?" she asked.

"Quite well as far as students go. But you must understand, that doesn't qualify me to pass any judgment on his past."

"His past. We'll come back to that. This may sound like a simple case of revenge based on what the media is pumping over the air, but I think it's more complicated than that. I think whoever's after Kevin sees his life as it is now and takes exception to it. That's where you come in. It appears that Kevin's a quiet man. Not a lot of friends. In fact, he evidently considers you his best. Maybe his only, other than Sam."

"Sam? You mean his childhood friend, Samantha? Yes, he's spoken of her. He seems quite taken with her."

"Tell me about him."

"You're looking for something in his life today that might elicit anger in someone from his past?"

She smiled. The psychologist in him was speaking. "Exactly."

"Unless Kevin comes forward with his confession, which he did, the man will extract a price."

"That's the basic story."

"But the confession missed the mark. So now you dig deeper, in search of that which so offends this Slater."

She nodded. Dr. Francis was a quick study. She decided to deal straight with the man. "On the surface it seems obvious. We have a student pursuing a holy vocation. As it turns out, his past is filled with mystery and murder. Someone takes exception to that dichotomy."

"We all have pasts filled with mystery and murder," Dr. Francis said.

Interesting way to put it.

"In fact, it's one of the aspects of the human condition Kevin and I have discussed before."

"Oh?"

"It's one of the first things an intelligent man like Kevin, who comes to the church later in life, notices. There is a pervasive incongruity between the church's theology and the way most of us in the church live."

"Hypocrisy."

"One of its faces, yes. Hypocrisy. Saying one thing but doing another. Studying to be a priest while hiding a small cocaine addiction, for example. The world flushes this out and cries scandal. But the more ominous face isn't nearly so obvious. This is what interested Kevin the most. He was quite astute, really."

"I'm not sure I follow. What's not so obvious?"

"The evil that lies in all of us," the professor said. "Not blatant hypocrisy, but deception. Not even realizing that the sin we regularly commit is sin at all. Going about life honestly believing that we are pure when all along we are riddled with sin."

She looked at his gentle smile, taken by the simplicity of his words.

"A preacher stands against the immorality of adultery, but all the while he harbors anger toward the third parishioner from the left because the parishioner challenged one of his teachings three months ago. Is anger not as evil as adultery? Or a woman who scorns the man across the aisle for alcoholic indiscretions, while she routinely gossips about him after services. Is gossip not as evil as any vice? What's especially damaging in both cases is that neither the man who harbors anger nor the woman who gossips seriously considers the evil of their own actions. Their sins remain hidden. This is the true cancer in the church."

"Sounds like the same cancer that eats away at the rest of society."

"Exactly. Although in the church it makes every attempt to

remain hidden, where it is left alone to grow in the dark. You ever wonder why incidences of divorce and gluttony and virtually all of evil's fruits are as high in the church as in society at large?"

"Actually, I didn't know that."

"Though being freed from sin, most remain slaves, blinded and gagged by their own deception. 'The good that I would, that I do not do and that which I would not, that I do.' Welcome to the church in America."

"And you're saying you've discussed this with Kevin?"

"I discuss this with every class I teach on the subject. Kevin, more than most students, understood it."

"Based on what you're saying, what Slater's doing isn't so different from what every old lady in the church does when she gossips?" *And killing Roy was no different either,* she almost said.

"Assuming that old ladies have a proclivity for gossip, a false assumption, actually. On the other hand, Saint Paul drew a distinction between some sins and others. Although he did place gossip in the most vile category."

Jennifer set down her cup on a cherry wood end table. "So you're suggesting that the Riddle Killer is interested in Kevin confessing his true nature, not necessarily some particular sin. Seems like a stretch. To what end? Why would Slater single out Kevin, unless Kevin somehow wronged him?"

"Now you're out of my league, I'm afraid."

"You're pushing theory way beyond what feels reasonable, Doctor. My brother was murdered. I hardly see any similarities between his killer and an old lady in a church."

"I'm so sorry. I didn't know." His compassion appeared thoroughly genuine.

"Even naysayers accept the brilliance of the teachings of Jesus," he said. "You do know what he said on the matter?"

"Tell me."

"That to hate a man is the same as killing him. Perhaps the gossipers are murderers after all."

The notion struck her as absurd. Jennifer sighed. "So Slater, who was once wronged by Kevin, studies him today and sees this great inconsistency—that Kevin lives a life of minor sins—anger, resentment, gossip. But Slater believes, as you seem to, that minor sins are no less evil than the greater sins. Kevin decides to become a priest. This upsets Slater and he decides to teach Kevin a lesson. That the gist of it?"

"Who's to say how a demented mind works?" The professor smiled. "Really, it's beyond me how anyone could do this to another man, especially a man like Kevin. Regardless of his past sins, Kevin is a walking testimony of God's grace. You'd think he's been through his share of difficulties. To have become the man he is today is nothing short of amazing."

She studied Dr. Francis. "He is quite unusual, isn't he? I didn't know his type still lived on the West Coast."

"His type?" the professor asked. "You mean his innocence?"

"Innocent, genuine. Maybe even naive, in a nonoffensive way."

"You're aware of his past?"

"Sketchy. I haven't exactly had the time to dig past his file these last two days."

The doctor's brow went up. "Perhaps you would do well to pay a visit to the home of his childhood. I don't know the entire story, but from what Father Strong told me, Kevin's childhood was anything but normal. Not necessarily terrible, mind you, but I wouldn't be surprised to find more there than Father Strong or any of the rest of us suspects, particularly in light of these recent events."

"So you don't know the details of his past. Still, you say he's been through his share of difficulties."

"His parents died when he was one. He was raised by an aunt who despises his pursuit of higher education. As you say, he acts like a man who has recently walked off an island to discover that there is a rest-of-the-world. Naive. I think there's something in Kevin's past that haunts him. It may shed some light on this man you call Slater."

"The boy," she said.

"I'm afraid I don't know about any boy."

She would take a trip to Baker Street as soon as she left. "Nothing else comes to mind? No other students or faculty might have any motive to hurt Kevin?"

"Heavens, no. Not unless all of our gossiping students are becoming murderers to flush out the truth." He grinned.

"You sound like a wonderful teacher, Dr. Francis. Do you mind if I call on you again?"

"Please." He tapped his chest. "There's a special place in here for Kevin. I can't place it or explain why I am so taken by the boy, but I think we all have something to learn from his story."

She stood. "I pray you're right."

"I didn't know you were a religious woman."

"I'm not."

15

THE YOUNG MEN WITH THE CHAINS didn't look like they were carrying any weapons. Not that criminals made a habit of hanging guns around their necks from shoestrings for all to see. Either way, Kevin gave them a pass and pulled back onto Western.

Maybe looking in less obvious spots would fare better. Side streets. Any beer-drinking slug wearing a wife-beater would be packing one, right? Or at least have a piece tucked under the mattress nearby. The fact was, Kevin had no clue what he was doing and the growing realization pushed his nerves into overdrive.

He drove several neighborhoods before working up the courage to park in one particularly seedy-looking lane and take to foot. Wouldn't it be ironic if he were held up at gunpoint minding his own business? Why play games with a serial killer when you could take a stroll down misery lane and get offed any day of the week? Just like in the movies. Or was the other more like a movie?

He walked down the street, past houses with prying eyes. Maybe now would be a good time to pray. On the other hand, considering his intentions, praying felt inappropriate. A ball rolled out on the sidewalk three feet in front of him. He glanced at the house to his right and saw a boy, maybe three feet tall, staring at him with wide brown eyes. A large, shirtless man covered in tattoos, bald except for a black goatee, stood in the doorway behind the boy, watching him from under bushy eyebrows. Kevin picked up the ball and tossed it awkwardly back into the brown lawn.

"You lost?" the man asked.

That obvious? "No," he said and turned away.

"You look lost to me, boy."

Kevin was suddenly too terrified to respond. He walked on, not daring to look back. The man humphed, but made no other comment. Half a block later he glanced back. The man had retreated into his house.

Now, that wasn't so bad. You go, boy. Kevin the player.

Kevin the fool. Here he was, wandering a strange neighborhood, pretending to have a clue, scheming nondescript plans, while the real game awaited its star player twenty miles south. What if Slater had called in the last couple hours? What if he'd called Jennifer or the police with the next threat? Or what if Sam had awakened, found him gone, turned on the phone, and received a call?

Kevin stopped walking. What on earth did he think he was doing? Sam. Sam had a gun. She'd never shown it to him, but he knew she carried it in her purse. Why not just take her gun? What was she going to do, throw him in jail for—

"Excuse me."

Kevin spun around. The man from the doorway stood five feet away. He'd pulled on a white T-shirt that barely managed to contain his bulging shoulders.

"I asked you a question."

Kevin's heart pounded. "I'm . . . I'm not lost."

"I don't believe you. I see a Wall Street punk walking down the sidewalk at ten in the morning and I know he's lost. You trying to score?"

"Score? No. Gosh, no."

"Gosh?" The man grinned and savored the word. "Gosh, no. Then what are you doing so far from home?"

"I'm . . . just walking."

"This look like Central Park to you? Not even the right state, boy. I can hook you up."

A cool sweat ran down Kevin's back. Ask him. Just ask him.

He glanced around. "Actually, I'm looking for a weapon."

The man's eyebrows went up. "And you think this is where weapons grow on trees, is that it?"

"No."

The man studied him. "You a cop?"

"Do I look like a cop?"

"You look like a fool. Is there a difference? What kind of idiot walks around a strange neighborhood looking for a piece?"

"I'm sorry. I should probably leave."

"I guess so."

The man was blocking the sidewalk, so Kevin sidestepped to the street. He took three steps before the man spoke again.

"How much you got?"

He stopped and faced the man. "Four hundred dollars."

"Let me see it."

What if the man robbed him? Too late now. He pulled out his wallet and spread it open.

"Follow me." The man turned and walked back toward his house without checking to see if Kevin followed.

He did. Like a puppy. How many prying eyes watched the sucker from Wall Street slinking along behind Biff?

He followed the man up to his porch. "Wait here." He left Kevin with his hands in his pockets.

Thirty seconds later he was back with something wrapped in an old white T-shirt. "Give me the money."

"What is it?"

"It's a thirty-eight. Cleaned and loaded." Biff glanced up the street. "Worth six, but it's your lucky day. I need the cash."

Kevin fished out his wallet with a trembling hand and handed the contents to the man. He took the bundle. Where was he going to put it? He couldn't just walk down the street with a bundle that had *gun* written all over it. He started to shove it down his pants—too bulky.

The man finished flipping through the bills and saw Kevin's dilemma. He grinned. "Boy, you are a case, aren't you? What're you gonna do, hold up your dog? Give me the shirt."

Kevin unwrapped a shiny silver pistol with a black handle. He gripped the butt with his fingertips and handed the shirt to the man.

The man looked at the gun and smirked. "What do you think you have there? A pastry? Hold it like a man."

Kevin snugged the gun in his palm.

"In your belt. Pull your shirt over it."

Kevin shoved the cold steel barrel past his bellybutton and covered it with his shirt. Still looked pretty obvious to him.

"Suck your gut in. For another hundred I'll show you how to pull the trigger." Grin.

"No thanks."

He turned and walked back out to the sidewalk. He had a gun. What on earth he was going to do with it, he still had no idea. But he had the piece. It was okay to pray now, maybe.

God, help me.

|||

Baker Street. It was the third time in two days Jennifer had driven down the narrow lane under the elms. The warehouse where they'd found the blood couldn't be seen from the street itself—it was in the second row of buildings. She imagined a young boy racing across the street toward the clustered warehouses with a bully at his heels. Kevin and the boy.

"What is here that you want to hide, Kevin?" she murmured. "Hmm?" The white house loomed to her left, immaculate, with the shiny beige Plymouth in its driveway. "What did Aunt Balinda do to you?"

Jennifer parked her car on the street and walked up to the porch. A slight breeze rustled through the leaves. The green lawn appeared freshly mowed and trimmed around the edges. She didn't notice until she stepped up on the porch that the red roses in the flower beds were imitation. For that matter, so were all the flowers. It seemed Aunt Balinda was too tidy a person to mess with the natural flaws of nature. Everything about the house was perfectly finished.

She rang the bell and stepped back. A curtain to her left parted; a middle-aged man with a crew cut looked out. Bob. Kevin's retarded older cousin. The face stared, smiled, and disappeared. Then nothing.

Jennifer rang the bell again. What were they doing in there? Bob had seen her . . .

The door cracked and filled with an old, heavily painted, saggy face. "What do you want?"

Jennifer flipped open her badge. "Agent Peters, FBI. Just wondered if I could come in and ask you a few questions."

"Certainly not."

"Just a few—"

"Do you have a search warrant?"

"No. I didn't think I would need one."

"We all make mistakes, dear. Come back with a search warrant." The woman started to close the door.

"Balinda, I presume?"

She turned back. "Yeah? So what?"

"I will be back, Balinda, and I'll bring the police with me. We'll turn the place inside out. Is that what you want?"

Balinda hesitated. Her eyelashes flapped several times. Ruby red lipstick glistened on her lips, like glossy putty. She smelled of too much talcum powder.

"What do you want?" Balinda asked again.

"I told you. Just a few questions."

"Then ask them." She made no move from the door.

The woman was begging to be properly engaged. "I don't think you understand me. When I come back in an hour, I'll have a half-dozen blue suits with me. We'll have guns and microphones. We'll strip-search you if we have to."

Balinda just stared.

"Or you can let me in now, just me. Are you aware that your son Kevin is in trouble?"

"Doesn't surprise me. I told him he'd end up in trouble if he went off."

"Well, it seems that your warning had some merit."

The woman made no move.

Jennifer nodded and stepped back. "Okay. I'll be back."

"You won't touch anything?"

"Not a thing." She lifted both hands.

"Fine. But I don't like people invading our privacy, you understand?"

"I understand."

Balinda walked inside and Jennifer pushed the door open. A single glance into the dimly lit house washed away her understanding.

She entered a hallway of sorts, formed by stacks of newspapers that ran nearly to the ceiling, leaving a passage just wide enough for a slight man to walk through without getting newsprint on his shoulders. Two faces peered at her from the end of the makeshift hallway—Bob's and another man's—both craning for a view.

Jennifer stepped in and closed the door behind her. Balinda whispered urgently to the two men and they retreated like mice. Grayed carpet had been worn to the wood subfloor. The edge of a newspaper to Jennifer's right stuck out far enough for her to read the headline. *London Herald.* June 24, 1972. Over thirty years old.

"Ask your questions," Balinda snapped from the end of the hall.

Jennifer walked toward her, mind swimming. Why had they stacked all these papers in tall neat stacks like this? The display gave eccentricity a whole new meaning. What kind of woman would do this?

Aunt Balinda wore a white dress, high heels, and enough costume jewelry to sink a battleship. Behind her, backlit by a window that overlooked a dirt yard, Eugene stood in riding boots and what appeared to be a jockey's outfit. Bob wore plaid knickers that revealed the tops of knee-high socks. A polo shirt hugged his thin frame.

The hall directed her into what appeared to be the living room, but again, its dimensions had been altered by floor-to-ceiling stacks of paper. Newspapers alternated with books and magazines and the occasional box. A foot-wide crack between two of the stacks allowed light in from what had once been a window. For all of its mess, the room had an order to it, like a bird's nest. The stacks stood several rows deep, allowing just enough room for old Victorian furniture placed just so between smaller mounds of paper in the middle of the floor. These appeared to be in the process of being sorted.

To Jennifer's right, a small kitchen table was piled high with dishes, some clean, most dirty. A collection of empty TV dinner packages sat on one of the chairs. The boxes had been cut with a pair of blue-handled scissors, which rested on the top box.

"Are you going to ask your questions?"

"I'm . . . I'm sorry, I just didn't expect this. What are you doing here?"

"We live here. What do you think we're doing here?"

"You like newspapers." They weren't complete papers, but sections and clippings from newspapers, she saw, categorized according to subject by placards set into the stacks. People. World. Food. Play. Religion.

Bob stepped away from where he'd cornered himself in the kitchen. "Do you like to play?" He held out an old Game Boy in his hand, a monochrome model that looked like it might play Pong with enough persuasion. "This is my computer."

"Hush, Bobby, honey," Balinda said. "Go to your room and read your books."

"It's a real computer."

"I'm sure the lady isn't interested. She's not from our world. Go to your room."

"She's pretty, Mom."

"She's a dog! Do you like dog hair, Bobby? If you play with her, you'll get dog hair all over you. Is that what you want?"

Bob's eyes widened. "The dog is gone."

"Yes, she will be. Now go to your room and sleep."

The boy started to walk away.

"What do you say?" Eugene said.

Bob turned back and dipped his head at Balinda. "Thank you, Princess." He flashed a grin, hurried off through the kitchen, and shuffled down another hall, this one stacked with books.

"I'm sorry, but you know children," Balinda said. "Minds full of mush. They only understand certain things."

"Do you mind if we sit?"

"Eugene, get our guest a chair."

"Yes, Princess." He grabbed two chairs from the table, set one beside Jennifer, and held the other for Balinda to sit. When she did, he lowered his head with the respect of an eighteenth-century butler. Jennifer stared. They had created a world out of their newspapers and all of this paraphernalia—shaped to fit their lives.

"Thank you."

"You're welcome, madam," Eugene said, dipping his head again.

It wasn't unheard of for adults to create their own realities and then protect them—most people clung to some form of illusion, whether it be found in an extension of entertainment or in religion or simply in a self-propagated lifestyle. The lines between reality and fantasy blurred for every human at some level, but this—this was a case study to be sure.

Jennifer decided to slip into their world. When in Rome . . .

"You've created your own world here, haven't you? Ingenious." She looked around, awed. Beyond the living room stood another doorway, maybe leading to the master bedroom. A stair banister ran along one wall. The same Sunday *Times* Jennifer had read earlier was spread out on the coffee table. The cover story, an article on George W. Bush, had been neatly cut out. The picture of Bush was at the bottom of a discard box. A stack two feet deep sat untouched next to the *Times,* topped by the *Miami Herald.* How many papers did they receive each day?

"You cut away what you don't like and keep the rest," Jennifer said. "What do you do with the clippings?" She turned to Balinda.

The old woman wasn't sure what to think of her sudden change. "What clippings?"

"The ones you don't like."

She knew with one look at Eugene that she'd guessed right. The man glanced nervously at his princess.

"What a brilliant idea!" Jennifer said. "You create your own world by clipping out only those stories that fit your idyllic world and then you discard the rest."

Balinda was speechless.

"Who's the president, Eugene?"

"Eisenhower," the man said without hesitation.

"Of course. Eisenhower. None of the others are worthy to be president. Any news of Reagan or the Bushes or Clinton just gets cut out."

"Don't be silly," Balinda said. "Everyone knows that Eisenhower is our president. We don't go along with the pretenders."

"And who won the World Series this year, Eugene?"

"Baseball isn't played anymore."

"No, of course not. Trick question. What do you do with all the baseball stories?"

"Baseball isn't played—"

"Shut up, Eugene!" Balinda snapped. "Don't repeat yourself like a fool in a lady's presence! Go cut something up."

He saluted and stood at attention. "Yes, sir!"

"Sir? What has gotten into you? You're losing your mind just because we have a visitor? Do I look like a general to you?"

He lowered his hand. "Forgive me, my princess. Perhaps I should save us some coin by cutting some coupons. I should love to take the carriage to the shop for stores as soon as I do."

She glared at him. He did an about-face and walked for the stack of fresh newspapers.

"Don't mind him," Balinda said. "He gets a bit strange when he's excited."

Jennifer glanced out the window. A thin ribbon of smoke drifted skyward from a barrel. The yard was black . . .

They burned them! Whatever didn't fit neatly into the world Balinda wanted went up in smoke. Newspaper stories, books, even pictures on TV dinner boxes. She looked around for a television. An old black and white sat dusty in the living room.

Jennifer stood and walked toward it. "I have to hand it to you, Balinda; you take the cake."

"We do what we are entitled to in the privacy of our home," she said.

"Of course. You have every right. Frankly, it would take tremendous strength and resolve to sustain the world you've managed to build around yourself."

"Thank you. We've given our lives to it. One has to find a way in this chaotic world."

"I can see that." She eased through the living room and peered over the banister. The staircase was filled in with reams of old papers. "Where does this lead?"

"The basement. We don't use it anymore. Not for a long time."

"How long?"

"Thirty years. Maybe longer. It frightened Bob, so we nailed it shut."

Jennifer faced the hall Bob had disappeared down. Kevin's room was down there somewhere, hidden behind piles of books—probably butchered—and magazines. She walked down the hall.

Balinda stood and followed. "Now wait a minute. Where—"

"I just want to see, Balinda. I just want to see how you managed it."

"Questions, you said. You're walking, not talking."

"I won't touch a thing. That's what I said. And I won't."

She passed a bathroom on her right, cluttered and filthy. The hall ended at the doorways of two rooms. The door on the right was shut—presumably Bob's room. The door on the left was open a crack. She pushed it open. A small bed sat in one corner, strewn with loose clippings from children's books. Hundreds of books stood against one wall—half with their covers torn off, altered, or trimmed to meet Balinda's approval. A small window with a pull-down shade looked into the backyard.

"Kevin's old room?" she asked.

"Until he abandoned us. I told him that if he left he'd end up in trouble. I tried to warn him."

"Do you even want to know what kind of trouble he's in?"

Balinda turned away. "What happens out of this house is not my concern. I told him he had no business running off with the serpent. Sss, sss, sss. It's lies, lies, all lies out there. They say we came from monkeys. You're all fools."

"You're right, the world is full of fools. But I can assure you, Kevin isn't one of them."

Balinda's eyes flashed. "Oh, he's not, is he? He was always too smart for us! Bob was the dumb one and Kevin was God himself, come to enlighten the rest of us poor idiots!" She took a breath through her nostrils.

She'd hit a button in the old hag. The adopted nephew wasn't retarded like her own son and Balinda had taken exception to the fact.

Jennifer swallowed and walked to the window. It was fastened down with one screw. What kind of mother would raise a boy in an environment like this? The thought of Kevin crying as they passed by the house yesterday came with new understanding. *Dear Kevin, what did she do to you? Who was the small boy who lived in this room?* The screw was loose in its hole.

Balinda followed Jennifer's stare.

"He used to crawl out of that window. He didn't know that I knew, but I did. Nothing happens around here without my knowing."

Jennifer turned back and brushed past Balinda. Nausea swept through her stomach. In a twisted way, Balinda had probably raised

Kevin with noble intentions. She'd protected him from a terrible world full of evil and death. But at what price?

Slow down, Jennifer. You don't know what happened here. You don't even know that this wasn't a wonderful environment for a child to be raised in.

She stepped into the living room and calmed herself.

"I knew he was sneaking out," Balinda was saying. "But I just couldn't stop him. Not without beating him raw. Never did believe in that kind of discipline. It may have been a mistake. Look at where it got him. Maybe I should have beaten him."

Jennifer took a shallow breath. "What kind of discipline *did* you use?"

"You don't need discipline when your house is in order. Life is discipline enough. Anything more is an admission of weakness." She said it all with her chest puffed, proud. "Isolate them with the truth and they will shine like the stars."

The revelation came like a cool balm. She looked around. So Kevin's rearing had been weird and distorted, but maybe not terrible.

"A man has been threatening Kevin," she said. "We believe it's someone your son—"

"He's my nephew."

"Sorry. Nephew. Someone Kevin might have known when he was ten or eleven. A boy who threatened Kevin. He had a fight with this boy. Maybe you remember something that might help us identify him."

"It must have been the time he came home all bloody. I do remember that. Yes, we found him in bed in the morning and his nose was a mess. He refused to talk about it, but I knew he'd been out. I knew everything."

"What kind of friends did Kevin have at that age?"

Balinda hesitated. "His family was his friend. Bob was his friend."

"But he must have had other friends in the neighborhood. How about Samantha?"

"That fool girl? They sneaked around. Don't think I didn't know. He let it slip a few times. She was the one who may have ruined him in the first place! No, we tried to discourage him from keeping friends outside the house. This is an evil world. You don't just let your children play with anyone!"

"You didn't know *any* of his friends?"

Balinda stared at her for a long time and then walked for the door. "You're starting to repeat your questions. I don't think we can help you more than we have." She opened the door.

Jennifer took a last look around the house. She pitied the poor boy who grew up in this distorted world. He would enter the real world . . . naive.

Like Kevin.

But Balinda was probably right. There was nothing more to learn here.

16

Sunday
Afternoon

SAMANTHA PACED THE FLOOR of the hotel room for the hundredth time. She'd anticipated almost every eventuality, but not Kevin's disappearance.

Roland had paged her and she'd called him from the room phone. He wasn't thrilled about her having turned off her cell but agreed that her plan had some merit. Meanwhile they had set up a meeting with the Pakistani, Salman, in Houston. This evening. Removing Kevin from the game by pulling him out of Slater's reach might have been the best way to stall the killer until her return tomorrow. But she hadn't considered the possibility that Kevin would disappear. Now she was due to catch a flight in a few hours, and Kevin was gone.

Jennifer Peters would be burning up the phone lines by now, trying to find them, but Sam couldn't bring herself to tip her hand—not yet. Something about the whole investigation bothered her, but she couldn't put a finger on it. Something wasn't right.

She reviewed the facts as she knew them.

One. Someone, probably a white male, had terrorized Sacramento over the last twelve months by selecting seemingly random victims, giving them a riddle to solve, and then killing them when they failed. He'd been dubbed the Riddle Killer by the media and the name had stuck with law enforcement. Jennifer's brother, Roy, had been his last victim.

Two. She had opened an undercover CBI investigation under the premise that the killer had or was an inside man. Nothing indicated that the killer knew of her investigation.

Three. Someone with almost the same MO as the Riddle Killer was now stalking both Kevin and her in a game of riddles.

Four. A concrete connection had been established between this same killer and a boy who'd threatened both her and Kevin twenty years earlier.

On the surface, it all made perfect sense: A boy named Slater takes to torturing animals and terrorizing other children. He's nearly killed by one of those children, Kevin, when Kevin locks him in a cellar to protect a young girl Slater intends to harm. But Slater escapes the cellar and grows up to become one of society's worst nightmares—a man void of conscience with a lust for blood. Now, twenty years later, Slater learns that the two children who tormented him so long ago are alive. He stalks them and devises a game to deal with both in one fell swoop. Obvious, right?

No. Not in Sam's mind. For starters, why had Slater waited so long to go after both her and Kevin? Did the small incident in the cellar just skip his mind for twenty years? And what was the likelihood that she, employed by the CBI, just happened to be assigned to a case involving the same person who tried to kill her twenty years ago?

And now, in the eleventh hour, this new lead from Sacramento—someone in Houston who claimed to know Slater. Or more accurately, the Riddle Killer. If she was right, they were all barking up the wrong tree.

Sam glanced at her watch. Two-thirty and still nothing. She had a plane to catch for Dallas at five. "Come on, Kevin. You're forcing my hand here."

She sighed and picked up her cell phone. She reluctantly switched it on and dialed Jennifer Peters's number.

"Peters."

"Hello, Agent Peters. Samantha Sheer—"

"Samantha! Where are you? Kevin's gone. We've been trying to track him down all morning."

"Slow down. I know Kevin's gone. He's with me. Or was with me, I should say."

"With *you?* This isn't your investigation. You have no right this side of hell to act without our approval! You trying to get him killed?"

Wrong, Jennifer, I don't need your approval. "Don't insult me."

"Do you have any idea how crazy things are down here? The media's gotten wind, presumably through that deadhead Milton, that Kevin's disappeared, and they're already suggesting Slater kidnapped him. They've got cameras on rooftops, waiting for the next bomb, for heaven's sake! A killer's loose out there, and the only man who may be able to lead us to him has gone AWOL. Why didn't you call? Where is he now?"

"Take a breath, Jennifer. I have called, against my better judgment. I've put in a request to share what we know with you, but only you, do you understand? What I share with you, no one else hears. Not Milton, not the FBI, no one."

"Put in a request with whom?"

"With the attorney general. We've been working this case from a new angle, you might say. Now you know, but no one else does."

Silence.

"Agreed?"

"I swear, the way these bureaucracies work, you'd think we still lived in caves. I've been busting my butt for a year on this case, and now I learn that some crackpot agency is doing an end run? Do you have any information that might be useful, or is that a secret too?"

"We have reason to suspect an inside link."

"Inside. As in law enforcement?"

"Maybe. We would have shared files a long time ago if we didn't suspect that someone inside may be tracking with Slater."

"Meaning?"

"Meaning we're not sure who we can trust. For reasons I can't go into today, I don't think Slater is who you think he is."

"You mean the boy? *I* don't even know who I think he is!"

"That's not what I mean. He probably is the boy. But who's the boy?"

"You tell us. He threatened you, didn't he?"

"That was a long time ago, and we have no ID. For all we know, he's the director of the FBI now."

"Please, don't patronize me."

"You're right. He's not the director of the FBI. All I'm saying is that we can't eliminate the possibility that he's someone on the inside. I'll know more tomorrow."

"This is ridiculous. Where are you now?"

Sam paused. She had no choice now. Withholding information from Jennifer would only hamper her investigation at this point. She needed the FBI to focus on their own investigation, not meddle in hers. And there was this little fact that Kevin was missing.

She explained her rationale for taking Kevin, and Jennifer listened patiently, interrupting occasionally with pointed questions. Sam's reasoning finally won her a grunt of approval. The news of Kevin's disappearance didn't.

"So as far as we know, Slater does have him," Jennifer said.

"I doubt it. But it does look like I've made a mistake. I didn't expect this."

Jennifer let the apology go, which from Sam was as good as an acceptance. The FBI agent sighed.

"Let's hope he comes in. Soon. How well did you know him when he was a boy?"

"We were close. I didn't have a better friend."

"I visited his aunt's house this morning."

Sam sat on the bed. How much did Jennifer know? Kevin had never shared the details of his life in the house with Sam, but she knew much more than he suspected.

"I never did see the inside of the house," Sam said. "His aunt wouldn't allow it. It was hard enough sneaking around the way we did."

"Was there abuse?"

"Physical, no. Not that I saw. But in my book Kevin suffered severe, systematic psychological abuse from the day he entered that twisted house. You talked to Balinda?"

"Yes. She's created a sanctuary for herself in there. The only realities that make it past the cutting floor are the ones she decides are real. God only knows what the house was like twenty years ago. Manipulation of a child's learning process isn't unheard of—it's even broadly accepted in some arenas. Military school comes to mind. But I've never heard of anything like Balinda's little kingdom. Judging by Kevin's reaction to the place, I would tend to agree. He suffered abuse in that house."

Sam let the phone line remain silent for a while.

"Be careful, Jennifer. This is a case about a hurting man as much as it is a hunt for a killer."

Jennifer hesitated. "Meaning?"

"There's more. There are secrets behind the walls of that house."

"Secrets he hasn't shared with you, his childhood sweetheart?"

"Yes."

By the sound of Jennifer's breathing, Sam knew she felt uncomfortable with the tone of the conversation. She decided to expand the agent's mind a little.

"I want you to consider something that's nagged me for the last two days, Jennifer. No one hears, understand? This is between us. Agreed?"

"Go on."

"I would like you to consider the possibility that Kevin and Slater are really the same person." She dropped the bomb and let Jennifer respond.

"I . . . I don't think that's possible." Jennifer chuckled nervously. "I mean that would be . . . the evidence doesn't support that! How could he pull off such a crazy stunt?"

"He's not pulling anything off. Please, understand me, I'm not suggesting it's true, and God knows even considering the idea terrifies me, but there are elements to this case that just don't sit right. I think the possibility is at least worth some thought."

"He would have to be calling himself. You're suggesting he was in Sacramento, blowing up victims three months ago?"

"If he is the Riddle Killer. I'm working on that."

"And if he is Slater, who's the boy? We found blood in the warehouse, consistent with this story. There was a boy."

"Unless the boy was really Kevin. Or there was no boy."

"You were there—"

"I never actually saw the boy, Jennifer."

"Your father forced the family to leave! What do you mean you never *saw* the boy?"

"I mean I told my father the boy was there—there was plenty of evidence at my window and I believed Kevin for the rest. Call it a white lie. Regardless, I actually never saw the boy. We forced the family of a bully to move, but thinking back on it, the boy ran off before my dad could apprehend him. He accused a local bully based on my testimony, and I based my testimony on Kevin's. But there was no definitive evidence that it was someone *other* than Kevin. I didn't even know Kevin had locked the boy in the warehouse until yesterday."

"The physical evidence for Kevin being Slater doesn't add up. He blew up his own car?"

"I'm not saying that he *is* Slater. I'm only positing a possibility. Considering his childhood, Multiple Personality Disorder may not be out of the question—the Kevin we know wouldn't necessarily even know that he's Slater. Everything that we have so far could fit the scenario; that's all I'm saying. There are no inconsistencies. Think about it."

"Neither is there any evidence to support it. Highly unlikely. MPD results only in very limited cases of severe childhood abuse. Almost always physical abuse. Balinda might be a witch, but she doesn't fit the profile for physical abuse. You said so yourself."

"You're right, there wasn't physical abuse. But there are exceptions."

"Not any that fit this scenario. At least not that I know of, and it is my field of study."

Probably right. Highly unlikely, but in cases like this every possibility had to be considered. Something was not what it seemed, and as disturbing as her suggestion was, Sam couldn't just discard it. If Kevin was Slater, exposing the fact would be the greatest favor she could do for her childhood friend.

On the other hand, hearing herself say it out loud, the notion sounded absurd. A simple voice or handwriting analysis would settle the matter.

"Have the lab run a handwriting comparison from the jug."

"We already have. Standard procedure. It was negative."

"It's technically possible for multiple personalities to have varying motor characteristics."

"In this case, I don't think so."

"Then start comparing it with everyone else connected to the case. Someone on the inside's working this, Jennifer. Someone's not who we think they are."

"Then get me your file."

"It's on the way."

"And if Kevin contacts you, call me. Immediately." To say that the agent sounded agitated would be like saying the sky was big.

"You have my word."

"As much as your plan to isolate Kevin may have made sense, having Slater's voice on tape could be invaluable. Particularly in light of your suggestion. Turn it on and leave it on."

Sam picked up Slater's silver phone and switched it on. "Done."

"The recording device is still active?"

"Yes."

A knock sounded on the door. Sam started.

"What is it?" Jennifer asked.

"Someone's at the door." She walked for the door.

"Who?"

She turned the deadbolt and pulled it open. Kevin stood in the hallway, blinking and haggard.

"Kevin," Sam said. "It's Kevin."

|||

Jennifer lowered the phone and sat hard. The notion that Kevin and the Riddle Killer might be the same man wasn't only absurd; it was . . . wrong. Sick. Deeply disturbing.

Galager walked by her desk, headed for the lab. She couldn't bring herself to look at him. Was it possible?

Her mind spun back to the scene of Roy's death. Was it possible that Kevin—

No! It made no sense.

And why is this such an infuriating prospect, Jennifer? You can't imagine Kevin killing Roy because you like Kevin. He reminds you of Roy, for heaven's sake.

Jennifer rehearsed the facts quickly. If Kevin was Slater, then he would have to be calling himself, possible but unlikely. He would also have to have an alter ego of which he was clueless. She had interviewed enough witnesses over the years to recognize sincerity, and Kevin had it in spades. He would have had to plant the bombs long ago, possible, but in both cases he would have had to detonate them without his own knowing.

No. No, this was too much. She began to relax. The man she had comforted in the park yesterday was no killer. The boy, whose blood they'd found in the cellar, on the other hand, could be.

Point was, she had panicked at the thought that Kevin might be the killer, hadn't she? She should have been ecstatic at the mere prospect of uncovering the killer's true identity. Which said that she cared far too much for Kevin, an absurdity in itself given the fact that she hardly knew him!

On the other hand, she was bound to him in a way few people ever are. They shared the death of her brother in common—she as the victim's survivor, he as the next victim.

Jennifer sighed and stood. She was too emotionally wrapped up in this whole thing. The bureau chief was right.

"Galager!"

The man paused at the door across the room. She motioned him back.

"What's up?"

"We found Kevin."

Galager pulled up. "Where?"

"Palos Verdes. He's okay."

"Should I get Milton?"

He was the last person she wanted to bring in. But she had her marching orders, didn't she? At least she didn't have to deal with him directly. She scribbled the information on a notepad, ripped the page off, and handed it to Galager.

"Fill him in. Tell him I'm tied up."

It was the truth. She was tied up, in knots that refused to loosen.

|||

They sat on the bed in a stalemate. Kevin was hiding something; that much Sam had known since she'd first talked to him. Friday night. Now his lying was more blatant, but try as she may, she could not coax the truth out of him. His story that he'd been wandering through his old neighborhood, thinking, for the past eight hours was simply unbelievable. True, given his circumstances, almost any behavior was possible. But she knew Kevin too well; she could read those clear blue eyes, and they were shifting. Something else was bothering him.

"Okay, Kevin, but I still don't think you're telling me everything. I have a plane to catch in a couple hours. With any luck, Slater will take the day to revel in his little victory yesterday. God knows we need the time."

"When will you be back?"

"Tomorrow morning." She stood, walked to the window, and pulled back the curtain. "We're closing in, Kevin. We're right on this guy's tail; I can feel it in my bones."

"I wish you weren't going."

Sam turned back. "Jennifer will be here. She'll want to talk to you."

He looked past her out the window. "Yeah."

Dark circles hung under his eyes. He seemed distracted.

"I need a drink," he said. "You want one?"

"I'm fine. You're not going to run off again, are you?"

He grinned. "Come on. I'm here, aren't I?"

"Yes, you are. Hurry back."

He opened the door to leave.

The beige phone on the nightstand rang shrilly. She glanced at the clock beside it—3 P.M. They had overstayed their checkout.

"Go ahead," she told Kevin. "It's probably the front desk."

Kevin left and she picked up the phone.

"Hello?"

"Hello, Samantha."

Slater! She whirled to the door. So Kevin *couldn't* be Slater! He'd been in the room when the killer had called.

"Kevin!" He was gone.

"Not Kevin. It's your other lover, dear."

How had Slater gotten their number? The only person who knew where they were was Jennifer. *Jennifer . . .*

"They want my voice, Samantha. I want to give them my voice. Have you turned the cell phone back on, or are you still playing your idiotic cat-and-mouse game?"

"It's on."

The line clicked. Slater's cell began to ring. She grabbed it and answered.

"There, that's better, don't you think? The game won't last forever; we might as well make this more interesting."

It was the first time she'd actually heard his voice. Low and gravelly.

"What good is a game that you can't lose?" she asked. "It proves nothing."

"Oh, but I can lose, Sam. The fact that I haven't proves that I'm smarter than you." Short heavy breath. "I came within a single pane of glass of killing you once. This time I won't fail."

The boy. She turned and sat on the bed. "So that was you."

"Do you know why I wanted to kill you?"

"No." Keep him talking. "Tell me."

"Because all nice people deserve to die. Especially the pretty ones with bright blue eyes. I despise beauty almost as much as I despise nice little boys. I'm not sure who I hate more, you or that imbecile you call your lover."

"You make me sick!" Samantha said. "You prey on innocence because you're too stupid to realize it's far more fascinating than evil."

Silence. Only heavy breathing. She'd struck a nerve.

"Kevin confessed, as you demanded," she said. "He told the whole world about that night. But you can't live by your own rules, can you?"

"Yes, of course. The boy. Was that me? Maybe it was, maybe it wasn't. Kevin still hasn't confessed his sin. He hasn't even hinted at it. The secret's much too dark, even for him, I think."

"What? *What* sin?"

He chuckled.

"The sin, Samantha. *The* sin. Riddle time. *What wants to be filled but will always be empty?* I'll give you a clue: It's not your head. It has a number: 36933. You have ninety minutes before the fireworks begin. And please remember, no cops."

"Why are you so afraid of the cops?"

"It's not who I'm afraid of; it's who I want to play with." The line clicked.

He was gone.

Sam stood still, mind reeling. He'd called on the hotel room phone. Could he have tracked them down so quickly? Or the phone—could he have a way of tracking it once she turned it on? Unlikely. She paced to the end of the bed and back. Think, Sam! Think! Where was Kevin? They had to—

"Sam?" Kevin's muffled voice sounded beyond the door. He knocked.

She ran for the door. Opened it.

"He called," she said.

"Slater?" His face went white.

"Yes."

Kevin stepped in, can of 7UP in his hand. "What did he say?"

"Another riddle. *What wants to be filled but will always be empty?* With some numbers. 36933." The most obvious solution had already run through her mind. She ran to the coffee table and grabbed the telephone book.

"Call Jennifer."

"How much time?"

"Ninety minutes. Threes. This guy's obsessed with threes and progressions of threes. Call her!"

Kevin set his drink down, jumped for the phone, and punched in her number. He relayed the information quickly.

"On the room phone," he said.

"No, he called back on the cell," Sam corrected him.

"He called back on the cell," Kevin relayed.

Sam spread the phone directory map open and searched the streets. Thirty-third. A warehouse district.

"No cops. Remind her no cops. If she has any ideas, call, but keep the others out of it. He was very clear."

She closed her eyes and took a deep breath. It was the only answer that made immediate sense. But why would Slater choose such an obvious riddle?

She looked up at Kevin. "Tell Jennifer that I was wrong about Slater. You were in the room when Slater called."

Kevin looked at her with a raised eyebrow, passed on the message, listened for a moment, and then addressed Sam. "She says she's on her way. Don't move."

Only Jennifer could know specifically where they were. She would have picked up the caller ID when Sam called her on the room phone. How had Slater tracked them down so quickly?

Sam stepped forward and took the phone from Kevin. "Don't bother coming, Jennifer. We'll be gone. Work the riddle. I'll call you as soon as we have something."

"How will leaving help you? I want Kevin back in my sights where I can work with him. You hear me?"

"I hear you. We're out of time now. Just work the riddle. I'll call you."

"Sam—"

She hung up. She had to think this through.

"Okay, Kevin. Here we go. Slater's into threes; we know that. He's also into progressions. Every target is larger than the one before. He gives you three minutes, then thirty minutes, then sixty minutes, and now ninety minutes. And he gives this number, 36933. The 369 follows the natural progression, but the 33 doesn't. Unless they're not part of the 369. I think we have an address: 369 Thirty-third Street. It's in a warehouse district in Long Beach, about ten miles from here. *What wants to be filled but will always be empty?* A vacant warehouse."

"That's it?"

"Unless you can think of anything better. Opposites, remember? All of his riddles have been about opposites. Things that aren't what they want or seem to be. Night and day. Buses that go around in circles. A warehouse that is designed to hold things but is empty."

"Maybe."

They stared at each other for a few seconds. They had no choice. She grabbed his hand.

"Come on, let's go."

17

THE WAREHOUSE IDENTIFIED AS 369 on Thirty-third Street stood among a dozen others in northern Long Beach, all constructed from the same corrugated tin, all two stories high, all addressed with the same large black numbers above the doors. Years of neglect had worn most of them down to a dull gray. The 369 was hardly more than a shadow. No sign identifying a business name. Looked vacant.

Kevin slowed the car and peered ahead at the looming structure. Dust blew across the sidewalk. A faded Mountain Dew bottle, the two-liter plastic variety, bumped up against a single-entry door to the right of the loading bay.

He stopped the car thirty yards from the corner and eased the gearshift into park. He could hear several sounds—the purring of the engine, the blower blasting air over their feet, the thumping in his chest. They all sounded too loud.

He glanced at Sam, who stared at the structure, searching.

"What now?"

He had to get the gun out of the trunk; that was what now. Not because he thought Slater would be here, but because he wasn't going anywhere without his new purchase.

"Now we go in," she said. "Unless the fire codes were nonexistent twenty years ago, the building will have a rear entrance."

"You take the back," Kevin said. "I'll take the front."

Sam's right eyebrow lifted. "I think you should wait here."

"No. I'm going in."

"I really don't think—"

"I can't sit around and play dumb, Sam!" The aggression in his tone surprised him. "I have to do something."

She faced 369 Thirty-third Street again. Time was ticking. Sixty-two minutes. Kevin wiped a trickling line of sweat from his temple with the back of his hand.

"Doesn't seem right," Sam said.

"Too easy."

She didn't respond.

"We don't have a key—how are we getting in?" he asked.

"Depends. Getting in isn't the concern. What if he's rigged it to blow upon entry?"

"That's not his game," Kevin said. "He said ninety minutes. Wouldn't he stick to his own rules?"

She nodded. "Has so far. Blew the bus ahead of schedule but only because we broke the rules. Still doesn't seem right." She cracked her door. "Okay, let's see what we have here."

Kevin got out and followed Sam toward the building. As far as he could see in both directions, the street was empty. A warm late afternoon breeze lifted dust from the pavement in a small dust devil twenty feet to his right. The plastic Mountain Dew bottle thumped quietly against the entry door. Somewhere a crow cawed. If Jennifer had figured out the riddle, at least she wasn't making the mistake of swarming in with the cops. They walked up to a steel door with a corroded deadbolt.

"So how *are* we getting in?" Kevin whispered.

Sam eased the plastic bottle aside with her foot, put a hand on the doorknob, and twisted. The door swung in with a creak. "Like that."

They exchanged stares. Sam stuck her head into the black opening, looked around briefly, and pulled back. "You sure you're up to this?"

"Do I have a choice?"

"I could go in alone."

Kevin looked at the dark gap and squinted. Black. The gun was still back in the trunk.

"Okay, I'm going around back to see what we have," Sam said. "Wait for me to signal you. When you go in, find lights and turn them on, but otherwise touch nothing. Look for anything out of the ordinary. Could be a suitcase, a box, anything not covered in dust. I'll work my way through the warehouse in the dark just in case someone's in there. Unlikely, but we'll take the precaution. Clear?"

"Yes." Kevin wasn't sure how clear it was. His mind was still on the gun in the trunk.

"Go easy." She edged to the corner, looked around, and then disappeared.

Kevin ran for the car on his tiptoes. He found the shiny silver pistol where he'd hidden it under the carpet behind the spare tire. He shoved it into his belt, closed the trunk as quietly as he could, and hurried back to the warehouse.

The gun handle stuck out from his belly like a black horn. He pulled his shirt over the butt and flattened it as best he could.

Darkness shrouded the warehouse interior. Still no signal from Sam. Kevin poked his head in and peered through the oil-thick blackness. He reached in and felt for a light switch along the wall. His fingers touched a cool metal box with a plastic switch on its face. He flipped the switch.

A loud hum. Light flooded the warehouse. He grabbed at his midsection and withdrew the gun. Nothing stirred.

He peeked again. A vacant foyer with a receiving desk. Lots of dust. The smell of mildewing rags filled his nostrils. But nothing like a bomb that he could see. Beyond the receiving area, stairs led up to a second floor. Offices. A panel of switches was mounted to the wall at the foot of the stairs. Marks broke the dust directly up the middle of the steps. Footprints.

He instinctively pulled his head from the door. Slater! Had to be. Sam was right; this was it!

Still no signal from her. Unless she'd called him and he'd missed it. With all these walls it was possible.

Kevin held his breath and slipped through the door. He stood still for a moment and then walked on the balls of his feet toward the receiving desk. Behind the desk—could be a place for a bomb. No, the footprints went up . . .

Clunk!

Kevin whirled around. The door had swung shut! The wind? Yes, the wind had—

Click. The lights went out.

Kevin started in the direction of the door, blinded by darkness. He took several quick steps, stuck out a hand, and groped for the door. His knuckles smashed into steel. He fumbled for the handle, found it, and twisted.

But it refused to turn. He gripped hard and jerked the handle first to the left and then to the right. Locked.

Okay, Kevin, stay calm. It's one of those doors that stays locked. Except that it had opened for Sam. Because she was on the outside.

Wasn't it normally the other way around?

He turned and yelled. "Sam?" His voice sounded muted.

"Sam!" This time the word echoed from beyond the stairs.

He'd seen a light panel by the stairs. Maybe they operated other lights? Kevin turned and walked toward the stairs, but his knees found the reception desk first. The crash sent a bolt of electricity through his nerves and he nearly dropped the gun. He stepped to the side and shuffled up to where he remembered the light switches.

"Samantha!"

He slapped the wall, found the switches, and palmed them on. No lights.

The floor above him creaked. "Sam?"

"Kevin!" Sam! Her voice sounded distant, from the back, as if she was still outside the building.

"Sam, I'm in here!"

His eyes had adjusted to the darkness. Light glowed from the upper level. Kevin glanced back toward the door, saw only darkness, and mounted the stairs. Light glowed faintly above him, a window maybe.

"Sam?"

She didn't respond.

He had to get to some light! Another floorboard creaked and he whipped around, gun extended. Was the weapon cocked? He snugged his thumb over the hammer and pulled it back. *Click.* Easy, Kevin. You've never shot a gun in your life. You shoot at a shadow and it might be Sam. And what if the gun doesn't even work?

He headed up the stairs on weak legs.

"Kevin!"

Sam's voice came from his right and forward, definitely outside. He paused halfway up the steps, tried to still his breathing so that he could hear better, but finally gave up and hurried toward the light at the top.

The glow came from a doorway at the end of a barely visible hallway. His breathing came hushed and low now. Something thumped down the hall. He held his breath. There it was again, a step. Boots. Directly ahead and to his right. From one of the other rooms along the hall. Sam? No, Sam was still outside! *Dear God, give me strength.*

He felt exposed standing in the hall. What was he thinking, waltzing up the stairs as if he were some kind of gunslinger?

Frantic, Kevin stepped to the faint outline of a doorway on his right. The floorboards protested under his feet. He cleared the doorway and slid back against the wall on his left.

Boots. There was definitely someone else on the upper floor with him. Could be Sam if the acoustics had misdirected her voice. Could it be her? Sure it could.

It is, Kevin. It's Sam. She's in the next room, and she's found the bomb. No, her voice had been distant. And she didn't walk like that. No way.

Her voice suddenly came again, faint. "Kevin!"

This time there was no mistake, Sam was yelling at him from below, out near the front door now. Her fist pounded on the steel door.

"Kevin, are you in there?"

He took one step back toward the doorway. The boot again. Thumping in the next room.

Someone was in there! Slater. He gripped the pistol tightly. Slater had lured him in. That's why the riddle was so simple. A dread spread through his bones.

Sam was at the front door. The deadbolt wasn't engaged—she should be able to either break it or pick it.

Another thought occurred to him. The bomb was probably set to go off—what if he was trapped in here when it did? What if the cops came and Slater detonated the bomb early? But Sam would never allow the cops anywhere near the warehouse now.

But what if she couldn't get the door open?

Panicked, Kevin slid along the wall, met a corner, and felt his way along the back wall. He put his ear on the plaster.

Breathing. Slow and deep. Not his. Slow shuffling.

A low voice reached through the wall. "Kevinnnn . . ."

He froze.

"Forty-six minutesss . . . Kevinnnn."

III

The difference between innocence and naiveté has never registered in Slater's mind. The two are synonymous. In fact, there is no such animal as innocence. They are all as guilty as hell. But he can't deny that some are more naive than others, and watching Kevin creep up the stairs like a mouse has reminded Slater of how utterly naive his nemesis really is.

He'd been sorely tempted to kick the man in the head then, while Kevin was still four steps from the top. Watching him tumble and break would have held its appeal. But place-kicking has always struck him as one of sport's more boring moments.

Welcome to my house, Kevin.

The man has gone and gotten himself a gun. He holds it like he might hold a vial of the Ebola virus and probably hasn't thought to cock it, but he's at least gathered the resolve to arm himself. And he is undoubtedly packing without Samantha's knowledge. She would never allow a civilian to stumble around with a loaded weapon. Kevin has found a sliver of manhood. How fun! The man may actually try to kill him, as if he's become the stalker instead of the victim.

In ways not even Kevin can yet know, this isn't such a new thing. Kevin has tried to kill him before. Their lives are inseparably intertwined, each bent on killing the other. To think that this man who's crept up the stairs holding his big shiny pistol has the stomach to pull the trigger, much less kill, is absurd.

Now the fool has wedged himself in the next room down and is undoubtedly wetting himself. If he only knew what lay in store for him in the hours to come, he might be lying in a puddle of his own vomit.

Here, kitty, kitty.

"Forty-six minutesss . . . Kevinnnn . . ."

|||

Kevin nearly pulled the trigger then. Not with calculated aim, but out of sheer terror.

"Sam?" His voice sounded like a wounded lamb's bleating. He was briefly revolted by his weakness. If this was Slater, he was getting exactly what he wanted. A face to face. A chance to blow him away.

The doorway stood opposite him, its gaping hole darker than the black surrounding it. If he were to run now, he could bound down the stairs and reach the front door, right?

A new sound reached into the room—the sound of something sharp scraping along the wall outside. Down the hall toward his door.

Kevin gripped the pistol in both hands, pointed it at the doorway, and slid down to his seat. If Slater stepped through that space, he'd do it. He'd see the dark form and start pulling the trigger.

The scraping continued, closer, closer. Closer.

"Kevinnn," a voice whispered.

God, help me! His mind started to go fuzzy.

Take him out, Kevin. Jennifer's voice echoed through his mind. Blow the scumbag away!

He could hardly see the gun in front of him to aim it, but he could point. And whoever walked through that door wouldn't be able to see him, right? Not in this darkness. Kevin would only see a shadow, but he had that advantage.

The scraping closed in on the door.

Sweat slipped into Kevin's eyes. He held his breath.

Sam's voice yelled distant. "Kevin, you stay put! You hear me?"

He couldn't respond.

"Stay right there."

She was going to get something to force the door. Pick the lock. A brick, a crowbar, a gun. A gun! She had a gun in her purse. *Hurry!*

The whisper came again. "Kevinnnn . . ."

The doorway suddenly filled with the dark shape of a man. Kevin's finger tightened on the trigger. What . . . what if it wasn't Slater? A bum, maybe.

The form stood still, as if staring at him. If it moved . . . If it even flinched, Kevin would pull the trigger.

Blood pounded through his head as if pumps had been shoved in his ears and were trying to suck him dry. *Whoosh, whoosh.* He couldn't move other than to tremble slightly in the dark. He was eleven years old again, facing the boy in the cellar. Trapped. *That'll cost you your eyeballs, punk.*

A metal object clanged against the front door. Sam!

The figure didn't flinch.

Now, Kevin! Now! Before he runs. Pull the trigger!

Clang!

"Why would I do something so senseless as blow up an old abandoned warehouse?" Slater's voice asked.

"It's so nice to meet you again face to face, Kevin. I like the dark, don't you? I thought about bringing candles for the occasion, but I like this better."

Shoot! Shoot, shoot, SHOOT!

"We've only been at this three days and I'm already tired of it. Practice is over. We start the real game tonight," Slater said.

The sound of steel against steel echoed from the front door.

"We'll be seeing you."

The figure moved.

The pressure Kevin had exerted on the trigger finally sprang the hammer at the same instant. The room ignited with a brilliant flash chased by a horrendous thunder. He saw Slater's black coat as he cleared the doorway.

"Aaaahhhh!" He fired again. A third time. He scrambled to his feet, leapt for the opening, and spun into the hallway. A door at the end of the hall swung closed. The man was gone. Darkness surrounded Kevin.

He whirled around, grabbed the railing, and stumbled down the stairs.

"Kevin!"

The door burst open to daylight before Kevin reached it. Sam jumped clear and he spilled out onto the sidewalk.

Sam had her weapon drawn. She took one look at Kevin and spun into the doorway, gun extended.

"He's gone," Kevin panted. "Out back. A window or something."

"Wait here." Sam ran to the corner, shoved her head around, and then disappeared.

The ground felt uneven under Kevin's feet. He gripped a telephone pole and steadied himself. Why had he waited? He could have ended the whole thing with one shot, right there in the room. On the other hand, he had no proof that the figure was Slater. Could've been an idiot playing . . .

No, it was Slater. Definitely. You spineless punk! *You let him walk. He was right there and you whimpered like a dog!* Kevin grunted and closed his eyes, furious.

Sam reappeared thirty seconds later.

"He's gone."

"He was just there! Are you sure?"

"There's a fire escape with a ladder. He could be anywhere by now. I doubt he's hanging around for an encore." She glanced back, considering.

"There's no bomb, Sam. He wanted to meet me. That's why the riddle was so easy. I saw him."

She stepped up to the door, looked inside, and flipped the switches. Nothing happened.

"How did the door lock?"

"I don't know. I was just in there and it slammed behind me."

She stepped just beyond the door and looked up. "It's rigged. He used a pulley with a string . . ." She followed the string with her eyes.

"What is it?"

"The string ends by the counter. He was down here when he pulled the door closed."

The revelation struck Kevin as absurd. "In the lobby?"

"Yes, I think so. String's pretty well hidden, but he was here. I don't want to contaminate the scene—we need to get some light in there." She walked back out and opened her cell phone. "You sure it was him?"

"He spoke to me. He stood right there and asked me why he'd be so senseless as to blow up an abandoned building." Kevin's legs felt like putty. He abruptly sat on the sidewalk. The gun hung from his right hand.

Sam eyed it. "This is what you found wandering your old neighborhood this morning?"

Kevin set the gun down. "Sorry. I can't just let him push me around anymore."

She nodded. "Put it back in the trunk or wherever you had it stashed, and please, don't use it again."

"I shot at him. You think maybe I hit him?"

"I didn't see any blood. But they'll find evidence of the shots." She paused. "They may want you to surrender the gun. I don't suppose it's legal."

He shook his head.

"Just get it out of sight before the others get here. I'll talk to Jennifer."

"Others?"

She glanced at her watch. "It's time for her to take over here. I have a plane to catch."

18

THERE WAS NO BOMB and Slater had met his objective forty minutes early. They had solved their first riddle within the allotted time, but it still had served the killer. He'd made contact with Kevin in person and escaped without a trace.

Sam had called Jennifer with the details while waiting for her cab to arrive. She was still unsettled about something—was even a little reluctant to call Jennifer, but she said that she had no choice. Of all the authorities, she trusted Jennifer the most. No cops until the ninety-minute mark had passed; that much she'd insisted on.

Jennifer was on her way with an FBI team to begin the investigation. Sam would be lucky to catch her flight; Kevin watched the cab's taillights as it sped down the street and around the corner.

Yes indeed, they had solved the riddle. Or had they? He should be swimming in relief about now—he'd come nose to nose with a madman and survived. Chased him away with a few shots to boot. Sort of.

But his head still felt like it was caught in a vise. He agreed with Sam; something wasn't right.

What was it about this appointment in Houston that was so important to her? And why wasn't she forthcoming on the actual nature of the meeting? She knew the Riddle Killer was here. What was there in Houston?

And why wouldn't she just tell him? Here in Long Beach the city was terrorized by the man the media had dubbed the Riddle Killer, but Sam was off on a tangent in another city. Made no sense.

A black car swung onto the street and roared toward him. Jennifer.

Two other agents climbed out with her, one with weapon drawn, both armed with flashlights. Jennifer spoke quickly to them, sending one around back and the other for the front door, which still stood open in a splintered frame. Sam had taken the car jack to it.

Jennifer approached him, dressed in a blue suit, hair flowing around her shoulders in the warm breeze. "Are you okay?" she asked.

She glanced at the warehouse, and for a brief moment Kevin imagined that her question was only a courtesy—her real interest lay in whatever awaited her prying eyes beyond the door. A new crime scene. Like all of them, she loved the crime scenes. As well she should—the crime scene led to the criminal, in this case Slater.

She turned her attention back to him.

"As okay as I can be, I suppose," he said.

She walked up to him and looked into his eyes. "I thought we understood each other."

He ran a hand through his hair. "What do you mean?"

"I mean we're on the same side here. I mean you tell me everything, or did our conversation yesterday not make an impression on you?"

He suddenly felt like a silly schoolboy standing in the principal's office. "Of course we're on the same side."

"Then make me a promise you can live by. You don't disappear unless we agree for you to disappear. In fact, you do *nothing* unless we agree you do it. I can't do this without you, and I certainly don't need you following someone else's lead."

An unreasonable sorrow swept over Kevin. He felt a knot in his throat, as if he might cry, right here in front of her. Again. Nothing would be so humiliating.

"I'm sorry. Sam said—"

"I don't care what Sam tells you. You're my responsibility, not hers. Heaven knows I need all the help I can get, but until you hear differently from someone besides Sam, you follow my lead. Regardless of whose idea it is, you talk to me. Okay?"

"Okay."

She sighed and closed her eyes momentarily. "Now what did Sam suggest?"

"That I should do everything you say."

Jennifer blinked. "She's right." She looked past him at the warehouse. "I want this creep as much as you do. You're our best shot . . ." She stopped.

"I know. You need me to get him. Who gives a rip about Kevin as long as we get what we need out of him; is that it?"

She stared at him, whether angered or embarrassed, he couldn't tell. Her face softened.

"No, that isn't it. I'm sorry you're living through this hell, Kevin. It's beyond me why innocent people have to suffer, but try as I have, changing the fact is beyond me." She held his eyes with her own. "I didn't mean to sound so harsh. I just . . . I'm not going to let him get to you. He killed my brother, remember? I lost Roy, but I'm not going to lose you."

Kevin suddenly understood. It explained her anger. Maybe more.

"And yes, as a matter of fact, I do need you," she said. "You're our best hope of apprehending a very demented nut case who happens to be after you."

Now Kevin felt more like a clumsy freshman than anyone who might be hauled into the school office for discipline. *Stupid, Kevin. Stupid, stupid.*

"I'm sorry. I'm so sorry."

"Apology accepted. Just don't run off again, okay?"

"Guaranteed." He lifted his eyes and saw the same strange look he'd seen in Sam's eyes at times. A cross between concern and empathy. *Stupid, stupid, Kevin.*

Jennifer dropped her eyes to his mouth and took a deep breath. "So. You saw him."

He nodded.

She glanced back at the door. "He's progressing."

"Progressing?"

"He wants more. More contact, more danger. Resolution."

"Then why doesn't he just come out and ask me for whatever it is he wants?"

She held a flashlight in her hand. "Are you up to walking through it with me? We'll wait until my men come out—I don't want to compromise any evidence. I realize you're frazzled, but the sooner I know how this went down, the greater our chances of using any information we come up with."

He nodded. "The cops know yet?"

"Not yet. Milton can't seem to keep his trap shut. He knows we found you and so does the media. As far as the public is concerned, this didn't happen. Tensions are high enough as it is."

She looked at her watch. "We still have eighteen minutes left in his ninety-minute window. Somehow that doesn't add up. Honestly, we were thinking library rather than warehouse."

"Library. *What wants to be filled but will always be empty?* As in empty knowledge."

"Yes."

"Hmm."

"We're getting evidence; that's what counts. We have his voice on tape; we have his presence in this building; we have more background. He's had several chances to hurt you and he hasn't. Sam told me that you spoke with him. I need to know exactly what he said."

"More background?" Kevin asked. "What background?"

An FBI agent walked toward them. "Excuse me, just wanted to let you know that the lights are back on. Fuse was pulled."

"No explosives?"

"Not that we can find. There's something here I think you should see."

She looked up at Kevin. "I'll be right back."

"Do you want me to show you what happened?"

"As soon as they're finished securing the scene. We don't want any more footprints or trace evidence than necessary. Hold tight." She hurried for the door and disappeared into the warehouse.

Kevin shoved his hands into his pockets and ran his fingers over Slater's cell phone. He was a klutz, no doubt about it. Maybe that was the sin Slater wanted him to confess. Kevin Parson is a fool and a klutz, a man incapable of entering society in any normal way because his Aunt Balinda beat his intellect against an imaginary wall for the first twenty-three years of his life. His mind is scarred beyond recognition.

He glanced back at the building, and the image of Jennifer walking for the door replayed itself. Sam was right; she liked him, didn't she?

Liked him? How could he know whether she liked him? *You see, Kevin. That's the way first-class losers think. They have no shame. They find themselves pinned down by an assassin's knife and their mind is drawn to the FBI agent they've known for all of three days.* Two days if he subtracted the day he ran off with Sam, the stunning CBI agent.

The cell phone vibrated at his fingertips and he jumped.

It went off again. Slater was calling and that was a problem, wasn't it? Why would Slater call now?

The phone rang a third time before he managed to unfold it. "H . . . hello?"

"H . . . hello? You sound like an imbecile, Kevin. I thought I said no cops."

Kevin spun to the warehouse. The agents were inside. There was a bomb in there after all, wasn't there? "Cops? We didn't call cops. I thought FBI were okay."

"Cops, Kevin. They're all pigs. Pigs in the parlor. I'm watching the news and the news says the cops know where you are. Maybe I should count to three and blow their guts to kingdom come."

"You said no *cops!*" Kevin shouted. There was a bomb in the warehouse and Jennifer was in there. He had to get her out. He ran for the door. "We didn't *use* the cops."

"Are you running, Kevin? Quick, quick get them out. But don't get too close. The bomb might go boom and they'll find your entrails on the walls with the others'."

Kevin shoved his head in the door. "Out!" he screamed. "Get out! There's a bomb!"

He ran for the street.

"You're right, there is a bomb," Slater said. "You have thirteen minutes left, Kevin. If I decide not to punish you. *What wants to be filled but will always be empty?*"

He slid to a stop. "Slater! Come out and face me, you . . ."

But Slater was gone. Kevin snapped the phone shut and whirled to the warehouse just in time to see Jennifer emerge, followed by both agents.

Jennifer saw the look on his face and stopped. "What is it?"

"Slater," he said dumbly.

"Slater called," Jennifer said. She rushed up to him. "We're wrong, aren't we? This isn't it!"

Kevin's head began to spin. He placed his hands on his temples and closed his eyes. "Think, Jennifer. Think! *What wants to be filled but will always be empty?* He knew we would come here so he waited for us, but this isn't it! What wants to be filled? What!"

"A library," the agent named Bill said.

"Did he say how much time?" Jennifer asked.

"Thirteen minutes. He said he may blow it early because the cops talked to the press."

"Milton," Jennifer said. "I swear I could wring his neck. God help us." She yanked a notepad from her hip pocket, stared at the page filled with writing, and began to pace. "36933, what else could have a number associated—"

"A reference number," Kevin blurted.

"But from which library?" Jennifer asked. "There's got to be a thousand—"

"The school of divinity," Kevin said. "Augustine Memorial. He's going to blow up the Augustine Memorial Library."

They stared at each other for a moment frozen in time. As one, the three FBI agents ran for the car. "Call Milton!" Bill said. "Evacuate the library."

"No cops," Jennifer said. "Call the school."

"What if we can't get through to the right people fast enough? We need a squad car over there."

"That's why we're going. What's the fastest way to the school?"

Kevin ran for his car across the street. "Down Willow. Follow me."

He slid behind the wheel, fired the engine, and squealed away from the curb. Eleven minutes. Could they reach the library in eleven minutes? Depended on traffic. But could they find a bomb in eleven minutes?

A horrifying thought strung through his mind. Even if they did reach the library, they would have no time to search without risking being caught inside when the bomb blew. There was this matter of seconds again. They could be forty seconds off and not know it.

A car was one thing. A bus was worse. But the library—God forbid that they were wrong. "You sick coward!"

They roared down Willow, horns blaring, ignoring the lights

completely. This was becoming a bad habit. He swerved out of the path of a blue Corvette and swung onto a smaller surface street to avoid the sea of traffic. Jennifer followed in the big black car. At each intersection the street dips pounded his suspension. He would make Anaheim Street and cut east.

Seven minutes. They were going to make it. He considered the gun in the trunk. Running into the library waving a gun would accomplish nothing but the confiscation of his hard-earned prize. He only had three bullets left. One for Slater's gut, one for his heart, and one for his head. *Pow, pow, pow. I'm gonna put a slug in your filthy heart, you lying sack of maggot meat. Two can play this game, baby. You picked the wrong kid to tick off. I bloodied your nose once; this time I'm gonna put you down. Six feet under, where the worms live. You make me sick, sick . . .*

Kevin saw the white sedan in the intersection ahead at the last possible moment. He threw his weight back into the seat and shoved the brake pedal to the floor. Tires screeching, his car slid sideways, barely missed the taillight of an ancient Chevy, and miraculously straightened. Hands white on the wheel, he punched the accelerator and sped on. Jennifer followed.

Focus! There was nothing he could do about Slater now. He had to get to the library in one piece. Interesting how bitter he'd become toward the man in the space of three days. *I'm gonna put a slug in your filthy heart, you lying sack of maggot meat?* What was that?

The moment Kevin saw the arched, glass face of Augustine Memorial Library, he knew that Jennifer's attempts to clear the place had failed. An Asian student ambled by the double doors, lost in thought. They had between three and four minutes. Maybe.

Kevin crammed the gearshift into park while the car was still rolling. The car bucked and stopped. He burst out and tore for the front doors. Jennifer was already on his heels.

"No panic, Kevin! We have time. Just get them out as quickly as possible. You hear?"

He slowed to a jog. She pulled up beside him, then took the lead.

"How many study rooms are there?" she asked.

"A few upstairs. There's a basement."

"PA system?"

"Yes."

"Okay, point the way to the office. I'll make an announcement; you clear the basement."

Kevin pointed out the office, ran for the stairs, and took them in twos. How long? Three minutes? "Get out! Everyone out!" He ran down the hall, spun into the first room. "Out! Get out now!"

"What's up, partner?" a middle-aged man asked lazily.

He couldn't think of a nonpanicky way to tell the man. "There's a bomb in the building."

The man stared for a second, then bolted to his feet.

"Clear the hall!" Kevin shouted, breaking for the next room. "Get everyone out!"

Jennifer's voice came over the PA, edgy. "This is the FBI. We have reason to suspect that there may be a bomb in the library. Evacuate the building calmly and immediately." She began to repeat the message, but yells echoed through the basement, drowning out her voice.

Feet pounded; voices cried out; panic set in. Maybe it was just as well. They didn't have enough time for order.

It took a full minute, at least, for Kevin to satisfy himself that the basement was clear. He was putting himself in danger, he realized, but this was his library, his school, his fault. He gritted his teeth, ran for the stairs, and was halfway up when he remembered the supply room. Unlikely anyone would be in there. Unless . . .

He stopped four paces from the top. Carl. The janitor liked to listen to his Discman while he worked. He liked to joke about how there was more than one way to fill the mind. Books were fine, he said, but music was the higher culture. He took his breaks in the supply room.

You're cutting it close, Kevin.

He whirled and ran back down. The supply closet was to his right, in the back. The building lay in silence now except for the urgent padding of his feet. What was it like to be caught in an explosion? And where would Slater have planted the charges?

He threw the door open. "Carl!"

The janitor stood by a stack of boxes with the words *New Books* written on pink sheets of paper.

"Carl! Thank God!"

Carl smiled at him and nodded his head to whatever music pumped into his ears. Kevin ran over to him and pulled the headphones off. "Get out of here! They've evacuated the building. Hurry, man! Hurry!"

The man's eyes widened.

Kevin grabbed his hand and shoved him toward the door. "Run! Everyone else is out."

"What is it?"

"Just run!"

Carl ran.

Two minutes. There was a second, smaller closet to his right—overflow supplies for administration, Carl had once told him. Mostly empty. Kevin leapt for the closet and pulled the door open.

How much explosive did it take to blow a building this size? Kevin was staring at the answer. Black wires protruded from five shoeboxes and met in a contraption that looked like the inside of a transistor radio. Slater's bomb.

"Jennifer!" he yelled. He twisted for the door and yelled again, at the top of his lungs. "Jennifer!"

His voice echoed back. The building was empty. Kevin ran his hands through his hair. Could he carry this thing outside? It'll blow there. That's where the people are. You have to stop it! But how? He reached for the wires, paused, and pulled back.

Pulling the wires would probably set it off, wouldn't it?

You're going to die, Kevin. Any split second it could go. He could set it off early.

"Kevin!" Jennifer's scream carried down the stairs. "Kevin, for God's sake, answer me! Get out!"

He fled the supply room in a full sprint. He'd seen the movies a hundred times—the explosion behind, the billows of fire, the diving hero rolling to freedom just out of the blast's reach.

But this wasn't a movie. This was real and this was now and this was him.

"Kevin—"

"Get out!" he yelled. "The bomb's in here!" He cleared the first four steps, and his momentum carried him to the top in two more bounds.

Jennifer was at the door, holding it open, face white. "What are you thinking?" she snapped at him. "It could go early. You'll get us both killed!"

He ran out and tore for the parking lot. Jennifer kept pace.

A huge arc of onlookers stood a hundred yards off, watching them run. "Get back!" she yelled, sprinting for them. "Farther back! Get—"

A deep, dull *whomp* cut her off. Then a louder, sharp blast and the crash of shattering glass. The ground shook.

Jennifer grabbed Kevin by the waist and pulled him down. They landed together and rolled. She threw her arms over his head. "Stay down!"

He lay smothered by her for a few long seconds. Screams rolled across the lawn. Jennifer pushed herself halfway up and looked back.

Her leg was over the backs of his legs and her hand pressed into his back for support. Kevin twisted and followed her gaze.

Half of the Divinity School of the Pacific's crown jewel lay in a heap of smoking rubble. The other half jutted to the sky, stripped of glass, naked.

"My God, my God, help us all," Jennifer said. "He blew it early, didn't he? I could kill Milton."

Still breathing hard from the run, Kevin dropped back down and buried his face in the grass.

19

Sunday
Night

THE LIBRARY EXPLOSION on the heels of the bus bomb put Long Beach at the world's center stage. All the networks played and replayed live footage of the library being blown to smithereens, courtesy of an alert student. Helicopters circled the hole that had been a building and relayed stunning images to millions of glued viewers. The world had seen this before and everyone had the same question on their minds: Terrorism?

But the explosion was the work of a madman known only as the Riddle Killer, the networks all said. Miraculously, no one had been hurt in the blast; in fact, no life had been taken by any of the three incidents. Nevertheless, they all knew it was only a matter of time. He'd killed in Sacramento; he would kill in Long Beach. Unless the authorities stopped him first. Unless his intended victim, Kevin Parson, confessed what the killer demanded he confess. Where was Kevin Parson? He'd last been seen running from the building with a woman, an FBI agent by some accounts. They had them on the student's video. Stunning footage.

The ATF had entered the fray after the first bomb; now they came in force. The state police, local police, sheriff, a half-dozen other task forces all poured over the library.

Jennifer did her best to keep Kevin beyond the reach of the media's long tentacles while making sense of the scene. She avoided Milton, for the simple reason that she didn't trust herself in his presence. He'd come within a few seconds of killing Kevin and countless others by talking to the press. If she'd been frustrated with him before, the sight of him running to and fro made her seethe now.

Still, he was an integral part of the investigation, and she couldn't avoid him once he finished his rounds with the press.

"You knew this was coming?" he demanded.

"Not now, Milton."

He took her arm and steered her away from the onlookers, squeezing with enough force to hurt her. "You were here. That means you knew. How long did you know?"

"Let go," she snapped.

He released her arm and glanced over her shoulder, smiling. "The word *negligence* mean anything to you, Agent Peters?"

"The word *carnage* mean anything to you, Detective Milton? I knew because he wanted me to know. You didn't know about the library because he said that if you were told, he'd blow the building early. In fact, he did blow it early, because you had to announce to the world that we'd found Kevin. You, sir, are lucky we got out when we did or you'd have *at least* two dead bodies on your hands. Don't ever touch me again."

"We could have put a bomb squad in there."

"Is there something with the air down here that messes with your hearing? What part of 'he told us he'd blow the building early' didn't penetrate that thick skull of yours? You almost killed us!"

"You're posing a danger to my city, and if you think I'm just going to stand by and let you, you're naive."

"And you're posing a danger to Kevin. Take it up with the bureau chief."

His eyes narrowed for a brief second, then he smiled again. "We're not through with this."

"Sure we are." She walked away. If not for the fact that half the world was watching, she might have taken the man's tie and shoved it down his throat. It took her thirty seconds to put the man out of her mind. She had more important things to dwell on than an overzealous fool. So she told herself, but in reality Milton sat in her gut like a sour pill.

Two questions soon preoccupied her mind. First, had anybody seen a stranger enter the library in the past twenty-four hours? And second, had anybody seen *Kevin* enter the library in the last twenty-four hours? Samantha had raised the question of Kevin's involvement, and although Jennifer knew the idea was ridiculous, the question raised others. Samantha's theory that someone on the inside might be somehow tied to Slater bothered her.

The Riddle Killer was remarkably elusive. The last three days were no exception. Sam was in Texas, flushing out something that had her hopes high. No doubt she'd come waltzing in tomorrow with a new theory that would set them back to square one. Actually, the CBI agent was beginning to grow on her, but jurisdiction had a way of straining the best relationships.

As it turned out, no one had seen a stranger around the library. And no one had seen Kevin. The front desk receptionist would have remembered Kevin—he was an avid reader. Short of bypassing the security system, of which there was no evidence, the likelihood of anyone entering the library unseen was small. Carl had been in the closet yesterday morning and there'd been no bomb, which meant Slater had found a way in since then, either at night or under their noses, unrecognized. How?

An hour after the explosion, Jennifer sat across from Kevin in a small Chinese restaurant and tried to distract him with small talk while they ate. But neither of them was good at small talk.

They went back to the warehouse at nine, this time armed with high-powered halogens that lit up the interior like a football field. Kevin walked through the scene with her. But now it was nearing midnight, and he was half-asleep on his feet. Unlike the library, the warehouse was still silent. No police, no ATF, only FBI.

She hadn't bothered to tell Milton about the incident at the warehouse. She would as soon as she was done with it. She'd explained the situation to Frank, and he'd finally agreed to her reasoning, but he wasn't happy with it. He was getting an earful from a dozen different sources. The governor wanted this tied up now. Washington was starting to apply pressure too. They were running out of time. If another bomb went off, they might take the case from her.

Jennifer glanced at Kevin, who leaned his head back against the wall in the reception area, eyes closed. She entered a ten-by-ten office storage room where they were compiling evidence for delivery to the lab. Under other circumstances, she would probably be doing this back at her desk, but Milton would be breathing down her neck. Besides, proximity favored the storage room, so Galager had transferred what he needed from the van and set up temporary shop here.

"Any conclusions, Bill?"

Galager leaned over a drawing of the warehouse floor plan, on which he'd painstakingly redrawn the footprints as they appeared.

"Best as I can tell, Slater entered and left through the fire escape. We have a single set of footprints coming and going, which correlates with the testimony. He walks up and down the hall a half-dozen times, waiting for Kevin to show, descends the stairs at least twice, springs his trap, and ends up in this room here." He tapped the room next to Kevin's hiding place.

"How did he lock the door? He shut it with the string, but Sam told me it was open when they first arrived."

"We can only assume that he had the lock rigged somehow. It's feasible that with a hard knock the lock could engage."

"Seems thin," Jennifer said. "So we have him entering and leaving through the fire escape. Kevin enters and leaves through the front door. What about the footprints themselves?"

"When all is said and done, there are only four clear prints, all of which we've casted and photographed. Problem is, they're all from the hallway and the stairs where both Kevin and Slater walked. Same size. Same basic shape. Both hard-soled and similar to what Kevin is wearing—impossible to visually determine which is which. The lab will break it down."

Jennifer considered his report. Sam hadn't entered the building, which was good thinking. But she hadn't seen Slater come or go either.

"What about the recording?" Galager had already transferred the data to a tape, which he had in a small recorder on the table.

"Again, the lab will have to tell us what they can come up with, but it sounds clean to me. This is the first recording from the hotel room." He punched the play button. Two voices filled the speaker. Slater and Samantha.

"There, that's better, don't you think? The game won't last forever; we might as well make this more interesting."

Low and gravelly. Breathy. Slater.

"What good is a game that you can't lose? It proves nothing."

She recognized Sam's voice. The tape played to the end of the conversation and clicked off.

"Here's the second recording, made while we were here earlier this evening." Galager punched it up. This time it was Kevin and Slater.

Kevin: *"H . . . hello?"*

Slater: *"H . . . hello? You sound like an imbecile, Kevin. I thought I said no cops."*

The recordings were clear and clean. Jennifer nodded. "Get them to the lab with the footprints immediately. Any word yet on the dagger tattoo or the blood work from the warehouse?"

"Blood's too old for anything but type. They're having trouble even with that, though. Twenty years is a long time."

"So it is twenty years old?"

"Best estimate, seventeen to twenty. Follows his confession."

"And the type?"

"They're having a hard time typing it. On the other hand, we do have something with the tattoo. A parlor in Houston says they have a large man with blond hair who comes in on occasion. Same tattoo as the one Kevin drew us. Says he's never seen a tattoo like it except on this man." Galager grinned deliberately. "The report came in about an hour ago. No current address, but the parlor says the man was in last Tuesday around ten o'clock."

"In Houston?" That's where Sam had gone. "Slater was in Houston last week? Doesn't sound right."

"Houston?" Kevin asked behind her. They turned to see him standing in the door. He walked in. "You have a lead in Houston?"

"The tattoo—"

"Yeah, I heard. But . . . how could Slater be in Houston?"

"Three-hour flight or a very long day's drive," Galager said. "Possible he's going back and forth."

Kevin's brow furrowed. "He has a dagger tattoo? What if this guy turns out to be the boy, but not Slater or the Riddle Killer? You pick him up and now he knows about me, where I live. All I need is another wacko after me."

"Unless this guy lives in a cave," Galager said, "he's heard the confession and seen your face on television. There's a chance he *is* Slater. And there's an even better chance that Slater is the boy. We have a man threatening you who all but admits that he's the boy; a boy who has reason to threaten you, identified with a very unique tattoo. And now we have a man with the same tattoo. Circumstantial, I realize, but it sounds pretty plausible to me. We make busts on less."

"But can you put someone behind bars with that?"

"Not a chance. That's where the physical and forensic evidence comes in. As soon as we have a suspect in custody, we measure him up against the evidence we've gathered, which is substantial. We have Slater's voice on tape. We have his shoe print. We have several bombs, all of which were made somewhere. We have six bugs—all this in three days. A virtual windfall in cases like this. I'd say Slater's getting sloppy."

And more so today than yesterday. "He's at least pushing the pace," Jennifer said. "Getting caught doesn't seem to concern him. Which isn't good."

"Why?" Kevin asked.

She looked at his haggard face. A blade of grass from the library lawn was still stuck in his shaggy hair. His blue eyes looked more desperate than enchanting now. He didn't tap his foot or rake his hair as frequently. The man needed rest. "Based on his profile, my guess is that he's closing in on his objective."

"Which is what?"

Jennifer glanced at Galager. "Good work, Bill. Why don't you wrap it up and call the locals?" She took Kevin's arm and led him out. "Let's take a walk."

Two of the streetlights nearest the warehouse were either shut down on energy conservation timers or burned out. A cool ocean breeze drifted over Long Beach. She'd shed her jacket and wore a sleeveless gold blouse with a black skirt—it was actually a bit chilly at this hour.

She crossed her arms. "You okay?"

"Tired."

"Nothing like fresh air to clear the mind. This way." She led him toward the fire escape in the back.

"So, what is Slater's objective?" Kevin asked again, shoving his hands in his jeans pockets.

"Well, that's a problem. I've been giving it a lot of thought. On the surface it seems simple enough: He wants to terrorize you. Men like Slater do what they do for a variety of reasons, usually to gratify some twisted need they've grown into over many years, but almost without exception they prey on the weak. Their focus is on their own need, not on the victim."

"Makes sense. And Slater's different?"

"I think so. His objective doesn't seem to be himself as much as you. I mean you specifically."

"I'm not sure I understand."

"Take your typical serial offender. Say a pyromaniac bent on burning down houses. He doesn't care whose house it is as long as it fits his needs. He needs to see the flame engulfing this structure—it excites him and gives him a feeling of power beyond his reach in any other way. The house is important—it has to be a certain size, maybe a certain build, maybe a symbol of wealth. In the same way a sex offender might prey on women he considers appealing. But his focus is on himself, not the victim. The victim is almost incidental."

"And you're saying that Slater hasn't chosen me for what I can do for him, but for what he can do to me. Like he did with your brother."

"Maybe. But this is playing out differently than Roy's murder. The Riddle Killer filled his thirst for bloodshed by killing Roy and killing him quickly. Slater is playing with you, over three days now. I'm beginning to question our initial assumption that Slater and the Riddle Killer are the same person." The Riddle Killer didn't seem to know his victims, other than Roy, whom he'd selected for her benefit. She rubbed her arms against the cold.

"Unless all that was just a cover-up for what he's doing now. Unless extracting revenge for what I did to him was the game all along."

"That's the obvious assumption. I'm not sure anymore. Revenge would be a simple matter. Assuming Slater is the boy you locked up, he could have found a hundred opportunities over the years to extract his revenge. His most obvious course would have been to hurt or kill you. I don't think Slater's interested in killing you. Not anytime soon, anyway. I think he wants to change you. He wants to force your hand somehow. I don't think the game's the device; I think the game's the objective."

"But that's crazy!" Kevin stopped and put both hands into his hair. "What is there about me? Who? Who would want to . . . to force my hand?"

"I know it doesn't all fit yet, but the sooner we narrow down Slater's true motivation, the higher our chances of getting you out of this mess."

They were at the back, by the fire escape. A ladder reached up to the second floor and curved into a window. Jennifer sighed and leaned against the tin siding.

"Bottom line is that if I'm right, then the only way to understand Slater's true motivation is to understand you, Kevin. I've got to know more about you." He was pacing, staring at the concrete, hands still in his hair.

"I want to know about the house," she said.

"There's nothing to know about the house," he said.

"Why don't you let me judge that?"

"I can't talk about the house!"

"I know you don't think you can, but it may provide our best clues now. I know it's hard—"

"I don't think you have a clue about how hard it is! You didn't grow up there!" He paced and smoothed his hair frantically, and then flung his arms wide. "You think any of this means anything? You think this is reality? A bunch of ants running around the globe, hiding their secrets in their deep dark tunnels? We *all* have our secrets. Who's to say that mine have anything to do with anything? Why don't the rest of the ants have to crawl out of their tunnels and broadcast their sins to the world?"

Kevin was baring himself, and Jennifer needed him to do just that. Not because she would ever exploit him, but because she needed to understand his secrets if she hoped to help him.

And she did hope to help him. More now than a day ago, even if Slater wasn't her brother's killer after all.

"You're right," she said. "We're all fallen, as my priest used to say. I'm not interested in your sin. I wasn't even in favor of the initial confession, remember? I'm interested in you, Kevin."

"And who am I?" He was desperate. "Huh? Answer me that. Who am I? Who are you? Who is anybody? We are what we do! We are our secrets. I *am* my sin! You want to know me, then you have to know my sin. Is that what you want? Every little dirty secret out on the table so that you can dissect it all and know Kevin, the poor tormented soul?"

"That's not what I said."

"You might as well have, because it's true! Why is it fair that I should spill my guts when the pastor next-door has as many nasty secrets as I do? Huh? If we want to know him, we have to know his secrets, is that it?"

"Stop it!" Her anger surprised her. "You're *not* your sin! Who ever told you that lie? Aunt Balinda? I've seen you, Kevin. You asked me what my profile for you was. Well, let me be more specific. You are one of the kindest, gentlest, most interesting, appealing men I know. That's who you are. And don't insult my intelligence or my feminine discernment by dismissing my opinion." She took a breath and a guess. "I don't know what Slater's up to, or why, but I guarantee you're doing exactly what he wants you to do when you start to believe that you're trapped. You've come out of that. Don't go back."

She knew by his blink that she was right. Slater was trying to pull him back to the past, and the thought so terrified him that he was breaking down. Which was exactly how Slater would accomplish his objective. He would trap Kevin in his past.

Kevin stared at her, stunned. It occurred to her then, looking back into his wide eyes, that she didn't merely like Kevin, she cared for him deeply. She had no business caring for him; she didn't even *want* to care for him, not in that way. Her empathy had risen to the surface, unbidden. She'd always been a sucker for the downtrodden. She had always had a soft spot for men who were hurting in some way. Now her soft spot had found Kevin.

But this didn't feel like a soft spot. She actually found him appealing, with his ragged hair and his charming smile. And those eyes. That wasn't empathy, was it?

She closed her eyes and swallowed. *God forbid, Jennifer. And when was the last time you dated a man, anyway? Two years ago? That hillbilly from Arkansas who came from good stock, so says Mom?* She'd never known the full meaning of boring until then. She would prefer a man with a goatee who rode a Harley and winked frequently.

Jennifer opened her eyes. Kevin was seated on the concrete, cross-legged, head in his hands. The man never ceased to surprise her.

"I'm sorry, I'm not sure where all that came from," she said.

He lifted his head, closed his eyes, and took a deep breath. "Please, don't be sorry. That was the nicest thing I've heard in a long time." His eyes fluttered open, as if he'd just heard himself. "Maybe *nicest* is the wrong word choice. It was . . . I think you're right. He's trying to pull me back, isn't he? That's his objective. So who is he? Balinda?"

Jennifer sat down beside him and folded her legs to the side. Her skirt wasn't exactly dress of choice for concrete sitting, but she didn't care.

"I need to tell you something, Kevin. But I don't want it to upset you."

He stared ahead and then turned to her. "You went to the house, didn't you?"

"Yes. This morning. It took a few threats to convince Balinda to let me in, but I saw the place and I met Eugene and Bob."

Kevin lowered his head again.

"I know it's hard, but I need to know what happened in that house, Kevin. For all we know, Slater could be someone Balinda hired. That would fit the profile. She wants to change you. But without knowing the whole story, I'm floundering here."

"You're asking me to tell you something no one knows. Not because it's so horrible—I know I'm not the only one who's had a few challenges along the way. But it's dead and buried. You want me to bring it back to life? Isn't that what Slater's trying to do?"

"I'm not Slater. And frankly, it doesn't sound dead and buried to me."

"And you really think this whole game has to do with my past?"

She nodded. "I'm assuming that Slater has an objective that is tied to your past, yes."

Kevin remained quiet. The silence stretched, and Jennifer sat beside him feeling his tension, hearing his breathing. She wondered if it would be appropriate to put a hand on his arm but immediately decided it wouldn't.

He suddenly groaned and rocked. "I don't think I can do this."

"You can't slay the dragon without luring it out of its hole. I want to help you, Kevin. I need to know."

For a long time he just sat there rocking. Then he stilled and his breathing slowed. Maybe it was too much too fast. He'd faced more than most could stomach these last three days and she was pushing him even further. He needed sleep. But she was running out of time. Slater was escalating.

She was about to suggest that they get some rest and consider it in the morning when he turned his face to the night sky.

"I don't think Balinda's intentions were necessarily evil." He spoke in a soft monotone. "She wanted a good playmate for Bob. He was eight when they adopted me; I was one. But Bob was retarded. I wasn't, and Balinda couldn't accept that reality."

He paused and took several deep breaths. Jennifer shifted and leaned on her arm so that she could watch his face. His eyes were closed.

"Tell me about Balinda."

"I don't know her story, but Balinda creates her own reality. We all do, but Balinda only knows absolutes. She decides what part of the world is real and what part isn't. If something isn't real, she makes it go away. She manipulates everything around her to create an acceptable reality."

He stopped. Jennifer waited a full thirty seconds before prodding him. "Tell me what it was like to be her son."

"I don't know it yet, because I'm too young, but my mom doesn't want me to be smarter than my brother. So she decides to make me retarded too because she's already tried to make Bob smarter but she can't."

Another stall. He was switching tenses, dipping into the past. Jennifer felt her stomach turn.

"How does she do that? Does she hurt you?"

"No. Hurting is evil in Balinda's world. She won't let me out of the house because the world outside isn't real. The only real world is the one she makes inside the house. She is the princess. She needs me to read so that she can shape my mind with what she makes me read, but she cuts up stories and makes me read only things she decides are real. I'm nine years old before I know there are animals called cats because Princess thinks cats are evil. I don't even know there is evil until I'm eleven. There's only real and unreal. Everything real is good and everything good comes from Princess. I don't do anything bad; I only do things that aren't real. She makes the things that aren't real go away by starving me of them. She never punishes me; she only helps me."

"When you do something that's not real, how does she punish you?"

He hesitated. "She locks me in my room to learn about the real world or makes me sleep so I'll forget the unreal world. She takes away food and water. That's how animals learn, she says, and we are the best animals. I can remember the first time because it made me confused. I was four. My brother and I are playing servant, folding dishtowels for Princess. We have to fold them over and over until they're perfect. Sometimes it takes all day. We don't have toys because toys aren't real. Bob asks me what one plus one is because he wants to give me two towels, but he doesn't know what to call it. I tell him that I think one plus one is two and Princess overhears me. She locks me in my room for two days. Two towels, two days. If Bob doesn't know how to add, then I can't either, because it isn't real. She wants me to be dumb like Bob."

An image of Balinda seated under a stack of clipped newspapers filled Jennifer's mind and she shivered.

Kevin sighed and changed tenses again. "She never held me. She hardly even touched me unless it was by mistake. Sometimes I went without food for days. Once a whole week. Sometimes we couldn't wear clothes if we did unreal things. She deprived us both of anything she thought might feed our minds. Mostly me, because Bob was retarded and he didn't do as many things that weren't real. No school. No games. Sometimes no talking for days. Sometimes she made me stay in bed all day. Other times she made me sit in the bathtub in cold water so I couldn't sleep all night. I could never ask her why, because that wasn't real. Princess was real, and if she decided to do something, anything else was unreal and couldn't be talked about. So we couldn't ask questions. Even questions about real things, because that would question their reality, which was unreal."

Jennifer filled in the blanks. The abuse wasn't primarily physical, not necessarily even emotional, although there was some of both of those. It was primarily psychological. She watched Kevin's chest rise and fall. She desperately wanted to reach out to him. She could see the boy, sitting alone in a bathtub of cold water, shivering in the dark, wondering how to make sense of his horrible world that he'd been brainwashed to think was good.

She fought back tears. *Kevin, dear Kevin, I'm so sorry!* She reached out her hand and put it on his arm. Who could do such terrible things to a little boy? There was more, details, stories that could undoubtedly fill a book to be studied by universities across the country. But she didn't want to hear more. If she could only make it all go away. She might be able to stop Slater, but Kevin would live with this past until the day he died.

A brief absurd image of her lying down beside him and holding him gently in her arms ran through her mind.

Kevin suddenly groaned and then chuckled. "She's a twisted, demented lunatic."

Jennifer cleared her throat. "Agreed."

"But you know what?"

"What?"

"Telling you about it makes me feel . . . good. I've never told anyone."

"Not even Samantha?"

"No."

"Sometimes talking about abuse helps us deal with it. Our tendency is to hide it, and that's understandable. I'm glad you're telling me. None of it was your fault, Kevin. It's not your sin."

He pushed himself up. His eyes were clearer. "You're right. That old goat did everything in her power to hold me back."

"When did you first realize that Balinda's world wasn't the only one?"

"When I met Samantha. She came to my window one night and helped me sneak out. But I was trapped, you know. I mean mentally. For a long time I couldn't accept that Balinda was anything but a loving princess. When Samantha left to study law, she begged me to go with her. Or at least somewhere away from Balinda, but I couldn't leave. I was twenty-three before I finally worked up the courage to leave. Balinda went ballistic."

"And you've done all this in five years?"

He nodded and grinned softly. "Turns out that I was fairly intelligent. It only took me a year to get my general education papers, and four years to graduate from college."

It occurred to Jennifer that she was treating him like a patient with these short, probing questions, but he seemed to want it now.

"Which is when you decided to become a minister," she said.

"That's a long story. I suppose because of my strange rearing the subject of good and evil held unusual fascination for me. Naturally I gravitated toward the church. Morality became somewhat of an obsession, I guess. I figured the least I could do was spend my life showing some small corner of the real world the way to true goodness."

"As opposed to what?"

"As opposed to the false reality we all create for ourselves. Mine was extreme, but it didn't take me long to see that most people live in their own worlds of delusion. Not so different from Balinda's, really."

"Observant." She smiled. "Sometimes I wonder what my delusions are. Is your faith personal?"

He shrugged. "I'm not sure. The church is a system, a vehicle for me. I wouldn't say that I know God personally, no. But my faith in a God is real enough. Without an absolute, moral God, there can be no true morality. It's the most obvious argument for the existence of God."

"I grew up Catholic," she said. "Went through all the forms, never did quite understand it all."

"Well, don't tell Father Bill Strong, but I can't say I do either."

Sitting next to him now, just a few minutes since his confession, Jennifer had difficulty placing Kevin in the context of his youth. He seemed so normal.

He shook his head. "This is incredible. I still can't believe I just told you all that."

"You just needed the right person," she said.

The sound of feet running on the pavement sounded behind them. Jennifer twisted around. It was Galager.

"Jennifer!"

She stood and brushed her skirt.

"We have another riddle!" Galager said. He held a sheet of notebook paper in his hand. "Mickales just found this on the windshield of Kevin's car. It's Slater."

"My car?" Kevin jumped to his feet.

Jennifer took the note. Yellow pad. The scrawling was black, familiar. The milk jug from Kevin's refrigerator. She read the note quickly.

3+3 = 6.

Four down, two to go. You know how I like threes, Kevin. Time's running out. Shame, shame, shame. A simple confession would do, but you force my hand.

Who escapes their prison but is captive still?

I'll give you a hint: It isn't you.

6 A.M.

Kevin gripped his hair and turned away.

"Okay," Jennifer said, turning for the street. "Let's get moving."

20

SAMANTHA WAS TIRED. The Pakistani had insisted they meet at a Mexican restaurant five miles out of town. The light was too low, the music was too loud, and the place smelled of stale cigarettes. She stared the witness directly in the eye. Chris had sworn that Salman would cooperate and he had. But what he had to say wasn't exactly what Sam wanted to hear.

"How do you know it was a dagger if you never saw it?"

"He told me it was. I have the tattoo on my back, and he said he had one like it on his forehead."

"Did you see any scarring or discoloration that might indicate he had the tattoo removed?"

"Perhaps. He wore his hair over his forehead. Didn't matter—he said he had it removed and I believed him."

They'd been over all of this at least once; he'd already described the tattooed man with remarkable detail. Salman was a tailor. Tailors notice these things, he said.

"And this was while you were in New York, four months ago. And you saw him five or six times at a bar named Cougars over the course of about a month?"

"That is what I have said. Yes. You may check with the bar owner; he may remember the man as well."

"So according to you, this man who had a dagger tattoo and who called himself Slater was in New York while the Riddle Killer was killing victims in Sacramento."

"Yes, definitely. I remember watching the news while I was in New York the very night after I had talked to Slater."

Salman had spilled enough details in the previous hour to make his testimony credible. Sam had been in New York four months ago. She knew the pub Salman referred to, a low-class joint frequented by your typical mix of unsavory characters. A CIA task force had set up a sting at the joint to flush out an Iranian whom they suspected had ties to a bombing in Egypt. The man had exonerated himself.

"Okay." She turned to Steve Jules, the agent who'd accompanied her from the Houston office. "I'm done. Thank you for your time, Mr. Salman. It was invaluable."

"Perhaps I could make you a suit," he said with a grin. "I have a new shop here. There aren't so many tailors in Houston as in New York."

She smiled. "Maybe next time I'm in Houston to escape the heat."

They left the bar in Steve's car. This wasn't what she'd wanted to hear. In fact, it was downright dreadful. What if she was right about the rest of it? *Dear God, dear God.*

She wanted only one thing now: to be with Kevin. Kevin needed her more now than ever. The despondent look on his face as she sped off to the airport haunted her.

Her childhood friend had grown into quite an incredible man, hadn't he? Tormented by his past, perhaps, but he'd escaped that hellhole he called a home and flourished. Part of her wanted nothing more than to run back to him and throw herself in his arms and beg him to marry her. Sure he had his demons; everyone did. Yes, he had a long struggle ahead of him; didn't they all? But he was the most genuine man she'd ever known. His eyes shone with the excitement and wonder of a child, and his mind had absorbed the world with stunning capacity. His progress was nearly superhuman.

On the other hand, she could never marry Kevin. Their relationship was too valuable to compromise with romance. He saw that too, otherwise he never would have allowed room for any attraction to Jennifer. Their occasional romantic innuendo was simply teasing. They both knew that.

She sighed.

"Tough interview," Steve said beside her.

She picked up her cell phone and punched in her boss's number. It would be late, but she had to get this to him. "I thought it went pretty smoothly," she said.

Roland picked up the phone on the fourth ring. "It's midnight."

"He was two hours late," Sam said.

"And?"

"And he knew Slater."

"Our guy?"

"Very possible. Tattoo like that is extremely unusual. But he claims to have known Slater in New York."

"So."

"So it was four months ago. Over a period of about a month. The Riddle Killer was in Sacramento then, killing Roy Peters."

"So Slater's not the Riddle Killer."

"That's right."

"Copy cat?"

"Could be."

"And if Slater is the boy, he's no longer walking around with a dagger tattoo on his forehead because he had it removed."

"So it seems."

Roland covered the phone and spoke to someone—probably his wife unless he was in a late meeting, which was entirely possible.

"I want you back in Sacramento tomorrow," he said. "If Slater isn't the Riddle Killer, he's not your concern."

"I know, sir. I have three days left on my leave, remember?"

"We called you back in, remember?"

"Because we believed that Slater was the Riddle Killer. If he's not, the trail's cold."

Roland considered her argument. He wasn't the most reasonable man when it came to time off. He put in eighty hours a week and expected his subordinates to do the same.

"Please, sir, I go way back with Kevin. He's practically family to me. I swear, three more days and I'll be back in the office. You have to let me do this. And there's still the chance that I'm wrong about Salman's testimony."

"Yes, there is."

"It's still possible that Slater knows the Riddle Killer."

"Possible."

"Then give me more time."

"You heard about the library?"

"The whole world heard about the library."

He sighed. "Three days. I expect to see you at your desk Thursday morning. And please, tread lightly down there. This is unofficial. From what I've heard the whole scene is one big snake pit. Every agency in the country has a stake in this."

"Thank you, sir."

Roland hung up.

Sam considered calling Jennifer but decided it could wait until morning. She could tell her only that Slater wasn't the Riddle Killer. She needed to satisfy herself as to the rest before she said anything that might do Kevin more harm than good.

She'd already checked on flights back. No red eyes, one at 6 A.M. and one at 9 A.M. She needed sleep. The nine o'clock United flight would have to do. It would take her through the Denver hub and put her in Long Beach at noon.

III

"Okay . . ." Kevin watched Jennifer pace the warehouse floor. They'd delayed plans to share details of the warehouse with the police and instead decided to use the place as a staging area. It was the only way to keep Milton off her back, Jennifer said.

"Let's review what we *do* know."

Agents Bill Galager and Brett Mickales straddled chairs by the table, chins in their hands, focused on Jennifer. Kevin leaned against the wall, arms crossed. It was hopeless. They were beat; they were clueless; they were dead. They'd rehashed a hundred ideas in the two hours since Slater's note had been discovered.

"We know that he's escalating. Car, bus, building. We know that all of his other threats made reference to damage of some kind. This one did not. We know that we have until 6 A.M. to solve or . . . or what we don't know. And we know the riddle. *Who escapes their prison but is captive still?*"

Jennifer spread her hands.

"You're forgetting the most crucial bit of knowledge," Kevin said.

"Which is?"

"The fact that we're toast."

They stared at him as if he'd just walked in and flashed his pecs. A wry grin crossed Jennifer's face. "Humor's good."

"People," Mickales said. "He's gonna do people this time."

"There were people every time."

"But he went after a car, a bus, and a building. This time he goes straight after people."

"Kidnapping," Kevin said.

"We've suggested that. It's a possibility."

"If you ask me, it's the best one," Mickales said. He stood up. "It fits."

Jennifer crossed to the table, eyes suddenly wide. "Okay, unless anybody has a better idea, we'll chase that."

"Why would Slater kidnap anyone?" Kevin asked.

"For the same reason he threatened to blow up a bus," Mickales said. "To force a confession."

Kevin stared at the man, suddenly overwhelmed. They'd been at it ad nauseam and they kept coming up with the same thing, which was essentially nothing. In the end it always came back to his confession.

"Look." He could feel the heat rising up his spine. He shouldn't be doing this—he was beyond himself. "If I had the slightest clue as to what this wacko wanted me to confess, you think I would hold out?"

"Easy, man. Nobody's suggesting—"

"I don't have the foggiest notion what his crazy confession is! He's nuts!" Kevin stepped toward them, aware that he'd crossed a line already. "They're out there screaming bloody murder for Kevin's confession. Well, I gave them one, didn't I? I told them I killed someone as a kid. But they want more. They want real blood. They want me to bleed all over their gossip columns! Kevin, the kid killer who brought down Long Beach!"

His fingers were trembling. They looked at him in silence.

He ran his fingers through his hair. "Man . . ."

"Nobody's screaming bloody murder out there," Jennifer said.

"I'm sorry. I'm just . . . I don't know what to do. This isn't all my fault."

"You need rest, Kevin," Jennifer said. "But if Slater's planning to kidnap someone, you may be a target. I know he said it wasn't you, but I'm not sure what that means." She turned to Galager. "Keep the watch on the house, but I want a transponder on him. Kevin, we're going to give you a small transmitting device. I want you to tape it where it won't be found. We'll leave it inactive—this guy's into electronics; he may scan for signals. Anything happens, you turn it on. The range is roughly fifty miles. Fair enough?"

He nodded.

She walked toward him. "Let's get you home."

Galager headed for the van, which was still parked on the street. Kevin walked outside with Jennifer. The weight of two days without sleep descended on him. He could hardly walk straight, much less think straight.

"I'm sorry. I didn't mean to blow up."

"No apology needed. Just get some sleep."

"What are you going to do?"

She looked off to the east. The helicopters were down for the night. "He said no cops. We could put a guard on likely targets, but for all we know, he's planning on kidnapping the mayor. Or it could be another bomb." She shook her head. "You're right, we're pretty much toast."

They stopped at the car. "It meant a lot," he said. "Talking to you tonight. Thank you."

She smiled, but her eyes were tired. How much sleep had she gotten in the last three days? He suddenly felt terrible for her. Flushing out Slater was more than a job for her.

"Go home and get some sleep," she said, squeezing his arm. "Galager will follow you home. We have someone outside. If Slater makes contact—if *anything* happens—call me."

Kevin looked up to see Galager pull up in the black car. "Somehow I doubt it'll be me. That's not what he wants. I'll be fine. The question is, who won't be?"

What if it was Jennifer? Sam was in Houston.

"What about you?" he asked.

"Why would he want to kidnap me?"

Kevin shrugged. "It's not like I have a lot of friends."

"I guess that makes me a friend. Don't worry, I can handle myself."

By the time Kevin finished with Galager's little lecture on the operational procedures for the transmitter and climbed into bed, the three o'clock hour had come and gone. His head was numb before it hit the pillow. He fell into an exhausted sleep within the minute, lost to the horrors of his new life.

For an hour or three.

|||

Slater stands by the fence, stock-still in the darkness. He's given them until six, but this time he will be done before six, before the first light grays the sky. He said six because he likes threes, and six is three plus three, but he can't risk doing this in the light.

No one has stirred in the house since his arrival thirty minutes ago. When he first conceived the plan, he considered just blowing up the house with all its occupants trapped inside. But after thinking very carefully about his ultimate objective, because that's what Slater does the best, he settled on this plan. Putting this woman in a cage will send the city through the roof. It's one thing to wonder which unnamed citizens might be the next to discover a bomb under their bed; it's far more disturbing to know that Mrs. Sally Jane who lives on Stars and Stripes Street and buys her groceries at Albertsons is locked up in a cage, waiting desperately for Kevin Parson to fess up.

Besides, Slater's never kidnapped anyone before. The thought brings a chill to his spine. The sensation of pleasure so intense that it runs up and down the spine is interesting. It is not boring like teenagers poking holes in their noses.

Slater looks at his watch. 4:46. Is 4:46 divisible by three? No, but 4:47 is. And that's one minute away. Perfect. Perfect, perfect, perfect. The pleasure of his brilliance is so intense that Slater now begins to shiver a little. He stands by the fence with perfect discipline, resisting a desperate urge to run for the house and drag her out of bed. He is perfectly disciplined and he is shivering. Interesting.

He's waited so long. Eighteen years. Six times three. Three plus three times three.

The two minutes crawl by very slowly, but Slater doesn't mind. He is born for this. He glances at his watch. 4:47. He can't stand it any longer. It's one minute early. Three is divisible by one. Close enough.

Slater walks up to the sliding glass door, pulls out the pick with a gloved hand, and disengages the lock in less than ten seconds. His breathing comes thick, and he pauses to still it. If the others wake, he will have to kill them, and he doesn't want to mess with that. He wants the woman.

He eases into the kitchen and leaves the door open. They have no dogs or cats. One child. The husband is Slater's only concern. He stands on the tile floor for a full minute, adjusting his eyes to the deeper darkness, breathing in the home's smells. The senses are the key to living life to its fullest. Tastes, sights, smells, feelings, sounds. Eat what you like, watch what you can, touch who you want. That's what he wants Kevin to do. To taste and touch and smell his true self. It will destroy him. The plan is perfect. Perfect, perfect, perfect.

Slater takes one deep breath, but very slowly.

He walks through the living room and puts his hand on the doorknob to the master bedroom. It opens without a sound. Perfect. The room is dark. Pitch-black. Perfect.

He walks slowly to the bed and stands over the woman. Her breathing is quicker than the man's. She faces him, mouth slightly parted, hair tangled on the pillow. He reaches out a hand and touches the sheet. Soft and smooth. Two hundred thread count at least. He could stand here over them for an hour and breathe in their smells without being seen. But the light is coming. He doesn't like the light.

Slater reaches into his shirt pocket and withdraws a note, which he sets on the dresser. For Kevin. He slips his hand into his coat and takes out a roll of gauze and a bottle of chloroform. He unscrews the bottle and dips the roll into the liquid. The smell fills his nostrils and he holds his breath. It has to be strong enough to put her under without a struggle.

He replaces the lid on the bottle, drops it into his pocket, and eases the roll of soaked gauze in front of the woman's nose, careful not to touch it. For a moment she doesn't stir, then she whimpers in her dreams. But she doesn't move. He waits twenty seconds, until her breathing slows enough to persuade him that she's unconscious. He shoves the roll into his jacket.

Slater settles to his knees, as if bowing before his victim. A sacrifice for the gods. He lifts the sheet and slips his hands under the body until his elbows are directly under her. She lies limp, like a noodle. He gently pulls her toward his chest. She slides off the bed and sags in his arms. The husband rolls half a turn and then settles. Perfect.

Slater stands and carries her out of the house without bothering to shut the doors. The clock in his car reads 4:57 when he settles behind the wheel with the woman breathing slowly in the backseat.

Slater starts the car and drives away. He could have carried her to the hiding on foot and returned later for the car, but he doesn't want to leave the vehicle in front of the house any longer than absolutely necessary. He's too smart for that. It occurs to him that this will be the first time he's ever brought a guest to the hiding. When she awakes, her eyes will be the first besides his own to see his world. The thought brings a moment of panic.

So then, all the more reason not to let her out. It's what will happen anyway, isn't it? Even if Kevin confesses, Slater has always known that she will have to die. His exposure to another human being will be temporary. He can live with that. Still, why hasn't this detail occurred to him earlier? It isn't a mistake, just an oversight. But oversight can lead to mistakes. He chides himself and turns down the dark street.

Slater doesn't bother with stealth now. The woman is stirring, so he gives her another healthy dose of chloroform, yanks the body out of the rear seat, and heaves it over his shoulder. He hurries for the door, opens it with a key, and enters the small room. Close door, feel for chain, pull on overhead light.

A dim light exposes the space. Down a flight of steps. Another chain, another light. Through the tunnel. Open the second door with a second key. The hiding. Home, sweet home.

The thought of sharing his home with another person for a little while suddenly doesn't seem so bad. In fact, it holds its own excitement. Everything he needs is here. Food, water, a bathroom, a bed, clothing, the electronics—of course, she won't be sharing any of those amenities.

The woman is stirring again.

He crosses to the room he's prepared. The walk-in closet once stored materials he's used in his games, but he's cleared it for her. Can't take the chance that she knows how to set off dynamite now, can he? The room is seven by seven and solid concrete all around except the ceiling, which is heavily insulated wood. The door is steel.

He places her onto the cement floor and steps back. She groans and rolls to one side. Good enough.

He closes the door, locks it with a deadbolt, and stuffs a rolled-up rug into the crack at the bottom. Lights out.

21

Monday
Morning

KEVIN HEARD THE RINGING long before he awoke. It sounded like a high-pitched laugh. Or an intermittent scream. Then there was the pounding, a thumping that could be his heart. But it sounded more like banging on the door.

"Sir?" Someone was yelling, calling him sir.

Kevin's eyes somehow managed to open. Light shone through the window. Where was he? Home. His mind started to drift. He would have to get up eventually and go to class, but at the moment he felt as though he'd met the wrong end of a rhino charge. He closed his eyes.

The muffled voice came again. "Kevin? The phone . . ."

His eyes snapped open. Slater. His life had been turned upside down by a man called Slater who called on the phone. The phone was ringing.

He spilled out of bed. The clock said 7:13. Slater had given them until 6 A.M. He ran to the bedroom door, twisted the lock, and yanked it open. One of the agents watching his house stood there, the cordless phone from the kitchen in hand.

"I'm sorry to wake you, but your phone's been ringing on and off for fifteen minutes. It's a pay phone. Jennifer told us to wake you."

Kevin stood in his pinstriped boxer shorts. "Has . . . has anything happened?"

"Not that I've heard."

Kevin took the phone absently. "Okay. I'll answer it this time."

The agent hesitated, expressionless, and then walked down the stairs for the door. Kevin didn't even know his name. He wore a dark navy jacket and tan slacks; black hair. Walked stiffly, like maybe his underwear were too tight. But the man had a name and maybe a wife and some kids. A life. What if Slater had gone after this man instead of Kevin? Or gone after someone in China, unknown to the West? For that matter, how many men or women were facing their own Slaters throughout the world? It was an awkward thought, standing there at the top of his stairs, watching the agent leave through the front door.

Kevin walked back into his bedroom. He had to call Jennifer. Six o'clock had come and gone—something had to have happened.

The phone suddenly rang. He picked up the receiver.

"Hello?"

"Kevin?" It was Eugene. Kevin felt himself shutting down immediately. The sound of that voice. They didn't have a phone in the house. He was calling from a pay phone.

"Yes."

"Thank God! Thank God, boy. I don't know what to do! I just don't know what I should do . . ."

You could start by drowning yourself. "What's wrong?"

"I'm not sure. It's just that Princess isn't home. I woke up and she was gone. She never leaves without telling me. I thought maybe she went down for some dog food because we threw it away, you know, but then I remembered that we burned the dog and—"

"Shut up, Eugene. Please, just shut up and try to make some sense for once. Her name is Balinda. So Balinda left without telling you. I'm sure she'll be back. You can live without her for a few hours, can't you?"

"This isn't like her. I have a very bad feeling, Kevin! And now I've gotten Bob worried. He keeps looking in all the rooms, calling for Princess. You have to come—"

"Forget it. Call the police, if you're so worried."

"Princess won't allow that! You know . . ."

He talked on but suddenly Kevin wasn't hearing. His mind had turned over a stone. What if Slater had kidnapped Balinda? What if the old hag was really gone?

But why would Slater take Balinda?

Because whether you like it or not, she is your mother, Kevin. You need her. You want her to be your mother.

A cold sweat broke out on his temples and he wasn't sure why. He had to call Jennifer! Where was Samantha? Maybe Jennifer had heard from her.

He interrupted Eugene's rambling. "I'll call you back."

"You can't call me! I have to go home!"

"Then go home."

Kevin hung up. Where was Jennifer's number? He ran downstairs, still in his boxers, snatched her card from the counter with a trembling hand, and dialed the number.

"Good morning, Kevin. I'm surprised you're not still sleeping."

"How did you know it was me?"

"Caller ID. You're on your home phone."

"Have you heard anything?"

"Not yet. I just got off the phone with Samantha. It seems we were wrong about Slater being the Riddle Killer."

"We may have a problem, Jennifer. I just got a call from Eugene. He says that Balinda's missing."

Jennifer didn't respond.

"I was just thinking, do you think Slater could have—"

"Balinda! That's it. It makes perfect sense!"

"It does?"

"Stay put. I'll swing by in ten minutes."

"What? Where are we going?"

She hesitated. "Baker Street."

"No, I can't! Really, Jennifer, I don't think I can go in there like this."

"Don't you see? This could be the break we need! If he took her, then Slater's tied to Balinda and Balinda is tied to the house. I know this may be hard, but I need you."

"You don't know that."

"We can't risk me being wrong."

"Why can't you just go?"

"Because you're the only one who knows how to beat him. If Slater did take Balinda, then we know that this whole thing goes back to the house. To the past. There has to be a key to it all, and I doubt that I'm the one who's going to find it."

He knew what she was saying, and it sounded more like psychobabble than truth. But she could be right.

"Kevin? I'll be there with you. It's paper and boards; that's all it is. I was there yesterday, remember? And Balinda's gone. Ten minutes?"

Balinda was gone. Bob wasn't the problem—he was a victim in this mess. Eugene was just an old fool without Balinda. The witch was gone.

"Okay."

III

The white house stood as ominously as always. He stared at it through the windshield, feeling silly next to Jennifer. She was looking at him, knowing him. He felt naked.

Balinda wasn't in the house. Unless she'd come back. If so, he wouldn't go in. Jennifer might want him to. She seemed pretty convinced that there was more to this than he'd told her, but in all honesty, he couldn't think of anything. Slater was the boy and the boy had nothing to do with the house.

"When is Sam coming?" he asked, stalling.

"She said noonish, but she has a few errands to run."

"I wonder why she didn't call me?"

"I told her you were sleeping. She said she'll call you as soon as she can." Jennifer looked at the house. "You didn't tell Sam about locking the boy in the cellar—how much does Sam really know about your childhood, Kevin? You two have known each other for years."

"I don't like to talk about it. Why?"

"Something's bothering her. She wouldn't tell me, but she wants to meet later this afternoon. She's convinced that Slater isn't the Riddle Killer. I can buy that, but there's more. She knows something else." Jennifer hit the steering wheel. "Why do I always feel like I'm the last to know what's going on here?"

Kevin stared at the house. She sighed. "I had to tell Milton about this. He wants to talk to you this morning."

"What did you say?"

"I said he would have to take it up with the bureau chief. We still have official jurisdiction. The rest are still running their investigations, but on the ground everything goes through us. The thought of Milton interviewing you gives me the creeps."

"Okay, let's go," Kevin said, distracted. They might as well get this over with. She would never know how much better he felt with her here. On the other hand, she was a psychologist—she probably *would* understand. He opened his door.

Jennifer put her hand on his arm. "Kevin, I need you to know something. If we discover that Slater did take Balinda, there's no way we can keep it from the media. They'll want to know more. They can be nosy."

"So then my whole life gets dissected by the press."

"Pretty much. I've done my best this far—"

"That's what Slater wants. That's why he took her. It's his way of exposing me." He dropped his head and ruffled his hair.

"I'm sorry."

Kevin stood from the car and slammed the door. "Let's get this over with."

Walking across the street and up the steps to the front door, Kevin made a firm decision. Under no circumstances would he blubber or show any more emotion in front of Jennifer. He was leaning on her too much already. The last thing she needed was a basket case. He would walk in, give Bob a hug, slug Eugene, do his I'm-looking-for-the-key-to-Slater routine, and leave without so much as batting an eye.

His foot crossed the threshold for the first time in five years. The tremble started in his fingers. It spread to his knees before the door closed behind him.

Eugene let them in. "I don't know. I just don't know where she could have gone. She should have been back by now!"

Bobby stood at the end of the hall, grinning wide, beaming. He started to clap and hop in place without leaving the ground. A lump the size of a boulder filled Kevin's throat. What had he done to Bob? He'd abandoned him to Princess. He'd been punished his whole life in part because of Bob, but that didn't make Bob guilty.

"Kevin, Kevin, Kevin! You came to see me?"

Kevin quickly walked to his brother and hugged the man tight. "Yes. I'm sorry, Bob. I'm so sorry." The tears were leaking already. "Are you okay?"

Eugene watched dumbly; Jennifer wrinkled her brow.

"Yes, Kevin. I'm very good."

He didn't seem so concerned about the old bat's disappearance.

"Princess has gone away," he said, smile suddenly gone.

"Why don't you show me your bedroom," Jennifer said to Eugene.

"My, my, my, my. I don't know what I'll do without Princess," Eugene said, heading off to the left.

Kevin let them go. "Bob, could you show me your room?"

Bob lit up and skipped through the narrow passage between the stacks of newspapers. "You want to see my room?"

Kevin walked down the hall on numb legs. It was surreal, this world he'd escaped. An issue of *Time* poked out of the stack to his right. The face on the cover had been replaced by a smiling image of Muhammad Ali. Only God, the devil, and Balinda knew why.

Bob hurried into his room. He snatched something off the floor. It was an old beat-up Game Boy, a monochrome version. Bob had himself a toy. Balinda had softened in her old age. Or was it because Kevin had left?

"It's a computer!" Bob said.

"Nice. I like it." Kevin peeked into the room. "Do you still read stories that Bal—Princess gives you to read?"

"Yes. And I like them a lot."

"That's good, Bob. Does she . . . make you sleep during the day?"

"Not for a long time. But sometimes she won't let me eat. She says I'm getting too fat."

Bobby's room looked just as it had five years earlier. Kevin turned back into the hall and pushed open the door to his old room.

Unchanged. Surreal. He set his jaw. The flood of emotions he'd expected didn't come. The window was still screwed down and the bookcases were still full of bogus books. The bed he'd spent half his childhood in was still covered by the same blanket. It was as if Balinda was waiting for him to return. Or maybe his leaving didn't fit into her reality, so she refused to accept it. With her mind there was no telling.

No keys to Slater here.

A wail—Eugene—carried through the house. Bob turned and ran for the sound. So it was true.

Kevin walked back out to the living room, ignoring the sounds of lament issuing from the back bedroom. He should take a torch to this place. Burn out the rat's nest. Add a few more ashes to the backyard. The stairwell to the basement was still choked off with a mountain of books and magazines, stacks that hadn't been touched for years.

Jennifer stepped out of the master bedroom. "He took her."

"So I gathered."

"He left a note." She handed him a blue slip of paper. Three words were scrawled in the familiar handwriting.

Fess up, Puke.

"Or what," he said. "You'll dump her in the lagoon?"

Kevin stared at the words, numb from four days of horror. Part of him didn't care, part of him felt sorry for the old hag. Either way, all of his deepest secrets would soon be on the table for the world to pick through. That was the point. Kevin wasn't sure how much he cared anymore.

"Can we go now?"

"Are you finished?"

"Yes."

She looked around. "The health department is going to have a field day once this gets out."

"They should burn it."

"That's what I was thinking," she said. Her eyes settled on his. "Are you okay?"

"I feel . . . confused."

"As far as the rest of the world is concerned, she's your mother. They may wonder why you don't seem to care. She may be a witch, but she's still human. Only God knows what he'll do to her."

The emotions came from his gut, unexpectedly and in a rush. He suddenly felt suffocated in the small, dark space. She was his mother, wasn't she? And he was horrified by the fact that he even *thought* of her as a mother, because in reality he hated her more than he hated Slater. Unless they were one and the same and she had kidnapped herself.

A confusing mixture of revulsion and sorrow overcame Kevin. He was falling apart. His eyes swam with tears and his face wrinkled.

Kevin turned for the door. He could feel their stares on his back. *Mommy.* Fire burned through his throat; a tear spilled from his left eye.

At least they couldn't see. He would never allow anyone to see this. He hated Balinda and he was crying for her and he hated that he was crying for her.

It was too much. He hurried for the door, crashed through with far more noise than he wanted, and let out a soft sob. He hoped Jennifer couldn't hear; he didn't want her to hear him acting this way. He was just a lost boy and he was crying like a lost boy and he really just wanted to be held by Mommy. By the one person who had never held him.

"Kevin?" Jennifer was running after him.

He only wanted to be held by Princess.

22

Monday
Afternoon

THE QUESTIONS HAD NAGGED at Samantha through the night. The scenario fit some unseen hand like a glove; the question was, which hand? Who was Slater?

She'd talked to Jennifer upon waking and heard about the note on Kevin's windshield. She should have taken an earlier flight! Jennifer suspected kidnapping, but as of seven this morning there had been no evidence of foul play.

Sam told Jennifer about Salman. If the Pakistani Salman had indeed met with Slater in New York, then whoever the FBI had located with a tattoo could not be Slater, because Slater's had been removed. Furthermore, Slater couldn't be the Riddle Killer—he'd been in New York at the time of Roy's murder. Jennifer hadn't been ready to accept her conclusion out of hand, but the two cases did have a few significant disparities that were obviously weighing on her mind. She talked about objectives. She was beginning to suspect that the Riddle Killer and Slater weren't similarly motivated.

As for the tattoo, they would know within a few hours.

Sam's plane landed at LAX at 12:35. She rented a car and headed south for Long Beach. Traffic on 405 was as bad as it got for a weekday. She called Jennifer. The agent answered on the first ring.

"Hi, Jennifer, it's Sam. Anything?"

"As a matter of fact, yes. The tattoo is a bust. Our man works on an oil rig six months a year. He's been out on one for the last three weeks."

"Makes sense. Any word on a kidnapping?"

Jennifer hesitated and Sam sat up. "Balinda was taken from her home last night," Jennifer said.

"Balinda Parson?" Sam's pulse spiked.

"One and the same. No contact, no leads, nothing but a note left in Slater's writing: 'Fess up, Puke.' Kevin took it pretty hard."

Sam's mind was already whirling. Of course! Taking Balinda would force media attention on Kevin's family. His past. "Does the media know?"

"Yes. But we're keeping them away from Baker Street under the claim that it could trigger Slater. There's wall-to-wall coverage on this thing. I've spent the last hour handling interagency concerns. The bureaucracy's enough to drive me nuts. Milton's ticked off, the ATF wants the evidence from Quantico—it's a mess. Meanwhile we're dead in the water."

Jennifer sounded tired. Sam braked and came to a stop behind a pickup truck billowing black smoke. "How is he?"

"Kevin? He's dead to the world. I left him at his house about two hours ago, sleeping. God knows we could all use some rest."

Sam pulled around the truck. "I have some ideas, Jennifer. Is there a chance we could meet sooner?"

"What is it?"

"I . . . I can't explain right now."

"Come by the station. Unless something breaks, I'll be here."

"Okay. But I have to chase something down first."

"If you have information that's pertinent to the investigation, I expect to be told. Please, Sam, I can use all the help I can get here."

"I promise you I'll call the second I know anything."

"Sam. Please, what's on your mind?"

"I'll call you," Sam said and hung up.

Without evidence her fears would have to remain the paranoia of a close friend, desperate for answers. And if she was right? God help them. God help Kevin.

She drove south, ticking off the facts. Slater had been in New York at the same time she'd been there. Slater knew her, a small detail she'd withheld from the CBI. Knowing Roland, he'd yank her from the case.

Slater was obsessed with Kevin's past; Slater was the boy; Sam had never seen the boy; all of the riddles had to do with opposites; all demanded a confession. Slater was trying to force Kevin back into his past. Who was Slater?

A chill snaked down her arms.

Samantha approached Kevin's house from the west, parked two blocks down, and took to foot, careful to keep yard fences between herself and the black car parked up the street. She had to do this without causing a fuss, and the last thing she wanted to do was wake Kevin if he was asleep.

Dread swelled in her chest as she neared. The notion that Kevin might indeed be Slater refused to budge from her tired mind.

She had to wait for the agent up the street to turn his head before crossing from the neighbor's fence into Kevin's backyard. She hurried up to the sliding glass door and knelt so that Kevin's picket fence blocked her head from the car's line of sight. Working quickly above her head, she inserted a thin pick into the lock and worked it with as much precision as she could from the awkward angle. The pin fell and she pried up the latch. She wiped a bead of sweat from her cheek, glanced back at the black car, slid the glass door open a foot, and slipped past the pulled blinds. She reached back through and closed the door.

If they'd seen her, they would be moving already. They hadn't.

Sam looked around the house. A two-by-four-foot travel poster of a bikini-clad native walking down a white beach said that New Zealand promised paradise. *Dear Kevin, you want so much. I should have known how badly you were hurting, even when we were children. Why did you hide it from me? Why didn't you tell me?*

The house's silence engulfed her. So peaceful, so quiet, asleep while the world crumbled. She crossed to the stairs and took them on her tiptoes. Kevin's bedroom was to the left. She eased the door open, saw him on the bed, and walked quietly up to him.

He lay sprawled on his belly, arms above his head, as if surrendering to some unknown enemy beyond the mattress. His head rested on its side, facing her, lower cheek bunched, mouth closed. His face didn't speak of surrender, only sleep. Deep, deep, sweet sleep.

He was dressed in street clothes; his tan Reeboks sat on the floor, nudging the bed skirt.

Sam briefly wondered if Jennifer had stayed with him until he fell asleep. Had she seen him like this? This sweet boy of hers? This stunning man who bore the weight of a hundred worlds on his shoulders? Her champion who'd slain the wicked boy on Baker Street?

What did Jennifer see when she looked at him? *She sees the same as you do, Sam. She sees Kevin and she can't help but to love him as you love him.*

Sam reached out, tempted to brush his cheek. *No, not as I love him. No one can love him as I love him. I would give my life for this man.* She withdrew her hand. A tear broke down her right cheek. *Oh, how I love you, dear Kevin. Seeing you these last three days has reminded me how desperately I love you. Please, please tell me that you will slay this dragon. We will, Kevin. Together we will slay this beast, my knight.*

The childhood role-playing reference flooded her with warmth. She turned away and walked into his closet. She wasn't sure what she was looking for. Something that Slater had left. Something that the

FBI missed because they wouldn't have guessed that it belonged to Slater.

Kevin had ordered his clothes neatly. Slacks and shirts hung in a row, jeans and cargo pants folded and stacked, shoes on a rack. Seminary dress to the right, casual dress to the left. She smiled and ran her fingers through the slacks. She smelled the shirts. His scent lingered. Amazing how she recognized it after so many years. He was still a boy. *A man, Sam. A man.*

She searched the closet and then slowly worked her way through the rest of his room, walking around him, careful not to make any sound. Other than the rise and fall of his back, Kevin did not move. Sam found nothing.

The bathroom proved no better, and her spirit lightened. She didn't want to find anything.

His study. Sam shut the door and sat at his desk. She ran a finger over his books: *Introduction to Philosophy. Sociology of Religion. Hermeneutics Revealed.* Two dozen others. He was in his first semester at the divinity school but he'd bought enough texts for two years, easily.

On the floor beside the desk she saw a small pile of paper, which she picked up. A paper he'd titled "The True Natures of Man." He was a true man.

Please, Sam, let's cut the romantic drivel and do what you came to do.

She was less concerned about noise; there were two doors between her and Kevin. She searched the drawers and removed the books one by one. This is where Slater would leave a clue. This was the room of the mind. He was obsessed with numbers and mind games. The mind. Somewhere, somewhere.

A small stack of business cards, topped by a slip of paper bearing her own number, sat by a calculator that looked fresh out of the box, perhaps never used. The first card belonged to John Francis, Ph.D.,

Academic Dean, Divinity School of the Pacific, South. Kevin had spoken at length about the man. Surely Jennifer had already interviewed him.

And what if she hadn't? The last four days rushed by without time for standard procedure or a thorough investigation. She picked up the phone and called the number on the card. A receptionist with a nasal voice asked her if she wanted to leave a message. No, thank you. She hung up, turned over the card, and saw that Kevin had scribbled another number with the same prefix. She dialed it.

"Hello, this is John."

"Hello, Dr. John Francis?"

"Yes, this is he."

"This is Samantha Sheer with the California Bureau of Investigation. I'm working with an agent Jennifer Peters on the Kevin Parson case. Are you familiar with it?"

"Of course. Agent Peters was here yesterday morning."

"Kevin speaks highly of you," Sam said. "You have a doctorate in psychology, isn't that right?"

"Correct."

"What is your assessment of Kevin?"

"That's a bit like asking which animals live in the sea. Kevin's a wonderful man. I can't say there's anyone else I'd rather tangle my wits with. Extraordinary . . . genuine."

"Genuine. Yes, he is genuine. Nearly transparent. Which is why it's strange he can't remember this sin Slater demands he confess, don't you think? I'm wondering, is there anything that's occupied him in these last few weeks? Any reoccurring themes, projects, papers?"

"As a matter of fact, yes. He was quite interested in the natures of man. You might say consumed with the subject."

Sam picked up the rough draft of the paper. "The true natures of man," Sam said. "And what are the natures of man? Or what would Kevin say are the natures of man?"

"Yes, well, that's the mystery, isn't it? I'm not sure I can tell you what Kevin would say. He told me he had a new model, but he wanted to present them cohesively in his paper."

"Hmm. And when is this paper due?"

"He was scheduled to turn it in this Wednesday."

"For what class?"

"Introduction to Ethics."

"One more question, Doctor, and I'll let you go. You're a religious man with an education in psychology; would you say that the natures of man are primarily spiritual, or psychological?"

"I know that Freud would turn in his grave, but in my mind there's no doubt. Man is primarily a spiritual being."

"And Kevin would agree to that?"

"Yes, I'm sure he would."

"Thank you for your time, Doctor. You sound like a reasonable man."

He chuckled. "They pay me to be; I do try. Anything else, don't hesitate to call."

She set the phone down. Ethics. She scanned the paper and saw that it was hardly more than the recitation of several theories on man's natures. It ended with a new heading: "The True Natures." She set the pages down. Where would Kevin keep his notes on the natures of man?

She stepped over to the bookcase and reached for a large gray book titled *Morality Redefined.* The book was used, frayed around the edges, pages yellowing. She lifted the cover, saw that it was a library book. Copyright 1953.

Sam flipped through the pages, but there were no notes. She was about to replace the book when the back cover fell open. Several loose sheets of white paper dropped to the floor. On the top of one in Kevin's handwriting: *The True Natures of Man, an Essay.*

Samantha withdrew the pages and sat down at the desk. They were only notes. Three pages of notes. She scanned them, a simple outline with headings that fit the subject. Summaries.

We learn as we live, and we live what we learn, but not so well.

How can a nature be dead and yet live? He is dead in the light, but thrives in the dark.

If Good and Evil could talk to each other, what would they say?

They are all pretenders, who live in the light but hide in the dark.

Insightful. But there was nothing here that Slater would have . . .

Sam froze. There at the bottom of page four, three small words.

I AM I.

Sam recognized the handwriting immediately. Slater! "I am I."

"Dear God!"

Sam set the pages on Kevin's desk with a trembling hand. She began to panic.

No. Stop. *What does "I am I" even mean, Sam? It means Slater is Slater. Slater snuck in here and wrote this. That proves nothing except that he has his nose in every part of Kevin's life.*

If Good and Evil could talk to each other, what would they say?

Then how had Kevin and Slater talked to each other? The FBI had a recording. How, how? Unless . . .

A second cell. He's using another cell phone!

Sam ran for Kevin's room. *Dear God, let me be wrong!* He hadn't moved. She crept up to him. Where would he keep the phones? The one Slater had left him was always in his right pocket.

There was only one way to do this. Quickly, before she awakened him. Sam slipped her hand into his right pocket. He wore cargo pants, loose, but his weight pressed her hand into the mattress. She touched the phone, felt the recording device on the back. Slater's.

She rounded the bed, crawled up for better access, and slid her hand into his left pocket. Kevin grunted and rolled to his side, facing her. She stayed still until his breathing returned to a deep slow rhythm and then tried again, this time with his left pocket exposed.

Her fingers felt plastic. Sam knew then that she was right, but she pulled it out anyway. A cell phone, identical to the one Slater had left for Kevin, except black instead of silver. She flipped it open and scrolled through the call history. The calls were to the other cell phone. One to the hotel room phone. Two to Kevin's home phone.

This was the cell phone Slater had used. To talk, to detonate the bombs. Sam's mind throbbed. There could be no doubt about it.

They would crucify him.

23

SAM ROLLED OFF THE BED, closed Kevin's door, and flew downstairs. She gripped the phone Slater had used to make his calls in her right hand—for now Slater wouldn't be making those calls, at least not on this phone. She didn't bother being discreet on her exit but walked right out the back, turned up the street, and ran for her car.

I, Slater, am I, Kevin. And that had been Samantha's greatest fear. That her childhood friend had a multiple personality disorder as she'd suggested to Jennifer a day earlier, and then immediately rejected because Kevin was in the room when Slater called. But it struck her as she lay trying to sleep last night that Slater had not *talked* to her while Kevin was in the room. The phone had only rung while he was in the room. Kevin was in the hall before she picked up and heard Slater. Kevin could have simply pushed the send button in his pocket and then talked to Sam once in the hall. Could multiple personalities work that way?

She'd been with Kevin in the car when Slater called, just before the bus blew. But she had no proof that Slater was actually on the line then. They had no recording of that call.

It was absurd. It was impossible! But try as she might in sleepless fits, Sam couldn't account for a single definitive situation that necessarily proved they couldn't be the same man. Not one.

Mere conjecture! It had to be coincidence!

Now this.

If Good and Evil could talk to each other, what would they say?

Sam reached her car, stomach in knots. This might not be enough. She'd been irresponsible to suggest the possibility to Jennifer in the first place. The man you think you might be falling in love with is insane. And she'd said it so calmly for the simple reason that she didn't believe it herself. She was only doing what she was trained to do. But this . . . this was an entirely different matter.

And Kevin *wasn't* insane! He was merely role-playing, as he had learned to do with Balinda for so many years. He had split into a divergent personality when he first began to comprehend true evil. The boy. He had been the boy! Only he didn't know that he was the boy. To Kevin at age eleven, the boy was an evil person who needed to be killed. So he killed him. But the boy had never died. Slater had simply remained dormant until now, when somehow this paper on the natures of man had allowed him to resurface.

She could still be wrong. In true cases of multiple personality disorders, the subjects were rarely conscious of their alternate personalities. Slater wouldn't know that he was Kevin; Kevin would not know that he was Slater. Actually they *weren't* each other. Physically, yes, but in no other way. Slater could be living right now as Kevin slept, plotting to kill Balinda, and Kevin wouldn't have a clue. Some things Slater did would be merely imagined; others, like the bombs and the kidnapping, would be acted out.

She tossed Kevin's phone on the seat and punched Jennifer's number into her own.

"Jenn—"

"I need to meet you! Now. Where are you?"

"Sam? I'm down at the PD. What's wrong?"

"Have you gotten the lab reports on the shoe prints and the recordings yet?"

"No. Why? Where are you?"

"I was just in Kevin's house and I'm headed your way." She pulled onto Willow.

"How's Kevin?"

Sam took a deep breath and let it out slowly. "He's asleep. I found a second phone on him, Jennifer. It was the phone used to call the cell with the recording device. I don't know how else to say this. I think Kevin is Slater."

"That's . . . I thought we'd already been over this. He was in the room when Slater—"

"Listen, Jennifer, I've come at this from a hundred different angles in the last twelve hours. I'm not saying that I can prove it; God knows I don't want it to be true, but if it is, he needs help! He needs you. And he's the only one who can take us to Balinda. Kevin won't know, but Slater will."

"Please, Sam, this is crazy. How could he have pulled this off? We've had people on the house. We've been listening to him in there! How did he get out to kidnap Balinda?"

"It's his house; he knows how to get out without your boys catching on. Where was he between 3 A.M. and 5 A.M. last night?"

"Sleeping . . ."

"Kevin may have thought he was, but was he? I don't think he's had six hours' sleep in the last four days. Trace it back. He hasn't gotten any phone calls while you were listening, at least not in the house. I hope I'm wrong, I really do, but I don't think you'll find a discrepancy. He's too intelligent. But he wants the truth out. Subconsciously, consciously, I don't know, but he's getting sloppy. He wants the world to know. That's the answer to the riddle."

"*What falls but never breaks? What breaks but never falls?* Night and day," Jennifer said. "Opposites. Kevin."

"Kevin. *Kevin* was the boy; that's why I never saw the boy when we were kids. He was in that warehouse cellar, but only him, no second boy. He hit himself. Check the blood type. The confession Slater wants isn't that Kevin tried to kill the boy, but that he *was* the boy. That Kevin is Slater."

"I am my sin," Jennifer said absently. There was a tremor in her voice.

"What?"

"Something he said last night."

"I'll be there in ten minutes," Sam said. "Don't let Kevin leave the house."

"But only Slater knows where he has Balinda? Kevin truly doesn't know?"

"That's my guess."

"Then we need Slater to find Balinda. But if we send the wrong signal, Slater may go into remission. If he does and Kevin doesn't know where Balinda is, we may have our first actual victim in this case. Even if we hold Kevin in a cell, she could starve to death." Jennifer was suddenly sounding frantic. "He's not the Riddle Killer; he hasn't killed anyone yet. We can't let that happen."

"So we let him walk out?"

"No. No, I don't know, but we have to handle this with kid gloves."

"I'll be right there," Sam said. "Just make sure Kevin doesn't leave that house."

|||

The sound of his bedroom door closing pulled Kevin from sleep. It was 3:00. He'd slept over four hours. Jennifer had insisted that he not be bothered unless absolutely necessary. So why were they in his house?

Unless *they* weren't in his house. Unless it was someone else. Someone like Slater!

He slid out of bed, tiptoed to the door, eased it open. Someone was opening the sliding glass door to the back lawn! *Just ask who it is, Kevin. It's the FBI, that's all.*

But what if it wasn't?

"Hello?"

Nothing.

"Is anyone here?" he called, louder this time.

Silence.

Kevin descended the stairs and stepped cautiously into the living room. He ran over to the window and peered out. The familiar Lincoln was parked half a block down the street.

Something was wrong. Something had happened. He walked to his kitchen phone and instinctively felt for the cell phone in his right pocket. Still there. But something wasn't right. What?

The cell phone suddenly vibrated against his leg and he jumped. He shoved his hand back into the pocket and pulled out the silver phone. The other phone, the larger VTech, was in his left hand. For a moment he stared at them, confused. Did I pick that up? So many phones, his mind was playing tricks on him.

The cell vibrated madly. Answer it!

"Hello?"

Slater's voice ground in his ear. "Who thinks he's a butterfly but is really a worm?"

Kevin's breathing smothered the phone.

"You're pathetic, Kevin. Do you have knowledge of this obvious fact yet, or am I going to have to beat it out of you?" Slater breathed heavily. "I have someone here who wants to hold you and for the life of me I can't understand why."

Blood flushed Kevin's face. His throat felt as though it was locked in a vise. He couldn't speak.

"How long do you expect me to play tiddlywinks, Kevin? You're obviously too dense for the riddles, so I've decided to up the ante. I know how conflicted you are about Mommy, but by now I have it under reliable advisement that you aren't so conflicted about me. In fact, you hate me, don't you, Kevin? You should—I've destroyed your life."

"Stop it!" Kevin screamed.

"Stop it? Stop it? That's all you can manage? You're the only one with the power to stop anything. But I don't think you have the guts. You're as yellow as the rest of them; you've made that abundantly clear. So here's the new deal, Kevin. *You* come and stop me. Face to face, man to man. This is your big chance to blow away Slater with that peashooter you obtained illegally. Find me."

"Face me, you coward! Come out and face me!" Kevin shouted.

"Coward? I'm petrified. I can hardly move, much less face you." Pause. "Do I have to chisel it on your forehead? You find *me!* Find me, find me! The game ends in six hours, Kevin. Then I kill her. You fess up or I slit her throat. Are we properly motivated now?"

The detail about the six hours hardly registered. Slater wanted to meet him. Kevin shifted on his feet. He actually wanted to meet him. But where?

"How?"

"You know how. It's dark down here. Alone, Kevin. All alone, the way it was meant to be."

Click.

For an endless moment Kevin stood glued to the linoleum. Blood throbbed through his temples. The black VTech phone trembled in his left hand. He roared and slammed it on the counter with all of his strength. Black plastic splintered and scattered.

Kevin shoved the cell phone in his pocket, whirled around, and flew up the stairs. He'd hidden the gun under his mattress. Three bullets left. Two days earlier the thought of going after Slater would have terrified him; now he was consumed with the idea.

It's dark down here.

He shoved his hand under the mattress, pulled out the gun, and crammed it behind his belt. Dark. Down. *I've got a few ideas about dark and down, don't I? Where the worms hide their nasty little secrets. He knew, he knew!* Why hadn't he thought of this earlier? He had to get out unseen and he had to go alone. This was now between him and Slater. One on one, man on man.

The FBI car was still somewhere down the street. Kevin ran out the back and sprinted east, the opposite way. One block and then he cut south. They would know that he'd left. In fact, they would have recorded Slater's last call to him through the home surveillance. What if they came after him? He had to tell Jennifer to stay away. He could use the cell phone, but the call would have to be short, or they would triangulate his position.

If *dark* and *down* was where he thought it might be . . . Kevin ground his teeth and grunted. The man was a pervert. And he would kill Balinda—empty threats weren't part of his character.

What if the FBI sent out helicopters? He turned west and hugged a line of trees by the sidewalk. The gun jutted into his back.

He started to jog.

III

"Now! I need some facts now, not in ten minutes," Jennifer snapped.

Reports normally came in from Quantico at intervals established by the agents in charge. The next report window was in ten minutes, Galager had explained.

"I'll call, but they've only had the evidence for a few hours. This stuff can take up to a week."

"We don't have a week! Do they know what's happening down here? Tell them to turn on the television, for heaven's sake!"

Galager dipped his head and left.

Her world had collapsed with the call from Sam two minutes ago. She still didn't want to accept the possibility that Kevin could have blown up the bus or the library.

From her corner station Jennifer could see the exit across a sea of desks. Milton barged out of his office, grabbed his coat, and headed for the door. Where was he going? He paused, glancing back, and Jennifer instinctively turned her head to avoid eye contact. When she glanced back, he was gone. An inexplicable rage flashed through her mind. But really none of this was Milton's fault. He was simply doing his job. Sure he liked the cameras, but he arguably had a responsibility to the public. She was directing her frustration and anger at him without appropriate cause—she knew this but it didn't seem to calm her.

It wasn't Kevin, she reminded herself. Even if Kevin was Slater, which hasn't been established, the Kevin she knew wouldn't blow anything up. A jury would take one look at his past and agree. If Slater was Kevin, then he was part of a fractured personality, not Kevin himself.

A thought smacked her and she stopped. Could Slater be framing Kevin? What better way to drag the man down than to frame him as the lunatic who tried to blow up Long Beach? She sat behind the desk, grabbed a legal pad, and penciled it out.

Slater is the boy; he wants revenge. He terrorizes Kevin and then convinces the world that he is Kevin, terrorizing himself because he is Slater. Kevin is ruined and Slater escapes. It would raise the bar for perfect crimes.

But how could Slater pull that off? Sam had found *two* phones. Why would Kevin be carrying around two phones without knowing it? And how could the numbers that Slater called be on that second phone? An electronic relay that duplicated the numbers to make it look like the phone had been used. Possible. And how could Slater have placed the phone in Kevin's pocket without Kevin's knowledge?

It would have had to be while Kevin slept, this morning. Who had access to Kevin . . .

Her phone rang and she snatched it up without thinking.

"Jennifer."

"It's Claude, surveillance. We have a situation at the house. Someone just called Kevin."

"Who?" Jennifer stood, knocking her chair back.

Static. "Slater. We're pretty sure. But that's not all."

"Hold on. You have the recording from Kevin's cell phone?"

"No, we have a recording from inside the house. Someone who sounded like Slater called Kevin from *inside* Kevin's house. I . . . uh, I know it sounds strange, but we have both voices inside the house. I'm sending the recording down now. He threatened to kill the woman in six hours and suggested that Kevin meet him."

"Did he say where?"

"No. He said Kevin would know where. He said it was dark down here, that's it."

"Have you talked to Kevin?"

"We made the decision to enter premises." He paused. "Kevin was gone."

Jennifer collapsed in her chair. "You let him *walk?*"

Claude sounded flustered. "His car's still in the garage."

She closed her eyes and took a calming breath. What now? "I want that tape here now. Set up a search in concentric circles. He's on foot."

She dropped her phone on the table and closed her fingers to still a bad tremble. Her nerves were shot. Four days and how much sleep? Twelve, fourteen hours? The case had just gone from terrible to hopeless. He was going to kill Balinda. Inevitable. *Who* was going to kill Balinda? Slater? Kevin?

"Ma'am?"

She looked up to see one of Milton's detectives in the door. "I have a call for you. He says he tried your personal line but couldn't get through. Wouldn't give his name."

She nodded at the desk phone. "Put it through."

The call transferred and she picked up. "Peters."

"Jennifer?"

It was Kevin. Jennifer was too stunned to respond.

"Hello?"

"Where are you?"

"I'm sorry, Jennifer. I'm going after him. But I have to do this alone. If you come after me, he'll kill her. You're recording the house, right? Listen to the tape. I can't talk now, because they'll find me, but I wanted you to know." He sounded desperate.

"Kevin, you don't have to do this. Tell me where you are."

"I *do* have to do this. Listen to the tape. It's not what you think. Slater's doing this to me. Don't bother calling me; I'm throwing this phone away." He abruptly clicked off.

"Kevin?"

Jennifer slammed the phone in its cradle. She ran her hands through her hair and picked up the phone again. She dialed Samantha's number.

"Hello?"

"Kevin's gone, Sam," Jennifer said. "He just received a call from Slater threatening to kill Balinda in six hours. He baited Kevin to meet him, said he would know where and that it was dark. As far as I know, that's it. The tape's on the way down."

"He's on foot? How could they let him walk out?"

"I don't know. The point is, we're now on a very tight time line and we've lost contact."

"Slater's cell—"

"He said he was getting rid of it."

"I'll go back," Sam said. "He can't get far."

"Assuming you're right about Kevin, Slater's drawing him to a place they must both know from their childhood. Any ideas?"

Sam hesitated. "The warehouse?"

"We'll check it out, but it's too obvious."

"Let me think about it. If we're lucky, we pick him up. Concentrate the search to the west—closer to Baker Street."

"There's another possibility, Sam. I know it may sound like a stretch, but what if Slater's framing Kevin?"

The phone was quiet.

"Forensics will give us a better picture, but the cell could have been planted and the call log duplicated by relay. The objective fits: Kevin is branded a psychopath who terrorized himself, he's ruined, and Slater skips free. Childhood grudge revenged."

"What a tangled web we weave," Sam said quietly. "Get the data on the recordings; hopefully it'll tell us more."

"I'm working on it." Galager walked in and sat down, file in hand. Jennifer stood. "Call me if you think of anything."

"One last thing," Sam said. "I talked to Dr. John Francis and he mentioned that you'd spoken to him already, but you might want to consider breaking this down with him. He knows Kevin well and he's in your field. Just a thought."

"Thank you, I will."

She set the phone down. Galager was back. "Well?"

"Like I said, not done. But I do have something. Ever hear of a seismic tuner?"

"A what?"

"Seismic tuner. A device that alters voice patterns."

"Okay."

"Well, I could record my voice and program this thing to match it to yours."

"So? The sample we sent them of Kevin's voice sounds nothing like Slater's—what's your point?"

"I talked to Carl Riggs at the lab. He says that even if they do determine that both Slater's voice and Kevin's voice have the same vocal patterns, someone who knew what they were doing could manufacture the effect with a seismic tuner."

"I'm not following. Bottom line, Galager." Her frustration was overflowing now.

"Bottom line is that Slater could have altered his voice to make it sound like a derivative of Kevin's voice. He could have obtained a sample of Kevin's voice, broken it down electronically, and then reproduced its vocal patterns at a different range and with different inflections. In other words, he could be speaking through a box that makes it sound like he's Kevin, trying not to be Kevin. Follow?"

"Knowing that we would analyze the recording and conclude that both voices were Kevin's." She blinked.

"Correct. Even though they aren't."

"As in, if he wanted to frame Kevin."

"A possibility. Riggs said there's an open case in Florida where a guy's wife was kidnapped for a ransom of a million dollars. The community came together in a fund drive and raised the money. But it turns out the kidnapper's voice was a recording of the husband's, manipulated by a seismic tuner. He evidently kidnapped his own wife. It's going to trial next month."

"I didn't know there was such a thing as a seismic tuner."

"There wasn't until about a year ago." Galager stood. "Either way, even if both voiceprints match Kevin's, we won't know if both really are his until we rule out the use of a seismic tuner. Riggs won't have the voice report until tomorrow. They're on it, but it takes time."

"And the shoe prints?"

"Should have that this evening, but he doesn't think it'll help us either. Not distinctive enough."

"So what you're telling me is that none of this matters?"

"I'm telling you none of this may matter. In the end."

He left and Jennifer sagged into her chair. Milton. She would have to depend on him now. She needed every available patrol car in the city to join the search for Kevin, and she needed the search conducted without risking a leak to the media.

Jennifer closed her eyes. Actually, none of that mattered. What mattered was the fact that Kevin was lost. The boy was lost.

She suddenly wanted to cry.

24

KEVIN KEPT TO THE SIDE STREETS, jogging as naturally as he could despite the pounding in his head.

When cars or pedestrians approached, he either changed directions or crossed the street. At the least lowered his head. If he had the luxury of a direct route, the crosstown jog would be half what it was with all of his side jaunts.

But Slater had said alone, which meant avoiding the authorities at all costs. Jennifer would have the cops out in force this time. She would be desperate to find him before he found Slater because she knew that Kevin didn't stand a chance against Slater.

Kevin knew it too.

He ran with the dread knowledge that there was no way he could face Slater and survive. Balinda would die; he would die. But he had no choice. Although he thought he'd freed himself, he'd really been slumping around in that dungeon of the past for twenty years. No longer. He would face Slater head-on and live, or die in this last-ditch effort to reach freedom.

What about Jennifer? And Sam? He would lose them, wouldn't he? The best things in his life—the only things that mattered now—would be ripped away by Slater. And if he found a way to escape Slater this time, the man would be back to hunt him down again. No, he had to end this once and for all. He had to kill or be killed.

Kevin swallowed hard and ran on through unsuspecting residential neighborhoods. Helicopters chopped through the sky. He couldn't quickly differentiate the police from others, so he hid from them all, which slowed his progress even more. Eleven police cars crossed his path, each time forcing him to alter direction. He ran for one hour and still was only halfway there. He grunted and pushed on. The hour stretched into two. With every step, his determination increased until he could almost taste his bitterness toward Slater, the coppery taste of blood on his dry tongue.

The warehouse district dawned on him without warning. Kevin slowed to a walk. His wet shirt clung to his torso. He was close. His heart began to pound, as much from his nerves as from exertion now.

Five P.M. Slater had given them six hours. Three plus three. The ultimate in this sick little game of threes. By now the whole city would be on a desperate manhunt to find Balinda before the nine o'clock deadline. The FBI would have listened to the surveillance from the house and, with Sam, they would be pounding their collective skulls against the wall trying to decode Slater's cryptic message. *You'll know, Kevin. It's dark down here.*

Would Sam figure it out? He'd never told her about the place.

Kevin crossed railroad tracks and slipped into a patch of trees sequestered away here on the outskirts of the city. Close. So close.

You're going to die, Kevin. His skin felt like a pincushion. He stopped and looked around. The city noise sounded distant. Birds chirped. A lizard scurried over dead leaves to his right, stopped, craned a bulging eye for a view of him, and then darted for the rocks.

Kevin walked forward. What if he was wrong? It could have been the warehouse where he'd trapped the boy, of course—that was dark down here. But Slater would never be so obvious. Cops would be crawling all over the place, anyway. No, this had to be it.

He caught sight of the old toolshed through the trees and stopped.

What little paint remained flaked gray with age. Suddenly Kevin wasn't sure he could go through with it. Slater was probably hidden behind one of the trees at this very moment, watching. What if he did run, and Slater stepped out from his hiding place and shot him? He couldn't call for help—he'd dumped the cell phone in an alley behind a 7-Eleven five miles east.

Didn't matter. He had to do this. The gun dug into his belly where he'd moved it when it rubbed him raw at his back. He touched it through his shirt. Should he pull it out now?

He eased the gun from his belt and walked forward. The shack sat undisturbed, hardly more than an outhouse. Breathing deliberately through his nose, Kevin approached the rear door, eyes glued to the boards, the cracks between them, searching for a sign of movement. Anything.

You're going to die in there, Kevin.

He crept up to the door. For a moment he stood there, shaking badly. To his right, deep tire marks ran through the soft earth. A rusted Master Lock padlock hung from the latch, gaping. Open. It was never open.

He eased the lock out of the latch and set it on the ground. Put his hand on the handle and pulled gently. The door creaked. He stopped. A small gap showed pitch-blackness inside.

Dear God, what am I doing? Give me strength. Did the light even work anymore?

Kevin pulled the door open. The shack was empty. *Thank God.*

You came to find him, and now you're thanking God that he isn't here?

But if he's here, he's under that trapdoor, down the stairs, through the tunnel. That's where "dark down here" is, isn't it?

He stepped in and pulled a chain that hung from a single light bulb. The bulb glowed weakly, like a dim lounge lamp. Kevin closed the door. It took him a full five minutes, trembling in the dim yellow light, to work up enough courage to pull the trapdoor open.

Wood steps descended into black. There were footprints on the steps.

Kevin swallowed.

|||

A mood of pending doom had settled over the conference room and two adjacent offices in the Long Beach police headquarters where Jennifer and the other FBI agents had worked feverishly over the past four days.

Two hours of methodical searching, both on the ground and from the air, had turned up nothing. If Slater's *dark down here* place was the warehouse cellar, he would walk in to find two uniformed policemen with weapons drawn. Sam had called in twice, the last time after giving up her ground search. She wanted to check into something that she didn't elaborate on. Said she would call back. That was an hour ago.

The forensic report on the shoe prints had come in—inconclusive. Jennifer had retraced every detail of the past four days, scrutinizing them for clues to which of the two new theories held more water. Either Kevin was Slater, or Slater was framing Kevin by seeding evidence to make it appear that he was Slater.

If Kevin really was Slater, then at least they had their man. No more games for Slater. No more victims. Unless Slater killed Kevin, which would be tantamount to suicide. Or unless Slater killed Balinda. Then they'd have two dead bodies lying in a place that's dark down here. Even if Slater didn't kill Balinda, Kevin would have to live with what he did as Slater for the rest of his life. The thought brought a lump to Jennifer's throat.

If Slater were someone else, Kevin would merely be the poor victim of a horrible plot. Unless he was killed by Slater, in which case he'd be the dead victim of a horrible plot.

The clock ticked on. 5:30. Jennifer picked up the cell phone and called Sam.

"Sam, we're dead down here. We don't have a thing. The shoe prints came back inconclusive. Please tell me you have something."

"I was just going to call. Have you talked to John Francis yet?"

"No. Why?"

"I've been at Kevin's house digging through his writings, papers, books, anything where he might have made reference to his past, a clue to a place that's dark. I knew Kevin was intelligent, but I never expected quite this—mind blowing. No obvious references at all to Slater or anything that even hints at multiple personalities."

"Which could support our theory that he was framed," Jennifer said.

"Maybe. But I did find this in a periodic journal he keeps on his computer. Listen. Written two weeks ago.

"'The problem with most of the best thinkers is that they dissociate their reasoning from spirituality, as if the two exist in separate realities. Not so. It's a false dichotomy. No one understands this more than Dr. John Francis. I feel like I can trust him. He alone truly understands me. I told him about the secret today. I miss Samantha. She called . . ."

"It continues about me," Sam said. "The point is, I think Dr. John Francis may know more than he may realize."

"The *secret*," Jennifer said. "Could be a reference to something he never told you. A place he knew as a child."

"I want to talk to him, Jennifer."

It was the only glimmer of light Jennifer had seen in two hours. "You have his address?"

"Yes."

Jennifer grabbed her coat. "I'll meet you there in twenty minutes."

III

The descent into the bomb shelter and through the tunnel had wrung a gallon of sweat from Kevin's glands. The door at the bottom of the stairwell into the basement stood wide open. Kevin leaned forward and peered into the room for the first time in twenty years, numb on his feet.

A shiny black floor with patches of concrete showing through. A chest freezer to the right, next to a white stove and a sink. A metal desk to the left, piled with electronics. Boxes of dynamite, a file cabinet, a mirror. Two doors that led . . . somewhere.

Kevin held the gun out with both hands, breathless. Sweat stung his eyes. This was it! Had to be. But the room was empty! Where was Slater?

Something bumped against the door to his right and Kevin jerked the gun toward it. Gray carpet had been rolled and stuffed into the crack at its base.

Thump, thump, thump. A muffled cry.

Kevin's body went rigid.

"Is someone there?" He could barely make out the words. "Pleeeease!"

Balinda. The room started to move. He shoved a foot forward and steadied himself. Frantic, he searched the room again. Where was Slater?

"Pleeeease, please." She sounded like a mouse. Kevin took another step. Then another, gun wavering before him.

"I don't want to die," the voice wept. "Please, please, I'll do anything."

"Balinda?" Kevin's voice cracked. The sounds stopped. A thick silence settled.

Kevin struggled to breathe. Slater had left Balinda here for him to find. He wanted Kevin to save his mommy, because that's what little boys do for their mommies. He had deserted her, and now he would rescue her to make up for the horrible sin. Kevin's world started to spin.

"Kevin?" The voice whimpered. "Kevin?"

"Mommy?"

Something scraped the concrete behind him. He whirled, gun extended.

A man stepped out of the dark shadows, sneering. Blond hair. *No shirt.* Beige slacks. White tennis shoes. *No shirt.* A tattoo of a heart over his left breast with the word *Mom* stenciled in black. He held a large silver gun at his side. *No shirt.* His naked torso struck Kevin as obscene. Slater, in the flesh.

"Hello, Kevin," Slater said. "I'm so glad you found us." He edged to his right.

Kevin followed him with the gun, finger tightening. *Do it! Shoot. Pull the trigger.*

"I wouldn't shoot just yet, Kevin. Not until I tell you how you can save Mommy. Because I swear if you kill me now, she's dead meat. Do you want Mommy to be dead meat?" Slater grinned and moved around slowly, gun still at his side. "Well, yes, I suppose you might want Mommy to be dead meat. That would be understandable."

A fist thumped into the door. "Kevin! Help me!" Balinda's muffled voice cried.

"Shut up, witch!" Slater yelled, face flushed red. He caught himself and smiled. "Tell her it isn't real, Kevin. That the darkness isn't really dark. Tell her that if she's a good girl, you'll let her out. Isn't that what she told you?"

"How do you know me?" Kevin asked, voice cracking.

"You don't recognize me?" Slater exposed his forehead with his left hand. "I had the tattoo removed."

He was the boy, but Kevin already knew that. "But . . . how do you know about Balinda? What are you doing?"

"You still don't get it, do you?" Slater edged closer to the door Balinda was thumping on. "Four days of crystal-clear clues and you still are as stupid as you look. Do you know how long I've waited for this? Hmm? Planned for this. It's brilliant. Even if you think you know, you don't. Nobody will know. Ever. That's the beauty of it."

Slater giggled. His face twitched.

"Drop the gun," Kevin said. He had to know what Slater meant. He wanted to shoot the man. He wanted to send a piece of lead through his forehead, but he wanted to know what Slater was saying.

"Drop the gun."

Slater reached for the doorknob, twisted it, pushed the door open. Balinda sat on the floor, hands bound behind her back, foot against the door. Slater calmly pointed his pistol at her white, stricken face.

"Sorry, Kevin," Slater said. "Toss me the peashooter, or I shoot Mommy."

What? Kevin felt his face flush with heat. He could still shoot and Slater would be dead before he could kill Balinda.

"Drop it!" Slater said. "I've got this trigger milled down to a hair. You shoot me and my finger twitches and she's dead."

Balinda started to cry. "Kevin . . . honey . . ."

"Now! Now, now, now!"

Kevin lowered the gun slowly.

"I know how fond you are of it, but when I say drop, I really do mean drop. Now!"

Kevin dropped the gun and stepped back, panicked.

Slater slammed the door shut on Balinda, stepped forward, and scooped up the gun. "Good boy. Mommy will be proud of you." He shoved Kevin's gun into his own belt, walked toward the door to the stairwell, and shut it.

"There."

Balinda's feet thumped the door again. "Kevin? Pleeeease . . ."

"Ahhhhh!" Slater screamed and ran at the door. He kicked it hard enough to put a dent in the steel. "Shut up! One more peep and I'll staple your mouth shut!"

Slater stood back, panting. Balinda quieted.

"Don't you hate these women who don't know how to keep their yappers shut?" Slater turned around. "Now, where were we?"

A strange resolve settled over Kevin. He was going to die down here after all. He really had nothing to lose. The twisted boy had grown up into a pathetic monster. Slater would kill both him and Balinda without a fleeting thought of remorse.

"You're sick," Kevin said.

"Now there's a novel thought. Actually, you're the sick one. That's what they suspect now and, believe me, by the time I'm done here, they won't have any reason to think differently."

"You're wrong. You've already proved your insanity. You've torn this city to shreds and now you've kidnapped an innocent—"

"Innocent? Hardly, but that's not the point. The point is, *you* kidnapped her." Slater grinned wide.

"You're not making sense."

"Of course not. I'm not making any sense to you because you're not thinking. You and I both know that I did all those nasty things. That Slater called Kevin, and Slater blew up the bus, and Slater is holding the old witch in a cement box. Problem is, they think that Kevin is Slater. And if they don't yet, they will soon enough. Kevin is Slater because Kevin is crazy." Grin. "That's the plan, puke."

Kevin stared, mind numb. "That's . . . that's not possible."

"Actually, it is. Which is why it'll work. You don't think I'd go for something implausible, do you?"

"How could I be you?"

"Multiple Personality Disorder. MPD. You're me without even knowing that you are me."

Kevin shook his head. "You're actually stupid enough to think that Jennifer—"

"Sam believes it." Slater walked over to the desk and touched a black box that looked like an answering machine. He'd lowered the pistol to his side, and Kevin wondered if he could rush him before he had a chance to lift it and shoot.

"She found the cell phone I used in your pocket—that alone's enough for most juries. But they'll find more. The recordings, for instance. They'll show that my voice is really your voice, manipulated to sound like a terrible killer named Slater." Slater feigned horror and shivered. "Oooo . . . chilling, don't you think?"

"There are a thousand holes! You'll never get away with it."

"There are no holes!" Slater snapped. Then he grinned again. "And I already *am* getting away with it."

He picked up a picture. It was a photograph of Sam, taken at a distance with a telephoto lens. "She's really quite beautiful," he said, lost in the image for a moment. He reached up and ripped down a large black sheet that hung on the wall. Behind it, fifty or sixty pictures had been affixed to the concrete.

They were all of Samantha.

Kevin blinked and took a step forward. Slater's gun came up. "Stay back."

Pictures of Sam on the street, New York, Sacramento, through a window, in her bedroom . . . Heat spread down Kevin's neck.

"What are you doing?"

"I wanted to kill her once." Slater slowly faced Kevin, eyes sagging. "But you know that. You wanted her, so you tried to kill me instead."

Slater's lips began to quiver and his breathing came in short quick drags. "Well, now I *am* going to kill her. And I'm going to show the world who you really are, because you're no better than I am. You're the pretty boy down the street she loves to play with. But does that make you better? No!" He screamed the last word and Kevin jumped.

"Hang out with me for a while and we'll see how sweet you are." He leaned forward and tapped Kevin's chest with the gun barrel.

"Deep down inside you're no different than I am. If you'd met me before you met Samantha, we'd both have been at her window, licking the glass. I know that, because I was just like you once."

"That's what this is about?" Kevin demanded. "A jealous schoolboy come back to butcher the boy across the street? You're pathetic!"

"And so are you! You're sick like the rest of them." Slater spat a thimbleful of saliva at the cement. It landed with a smack. "Sick!" He took two steps forward and shoved the gun into Kevin's cheek. Pain flashed up his jaw. "I should just end this now. You and all the freaks who pretend to be so sweet on Sundays! You may not be me but really you are me, you slug."

Slater's body shook against Kevin's.

Kevin's mind began to shut down. *You're going to die, Kevin.*

III

Slater fights a desperate urge to pull the trigger. He knows that he can't do it. This isn't the plan. Not this way. Not yet.

He stares at Kevin's round eyes. The smell of fear and sweat wafts through his nostrils. Impulsively he sticks out his tongue and presses it firmly against Kevin's jaw. He draws it all the way up his cheek to his temple, as if he's licking an ice-cream cone. Salty. Bitter. Sick, sick, sick.

Slater shoves Kevin and steps back. "Know what I taste? I taste Slater. I'm going to kill her, Kevin. I'm going to kill both of them. But that's not what the world will think. They're going to think that you did it."

Kevin straightens and glares at him. The man has more spunk than Slater estimated. Enough to come here, he'd guessed as much. But he can't forget that this man also locked him in that cellar once, when he was still a boy. They might be more alike than even Slater realizes.

He takes a deep breath. "Now, let's calm down, shall we? I have a new game I would like to play."

"I'm not going to play any more games," Kevin says.

"Yes, you are. You'll play more games or I'll cut up Mommy, one finger at a time."

Kevin glances at the door that holds the old woman.

"And if we still aren't properly motivated, I'll start on *your* fingers. Are we still all stuffed and cocky?"

Kevin just stares at him. At least he isn't whimpering and crying like the old hag.

"Let's face it, Kevin. You came here with one thing on your mind. You wanted to kill. Kill, kill, kill. That's another way you and I are alike." Slater shrugs. "True, the object of your blood lust is me, but when you cut away all the face-saving, it's the same instinct. Most humans are truly murderers, but I didn't bring you here to lecture. I brought you here to kill. I'm going to give you your wish. You came to kill me, but that doesn't suit my tastes, so I've chosen to flip things a bit."

Kevin doesn't flinch.

"We already have one, but we need the other." Slater looks at the wall, the collage of pictures. It's in part her beauty that he hates so much. It's why he keeps the photographs covered. By nine o'clock she will be dead.

"Kill me," Kevin says. "I hate you." He speaks the last words with such contempt that Slater feels a sliver of shock.

But Slater doesn't show shock. He shows anger and hatred, but not shock, because shock is weakness.

"So courageous. So noble. How can I refuse such a sincere request? Consider yourself dead already. We all die; yours will be a living death until you finally do kick the bucket. In the meantime, we must lure in our second victim. She will fly to your rescue. Her knight is in peril."

"I despise you."

"You will help me or Mommy will begin to scream!" Slater says.

Kevin glares at him and then closes his eyes slowly.

"Just a simple call, Kevin. I would do it, but I really need her to hear your voice."

Kevin shakes his head and is about to speak, but Slater doesn't want to hear it. He steps forward and slams the gun against the side of Kevin's head.

"I'll kill her, you perverted little brat!"

Blood oozes down Kevin's face. This excites Slater.

Kevin's face wrinkles and he begins to cry. Better, much better. He sinks slowly to his knees and for the first time since his nemesis entered the room, Slater knows he will win.

III

Samantha raced through Long Beach. Secret. What secret? Kevin had hidden his dealing with Slater as a boy and he'd remained quiet about his home life, but the journal entry had to be something else. Something the professor knew.

She was a block away when her cell phone rang. She couldn't imagine how investigators had managed before the advent of cellular technology. On the other hand, criminals took advantage as well. Slater certainly had.

"Sam."

"This is Kevin."

"Kevin!"

" . . . no one else. Do you understand?" His voice sounded flat—horrible. He was reading, being forced. Sam veered for the curb, ignoring a honk behind.

"Kevin, if you're with Slater keep talking and don't cough. If you're not, cough. Yes, I do understand." Actually, she'd missed what she was supposed to understand. And she quickly considered asking him to repeat it, but that might endanger him.

Kevin didn't cough.

"We're playing a new game," he said. "This game's for you, Sam. If you can find us before nine, he'll set me and Mommy free." His voice wavered. She heard a muffled voice in the background. Slater.

"I will give you the first clue. If you find it, there will be another one. No authorities can be involved, including that wench, Jennifer." Slater chuckled in the background. His voice suddenly filled the phone, loud and eager.

"First clue: *Who loves what he sees, but hates what he loves?* You might find a clue in his house; you might not. Hurry to the rescue, Princess." The phone went dead.

"Slater? Kevin!" Sam threw the phone against the windshield. "Aaaahh!"

Who loves what he sees, but hates what he loves? Her mind was blank. 6:27. Less than three hours. She had to get back to Kevin's house. The answers had to be in his papers. His journal. Somewhere!

She roared through a U-turn and headed back north. What was the chance that Slater had found a way to monitor her phone calls? If he knew electronics well enough to pull off a frame on Kevin, he knew more than she. No authorities involved, he'd said.

Sam bent for her cell on the floor and swerved badly enough to force a second attempt. She caught the phone, fumbled with the battery, which had jarred loose. Power on. Redial.

|||

"Thank you again for your time, Dr. Francis. As I explained on the phone—"

"Yes, yes, of course." The professor waved her in. "Please come in, dear. Believe me, I will do whatever I can for that boy."

Jennifer paused. "You understand why I'm here? It seems that you know more about Kevin than you first suggested. At least Kevin believes you do."

"I know him better than most, yes. But nothing that I haven't told you."

"That's what we're going to find out. With your help." She stepped into the house. "We're running out of time, Professor. If you can't help us, I'm afraid no one will be able to. You talked to Samantha Sheer from CBI earlier today; she'll be here shortly." Her cell went off and she pulled it from her waist. "Excuse me."

It was Sam. She'd heard from Kevin. Jennifer instinctively turned back toward the door and listened while Sam ran through the details.

"So you're headed *back* to the house?"

"Yes. Review the clue with Dr. Francis. *Who loves what he sees, but hates what he loves?* You got it? Review *everything* with him. He has to know something."

"I have to report this."

"Slater said no cops, and he mentioned you by name. You won't be out of the loop. Just stay where you are. Don't brief Milton. Let me work alone; that's all I ask. If you think of anything, call me. But this is between us now. Kevin, Slater, and me. Please, Jennifer."

Jennifer hesitated. "Okay. I'll give you an hour. Then I call this in, understood? I'm over my head here."

"I'll call you."

"One hour." She closed the cell.

"Anything wrong?" Dr. Francis asked.

"Everything's wrong, Doctor."

25

Monday

6:37 P.M.

WHO LOVES WHAT HE SEES, but hates what he loves?" Dr. Francis said. "Every man, every woman, every child beyond the age of accountability."

"He loves the ice cream, but hates the fat it puts on his waist," Jennifer said.

"Yes. She loves the wrong man, but hates what he does to her life. The dilemma goes back to Eve and the apple in the garden. Sin."

"I don't see how that helps us," Jennifer said. "The reference has to be personal, something that only Sam or Kevin might know. Something the three of them knew when they were children."

"Three children? Or two? Sam and Kevin, who had his alter ego—the boy?" Dr. Francis sat in a large leather recliner and leaned forward. "Tell me everything. From the beginning. Time is slipping."

He listened, eyes sparkling, with only the occasional frown to betray his anxiety over Kevin's predicament. In many ways he reminded Jennifer of Kevin, genuine to the bone and thoroughly intelligent. It was the first time she'd run through the last four days aloud and with such comprehensive minutiae with anyone except Galager. The first call, the car bomb, the second call regarding the doghouse. Then the bus, Kevin's flight with Sam to Palos Verdes, the warehouse, the library, the kidnapping, and now this death threat.

She told it all in one long run-on, interrupted only by his prodding for further detail. He was a thinker, among the best, and he seemed to like playing detective. So did most people. His questions were insightful. How do you know that Kevin was inside his house when the second phone call was made? Is there a way to intercept a laser signal? All the questions lent themselves to whether Kevin could logically be Slater.

Twenty minutes and Sam still hadn't called. Jennifer stood and paced, hand on chin. "I can't believe it's coming down to this. Kevin's out there somewhere in the dark with a madman and we're . . ." She ran her hands through her hair. "It's been like that since I got down here. Slater's always one step ahead, and we're running around like a bunch of toy monkeys."

"You remind me of Kevin when you do that."

He was looking at her hands, still in her hair. She sat down on the couch and sighed. "So now I'm Kevin as well."

He chuckled. "Hardly. But I do agree that the primary question is who, not what. Who is Kevin? Really."

"And?"

He leaned back and crossed his legs. "Multiple Personality Disorder. It's referred to as Dissociative Identity Disorder these days, isn't it? Where two or more personalities inhabit a single body. As you know, not everyone acknowledges such an animal. Some spiritualize the phenomenon—demon possession. Others discount it outright or think of it as commonplace, a gift even."

"And you?"

"While I do believe in spiritual forces and even demon possession, I can assure you that Kevin is not possessed. I've spent many hours with the boy, and my own spirit isn't so callous. The fact of the matter is, all of us experience some level of dissociation, more so with age. We suddenly forget why we walked into the bathroom. Or we have strange déjà vu. Daydreaming, highway hypnosis, even losing yourself in a book or movie. All forms of dissociation that are thoroughly natural."

"A far cry from the kind of dissociation that would be required for Kevin to be Slater," Jennifer said. "As you said, you've spent time with him, so have I. Kevin doesn't have a trace of Slater in him. If both personalities share the same body, they are completely unaware of each other."

"*If.* That is the operative word here. If Kevin is also Slater. Frankly, your theory that Slater may be framing Kevin makes as much sense. But . . ." Dr. Francis stood and paced to the fireplace and back. "But let's assume Kevin is Slater for the moment. What if there was a child, a boy, who from a very young age was isolated from the real world."

"Kevin."

"Yes. What would that child learn?"

"He would learn whatever he was taught from his surroundings: the environment he could touch, taste, hear, smell, see. If he were alone on an island, he would think the world was a small piece of dirt floating on the water, and he would wonder why he didn't have fur like the rest of his playmates. Like Tarzan."

"Yes, but our child does not grow up on an island. He grows up in a world of shifting realities. A world where realities are merely slips of paper cut up into truth. There are no absolutes. There is no evil and, by extension, there is no good. Everything is pretend, and only that which you decide to be real is actually real. Life is merely a string of role-playing adventures."

Dr. Frances lifted his hand to his beard and pulled lightly at the gray strands. "But there *is* an absolute, you see. There is good and there is evil. The boy feels a void in his soul. He longs for an understanding of those absolutes, good and evil. He is abused in the most mentally strenuous ways, causing his mind to separate into dissociative realities. He becomes a master role-player, and finally, when he is old enough to understand evil, he subconsciously creates a personality to play the part. Because that's what he's learned to do."

"The boy. Slater."

"A walking, living personification of man's dual nature. The natures of man could be playing themselves out through personalities he's created. It does follow, doesn't it?"

"Assuming man has more than one nature. It could also be a simple fracture—common dissociation."

"Man does have more than one nature," the professor said. "The 'old man,' which is our flesh, and the fingerprint of God, the good."

"And for those of us who don't necessarily believe in the spirit of God? Who aren't religious?"

"A person's inner natures have nothing to do with religion. They are spiritual, not religious. Two natures battling. Good and evil. They are the good that we would do but do not do, and they are that which we would not do, but still do. The apostle Paul. Romans chapter seven. The capacity for good and evil is within every person from birth, I think. The spirit of God can regenerate man, but it is the human spirit I'm talking about here. Not a separate nature, although I would say that the struggle between good and evil is hopeless without divine intervention. Perhaps that's what you think of when you say 'religious,' although really religion has little to do with divine intervention either."

He offered a quick smile. For the second time in as many days he was tempting her to discover his faith. Right now, however, she didn't have the time.

"So you're thinking Kevin, as a young boy, simply struggled to make sense of the conflict within him, between basic good and evil. He dealt with it the way he learned to deal with all reality. He creates roles for each persona and plays them out without knowing that he's doing it."

"Yes, that's exactly what I'm thinking," the professor said, standing and pacing to his right. "It's possible. Entirely possible. It may not even be classical Dissociative Identity Disorder. Could be Posttraumatic Stress Disorder, which is even more likely for this kind of unconscious role-playing."

"Assuming Kevin is Slater."

"Yes, assuming Kevin is Slater."

III

Sam poured through Kevin's journal, searching desperately for a key to the riddle. *Who loves what he sees, but hates what he loves?* When that yielded no answer, she paged through his class notebooks.

The most obvious answer was mankind, of course. Mankind looks and sees and loves and then hates. The story of humanity in one sentence. Not quite up there with Descartes's "I think therefore I am," but obvious enough.

Who loves what he sees, but hates what he loves? Who, who? Slater. Slater was who. Despite Jennifer's theory, Kevin had to be Slater. If so, Slater was the hater of the two.

She sighed. Something common to all three of them triggered this riddle. But what? She had only two hours to win this mad game. And even if she did find them, Slater surely wouldn't let them all go. Someone would die in the next two hours. Kevin had saved her from the killer once; he'd risked his life. Now it was her turn.

6:59. And this riddle was only the first clue.

She mumbled through gritted teeth. "Come on, Kevin! Tell me something."

III

"Then Slater's the boy, stalking Sam, but he's really Kevin's evil alter ego," Jennifer said.

"And Kevin doesn't like the evil boy, so he kills him," the professor said.

"But isn't that evil? To kill?"

"God killed a few men in their time. Read the Old Testament. Kevin tries to kill the boy because the boy threatens to kill his childhood friend."

"But the boy is really Kevin. So Kevin would have killed Samantha if he hadn't dealt with the boy?"

"Think of it—a personality that embodies only evil would be quite a little monster. Slater, the evil in Kevin, sees that Samantha favored Kevin over him. Slater decides he must kill Sam."

"And now that monster has come back to life and is stalking Kevin," Jennifer said. "In this scenario of yours."

"That monster never died. That would require more than Kevin was capable of on his own. Death to the old self." Dr. Francis paused and then continued. "As Kevin matured, he recognized Balinda's folly, but he didn't recognize his dual nature. He did, however, successfully climb out of his past, leave the house, and embrace the real world."

"Until three months of seminary and discussions of his one obsession, the natures of man, finally brings Slater back to the surface," Jennifer finished.

The professor lifted an eyebrow. "It's possible."

As a clinical theory the possibilities were interesting, but Jennifer was having difficulty accepting it as reality. Theories abounded in the study of the mind, a new one every month, it seemed. This was a theory. And time was still ticking away, while the real Kevin possibly sat at the real Slater's gunpoint, praying desperately for someone to burst through the doors and save him.

"But why the game? Why the riddles?"

"I don't know." His eyes glimmered mischievously. "Perhaps the whole thing was really Kevin's idea."

"I don't follow."

"Evil only survives in the dark. This isn't religious either, by the way. The simplest way to deal with evil is to force it into the light of truth. Expose its secret. Sun on the vampire. Sin thrives in the dungeon, but slap it on the table for all to see, and it withers rather quickly. It was one of Kevin's greatest complaints about the church, actually. That everyone hides their evil. Their sin. Pastors, deacons, bishops—they perpetuate the very nature they are in business to destroy by covering it up. No confession allowed except in secret."

"Now you sound like a skeptic."

"I'm a skeptic of religious systems, not of the faith. Someday I will be happy to discuss the difference with you."

"How does this make the riddles Kevin's idea?"

"Perhaps subconsciously Kevin knows that Slater still lurks. What better way to destroy him than to expose him? Kevin could be forcing Slater's hand, forcing him to reveal himself. Ha! I'm telling you, Kevin is genuine enough to conceive of just such a plan! Slater thinks he has Kevin where he wants him by forcing a confession, when it's the very confession that will destroy Slater, not Kevin! It's like the cross all over again."

Jennifer rubbed her temples. "I can just hear the court case now. This all assumes Slater isn't framing Kevin."

"Yes. But either way, we've pieced together his framework. At least the logic of it." Dr. Francis sat and faced her with his fingers touching each other in a tepee. "My goodness. You came here to find out who Kevin really is. I think I've just stumbled on it, my dear."

"Tell me, who is Kevin?"

"Kevin is every man. And woman. He is you; he is me; he is the woman who wears a yellow hat and sits on the third pew every Sunday. Kevin is the natures of humanity personified."

"Please, you can't mean that everyone's a Slater."

"No, only those who do as Slater does. Only those who hate. Do you hate, Jennifer? Do you gossip?"

III

Who loves what he sees, but hates what he loves? The simplicity of it hit Sam midstride, as she paced Kevin's living room, staring at the travel posters. The windows to the world. It wasn't *who;* it was the *seeing!* Who had *seen?* Slater had seen her and wanted her. But where had he seen her?

The window. Her window! The boy Slater had watched her from the window and seen what he desperately wanted but could not have. And he hated her.

The answer to the riddle was her window!

Sam stood still, stunned, then ran for her car. She fired the engine and roared down the street. 7:23.

Sam punched in Jennifer's cell number.

"This is—"

"I think I have it! I'm on my way now."

"What is it?" Jennifer demanded.

Sam hesitated. "This is for me—"

"Just tell me where, for heaven's sake! I know it's for you, but time's running out here!"

"The window."

"Kevin's window?"

"My window. That's where Slater saw me. That's where he hated me." She glanced in her rearview mirror. Clear. "I need more time, Jennifer. If Slater even gets a whiff of anyone else snooping around this, he may pull the trigger. You know that."

No response.

"Please, Jennifer, there's no other way."

"We could have a dozen of the best minds on this."

"Then get them on it. But no one from the investigation and, without question, no locals. We can't risk a leak. Besides, no one's going to know these riddles like I do. This is about me now."

Silence.

"Jennifer—"

"Just hurry, Samantha."

"I'm doing sixty in a thirty-five as it is." She hung up.

Hold on, Kevin. Please don't do anything stupid. Wait for me. I'm coming. I swear I'm coming.

26

Monday
7:25 P.M.

WHETHER THE BOY WAS IMAGINARY OR REAL, he knew Sam and he wants her to come," Dr. Francis said as Jennifer closed her phone. "He's luring her in. You see that, don't you? The riddles are only to continue the game."

Jennifer sighed. "And if Sam finds them? He'll kill them all and I'll have done nothing."

"What can you do?"

"Something. Anything! If I can't save him, then I should report this."

"Then report it. But what can any of your colleagues do?"

He was right, of course, but the idea of sitting here in his living room discussing the natures of man was . . . impossible! Roy had been killed in similar circumstances by the Riddle Killer. True, Slater probably wasn't the same man who'd killed Roy, but he represented the same kind of man. Unless Kevin was Slater.

Did Slater live in her? Do you hate, Jennifer? Milton?

"Perhaps the most you can do is try to understand, so that if an opportunity does come, you're better equipped," the professor said. "I know how frustrating it must be, but now it's up to Sam. She sounds like someone who can handle herself. If I'm right, Kevin will need her."

"How so?"

"If Kevin is Slater, he'll be powerless to overcome Slater on his own."

Jennifer looked at him and wondered what movies he watched.

"Okay, Professor. We still don't know if Kevin is Slater or not. Theories are fine, but let's try the logistics on for size." She pulled out her notebook and crossed her legs. "Question: From a purely logistical and evidentiary perspective, could one person have done what we know to have happened?"

She opened the book to the list she'd made two hours earlier, after Sam's call suggesting for the second time that Kevin was Slater. She ticked the first item with her pencil. "Kevin gets a call in his car."

"Although you said there's no evidence of that first call, correct? The cell phone was burned. The entire call could have been in Kevin's mind, two voices talking. Same with any unrecorded conversation he had with Slater."

She nodded. "Number two. The car blows up three minutes after the call, after Kevin has escaped."

"The personality that is Slater carries a sophisticated cell phone in his pocket—Kevin's pocket. This device is a secure telephone and a transmitting device. After the imaginary conversation giving him three minutes, the Slater personality triggers a bomb he's planted in the trunk. It explodes, as planned. He detonates all of the bombs in similar fashion."

"The second phone Sam found."

"Follows," Dr. Francis said.

"Where does the Slater personality make all these explosives? We found nothing." Jennifer had her own thoughts but she wanted to hear the professor.

He smiled. "Maybe when I'm done playing scholar, I'll apply for a job with the FBI."

"I'm sure we would welcome you. Understanding of religion is a hot recruitment criterion these days."

"Slater obviously has his hiding place. Likely the place he's hidden Balinda. Kevin takes frequent trips to this location as Slater, totally unaware. The middle of the night, on the way home from class. He remembers nothing of them because it is the Slater personality, not Kevin, who is actually going."

"And his knowledge of electronics. Slater learns, but not Kevin."

"So it would seem."

She looked at her list. "But the warehouse is different because he calls the room phone and talks to Samantha. It's the first time we have him on tape."

"You said the phone rang while he was in the room, but Slater didn't speak until Kevin was out. He reaches into his pocket and presses send on a number he's already entered. As soon as he's in the hall, he begins to speak."

"Sounds far-fetched, don't you think? Somehow I don't see Slater as a James Bond."

"No, he's probably made his mistakes. You just haven't had the time to find them. For all you know, the recording will bear that out. We're just reconstructing a possible scenario based on what we do know."

"Then we can assume he planted the bomb in the library the night before last somehow, while he was supposedly in Palos Verdes with Samantha. Maybe he slipped out at night or something. The library's not exactly a high-security facility. He, meaning Slater, did everything either while our eyes were off him or remotely using the cell phone."

"If Kevin is Slater," the professor said.

She frowned. The scenario was plausible. Too plausible for her own comfort. If it bore out, the scientific journals would be writing about Kevin for years.

"And the Riddle Killer?" she asked.

"As you said earlier. Someone Slater imitated to throw the authorities off. What do you call it—copy cat? It's only been four days. Even the wheels of the FBI can turn only so fast. Perpetuating the double life beyond a week might be impossible. Four days is all he evidently needed."

Jennifer closed the notebook. There were a dozen more, but she saw with a glance that they weren't so unique. What they really needed was the analysis of the two recordings from Kevin's cell phone. It was the second call that interested her. If this theory held water, the same person had made and received the call that had sent them running for the library. It couldn't have been imagined by Kevin because it was recorded.

She sighed. "This is way too complicated. There's something missing here that would make all of this much clearer."

The professor ran his fingers over his bearded chin. "Maybe so. Do you rely on your intuition very often, Jennifer?"

"All day. Intuition leads to evidence, which leads to answers. It's what makes us ask the right questions."

"Hmm. And what does your intuition tell you about Kevin?"

She thought about it for a moment. "That he's innocent, either way. That he's an exceptional man. That he's nothing like Slater."

His right eyebrow went up. "This after four days? It took me a month to conclude the same."

"Four days of hell will tell you a lot about a man, Professor."

"'Yea, though I walk through the valley of the shadow of death, I will fear no evil.'"

"If he is Slater, do you think Kevin's afraid?" she asked.

"I think he is petrified."

|||

Baker Street was black and still, shrouded in the long line of elms standing like sentinels. The drive had sliced twenty-one minutes off the clock, thanks to an accident on Willow. 7:46. She passed Kevin's old house—light glowed behind the drapes where Eugene and Bob might very well still be crying. Jennifer had kept the media at bay for the day, but it wouldn't last. By tomorrow there would probably be at least a couple vans parked out front, waiting for a snapshot of the crazies inside.

What loves what it sees? She slowed the car to a crawl and approached her old house. A porch light glared angrily. The hedges were ragged, not trimmed like her father had kept them years earlier. She'd already decided that she wouldn't bother the residents for the simple reason that she couldn't think of a decent explanation for why she would want to snoop around the bedroom window without causing alarm. She hoped they didn't have a dog.

Sam parked the car across the street and walked past the house, then cut into the neighbor's yard. She rounded the house and headed for the same old fence she and Kevin had wriggled through on a hundred occasions. Unlikely the boards were still loose.

She crouched by the fence and ran along it toward the east side of the yard, where her old bedroom faced. A dog barked several houses down. *Settle down, Spot, I'm just going to take a peek.* Just like Slater used to take peeps. Life had come full circle.

She poked her head over the fence. The window was opaque, slightly obscured by the same bushes she'd crawled over as a child. Vacant? No dog that she could see. The boards she'd once been able to slip through wouldn't budge. Up and over—the only way.

Sam grabbed the fence with both hands and vaulted it easily. She had a body built for gymnastics, a coach had told her in law school. But you don't start taking gymnastics at age twenty and expect to make the Olympics. She had opted for dance classes.

The lawn was wet from a recent watering. She ran for the window and knelt by the hedge. What was she looking for? Another clue. A riddle maybe, scratched in the ground. A note taped to the brick.

She slid in behind the bushes and felt the wall. The musty smell of dirt filled her nose. How long had it been since anyone had climbed through this window? She eased her head up and saw that the window not only was dark, but had been painted black on the inside.

Her pulse spiked. Did Slater live here? Had he taken residence in her old house? *I can't have you, so I'll take your house.* For a moment she just stared at the window, caught off guard. Someone laughed inside. A man. Then a woman, laughing.

No, they'd probably just turned the room into a darkroom or something. Photography buffs. She exhaled and resumed her search. Time was ticking.

She felt along the ledge, but there was nothing she could feel or see. The ground was dark at her feet, so she knelt and groped around in the dirt. Her fingers ran over a few rocks—he could have written a message on a rock. She held them up to what little light reached her from the warehouses across the street. Nothing. She dropped the rocks and stood again.

Had she been wrong about the window? There was a message here; there had to be! The dial on her watch glowed green, 7:58. She felt the first tendrils of panic tickle her spine. If she was wrong about the window, she'd have to start over—the game would be lost.

Maybe she shouldn't be looking for a written message.

She groaned and stepped back into the lawn. The panic was growing. *Take a breath, Sam. You're smarter than he is. You have to be. For Kevin's sake. Play his game; beat him at his own game.*

She paced the lawn, uncaring of her exposure now. She wore black slacks and a red blouse, dark colors that wouldn't easily be seen from the street. Time was running out.

Sam walked to the fence and faced the window. Okay, is there something in the bushes? An arrow? That was stupid movie stuff. She followed the roofline. Did it point anywhere? There were two second-story windows above the one down here, forming a triangle of sorts. An arrow.

Enough with the arrows, Sam! This is something that you couldn't mistake. Not something cute out of a Nancy Drew mystery. What's changed here? What is altered to make a statement? What's altered that could *make a statement?*

The window. The window is painted black, because it's now a darkroom or something. So really it's not a window any longer. It's a dark sheet of glass. No light.

It's dark down here, Kevin.

Sam let out a small cry and immediately swallowed it. That was it! *No* window. What used to have light but does no more? What has no window?

Sam ran for the fence and slung herself over it, spilling to the ground on her landing. Was it possible? How could Slater have pulled it off?

She felt for her gun. *Okay, think. One hour.* If she was right, she didn't need five minutes, much less sixty, to find Kevin.

|||

"And how is a man or a woman set free from this hideous nature?" Jennifer asked.

"You kill it. But to kill it you must see it. Thus the light."

"So just like"—Jennifer snapped her fingers—"that, huh?"

"As it turns out, no. It needs a daily dose of death. Really, the single greatest ally of evil is darkness. That is my point. I don't care what faith you have or what you say you believe, whether you go to church every Sunday or pray to God five times a day. If you keep the evil nature hidden, like most do, it thrives."

"And Kevin?"

"Kevin? I don't know about Kevin. If he is Slater, I suppose you would need to kill Slater the way you kill the old self. But he can't do it alone. He wouldn't even know to kill him. Man cannot deal with evil alone."

III

Kevin had never shown her the inside of the old shed because he said it was dark inside. Only he hadn't just said inside, he said *down* there. She remembered that now. Nobody used the useless old shack in the corner of the lawn. The old bomb shelter turned toolshed on the edge of the ash heap.

The window that wasn't really a window had to be Kevin's window. In Slater's mind he might have used another riddle: *What thinks it's a window but really isn't?* Opposites. As a boy, Kevin thought he'd escaped his tortuous world through his window, but he hadn't.

The old toolshed in the corner of Kevin's lawn was the only place Sam knew of that had a basement of sorts. It was dark down there and it had no windows, and she knew that she knew that she knew that Slater was down in that bomb shelter with Balinda.

Sam held the nine millimeter at her side and ran for the shack, bent over, eyes fixed on its wood siding. The door had always been latched and locked with a big rusted padlock. What if it still was?

She should call Jennifer, but therein lay a dilemma. What could Jennifer do? Swoop in and surround the house? Slater would do the worst. On the other hand, what could *Sam* do? Waltz in and confiscate all illegally obtained firearms, slap on the handcuffs, and deliver the nasty man to the county jail?

She had to at least verify.

Sam dropped to her knee by the door, breathing heavily, both hands wrapped around her gun. The lock was disengaged.

Just remember, you were born for this, Sam.

She stuck the barrel of her gun under the door and pulled, using the gun sight as a hook. The door creaked open. A dim bulb glowed inside. She pushed the door all the way open and shoved her weapon in, careful to stay behind the cover of the doorjamb. Slowly, the opening door revealed the shapes of shelves and a wheelbarrow. A square on the floor. The trapdoor.

How deep did the shelter go? There had to be stairs.

She stepped in, one foot and then the second. The trapdoor was open, she could see now. She edged over to the dark hole and peered down. Faint light, very faint, from the right. She pulled back. Maybe calling Jennifer would be the wisest course of action. Just Jennifer.

8:15. They still had forty-five minutes. But what if she waited for Jennifer and this *wasn't* the place? That would leave them with less than half an hour to find Slater. No, she had to verify. Verify, verify.

Come on, Sam, you were born for this.

Sam shoved the gun into her waistband, knelt down, gripped the edge of the opening, and then swung one leg into the shaft. She stretched her foot, found a step. She mounted the stairs and then swung back up. The shoes might make too much noise. She took them off and then settled back on the stairs.

Come on, Sam, you were born for this.

There were nine steps; she counted them. Never knew when she might have to run back up full tilt. Knowing when to duck to avoid a head-on with the ceiling and when to turn right to exit the shack could come in handy. She was telling herself this stuff to calm her nerves, because anything in the dread silence was better than facing the certainty that she was walking to her death.

Light came from a crack below a door at the end of a concrete tunnel. The tunnel led to a basement below Kevin's house! She'd known that some of these old bomb shelters were connected to houses, but she'd never imagined such an elaborate setup beneath Kevin's house. She'd never even known there *was* a basement in his house. Wasn't there a way to the top floor from the basement? Jennifer had been in the house, but she hadn't said anything about a basement.

Sam withdrew her gun and tiptoed down the shaft.

"Shut up." Slater's voice sounded muffled behind the door. Sam stopped. Verified. She could never mistake that voice. Slater was behind that door. And Kevin?

The door was well insulated; they would never hear her. Sam walked to the door, nine millimeter up by her ear. She reached for the doorknob and slowly applied pressure. She didn't plan on bursting in, or entering at all, for that matter, but she needed to know a few things. Whether the door was locked, for starters. The knob refused to turn.

She backed up a foot and considered her options. What did Slater expect her to do, knock? She would if she had to, wouldn't she? There was only one way to save this man, and it was on the other side of that door.

Sam eased down to her belly and pressed her left eye to the crack beneath the door. On the right, white tennis shoes walked slowly toward her. She stilled her breathing.

"Time is most definitely winding down," Slater said. The feet were his, white tennis shoes she didn't recognize. "I don't hear your lover breaking down the door."

"Sam's smarter than you," Kevin said.

The tennis shoes stopped.

Sam jerked her eye to the left, where the voice had come from. She saw his feet, Kevin's shoes, the tan Reeboks she'd seen by his bed a few hours ago. Two voices, two men.

Sam pulled back. Kevin and Slater weren't the same person. She'd been wrong!

Sam flattened herself again and peered, breathing too loudly but not caring now. There they were, two sets of feet. One to her right, white, and one to her left, tan. Kevin tapped one foot nervously. Slater was walking away.

She had to tell Jennifer! In case something happened to her, she had to let Jennifer know who stood behind that door.

Sam slid back and stood. She hurried to the end of the hall. Going up the stairs might be prudent, but at this distance, there was no way Slater could hear. She lifted her phone and hit redial.

"Jennifer?"

"Sam! What's going on?"

"Shh, shh, shh. I can't talk," Sam whispered. "I found them."

A barely audible ring pierced the silence, as if a gunshot had discharged too close to her ear within the last half-hour.

Jennifer seemed incredulous. "You . . . you found Kevin? You actually located them? Where?"

"Listen to me, Jennifer. Kevin's not Slater. Do you hear me? I was wrong. It has to be a frame!"

"Where are you?" Jennifer demanded.

"I'm here, outside."

"You're absolutely positive that Kevin isn't Slater? How—"

"Listen to me!" Sam whispered harshly. She glanced back at the door. "I just saw them both; that's how I know."

"You have to tell me where you are!"

"No. Not yet. I have to think this through. He said no cops. I'll call you." She hung up before she lost her nerve and dropped the phone into her pocket.

Why didn't she just call Jennifer in? What could she possibly do that Jennifer couldn't? Only Slater knew the answer to that. The boy she'd never seen. Until today. *Kevin, dear Kevin, I'm so sorry.*

A shaft of light suddenly cut through the tunnel. She whirled around. The door was open. Slater stood in the doorframe, bare-chested, grinning, gun in hand.

"Hello, Samantha. I was getting worried. So nice of you to find us."

27

Monday
8:21 P.M.

SAM'S FIRST INSTINCT WAS TO RUN. Up the stairs, duck, to the left, into the open. Come back with a flamethrower and burn him out. Her second instinct was to rush him. The rage that flooded her mind seeing him backlit by the light surprised her. She could feel her gun at her waist and she grabbed for it.

"Don't be so predictable, Sam. Kevin thinks you're smarter than me. Did you hear him say that? Prove it, darling." He brought the gun up and aimed it inside to his right. "Come on in here and prove it to me, or I'll cap the kid where he stands."

Sam hesitated. Slater stood with a cocky grin. She walked down the hall. *You were born for this, Sam. You were born for this.*

Slater backed up, keeping his gun aimed to his right. She stepped past the steel door. A single bulb cast dim light over the basement. Shades of black and gray. Stark. Kevin stood in front of a wall of pictures, face ashen. Pictures of her. He took a step toward her.

"Not so fast," Slater snapped. "I know how badly you want to be the hero again, boy, but not this time. Take the gun out slowly, Samantha. Slide it toward me." There wasn't a trace of doubt on Slater's face. He had them precisely where he'd intended.

Sam slid the gun across the concrete, and Slater scooped it up. He walked to the door, closed it, and faced them both. It struck Sam, staring at the man's smirk, that she'd committed a kind of suicide.

She'd stepped into the lair willfully, and she'd just given the dragon her gun.

You were born for this, Sam. Born for what? Born to die.

She turned from him purposefully. *No, I was born for Kevin.* She looked at him, ignoring Slater, who stood behind her now.

"You okay?"

Kevin's eyes darted over her shoulder and then settled on hers. Trails of sweat glistened on his face. The poor man was terrified.

"Not really."

"It's okay, Kevin." She smiled. "I promise you, it'll be okay."

"Actually, it won't be okay, Kevin," Slater said, walking briskly to her right. He wasn't the monster she'd imagined. No horns, no yellow teeth, no scarred face. He looked like a jock with short blond hair, tight tan slacks, a torso cut like a gymnast's. A large, red tattoo of a heart branded over his breast. She could have met this man a dozen times over the years and not taken notice. Only his eyes gave him away. They were far away, light gray eyes, like a wolf's. If Kevin's eyes swallowed her, Slater's were the kind she might bounce off of. He even smiled like a wolf.

"I'm not sure you're aware of what we have here, but the way I see it, you're both in a bit of a pickle," Slater said. "And Kevin is fit to be tied. He's made three phone calls to his FBI girlfriend, and I just sat back and let him do it. Why? Because I know how hopeless his situation is, even if he doesn't. No one can help him. Or you, dear Samantha."

"If you wanted to kill Kevin, you could have done it a dozen times," Sam said. "So what *is* your game? What do you hope to accomplish with all of this nonsense?"

"I could have killed you too, my dear. A hundred times. But this way it's just so much more fun. We're all together like a happy little family. Mommy's in the closet, Kevin's finally come back home, and now his little girlfriend has come to save him from the terrible boy down the street. It's almost like old times. We're even going to let Kevin kill again."

Slater's lips fell flat. "Only this time he's not going after me. This time he's going to put a bullet in your head."

Sam took this in and faced Kevin. He looked so frail in the yellow light. Afraid. Slater was going to force his hand to kill. Her. It all made perfect sense now, although exactly what Slater had in mind, she didn't know.

Surprisingly, Sam felt no fear. In fact, she felt somewhat buoyed, even confident. *Maybe this is how you feel just before you die.*

"So. He's the boy, after all," Sam said to Kevin. Both men were watching her. "How does a big, strong, handsome man like this become so jealous of you, Kevin? Think about it. How could such a powerful, intelligent man be driven to such insane fits over one man? Answer: Because underneath that big, bold, red tattoo and all that bulging muscle, he's only a pathetic little weasel who's never managed to make a friend, much less win a girl."

Slater stared at her. "I'll keep your predicament in mind and forgive the rest of your desperate insults, but I don't think *jealous* is the right word, Samantha. I am not jealous of this piece of meat."

She faced him slowly, wildly bold and unsure why. "Then forgive me for such poor word choice. You're not insanely jealous; you're delighted with the sweet bond of love that Kevin and I have always shared. The fact that I would have shoved a toilet plunger into your face if I'd ever caught you peeping and licking at my window doesn't bother you, does it?"

His mouth was a thin, straight line. He blinked. Again.

"The fact is, *I chose Kevin,*" Sam said. "And Kevin chose me, and neither of us wants anything to do with you. You can't accept that. It drives you crazy. It makes you see red."

Slater's face twisted. "And Kevin doesn't see red?"

Silence settled. Balinda was in the closet. A clock on the wall read 8:35. She should have told Jennifer where they were. Her cell phone was still in her pocket, and she didn't think Slater knew. Could she call Jennifer? If she could slip her hand into her pocket and press the send button twice, it would automatically dial the last number. Jennifer would hear them. A tingle ran through her fingertips.

"You really think Kevin is any different than me?" Slater waved the guns around absently. "You really think this little puke here doesn't want exactly what I want? He'll kill and he'll lie and he'll spend the rest of his life pretending he won't, just like the rest. That's better than me? At least I'm honest about who I am!"

"And who are you, Slater? You're the devil. You're the sickness of this world. You're vile and you're vomit. Go on, tell us. Be honest—"

"Shut up!" Slater screamed. "Shut your disgusting pie hole! This little piece of trash sits in the pew every Sunday, swearing to God that he won't keep doing his secret little sins when he knows as well as I that he will. We know he will because he's made this promise a thousand times and breaks it every time. He's the liar." Spittle flew from his lips. "*That's* the truth!"

"He's nothing like you," Sam said. "See him? He's a terrorized victim whom you've tried desperately to pound to a pulp. See you? You're a revolting monster pounding whoever threatens you into a pulp. See me? I'm neither terrorized nor frightened, because I see you and I see him and I see nothing in common. Please, don't be such a snail."

Slater stared at her, lips parted, stunned. She had pushed him beyond himself with the simple truth, and he was writhing inside already. She shoved her fingers into her pockets and confidently hooked her thumbs.

"Where do they breed your kind, Slater? Is that a mask you're wearing? You look so normal, but I have this unshakable suspicion that if I pulled your ear, the whole mask would come off and—"

Gunfire crashed through the room and Samantha jerked. Slater had fired the gun. A muffled wail cried through the door. Balinda. Sam's pulse quickened. Slater stood without flinching, gun ex-tended to the ground where his bullet had chipped a divot from the concrete. "That hole below your nose is starting to bother me," he said. "Maybe you should think about closing it."

"Or maybe you should consider putting a hole in your head," Sam said.

Slowly a smile formed on his lips. "You have more spunk than I would have guessed. I really should have broken your window that first night."

"You're demented."

"How much I loved to hurt little girls like you."

"You make me very, very sick."

"Take your hands out where I can see them."

He'd noticed. She pulled her hands out of her pockets and returned his glare. Neither backed down.

"Enough!" Kevin yelled.

Sam faced him. Kevin scowled at Slater, whose face was red and quivering. "I've always loved her! Why can't you just accept that? Why have you hidden away all these years? Why can't you find some other poor sucker and leave us alone?"

"Because none of them interests me like you do, Kevin. I hate you more than I hate myself, and that, puke face, is quite interesting."

III

Slater sounds confident, but he's never felt so much unease in all of his life. He has underestimated the strength of the girl. If his plan depends on bending her will, he will have significant challenges ahead. Fortunately, Kevin is more pliable. He'll be the one pulling the trigger.

What is it about her? Her nerve. Her unyielding conviction. Her arrogance! She really does love the fool and she flaunts that love. In fact, she is all about love and Slater hates her for it. He'd seen her smiling, combing her hair, bouncing around her bedroom as a child twenty years ago; he'd seen her run around, locking up criminals in New York, like some kind of superhero on steroids. Happy, happy and snappy. It makes him sick. The look of disdain in her eyes now brings small comfort—it's born out of her love for the worm to his right. So then, all the more reason for Kevin to put a bullet through her pretty white forehead.

He glances at the clock. Nineteen minutes. He should forget the timing and just do it now. A bitter taste pulls at the back of his tongue. The sweet taste of death. He should do it!

But Slater is a patient man, most excellent in all of the disciplines. He will wait, because it is his power to wait.

The game is down to the last test. The last little surprise.

Slater feels a surge of confidence sweep through his bones. He chuckles. But he doesn't feel like chuckling. He feels like shooting his gun again.

Say what you want now, little girl. We'll see who Kevin chooses.

III

Kevin watched Slater, heard him chuckle, knew with awful certainty that things were going to get worse.

He couldn't believe that Sam had actually come in and given up her gun like that. Didn't she know that Slater would kill her? That was his whole point. Slater wanted Sam dead, and he wanted him to kill her. Kevin would refuse, of course, and then Slater would just kill her himself and find a way to frame Kevin. Either way, their lives would never be the same.

He looked at Sam and saw that she was watching him. She winked slowly. "Courage, Kevin. Courage, my knight."

"Shut up!" Slater said. "Nobody talk! My knight? You're trying to make me gag? *My knight?* What rubbish!"

They stared at him. He was losing himself in this game.

"Shall we begin with the festivities?" Slater asked. He shoved Samantha's gun into his waistband, took two long steps to Balinda's door, unlocked it, and threw it open. Balinda sagged against a wall, bound and wide-eyed. Black smudges covered her white lace nightgown. Stripped of makeup, her face looked quite normal for a woman in her fifties. She whimpered and Kevin felt a pang of sorrow knife through his chest.

Slater bent down and hauled her to her feet. Balinda stumbled out of the room, lips quivering, squeaking in terror.

Slater shoved her against the desk. He pointed to the chair. "Sit!"

She collapsed to her seat. Slater waved his gun at Sam. "Hands up where I can see them." She lifted her hands from her waist. Keeping his gun pointed in Sam's general direction, Slater pulled a roll of duct tape from the top drawer, ripped off a six-inch slab with his teeth, and plastered it over Balinda's mouth.

"Keep quiet," he mumbled. She didn't seem to hear. He shoved his face up to her. "Keep quiet!" he yelled. She jumped and he chuckled.

Slater removed the second gun from his pants and faced them. He cocked the guns, raised them to his shoulders. Sweat covered his white chest like oil. He grinned, lowered his arms, and twirled each pistol like a gunslinger.

"I've thought about this moment for so long," Slater said. "The really big moments in life are never as inspiring as you imagine them—I'm sure you've both figured that out by now. What happens in these next few minutes has run so many laps around my mind that I swear there's a groove an inch deep in there. I've taken way too much pleasure from the thoughts already; nothing can possibly compare. That's the downside of dreaming. But it's been worth it. Now I'm going to make it happen, and of course I'll try to spice it up as much as possible to keep things interesting."

He spun each gun again, the left, then the right. "I've practiced, can you tell?"

Kevin looked at Sam, who stood five feet from Slater, staring at the madman with a quiet fury. What was going through her mind? Slater had shifted his focus to her the moment she'd come in. With Kevin, the man showed no fear, but now facing Sam, Slater was trying to hide his fear with this show of his, wasn't he? He was actually afraid. Sam just stared at him, undaunted, hands limp by her hips.

Kevin's heart swelled. She was the true rescuer, always had been. He wasn't the knight; she was. *Dear Sam, I love you so. I've always loved you.*

This was the end; he knew that. They couldn't save each other this time. Had he told her how much he really did love her? Not with romantic love—with something much stronger. A desperate need. The need to survive. The way he loved his own life.

Kevin blinked. He had to tell her how precious she was to him!

"The game is simple," Slater said. "No need confusing the common folk. One out of two people will die"—he glanced at the clock—"seventeen minutes from now. The old woman"—Slater shoved one of the guns to her temple—"who has evidently mistaken life for a Froot Loops commercial. Actually, I like that about her. If you're going to pretend, you might as well do the whole enchilada, right?"

He smiled and slowly aimed the other gun toward Samantha. "Or the bright young maiden." Both arms were fully extended at right angles now, one toward Balinda, the other toward Sam. "Our executioner will be Kevin. I want you to begin thinking about which wench you'll kill, Kevin. Killing neither isn't an option; that would ruin the fun. You must choose one."

"I won't," Kevin said.

Slater tilted the gun and shot him in the foot.

He gasped. Pain throbbed through to his sole and then spiked up his shin; nausea rolled into his gut. The Reebok on his right foot had a red hole in it and was trembling. His horizon tipped.

"You will." Slater blew imaginary smoke from the barrel. "I promise you, Kevin. You most definitely will."

Sam ran for him and caught his sagging body. He let her support him and adjusted his weight to his left foot.

Sam jerked her head toward Slater. "You're sick . . . You didn't need to do that!"

"A hole in the foot, a hole in the head; we'll see who ends up dead."

"I love you, Sam," Kevin said softly, ignoring the pain. "No matter what happens, I want you to know how lost I am without you."

III

Jennifer paced. "I could *strangle* her!"

"Call her," Dr. Francis said.

"And risk exposing her? She could be right outside his door and her cell goes off? Can't do it."

He nodded. "Something doesn't sit right."

She picked up her phone. "I had myself firmly convinced that Kevin was Slater."

"And he isn't."

"Unless—"

Her cell phone chirped. They both looked at it. Jennifer flipped it open.

"Hello?"

"We have the report from Riggs," Galager said. But Jennifer already knew that Slater and Kevin weren't the same person.

"Bit late. We already know. Anything else?"

"No. Just that."

She sighed. "We have a problem, Bill. What's the mood over there?"

"Gloomy. Frantic without direction. The director just called for you. He's getting an earful from the governor. Expect a call any second. They want to know."

"Know what? We don't know where he's stashed Balinda. We're down to a few minutes and we don't have the faintest idea where he's taken her. Tell them that."

Galager didn't respond right away. "If it's any consolation, Jennifer, I think he's innocent. The man I talked to wasn't a killer."

"Of course he isn't a killer," Jennifer snapped. "What do you mean? Of course . . ." She turned to the professor. His eyes were fixed on her. "What did the report say?"

"I thought you said you knew. The voices on the recording are from the same person."

"The seismic tuner—"

"No. The same person. In Riggs's estimation, if the recording is Kevin and Slater, then Kevin is Slater. There's an echo in the background that barely surfaces on the second tape. Both voices are from the same room. Riggs's guess is he's using two cell phones and the recording picks up a faint reproduction of what he's saying on the other phone."

"But . . . that's impossible!"

"I thought it was the prevailing theory . . ."

"But Sam's with them, and she called us. Kevin isn't Slater!"

"And what makes you think you can trust Sam? If she's with them, didn't she tell you where they are? I'd bank on Riggs."

Jennifer stood frozen to the carpet. Was it possible? "I have to go."

"Jennifer, what do I—"

"I'll call you back." She snapped the phone closed and stared at the professor, dumbstruck.

"Unless Sam *didn't* see them both."

"Did you ever meet with Sam?" Dr. Francis asked. "Actually see her with your own eyes?"

Jennifer thought. "No, I didn't. But . . . I talked to her. So many times."

"So did I. But her voice wasn't so high that it sounded necessarily female."

"Could . . . he do that?" Jennifer scrambled for understanding, searched for something, anything Sam had done that might contradict the notion. None came immediately to mind. "Cases of many more than two personalities have been documented."

"What if Slater isn't the only one who's Kevin? What if Samantha is also Kevin?"

"Three! Three personalities in one."

28

SAMANTHA WATCHED THE SECOND HAND tick relentlessly through its slow arc. Kevin sat on the floor, head in hands, distraught. Balinda slumped in her chair five feet to his left, mouth taped gray, eyes flittering over Kevin. If Kevin's aunt could talk now, what would she say? *I'm so sorry, Kevin! I beg your forgiveness! Don't be a coward, Kevin! Get up and kick that man where he'll remember it!*

Balinda never looked at Slater. It was as if he didn't exist. Or she couldn't bear to look at him. For that matter, the woman didn't look at Sam either. Her attention was consumed by Kevin and Kevin alone.

Sam closed her eyes. *Easy, girl. You can do this.*

But in all honesty she was no longer feeling like she could do this or anything. Slater had two guns and a big smile. She had only her cell phone.

"Uh, uh, uh, hands where I can see, darling."

| | |

Jennifer ran her hands through her hair. "This is crazy!" Her head hurt and time was running out. *Think!*

"She was always disappearing! She—he could have made it all up. The CBI, the task force, the interview with the Pakistani, all of it! They were all things she could have created in her mind based on information Kevin already knew."

"Or that Kevin simply fabricated," Dr. Francis said. "Kevin concludes that Slater can't be the Riddle Killer because deep in his subconscious he knows that *he* is Slater. Sam, his alter ego, concludes the same. She's working to free Kevin without knowing that she *is* him."

"She kept suggesting that there was someone on the inside! There was—Kevin! He was on the inside. And she was the one who first concluded that Kevin was Slater!"

"And to Kevin, both Slater and Samantha are as real as you and me."

They were running over each other with their words now, connecting dots that formed a perfect picture.

Or did they?

Jennifer shook her head. "But I just talked to Sam and she saw Kevin and Slater while she was *outside* the door. You're saying that I was actually talking to Kevin, and that he was simply imagining himself as Samantha, sneaking up on him and Slater?"

"It's possible," the professor said, excitedly. "You've read the case studies. If Kevin is truly split, Sam would have her own personality. Everything she's done has been done completely in Kevin's mind, but to both of them, it has been completely real."

"So it was Kevin I just talked to."

"No, it was Sam. Sam is distinct from Kevin in his mind."

"But physically, it was Kevin."

"Assuming she is him, yes."

"And why didn't Slater stop him? If Slater was there as well? Kevin picks up the phone and calls me, and in his mind he's really Samantha, outside the door. Makes sense. But Slater's there too. Why doesn't he stop the phone call?"

"I don't know," the professor said, turning with hand on chin. "You'd think he'd stop Kevin. So we could be wrong."

Jennifer massaged her temples. "But if they *are* all Kevin, it would mean he never even had a childhood friend named Samantha. He created her as an escape to fill the void in his life. Then he created Slater, and when he discovered that Slater hated Sam, he tried to kill Slater. Now Slater's come back and so has Sam." She turned. "But her father was a cop! He lived in the house three down from Kevin's."

"Kevin could have known that a cop named Sheer lived in that house and simply built Samantha's reality on that. Do you know whether Officer Sheer even had a daughter named Samantha?"

"Never checked." Jennifer paced, sorting through the tide of thoughts. "It does make sense, doesn't it? Balinda wouldn't let Kevin have a best friend, so he fabricated one. He role-played her."

"This is what Kevin could have meant when he told me he had a new model for the natures of man," Dr. Francis said. "The three natures of man. Good, evil, and the man struggling between! 'The good that I would, that I do not, but that which I would not, that I do.' There are really three natures in there! One, *the good.* Two, *that which I would not.* And, three, *I!*"

"The struggle between good and evil, embodied in a man who is role-playing both good and evil and yet is still himself as well. Kevin Parson."

"The noble child. Every man."

They stared at each other, transfixed by the enormity of it all.

"It's a possibility," the professor said.

"It almost makes perfect sense." Jennifer glanced at her watch. "And we're almost out of time."

"Then we have to tell her," Dr. Francis said, walking for the kitchen. He turned back. "If Sam is Kevin, then she has to be told! *He* has to be told! He can't deal with this on his own. No one can deal with evil on their own!"

"Call Sam and tell her that she's Kevin?"

"Yes! Sam's the only one who can save him now! But she's powerless without you."

Jennifer took a deep breath. "What if we're wrong? How do I tell her without sounding like an idiot? Excuse me, Sam, but you're not a real person. You're just part of Kevin?"

"Yes. Tell her as if we know it's a fact, and tell her quickly. Slater may try to stop the call. How much time?"

"Ten minutes."

III

"This is going to be delightful, Samantha," Slater said, clicking the barrels of the two pistols together like drumsticks. He squirmed. "It's starting to give me shivers all over."

The phone was her only hope, but Slater kept insisting that her hands remain where he could see them. If he knew about the phone, he would have insisted she give it up. Either way, it sat like a useless lump in the folds of her slacks. She'd thought through a dozen other possibilities, but none presented themselves as viable. There would be a way—there was always a way for good to triumph over evil. Even if Slater did kill her . . .

A high chirping sound cut through the silence. Her cell!

Slater spun, glaring. She acted quickly, before he could respond. She snatched it from her pocket and flipped it open.

"Hello?"

"Sam, listen to me. I know this may sound impossible to you, but you're one of Kevin's personalities. Both you and Slater, do you hear me? That's why you can see them both. You—we—have to save Kevin. Tell me where you are, please, Sam."

Her mind rocked crazily. What had Jennifer said? She was one of Kevin's . . .

"What . . . what do you think you're doing?" Slater demanded.

"Please, Sam, you have to believe me!"

"You saw me in the car at the bus explosion," Sam said. "You waved."

"The bus? I saw Kevin. I waved to Kevin. You . . . you'd already left for the airport. Listen to me . . ."

Sam didn't hear any more. Slater had recovered from his shock and bounded for her.

"Below the screw," Sam said.

Slater's hand crashed against the side of her head. The cell phone dug into her ear and clattered to the concrete. She instinctively reached for it, but Slater was too quick. He slapped her arm away, scooped up the cell phone, and threw it across the room. It skipped off the floor and shattered against the wall.

He faced her and shoved a pistol under her chin. "Below the screw? What does that mean, you filthy little traitor?"

Sam's mind hurt. *You are one of his personalities,* isn't that what Jennifer had said? *I am one of Kevin's personalities? That's impossible!*

"Tell me!" Slater yelled. "Tell me or I swear I'll put the hole in your head myself."

"And forgo the pleasure of seeing Kevin do it?" Sam asked.

Slater looked at her for a moment, eyes working over her face. He jerked the pistol back and grinned. "You're right. Doesn't matter anyway; they're out of time."

|||

"It was her?" Dr. Francis asked.

"Sam. Call was terminated. Sure didn't sound like Kevin to me. She said she saw me at the bus, but I never saw her." Jennifer swallowed. "I hope we didn't just put a bullet in Sam's head."

Dr. Francis sat slowly.

"She told me they were below the screw," Jennifer said.

"The screw?"

Jennifer whirled to him. "The screw that held Kevin's window closed. Below the window, below the house. There's . . ." Could it be so close, right under their noses? "There's a stairwell in the house, clogged with piles of newsprint now, but it leads to a basement."

"Below the house."

"Kevin has Balinda in the basement of their house! There has to be another way in!" Jennifer ran for the door. "Come on!"

"Me?"

"Yes, you! You know him better than anyone else."

He grabbed his coat and ran after her. "Even if we find them, what can we do?"

"I don't know, but I'm done waiting. You said he can't do this without help. God, give us help."

"How much time?"

"Nine minutes."

"My car! I'll drive," the professor said and veered for the Porsche in the driveway.

III

Samantha had never felt more distracted from the mission at hand than now. What was the mission at hand? Saving Kevin from Slater.

She thought back to her years in college, to her law enforcement training, to New York. It was all fuzzy. Broad sweeps of reality without detail. Not the kind of detail that immediately surfaced when her mind wandered to the past, as a child, sneaking around with Kevin. Not the specifics that flooded her mind when she considered these past four days. Even her investigation of the Riddle Killer now seemed distant, like something she had read, not actually engaged in.

If Jennifer was right, she was really Kevin. But that was impossible because Kevin sat on the floor ten feet away, rocking, deeply withdrawn, holding a red foot, bleeding from his left ear.

Bleeding from his ear. She took a step around for a better view of Kevin's ear. Her cell phone lay in several pieces twenty feet away on the concrete where Slater had hurled it. That was real enough. Was it possible that Kevin had made her up? She looked at her hands—they seemed real, but she also knew how the mind worked. She also knew that Kevin was a prime candidate for multiple personalities. Balinda had taught him how to dissociate from the beginning. If Kevin was Slater, as Jennifer insisted, then why couldn't *she* be as well? And Sam could see Slater because she was there, in Kevin's mind where Slater lived. But Balinda was real . . .

Sam walked up to Balinda. If Jennifer was right, there were only two bodies here—Kevin's and Balinda's. She and Slater were only personalities in Kevin's imagination.

"What's with you?" Slater snapped. "Back off!"

Sam turned to face the man. He had the barrel of his weapon trained on her knee. Did he really have the gun if he was just in her mind? Or was that Kevin, and he only looked like Slater to her?

Slater grinned wickedly. Sweat wet his face. He glanced at the clock behind her. "Four minutes, Samantha. You have four minutes to live. If Kevin chooses to kill his mother instead of you, then I'm going to waste you myself. I just decided that, and it feels pretty good. How does it feel for you?"

"Why is Kevin bleeding from the ear, Slater? You hit me in the ear, but did you hit him in his ear?"

Slater's eyes shifted to Kevin and then back. "I love it. This is the part where the clever agent begins to play mind tricks in a last-ditch effort to confuse the nasty assailant. I really do love it. Back away from the bait, precious."

Sam ignored him. Instead she reached out and pinched Balinda on the cheek. The woman clenched her eyes and made a squeak. Thunder crashed through the chamber; white-hot pain seared through Sam's thigh. Slater had shot her.

Sam gasped and grabbed her thigh. Blood spread through her black capris. Her head swam. The pain was real enough. If she and Slater weren't real, then who was shooting whom?

Kevin jumped to his feet. "Sam!"

"Stay!" Slater said.

Sam's mind climbed from the pain. Kevin was shooting himself? Any normal person viewing this would see that he'd just shot himself in the thigh.

The details began to fall into order, like dominoes slowly toppling in a long line. So then if Kevin shot Sam in the head, he'd really kill whom? Himself? He was going to kill either Balinda or himself! And even if Slater killed Sam, he would really be pulling the trigger on Kevin, because all three of them occupied the same body. No matter who shot whom, Kevin's body would receive the bullet!

Sam felt a swarm of panic. Tell Kevin, Jennifer had said.

"When I say back off, I mean back off—not pinch her, not lick her, not spit on her," Slater said. "Back off really does mean back off. So . . . *back off!*"

Sam took a side step away from Balinda. *Hurry, Jennifer, please hurry! Beneath the screw. That means the basement; you know about the basement, don't you? Dear God, help them.*

"Hurts, doesn't it?" Slater's eyes danced around. "Don't worry, a bullet to the head does wonders for the odd surface wound. *Pow!* Works every time."

"He's bleeding in the ear because you hit *me* in the ear," Sam said. "He's bleeding in the leg too, isn't he?" She followed Slater's glance. Kevin stood, weaving on his feet, stricken with empathy. Blood soaked both his shoe and his right pant leg. He didn't feel the pain because in his mind it hadn't happened to him. Their personalities were completely fragmented. And what about Slater? She dropped her eyes to his thigh—a red spot was spreading on his tan slacks. Slater had shot Sam, but the wound appeared on both Kevin and Slater. She looked at Slater's ear. Then at his shoe. Blood there too.

"I'm so sorry, Sam," Kevin said. "This isn't your fault. I'm sorry I got you into this. I . . . I shouldn't have called you."

"You called her because I told you to call her, you idiot!" Slater said. "And now you're going to kill her because I'm telling you to kill her. Don't slip into Mommy's land of Froot Loops on me, Kevin. I swear I'll kill every one of you if you don't play nicely."

The truth of the matter struck Sam as she watched the deepening lines of sorrow in Kevin's face. This was the confession that Kevin had to make. The whole game was really *Kevin's,* a desperate attempt to flush his evil nature out of its hiding place. He was trying to expose the Slater in him. He'd reached out to her, the Samantha in him, the good in him. He was exposing the good and the bad in him to the world, in a desperate attempt to be rid of Slater. Slater thought he was winning, but in the end Kevin would be the victor.

If he survived. He'd already shot himself twice, once in the foot and once in the thigh.

"I have a theory," Samantha said, voice unsteady.

"The old Colombo trick," Slater said. "Let's stall the nasty man with the I've-got-a-theory routine. Can it! Time's ticking."

Sam cleared her throat and pressed on. "My theory is that I'm not really real."

Slater stared at her.

"I'm a childhood friend Kevin created because that's what he learned to do when he was a child." She looked into his eyes. "You made things up, Kevin. Only I'm not really made up—I'm part of you. I'm the good part of you."

"Can it!" Slater said.

"Slater isn't real either. He's another personality, and he's trying to trick you into killing either me or your mother. If you choose me, you'll be killing the good in you, maybe even yourself. But if you choose Balinda, you'll be murdering another living person. Your mother, for all practical purposes."

"That's a lie, you foul-mouthed, sick . . ." Slater's tirade sputtered short. His eyes bulged from a red face. "That's the stupidest thing I've ever heard!"

"That's not possible," Kevin said, face round in confusion. "That can't be, Sam! Of course you're real! You're the most real thing I've ever known."

"I *am* real, Kevin. I'm real and I love you desperately! But I'm part of you." Hearing herself say it, she sounded foolish. How could she possibly not be real? She felt and looked and even smelled real! But it did make sense on some unspeakable level.

"Look at your leg. You're bleeding because I was shot," she said. "I'm you. And so is Slater. You have to believe me. You've taken the good and the evil in you and turned them into imaginary people. Personalities. It's not really that strange, Kevin. You're acting out the struggle between good and evil every human being engages in. Slater and I are only the players in your own mind. But neither of us can do anything unless you give us the power to do it. He can't pull that trigger unless you do. Do you—"

"Shut up! Shut up, you lying piece of trash!" Slater jumped across the room and shoved a gun into Kevin's hand. He lifted the hand and pointed it toward Samantha.

"You have fifty seconds, Kevin. Fifty, tick, tick, tick." He lifted his own pistol and pressed the barrel against Balinda's temple. "Either you shoot Sam or I shoot Froot Loops."

"I can't shoot her!" Kevin cried.

"Then Mommy dies. Of course you can! You pull that trigger, or I swear I'm going to take care of Mommy and then finish you off for being a bad sport, you hear me? Forty seconds, Kevin. Forty, tick, tick, tick."

Slater's face glistened in the dim light. Kevin held the gun by his side. His face wrinkled; tears hung in his eyes.

"Point the gun at Samantha, you idiot! Lift it up. Now!"

Kevin lifted it slowly. "Sam? I can't let him kill Balinda, right?"

"Please don't get all sentimental on us," Slater said. "It's good for the mood, I realize, but it makes my stomach turn. Just put a bullet through her forehead. You heard her, she's not real. She's a figment of our imaginations. Of course, so am I; that's why you have two bullet holes in your leg." He chuckled.

Sam's mind hurt. What was really happening? What if she was wrong? Never before had she held a notion to be so utterly impossible and so utterly true at once. And she was now telling Kevin to gamble his very life on that notion. *Dear God, give me strength.*

"Look at your leg, Kevin," Sam said. "You shot yourself. Please, I'm begging you. Don't let Slater kill her. He can't shoot unless you give him the power. He's you."

29

THE DOOR at the end of the tunnel was unlocked. Jennifer could hear Sam's voice begging inside. She wasn't sure what she would find when she crashed in, but time was gone. Dr. John Francis breathed raggedly behind her.

They'd come to the house, barged past Eugene to find the stairwell still blocked with books. After frantically searching the perimeter, they found the stairs in the old bomb shelter. No telling how often or how long Kevin had been here over the years thinking he was Slater.

"Here we go."

She twisted the knob, took a deep breath, and threw her weight forward, gun extended.

The first thing she saw was Balinda, seated in a wooden chair, bound and gagged with gray duct tape. The second was the man standing over her. Kevin.

Kevin had a gun in each hand, one outstretched and pressed into Balinda's temple, and the other crammed against his own head like a man about to commit suicide. No Samantha, no Slater. Just Kevin.

But she knew that Kevin wasn't seeing what she saw. His eyes were clenched tight and he was hyperventilating.

"Kevin?"

He jerked his head toward her, eyes wide.

"It's okay, Kevin," Jennifer said. "I'm here." She held out a hand, urging calm. "Don't do anything. Please, don't pull that trigger."

Sweat covered his upper lip and cheeks. He stood, torn, terrified, furious. Blood leaked from wounds on his right thigh and foot. He'd shot himself! Twice.

"Kevin, where is Samantha?" Jennifer asked.

His eyes jerked to his left.

"Shut up," he snarled. Only it was in Slater's voice, which she now clearly recognized as Kevin's voice, but lower and grating.

"You're not real, Slater," Jennifer said. "You're only a personality Kevin created. You have no power on your own. Sam, do you hear me?"

"I hear you, Jennifer," Sam said—only it wasn't Sam; it was Kevin speaking in a slightly higher voice. Unlike over the phone, Jennifer heard the resemblance now.

"You don't see me, do you?" Sam asked.

"No."

"Listen to her, Kevin," Sam said. "Listen to me. I would die for you, my knight. I would gladly give my life for you, but it's Slater you have to kill, not me. Do you understand? We are you. Only you. And now that you've flushed him out, you have to kill him."

Kevin clenched his eyes and began to shake.

"Shut up!" Slater screamed. "Everyone, shut up! Do it! Do it, Kevin, or I swear I'll put this round in Mommy's forehead! Time's up!"

Jennifer felt frantic. "Kevin—"

"Shoot Slater, Kevin," the professor said, stepping past her. "He can't kill you. Put the weapon on Slater and kill him."

"Won't he shoot himself?" Jennifer demanded.

"You have to separate yourself from Slater, Kevin."

Kevin's eyes fluttered open. He'd recognized the professor's voice. "Dr. Francis?" Kevin's normal voice.

"There are three natures, Kevin. The good, the bad, and the poor soul struggling between them. Remember? You're role-playing those three roles. Listen to me. You have to kill Slater. Take your gun off Sam and point it at Slater. He can't do anything to stop you. Then, when you are sure that you have your gun on Slater, I want you to shoot him. I'll tell you. You have to trust me."

Kevin turned his head, staring to his left and then back to his right. From Kevin's perspective he was looking between Samantha and Slater.

"Don't be a fool!" Slater said. Kevin swung the gun that was on Balinda toward Jennifer. "Drop the gun! Out!" It was Slater and he was frantic.

"Do what the professor says, Kevin," Sam said. "Shoot Slater."

III

Kevin stared at Slater and wondered why he hadn't fired. The man had swung his gun from Balinda and aimed it at Jennifer, but he wasn't pulling the trigger. The time had come and gone and still Slater hadn't shot.

It occurred to him that he still had the gun in his hand, trained on Sam. He lowered his arm. They wanted him to shoot Slater.

But . . . if Sam and Jennifer were right, that was him over there, threatening Jennifer. And they wanted him to shoot himself? He'd flushed the man out of his hiding and now he was to kill him.

Kevin turned to Sam. She looked so tender, so lovely, eyes drawn with sympathy. *Dear Sam, I love you so.* Her eyes reached into his mind, his heart, melting him with their love.

She took a step toward him. "I should go now, Kevin."

"Go?" The thought frightened him.

"I won't be gone. I'll be with you. I *am* you. Shoot Slater."

"Stop!" Slater screamed. "Stop!" He stepped out and swung his gun on Samantha.

"I love you, Kevin," Samantha said. She stepped up to him, smiled gently, knowingly. "Shoot him. His kind is powerless when you understand who holds the true power. I know you're the one who feels powerless, and on your own, you are. But if you look to your Maker, you'll find enough power to kill a thousand Slaters, wherever they crop up. He will save you. Listen to Dr. Francis."

She reached out and touched his hand. Her finger went through his skin, into his hand. Kevin watched, mouth gaping. Samantha stepped into him, her knee into his knee, her shoulder into his shoulder. He couldn't feel her. Then she was gone.

Kevin gasped for air. She was him! She'd always been him! The realization fell into his mind like an anvil dropped from heaven. And she was gone, wasn't she? Or maybe closer than ever. A buzz circled his mind.

And if Sam was him, then Slater . . .

Kevin turned to his right. Slater shook from head to foot, gun aimed at Kevin's head now. But that wasn't a real person over there; it was only his evil nature, right?

Kevin looked at Jennifer. Her eyes were begging him. She couldn't stop Slater because she couldn't see him. She only saw him—Kevin.

If he was Slater, then the gun was really in his hand, wasn't it? He could force Slater to lower the gun by lowering it himself, in his mind.

Look to your Maker, Sam had said.

Open my eyes.

Kevin looked at the pathetic man who called himself Slater. He closed his eyes. It occurred to him then that he had two guns in his hands—one at his side and one at his temple. That would be Slater. He lowered the gun; now he had two guns by his side, one in each hand. He opened his eyes.

Slater faced him, gun lowered, face twisted with fury. "You'll never succeed, Kevin. Never! You're just like me, and nothing will ever change that. You hear me? Nothing!"

"Now, Kevin," Dr. Francis said. "Now."

Kevin lifted his right arm, pointed the nine millimeter at Slater's head, and pulled the trigger. The shot echoed loudly. At this range he could hardly miss.

But he did miss. He missed because suddenly there was no target to hit. Slater was gone.

Kevin lowered the gun. The bullet had buried itself in the metal desk behind the spot where Slater had stood, but it hadn't penetrated any flesh and blood. Slater wasn't flesh or blood. He was dead just the same. At least for now.

For a few long seconds the room rang in the aftermath of the detonation. Balinda began to sob. Kevin looked at her and pity, not anger, washed through his mind. She needed help, didn't she? She was a wounded soul, like him. She needed love and understanding. He doubted she would ever be able to return to the false reality she'd created.

"Kevin?"

The world seemed to collapse at the sound of Jennifer's voice. He wasn't certain what had just happened, but if he wasn't mistaken, he'd blown up a bus and a library and kidnapped his aunt. He needed help. Dear God, he needed help!

"Are you all right, Kevin?" Jennifer's voice broke.

He lowered his head and began to cry. He couldn't help it. *Dear God, what have I done?*

An arm settled on his shoulders. He could smell the musty scent of her perfume as she pulled him close.

"It's okay, Kevin. Everything's okay now. I won't let them hurt you, I promise."

He dissolved in sobs at her words. He deserved to be hurt. Or was that Slater's old voice?

Listen to Dr. Francis, Samantha had said. He would. He would listen to Dr. Francis and let Jennifer hold him. It was all he had now. Truth and love.

30

One Week Later

JENNIFER LOOKED THROUGH the glass door at Kevin, who stood by the flowers in the professor's lawn, touching and smelling the roses as if he'd newly discovered them. Dr. John Francis stood beside her, gazing out. Kevin had spent the last seven days in a prison cell, awaiting an extended bail hearing that had ended three hours earlier. Persuading the judge that Kevin wasn't a flight risk was a simple matter; convincing her that Kevin wasn't a threat to society wasn't. But Chuck Hatters, a good friend to Jennifer and now Kevin's attorney, had managed.

The press had slaughtered Kevin that first day, but as the details of his childhood leaked out over the next week, their tenor had changed—Jennifer had seen to that. She'd held a news conference and revealed his past in all of its horrifying detail. Kevin was simply role-playing as only a child who'd been severely abused and fractured could role-play. If even a single person had been hurt or killed, the public would probably have continued screaming retribution until another earth-shattering event distracted them. But in Kevin's case, pity quickly took precedence over a few destroyed buildings. The Slater personality would never have blown up any bus before it had been evacuated, Jennifer argued. She wasn't sure she believed it, but enough of the public did to swing the tide of outrage. Kevin still had his significant detractors, of course, but they no longer dominated the airwaves.

Was he insane? No, but she couldn't tell them that yet. The courts would put him through the wringer, and legal insanity was his only defense. In many ways, he *had* been legally insane, but he seemed to have emerged from the basement with a full grasp of himself, perhaps for the first time in his life. Patients who suffered from Dissociative Identity Disorder typically required years of therapy to pull themselves free of their alternate personalities.

For that matter, even the diagnosis would take some time. Kevin's admittedly enigmatic behavior didn't fit any classical disorder. Dissociative Identity Disorder, yes, but there were no cases of three personalities carrying on a conversation as she herself had witnessed. Posttraumatic Stress Disorder, perhaps. Or a strange blend of Schizophrenia and DID. The scientific community would undoubtedly argue over this one.

The good news was that Kevin could hardly be better. He would need help, but she'd never seen such a sudden shift.

"I'm curious," Dr. Francis said. "Have you unraveled Samantha's part in all this?"

Samantha? He spoke as if she were still a real person. Jennifer looked at him and caught the smile in his eyes. "I think you mean how Kevin managed to play Samantha without tipping his hand, don't you?"

"Yes. In the public places."

"You were right—another day or two and we'd have caught on. There were only three places where Sam was supposedly exposed to the public. The Howard Johnson hotel, the hotel in Palos Verdes where they spent the night, and when they cleared the bus. I talked to the clerk at the Howard Johnson where Sam stayed. She did remember Sam, if you recall, but the person who she remembers was a man with brown hair and blue eyes. Sam."

"Kevin," the professor said.

"Yes. He actually went over there and checked in as Sam, thinking he really was her. If he'd signed in under Samantha instead of Sam, the clerk would have raised a brow. But to her he was Sam."

"Hmm. And Palos Verdes?"

"The maître d' from the restaurant will be a good witness. Evidently some of the customers complained about the strange behavior of the man seated by the window. Kevin. He was staring directly across the table and speaking to an empty chair in hushed tones. Raised his voice a couple times." Jennifer smiled. "The maître d' approached and asked if everything was okay, and Kevin assured him it was. But that didn't stop him from walking to the dance floor a few minutes later and dancing with an invisible partner before leaving the room."

"Sam."

"Sam. According to Kevin, the only other time they were together in public was when they cleared the bus that blew up. Kevin insisted that Sam was in the car, but none of the passengers remember seeing another person in the car. And when I drove by a few minutes after the explosion, Kevin was alone, although he clearly remembers Sam sitting beside him, talking on her phone to her superiors. The California Bureau of Investigation has no record of her, of course."

"Of course. And I suppose Kevin chose to imitate the Riddle Killer because it offered him a fully fleshed persona."

"Don't you mean *Slater?*"

"Pardon me—Slater." The professor smiled.

"We found a stack of newspaper clippings on the Riddle Killer in Slater's desk. Several were addressed to Kevin's home. He never remembers receiving them. He can't remember how he got into the library undetected or how he planted the bombs in his car or the bus, although the evidence in the basement leaves no doubt that he built all three bombs."

Jennifer shook her head. "Kevin himself, as himself, wasn't aware that he was carrying both Sam's and Slater's cell phones most of the time. You'd think when he wasn't in their personas, he'd be aware of that much, but somehow the alter egos managed to shut off his mind to those realities. Amazing how the mind works. I've never heard of such a clear fragmentation."

"Because the personalities Kevin spun off were so diametrically opposed," Dr. Francis said. "*What falls but never breaks; what breaks but never falls?* Night and day. Black and white. Evil and good. Kevin."

"Night and day. Evil. Some in your camp are calling him possessed, you know?"

"I've heard."

"And you?"

He took a deep breath and let it out slowly. "If they want to attribute his evil nature to a demonic presence or a stronghold, they may do so without argument or endorsement from me. It sounds quite sensational, but it doesn't change the fundamental truth. Evil is evil, whether it takes the form of a devil with horns or a demon from hell or the gossip of a bishop. I believe Kevin was merely playing out the natures that reside in all humans from birth. Like a child might play Dorothy and the Wicked Witch of the West. But Kevin really believed he was both Slater and Samantha, thanks to his own childhood."

The professor crossed his arms and looked back out at Kevin, who was staring at a cloud formation now.

"I do believe that we all have Slater and Samantha living within us as part of our own nature," he said. "You could call me *Slater-John-Samantha*."

"Hmm. And I suppose that would make me *Slater-Jennifer-Samantha*."

"Why not? We all struggle between good and evil. Kevin lived that struggle out in dramatic fashion, but we all live the same struggle.

We all struggle with our own Slaters. With gossip and anger and jealousy. Kevin said his term paper was going to be a story—in more ways than one, I think he just lived his paper out."

"Forgive my ignorance, Professor," Jennifer said without looking at him, "but how is it that you, supposedly a 'regenerated' man, devoted servant of God, still struggle with evil?"

"Because I am a creature of free will," Dr. Francis said. "I have the choice at any given moment how I will live. And if I choose to hide my evil in a basement, as Kevin did, it will grow. Those who populate America's churches may not be blowing up buses and kidnapping, to be sure, but most hide their sin just the same. Slater lurks in their dungeons and they refuse to blow the lid off them, so to speak. Kevin, on the other hand, most certainly blew the lid off, no pun intended."

"Unfortunately, he took half the city with him."

"Did you hear what Samantha said in the basement?" the professor asked.

Jennifer had wondered if he would bring up Samantha's words. "'You are powerless on your own. But if you look to your Maker, you'll find enough power to kill a thousand Slaters,'" she said. The words Samantha spoke to Kevin had haunted Jennifer for the last week. How had Kevin known to say that? Was it really as simple as his good nature crying out the truth?

"She was right. We are all powerless to deal with Slater on our own."

He was talking about man's dependence on God to find true freedom. He'd spent long hours with Kevin in his prison cell—Jennifer wondered what had passed between them.

"After seeing what I've seen down here, I'm not going to even try to argue with you, Professor." She nodded at Kevin. "You think he's . . . okay?"

"Okay?" Dr. Francis's right eyebrow went up. He smiled. "I'm sure he'll be delighted to hear the news you have, if that's what you mean."

Jennifer felt exposed. He could see more than she meant for him to see, couldn't he?

"Take your time. I have some calls to make." He walked for his study.

"Professor."

He turned back. "Yes?"

"Thank you. He . . . we . . . *We* owe our lives to you."

"Nonsense, dear. You owe me nothing. You may, however, have a debt to Samantha. And to Samantha's Maker." He grinned deliberately and entered his study.

Jennifer waited until his door closed. She slid the glass door open and stepped onto the patio. "Hello, Kevin."

He turned, eyes bright. "Jennifer! I didn't know you were here."

"I had some time." As much as she tried to ignore the fact, there was a unique bond between them. Whether it was her natural reaction to the sympathy he engendered or her own generous spirit or more, she didn't know. Time would tell. The Riddle Killer was still at large, and yet she somehow felt she'd found herself for the first time since Roy's death.

Kevin glanced back at the roses. His eyes couldn't hold hers unwaveringly as they had before—he'd lost a certain innocence. But she preferred him this way.

"I'm taking a sabbatical," she said.

"From the FBI? You are?"

"I am. I just came from a hearing with Judge Rosewood." Jennifer couldn't contain herself any longer. She smiled wide.

"What?" he asked. Her elation spread to him. "What's so funny?"

"Nothing. She's going to consider my request."

"The judge? What request?"

"You do know that I'm a licensed psychotherapist, don't you?"

"Yes."

"Even if we win your acquittal, which I think we will, the court will insist on therapy. In fact, your treatment will likely begin much sooner. But I don't think we can trust just any psychotherapist to pry around your head."

"Psychobabble," he said. "They . . ." His eyes widened. "You?"

Jennifer laughed. If the judge could see her now, she might reconsider. But she couldn't. In fact, no one could. The professor had retired to his office.

She walked up to him, pulse quickening. "Not your psychotherapist, exactly. But I'll be there, every step of the way, monitoring. I don't intend to let anyone mess with your mind any more than they have to."

He stared into her eyes. "I think I'd let you mess with my mind."

Everything in Jennifer's being wanted to reach out to him then. To touch his cheek and tell him that she cared for him more than anyone she'd cared for in a very long time. But she was an FBI agent, for heaven's sake. The agent in charge of his case! She had to remember that.

"Do I really need a psychotherapist?" he asked.

"You need me." That sounded a bit forward. "I mean you need someone *like* me. There are a lot of issues . . ."

Kevin suddenly leaned forward and kissed her on the cheek. "No, I don't need someone like you," he said. "I need you."

He pulled back, then looked away and blushed.

She couldn't help herself anymore. She stepped forward and kissed him very lightly on his cheek.

"And I need you, Kevin. I need you too."

I do not understand what I do. . . . It is no longer I myself who do it, but it is sin living in me. . . . For what I do is not the good I want to do; no, the evil I do not want to do—this I keep on doing. . . . I find this law at work: When I want to do good, evil is right there with me. . . . I delight in God's law; but I see another law at work in the members of my body, waging war against the law of my mind and making me a prisoner of the law of sin. I myself in my mind am a slave to God's law, but in the sinful nature a slave to the law of sin.

From a letter written by Saint Paul to the church in Rome, A.D. 57.
ROMANS 7:15–25

PLAGUEMAKER

Tim Downs

THOMAS NELSON
Since 1798

NASHVILLE DALLAS MEXICO CITY RIO DE JANEIRO BEIJING

For my beautiful Joy

*"Many women do noble things,
but you surpass them all."*

Published in Nashville, Tennessee by Thomas Nelson. Thomas Nelson is a trademark of Thomas Nelson, Inc.

Thomas Nelson, Inc. titles may be purchased in bulk for educational, business, fund-raising, or sales promotional use. For information, please e-mail SpecialMarkets@ThomasNelson.com.

Library of Congress Cataloging-in-Publication Data

Downs, Tim.
Plaguemaker / Tim Downs.
p. cm.

ISBN 1-59554-022-9 (hard cover : alk. paper)

1. Bioterrorism—Prevention—Fiction. 2. Government investigators—Fiction. I. Title.
PS3604.)954P58 2005
813'.6—dc22 2005012627

Printed in the United States of America
07 08 09 QW 5 4 3 2 1

CHAPTER ONE

SPECIAL AGENT NATHAN DONOVAN lifted his tray table and peered down at the small plastic case wedged between his feet, just as he had done a hundred times before. It was a beverage cooler, really, nothing more, the kind he might have smuggled into a Mets game or taken to the Jersey shore. The simple red lid was unceremoniously duct-taped to the chalky white body, giving it an altogether unassuming appearance—as though it might contain nothing more than a frigid six-pack or a picnic lunch for two.

Well-meaning scientists at the University Hospital in Kuala Lumpur had plastered the thing with every cautionary label imaginable. Long strips of neon-green tape flashed the word *BIOHAZARD* at regular intervals; fluorescent orange stickers warned of CORROSIVE MATERIALS and CHEMICAL HAZARD; even the Radiology Department chipped in, adding a series of triangular black-and-yellow labels declaring: DANGER! THIS EQUIPMENT PRODUCES IONIZING RADIATION WHEN ENERGIZED.

Donovan had carefully removed all of them, for the same reason that half of his fellow counterterrorism agents in New York City declined to wear their FBI windbreakers: It just doesn't pay to advertise. The Malaysian authorities thought the shrieking labels would hold the curious at bay—Donovan knew they would have just the opposite effect. He might as well hang a sign around his neck that says, "Look what I've got!" Only a fool or a novice stamps SECRET on the front of a secret document. A professional will take a plain blue cover every time.

At the University Hospital, words had buzzed around Donovan's head like Malaysian fruit bats. Microbiologists and disease specialists tossed around terms that he could barely pronounce, let alone comprehend—words like *panenterovirus*, *cytomegalovirus*, and *respiratory syncytial virus*. All he understood—all that was explained to him—was that Malaysian pig farmers were dying by the hundreds and no one knew why. The disease began with raging fever, followed by delirium, then sudden and irreversible coma. Those were the lucky ones; the less fortunate were left conscious to face the wasting agonies of vomiting, diarrhea, and internal hemorrhaging. Each path was different, but the destination was ultimately the same: a violent and certain death.

No one knew what it was, how it was carried, or how it was transmitted. The disease resisted all known antibiotics, even the big guns like streptomycin. That's what set off all the bells and whistles at the Centers for Disease Control in Atlanta: That kind of antibiotic resistance rarely occurs in nature. It suggests intentional genetic manipulation, and that raises the possibility that some idiot, or group of idiots, might be trying to play dice with the universe again.

No one knew what to do. On Malaysian hog farms, gas-masked soldiers trained their assault rifles on squealing pigs, decimating entire herds, while across town other farmers smuggled their own pigs past roadblocks to markets in other states, allowing the disease to leapfrog from region to region and, inevitably, from country to country. That's why the CDC wanted a look. It was only a matter of time; in the global village of the twenty-first century, there is no such thing as a local outbreak.

A local pathologist had managed to isolate the virus from the blood and spinal fluid of two cadavers before becoming one herself. Before her own brutal demise, she succeeded in growing a fist-sized lump of the stuff in a culture of porcine kidney cells. Scientists at the University Hospital placed the mucosal mass in an airtight metal container, surrounded it with dry ice, and packed it carefully in a simple red-and-white cooler, addressing it to the CDC's Division of Vector-Borne Diseases in Fort Collins, Colorado.

But one courier company after another turned the shipment down. No one would take the risk. No one was willing to say, "We'll absolutely, positively have it there by 10:30 tomorrow morning—unless we happen to drop it, in which case half the western U.S. will begin vomiting blood." That's why the CDC called the Joint Terrorism Task Force, and that's why they called New York: because N.Y. agents are known as the best and the toughest in the Bureau. And that's why the job went to Nathan Donovan: because no one was better, and no one was tougher.

He glanced down at the box for the hundred-and-first time. *Maybe no one was dumber,* he thought.

At the hospital, they had handcuffed Donovan to the cooler like a diplomatic courier. For most of the flight from Kuala Lumpur to Los Angeles, he sat with the box in the center of his lap, clutching the handle with both hands like an old woman in Battery Park. But it occurred to him that a single inadvertent gesture, like reaching out to a flight attendant for a bag of peanuts, could jerk the cooler off his lap and onto the floor. *But it can't fall off the floor,* he decided, so he removed the handcuff and slid the cooler between his feet.

He felt the aching stiffness in his back and legs again. He arched backward, and his 220-pound frame flexed the back of his seat like a beach chair. Behind him he heard an expletive in some unknown tongue, like the bark of a small dog.

For eighteen hours he had unconsciously squeezed the cooler between his legs, as if it might somehow squirt out and slide down the aisle like a wet bar of soap. Only now, on the final leg of his journey, did he begin to relax—but only a little.

The 737 lifted off from a westbound runway and headed out over the Pacific one last time before turning northeast on its two-and-a-half-hour route to Denver. Donovan surveyed the sea of heads around him: Some slumped back in restless slumber; others nodded together in intimate conversation. Some seats appeared empty, until a tiny pair of hands gripped the top of the seat and then quickly vanished again. There were heads of all shapes and colors and sizes; there was long hair, short hair, and hair long gone; there were streamlined ears tucked tightly back against skulls, and large, curling ears that jutted out like diving planes on a submarine.

Donovan didn't care. He was looking for eyes—eyes that turned away when he looked at them, eyes that lingered a little too long. He turned his left leg slightly and raised it until it bumped the seat above; he felt a reassuring metallic tap from the Glock beneath his pant leg. He hated the ankle holster; it made the gun too hard to reach. But in the current social climate, allowing fellow passengers to catch a glimpse of gunmetal from beneath a blazer was a definite faux pas, and Donovan found himself wearing the ankle holster more and more. *Better than no gun at all,* he thought.

They were passing directly over Santa Monica now. Out his window, in the distance, he could just catch a glimpse of the cliffs at Malibu. They continued to climb over the sprawling San Fernando Valley, gaining altitude for the hop over the San Gabriel Mountains ahead.

Then it happened.

Donovan heard the blast before he felt the concussion—from somewhere in the forward baggage compartment, he thought. The floor in the first-class galley buckled wildly and then flattened again. The shock wave traveled back the full length of the plane, causing the entire fuselage to ripple visibly. Donovan was astonished that the airframe could contort that far without disintegrating—yet somehow, the plane was still intact. Overhead compartments sprang open like a line of mousetraps, vomiting out carry-on luggage, briefcases, shopping bags, and a blizzard of coats and sweaters. Above each row of seats a rectangular door dropped open, and a tangle of tubing and bright yellow plastic dangled down like a sea of jellyfish.

In his mind, Donovan could see the bomb: a small device, probably homemade, nothing more than a few feet of wire with a timer attached to an explosive charge. No, not a timer, an altimeter—set to go off at cruising altitude to maximize the loss of life and disperse the wreckage as widely as possible. It was a small blast in relative terms—definitely not C4, probably not even TNT. Probably just a canister of gunpowder embedded in a cocktail of nails and ball bearings for shrapnel. A simple bomb, really, a beginner's bomb—the kind you could build for twenty-five bucks with parts from a local Radio Shack.

They were lucky, he thought. The blast had blown downward, away from the passenger compartment—but it must have ripped the belly out of the ship, and there were things down there you didn't want to lose, things like hydraulics, and landing gear, and fuel lines . . .

For an instant the entire plane was silent and still, a freeze-frame before the panic to come. Bodies were rigid, faces frozen in disbelief. Arms angled everywhere, with white-knuckled fists clutching at seat backs, armrests, fellow passengers—*the way a man grabs on to a limb when it breaks away from a tree,* Donovan thought. And it would do them just as much good—because outside the plane, he heard the trailing whine of the engines as they began to lose power.

Then the nose tipped forward, and the plane started down.

Donovan watched stone-faced as the image before him erupted into motion. There were shrieks and sobs and mournful wails, some more animal than human. Long-unsaid prayers were dredged up from childhood memories; complete strangers embraced; mothers clutched at wild-eyed children, combing hair and straightening collars as if they were preparing for school photos and not death. Some wept quietly, some spoke aloud to no one in particular, and some sat in peaceful serenity. And over the intercom, through tearful sobs, a flight attendant offered insane instructions on how to "prepare for an emergency landing."

Donovan looked out the window and measured the angle of their descent against the horizon; they were coming down like a mortar shell. It wouldn't be a landing; it would be a detonation, with six thousand gallons of high-octane jet fuel erupting on impact—half of it vaporizing in a roiling fireball and half of it spewing like napalm over whatever godforsaken neighborhood or trailer park happened to be nearby. The debris would be spread over half a mile; a week from now a DMORT team would be sifting through the wreckage, searching for bits of bone and tooth, fragments of DNA to offer comfort to grieving families. *They'll be mailing us home in envelopes,* Donovan thought. *That's all that will be left.*

He listened for the feeble voice on the intercom again and slowly shook his head. You can put your seat back in an upright and locked position, you can put your head between your knees, but you're still going to *die.* That's all there is to it; that's how it is. The good people of United flight 296 to Denver were dead, every last one of them, and there was nothing they could do.

Then Donovan looked down at his feet.

There sat the little red-and-white cooler nestled between his feet, blissfully unaware of its impending destruction. But—*would* the crash destroy the cooler utterly and completely? Inside that cooler was a life-form, and like all living things, it would do everything in its power to survive. He visualized the crash again: the nose-first impact, the pulverizing momentum of eighty-five tons of imploding metal, the incinerating belch of fire—no living thing could survive that.

Or could it? The virus was a living thing, yes, but it was a living thing sealed in an airtight container, packed in dry ice, cradled in thick foam, shielded by plastic armor . . . Was the cooler fireproof, he wondered? Would it disintegrate on impact? Would it melt? Would the plastic crumble, the dry ice vaporize, and the canister rip apart like a tin can in a campfire? Or would the plastic casing only fracture? Would it bounce and roll and ricochet, but still survive the impact?

Or would the blast throw the cooler free of the plane? Donovan had worked crash sites before; he remembered picking his way through the utter annihilation, every fragment of the plane and its contents reduced to inches—and then suddenly finding a handbag or an attaché completely intact, as though it had been gently set aside before impact. Would the cooler be the handbag this time? Would it crack, and split apart, and dump its living contents onto the surrounding debris?

And when the DMORT team worked its way through the wreckage, would some hapless deputy coroner lift the empty canister and peer inside? Would he casually toss it aside, then wipe the sweat from his forehead or rub the smoke from his eyes? And when he went home that night, would he kiss his wife? Would he hug the kids? Would he pat the dog and shake hands with a neighbor?

Donovan looked around the plane. It was a ghost ship, filled with specters already beginning to fade away. They were already beginning to grow quiet, already acquiescing to their inevitable doom. They were already dead, every one of them. There were maybe two hundred on the plane—but on the ground, there were millions.

Donovan looked out the window. He had about a minute, no more.

He jerked the cooler up onto his lap and began to tear away the long gray strips of tape. When he opened the lid, a silent mist poured over the sides and down onto his legs. From the center of the ice he slid a tall silver canister and began to tug at its lid. It opened with a dull pop. He held his breath and peered down into the black interior.

Then he turned to his right and dumped the gelatinous blob in the center of the aisle.

He watched: The mass seemed to hesitate for a moment, then dissipate into the carpet. It seemed to spread and grow, putting out feelers like a vine, reaching out just like the rest of the passengers for someone, something, to hold on to. But it didn't matter—it was unprotected now, and it had no more chance of surviving than they did.

Than *he* did. The thought crossed Donovan's mind for the first time. He took a deep breath and leaned back in his seat. He had never been afraid of anything in his life, and he was not about to start now. He closed his eyes and put death out of his mind. Why not? He'd never feel it anyway.

Then, from outside the window, he heard the rising drone of the engines, followed by a heavy, sinking tug in his gut. Everywhere around him people gasped and stiffened, anticipating the impact—but the impact never came. Instead, the nose of the plane began to turn upward. As the engines continued to accelerate, the 737 leveled off, then once again began to climb.

From everywhere on the plane came astounded gasps and great, heaving sobs of relief. Passengers stared out the windows in astonishment; they stared at one another in unspeakable joy; they stared at the ceiling and uttered silent thanksgivings.

But not Nathan Donovan. He stared at a fist-sized stain in the center of the aisle.

Then he heard a voice say, "What did you do?"

He looked up. There was a young boy standing in the aisle, staring with him at the spotted carpet. The boy looked up into Donovan's eyes; the eyes were dark and wet and sunken deep into the pale little face. He was terribly thin, and the sagging neck of his blue hospital gown draped down over one bony shoulder. On both elbows, white strips of surgical tape secured pads of folded gauze.

Donovan couldn't bear to look at the boy. He shut his eyes hard. "I'm sorry," he said in a whisper.

"I don't feel so good, Daddy."

When Donovan looked again, the boy was backing slowly away down the aisle. His hair was gone now, and tiny veins coursed over his head like pale blue threads. The skin of his face was sallow, almost transparent, and his skull was clearly visible beneath.

"Wait," Donovan pleaded.

But the boy kept getting smaller, and thinner, and farther away.

"Wait!" Donovan shouted after him. "I can help! I can fix this!" He dropped to his knees in the center of the aisle and began to furiously scrape at the spot with his fingernails—but the spot only grew larger. It spread to the edges of the aisle now and sent ominous tendrils creeping up the sides of the seats.

The boy spoke one last time in a distant voice.

"Why won't you help me, Daddy? Why don't you love me anymore?"

NATHAN DONOVAN SAT BOLT upright in bed and stared into the darkness. He ran his fingers through the cold, damp mat on his chest and wiped his hand on the sheet. He turned and looked at the clock.

It was 4:00 a.m.—the usual time for the dreams.

CHAPTER TWO

DONOVAN SQUINTED AT THE spots on the man's forehead. They were on the right side, just above his temple, but well below the graying edge of his hairline. They were fleshy little things—what did you call them? Not warts—they were the color of warts, but they stuck up too high, and they had little dark tips like mushrooms. That was it, just like mushrooms—but they couldn't be called mushrooms. Polyps, maybe? Cysts?

Donovan found them annoying and fascinating at the same time. What makes a man grow his own little mushroom farm on his forehead? Surely he could cut them off—one swipe with a straight razor and a few days with a Band-Aid would take care of them. But no, he had to keep them—not in some nether region where fungus belongs, but on his *head*—and just an inch above his brow, making eye contact with the man virtually impossible. *Maybe it was a test,* he thought; maybe it was something that psychiatrists regularly do to see what kind of response they get from their patients. It could be—he'd never been to a psychiatrist before. Maybe after he left, the man would peel them off one by one and place them in a little box—

"Mr. Donovan, can we try to focus?"

"Sorry." Nathan shifted in his chair and resettled himself. But he didn't try to make eye contact—that was futile. He tried to focus instead on the open manila folder on the man's desk.

"You were a Marine," the psychiatrist said.

"Yes."

"You were in ordnance removal. Tell me about that."

Donovan shrugged. "People made bombs. I took them apart."

"Did you enjoy the work?"

"It fit me."

"How so?"

"I'm analytical," he said, carefully measuring his words. "I like problem solving."

"Do you like explosions?"

"If you like explosions, you join the artillery. In ordnance removal you only get one."

The man looked down at the folder and turned a page. Donovan leaned to the left slightly, trying to catch a glimpse of his opposite temple.

"I see you grew up in Ohio."

Donovan rolled his eyes. "Look, let me save you some time here. I grew up on a farm in Ohio. Some people spend their lives trying to escape small towns; some people spend their lives trying to get back. I wanted out. I enrolled at Ohio State to study engineering, but I switched to criminology because I was nineteen and I found the exams were easier to take when I was drunk. I joined the Marines because you can't do squat with a criminology degree, and besides, I liked their dress uniforms—still do. I went with ordnance removal because I spent my whole childhood blowing things up, and it sounded like a great career. I must have done okay, 'cause after a few years they sent me to the Academy as an instructor. That's where the Bureau found me; they do a lot of recruiting there. I was just the kind of guy they were looking for: I had a college degree, command experience, and I could make things go boom—or not go boom—whatever they needed."

The psychiatrist smiled slightly and closed the folder.

"Mr. Donovan, do you know why you're here?"

"Of course."

"Tell me."

"I'm here at the request of my supervisory special agent."

"That's it? Just a casual request to drop by and pay the psychiatrist a visit?"

"I'm here under my supervisor's orders."

The man paused. "Do you think you need to be here?"

Donovan felt a knot tighten in his stomach. He hated questions like this—they made him feel silly and childish. It reminded him of his basic training in ordnance removal, when the instructor asked, "Do you think you should cut the blue wire or the red wire?" How should he know? Tell me what to do or let me blow myself up, but don't ask stupid questions.

"You tell me," Donovan said evenly.

The psychiatrist opened the folder again and took out a multipage report. "You joined the FBI in 1996. You requested assignment in New York. Why New York?"

"They had the reputation—the best and the brightest. Besides, they told me I could have any assignment I wanted, as long as I picked New York. Nobody wants it—too expensive, lousy hours. You get up at 4:30 just to beat the traffic through the tunnels."

"But that didn't deter you."

"I'm a Marine. I'm used to the hours."

He returned to the report. "Sixteen weeks at Quantico," he said. "And then?"

"The usual freshman runaround. Six months on the 'Applicant Squad'—running background investigations, manning the call center, working surveillance."

"And then you moved to counterterrorism. Why counterterrorism?"

"Like I said: I like solving problems."

"You can solve problems sitting behind a desk."

You're right, Donovan thought. *You can solve little paperbound problems while you sit behind a desk growing mushrooms on your forehead.*

"I enjoy activity."

The man looked up. "Do you enjoy violence?"

Donovan didn't reply.

The psychiatrist turned a page of the report and slowly scanned the text. "In April of last year, you were involved in a hostage situation in Brooklyn. Tell me about that."

Donovan studied the ceiling while he organized his thoughts. "It was in Dyker Heights," he said, "a few blocks off Eighth Avenue. Italian couple, single-family dwelling. The wife heard a noise downstairs, sent her husband down to take a look. He walked into the living room, found a guy carrying out his TV—the guy shot the husband dead on the spot. The wife heard the gunshot, called NYPD. They arrived before the guy could get away, so he took the wife hostage. He told the cops he had a bomb, threatened to blow the whole place up. That's when NYPD called us—a bomb is considered a weapon of mass destruction, and that automatically involves the Joint Terrorism Task Force. We sent out a WMD squad; I was first on the scene."

The man nodded, verifying Donovan's account against the text. "And what happened when you got there?"

"I took up position on the front porch of the house, just to the left of the front door."

"Is that standard procedure in a situation like this?"

Donovan shifted uneasily. "It's a little difficult to define 'standard procedure' in a situation like this."

"Well, let's try. Who was in charge that night? Who had jurisdiction?"

"NYPD was the first responder, so it was their ball game—until we showed up, that is. In a WMD scenario, the FBI always has jurisdiction."

"So as the first FBI agent to arrive on the scene, you assumed command."

"No, not exactly. It's not that simple; we don't always just take over. If NYPD has things under control, we sometimes let them handle it."

"And in your opinion, did NYPD have things under control?"

Donovan paused. He began to construct his sentences more carefully now, like a man stacking high explosives.

"They had the basics covered. They established a perimeter, they set up a command center, and they had a hostage-negotiation team on the way. I felt, however, that they were failing to capitalize on certain tactical advantages."

"Such as?"

"Speed. The element of surprise."

"And in your experience with hostage situations, have you found *speed* to be a great advantage? You know, of course, that the first fifteen minutes of a hostage situation are the most dangerous. Time is almost always on the side of the hostage negotiator."

"*Almost* always. In this situation, time was working against us."

"How so?"

"The shooter had already killed once—he would be much quicker to kill the second time. What did he have to lose?"

"What about the bomb?"

"I didn't believe there was a bomb."

"Why not?"

"There was no purpose for a bomb. It didn't fit. A bomb requires forethought; a bomb requires planning. Nobody walks around with a bomb just in case they need one—I know something about this."

"And the NYPD officer in charge—did he agree with your assessment?"

Donovan paused. "He did not."

The psychiatrist turned back to the report again. "And so, against the wishes of the commanding officer, you broke perimeter and, gun in hand, simply walked up to the front door—'cowboylike' is the term the officer used."

"Too bad—I was going for Dirty Harry." Donovan bit his lip the instant the words left his mouth. This was no place for humor. The mushroom-man was not his bar buddy or his locker partner; he was a Midtown shrink hired by the Bureau to evaluate his mental and emotional stability. He cursed his own stupidity and lack of judgment and pulled the reins in tight again. The psychiatrist made a small note on a legal pad before continuing.

"According to the report—correct me if I'm wrong—there was a large picture window to the left of the door. You heard sounds from the shooter and the hostage in the living room, so you simply stepped in front of the window and took aim. The shooter fired first, shattering the glass, at which time you fired twice, striking him once in the head and once in the abdomen."

"Yes."

The psychiatrist paused. "Mr. Donovan, can you understand why this behavior might be described by some as 'cowboylike'?"

"I considered it an acceptable risk."

"An interesting term. Perhaps we can explore what you mean by 'acceptable risk' at a later time. Mr. Donovan, you seem to make a habit of taking risks no one else would find acceptable."

Donovan drew a breath and spoke slowly. "I heard the shooter and the hostage in the living room. I could hear the woman speaking—whimpering is more like it. The shooter's voice sounded agitated, confused, unstable. In light of that, I felt that the best approach was to distract him suddenly, try to throw him off guard. In his confused state of mind, I felt confident that he would release the hostage and confront me, giving me a firing opportunity."

The man nodded thoughtfully, considering the rationality of Donovan's account. "But according to witnesses, several seconds elapsed between the time you stepped in front of the window and the shot that broke the glass."

"I had to give the shooter time to spot me, release the hostage, and give me a clear line of fire."

"Did you have to give him time to shoot first?"

Donovan shrugged. "It only seemed fair."

The words seemed to remain in the air and float, like little globules of nitric acid injected into glycerin. To Donovan's surprise, the statement shocked even him.

"It only seemed fair," the psychiatrist repeated slowly. "Mr. Donovan, I'd like to give you a minute to reflect on those words."

Donovan thought it was just a figure of speech, but true to his word, the psychiatrist delayed a full minute before speaking again. It was a heavy, plodding, torturous minute.

"Have you ever actually been shot?" the psychiatrist asked at last.

"No."

"Do you have a desire to be?"

Stupid, idiotic question. "Of course not."

"Mr. Donovan," the psychiatrist said, squinting at him, "do you have any delusions of personal invulnerability?"

Donovan felt the knot in his gut spreading out over his body, filling his limbs with an aching restlessness. He felt adrenaline beginning to chew at the ends of his nerves until the tips of his fingers began to tremble like tuning forks. His throat twisted into a sodden, knotted rope, and the hair on his neck stood out like wire.

He continued to stare straight ahead, motionless, expressionless, smothering his growing anger like a leaden blanket wrapped around a pipe bomb. For weeks at a time he kept the demon locked safely in the basement, but from time to time he heard the familiar footsteps on the wooden stairs and he knew it had to come out. He had learned to conceal its presence, and it was an almost perfect disguise; but the demon was like a man buried alive, locked in a coffin, clawing at the lid and begging to be released. To hold it inside took everything Donovan had.

The psychiatrist rose from his chair, stepped slowly around to Donovan's side of the desk, and leaned back against the edge. He crossed his legs at the ankle; the move brought his right foot within inches of Donovan's own. Donovan felt a blue-white spark arc between them.

"You married in 1998," the psychiatrist said with an infuriating softness. "Tell me about that."

"The bride wore white; I wore black," Donovan said.

"Are you uncomfortable talking about your marriage?"

"Do you know anyone who's *comfortable* talking about a divorce?" Donovan imagined himself making a quick, sweeping motion with his right foot, taking the man's legs out from under him and sending him crashing to the floor.

"Tell me about your wife," the man continued.

"My *ex*-wife is a professor of political science and international relations at Columbia. She's an expert in the psychology of terrorism. She does piecework for the Bureau—that's how we met."

"Two professionals working in demanding careers," the man said thoughtfully. "That can put a lot of stress on a relationship."

Don't play head games with me, Donovan thought. *And for God's sake don't sympathize! You don't know me, and you don't know my life—just write me a hall pass and let me get back to class.*

"There was a lot of stress," Donovan said, parroting the man's own words.

"What would you say was the cause of your divorce?"

"Irreconcilable differences."

The psychiatrist shook his head. "That's just a legal term. What would you say was the *cause*?"

Donovan slowly looked up. He knew when their eyes met, his rage would become evident, but he didn't care anymore. He felt humiliated, he felt violated, and he wanted it to stop. "Does anybody really know?" he said in his lowest voice.

"I think you do."

Donovan glared at the man. There he stood, leaning against the desk, arms neatly crossed, waiting patiently—*pleasantly*—for Donovan's reply. He was just like the guy in Dyker Heights, an intruder in somebody else's home, knocking over furniture that didn't belong to him and dumping out drawers filled with secret and intimate things. What did he care? It wasn't *his* garbage. He could go home at the end of the day and leave somebody else to clean up the mess.

Donovan set his jaw and said nothing. The psychiatrist noted the stillness and changed his tack.

"Tell me about these dreams you have."

"What dreams?"

"It's in your file. A friend mentioned it."

Some friend, he thought. "Everybody has dreams."

"I'm talking about dreams of futility, dreams involving unsolvable problems, recurring dreams, dreams that won't let you sleep at night."

"Who doesn't have dreams like that?"

"Healthy people," he said.

"You know any?"

"Tell me—how do these dreams end?"

"I wake up."

He nodded. "Are you still having them?"

Donovan locked eyes with him. "No."

The psychiatrist held his gaze for a moment, then slowly turned away and took a seat behind the desk again.

"You're just the kind of guy the Bureau likes," he said, scribbling illegible notations on his legal pad. "You can dismantle a bomb without breaking a sweat. You can stand in front of a terrorist and let him take the first shot. I'll bet you didn't even flinch, did you?"

"You make it sound like some kind of neurosis."

"It is—but for the Bureau it's a very useful neurosis. They know you'll approach any situation with total abandon, with utter fearlessness. You'd walk through fire if they asked you to. That makes you a useful guy, Mr. Donovan; you get the job done—that is, as long as those qualities of yours are directed at the bad guys."

"I received a commendation for my actions in Dyker Heights—for courage under fire."

"Publicly, the Bureau calls it 'courage.' Privately, you've got them worried—*that's* why you're here, Mr. Donovan. They're wondering if this exceptional courage of yours isn't really something else. Over the last two years you have been unnecessarily placing yourself—and others—in harm's way. Don't worry, the Bureau will continue to present you with nice little awards and commendations right up until the moment you get yourself killed—and you will get yourself killed, Mr. Donovan; it's only a matter of time. The Bureau knows that—they're just hoping you'll be a good boy and die alone."

Donovan made no reply. He just sat in silence as the psychiatrist completed his notations. When he did, he tore off the top sheet from the legal pad, placed it in the folder, and smoothed it shut.

"The Bureau is paying me to do a psychological evaluation on you," he said. "Okay, here it is: I think you've got two problems, Mr. Donovan. You're angry, and you're afraid."

Donovan pinned him with a searing stare. "I've never been afraid of anything in my life."

"Interesting," the man replied. "I say you're angry and you're afraid—you say you're not afraid of anything. You ignored my comment about anger, Mr. Donovan—why is that? It's because you can't deny the anger; you feel that every day. You feel it right now, don't you? I can see it in your face: I get a little too close, and you light up like a highway flare. It's your fears that you don't recognize, and I think you have a whole closet full—and not just the ordinary bogeymen. Why don't you feel fear, Mr. Donovan? That's the question you need to ask yourself; that's the question only you can answer. But let me give you a clue: Fear and anger work together. Anger is like a roadblock; it's like a barricade. It tells you where you can go and where you can't. When you begin to feel fear, anger blocks the way—it says, 'No more.' When someone gets a little too intimate, anger steps in and says, 'That's close enough.'"

Donovan had no idea what to say in reply—but he knew he had to throw this dog a bone or he'd never let go of his leg. "Okay," he said with a sigh. "You're right. I do feel anger. I guess I—"

"Don't patronize me, Mr. Donovan. I've treated you with respect today; you can at least do the same for me. You and I both know you are light-years away from dealing with this problem. To do that, you have to go to a dark place—and you're not ready for that."

Donovan stood up. "Enough of this crap," he said. "You want to help me? Then let me get back to work. Look, you say this is something I have to work out for myself, right? Well, I can't do that by crawling off in some corner and contemplating my navel. If you really want to help me, help me get back to *work*."

The psychiatrist seemed lost in thought for a moment—then he flipped open the folder again and made a quick inscription on the top page, adding his signature with a flourish.

"Do you prefer the Jets or the Giants, Mr. Donovan?"

"I'll take the Jets."

"I figured. Do you know what I think whenever I watch the Jets play? I think, *Thank God for the NFL! There go a dozen men who might otherwise be in prison.* That's you, Mr. Donovan. You're a very dangerous man—but I suppose you're less dangerous on the job than off."

The psychiatrist extended his hand. Donovan shook it quickly, then headed for the door.

"You said something," the psychiatrist called after him. "You said, 'Nobody walks around with a bomb just in case they need one.' Funny thing."

"What's funny?"

"You do."

CHAPTER THREE

THE BODY LAY HALF on the carpet, half on the white ceramic tile. It lay faceup, with its eyes half-closed in a dreamy, faraway stare, as though the victim had been utterly bored by the details of his own violent death. There was a single bullet hole near the center of the forehead—*a 9mm, maybe a .357,* Donovan thought. The flesh around the entry wound was smooth and even, and there was no powder tattoo, indicating that the shot was fired from at least a couple of feet away. The bullet had exited at the back and disappeared. Donovan looked across the sprawling loft to his right, where a couple of NYPD forensic techs searched the walls and ceiling for a telltale hole or crack. He shook his head; they could be looking for an hour in a place this size.

The exit wound itself was invisible, concealed by the skull, but the hole had allowed a crimson liquid to form a remarkably symmetrical puddle under the head. *Just like the halos on the angels in those old paintings,* he thought.

Donovan looked to his left; there were no old paintings here. The carpeted portion of the loft comprised an extensive private art gallery, dotted with objects of every conceivable size and shape and color, but nothing recognizable—nothing "objective," the art people would say. The loft was in TriBeCa, the old industrial section below Canal Street, where the exorbitant rents of SoHo a few blocks to the north once forced less-affluent artists and gallery owners to take up residence—that is, before TriBeCa became equally prohibitive. The loft still showed traces of its garment factory roots, with plumbing stacks and gas conduits snaking across the smoky walls like a map of the Manhattan subway. Throughout the room, freestanding panels of teak or pecan stood awash in brilliant light, each bearing a canvas screaming its own colorful obscenities. In front of each panel, acrylic display stands offered gifts of bronze and chrome and twisted glass. An electrical grid hung suspended from the black ceiling, where the blue-and-white rims of glowing halogen spotlights glowed like planets at sunset.

In the center of the far wall, under the brightest spotlights of all, stood a single display stand. It was square and large, about eighteen inches on a side. It rose no more than six inches from the carpet—and it was empty.

There was a sharp rap on the open door frame.

"Hey, Donovan."

"Hey, Poldie. You just getting here?"

"Nah, I was talking to the neighbors. Upstairs, downstairs, across the hall." The man started into the room.

"Hold it—put these on first," Donovan said, pointing to the blue surgical booties covering his own shoes. "There, by the door."

He was a heavy, thick-chested man. As he lowered himself, he extended his arms back toward the floor, then froze for an instant before dropping the final six inches like a sack of wet laundry. He landed with a huff and reached into a nearby box for a pair of the elastic coverings.

Leopold Satwyck—"Poldie" to everyone who knew him—was in his midfifties, a thirty-year veteran of the NYPD. He was not Polish; he was a Polack—there's a difference, Poldie said. He was a proud representative of one of the still-distinct ethnic communities that surround the East and Hudson Rivers. His features were thick and rough. His eyes were permanently underscored by purple-gray parentheses, and his nose was a bulbous lump of paste-colored orange peel with a lacework of intricate red and blue threads. His chin had long ago doubled and was in the process of multiplying again. If Poldie had a trademark, it was his hair; it was as thick as piano wire. No matter how hard he tried to plaster it down on the sides, it simply refused to be tamed. By the end of the day, rebellious gray strands stood out from his head in proud defiance—the Polish Rebellion, Poldie called it. In bad weather, Poldie looked like a cat in a wind tunnel.

They were an odd couple, Poldie in his starched white button-downs and Windsor-knotted ties, and Donovan in his navy crewnecks and Dolce & Gabbana shades. But then, that was the point of the JTTF—thirty different agencies joining together, old eyes paired with young, so that together they might spot things that a single pair of eyes could miss.

Donovan watched Poldie's face redden as he stretched to pull a bootie over the tip of his shoe.

"Hey, Poldie, you need some help there?"

Poldie looked up with a smoldering stare. Donovan loved it—it was Poldie's patented look, the one that said, "I'd shoot you, but I wouldn't want to waste the bullet." The look was a legend at headquarters; it was said to have the power to wither desk plants and cause computers to freeze. Subordinates and clerical workers steered well clear of Poldie just to avoid "the Look," but Donovan considered it an off night when he failed to merit at least one.

Poldie struggled to his feet again and started across the carpet, stopping to examine the various objets d'art along the way.

"You like this stuff?" he said, leaving no doubt as to his own opinion. "My dog leaves better art than this."

"Don't knock it. This is expensive stuff."

Poldie shook his head. "*Artists* are supposed to suffer, not viewers." He padded across the carpet to Donovan's side.

Donovan glanced at him. "Hey. Did you tell somebody about the dreams?"

"What dreams?"

"You know what dreams—my dreams. Who did you tell?"

"Nobody. Mayer, maybe. He asked me."

"He asked you. He says, 'Is Donovan having dreams?'"

"No, he asks me if you're okay. I say, 'Sure.' He asks, 'Is he sleeping enough?' I say, 'Who sleeps enough?' But he just stands there, looking at me—you know how he does. So I say, 'Maybe he has dreams sometimes. Maybe he wakes up a lot.'"

"*Maybe*," Donovan said. "Poldie, you got a mouth like the Holland Tunnel."

Poldie's one irredeemable quality was his tendency to talk—to anyone, at any time, about anything crossing his mind at the moment. Poldie was like a man with a Plexiglas skull; you could actually see the workings of his mind. He formed his thoughts right in front of you, darting down one mental alleyway after another, spitting out words and then searching for thoughts to fit them. Poldie liked to say, "Sometimes I talk so fast I say things I haven't even thought of yet." It was funny—most of the time.

Poldie looked at the body. "He's the best-looking thing in here. How much you asking?"

"A neighbor called it in," Donovan said. "He says there was a big party here night before last, some kind of gallery event—an opening or something. Says he dropped by the next day to pay a visit, but there was no answer. Tried a couple more times, then he got suspicious, so he called NYPD. This is how they found him."

He gestured to the left and right, outlining the basic layout of the unit. "The gallery is the carpeted area. Over there, the ceramic tile, that's a kitchen and foyer. Down that hallway, there's a bedroom and an office. No sign of forced entry. Might have been somebody he knew—maybe somebody from the party."

"Maybe somebody who likes art," Poldie offered. "So who called the JTTF? Homicides are NYPD's job. This one should belong to Manhattan South."

"That's who called us."

"How come?"

Donovan motioned to one of the forensic technicians still searching for the elusive bullet. "Lieutenant, would you please explain to my big-mouthed partner why Manhattan South thinks a regular homicide might be of interest to the JTTF?"

The technician carefully knelt down by the victim's head. "It's this," he said, outlining a spray of tiny red dots that radiated outward from the head. "We might not have seen them if it wasn't for the white tile."

Poldie shrugged. "Blood spatter."

"It's not blood spatter. Blood spatter occurs when a bullet or weapon causes blood to spray on surrounding surfaces. But this victim was standing when he was murdered—he fell backward and landed in this spot. But these little dots, what you called 'blood spatter,' surround the head as if he were shot lying down."

"So it happened when the head hit the ground."

"Look at the little dots," the technician said. "Look how even they are—almost as if they were airbrushed. Blood just doesn't splatter that way. It's too viscous—the dots would be larger, and all different sizes."

"Then what is it?"

"I can answer that," said a voice from the hallway.

They looked up to see a man rounding the corner from the back bedroom. He was tall and angular with broad shoulders and large hands. His clothes looked somehow unsettled, as if they had stopped by for a visit but were deciding whether or not to stay. He wore sagging khakis that puddled around a pair of broken-down Reeboks. He wore a gray Penn State Athletics shirt under an open-fronted button-down that didn't match in any conceivable way. His head was an inverted triangle, with a broad, contemplative brow. Under that thoughtful brow stood the largest pair of spectacles that Poldie had ever seen—and he said so.

"Holy—look at the specs! They look like Coke bottles."

The man stopped directly in front of Poldie and looked at him. Through the massive lenses his eyes were the size of brown chestnuts. When he blinked they momentarily vanished, then reappeared an instant later even larger than before.

"They're the size of boccie balls," Poldie said.

"Boccie balls," the man repeated. "Only in New York."

"Can I try them on?"

"Can I hold your gun?"

Donovan decided it was time to step in; there was an outside chance that Poldie might make the trade. "Poldie, I want you to meet a friend of mine—Dr. Nick Polchak. Nick, this is Detective Leopold Satwyck. Just call him Poldie—and whatever you do, don't tell him any secrets."

The two men shook hands, but Poldie never took his eyes off Nick's glasses. "Can you see through those things?"

"That would be the general idea, now, wouldn't it?"

"Poldie, Nick is a professor at N.C. State down in Raleigh. I asked him to fly up this afternoon when I got the call from Manhattan South. We've worked together before. Nick is a forensic entomologist."

"You're a bug guy!" Poldie said in amazement.

"I used to be a bug guy, but I grew up. Now I'm a bug man."

"How do you guys do it? I mean, all the flies and maggots and decomposing bodies?"

"We're shaking hands over a dead man," Nick said. "Do you detect a little irony?"

"Yeah, but we usually work with *new* dead guys."

Nick stared at him for a minute, then turned and looked at Donovan. "I'm assuming he's with you."

"Tell him about the blood spots," Donovan said. "Tell him what they are."

Nick squatted down by the legs of the corpse and gingerly slid up its right pant leg. "Look at this," he said.

Poldie grimaced. "Geez—he shaved his legs."

Nick looked up at him. "May I see your badge?"

"Poldie, look at the red spots," Donovan said, pointing. "See? They're on the other leg too."

"And also around the waist," Nick added. "That's the giveaway—fleas like to bite around the waist."

"The guy had *fleas*?"

"Let me show you something." Nick turned to his right and crawled on all fours to the center of the carpeted area; he motioned for Donovan and Poldie to follow. Donovan dropped to his knees beside him. Poldie lowered himself a good deal more slowly, and his knees made a sound like crunching cornflakes. Nick took a sheet of white paper from his shirt pocket, unfolded it, and smoothed it out on the carpet's surface. To the side of the paper he made a few quick brushing motions, and tiny gray dots began to appear magically.

"There are thousands of them," Nick said.

Poldie lifted his hands from the carpet.

"Don't worry, Detective, they're all dead—every last one of them."

"How come they're all dead?"

"They were purposely exterminated. If we had a sample of carpet fiber analyzed, I'm betting we'd find traces of permethrin or hydroprene. Or they may have used an aerosol."

"But if he had the place exterminated, how come he's still got flea bites?"

Nick looked at Donovan. "He's good at questions."

Donovan nodded. "It's his specialty. What did you find in the bedroom and office, Nick?"

"Nothing—not a single flea. And look at this." Nick crawled forward on the carpet, sliding the paper to a spot near the empty display stand. He brushed at the carpet again, and the gray spots began to reappear—but more than twice as many as before.

"There's a definite distribution pattern here," he said. "The flea population is densest here, by the wall. The number decreases as you move across the carpet toward the body. That means, of course, that the fleas were purposely released in the room."

"How do you know that?"

"This is not your ordinary flea infestation," Nick said. "Think about it: Over time, the fleas would spread out and become fairly evenly distributed. But here, they're concentrated all in one place—and I found none at all in the bedroom. Isn't that a little odd? The only way to explain this fan-shaped distribution is if the fleas were released from a single point—my guess would be from right over there," he said, pointing to the empty display stand. "That seems to be the locus. From that point, they worked their way across the carpet toward the foyer."

"Why would they do that?"

"Fleas are attracted by motion. They probably sensed activity in the busier part of the room and went after it. It wouldn't be an easy trip—this is thick carpet, and a flea's hind legs are shaped like little jigsaw blades. Most of them never made it; apparently some of the more aggressive ones did."

"The fleabites on the legs?"

"And the dots of blood around the head. It's fecal matter, Detective. Fleas feed on blood, but most of it passes through them undigested. It gets left behind in tiny red dots. Your forensic guys are sharp; beginners usually mistake it for blood spatter."

Donovan elbowed Poldie, earning him his second Look of the evening.

Nick stepped to the center of the room and looked around. "So here's the scenario," he said. "Someone purposely released thousands of fleas in this room."

"Why?"

"Your guess is as good as mine."

"A prank, maybe? A competing gallery owner? A disgruntled buyer, somebody who thought he got ripped off and wanted to get even?"

"I doubt it," Nick said. "We're talking about thousands and thousands of fleas here. You don't just have your dog roll around on the carpet to create an infestation like that. Rearing an insect population this large is a laboratory procedure. It takes time, and money, and expertise—trust me on this. Somebody went to a lot of trouble to do this. Besides, you've got a dead man here. It would be naive to consider the fleas and the murder as two separate events—especially when you consider that the fleas were exterminated *after* the murder took place."

Poldie held up both hands. "Whoa—you're way ahead of me here."

Nick looked at him. "Now, there's a surprise."

"How do you know that?"

Nick stepped to the empty display stand, turned, and started slowly across the carpet toward the body. "The fleas worked their way through the carpet, attracted by motion and exhaled carbon dioxide. When they got here, they found the victim already dead."

"Why dead?" Donovan asked. "How do you know he wasn't still alive?"

"The bites on the waist," Nick said. "Fleas like the waist area, but it's a matter of access. A flea can jump maybe eight inches, no higher. That gives it access to the ankles and legs of a standing figure—but to reach the waist, it needs to find someone lying down."

"In the bedroom," Poldie said. "You know, 'Don't let the bedbugs bite.'"

"There are no fleas in the bedroom, remember? They're all out here. This is where the fleas found him—he had been murdered just a few minutes before."

"Now, wait a minute," Poldie complained.

"It's the bites," Nick said. "A flea is something like a mosquito—when it bites, it injects a little saliva into the wound. That's what creates the red bump—it's a histamine reaction. But histamine reactions occur only when a person is living—and for a few minutes after death. Your boy here died instantly; the fleas arrived when he was lying down; ergo, immediately after death. And one more thing: Fleas feed only on *warm* blood. They were attracted to the blood around the head—but only while it was still warm. That wasn't long."

"But the fleas are all dead," Donovan said. "Are you saying someone came in and exterminated *after* the murder?"

"That would follow."

"But why?"

"The only possible conclusion is that someone didn't want us to find the fleas—which only strengthens my premise that the two acts are connected."

Donovan stepped to the display stand himself and retraced Nick's path across the carpet. "Somebody dumps the fleas," he said, "then somebody—maybe the same guy—shoots the victim in the head. The fleas cross the carpet, find the body, and help themselves. Then somebody comes back and exterminates the place. Who would do that?"

"Not him," Poldie said, nodding at the body.

"I'd say that's what you're investigating," Nick said. "Lucky for you, the detective has already narrowed the search."

Poldie looked at Nick with undisguised admiration. "You guys are amazing," he said. "You're worth whatever they pay you."

Nick turned to Donovan. "The detective mentioned money. We're friends now."

Donovan shook his head. "Nick and I have an agreement. He's here as a professional courtesy."

"*Courtesy,*" Nick said. "That means two weeks from now the FBI will mail me a certificate and a Junior G-Man badge. Gee willikers."

There was another knock on the door. An NYPD officer leaned in the doorway and said, "There's a *Times* reporter downstairs. He wants to talk to someone."

"I'll go," Poldie said.

"Just the basics, Poldie," Donovan reminded him. "Until we know more. When you're done, follow up with the neighbors again. Ask about anybody unusual entering or leaving the building. Look for personal angles. Ask about anybody with a grudge against the deceased—you know the routine. And check with the super; see if the building has a surveillance system—there may be videos."

"Got it." Poldie started off toward the door.

"Hey, Poldie," Donovan called after him. "Keep the JTTF out of it, okay? Just tell the reporter it's an NYPD case."

"That reminds me," Poldie said. "Why *did* they call the JTTF on this one? What's the big deal about a bunch of fleas?"

"They're all the same species," Nick responded. "*Xenopsylla cheopis,* the Oriental rat flea."

"So?"

"They should be *Ctenocephalides felis*—cat fleas. That's the most common flea in the U.S. The Oriental rat flea is common to Europe and the tropics—not New York."

"Is that important?"

"Could be. They can carry bubonic plague."

CHAPTER FOUR

MACY APPROACHED THE FIRST uniform she saw and flashed her credentials.

The officer shook his head. "Uh-uh. Nobody allowed inside the perimeter. Take the detour around to the—"

"You people sent for me," she said. "Check with your boss."

The officer slipped the radio from his belt and held it diagonally across his mouth. "LaGambina," he said, holding the credentials at eye level. "I got a Dr. Macy Monroe here, professor of political science and international relations at Columbia University. Somebody send for a tutor?"

There was a crackle of static and a distorted voice—an urgent, emphatic voice.

"Yes sir. Right away." The officer turned back to Macy with a good deal more decorum. "My apologies, ma'am. Captain says I'm to escort you immediately to the command post. If you'll follow me, please."

"I can find it," she said, stepping across the yellow barrier tape. "A bunch of big guys in uniforms, right?"

Macy had been surrounded by books in the Graduate Reserve section of Low Library when her cell phone went off. She had an office, of course, but she preferred the solemn atmosphere of the old place with its spectacular view across the quad. Her office was just too quiet; she needed a little distraction to stay focused, and a few rustling pages and muffled coughs were just the thing to occupy her peripheral thoughts. She loved the long wooden tables and the intimate, eye-level lighting. She always surrounded herself with stacks of books, the older and thicker the better, a forbidding mountain of knowledge just waiting to be conquered.

She had meant to set her cell phone to vibrate, but she always seemed to forget, despite glaring reminders plastered throughout the library. When the piercing trill went off, shattering the tomblike atmosphere, she had to flash an apologetic grin at a dozen pairs of condemning eyes.

"Hold on," she whispered into the phone, then scurried down the stairs and into the bustling lobby to take the call.

Now, just thirty minutes later, she found herself in a residential/commercial section of Forest Hills, a proudly Jewish section of Queens. It was a beautiful street, lined with tightly packed buildings sporting colorful awnings and cascading flower boxes. It had a village atmosphere, as serene in its own way as any library. On the ground floor of each building was a clothier, or deli, or market; the two or three floors above were invariably residential, occupied by business owners and their extended families. The pristine sidewalks were ordinarily crowded with shoppers, strollers, and scurrying children—but not today. Inside the police perimeter the streets were as quiet as the southern Negev.

Rounding a corner, Macy saw a group of officers gathered around a Technical Assistance Response Unit. Most of them wore NYPD black, but a handful of navy FBI windbreakers mingled among them. *A WMD squad,* she thought, feeling a sudden twinge of anxiety that bordered on nausea. She quickly scanned the heads for a familiar face; he wasn't among them, and Macy relaxed again.

A senior NYPD officer spotted her first and waved her over. He looked over her shoulder as she approached.

"I told LaGambina to escort you," he growled.

"I told him not to. What can I do for you, Captain?"

The group closed in around her, and quick introductions were made. Someone shoved a steaming Styrofoam cup into her hand.

"Macy—like the department store?" someone asked.

"Only younger," she said. "Younger and cheaper" was the line she used with girlfriends, but not with black shirts and Bureau boys. She liked to get a laugh as much as the next person, but not at her own expense. Respect was hard to come by with these people; she wasn't about to give it away.

"Where's our boy?" she asked.

The commanding officer pointed across the street. There stood a Jewish grocery with a green-and-white awning overshadowing a red-trimmed door. Beside the door was a long display window, with the ends of crowded white shelves just barely visible through the glass.

"He's an Arab boy," the commanding officer said. "Fifteen, maybe sixteen years old tops. He charged in wearing a standard bomb vest. Witnesses tell us it was gray and bulky and had a series of pouches in it—all of them full. Looks like a manual detonator; he held it in his right hand."

"Hostages?"

"None. He rushed straight to the back of the store, shouted something in Arabic, then froze. For some reason he hesitated; that gave everyone in the store a chance to get out."

"So we've got a barricaded suspect. How long has he been in there?"

"We got the call about forty-five minutes ago. We were here and set up in fifteen. We've got a TARU and a hostage-negotiation team from the 112th Precinct. We've got a tactical unit setting up over in that alley—we like to keep those fellas out of sight until we need them. They're studying the building blueprints now."

"Let's hope we don't need them. Have you been able to make contact with the boy?"

"No. We captured the phone line going into the store, and we keep ringing him, but he won't answer the phone. He could be dead."

"Could be—we have to assume otherwise. Maybe the phone is in a bad place—maybe it puts him in a line of fire."

"We thought about throwing in a cell phone. We decided to wait until you got here."

"Good idea. People wearing bombs don't like to see small objects rolling across the floor toward them."

Macy turned to one of the men with bright yellow letters emblazoned across his back. "You must be the WMD guys," she said. "What can you tell us about this bomb?"

"Not much." The man shrugged. "We can't get a look at it—all we've got to go on is what witnesses have told us. Sounds pretty standard—probably eight kilos of C4 in a series of vest pockets."

"How bad is that?"

"It could bring the building down—maybe the ones on each side with it."

"Maybe we should let him," another agent said.

"Excuse me?"

"He's alone in there. If he wants to go out with a bang, I say let him. It's better than risking any of our people trying to walk him out. Sort of an unscheduled urban-renewal project. I'll bet these old buildings are insured for twice what they're worth anyway. What do we have to lose, a few knishes and some blini?"

They looked at the grocery store again—still no sign of movement in the shadows behind the glass. They could hear the ring of the telephone inside the TARU van. "Still no answer," a uniformed woman called out.

From around the corner came the muffled sound of struggling, shouting, pleading. An instant later a young, dark-haired woman broke into view, running toward them with an NYPD officer in close pursuit. He grabbed her by the left arm and spun her around, momentarily halting her advance, but she tore away and started forward again, running directly for the store. This time the officer tackled her from behind, breaking her down like a Giants linebacker. She hit the street headlong with her arms pinned to her sides, but she lifted her face toward the store and continued to scream uncontrollably. Macy took a step forward.

"I can't understand a word she's saying!" the officer shouted, pulling one of her arms behind her back and positioning the handcuffs.

"It's Yiddish!" Macy called back. "Let go of her hands!"

"Are you nuts? I've been trying to—"

"Do it!" Macy shouted.

The officer released the woman's left arm; she began to point frantically at the grocery store front. Macy's eyes followed her hand to one of the second-floor windows. At the sound of the woman's desperate screams, the draperies swung aside and two tiny faces pressed against the glass. One smiled, and a little hand waved from side to side.

"Let her go!" Macy shouted to the officer. "Get her out of here, but let her go!" She turned to the ashen-faced FBI agent. "He's got two hostages now—still want to let him blow the place up?"

She turned to the NYPD commander. "Get me your tactical commander—I need to know if there's a way to reach those kids without being seen."

Now she charged to the TARU van and looked inside. "Who's the chief negotiator? Who's in charge here?"

A detective from the 112th raised his hand.

"May I have a word with you, please?"

He stepped out of the van. Macy took him by the arm and turned him quickly aside.

"I need your help," she said. "I need a good secondary negotiator out here. I need somebody who's had training in this, somebody who knows the ropes."

"In other words, you're taking over."

She took a step closer and spoke in a low, even voice. "Look—I've got a doctorate in international relations. My field of study is the psychology of terrorism. I've got two areas of regional expertise—one is the Middle East. I'm fluent in Arabic. That's why they sent for me, okay? Nothing personal—it's not about you."

He tried to look as indifferent as possible. "It's your show. What do you want to do?"

"Get me a throw phone. I'm going in."

The tactical and NYPD commanders approached from behind. "You're going to *what*?"

"It's the only way," Macy said.

"Not a chance," the NYPD commander replied. "I asked you here to advise, not to get yourself blown up."

"I don't want that either. I've got vacation coming."

"I'm not giving this boy a hostage."

"He's got two already—he just doesn't know it yet." She turned to the tactical commander and shook his hand as she spoke. "Have you had a look at the building? Can you get to those kids?"

"The front door leads directly to a stairway," he said. "It's visible to the entire store. There's a fire escape in the back—but there's a big security window in the back of the store too. We don't know where this kid is holed up; there's a chance he could see us approaching from any angle."

"What about the roof?"

"We could come up through an adjacent building and cross over, then rope down through a third-floor window. But there's a problem with sound—this place is as quiet as a church. If a window breaks, if the floor creaks, this kid could hear us coming a mile away."

"Then you need a distraction inside."

"Wait," the commander said. "We could call the second-floor apartment—get the kids to open a window, maybe even sneak down the stairs and make a break for the front door."

"No," Macy said. "The last thing we want is a phone ringing on the second floor. There's a chance the boy hasn't even thought about who might be upstairs. Make sure your people secure *all* the lines going into the building—we don't want some worried relative trying to call in."

Now the hostage negotiator spoke up. "If somebody's going in, it should be me. That's my job; that's what I'm trained for."

Macy thought about the NYPD hostage negotiator training process: A few weeks of classroom training and you get a certificate allowing you to intervene in domestic squabbles and disturbances involving disgruntled employees and people who stopped taking their medication too soon. She should know; she wrote the training manual.

"No," she said. "It's got to be me."

"Why?"

"Look, I speak Arabic. He may not be answering the phone because he doesn't speak a word of English. If you walk in there and the first word you say is in a foreign tongue, that may be all he needs to remind him that you're the enemy."

"I don't have to say a word. I can just take in a phone and back out."

She shook her head. "There's another reason. You're a man."

The three men glanced at one another, but no one knew what to say in response.

"It's like this," Macy said. "An Arab culture is a patriarchal culture. That means men control most of the ostensible power. That boy is in there ready to blow himself up because he believes that's how you get yourself a river of honey, a river of wine, and seventy-two virgins. A *man* told him that; in Arab cultures, the relationships between men and boys are very complex and very powerful.

"But in patriarchal cultures, women also exert enormous influence—but they learn to do it in indirect ways. In fact, some cultures are patriarchal in form only. The women have the real power; they just allow their men the appearance of control."

Macy stopped. The men's eyes were beginning to glaze over. *This is the problem with critical-incident teams,* she thought. *There's an extreme prejudice toward action. Everybody wants to do something, but nobody wants to talk theory.*

"Here's the bottom line," she said. "If a man walks in that door, no matter what he says or does, he will be a visible reminder of duty, and courage, and *shame*—and that's when things go boom. An Arab boy will die for his father—but he will live for his mother. Get it?"

She took a handkerchief from her purse and scrubbed at her mouth and eyes. She pulled off her earrings and a bracelet and took a silver brooch from her left lapel. She instinctively reached for her ring finger, but it was already bare. She dropped all of it into her purse and pulled her hair back with a simple rubber band.

"How do I look?" she asked.

"Plain enough."

"Like a mom?"

"Not like *my* mom."

"Flatterer."

"If you're going in," the commander said, "then put this on." He held out a bulky black Kevlar vest.

Macy almost laughed. The gesture reminded her of her aunt Jean, who always brought a jar of her homemade preserves to a funeral. *It's human nature*, she thought. *When people feel powerless they always seem to offer the most ridiculous and useless things.*

"No thanks," she said.

"I'm afraid I have to insist. It's policy."

"Look, Captain. You and I both know that if the boy pushes the button, the only thing that vest will do is allow your cleanup squad to find a larger piece of my torso intact. No thanks—I can't go in there looking like one of your ninjas. I'm going in as a woman, and I need to look like a woman."

A TARU officer handed her a silver throw phone. "It's always on," he said. "Even when it's in the cradle it broadcasts. We'll hear everything you say."

Macy nodded. "Listen closely," she said. "When I'm talking to him, I'll be talking to you too. If I need anything, if I want you to do something, you'll know it." She turned toward the street.

"One thing," the tactical commander said. "I'm putting two shooters on the second floor across the street with a clear view of the store window. If things aren't working, if you can't talk him out, just lure him in front of the window. We'll do the rest."

Macy winced. If things didn't go well, she was to lure the boy out into the open where he could be neatly and efficiently murdered. *Some mother*, she thought.

At the door of the grocery, she paused. Her first words in Arabic needed to be flawless, without a hint of foreign accent or a trace of hesitation. She mouthed the words silently until the rhythm and cadence came back to her.

She reached for the door and then stopped. This was the hardest moment of all, like the first step into a dark cellar, when all the old fears come rushing out at once. For the police she put on an air of perfect confidence, but she had learned the hard way that dealing with terrorists is not a science; it's an art—a very imperfect art. Despite all her training and experience, she had no way of knowing what would happen when she opened that door. For all she knew, the boy might hate his mother; he might push the detonator at the first sight of her. A voice in the back of her mind asked her if she was prepared to die today. She shook off the thought and tried to refocus. There are some places your mind just can't go—not at a time like this.

She slowly opened the door. A bell jingled, and her heart jumped into her throat.

"Hello," she called out in Arabic. "May I come in, please?"

There was no response.

She slowly tiptoed down an aisle toward the back of the store, letting her words go before her. "May I come in? It's only me. I'd like to speak with you for a moment, if you'll allow me."

Still nothing.

"I'm a friend. I just came to talk. I've brought you something—may I show you?"

She rounded the end of an aisle. There was the boy, sprawled back against the glass of the deli counter, staring at her through eyes as black as Saudi oil. He held the detonator aloft in his right hand; his thumb stood poised above the button, and his hand trembled with uncertainty.

Don't look at the detonator, she reminded herself. *It's just a friendly visit.*

"Get out of here, woman!"

Macy bowed her head slightly in a display of womanly deference. She looked at him from the tops of her eyes. His skin was bronze, and his hair was thick and black. He was slender; his joints seemed larger than the adjoining limbs. A sparse tangle of facial hair sprouted from his chin, longer on the left than the right. *Just a boy,* she thought. *Not a foal, and not a stallion.* She wanted to shake her head. She wanted to say, "You sad little fool. What would you do with seventy-two virgins?"

"I brought you this," she said gently. "We thought the phone in here might be broken. This is for you, in case you want to talk to us."

"The time to talk is over," he said with angry defiance, but his voice was an octave too high to make it work.

"There is always time to talk," she said simply. She glanced around the room; beside the deli counter were a half dozen tables with wire-backed chairs. "May I sit?" she asked, pulling out one of the chairs.

"No!" he shouted back.

She showed him a look of injury and affront that bordered on anger. *Try a little guilt, kiddo. You don't talk to your mother that way.*

He lowered his eyes. "Sit," he grumbled.

She set the phone on the table nearest him and took a seat.

"Do you speak any English?" He shook his head. *Then he hasn't been here long,* she thought. *The Arabs in New York know they're a minority, and they pick up English fast.* "I apologize for my Arabic. Your language is so beautiful, and I speak it so poorly."

"It's not bad," he said reluctantly.

"My name is Macy. What may I call you?"

"Call me Shahid," he said—the Arabic word for "martyr."

She looked around the store. "You're all alone," she said for the throw phone. "May I ask where you're from?"

He glared at her. "You are with the police."

"I am not with the police—I am a schoolteacher."

"Then why are you here?"

"I speak Arabic. I've been to Jordan; did you know that? I've been to Lebanon and to Syria too." She left Israel out of it; no sense spoiling their little reunion. "I've been to Kuwait, and to Yemen, and to Saudi Arabia. I think I liked Saudi Arabia best—I love Medina." She watched for some sign of recognition, some hint of "Me too" in his eyes—but he showed her nothing.

"Are you hungry?"

The boy seemed taken aback. "I will not require food."

"Nonsense—you must eat to stay strong. I know a place not far from here—in Brooklyn Heights. Have you been there yet? You must go. There is a restaurant there; they serve a wonderful *shawarma*—you can have beef or lamb. I can send for some. May I?"

The boy said nothing. *At least he didn't say no,* Macy thought. She gently lifted the throw phone and looked at him as she spoke. "Did you get that?" she said in English. "*Shawarma*—they know what it is. Bedouin Tent on Atlantic Avenue. Take your time—and don't send it in unless I ask for it."

She hung up the phone and smiled.

"Do you have a sister at home? Someone like me?"

"You are much older than my sister."

"Your mother, then—is she about my age?"

"How old are you?"

"It's rude to ask," she scolded. "I'd like to meet your mother."

The boy sneered. "Perhaps she can clean your house."

Macy frowned. "You insult me *and* your mother. Still, I would like to meet her."

"Why?"

"Because I have met her son—and I would like to show her a picture of mine. Would you like to see?" She lifted her purse; the boy straightened and extended the detonator menacingly.

"It's just a purse," she said softly. She slowly turned and inverted it, spilling its contents across the table.

"You carry too many things," the boy grumbled.

"Women always do." She picked out her wallet and opened it to a section of small photographs in glossy plastic sleeves. The first was empty, but the faint contour of two heads was still visible on the plastic. She opened to the second photo, an image of a small boy no more than three. She slowly stood up from her chair, holding the wallet in front of her. *Either you come to me or I come to you,* she thought.

The boy measured the distance between them, then impatiently gestured for her to approach. She held the wallet at arm's length and approached until the wallet was within reach; he quickly reached out and snatched it from her hands. He gave the photograph a cursory glance and offered the wallet back, but Macy shook her head.

"Look at the next one," she said.

The boy flipped the plastic sleeve. The next photograph was an image of the same child—only this time he appeared tired, and frail, and bald-headed.

"What's wrong with him?" the boy asked.

"He had cancer. He's dead now."

The boy looked at her, unsure of what to say. For an instant, his countenance softened—then anger reclaimed him again. "What do I care about your son?" he said, tossing the wallet back to her. Macy let the wallet bounce off her chest and fall to the floor. She stood looking at it for a moment; when she lifted her eyes again, they were filled with anger of her own.

"What do you *care*?" she repeated. "How dare you. That was my son—and you throw him on the ground as if he were dirt. His life meant nothing to you—*nothing*. Well, it meant everything to me, because I was his *mother*. You know nothing about that, do you? Nothing about what it means to be a *mother*. You have no idea what it's like to watch your son waste away and die, to know that all your love and all your service were for nothing. You don't care about my son—but your mother would care. She would weep with me and hold me, because she is a mother too. She has a son, and she knows how it would break her heart to hear that he was dead—and not for something important, but for *nothing*.

"Men throw their lives away," she said with contempt, "and all women can do is watch and weep. No one thinks about the mothers—no one asks us how *we* feel."

She watched him as she spoke, waiting for his eyes to begin to soften, for his shoulders to round and droop. The anger was hers now; the power was hers. All that was left was his shame—but she knew that shame was still enough to kill them both.

The boy stared into space. "I have no choice," he said quietly.

"There is a saying in English," she said, holding up one finger. "He's in the back right corner. He has no weapon other than the bomb." The boy waited for the translation.

"It means, 'It's never too late to change your mind. There is always a choice.'"

"I cannot go back."

"Then you will have to kill me too." She held her breath. In her mind, she saw him shrug and press the detonator; she felt the heat and the impact and imagined her body catapulted backward across the store.

"You can go." The boy glared at her as he spoke. "I did not ask you to come."

"I will not go. You will throw away your life *and* mine—and then you will stand before the holy one and say to him, 'Let me into your Paradise. I am a *shahid*; I killed myself and *one woman*.'" Macy sneered. "How great will be your reward."

The boy just stared at the floor now. His anger and his power were gone; even his shame had been trumped by a greater shame. He was naked and alone, just a boy again, with no idea what to do next.

Macy took a step toward him. She lowered her eyes to the floor with his and spoke under her breath, as women do in the marketplace when they speak of intimate things. She prayed that he would not detect the trembling in her voice.

"There is a way," she said. "Outside there is a team of men. They are very large and very strong. They are highly trained, and they carry powerful weapons. They are known as a Special Weapons and Tactics team."

"Special Forces?" the boy said in awe.

"Yes, like Special Forces. They move very quickly and without a sound. If you were distracted—for even a moment—they would move in like shadows and overcome you. And who could blame you? Not even a great warrior could resist them."

Who could blame you? They were words of salvation, and they called to the boy like a crier from a minaret.

"I must ask one thing," Macy said even more softly. "The men outside, they have wives and children who wait for them at home. Before they come in, I must ask you to remove . . . this." She nodded, almost imperceptibly, toward the vest.

The boy stood silently, his mind racing.

Macy leaned forward until their heads were almost touching. "No one thinks of the mothers," she said.

The boy stepped back and began to fumble dumbly with the straps of the vest. "Yes," she said softly as he released each strap, soothing him like a groom with a nervous thoroughbred. She said, "Thank you," as he slid off the vest and set it on the floor beside him. Then she took him gently by the arm and walked him several feet away.

"Now *I* must ask one thing," the boy said. "I will not surrender to these men. They must *take* me."

"I understand," she said. "This is how it will happen: When I signal them, six men will enter this room. They will make a great deal of noise, and they will fire several shots into the wall. Do you understand? Not at you—at the wall. They will bend your arms behind your back, and they will bind your wrists with a plastic strap. Then they will help you to your feet and lead you out to a vehicle waiting outside." She paused. "Do you understand?"

He nodded fiercely.

"Then I will signal the men." She lifted the phone from its cradle and repeated the instructions in English. "Did you get all that?" she asked.

"We're on our way," said the voice on the other end.

She hung up the phone again and they stood in silence, waiting.

"Do you think I'm a coward?" the boy whispered.

Macy looked at him. "You did the hard thing. That's what courage is."

A moment later the door burst open, and six heavily armed men poured through and charged toward the back of the store. Macy could see their black ballistic helmets bobbing toward them like sea buoys. Three of the men pointed their Heckler & Koch submachine guns at the base of the wall and squeezed off a handful of single rounds. Macy stood perfectly still; better to let these men work around you.

She looked at the boy. "It will go easier for you if you lie down."

"They must *take* me," the boy repeated defiantly.

The men were happy to comply. One sweep of a boot took the boy's legs out from under him; a second man pinned him to the floor with a knee in the center of his back, while a third banded his wrists in a matter of seconds. They jerked him to his feet again; in their hands, the boy seemed to possess no weight at all.

"Easy, guys," Macy said. A lot of adrenaline was flowing in there—a lot of testosterone too—and it wouldn't take more than a kick or a jab from the boy to earn him a broken jaw or a rifle butt to the side of his head. *Maybe he'd like that,* Macy thought. *Something to show his friends—if he'll have any left.*

Three of the men searched under every table and counter in the store, while one gingerly disconnected the curling red wires from the bomb vest. The remaining two hustled the boy down the center aisle to the door; Macy followed close behind. Directly in front of the doorway, an NYPD van waited with its side door yawning wide. Macy stood in the doorway, watching as they turned the boy, tucked his head down, and shoved him into the center seat.

The boy stared at Macy with burning eyes. "I am Ali bin Ahmad bin Saleh Al-Fulani," he said.

Macy nodded as the door slid shut, and she watched as the van pulled away.

CHAPTER FIVE

"EXPLAIN AGAIN ABOUT THE fleas," Mayer said slowly.

Nathan Donovan sat across from his supervisory special agent, the next man up the totem pole in the FBI's convoluted administrative hierarchy. Reuben Mayer was an old man, a veteran of countless reorganizations and regime changes at the Bureau, and nothing ruffled or surprised him anymore. He had seen it all, and there was simply nothing left to get all in a huff about. Mayer was like a man in slow motion, as if over the years he had learned to perform every thought, every word, and every motion with an absolute minimum of exertion.

He even looked slow. His shoulders were slightly rounded, the beginning of osteoporosis, and it caused him to slump slightly over his desk. The sacks under his eyes hung with such weight that his lower eyelids seemed to pull away from his eyeballs, leaving dark little pockets above. His face was long and drawn, and it widened at the bottom, where great sagging jowls bagged around his neck. It gave him the overall appearance of a melting candle, drooping under its own weight, as if at any moment his face might ooze over his collar and onto the desk.

To his reporting agents, Mayer's pace was maddeningly slow. They all searched for ways to speed along the weekly reporting process, but nothing seemed to help. At the Christmas party, they all chipped in and bought the old man a plaque for his office that read: "I have only two speeds: If you don't like this one, you'll hate the other." The gift was given anonymously; it had not been seen since. Reuben Mayer ran on his own timetable, and anyone trying to hurry him along simply earned a long, slow, forlorn glare—which only made the meeting longer.

Donovan sat impatiently while Mayer read his summary of the TriBeCa murder, his eyes sweeping back and forth over the text like weighty pendulums.

"There were thousands of fleas," Donovan said. "The Manhattan South forensic guys spotted them. They thought it was a red flag, so I brought in a bug man from North Carolina to take a look. He says no doubt about it, somebody dumped the fleas there on purpose."

"How does he know that?"

"By the number and distribution—but most of all, by the species."

"Species?"

"Yes sir. The way I understand it, fleas are named after the animal they feed on—so there are cat fleas, dog fleas, even people fleas. But these were Oriental rat fleas; they don't belong in New York, and—"

"So why do we care about fleas?" Mayer interrupted. His voice was a perfect monotone; it didn't even make the effort to rise for a question.

"Because Oriental rat fleas are known to be carriers of bubonic plague," he said. "That's why the forensic guys flagged it."

"Bubonic plague."

"Yes sir."

"Like in the Middle Ages, bubonic plague."

"I think so, sir, yes."

"Any of these fleas have plague?"

"No sir."

"And how do we know that?"

"My bug man. Apparently there's a way to tell just by looking at them under a microscope."

"He's sure about that?"

"Yes sir."

He looked down at the report again. A full five seconds passed before he added, "We should make sure about that." He closed the folder and extended it toward the out-box on the corner of his desk; he paused before letting it drop, as if his shoulder had suddenly locked or his sleeve had snagged on a hook.

"How do you want to proceed?" he asked.

"I think we should treat it like an ordinary homicide—because it probably is. Detective Satwyck is following up with neighbors, looking for people who attended the party, trying to find somebody with motive. I suggest we let NYPD find a perp; then we can ask him about the fleas."

Mayer nodded; no sense wasting a word. He dragged another folder in front of him now and lifted the cover as if it were a sheet of plywood. He began to read again, leaning on his elbows and rubbing his temples in long, slow circles.

"Tell me about the psychiatrist," he said without looking up.

Donovan hesitated. "I think it went well."

"Tell me about it."

"Well, he said . . . He thinks that I . . . You probably have it all right there in his evaluation, sir."

"You tell me."

Donovan could feel his teeth grinding. "He said I'm fit for duty."

Mayer's brown eyes turned up to Donovan like a Central Park swing. "He says you're angry."

Donovan shrugged. "Hardly worth the money."

"He says you might get yourself killed—or you might kill somebody." He paused. "Which is it?"

Donovan said nothing. Seconds went by.

The old man slowly closed the folder again. "He says you're fit for duty. That's good enough for me—for now."

Behind them, there was a knock on the glass panel of the door. Donovan turned and looked, grateful for the reprieve. A young administrative assistant stuck her head in the door.

"Sorry to interrupt. Mr. Donovan, you've got a call from overseas—I thought you might want to take it."

"Are we done here?" Donovan asked. He was halfway to the door before the old man completed his nod.

"I love you, marry me, bear my children," Donovan said to the woman as they walked down the hall toward his cubicle.

"I'll check with my husband," she said. There was no real reason for the interruption. Agents received calls from all over the world; it was standard practice for administrative assistants to take messages so that agents could respond at their leisure. But when Donovan was reporting to Mayer, his standing order was to be interrupted even for a wrong number.

"This is Donovan," he said, pulling on a wireless headset and flopping down in his desk chair.

"Well, hello," a voice said brightly on the other end. "This is London calling. Can you hear me clearly?"

"Yeah, they've got these things called 'satellites' now. They really do the job."

There was a chuckle on the other end. The voice was that of an old man, distinctly British.

"You'll forgive me," he said. "I never quite get used to the technology. I always imagine I'm speaking into a tin can with a long string stretched across the ocean."

Donovan smiled. He couldn't help imagining Batman's butler, Alfred, or Colonel Pickering from *My Fair Lady*—some quintessential British stereotype as seen through American eyes. The voice was the virtual opposite of Mayer's—it was lively and rich, and it had a musical quality that made you want to listen if only for the sound.

"I didn't get your name," Donovan said, reaching for a legal pad. He jotted down a single word: *Lee.* "So, Mr. Lee, why is the Queen calling the colonies today?"

"This is a private concern," the old man said. "Well, that's not precisely accurate; the matter I wish to discuss with you is of the utmost public importance. But I make no claim to represent the Crown or any governmental agency. I'm calling you purely as a private citizen."

"All right, then what can I do for you?"

"A most interesting newspaper article was brought to my attention just this morning. It appeared the day before last in your *New York Times*; it concerns an apparent homicide that occurred in a section of Manhattan known as *TriBeCa.* Am I saying that correctly?"

"Close enough. Why would a homicide in Manhattan concern you, Mr. Lee? Were you acquainted with the deceased?"

"I'm afraid I have no information that might help with your direct investigation, Mr. Donovan. No, the thing that caught my eye was the mention of . . . fleas."

"I'm sorry, did you say *fleas*?"

"Quite a number of them, I would imagine."

Donovan rolled his eyes; Poldie did the interview with the *Times* reporter. *Just the basics*, Donovan had told him. The big Polack—he managed to remember the fleas, but he couldn't remember to keep his big mouth shut.

"You'll have to excuse me, Mr. Lee; I haven't seen the story in the *Times* yet. What else does it say?"

"Is the newspaper account correct, Mr. Donovan?"

"I'm afraid I can't comment on that. The thing is, that information was never supposed to be released to the public."

"We may both be very glad it was."

Donovan paused. "How did you get my name, Mr. Lee?"

"The officer quoted in the *Times* article was a Detective Leopold Satwyck of the New York Police Department. I spoke with him this morning; he was most helpful."

"I'll bet he was."

"Tell me, Mr. Donovan, why is the FBI taking an interest in an ordinary homicide?"

"Again, no comment."

"Unless, of course, you suspect that it's not an ordinary homicide."

Donovan didn't reply.

"I suppose there are a number of reasons a case like this might fall under your agency's jurisdiction: It might involve organized crime, or drug trafficking, or interstate travel—"

"Look, Mr. Lee, let me save you some time here. I'm not at liberty to discuss an open investigation, okay?"

There was a pause. "If you're not at liberty to answer my questions, perhaps you'll allow me to simply make a few observations. You have no restriction against listening, do you? Trust me, Mr. Donovan, you may find my comments most helpful."

"I'm listening."

"As I see it, there are only four reasons an infestation of fleas at a crime scene might merit mentioning at all. First, if the fleas were discovered in an unusual environment—say, in an upscale neighborhood like your own TriBeCa. This suggests, of course, that the fleas were purposely introduced. Second, if the fleas were present in unusual number. Again, this raises the possibility that someone purposely interfered with the natural course of things."

"And why would someone want to do that?"

"Oh, you're allowed to ask me questions?"

Donovan said nothing.

"Are you still there, Mr. Donovan?"

"Still here."

"Very well, the third possibility is that the insects had an unusual distribution—say, a large population in one corner but nowhere else. This would suggest that the fleas had not been present long—and once again, that they were purposely introduced." He paused. "How am I doing?"

"No comment. This is fascinating, Mr. Lee, but we're talking about fleas here. A pile of fleas is hardly a threat to the city of New York."

"No. But an epidemic of bubonic plague just might be."

Donovan straightened. "Excuse me?"

"That's the fourth possibility, Mr. Donovan—that all of the fleas represented a single species, a species not common to New York. I assume you are aware that the Oriental rat flea is capable of transmitting plague?"

He paused. "We're aware."

"Then the species was indeed *Xenopsylla cheopis*?"

No reply.

"I see no other reason the Federal Bureau of Investigation would concern itself with these events," the old man said. "Especially the Office of Counterterrorism."

"Mr. Lee, are you some kind of insect expert? We already asked a forensic entomologist to consult on this case."

"That was very wise. And what did he have to say?"

"Are you an epidemiologist or an infectious disease specialist?"

"I am not."

"Then, Mr. Lee, I have to ask you: What is your interest in this case?"

There was a pause on the other end. "You might say I have a lifelong interest in this case."

Donovan waited, but there was nothing more. "Look," he said, "if you have information that bears directly on this case, the FBI would greatly appreciate any assistance you can give us."

"And I, for my part, am most eager to help. The question is how to best convey this information to you."

"Overnight it to us; I'll give you a billing number. Or you can fax it. If it's in electronic form, we can do it by encrypted e-mail."

"The issue is not a technical one," the old man said. "The information I have is of a rather . . . personal nature."

"If you consider it sensitive, I'll contact the U.S. Embassy and we can black-bag it."

"No, I mean *personal*—the kind of information best imparted face-to-face."

Donovan paused. "You want to meet?"

"I plan to be in New York the day after tomorrow. Would it be convenient to arrange a meeting then?"

"Give me a time and a place."

"Oh, let's do lunch," the old man said enthusiastically. "I never pass up a chance to dine in New York City."

"Lunch it is. Do you have a place in mind?" The old man spoke slowly while Donovan took down the address.

"Do you know it?"

"I know the general area."

"It's a date then. The day after next for lunch."

"One more thing, Mr. Lee. How will I know you?"

"Not to worry," he said. "Everyone on the block will know you."

CHAPTER SIX

NEW YORK HAS BEEN the most ethnically diverse city in the world since the 1600s, when barely a thousand residents already spoke fifteen different languages. Some think of the city as a tapestry, with hundreds of bright-colored threads woven tightly together in a seamless social fabric. In reality, New York is more like a mosaic, with hundreds of glittering tiles precariously held together by some invisible cement. On the Lower East Side of Manhattan lies the most enigmatic piece of this puzzle, a two-square-mile section of decaying tenements known as Chinatown.

The intersection of Mott and Canal Streets marks the financial center of Chinatown, where the jewelers and grocers of Canal Street join Mott Street's teahouse proprietors and restaurateurs. Nathan Donovan stood staring at a multistory concrete building with brightly lacquered balconies and a tiled roof that curled up at the corners like a pair of old slippers. *Pagoda,* he remembered, *that's the name for it.* He recalled the word with a sense of satisfaction, though he had few others in his vocabulary to describe the melee of otherworldly sights and sounds and smells that engulfed him. Canal Street stretched out before him, its sidewalks impossibly crowded with a sea of disembodied heads pulsing back and forth like corpuscles in an artery. Pedestrians dodged between narrow storefront merchants and sidewalk vendors hawking everything from firecrackers and baseball caps to fish balls and peanut cakes. Above them, a confetti of red and yellow banners displayed inscrutable Chinese pictographs; higher still, aging brick facades wearily supported black-iron balconies and rickety fire escapes.

One tiny shop, scarcely more than a flea-market stall, featured "genuine" Prada and Louis Vuitton. Above the open doorway a metal security shutter hovered, ready to crash down at the first hint of government interference. Donovan, a head taller than anyone on the sidewalk and dressed entirely in black, had caused more than one thriving business to close early for lunch that day.

Donovan hated to leave his Buick behind, and it was against company policy to do so; but parking in Chinatown was virtually impossible, and if his services were unexpectedly called for, he could travel on foot faster than he could retrieve his car from some subterranean parking garage. Instead, he took the subway to the Canal Street exit, where he worked his way past the fishmongers and apothecaries to the agreed-upon meeting place.

He glanced around, searching the passing throng for Western faces. He kicked himself for not insisting on a basic description; he just assumed that an elderly British gentleman would stand out in this crowd as clearly as he did. He looked to his right; just a few yards away, a man squatted by the curb, piling a heap of crumbling pork into a square of floured dough, then squeezed it in his fist until it resembled a wadded white napkin.

"It's called *wonton,*" a voice said behind him. "Have you tried it? It's very good."

Donovan turned, but no one was there—at least, no one to account for the unmistakable British inflection. He searched the faces; there, at a small table at a crowded sidewalk café, sat an elderly Chinese man looking directly into his eyes.

The old man smiled.

"You can order off the menu if you like," he said. "They have exquisite seafood here, flown in fresh daily. But I suggest the *dim sum*—sort of like your American 'brunch.' That way, you can sample a whole variety of dishes."

Donovan just stared. He understood the words, but the accent was so incongruous with the face that it was like watching an old movie with the sound out of sync. The old man motioned him over and gestured to the chair opposite.

"You could have told me," Donovan said, pulling out the chair.

"What fun would that have been? You know, if I hadn't made eye contact, I'll bet I could have kept you guessing for quite some time."

"A whole afternoon of fun," Donovan said.

"Tell me, I'm curious: What were you expecting to see? Some dusty old Londoner, I imagine?"

"Something like that, yes."

"And instead you find?"

"Some dusty old mandarin."

The old man clapped his hands in delight. "I can't tell you how relieved I am to see that you have a sense of humor. It's something that I find Westerners lack—not the bawdy, barroom type of humor, but a sense of irony—of *subtlety.* You know, I have never met a truly wise man who lacked a sense of humor."

"I know some pretty smart people who are drop-dead dull."

"I'm referring to wisdom, not simple intelligence. The failure to distinguish between knowledge and wisdom is a common Western error. To you, it's all just 'smart' or 'dumb.' In the East we know better. Smart people are sometimes the biggest fools."

Donovan extended his hand across the table. The old man's grip was more vigorous than he'd expected. "I'm Nathan Donovan. You know who I work for; better not to say it out loud."

"Another sign of wisdom," the old man said. "And by now you have surmised that my name is spelled L-i, not L-e-e. Please, call me Li."

"And your first name?"

The old man's lips reverted effortlessly to his mother tongue. The name poured out like water; it was soft and flowing, with none of the abrasive consonant sounds common to the English language. It sounded something like "Shee Dong Lee," or maybe "Gee Dung Lean." It didn't matter—Donovan was lost after the first syllable.

"Li it is," he said.

A waitress arrived, and after a quick glance at Donovan, she exchanged prolonged pleasantries with Li. There was a rapid-fire volley of words—*like a series of bursts from an automatic weapon,* Donovan thought. Then there were smiles and quick nods, and then both of them turned to Donovan.

"If you insist on ordering à la carte," Li said, "then I recommend the honey-glazed garlic shrimp or the hot-and-pepper soft-shell crabs—but really, the *dim sum* here is not to be missed."

"Something simple," Donovan said. "Maybe some chow mein."

Li blinked. "Perhaps I should explain *dim sum* a bit more. The waitress will bring a cart to our table, filled with indescribable delicacies, and you may sample whatever your heart desires. Lighter, steamed dishes come first, followed by more substantial fare—my personal favorite is shrimp dumplings wrapped in seaweed and topped with a dollop of salmon caviar. After that comes dessert; you absolutely *must* try the custard tarts or the almond pudding."

"Chow mein," Donovan said to the waitress.

The waitress lowered her eyes. "*Low faan,*" she said under her breath.

Li nodded. *"Guey low."* The two men watched until the waitress disappeared through a doorway.

"What did she say?"

"She called you a 'barbarian.'"

"And what did you say to her?"

"I quite agreed—and I added that you are a 'foreign devil.'"

"Thanks a lot," Donovan said.

"I hope you're not offended. I assure you, the word *barbarian* has lost its pejorative sense—most of it, anyway. In this case, some of it is deserved. I mean, ordering chow mein in Chinatown—really now. It isn't even Chinese, you know."

"And that makes me a barbarian?"

"The Chinese have used the term 'barbarian' for centuries to refer to all outsiders. It isn't just you; it's everyone. The fact is, the Chinese have always considered their culture to be superior to all others—an island of culture in a sea of mediocrity, you might say. It's hard to blame them; after all, the

Chinese were the first to introduce the abacus, the compass, the seismograph—even gunpowder. By the twelfth century our ships were already sailing the world; by the thirteenth we were using multistage rockets in naval warfare. We were the first to use paper, just a hundred years after Christ; Europe didn't catch on for another thousand years. We employed movable type four hundred years before Gutenberg did. And let's not forget silk—we managed to keep that our little secret for three millennia."

"You must be very proud," Donovan said.

"We are—and deservedly so, don't you think? Until quite recently, China was always centuries ahead of the West. In fact, when England sent its first ambassador to China in 1793 to request trade between our nations, the emperor replied that China 'possessed all goods in prolific abundance' and had no desire to sample barbarian merchandise. I'll bet that put the burn on some British ears, don't you think?"

"I can't figure you," Donovan said. "Are you Chinese or British?"

"I like to think of myself as a citizen of the world—Chinese by birth and ancestry, British by training and tenure. I lived in China until shortly after the war, when I moved to England and matriculated at Oxford. I've been there ever since—though I have traveled extensively."

The waitress returned now with a two-level rolling tray packed with an assortment of colorful dishes. Li selected several with gusto; when he finished, the waitress pulled a plate of rice and vegetables from the lower tray and set it unceremoniously before Donovan.

"The *low faan* needs a fork," he said.

"*Bot guey,*" she whispered, then departed again.

Donovan looked at Li.

"'White devil,'" the old man translated. "What did you expect?"

Li's face suddenly straightened. He looked over Donovan's shoulder at the street behind him. Donovan turned; from the crowded sidewalk, half a dozen young men approached and gathered slowly around their table. They were young—eighteen, maybe twenty years old. They were all Oriental, and similarly dressed—like Americans, like teenagers, but five to ten years behind the current style.

The tallest of the young men fixed his eyes on Donovan, slowly rolling a wad of gum from one side of his mouth to the other as he stared. He said something quickly in Chinese; it sounded somehow more guttural than Li's fluid tongue. Li responded calmly with just a word or two.

"What did he say?" Donovan asked.

"He says he would like to sit down."

"Tell him to pull up a chair."

Li translated Donovan's words, and the young man responded—but this time his voice sounded lower and more menacing.

"Well?"

Li hesitated. "He says he would like to sit in *your* chair."

Donovan stared back at the man without flinching. He slowly pulled back the left lapel of his blazer, reached into the inside pocket with two fingers, and pulled out his FBI credentials. He opened the leather folder, set it on the table, and slid it forward.

The young man picked up the credentials, slowly took the wad of gum from his mouth, and pressed it onto the center of the photograph on the lower left. Then he closed the folder, squeezed it tight, and tossed it back on the table.

Donovan felt his face flush. He slowly brought his left foot up to rest on his right knee. He put his right hand on his ankle, feeling for the leather ankle holster and the Glock within. He began to calculate the time necessary to draw the weapon, release the safety, chamber a round, and fire. He brought his left hand to rest beside his right and casually grasped the edge of his pant leg.

Suddenly Li jumped to his feet and began to bark at the men, scolding them in contemptuous tones and dressing them down in words that required no translation. He glared at each of them in turn until their eyes broke away and lowered to the ground; then one by one they slowly turned and swaggered back toward the street.

Li glared after them until they were a safe distance away; then he slowly took his seat again and looked at Donovan.

"They were Vietnamese," he said. "Did you notice the darker skin?

They're known as *sai low*—'little brothers' in the vernacular. The local tongs hire them as a sort of private police force."

"I thought they sounded different."

"They spoke Cantonese, not Mandarin. Cantonese is the language of southern China. Like many educated Chinese, I speak both."

"What did they want?"

"They wanted to know if you were bothering me. You must understand, your presence here is unwelcome—even an act of aggression."

"Why?"

"You are a *low faan*, you are rather large and imposing, and you are clearly a government official."

Donovan looked down at himself. "Is it that obvious?"

"When I arrived this morning, I stopped a *chong you bing* vendor and asked him, 'Have you seen an FBI agent today?' He said, 'At the corner of Mott and Canal. Be careful.' These people are used to being betrayed and abused by government officials, Mr. Donovan. To them you represent cruelty, fear, and corruption. They can spot a policeman a mile away. The 'little brothers' recognized you immediately."

"So they were just protecting you."

"Perhaps. Or perhaps they were trying to run you off so I would make easier prey. An old man in Chinatown is an easy target for the *sai low*. It's hard to tell with the Vietnamese; some are very ruthless. They have no problem with violence."

"Neither do I," Donovan said.

Li studied him. "I thought not. I had the impression that you were about to do something quite foolish—something that both of us might have regretted later."

Donovan said nothing.

Li frowned. "Mr. Donovan, you may hold your life lightly, but I want you to understand something: I am here because I have a mission to fulfill, and I do not wish to endanger that mission by associating with a man who cannot control his passions."

Donovan glared. He didn't like having his hand slapped; it made him want to slap back. But he held his tongue because the old man might have information he needed—and because somewhere inside, he knew the old man was right.

"What did you say to them?" Donovan grumbled.

"I rebuked them—something only an older man can do. I told them they were rude and lacked good breeding; that they were insulting my guest and dishonoring me. In the East, the elderly are still respected. When they are not, it is a source of shame. They thought to take advantage of me because of my age; I turned my age against them. I used my most powerful weapon, Mr. Donovan—I used *wisdom.* As a result, we are able to continue with our lunch—me with my assortment of Eastern delicacies, and you with your mockery of Chinese cuisine."

Li leaned closer now and lowered his voice. "And you, Mr. Donovan—how would *you* have dealt with the young men?"

"Given a choice? I would have beat the snot out of them."

"'Beat the snot out of them'—what a very American thing to say. You would have engaged in fisticuffs with six men?"

"I've done it before."

"Yes, I can imagine—you're quite a formidable-looking fellow. And what would have happened when the first of the young men reached for his weapon? Then you would have been forced to reach for yours. I assume you are armed; I assure you they are."

The old man reached across the table and picked up Donovan's credentials. He pulled the leather folder open, and long pink filaments stretched between the covers. He grasped the wad of gum with his fingers and began to pull it away.

"You don't have to do that," Donovan said.

The old man ignored him and continued working. He scraped the remaining traces away with his fingernails, then polished the photograph and the seal of the attorney general with his napkin.

"I said, 'You don't have to—'"

"It had to be done," Li said matter-of-factly. "I did what was necessary, and nothing more." He held out the folder to Donovan—but when he reached for it, Li held on until Donovan looked into his eyes. "That is the lesson you must learn," he said. "To do what is necessary—and nothing more."

Donovan dropped the credentials back into his pocket. "Look, Mr. Li—"

"Just Li, please."

"Li—I didn't come here for a lecture on anger management, okay? I get that from my psychiatrist."

Li raised one eyebrow. "Oh?"

"Which is none of your business. I came here because of a phone call—a phone call that interrupted a very important meeting, by the way. You said you had information for me—okay, here I am. I'd like to know why a man like you is interested in fleas."

"Oh, not just fleas," he said. "I employ a clipping service in London whose job it is to scan several of the world's major newspapers. They are instructed to alert me whenever certain words appear—like the word *flea*."

"You get a call every time somebody uses the word *flea*?"

"Only when it occurs in an unusual context—say, in the Metro section of the *New York Times*. That's a bit unusual, don't you think? Tell me something, Mr. Donovan: The fleas you discovered in TriBeCa—they were Oriental rat fleas, were they not?"

Donovan hesitated.

"Come now," Li said. "I've come all this way at my own expense—surely you can tell me that much."

"Okay—they were Oriental rat fleas."

Li nodded. "Just as I feared."

"Because of their ability to spread bubonic plague?"

"Yes. More than a hundred species of fleas are capable of transmitting the disease, but *Xenopsylla cheopis* is particularly adept at it."

"On the phone you mentioned an epidemic of plague in New York City. What did you mean by that?"

"How much do you know about bubonic plague, Mr. Donovan?"

He shrugged. "I know it's on the CDC's list of the five most dangerous pathogens. It's considered a major bioterrorism threat."

"A wise assessment."

"You think somebody tried to purposely spread plague with those fleas?"

"I believe it was some kind of failed experiment—a test of sorts."

"What makes you think so?"

"There are other words I search the world's newspapers for. Some of them are technical terms you would not be familiar with; a few of them are proper names. Are you familiar with the names 'Harbin' or 'Ping Fan'?"

Donovan shook his head.

"They are villages in Manchuria. What about the name 'Sato Matsushita'? Have you ever heard that name before?"

"Should I have?"

"I would be quite surprised if you had."

"Who is he?"

"I believe he is the one responsible for your flea infestation in TriBeCa."

"Why?"

"Because it is his life's mission to destroy the United States with an epidemic of bubonic plague."

Donovan slumped back in his chair and watched as the old man relished a bite of something that looked like a steaming dumpling with translucent skin.

"You don't seem too excited about it," Donovan said.

Li glanced up. "I can understand your alarm—but you must understand, what I'm telling you is hardly news to me."

Donovan took a moment to collect his thoughts. "Okay," he said, "let's assume for a minute that the fleas were put there on purpose. And let's assume they have something to do with bubonic plague—and those are both *big* assumptions. What makes you think this man had anything to do with it?"

Li carefully wiped his mouth and folded the napkin again before setting it beside his plate. "I understand that criminals sometimes have a modus operandi," he said. "A unique way of doing things that connects them to specific crimes—like the jewel thief who leaves a rose on the pillow beside his victim."

"You've been watching too many old movies on the BBC."

"But these identifying 'trademarks' do exist, do they not?"

"Sometimes."

"Very well, then. I believe what you have discovered in TriBeCa is the modus operandi of only one man—Sato Matsushita."

"Li, you keep saying you *believe.* Can you prove any of this?"

"No—but neither is it my imagination. What I am telling you is the result of six decades of careful research and investigation. I have been searching for Sato Matsushita for over sixty years," he said. "I need you to help me find him."

"You need *us* to help *you* find him? Li, the FBI is not a bunch of private investigators. If you wanted to find this man, why didn't you contact your own people? Why not talk to Scotland Yard or MI6?"

"Because Sato Matsushita has no interest in the British Isles. I contacted you because our interests overlap. My goal is to find Sato Matsushita, and your job is to protect the people of the United States."

"Why do *you* want to find this man?"

Li paused. "For personal reasons."

"I'm sorry, that's not good enough."

"It will have to do for now—until I know you better."

"Li, the FBI is not going to help *you* find somebody. If we determine that this Sato Matsushita represents a legitimate threat to the United States, then *we* will find him. The Bureau is not in the habit of allowing civilians to participate in official investigations."

"I think you have it backward," Li said. "*I* am allowing *you* to 'participate.' The search for Sato Matsushita will be just another case number for the Federal Bureau of Investigation—for me, it is my life's work. Besides, without my help you will never find him."

"Why not?"

"After World War II he effectively disappeared. I have been collecting information on him ever since. Much of my research cannot be duplicated; many of my interviews were conducted with sources long since dead."

"Do you have a photograph of this man?"

"None exist."

"Then how would you know him if you found him?"

"I have met him," Li said. "If I saw him again, I would know him."

"A man can change a lot in sixty years."

"I would know him, Mr. Donovan. I am probably the only man on earth capable of identifying him. That is why you must help *me* find him. If you do not allow me to 'participate,' you will not find him. And if you do not find him, millions of your people may die—beginning right here in New York."

"Look," Donovan said, "if you have information pertaining to this individual, then we'd like to see it. Give us your research—names, dates, historical records, whatever you have."

"You want my research without *me*," Li said. "I *am* the research, Mr. Donovan."

The two men sat in silence for a moment, eyeing each other. *Whatever the old man knows,* Donovan thought, *he isn't going to hand it to me in a gift-wrapped box.*

"You'd only slow us down," Donovan said.

"I assure you, I'm quite spry for my age. You'd be surprised."

"Look—if there's any chance at all that somebody wants to attack the United States, then you can understand that we need to check this out fast. Time is kind of important here."

The old man screwed up his face. "Time? Are you going to lecture a man on a sixty-year journey about the value of time? A man your age knows nothing about time, Mr. Donovan. That's the problem with you Westerners—you're so impatient. You want everything *right now.* That's what makes you Americans so superficial, like ducks that skim across a pond but barely touch its surface. Life is like a book, Mr. Donovan; it has great themes to be reflected upon and deep meanings to be rooted out. But you Americans think it's all about plot; you always want to skip ahead to the end to see how it all comes out, and so you miss all the richness; you miss all the subtleties. You have no sense of *story*; you have no—"

"*Okay,*" Donovan said, throwing up both hands in surrender. "Then let's do it your way. I need to know about this Sato Matsushita, okay? So tell me about him."

The old man smiled. "That's *much* better."

CHAPTER SEVEN

Kyoto Imperial University, Japan, April 1942

NINETEEN-YEAR-OLD SATO MATSUSHITA stared at the thick manila folder that lay on the table before him. It was closed, with its label facing away. It was easy enough to read, though; it bore the name of Sato Matsushita.

He had never seen the folder before, though he knew what it had to contain—it was his school transcript, a summary of his entire life to date in a single stack of documents. It would contain a list of all of his coursework, from the elementary level to the present day, with the results of each major examination and each teacher's summary evaluation. "Brilliant," one had told him. "A born scientist," said another—but those were words spoken to his face. He wondered what private doubts and criticisms the folder might also contain, and he longed to look for himself—but such a breach of propriety would be inexcusable, and so he sat with his hands folded, waiting for someone with enough authority to open the folder and weigh his life in the balance.

The room was as silent as a temple. He looked out the second-floor window; it was spring in Kyoto, and he could see the tissue-paper tips of the cherry blossoms in full bloom. Golden sunlight poured through the window; he longed to move his chair in front of it just to feel the warmth. But the sunlight fell in the opposite direction, and in the shadow where he sat, there was still the chill of winter in the air.

The door opened abruptly, and a solitary figure briskly entered. Sato snapped to his feet, lowering his eyes in his most officious bow, awaiting permission to breathe again. The figure before him wore the uniform of a full colonel in the Kwantung Army.

"Sit," the officer said without courtesy.

Sato returned to his seat and raised his eyes for the first time. The man was tall, with a long face and nose. A sweeping mustache covered his upper lip, turning up slightly at the ends in a nod to Western fashion. When he removed his hat, Sato saw that he was bald. The face was altogether as sterile as a surgeon's table, except for the eyes—they were wide and black, and as piercing as a sword. The colonel said nothing for a moment; he silently studied the details of Sato's face, without ever meeting his eyes.

"Do you know who I am?"

"Sir, everyone at Kyoto knows who you are," Sato said. "You are Shiro Ishii, chairman of the Department of Immunology at Tokyo Army Medical School."

Ishii grunted. "But I am an alumnus of Kyoto Imperial University."

"Yes sir. I read your dissertation: 'Research on Gram-Positive Twin Bacteria.'"

The comment earned Sato a small nod. Sato knew he had to be careful; Ishii was known as a man with an insatiable ego, and such a man expected to be fondled—but not without art.

Ishii opened the folder and began to scan the pages within. "You are only nineteen, and yet you are in your fourth year."

"Yes sir."

"You have completed coursework in bacteriology? Serology? Pathology?"

"Yes sir. And I have done graduate research in both epidemiology and preventive medicine."

"Preventive medicine," Ishii said. "Are you aware of the water filtration system I developed while serving as chief of the Water Purification Bureau?"

"A brilliant invention, sir. It single-handedly stopped the spread of cholera among our troops in China." Sato was also aware that Ishii had profited handsomely from his invention. Word around the university was that the manufacturer had paid Ishii more than fifty thousand yen in "thank-you money" for exclusive manufacturing rights.

"And do you know the source of the cholera outbreak?"

Sato said nothing. Cholera and typhus had been the bane of armies since ancient times. The source was simply tainted drinking water or poor sanitation.

"The Chinese," Ishii said decisively.

"The Chinese, sir?"

"Do you not find it curious that in a single year *six thousand* of our finest troops contracted cholera?"

Hardly our "finest troops," Sato thought. The soldiers assigned to China were widely considered the dregs of the Imperial Army. Who knew what primitive sanitation practices prevailed among those peasants?

"That does seem odd, sir."

"Our intelligence sources tell us that the Chinese purposely polluted their wells, rivers, and streams with the cholera pathogen."

It seemed unlikely. Both cholera and typhus were fragile organisms; the Chinese would almost have to dump them in the river on one side while the Japanese troops drank from the other.

"It was a deliberate attempt at biological warfare, Mr. Matsushita. And since that time, I have been responsible for the development of a top secret counterbiological program known as Unit 731."

It was hardly a secret. Every graduate student at Kyoto had heard of Unit 731, and most of the undergraduates as well. But its daily activities and the focus of its research were largely unknown; for security purposes, the facility had been established in rural Manchuria, far from prying eyes. All that was known about Unit 731 was that it was assigned some of the best and the brightest of Japan's medical researchers—and that once assigned there, they virtually disappeared.

"But—biological warfare was outlawed by the Geneva Convention of 1925," Sato said. "China was a signatory to this convention."

"And why do you suppose biological warfare was forbidden?"

Sato hesitated. "Because it is immoral."

"No—because it is *powerful.* In 1928 I undertook a two-year inspection tour of Western nations: Italy, France, Germany, Russia, the United States—and many others. I assure you, our enemies are actively engaged in biological warfare research. They pursue this knowledge in secret, hiding behind a false and worthless agreement. The Geneva Convention was intended for *us,* Mr. Matsushita—nations of honor and integrity. Just as our enemies seek to deny us access to steel and petroleum and rubber, they wish to deny us access to *knowledge.* The Geneva Convention was intended to keep us in helpless ignorance while our enemies gained a strategic advantage."

Ishii rose from his chair and stepped to the window. In the sunlight his skin looked pale and uneven, revealing a man who had spent too many hours under laboratory light. He stood with his hands folded behind his back, rocking slightly from heel to toe. It was not a posture; it was a pose—like everything Ishii seemed to do.

"Since the turn of the century, Japan has led the world in military medicine," he said. "In America's war with Spain, fourteen men died of disease for every one killed by a bullet. Just ten years later, in our struggle against Russia, we reduced the death toll from disease and infection to just 1 percent. Now we must put this knowledge to use in defense of our nation." He turned and looked at Sato. "It is my privilege to present you today with your military commission. You will enter the Kwantung Army under my command at the rank of physician second-class—first lieutenant, if you will."

Sato was incredulous. "Sir, I have a semester of school left—and then there is graduate school."

"An unnecessary luxury," Ishii said with a wave of his hand. "You have precisely the qualifications I require. You will complete your medical education in the field, under my command."

"But, sir, I—I have a younger sister. I am her only family."

Ishii shrugged indifferently. "We are all orphans, are we not? Sons and daughters of the emperor, but orphans nonetheless. I take from your sister a humble student, but I will return to her a hero in the battle for the Greater East Asia Co-Prosperity Sphere. A worthy trade, I'm sure she will agree."

Then Ishii turned and exited as abruptly as he had arrived.

THAT EVENING, SATO'S SISTER watched him, wide-eyed, as he packed a bag with his few belongings.

"Where are you going?" she asked.

Sato paused. "A school assignment."

"What kind of school assignment? Where?"

"It is a research project. Not here, not in Kyoto—in the field."

"In the war?"

"No, not in the war—but for the war." He turned and looked at her, and he saw the look of terror and abandonment in her eyes. He felt sick to his stomach. He sat down on the cot and took her by both arms.

"You have heard about the American Doolittle? You know what happened in Tokyo just last week?" News of the first assault on Japanese soil was everywhere. It involved just a handful of bombers, causing very little damage and only a few civilian casualties—but the psychological impact was enormous. The Japanese thought of their homeland as an impregnable island fortress, but just five months into the war, their sacred walls had already been breached. Some said it was an accident; some said it was an omen—but throughout the islands the fear was tangible.

"I have heard," she said.

"Japan is an island nation," Sato said. "Our enemies' homelands are far larger and richer in resources. We must find creative new ways to defend ourselves. That is my assignment. Do you understand, little one?"

She nodded. "*Wakari masu.*"

Sato returned to his packing. A minute later, he felt a hand tugging on the hem of his white *hadajuban.*

"When can I come to you?" the little girl whimpered.

Sato wheeled around. "Why must you be so selfish? Are you the only one to sacrifice? Shall I tell the emperor, 'We must lose the war, Imperial Majesty—Emiko cannot be inconvenienced'?"

The little girl began to weep. Sato longed to embrace her, but it was better for her to be strong now. "Wipe your eyes," he said. "You are a very lucky girl, you know. I have a friend at the university; his family has agreed to take you in. Do you know where they live, Emiko? At the *seashore.* Think of it—you may even have your own boat."

The little girl wiped at her eyes with the backs of her hands. "When will you come back?" she asked.

"I will come back," he said. "This will be good for both of us—you will see. '*Ame futte ji katamaru,*'" he quoted. *Ground that is rained on becomes hard; adversity builds character.*

"Promise you will come back."

Sato smiled. "Don't I always come home from school?"

Two days later, Sato found himself on a military transport bound from Tokyo to Manchuria. Out the window, he watched the endless green-and-brown patchwork of fertile farmland rolling by below. A single black line cut like a stitched wound through the center of the quilt; it was the South Manchurian Railway, stretching eleven hundred kilometers from the coastal ports into Manchuria's hinterland.

The plane began to descend now. Sato looked up ahead and let out a gasp. Coming into view was an enormous industrial complex, as large as the sprawling steel mills of Osaka. No, it was even larger—he counted sixty or seventy buildings covering five or six kilometers of land. Some of the buildings were long and narrow, like boxcars on a track; others were enormous rectangles surrounding grassy courtyards. A central building, one of the largest, was encircled by a wide moat and a towering brick wall topped with rolling razor wire.

He roused a sleeping soldier beside him. "Ping Fan?" he shouted over the drone of the engines.

The soldier peered out the window. "That's the lumber mill. See the little square buildings? *Ro* buildings, we call them. They're for the *marutas*—you know, the logs."

"There's a lumber mill here?"

The soldier shook his head, pulled his cap down over his eyes, and settled back to finish his nap.

To Sato's surprise, the transport plane did not land at Ping Fan, but continued north another hundred kilometers or so before settling down on a macadam runway in an expanse of empty pastureland.

When Sato climbed unsteadily through the exit hatch, an enlisted man twice his age awaited him with a thick white garment folded under one arm.

"Mr. Matsushita," he said with a cursory bow. "Welcome to Anda Proving Ground. You will need this. The colonel instructs you to suit up immediately."

Sato held up the heavy garment. He had never worn a complete biological suit before; the midlevel pathogens he had handled at Kyoto required nothing more than latex gloves and a mask. He looked up at the soldier, who was half-concealing a grin.

"I will require your assistance," Sato grumbled.

"*Hai.*" The soldier snapped a quick salute, then quickly and expertly guided Sato through the convoluted series of zippers, seals, and linings. Before pulling on the heavy cylindrical hood, he glared at the soldier one last time.

"That is all I require," he said. "Return to your duties." It was his first order as an officer in the Imperial Army; he was certain the story would be recounted with particular glee in the enlisted men's quarters that night.

The narrow rectangular window of his hood provided only a limited range of vision. He turned from side to side; it was like looking through a magnifying glass, with only what was immediately before him coming into focus. Across the field, he saw a group of standing figures. He started toward them, watching the ground at his feet and thinking how much it was like peering out the window of the airplane.

He thought about Emiko; he had thought about little else the last two days. To have to send her by train, to have to send her *alone* . . . They had never been apart for more than a day since Emiko was a little child. That was the benefit of a student's life—the structure, the schedule, the predictability. He had hoped to finish his graduate education, then take a position there in Kyoto—perhaps at the university. It was a simple, unambitious plan, but it would have allowed them to be together. Now here he was, across the sea and a thousand kilometers beyond. Surely the officers at Unit 731 brought wives and families with them—why not a sister? But how could he make such a request—please, can my sister come along? They would think him a fool; they would call him a *boy*—and in his heart, he knew that's what he was. He was a boy who needed an idiot corporal to help him dress.

Lost in thought, Sato bumped headlong into a standing figure and stumbled backward.

"I'm sorry," he stammered, "I didn't see—"

He focused the narrow window on the figure before him. It was a Chinese peasant, a man, perhaps twenty-five or thirty years of age. He was tied against a tall board set vertically into the ground. His hands were bound behind him, and his knees were wrapped tightly together to prevent his body from slumping. He wore some kind of primitive headgear, and a simple sheet of rusting boilerplate hung from a rope around his neck to cover his chest. Other than that, he was completely naked—and he was dead.

"It protects the vital organs from shrapnel," Colonel Ishii said with a rap on the iron plate.

Sato looked up, startled.

"When the bomb explodes, pieces of the casing fly everywhere," Ishii said. "We can hardly test the efficacy of the pathogen if the subject dies in the initial blast."

Sato looked around him; he was standing in a ring of concentric circles. In the center was a small stand surrounded by a halo of soot and debris. In each of the surrounding circles stood at least one vertical board, to which a Manchurian villager was bound, radiating outward from the center like planets around a sun. The top of the first board was marked "30 meters," the second read "40," and so on back at ten-meter intervals. There were fifteen figures all together. Most were men of various ages, but a few were women. All were dead. From one silent figure, viscera hung from a gaping incision like sausages in a butcher's window.

"Most disappointing," Ishii said. "There is no sign of infection at any distance. The pathogen is apparently being destroyed in the initial explosion. This will be your challenge, Mr. Matsushita: to perfect a means of distributing the pathogen alive and in a virulent form. I have every confidence in you." Ishii whirled and headed off across the field.

Sato wrestled off his hood and dropped to his knees.

THE STORY WAS INTERRUPTED by the trill of Donovan's cell phone. He held up one finger to the old man while he took the call.

"Sorry," he said, folding the phone shut again with a dull click.

"I detest those things," Li said. "It interrupted the flow of a perfectly good story."

"My partner found something he thinks I should see. I need to break this off—but I want to get the rest of this story. Where are you staying?"

"Right here."

"In Chinatown?"

"Why not? The food is excellent." He glanced at Donovan's uneaten lunch. "Most of it, anyway."

"Let's meet again—but let's pick a different place next time, okay?"

"Where did you have in mind?"

"I don't know," Donovan said, glancing around. "How about America?"

CHAPTER EIGHT

"Where you been?" Poldie asked. "I can't keep this guy on hold all day."

"Sorry," Donovan said. "Took me half an hour to work my way up Canal." He stepped inside, and Poldie shut the door behind him. "What's up?"

"I talked to the neighbors," Poldie said. "I found a guy who was at the party. I asked him if he had a guest list, if he knew anybody else who was there; you can guess how that went over. He didn't know anybody; he was a total stranger—but I pressed him on it, and he finally produced a couple of names—this guy was one of them."

"Where is he?"

"In the kitchen—making us some cappuccino," he said with a lift of his little finger. Poldie was the type who thought coffee tasted better from a Styrofoam cup, but he wasn't stupid. A cop knows never to refuse an offer of hospitality. He would have said, "Yes, please," if the man had offered him tea and crumpets.

The address was in the historic Cast-Iron District of SoHo. The sprawling living room was done entirely in neutral tones to highlight the undoubtedly original artwork that dotted the room. On one wall hung a triptych of glossy panels with slashes of blinding color across each. On a glass coffee table, a twisting pile of polished chrome spiraled up toward the ceiling. *Very posh,* Donovan thought, *very expensive*—the kind of place that made you want to stuff your hands in your pockets and stand in a corner of the room.

"How did it go with the English guy?" Poldie asked.

"Chinese guy."

"Huh?"

"It was L-i, not L-e-e. He's Chinese, but he lives in England. That's why he wanted to meet in Chinatown—he likes the food."

"I can't eat that stuff—eel brains and turtle heads and all. Turns my stomach."

"No, you like kielbasa—mystery meat stuffed in a pig intestine."

"Now you're talking."

"You know, the guy was eighty years old."

"No kidding—and he still eats that garbage?"

Donovan glanced down at Poldie's abundant girth. "He was skinny too. Maybe you should try a few eel brains."

"Let's not get personal. What did the old man want?"

Donovan hesitated. "It sounds crazy."

"Try me."

"He says the fleas were no accident. He claims there's a guy who wants to attack the U.S. with bubonic plague—some old Japanese scientist. Says he developed the process during World War II, but he never got to use it—so he's still trying. Li says he's been tracking this guy for sixty years."

Poldie rolled his eyes. "Too many turtle heads," he said.

"Maybe."

"C'mon, Donovan, that's the biggest tall tale I've ever heard."

"Have you heard the one about the two airliners that flew into the Twin Towers and knocked them down?"

"Let's not get paranoid here."

"Did you ever talk to a crazy person, Poldie? This guy wasn't like that."

"I've talked to a lot of liars. Maybe he's a good one; he's had eighty years to practice."

"Maybe."

"You believe this cock-and-bull story?"

"No—but he seems to believe it. I mean, why did he fly all the way over here—just to tell me a lie? I think it's worth running a background check on him."

"Good idea. Get the name of his retirement home. Find out if there's an old Japanese guy who's been stealing his slippers."

Just then an enameled doorway swung silently open, and a man appeared carrying a teakwood tray and two silver-rimmed cups. He was a slender man, immaculately dressed, with close-cropped gray hair and hollow blue eyes. He glanced from Poldie to Donovan and back again, as if estimating the two men's combined weight.

"I thought I heard the door," he said meekly.

Poldie stepped forward. "Let me take that for you. Thanks, that looks just great. Mr. Hollister, I'd like you to meet my partner—this is Special Agent Nathan Donovan."

The man blanched. "You're with the FBI?"

Donovan extended his hand. "Don't let it throw you," he said. "We're just like the NYPD, only with better-looking wives." The attempt at humor was in vain. The man had a look of ominous foreboding, as if his doctor had just summoned an associate to the examining room. "Seriously," Donovan said, "there's been an ongoing partnership between the Bureau and NYPD ever since 9/11. It's a regular thing."

Poldie looked at Donovan. "Mr. Hollister has something I thought you should see. He's been a big help here, no kidding." Poldie plopped down at one end of the sofa; he sank into the cushion like a rock in a sling. On the coffee table in front of him was a scattered pile of glossy photographs. Poldie patted the cushion beside him, and Mr. Hollister eased his way over and gently took a seat. Donovan considered taking the other end of the sofa, but he decided against it; being surrounded by the NYPD and the FBI might have been more than this guy could handle. He pulled up a chair across from them and sat down.

"These are photos Mr. Hollister took at the party," Poldie said.

"No kidding," Donovan replied. "What kind of a party was it, Mr. Hollister?"

"What kind?"

"You know—was there a specific purpose for it? Somebody's birthday? Some kind of celebration?"

"Just a social gathering, as far as I know."

"Maybe a gallery event of some kind?"

"I really wouldn't know."

"Was there a printed invitation?"

"We covered that," Poldie said. "It was just word of mouth."

Let him say it, Donovan thought. *I want to hear his voice.* He gave Poldie a quick look, then began to pick through the photos on the coffee table.

"Did you know the deceased, Mr. Hollister?"

"Well, yes, of course. He was the host, after all. We were casual acquaintances, that's all."

"Did you know anyone else at the party?"

"No."

"You're sure about that?"

"Quite sure, yes."

Donovan held up one of the photographs. "You're in this one."

The man blinked twice. "I'm sure I loaned the camera to a stranger. You know—just to get into a picture." If he had been hooked to a lie detector, the stylus would have gone off the paper and up the wall. Donovan gave him his most reassuring nod.

"This is what I wanted you to see," Poldie said. He collected half a dozen photos from the table and began to place them in front of Donovan one by one. Each was a crowded shot of partygoers huddled in the same section of the room. In each photo the faces changed, but the setting remained the same.

"So?" Donovan said.

"Now look at this one." In the final photograph, the group had divided—

some to the left, some to the right. In the center of the photo, visible for the first time, was the square display stand—and it was not empty.

On the display stand stood a tall earthenware vase of some kind. It was a good three feet tall, reddish brown in color, with faded black symbols and images around the neck. It was ancient looking; there were two ear-shaped handles, but one was broken in half, and the other looked chipped and eroded—*like iron in seawater,* Donovan thought. He looked up at Mr. Hollister with his best poker face.

"You seem to be an art collector yourself, Mr. Hollister."

"It's just a hobby."

"You have some nice pieces here. Tell me, how do you decide what to buy? I mean, a guy like me would get taken for sure."

"Well, a collector has to ask a lot of questions. You seek professional advice. You never make the decision to purchase alone."

"You must have learned quite a bit over the years about painting, and sculpture, and—what do they call those scratchy-looking prints?"

"Intaglio."

"Say—you sound like a professional yourself, Mr. Hollister."

"Not really. I guess you could say—that is—in some circles I'm considered something of an expert."

"I thought so." Donovan held up the photo of the earthen vase. "Can you identify this object, Mr. Hollister?"

"No."

Donovan glanced at Poldie, who nodded with his eyes.

"As 'something of an expert,' can you describe it for me?"

Hollister took the photo and studied it nervously. "It looks very old," he began.

"Yes, it does. How old would you say?"

"I have no way of knowing."

"It looks like it's made of clay, like a flowerpot. Would you agree?"

"It would appear so. It's hard to say from the photograph."

"But you saw it in person."

"Yes, well, I—it was an entire gallery of artwork, you know. It's hard to remember any single piece."

"Even for an expert like you?"

"Even for me."

"Mr. Hollister, do you suppose this particular piece was valuable?"

"I would think so, yes."

"More valuable than any of the other items in the gallery?"

"It's impossible to say."

"Funny thing," Donovan said. "The day after the murder, when we examined the gallery, this piece was missing. As far as we can tell, it was the only object missing. Any idea who might take it?"

"Of course not."

Donovan glanced around the room at the man's own extensive collection. "I'll bet these were all expensive," he said. "Are they insured?"

"Certainly."

"With a single company?"

"Yes."

"So if I contacted your insurance company, they could show me an inventory of your entire collection."

"I suppose so. Why?"

"We checked with the company that insured the TriBeCa gallery. They gave us an inventory. Every item on the list was accounted for—but this vase was not on the list. What do you make of that?"

"I have no idea."

"Make a guess. Give us an expert opinion."

He paused. "I can only surmise that it was a recent acquisition—something he had not yet had time to insure."

"That's a good thought. Any other ideas?"

"None at all."

"Poldie, any thoughts? Help us out here."

Poldie rubbed at his chin. "One possibility," he said. "Maybe it was stolen. You can't insure merchandise that's illegally obtained."

"Now, see here," Hollister protested. "I attended a simple social gathering and that's all. I know nothing about stolen merchandise or artwork that was illegally obtained."

Donovan smiled. "Of course you don't," he said in a tone that clearly implied, "Who are you kidding?" He paused for a beat and then said, "Well, Detective, I think we've taken enough of this gentleman's time. I don't think we'll be needing to bother Mr. Hollister again." Donovan began to rise from his chair; the look of relief on Hollister's face was evident.

"Oh—one small favor," Donovan said, picking up the photo of the earthen vase. "May I borrow this? I promise I'll return it."

CHAPTER NINE

Special Agent Elizabeth Mowery pressed a key on her laptop computer, and the photographic image on the screen changed. "Now, here's an exemplary piece," she said.

Donovan studied the image. It was a mask of a woman's face—at least, he thought it was a woman. More like a woman than a man, anyway. The face had no expression. A rich woman, he thought, one with enough money to have herself carved in stone—but not enough money to have it done right. Maybe her kid did it. Yeah, that's what it looked like, a kid's third-grade art project. The lips were just two little snakes of clay, pressed on and smoothed out flat. The eyes were just two almond-shaped holes—"I can't do eyes," the kid probably said. The eyebrows were a pair of arching curves that joined in the center, like a giant bird landing on her forehead. The hair is where the kid got bored—just a series of flat smudges parted down the center. The cone-shaped nose was broken off at the end—probably dropped it on the way home. *It was a joke,* Donovan thought, the kind of project any six-year-old could whip up with a can of Play-Doh and a half hour to kill.

Agent Mowery sighed. "Beautiful, isn't it?"

"Fabulous." Donovan nodded.

"This is from Uruk. It's Mesopotamian, more than five thousand years old."

Mommy, look what I made you. How nice, honey—what is it? It's you! Oh, thank you, I'll put this in a special place. Then the kid runs off to play in the Euphrates and the mom thinks, Geez, do I look this bad? I've got to get down to the spa. *She hides the thing in the back of a drawer somewhere, and five thousand years later it turns up as great art.*

They sat side by side in a darkened conference room at the FBI's New York headquarters at 26 Federal Plaza. Elizabeth Mowery was assigned to the Bureau's Art Theft Program, a part of the Major Theft/Transportation Crimes Unit. The laptop was connected by wireless network to the National Stolen Art File, a photographic database of stolen art and cultural artifacts from all over the world.

Mowery pressed another key. "Now, this is a fragment of a limestone stele, showing the king hunting lions."

"Swell," Donovan said. "Did you recognize the object in the photo I sent you?"

She clicked back to the index and searched for that particular image. "Here it is."

Donovan looked at the image: a tall earthen vase with ear-shaped handles—one broken, one still intact.

"That's the one," he said. "What can you tell me about it?"

"It's Babylonian, sixth century BC. A terra-cotta funerary jar from the time of Nebuchadnezzar."

Donovan stared at her blankly.

"Didn't you ever take a class in art history?" she asked.

Why would he want to do that? In college, Donovan's policy was to avoid any class that dealt with names, dates, or places—in fact, any class that required a state of complete consciousness. "Never could squeeze it into my schedule," he said.

"*Mesopotamia* means 'between the rivers,'" she began with irritating simplicity. "It describes the area between the Tigris and Euphrates

Rivers—modern-day Iraq. It's home to one of the oldest continuous cultures in the world—maybe *the* oldest. First the Sumerians lived there, then the Assyrians, then the Babylonians—that was their heyday, around the sixth century BC. Nebuchadnezzar was the most powerful king in the world at the time. He built the Hanging Gardens of Babylon, remember?"

"Sure," he lied. "What about the jar?"

"It's a funerary jar—where the ashes of a famous person or a beloved family member would be stored. It's made of terra-cotta—a reddish clay that's hard-fired in a kiln. Mesopotamia is famous for its clay; Babylon was built almost entirely out of glazed mud-brick. Have you ever seen the Ishtar Gate? It's incredible. I think I have a photograph of it here somewhere—"

"Boring an FBI agent is a federal crime," Donovan said. "Tell me about the jar."

"It was stolen from the Iraqi National Museum of Antiquities in April of 2003. Remember?"

Donovan did remember. When American troops first entered Baghdad and Iraqi forces retreated, the Iraqi people looted the museums, the hospitals, the government offices—even Saddam Hussein's palace. CNN broadcast images of smiling Iraqi citizens carting off beds, office furniture, ornate fixtures, even a porcelain bathtub. They took everything that was not tied down.

"The museum was stripped bare," Mowery said. "More than fifteen thousand artifacts were stolen and twenty thousand more damaged. It was a national tragedy—an entire cultural heritage just disappeared. And it could have been prevented, if we hadn't been so busy protecting our interests in Iraqi oil."

Donovan had a different perspective. An invading force was like the tip of a spear—pointed at the end. The first troops into Baghdad were concerned with nothing more than dodging enemy sniper fire; the second units in were responsible for securing the city's critical assets, and museums just weren't very high on the list. It wasn't just museums that were looted; it was libraries, shops, and businesses too. In virtually every part of the city, Iraqis robbed Iraqis blind. There was simply no way to protect all of Baghdad from itself. As an ex-Marine, Donovan knew that "strategic objectives" were all a military force could ever hope to achieve. The National Museum was Iraq's past, but the oil fields and refineries were its future. For Donovan's money, they got it right—but this wasn't the time to argue politics.

"How much of the stuff has been recovered?"

"Most of it," she said. "When the looting began, it was like a fever—people just grabbed anything that looked valuable. They didn't give much thought to what they were going to do with it later on. I mean, where does an average citizen sell a three-thousand-year-old relief carving? It's not like you can scalp it in a back alley somewhere—and there are international laws prohibiting the sale of stolen archaeological and ethnological artifacts. I think the Iraqi people realized that they had only robbed themselves, and the stolen pieces began to mysteriously reappear again."

"But not this one."

"No. This one and a handful of others are still out there."

"How valuable is it?"

"To the Iraqis, it's priceless. It has no real value, of course—no precious metals or inlaid gems. Its value is completely symbolic. Remember, Babylon represents Iraq's glory days—the time when they ruled the known world. It's a little like us losing the Liberty Bell."

"Any idea where it went?"

"Sure," she said. "Want to see it?"

Donovan wasn't sure he heard correctly—but before he could ask for a clarification, Mowery rose and headed for the door, beckoning for Donovan to follow. He pursued her down a series of short hallways, past intricate mazes of cubicles defined by fabric-covered panels with metal trim. Donovan didn't mind his own cubicle once he was seated at his desk; it was only when he stood and looked across the office that he felt like a drone in an endless beehive.

Mowery opened a door and entered. Donovan looked at the doorway before stepping in behind her. *How does she rate a door?* He looked around the tiny office, packed with bookshelves and paper. *At least she has no window*, Donovan thought, and he felt a little better about his own cell in the hive.

Mowery sat down at her desk, picked up a handful of messages, and began to shuffle through them. Donovan stood across from her, waiting. She looked up at him as though she were seeing him for the first time.

"Oh," she said casually, pointing to the corner. "There you go."

Donovan turned. There, in a crowded corner, sat the funerary jar with a stack of magazines and a small green plant resting on top.

"Where did you find it?" he asked.

"In a private showroom in the back of a gallery on the Upper East Side. Very posh, very respectable, very illegal. We had been watching the place for quite a while. We picked it up about two months ago."

"Two months? But the photo I gave you was taken just a week ago."

She pointed to a spot behind Donovan. He turned again; there, in the opposite corner of the office, sat another funerary jar identical to the first.

"They're fakes," she said. "We've uncovered three so far—the one in your photo makes four."

Donovan said nothing.

"Look," she said. "Not everyone looting the Iraqi museum was an amateur. There were people there who knew what they were doing. The amateurs, they grabbed the shiny things—the jewelry, the ivories, the bronzes. The professionals went for things like this—things of real value, things worth the risk of selling on the black market—things that can be *copied*."

"Copied?"

"Why sell one when you can sell half a dozen? Think about it—it's the perfect scam. You steal a priceless artifact, a remnant of King Nebuchadnezzar himself, and you let it be known that it might be available for sale—at the right price."

"What's the 'right price'?"

"Half a million, maybe more. But there's no negotiation, because it's a once-in-a-lifetime opportunity and a one-of-a-kind object—or so the buyer thinks. Before the sale, you hire a local artisan to make a few copies.

After all, what does it take—a pile of Iraqi clay and a pottery wheel? Then you sell the copies, but you keep the original.

"New York is the perfect mark for a scam like this: The city is filled with unscrupulous private gallery owners who would jump at the chance to add a piece of Babylonian history to their personal collection—illegally or not. So the gallery owner makes the purchase, and he finds some clever way to sneak it past Customs. And if he somehow later discovers that his prize acquisition is a fake, what's he going to do? He can't exactly go to the authorities, now, can he? What would he say? 'In violation of Title 18 of the U.S. Penal Code, I have knowingly purchased a stolen artifact from the Iraqi National Museum—and I want my money back.' Like I said—it's the perfect scam."

"So that's it? It's just about money?"

"Three million bucks for half a dozen clay pots? Pottery Barn should do so good."

"Where do these fakes originate? Do we know?"

"We're working on that. Probably not Iraq—too much risk of discovery there. Our best guess is Syria; a lot of things crossed the border there at the start of hostilities."

"Syria?"

"Could be. We're pretty sure the fakes are made somewhere near the original area. A Middle East return address is important in a sale like this. A genuine Babylonian relic can't exactly arrive from Tijuana, now, can it?"

Donovan thought for a minute. "The vase in my photo—what did you call it? The 'funerary jar.' It was there one day and gone the next. When we showed up to investigate the murder of the gallery owner, the jar had been taken. Any thoughts?"

"Stolen art makes good stealing," she said. "It's uninsured, and the theft can't be reported. Maybe your gallery owner did one private showing too many."

Donovan nodded. "These funerary jars—are they always empty?"

Mowery paused. "I've never been asked that before."

"Ignorance is my specialty."

"They're almost always empty," she said. "The jar itself is fired in a kiln to harden it, but the top is just a clay plug left to air-dry. It's much more fragile, so it tends to break apart over time. Somewhere along the way, the contents always seem to get dumped out. People want the jar, not a bunch of ashes."

"Would a gallery owner know that?"

"Hard to say. A lot of them have more money than experience."

Donovan started for the door, then turned back. "Oh, one more thing: Could you use these jars to transport fleas?"

"Fleas?"

"You know—little jumping things."

"I guess so. But why in the world would you want to?"

CHAPTER TEN

THE WOMAN BEHIND THE information counter was young. Her hair was short and artificially black, with bangs cut straight just above her eyes. Her lipstick was purplish-red, so dark that it made her skin look like plaster. From the left side of her nose, a tiny silver post protruded. A book was open in front of her on the counter: Chaucer's *Canterbury Tales. Probably a college student,* Donovan thought, *maybe from Columbia.* He cleared his throat, and the young woman looked up.

"I'm looking for some place called the Cuxa Cloister," he said. "Can you help me out?"

"Through that doorway and to the left," she said. "You can't miss it."

Give me a break, he thought. *This is New York—you can miss anything here. You can miss a turn and spend the next fifteen minutes honking at taxicabs. You can miss a whole neighborhood if you blink at the wrong moment. You can miss your subway stop and end up on the wrong side of town—or even worse, in Jersey.* Donovan could easily miss the Cuxa Cloister, because he had no idea what a "cloister" was—but he wasn't about to look stupid in front of some twenty-year-old nymphet.

"Isn't this whole museum called the Cloisters?" he asked.

"That's right."

"So—I'm looking for a cloister inside a cloister."

"Basically, yes."

"How many cloisters do you have here?"

"Five altogether. The Cuxa is the largest."

"The largest in what way?"

"Size."

Donovan frowned. "I'm looking for an old man," he said.

"We get a lot of them here."

That figures, he thought. "They do love their cloisters, don't they?"

"They do."

"This is a Chinese man. He's in his eighties, but he looks younger. He's about five foot three, speaks with a British accent. Have you seen him?"

"Yes."

"Where is he?"

"In the Cuxa Cloister. Through the doorway and to the left."

Donovan glared at her and started for the doorway.

"Hey," the young woman called after him.

He turned.

"A cloister is a courtyard surrounded by covered hallways on all four sides. Each hallway has an open colonnade facing the courtyard."

She winked.

"Thanks," Donovan grumbled.

She was right—he couldn't miss it. Through the doorway and to the left, Donovan found himself in a long passageway. To his left, the wall was solid stone. The roof above him sloped down from left to right, where it was supported by a series of rounded stone columns joined by semicircular arches. The archways looked out on a kind of central garden; two narrow sidewalks crossed in the center, dividing the garden into grassy quadrants dotted with coarse, untrimmed shrubberies. At the far corner, he saw an old man sitting quietly atop a low wall. Donovan waved; there was no response. *Who knows,* he thought, *the old guy could be almost blind.*

"Li," he called out as he rounded the corner. There was no answer. *Maybe he's deaf too.* "Li!" he shouted. Still no response.

Donovan was standing right beside the old man now. Li sat with his head bowed and his eyes closed with an almost deathlike stillness. Donovan reached out and shook him gently. The old man slowly opened his eyes and looked up.

"Do you have any idea what a cloister is?" Li asked.

"Of course. It's a courtyard surrounded by covered hallways on all four sides."

"A cloister is a place of solitude, a place of quiet reflection—which you just managed to shatter. This cloister was brought here stone by stone from a monastery in France. Eight hundred years ago, Benedictine monks used to sit on this very wall in a discipline of silence."

"Sorry. I thought you dozed off."

"I was meditating."

"On what?"

"On life. On death. On the universe and my small but meaningful part in it. Don't you ever meditate?"

"Never had much time for it."

"You mean you've never had much use for it."

"Life is busy, Li."

"Life is too busy to have time to think about life—ironic, isn't it? You know, Blaise Pascal once said that the distinguishing characteristic of humankind is *distraction.* We don't like what we see when we slow down long enough to look at our lives, and so we keep ourselves distracted—we fill our lives with all sorts of trivial stuff and nonsense. That way, we never have to confront our emptiness or longing; we simply don't have time for it. How very convenient."

Li studied him for a moment. "What about you, my busy young friend? Suppose you closed your eyes for a moment and shut out all the busyness and noise and distraction—suppose you looked into your *soul.* What would you find?"

"I think I'd fall asleep."

"Excellent. It requires peace to fall asleep. Is that what you'd find there, Nathan—peace?"

"Look, Li—"

"I know"—the old man sighed—"you don't have time for this."

"Next time, I pick the meeting place."

"What do you mean? This is the perfect meeting place."

"A museum?"

"Not just any museum. This is the Cloisters—the largest collection of medieval art and architecture in the Western Hemisphere. I thought it would be the perfect setting for today's discussion."

"Okay, fine. Now can we get to the subject?"

"I'm sorry. What is the subject?"

"Bubonic plague in New York City."

"Oh, no, that's not the subject at all. That's just a subplot of a much grander story I was unfolding—before I was rudely interrupted, that is."

"Then let's get back to your story. You were telling me about Sato Matsushita, remember? A scientific whiz kid at nineteen, drafted into the army in 1942, assigned to a biological warfare unit in Manchuria. He shows up, discovers that they're doing human testing."

Li frowned. "You've stripped all the flesh off my beautiful story. You've left nothing but bones."

"That's my job. What happened next?"

"Over the next three years, Sato was exposed to the full range of Unit 731's activities. There were 150 buildings eventually constructed at Ping Fan. Buildings Seven and Eight were used to house the *marutas*—the logs for their sawmill, you see. In Building Seven males were imprisoned; in Building Eight, females and infants. Rural Manchuria provided an inexhaustible supply of human beings for experimentation; about two hundred unfortunate Chinese or Koreans were kept there at any given time. They were all 'criminals,' of course—convicted of espionage, or anti-Japanese sentiment, or some other trumped-up charge. They were sent to Ping Fan on 'special consignment,' and they were never heard from again. Buildings Seven and Eight were connected by tunnel to the experimental laboratories and the crematorium. That's where they all ended up, of course—every last one of them."

Donovan shook his head. "How many people are we talking about?"

"Well, now, that's a very interesting question. During the years that Matsushita was present, about three thousand souls. That's just at Unit 731; at other laboratories around China, perhaps six thousand more. But those were just the laboratory casualties; the real horror resulted from the field experiments."

"Field experiments?"

"A laboratory can only produce theories; theories have to be tested in the real world. Beginning in 1939, Unit 731 began to conduct field experiments in selected Chinese provinces. Wells were infected with cholera. Sweet cakes laced with paratyphoid bacteria were left near fences and trees for children to find. And in the most effective experiment of all, plague-infected fleas were released from airplanes to rain down on unsuspecting villages. The epidemics that resulted spread like wildfire to neighboring areas. You know, there are areas of China where plague outbreaks still occur to this very day.

"So—how many people are we talking about? To make an accurate assessment, we must include both the laboratory deaths and the field trials; we must also include the deaths that resulted from ongoing epidemics. In total, the best estimate is a quarter of a million people."

Neither of them said anything for a minute.

"And Matsushita participated in all this?"

"Unwillingly at first. I think it troubled him greatly, the whole concept of biological warfare. He was in many ways a moral person, you see—at least at the beginning. But evil has a hardening effect; the conscience can be seared until the scar tissue that remains has no nerve endings at all. At first, it was all unthinkable; then it became a necessary evil; after that, it was just his job. I believe more evil has been committed under that rubric than any other: 'I was just doing my job.'"

"Li—how do you know all this?"

"Much of it is a matter of public record. By the end of the war, both the Allies and the Soviets were well aware of the activities of Unit 731. If you remember your history, the Soviet Union waited to declare war on Japan until the very last days of World War II. Their intention was not to assist in the fighting but to seize some of the spoils of war for themselves. The situation in Manchuria was much like that in Berlin: The Allies and the Soviets paired off around the plunder, seeking every opportunity to strengthen their position in the postwar world. That included, of course, a grab for the best Japanese scientists."

"Including Unit 731 scientists?"

"Why not? Your own space program was made possible by Nazi rocket scientists. One day they were raining V-2 rockets down on London; the next day they were respectable engineers working for NASA."

"But after the war there were trials for Nazi war criminals."

"Yes—but Europe was very different from China. The chief victims of the Holocaust were the Jews, a cohesive and homogeneous people. They pursued their assailants; they championed the cause of justice. America has a large Jewish population who felt personally aggrieved by the Nazi atrocities; the Russian people suffered greatly at the hands of the Nazis as well. There were several parties who were unwilling to allow Nazi war criminals to escape unpunished.

"But in China, neither the U.S. nor the Soviet Union were the victims. *We* were the victims—the Chinese. But postwar China was not a unified society—it was just a collection of isolated farms and villages. We had no champion; we had no one to pursue justice for us."

"So the Unit 731 scientists went unpunished?"

"The Allies had more important things to worry about. After all, the end of World War II was the beginning of the Cold War. And what was more important, raking up the muck of a war that both sides wanted to forget, or looking to the future? Besides, China was about to turn Communist—that didn't win us any sympathy from the West. And Japan, America's old enemy, was now a critical ally in the war against Communism. The Americans decided that it was not in their best interest to reopen old wounds. Instead, they struck a deal with the devil: In return for their biological warfare research, the Unit 731 scientists were granted immunity from prosecution."

"You're joking."

"The commander of Unit 731, Shiro Ishii, died of throat cancer in

1959. Some of the scientists became captains of industry; others went on to hold esteemed positions in government or academia. All died peacefully in their beds."

"And Sato Matsushita?"

Li smiled. "What do you say we stretch our legs? I want to show you something."

CHAPTER ELEVEN

HERE WE ARE," Li said. "These are known as the Nine Heroes Tapestries." In a rectangular room just off the cloister's west wall, four ancient tapestries hung from floor to ceiling. They were black and red and gold mostly, with occasional patches of bright blue interspersed throughout. Each one featured a series of royal-looking figures—*sort of like the characters on playing cards,* Donovan thought, all seated in some kind of ornate cathedral setting. The tapestries were in pieces, each one patched together from variously sized fragments to create a single panel.

Li studied them admiringly. "So tell me, what do you think of them?"

"Big," Donovan said.

"A profound observation. Anything else?"

"Old."

"They are indeed. They were made in the late 1300s for the brother of the king of France. They portray nine great heroes from the past: three pagan, three Hebrew, and three Christian. There are Hector, Alexander, and Julius Caesar; Joshua, David, and Judas Maccabaeus; Charlemagne, King Arthur, and Godfrey of Bouillon. I'm proud to say that one of them was a fellow servant of the Crown. None of them, I might add, were American."

"King Arthur was just a legend."

"Bite your tongue." Li stepped back and gestured to the set of tapestries with open arms. "Tell me, seriously—what do you think?"

Donovan looked again. Black backgrounds and bad drawing—to him they looked like the black velvet paintings of tigers and bullfighters he used to see for sale at gas stations in Queens—"$9.99 with fill-up."

"Stunning," he said.

Li grinned from ear to ear. "You see? I knew you were not the barbarian you pretend to be."

"Look, Li, I've had enough art history for one week."

"Oh, this is not about art. I brought you here for a different reason. You see, tapestries like this served a practical function in the Middle Ages. They were used to cover windows—to keep out the Black Death."

"The plague?"

"Or the Pestilence, as it was known then. In the late 1340s, plague took the lives of twenty-five million people in Europe. That was one-third of the population—a quarter of a billion people in today's terms. The Black Death was unique in all of human history. It's no exaggeration to say that it changed the path of Western civilization.

"Let's walk," he said. They exited the same way they came in and began to amble slowly down the cloister's empty halls.

"The Black Death actually began in China. Did you know that? The Tartars brought it with them from the steppes of central Asia. In 1345 they laid siege to the city of Kaffa on the Black Sea. The siege lasted two years; during that time, the plague broke out among the Tartar troops. According to eyewitnesses, thousands died every day—like arrows raining down from heaven, they said.

"The symptoms were easy to recognize: First there was a sudden fever, then chills and weakness, followed by enormous and painful swelling in the armpits or groin—those are the 'buboes' from which the disease takes its name. Next came exhaustion, lethargy, and delirium; after four days of this agony, the poor wretch would perish from respiratory failure. This manner of death produced an overall purplish color—thus the 'Black Death.'

"The Tartars had a problem on their hands—how to deal with thousands upon thousands of diseased and decomposing corpses. Then someone came up with a bright idea: They decided to catapult the bodies over the walls of Kaffa and into the city. Soon there were mountains of dead within the walls, witnesses said. In no time at all the plague broke out among the Venetian traders who inhabited the city.

"Now the Tartars had blockaded the land in front of the city, but not the sea behind it. So when the Venetians saw the plague erupting, they fled to their ships and put out to sea—and they took the plague with them. By 1348 the plague had reached Italy—first Sicily, then Genoa, and then it spread from harbor to harbor all over the Mediterranean. The seaports were the key; there are ghastly stories of plague ships sailing into port with no one on board alive. Eerie, don't you think?

"From the seaports, the plague spread like a flame across the continent. England was hit as hard as any; the population of England didn't return to its preplague level for more than four hundred years. All told, more than twenty-five million died: the rich and the poor, the nobleman and the peasant, the priest and the pagan. The plague, you see, is not a respecter of persons."

"And the Tartars started it all with their catapults," Donovan said.

"In a way, yes. They made an intentional effort to spread the disease to the enemy. It was one of the first deliberate attempts at biological warfare."

"It sure worked."

"Actually, it did not—they just thought it did. You see, the mechanism of bubonic plague was not clearly understood for another five centuries. Plague is *enzootic*. That means its natural home is in certain types of animals—voles, gerbils, even the prairie dogs of your American Southwest. That's why plague can never be eradicated; it will always survive in some rodent population, hidden away in vast underground burrows.

"Now, from time to time the plague decides to move up the zoological ladder—no one really knows why. From a gerbil host, it may jump to a wild grass rat; from the grass rat, it moves on to the urban brown rat; from the brown rat, it attacks humankind. But the intermediary in this whole process—the truly responsible party—is the *flea.* That's what the Tartars didn't understand."

"So the Venetians weren't really infected by the bodies," Donovan said. "They were infected by fleas *on* the bodies."

"Most likely, yes. As strange as it may sound, bubonic plague itself is not all that contagious. But certain kinds of fleas are especially adept at transmitting the disease. Fleas feed on blood, you see, and fleas are a common parasite found on rodents. When a flea bites a plague-infected rodent, it draws in the bacteria with the blood. The bacteria begin to multiply wildly in the flea's foregut, blocking off its stomach entirely. Now the flea, infected with plague bacteria, begins to starve. Its hunger becomes insatiable; try as it may, it cannot take in more blood—so it frantically jumps from host to host, taking the disease along with it. Every time it bites, it injects a little saliva—and twenty thousand bacteria along with it.

"When those catapulted bodies landed, the fleas fled in search of another host, and the Venetians were close at hand. That's how the disease was spread in Kaffa; that's how the bubonic form of plague is always spread."

"And that's why you picked up on the fleas in the TriBeCa story."

"Yes—because fleas can be purposely employed to spread plague. Your entomologist identified the fleas in TriBeCa as *Xenopsylla cheopis*—the Oriental rat flea. That is the species that was responsible for the carnage in medieval Europe. Sato Matsushita knows that; Unit 731 did extensive study on Oriental rat fleas—how to rear them, how to artificially infect them with plague, how to successfully introduce them into a human population. The Oriental rat flea is precisely what one would employ to create an epidemic of bubonic plague—if one were so inclined."

"And you think Sato Matsushita is so inclined."

"I'm certain of it."

Donovan stopped and waited until the old man turned to look at him. "Why, Li? Why would an eighty-year-old Japanese man want to launch an attack of bubonic plague against the United States?"

"Because he didn't have the opportunity sixty years ago."

"So? There's unfinished business in every war: bombs that don't get dropped, shots that don't get fired—"

"And shots are always fired *after* the surrender is signed. There is always unresolved anger; there is always the desire for revenge."

"Sixty years later?"

"In this case, yes."

"Come on—nobody carries a grudge that long."

"Sato Matsushita was assigned to Unit 731's plague program. The program was fraught with problems; chief among them was finding a way to distribute plague-infected fleas alive and unharmed. They tried different types of bombs, but the fleas were always destroyed by the blast."

"They should have tried a shaped charge—it would have directed the blast away from the payload."

Li paused. "You seem to know something about bombs."

"I was in the Marine Corps—in ordnance removal."

"You made bombs?"

"I made them; I took them apart."

"That must have taken a great deal of courage."

"We called it 'controlled insanity.' Some days required more control, others more insanity."

Li thought for a moment. "Which do you possess more of now?"

"Li—the story."

"Oh, yes. Well, as an expert in this area, you'll appreciate Sato's solution to the problem. He developed an entirely different type of bomb. It was a hollow ceramic shell, designed to be dropped from an airplane by parachute. The nose cone fell away and dropped to the ground; when it struck the ground, it sent back a radio signal, setting off a charge just powerful enough to shatter the ceramic shell and release the thirty thousand fleas within. With this technique, over 80 percent of the fleas survived."

"A ceramic bomb. Very clever."

"Yes—and so successful that it was decided to employ the bomb against the city of San Diego."

"You're kidding."

"The plan was code-named Operation Cherry Blossoms at Night, and it was slated for September 22, 1945. They had only one problem left to solve: how to get an airplane close enough to America's West Coast to deliver the bomb."

"How about a carrier?"

"There were none left—by 1945 the Imperial Navy had been decimated. There was only one possibility: a top secret submarine developed by the Japanese navy. It had a large cylindrical compartment on top—a kind of hangar if you will, capable of stowing a folding-wing aircraft inside. The submarine could sail undetected within striking distance of the coast, then surface and launch its airplane. It was just the ticket."

"But."

"But the Japanese navy would not risk exposing one of its few remaining vessels in a frivolous attack on a civilian population center. They knew an American invasion was imminent, and they wanted to save the submarines to launch kamikaze attacks against U.S. carriers."

"So Operation Cherry Blossoms at Night never happened."

"No. The war came to an end in August, just six weeks before the scheduled attack."

"And you think Sato Matsushita still wants to carry it out?"

"Some form of it, yes."

"Are you sure this guy is still alive?"

"No."

"But you think he is—even though he would be over eighty years old."

"*I* am over eighty years old."

Donovan paused. "It all sounds crazy to me. But the way I see it, there's no way to know whether there's anything behind this theory of yours unless we find this guy and talk to him."

"An excellent idea—and as I told you before, I have been trying to 'find this guy' for more than sixty years now. I will require your resources to help me do so."

"No offense, Li, but why should we help you when we can do it ourselves? You said yourself that all this is a matter of public record."

"That's quite true. Everything I've told you today can be gleaned from any university library—but you won't be able to learn anything more."

"Why not?"

"As the end of the war approached, the Unit 731 scientists saw the handwriting on the wall. Each one knew he had to strike some kind of bargain in order to save his own skin. Shiro Ishii, for example, went to the Allies—but how many sources of information did the Allies require? Sato Matsushita understood this, so he went to the Soviets. After the war, Matsushita disappeared behind the Iron Curtain. That is where his trail ends."

"But somehow you were able to track him."

"Yes."

"Then so can we."

"If your people attempt to locate him without my help, they will reach a dead end. Try if you wish; it's a waste of valuable time. You'll find that Sato Matsushita simply vanished from the face of the earth."

Donovan shook his head. "You underestimate the FBI."

The old man raised one eyebrow. "You underestimate me."

Li turned and continued down the corridor. Donovan watched him for a moment before following. He was an old man, but he stood perfectly erect; no slight hanging of the head, no rounding of the shoulders, no sign at all of brittleness or osteoporosis. He looked ten years younger than most Americans his age—maybe twenty. *Maybe that's what you get from eating eel brains and turtle heads*, Donovan thought. There was an energy about the old man, a self-assurance, a sort of lightness in his step—almost a swagger. Donovan wondered if he would have the same quality when he was eighty; he wondered if he had the quality now.

And his mind—no doubt about it, the old man was as sharp as a razor. But this story of his, it was so—*unbelievable.* That was the problem: The story was incredible, but the man himself almost compelled belief. Could it be true? Could there be something to this bizarre story of his? And did this eighty-year-old man have knowledge that the Bureau could never attain on its own? Donovan looked at him again—*sixty years is a long time to collect newspaper clippings . . .*

Maybe the old guy's right, Donovan thought. *Maybe I do underestimate him.*

The old man had reached the corner now; Donovan started after him. "Li," he called, "I want to show you something." He reached into his blazer pocket and removed a glossy four-by-six photo. "Can you identify this object?"

Li studied the photo. "It looks like an urn of some sort."

"That's right—it's called a funerary jar."

"It's very old—Mesopotamian, if I'm not mistaken. The relief work around the neck—the images of the lion, the bull, and the ram—they're all symbols of Near Eastern royalty. It might be Assyrian—perhaps Persian."

"You really know your art history."

"Well, it's more artifact than art. At my age, one takes an interest in older things—since I'm rapidly becoming an artifact myself. What is the significance of this object?"

"It's a copy of an item stolen from the Iraqi National Museum of Antiquities. It turned up in that gallery in TriBeCa; then it disappeared again. The fleas in the gallery—they spread out from a definite point, from the exact spot where this was on display. Li—there's a good chance the fleas were transported in this funerary jar."

Li examined the photo more closely.

"It's made of clay," Donovan said.

"Yes." Li nodded. "One might call it *ceramic.*"

CHAPTER TWELVE

Damascus, Syria, present day

SATO MATSUSHITA STROLLED QUIETLY down the long, high corridor of *Souk al Hamidiyeh*, the ancient marketplace that stretched five hundred meters from west to east across the old city of Damascus. For five thousand years Damascus has been a crossroads of civilization, and the old bazaar still reflected it. Arabs, Kurds, Armenians, and Turks mingled together with Western tourists. Styles of dress ranged from Europeans in haute couture to bearded Bedouins in flowing robes and traditional checkered headgear. Half a dozen languages could be heard, but Arabic rose above them all; it was an Arab market after all, and in the *souk* the Arab tongue is still the language of commerce.

The corridor's walls were a beehive of tiny shops, booths, and stalls, offering wares of every imaginable kind: richly colored carpets woven from goat or camel hair, woven baskets and raffia, embroidered silk brocades, copper pots engraved with intricate arabesques, and wooden boxes delicately inlaid with exotic woods. Shoppers and browsers crowded around the stalls, while eager tradesmen wandered the aisles, holding their wares aloft and recounting their virtues. European tourists haggled clumsily with seasoned vendors, shaming them into settling for only twice what each item was worth. Hard-won treasures traded hands with a flourish, while euros and dollars and pounds flowed invisibly under tables and behind backs.

The bazaar was centuries old. It had been built and rebuilt many times; this incarnation dated from the thirteenth century, built atop the ruins of an old Roman fortress. That's what Sato liked about the *souk*; that's what he liked about the city itself. Damascus is one of the oldest continuously inhabited cities on earth, and one of the most frequently conquered. First the Egyptians, then the Israelites, then Assyrians, Greeks, Romans, Turks, Ottomans, and French—and each one built their palaces and markets atop the civilization that came before it, like a deck of shuffled cards. That's what the old man liked; all of Damascus was built on the ruins of something else. It seemed somehow appropriate, and it served as a reminder of what could be.

Sato passed directly down the center of the aisle, looking neither to the right nor to the left. He wasn't there to shop. He took this path almost every afternoon, using the jostling crowds and the cacophony of voices to help him transition from the solitude and silence of his research at the Scientific Studies and Research Center. For Sato it was a kind of cleansing ritual, a sort of bathhouse for the soul. The noisy, crowded bazaar was the soaping-up; the rinsing-off came at the eastern end, where the bustling market gave way to the magnificent Umayyad Mosque.

The sprawling, marble-covered courtyard was the atmospheric opposite of the *souk*. It was peaceful and serene, surrounded by stone colonnades and intricate mosaics. In the center of the courtyard was the ablutions fountain, marking the midpoint between Istanbul and Mecca, the meeting point between East and West. Like most of the buildings of Damascus, the mosque was only the most recent occupant of its location. Its courtyard had been a place of reflection for three thousand years: first by the Aramaeans, then the Romans, then the Christians, and finally the Muslims just a scant millennium ago. Sato walked slowly and silently across the courtyard, breathing the ancient air and remembering the past. That's what Damascus allowed him to do—*remember*. Moscow did not; Baghdad did not. Modern cities were so forward-looking, always in a hurry to forget the past; but Damascus *was* the past, a place where everyone lived among the ruins.

He exited the courtyard now, cleansed and refreshed, and circled behind the mosque to one of the city's better coffeehouses, the Alsham Alkadima. The café was crowded but relatively quiet. Small groups of men huddled around tables, sipping tea and coffee and drawing on old pipes, playing backgammon and dominoes and nodding their heads gravely about politics and business and war.

Sato took a table where he could be seen from the door. A waiter approached and made a slight bow.

"*Ahweh,*" Sato said. "For two."

"How do you take it?"

"*Murrah,*" Sato said. "I prefer my coffee bitter. *Mazbuta* for my friend."

"Cardamom? Orange blossom water?"

Sato shook his head, and the waiter left.

A few moments later, an Arab approached Sato's table. He looked half Sato's age, though his skin was rough and weathered and his precise age was difficult to determine. He was dressed simply, in a khaki jacket with a coarse wool sweater underneath. A thick mustache jutted forward from his upper lip, streaked with threads of gray. He had coarse black hair peppered at the temples. On his left cheek was a horizontal scar; it started as a tiny slit just below his eye and widened as it went back like a gash on a melon. It slashed back around the side of his face, cutting a barren swath through the middle of his sideburn. The scar stopped just before his left ear, which was missing except for a curling twist of flesh.

His name was Raheem Khalid. He was Syrian by birth and had been a soldier since boyhood. Khalid had crossed many borders since his youth to add his weight wherever the Arab balance of power was threatened in the Middle East. He fought against the Israelis in southern Lebanon; he joined guerrilla raids against the West Bank and the Golan Heights; he fought against the Kurds in northern Iraq. In 1991 he joined with the Iraqis in their battle against the American-led coalition. He lost a brother and his left ear to an American M16, and in the process gained a lifelong foe.

Khalid nodded a greeting. "Dedushka," he said simply—the Russian word for "grandfather."

Sato looked up. "I've ordered us a Turkish coffee."

Khalid grunted and took a seat. "*Turkish* coffee—the name is insulting. Syrian traders brought coffee to Istanbul four hundred years ago—now they send it back to us with their name on it. They are worse than the Americans."

"No one is worse than the Americans."

The man lowered his eyes. "No."

The waiter returned now with a steaming *Rakweh.* He placed a demitasse cup before each of them, but no spoon. He poured slowly into each cup to evenly distribute the thick sediment. The two men waited in silence until he left.

"This place is too crowded," Khalid said. "Too many ears."

"Too many is enough," Sato said. "If you listen carefully, Khalid, you will hear all sorts of intrigue in here. Our voices will not stand out."

"I don't like it."

"That's what coffee is for, is it not—striking deals and hatching plots? That's why the Turks liked your coffee; that's why the custom caught on. Now—tell me about New York. I have already been briefed; I know that your test has failed."

"It appears that you were right," Khalid said.

"Tell me."

"We found buyers for four of the jars," he said. "All made it past U.S. Customs successfully—all were delivered to their respective buyers. We made an enormous profit—almost two million dollars U.S."

Sato frowned. "This is not about money."

"It takes money to accomplish so great a task, Dedushka."

"It also takes a successful delivery system. Tell me about the test."

"We sent the first three jars empty—just to test the waters, just to make sure they would make it across the border. We sent the fourth jar with the—" He glanced around for listening ears. "We sent the fourth jar full."

"And?"

"It, too, arrived safely."

"Then the test was a success—yes?"

Khalid hung his head. "We sent an operative to retrieve it. He was to steal back the jar so we could verify that the contents had survived the trip. When our operative got there, he found that the jar had been somehow damaged, and the contents had been allowed to escape."

"So he silenced the buyer with a gunshot to the head and left thousands of fleas behind," Sato said, glaring at Khalid. "Yes, I know—I read all about it in the *New York Times.*"

"He exterminated the fleas before he left," Khalid grumbled. "The Americans should never have found them."

"The Americans *did* find them."

"No one will make the connection to you," Khalid said.

"Do I have your assurance of that? Just as I had your assurance that this ridiculous plan of yours would work?"

"It was not my plan. It isn't my money, so I don't make the decisions."

"No, your superiors do—but they are not *my* superiors, Khalid. They have made an inexcusable error in judgment; they have risked exposure of my entire strategy. So I ask you, in what sense are they superior? No. From now on, we will do it my way—just as I have said from the beginning."

"It's their money," Khalid said. "They want to do it their way."

"Perhaps we'll find them more humble and teachable after this embarrassing failure," Sato replied. "Tell them I will make no further concessions; tell them I will allow no more outside interference."

"They won't like it."

"Remind them what I offer in trade: a true weapon of mass destruction with an efficient and utterly untraceable delivery system. It will claim a minimum of a million lives—perhaps twice that many. The economic and social impact on America will be irreparable. I offer your superiors what they have always sought—what they attempt to gain for themselves with their silly little bombs and devices. I have spent sixty years perfecting this system, Khalid—should I now let them alter my plan with their foolish and ignorant suggestions? No more; never again. Tell them I offer them my weapon, my way—or no weapon at all."

"I will tell them," Khalid said.

"Tell them also why this foolish plan of theirs failed. A flea is a fragile animal. It must feed on blood—warm blood—and it requires oxygen and specific environmental conditions to survive. To pack thousands into a tiny container and then expect them to survive in uncertain conditions for an extended period of time is sheer folly. It did not work sixty years ago, and it will not work today. I must accompany the fleas, Khalid. I must feed them and nurture them until the moment before they are employed."

"They did not want to risk you," Khalid said. "They thought it safer to attempt to send the fleas alone."

Sato let out a snort. "Do they not strap bombs on their zealots and send them into Jerusalem cafés? If they want a hundred dead, do they not sacrifice one? I offer them ten thousand times a hundred—are they not willing to risk one to get it? You and I know the real reason for their fear, Khalid. They are more than willing to risk me; it is their own cowardly necks they are unwilling to risk. If I am captured, I could expose them all. Tell them that is the chance they must take. Tell them that without great risk, there is no great glory."

"I will tell them as you say."

"Good. They will listen to you."

"You overestimate me, Dedushka. I am just a soldier."

"You are more than that, Khalid. We have been associates now for more than a decade—since I first came to Iraq from the Soviet Union, when you were just a young lieutenant in the Republican Guard. We almost persuaded them then, didn't we? We almost had our chance. But it was not to be—not then, not there. When the Iraqi army was destroyed, when the situation there became unstable, it was you who invited me here. You arranged my sponsorship, my housing, my laboratory at the Scientific Studies and Research Center. It was you who saw me safely across the border into Syria, along with the seeds of my research. If I have neglected to say so, I want you to know that I am grateful. I consider you almost a friend."

Sato finished his coffee and turned the cup upside down on the saucer. "Now we must send for a fortune-teller. That is the Turkish custom: When the cup cools, the fortune-teller will read the grounds that remain in the cup. She will tell us our futures."

"I don't need a Turk to tell me my future—I will make my own future."

"Yes," Sato said. "We will make the future." He leaned forward now and spoke in a somber tone. "Listen to me, Khalid—I want to remind you of something. This strategy, this system of mine—you know that it is more than a weapon; it is my life's mission. I have spent sixty years in pursuit of this single goal. Please understand that I accept the assistance of your superiors only because they serve my mission. Your superiors, your country, even you, Khalid—everything is secondary to my mission."

"And I serve you because your mission and my mission are the same."

Sato nodded. "A common purpose. Is that not the source of all true friendship?"

CHAPTER THIRTEEN

Brookhaven, New York

Danny Cardello paced the floor of his office, staring out the big glass window at the chaos on the factory floor. His young fireworks company, Pyrotech, had doubled in size in only three years—then doubled again in just the last three months. His headaches had doubled, too, and the Italian sausage he'd wolfed down for lunch was burning a hole in his gut like a Roman candle. He looked again. There were bodies everywhere, people he didn't even know, scurrying across the factory floor like so many ants. *Some family business,* he thought. *Growth is good, but this is like cancer.*

Danny's company was just a young upstart in the competitive, family-dominated fireworks display industry, but less than a year ago, *Pyrotech* became an industry buzzword when Danny managed to accomplish a startling coup de grâce. In a spectacular demonstration of overpromising and underbidding, he had managed to wrest away New York City's Fourth of July Fireworks Spectacular from the legendary Souza family, which had held the concession for more than twenty consecutive years. Danny found it surprisingly easy; all he needed to do was grossly exaggerate the capabilities of his company and promise magnificent, never-before-seen effects—never-before-seen because they didn't yet exist.

And there was one more little hitch: To pull off the New York display as promised, Pyrotech would have to take a loss. The event would be a major financial hit, almost enough to sink the company—but it could be worth it for the promotional value alone. Live from New York, broadcast all over America on NBC, the Fourth of July Fireworks Spectacular—brought to you by Pyrotech, the little company that could. Danny knew that all the premier fireworks displays in the U.S. were dominated by a handful of "fireworks families"—the Souzas in California, the Gruccis in New York, the Zambellis in Pittsburgh. You don't make money in the fireworks business by selling bottle rockets to kids. You go for the big events—New York, Boston, Philadelphia, San Francisco. Danny had managed to snatch the goose while the giant was sleeping; now all he had to do was hold on until one event led to another, and then came the golden egg. Then he could charge what he was worth.

But first he needed to deliver the goods in New York. It wasn't enough just to land the contract—that was just a business deal. He had to beat Souza soundly—he had to put on a show no one had ever seen before. If he didn't—he could just see the headlines: "Pyrotech Bombs in the Big Apple"; "Pyrotech Fizzles—City Regrets Change, Begs Souza to Return"; "Pyrotech Announces Plan to Sell Variety Packs in Wal-Mart Parking Lots." He felt the ball of fire burning in his gut again. He opened a desk drawer and took out a bottle of Mylanta.

He mentally reviewed the terms of the agreement: forty thousand shells—did he promise *forty*? That was five more than Souza ever did. He promised four separate firing locations—Souza offered only three: on the East River, just south of the Brooklyn Bridge, and across from Liberty Island. Danny threw in the Hudson River too. Now people would be able to watch the fireworks from all five of New York's boroughs—even the Bronx. Twelve hundred shells going off every minute, all perfectly synchronized with the music—it would take thirteen miles of wire to pull it off, eight separate barges, and seventy thousand feet of steel and plastic mortar pipe.

But the logistics he could handle; the logistics were just business too. His biggest headache was the finale. To land the contract, he had to promise the biggest, baddest slam-bang finale in the history of fireworks, one that would make old people coo like pigeons and babies pop out their pacifiers. *What is it with finales?* he wondered. You could detonate a nuclear warhead and people would still ask, "When's the finale?" *But that's the way it works,* Danny thought. In fireworks, you live or die by your finale—and Danny's Fourth of July Fireworks Spectacular was currently on life support, because Danny had no finale.

He had spent the last eight months traveling the world in search of something new, something never before seen. He hit all the major pyrotechnics markets—Italy, Portugal, China, Japan—but all he found was more of the same. There were chrysanthemums, peonies, starbursts, and showers; yellow ribbons for the troops and smiley faces for the kids. Just the same old, same old—maybe a little louder or brighter, but certainly nothing that would impress the been-there-done-that citizens of New York. Danny looked out the window again. Maybe he could just invite everyone to Brookhaven, then torch the whole warehouse at once—maybe that would do it.

"Danny, you have a call on line one."

"No calls," Danny said.

"It's from overseas."

"Where overseas?"

A pause. "Syria."

Syria? Who did he know in Syria? "Take a number."

Another pause. "He's very persistent. He says you'll want to talk to him."

"Who is it?"

"How should I know?"

"What does he want?"

"You want to have this whole conversation through me, or you want to take the phone call?"

"You're fired," Danny said.

"Then you can make your own dinner tonight. He's on line one."

Danny lifted the receiver. "Yeah, Danny Cardello."

"Mr. Cardello, thank you for taking my call."

It was some old guy; he sounded Japanese. "Look, you caught me at a bad time here," Danny said.

"I understand. With the New York City display just weeks away, I imagine things are very busy there—*very* busy."

"I didn't catch your name, Mr.—"

"Mr. Ogatsu. Is my family name familiar to you?"

Was he kidding? The Ogatsus were the oldest fireworks family on the planet. The Souzas had been in the business for only a century, the Gruccis a little longer; the Ogatsus of Japan got their business license in the seventeenth century. Their modern-day company, Marutamaya, was known all over the world.

"My wi—my secretary said this call was from Syria."

"Yes, that's right."

"Marutamaya is based in Tokyo."

"And also Ibaraki and Yamanashi. We have thirty-two factories all together. Have you visited us?"

"Sure, just a few months ago. Have we met?"

"No, sorry to say. The Ogatsu family has dispersed over the years. I now reside in Damascus. Though many of our family now live abroad, some of us still maintain an interest in the family business. My particular interest is in research and development."

"Good for you." Danny didn't have time to trade fireworks stories with some old coot who made his own sparklers at the retirement home.

"It's unfortunate," the man said. "Because I no longer live in Japan, buyers don't bother to visit me. They assume that one man alone could offer nothing that an entire factory could not. But I believe the creative process is always individual in nature. Great discoveries are made by gifted individuals, not by committees. Don't you agree?"

"Uh-huh." Danny was shuffling through paperwork, waiting for an opportune moment to end the call.

"Tell me, please: Is your program for the New York display complete yet?"

"What? Oh, sure, months ago."

"That's too bad. I had something quite unusual to show you—something that might have made a significant contribution to your presentation."

Danny stopped what he was doing. "What are we talking about here?"

"Are you at a computer?"

"Sure. Just a minute." He swept a pile of papers onto the floor.

"I'm going to give you an Internet address. You'll find a link to a compressed video file there. The video was taken in the Syrian Desert not far from here. Do you have a moment to view it? It will only take a minute of your time. I'll hold on while you look."

Danny entered the URL and waited. The screen that appeared was practically empty. *I hope his pyrotechnics are better than his Web design*, he thought. There was a single link in the center of the page; Danny clicked it, and a smaller window appeared. He enlarged it to fill the screen.

The screen was completely black. Danny was about to say, "It's not working," when a flash of light at the bottom of the screen revealed a single steel mortar against a desert backdrop. The flash was followed by a thundering boom, then darkness again—but a few seconds later the screen erupted in light.

In the center was a slow-rising column of glittering silver and gold, so bright and so full that it looked solid to the touch. As the column reached its peak, it suddenly exploded, sending tendrils of brilliant green sprawling across the sky, dripping like watercolors as they went. From the tendrils, curling leaves of yellow began to appear, beginning at the center and spreading out toward the tips. There were hundreds of them, and they were crisp and clearly defined, not just the usual quick streaks of light that disappeared almost before they could be seen.

An instant later, leaves of the deepest blue began to appear, and Danny's jaw dropped open. He understood the chemistry of fireworks: Strontium gives you red; barium, green; sodium, yellow—but nothing gives you blue. A true blue was the holy grail of pyrotechnic chemists all over the world—and yet here it was, the deepest blue he had ever seen. The blue leaves gave the image depth, making it appear almost three-dimensional.

Now the tips of the tendrils exploded into dazzling clusters of pink and red, and the figure was complete. It was a cherry tree—the image was clear and sharp and unmistakable. It was nothing like other patterned shapes, the primitive hearts and stars and circles common to fireworks displays all over the world. There was no guesswork here—no one would ever say, "Was that a bow tie? I thought it was a dog bone."

And it *lasted*—that was the most remarkable effect of all. The chemical pellets that fill an aerial shell are consumed in less than a second; the first sequence of an effect disappears long before the last ever takes place. But *this*—it was as though the image were painted on the sky. The column, the tendrils, the leaves, the blossoms—they were all still there, just sitting and glittering like jewels in the desert sky.

An instant later, the entire image disappeared all at once.

Danny just blinked at the screen. The kid in him wanted to shout and cheer; the fireworks expert wanted to sing praises; but it was the businessman who spoke into the phone. "Very interesting," he said.

"Have you ever seen anything like it?"

"There was one in Lisbon," he started to say, but he caught himself. What was he doing? This man knew things about fireworks that Danny had only dreamed of. All he had to do was offend the man, all Mr. Ogatsu had to do was hang up his telephone, and Danny would lose this masterpiece forever. "Never," he said. "Mr. Ogatsu, I have been to fireworks demonstrations all over the world in the last few months, and I guarantee you there is nothing like this anywhere."

"I'm so glad you like it."

"I have to ask you something. Has this video been altered in any way?"

There was a pause on the other end. "You insult me."

"No—wait. I'm not suggesting that you did anything, Mr. Ogatsu; it's just that—well, put yourself in my place. This is so different, I just have to know for sure."

"I assure you, the video was not edited or retouched in any way. The effect you saw was exactly as it appears."

"How did you get the blue? I've never seen a color like that before."

"You understand, of course, that I cannot reveal family secrets. I will tell you that I have personally made discoveries I do not even share with the rest of the Ogatsu family."

Danny could barely contain himself.

"I was hoping you could make use of this effect in your New York display—but as you said, your program was completed months ago."

"No! I mean, it was—except for the finale. And the finale is everything, you know. I've been looking for something really different, something that would really cap off the show. Mr. Ogatsu, this is exactly what I've been looking for."

"You can still include it, then?"

"Absolutely."

"I'm so glad. I'm very proud of it. I was hoping it could be introduced at some larger event, and not just at closing time at some minor amusement park."

"Well, the Fourth of July in New York is the biggest event of all. I'd be proud to include your effect in my show." He took a breath and held it. "Let's talk about price."

"I was thinking about a thousand dollars per shell. That seems reasonable."

Danny wanted to do handsprings. A thousand per shell for his finale? It wasn't possible—he couldn't get off that easy. "That's more than fair," he said. "In fact, I think you're undercharging. Let's make it fifteen hundred a piece."

"Very well, if you insist. How many shells will you require?"

"Eight—one for each of the barges."

"Yes—I think that will cover things quite nicely."

"And I'd like to talk to you about an exclusive arrangement."

"Exclusive?"

"Yes—I'm willing to pay a premium if you'll agree not to sell this shell to anyone else until after the New York show."

"I'm aware of no other major displays before your own."

"Still, just to make sure. You understand—this is something completely different, and I don't want anyone else to steal our thunder."

"I agree—this is something that should be reserved for New York. Very well, it will be an exclusive arrangement."

"Done," Danny said with finality, hoping to block any possible escape.

The old man paused. "There are a couple of conditions I would like to mention," he said. "They must be considered a part of our agreement, and they are not open to negotiation."

Danny's heart sank a little. "Such as?"

"First, I must accompany the shells. I will not ship them; I will bring them to you in person. You can arrange the technical details—the placement of the mortars, the wiring, and so on—I will send you whatever specifications you require. The shells themselves will not arrive until one day before the event."

"That's acceptable."

"Please understand, the workings of this shell are a closely guarded secret. I do not wish to insult you, but you and I both know that if I allow my shell to travel unaccompanied, it will be a very brief time before my effect finds its way into another family's recipe book."

"I understand your concern," Danny said. "What else?"

"Second, I must accompany my shells to your barges, and I must personally oversee their loading and launch."

"Ignition is all done by computer."

"Of course. I simply wish to make sure that each of the eight shells is successfully launched. I must be certain that none remain behind; a failed shell can still reveal its secrets."

"That makes sense. Agreed."

"Finally, no one is to touch the shells but me. No one is to examine them. No one is to assist me in any way unless I specifically request his help. I hope I do not appear overly cautious, Mr. Cardello; as you know, in this business a secret has a very short life span. I simply wish to preserve my secret as long as possible."

"I'd feel the same way. Is that everything?"

"Those are my terms."

"Great! I'll get a contract together before the day is over and have it on your desk the day after tomorrow."

"There is no hurry. I consider our verbal agreement binding."

"One more question, Mr. Ogatsu. I was amazed at the way your effect extinguished all at the same time—almost like a sign switching off."

"Thank you. That was not an easy task."

"I want to use your shells as my grand finale—fire them off from all eight barges at the same time. My question is: Can they *all* be synchronized? Can they all be timed so that everything goes black at once?"

"I promise," the old man said. "Everything will go black at once."

Sato waited a moment before dialing again.

"Khalid," he said. "Have you spoken yet with your superiors? Ah, good. When you do, please inform them that I have already reinstated my original plan. I have made the necessary contact in New York, and everything has been arranged. Yes, I know, Khalid—please forgive my apparent haste. Our friends will understand that if we allow this opportunity to pass, we must wait another full year—and they do not wish that delay any more than I do.

"Please inform your superiors that I will require the form of transport specified in my original plan—I'm certain they have the resources to arrange this on short notice. I will wish to set up a temporary lab in the lower cargo hold. It will require adequate ventilation and an air-filtration system—I will send them all of the specifications they need.

"And, Khalid—remind them to follow my instructions to the letter. We do not want a ghost ship arriving in New York Harbor."

CHAPTER FOURTEEN

THE CLOCK ON THE wall was the old-fashioned mechanical kind, the kind with a ticking second hand. It would have been bearable in a noisy cubicle, or hanging in some busy hallway. But in an office like this—four walls, door closed, quiet as a crypt—it was maddening. Donovan sat across from Reuben Mayer, waiting in concealed agony while the old man studied his weekly report. Mayer sat hunched over the folder, utterly motionless except for an almost imperceptible swinging of his head from side to side. From the corner of his eye, Donovan watched the clock's second hand advance. It made a hollow clicking sound that echoed off the walls, and the pitch seemed to change slightly from tick to tick—that particularly annoyed him. The second hand seemed to hesitate before jumping on to the next black hash mark—it seemed like two or three seconds at least. *What kind of a clock is that? What's wrong with a nice electric clock with a sweeping second hand—or better yet, an LCD with no hands at all?* Donovan wondered if it really wasn't a clock at all. Maybe it was some kind of voodoo metronome, casting a spell over Reuben Mayer, making sure that he could never move faster than a lava flow—

"You think he's nuts?"

"I'm sorry?"

"The old man—this Li character—do you think he's nuts?"

"No sir, I don't. Eccentric maybe, but not crazy."

Mayer glanced up. "'Eccentric' can get you put in a home. Is he senile?"

"I don't think so. He's highly educated—he's got a PhD in biochemistry."

"I'm talking about his rational processes. Any gaps in memory? Signs of confusion? Loss of concentration?"

"He's as lucid as you are, sir."

One slow blink from Mayer. "Maybe it's just an old man's fantasy," he said. "A story he tells to get some attention. A tall tale, a fish story, the one that got away."

"He flew all the way from London to tell this story."

"Why not? He meets with the FBI; he consults with the CIA. Something to tell his friends back home."

"It's possible—but I don't think so."

"Why?"

"I ran a background check on him after our first meeting. His full name is *Zhong Ren Li*—I'm not sure how to pronounce it. He immigrated to Great Britain after the war and enrolled at Oxford. When he finished his degree, he moved to Linz, Austria, and went to work for a man named Simon Wiesenthal. Wiesenthal was a survivor of the Mauthausen concentration camp. When the war ended, Wiesenthal started collecting evidence against Nazi war criminals. He opened the Jewish Documentation Center in Linz, staffed by thirty volunteers—apparently Li was one of them. Remember Adolf Eichmann?"

Mayer slowly cocked his head to one side. Donovan winced; he had just asked a Jew if he remembered Adolf Eichmann.

"I believe so, yes," Mayer replied coolly.

"Well, Eichmann was hiding in Buenos Aires under the name of Ricardo Klement when Wiesenthal's group tracked him down. It turns out Li played a big part in that capture."

"A Nazi hunter," Mayer said. "I'm impressed."

"That's my point, sir. Li's not the sort of man who needs to make up stories—he's got plenty of his own. And his record shows that he has the knowledge and experience to track a man over time and across continents. Whether Li's story turns out to be true or not, Li himself is a credible source."

Mayer studied the report again. "Tell me about this plague-maker fellow. What's his name—Santo?"

"Sato, sir. It's Japanese."

"I saw it here somewhere." Mayer slowly spread the pages of the report.

"It's Sato, sir."

"Here it is. *Sato.*"

Donovan gripped the arms of his chair.

"It says here that at the end of the war, this Sato went over to the Russians—then all trace of him disappeared."

"According to Li, yes."

"According to Li. Have you checked that out?"

"Yes, sir. There was definitely a Unit 731 in Manchuria, just as Li said, and it was as bad as anything the Nazis handed out—human testing, medical experiments, the whole nine yards. It's a matter of historical record."

"And what was Sato's role in all this?"

"That's hard to say. In the documents seized after the war, there's only one mention of Sato Matsushita—in a roster of scientists employed at Unit 731. But there are no records of his research or activities while he was there."

"So as far as we know, Sato Matsushita is just a name," Mayer said. "Everything else your boy has told us could be legend. He could be making it all up."

"It's possible. I don't think so."

"Why?"

"Because Li has spent the last sixty years searching for this man."

"According to Li."

Donovan didn't reply.

"And after Sato went over to the Soviets, what happened then?"

"Like Li said—he disappeared from the face of the earth."

"But Li has further information."

"He says he does, yes."

"Information that only he possesses."

"Yes."

Mayer paused. "That makes him a very important fellow, doesn't it?"

Donovan felt his face flush. He knew what Mayer was saying—that Li might very well be nothing but a lonely old man seeking attention, a one-time Nazi hunter reliving the glories of days gone by. It could all be a fantasy—a story—a *lie.* The only reason Donovan had to believe Li was the power of the old man's personality—but Mayer had never met Li, and with nothing to consider but the pathetic handful of facts in Donovan's report, Mayer had no reason to believe at all. Donovan suddenly felt stupid; no, it was worse than that—he felt *naive.* But for a reason he couldn't fully understand, he did believe Li—and the fact that Mayer did not made him angry.

"So you think the old man is nuts?"

"I think this whole thing is nuts," Mayer said. "I think this Li is a bored old man jerking your chain. I think this Sato character might be just a figment of his imagination—some old bogeyman left over from the war. I think his trail disappeared because *he* disappeared a long time ago."

"You want me to tell the old man to pack up and go home?"

"Yes—but the ADIC doesn't."

"The assistant director in charge?" Donovan sat up a little straighter; the ADIC was the Bureau chief over all of New York City.

"I passed your report upstairs," Mayer said. "The ADIC thinks we should follow it up."

"Why?"

"Because it's a post–9/11 world, Mr. Donovan. You know all the flak we took after the Trade Center—the FBI should have seen it coming; there were clues, but we didn't follow them up. In the current political climate, we can't afford to leave any stone unturned. Your orders are to stick with the old man—at least until we can *prove* he's nuts. Let's find out if this Li really has anything we want. Tell him that we welcome his cooperation, and collect whatever information he has."

Donovan paused.

"Problem, Mr. Donovan?"

"The situation is a little—tricky."

"Tricky?"

"Yes, sir. Li says it's his life mission to find Sato Matsushita. *He* wants to find him. He's not offering to assist us; he wants the FBI to assist him."

"Now, that *is* nuts."

"That's what I told him—but he's determined."

"So apply some leverage. Tell him he's impeding a federal investigation."

"He's a British citizen, sir. And he approached us, remember?"

"What are we supposed to do, give him a badge and swear him in?"

"No—I just think we have to play it his way for a while. What do we have to lose?"

"Time," Mayer said. "The ADIC wants to expedite this. If the old man really is nuts, we've got all the time in the world. But if there really is anything behind this story of his, then time could be critical."

"What do you want me to do?"

"Get an expert opinion."

"On what?"

"The old man's mental condition. His psychological makeup and motivation. The feasibility of this plague scenario of his."

"You want to use somebody inside the Bureau or take it outside?"

"Outside."

"Any recommendations?"

"I've got a name for you." Mayer slid a second folder across his desk and opened it. "Dr. Macy Monroe," he read from the top page, "Professor of Political Science and International Relations at Columbia University."

Donovan felt the floor drop away beneath him like the Parachute Jump at Coney Island. If he had a penny in his open palm, he was sure it would have floated into the air.

"You gotta be kidding."

"'Ongoing consultant to the CIA, the State Department, and the

Office of Technology Assessment,'" he read. "'Specializes in the psychology of terrorism and international terrorist threat assessment.'"

"Wait a minute—the Bureau can't require me to work with a family member."

Mayer looked up. "What family member?"

"Come on, Reuben—you know Macy's my ex-wife."

"That makes her an ex–family member. More like a friend."

Since when is an ex-wife like a friend? Donovan thought. He felt sick to his stomach.

Mayer continued to read. "'Past lecturer in Foreign Policy Studies at the Brookings Institution. Member of the Livermore Study Group. Adviser to NYU's Center for Catastrophe Preparedness and Response.' Quite a pedigree," he said.

"I'm not questioning her qualifications. I'm saying I can't work with her."

"Why not?"

Donovan fumbled for an explanation. "What I mean is, she can't work with me."

"So if we ask her, she'll turn us down."

"Yes. No—I don't know what she'd say."

"Let's find out," Mayer said.

"Since when is it Bureau policy to go around hiring ex-spouses?"

"It's Bureau policy to hire the best people we can find," he said. "Always has been." He turned back to the folder again. "'Regional expertise in both the Middle East and Japan.' Now, there's a coincidence." He glanced up. "This says she speaks both Arabic and Japanese."

"Plus some French," Donovan grumbled.

"Four languages," he said. "Did you ever win an argument?"

"Reuben, I'm begging you—don't make me do this."

"It's done," Reuben said. "Her name came down from the ADIC himself. The most qualified person in this city—maybe in the country—just happens to be your ex. Sorry," he said. "I'd get over it if I were you."

Donovan glared at him. “Did you ever try to ‘get over’ an ex-wife?”

“Do you call her, or do I?”

“I do.”

“Good. Questions?”

“Just one,” Donovan said. “Who do I shoot?”

“Anybody but your ex-wife,” Mayer said. “She’s on the payroll now.”

CHAPTER FIFTEEN

THE CHALK ON THE blackboard made a quick clicking sound, like a mouse with a piece of hard candy. Macy's right hand moved in large, brisk strokes, spelling out the words *ASYMMETRICAL WARFARE* in capital letters.

"Who can tell me what this means?" she asked, turning to the class.

"Fighting on your own turf," one student offered.

"Give me an example."

"David meets Goliath," said another.

"Good—let's talk about that one. Who remembers the story?"

A dozen hands went up.

"Okay. This was a Middle Eastern territory dispute, with Israel in one corner as usual. Who was in the opposite corner?"

"Palestine?"

"No—but you're not far off. Anybody else?"

"The Philistines."

"There you go. Here's a piece of historical trivia for you: The name Palestine is derived from the word *Philistine.* Now the Philistines occupied the coastal region of Israel, what we now call the Gaza Strip. The armies of Israel and Philistia were about equal in number and strength, so nobody wanted to make the first move. It was a standoff, and it lasted for a month and a half.

"Then one of the Philistines suggested a way to break the tie: Each army would pick a champion and the champions would slug it out, winner take all. So—who went to bat for the Philistines?"

"Goliath," someone said in his best Darth Vader voice.

"And for the Israelites?"

"David!" Scattered applause from the classroom.

"Right. Now, David was just a boy—maybe fifteen or sixteen years old. The king at the time was a man named Saul. Saul called David into the locker room to help him suit up for the big game. Saul gave David his helmet, his armor, his sword—but they were so big on David that he couldn't even walk. He looked like that character from the Looney Tunes—you know, the little guy with the big Roman helmet. What was his name?"

A hand shot up in the first row. "Marvin the Martian," a young man said, grinning. "His sidekick was Commander K-9 the space dog, and his favorite weapon was the Illudium PU-36 Explosive Space Modulator."

Macy looked at him. "What year did World War I begin?"

The student's face went blank.

"I thought so," she said. "Anyway, David couldn't fight in Saul's armor. Somebody tell us what was going on here—describe the situation for us."

"Goliath wanted David to fight on *his* terms," a woman said.

"What terms were those? What were Goliath's assets?"

"Size. Strength."

"Exactly. He was over nine feet tall, and he was covered with armor from head to foot. Like our Third Armored Division—he was big, armed to the teeth, and practically invulnerable. Those were his assets; what were his liabilities?"

"He was dumb."

"Maybe," Macy said. "Or maybe he was just used to people doing things his way. You can get careless that way, can't you? What else—what were his weaknesses?"

"He was slow."

"Ah," Macy said. "He was *slow*—and in warfare, speed is a critical advantage. Now—what were David's assets?"

A muffled voice from the back of the room: "Rocks."

Through the laughter, Macy made a slight bow. "A double entrendre at eight o'clock in the morning," she said. "I don't know what you ordered at Starbucks this morning, but keep it coming. Okay, David had courage—another critical advantage. But he had something else too. What was it?"

Silence.

Macy stepped back to the blackboard and tapped her chalk by the large white letters. "He had *this*," she said. "David had the ability to think outside the box. Goliath wanted him to fight a traditional battle; Saul wanted him to fight a traditional battle. But David knew that would be suicide. He could never defeat Goliath on Goliath's own terms. He had to fight *his* way; he had to capitalize on the assets he had. David had speed, and quickness, and expertise with a nontraditional weapon: the sling. Goliath's armor was designed to withstand the point of a spear and the edge of a sword—but not a rock to the forehead."

Just then the door at the back of the classroom opened. The hinges were silent, but the glass panel made a brittle, rattling sound. Nathan Donovan slipped into the back of the classroom as inconspicuously as any tall, dark-suited federal agent could. He took a seat and nodded for Macy to continue.

Macy rarely broke stride in the middle of a lecture. She slowly gained momentum when she taught, like a locomotive building up steam, and she was just as hard to stop. She sometimes continued her lecture right through the bell, while sheepish students with next-hour classes collected their books and crept quietly away until only a single listener remained—some sympathetic soul who couldn't bear to be the last to go and leave Macy talking only to herself. Once the train was up to speed, Macy was oblivious to all interruptions: raised hands, late arrivals, coughing fits, even fire alarms. But when Donovan entered the room, she stopped and looked; it was enough to turn half of the heads in the classroom.

Macy attempted a recovery by returning to her lecture with renewed enthusiasm, which only made the few who were still oblivious turn and study Donovan as well. When Macy realized there was no use fighting it, she stopped.

"By now you've all noticed that we have a visitor," she said. "The 'Man in Black' in the back of the room is Special Agent Nathan Donovan of the FBI. Relax, he's not here because of anything you did—not yet, anyway."

Donovan cupped his right hand and did his best Miss America wave.

Macy pointed to the blackboard. "Mr. Donovan graduated from the Big Ten, so this may be asking a lot of him, but—can you tell us how the Bureau would define this term, Mr. Donovan?"

"Terrorism," Donovan said.

"I'll bet that's the term Goliath used when David pulled out his sling."

Donovan shook his head. "I'll bet the term was 'Uh-oh.'"

The class laughed; Macy kept a straight face. "The term 'terrorism' isn't particularly helpful," she said. "It describes the effect an attack has on its victim, but not the motivation for the attack. And if we never understand the cause, we won't be able to prevent it from happening again."

"You understand the cause of terrorism?" Donovan asked.

Macy glared back. "I understand the reason for asymmetrical warfare. So do the Palestinians; so does al-Qaeda; so does every outgunned and outnumbered guerrilla force in the world." Her countenance softened now. "And so does this class," she said. "So what does the story of David and Goliath have to do with the military situation in the modern world? Anybody?"

"It's David versus Goliath everywhere we look," someone said.

"And who represents Goliath in your scenario?"

"We do—the U.S."

"We're the bad guys?" Donovan said from the back of the room.

Macy took the comment in stride. "No, we're the *big* guys. And who represents David?"

"Everyone smaller," a young man said. "Everyone who lacks our technology; everyone who can't match our level of military spending. Just about everybody."

Macy nodded. "This is the important point here, people: *David can't fight in Saul's armor.* In today's world, America is unparalleled in military technology, training, and supply. No one is even close. So we roll in with our Third Armored Division and we call out to the enemy, 'Bring out your guns! Line up your tanks! Come on out and fight like a man!' By which we mean, 'Come on out and fight *our* way.' And when anyone is actually stupid enough to try it—like Saddam Hussein in the first Gulf War—it ends up looking more like a video game than an actual battle. And we love it—why shouldn't we? It demonstrates our absolute superiority, and it holds our losses to a bare minimum.

"But the enemy isn't stupid—that's what Goliath forgot, and that's what got him killed. If the enemy doesn't have guns and tanks, he'll come at you with a sling and a stone."

"What if you take away his sling?" Donovan asked.

"Anybody can make a sling," Macy said, "and rocks are everywhere. You can't take away all the world's slings—that's a waste of time. If a man wants to kill you, he'll find a way to try."

"Then what do you do?"

Macy looked at him. "You find the man first."

The bell rang, releasing the palpable tension; there was an almost audible sigh of relief from the class. When the doors crashed open, it was like pricking a balloon; students poured out like escaping air. Only one student remained, carefully repacking her books and papers into a backpack. She stopped abruptly and glanced around, mortified to find herself alone. She quickly scooped the rest of her belongings under one arm and hurried out.

Donovan rose and came forward.

"Thanks for your contribution to the class today," Macy said, returning her own books to a leather attaché.

"I love 'Bible Hour,'" Donovan said. "Did I miss the snack?"

"What do you want, Nathan?"

He paused. "Can we sit down?"

"Is it necessary?"

"It would help," he said. "Please?"

They both took seats on the folding wooden amphitheater chairs.

"I never did like these seats," he said.

"You never liked classrooms."

"That's true. I guess I never was much of a student. At least you get to stand up and teach."

"You have to pass a couple of classes before they let you teach," she said. "It's sort of a requirement."

Donovan tried to slow things down. "How are you doing?" he asked.

"In what capacity?"

He rolled his eyes. "Come on, Macy, it's a simple question. I ask, 'How are you doing?' and you say, 'I'm doing fine.'"

"Is that what you want to hear?"

"I want to hear how you're doing."

"I'm doing fine. Anything else?"

The door suddenly opened, and a student stepped inside. He glanced at Macy and Donovan and instantly read the expressions on their faces; he looked like a mosquito caught in a bug zapper. He backed out quickly and shut the door behind him.

"This is not a personal visit," Donovan said.

"That's good. I haven't seen you in, what—almost a year? And then, without any advance notice, you drop in on my classroom. I'd hate to think this is your idea of a personal visit."

"I thought about calling," he said.

"But you didn't."

"I thought it would be too hard."

"Lots of things are hard, Nathan. Life is hard sometimes—"

"Let's not go there, okay?"

There was a moment of awkward silence.

"So if this is not a personal visit, why are you here?"

"I need your help," he said.

She paused. "You need me to *help* you."

It was a simple sentence, but it was like an iceberg; a tiny, innocent tip concealing a thousand tons of coldness below.

"I've got a lot on my plate right now," she said.

"This is not a personal request," he said. "The Bureau wants your opinion on a case we're working on—a case *I'm* working on."

"They want *me* to work with *you*?"

"Well . . . yes."

"Don't they know about us?"

"Of course they know. They don't care. You're the most qualified person for the job, that's all."

Macy squinted. "They want *me* to work with *you*?"

Donovan groaned. "I told them it wouldn't work."

"You told them you couldn't work with me?"

"No, I told them *you* couldn't work with *me*."

"Where do you get off telling them that?"

"What?"

"If you can't work with me, that's one thing—but don't try to make this out to be my problem."

"Macy, how are we supposed to work together? We couldn't even stay married."

"That's a little different, don't you think? Did they say I have to love you?"

"Of course not."

"Did they say I have to respect you?"

Donovan glared at her. "All they told me is that I can't shoot you."

"Well, do you think you can manage that?"

"Right now I'm not so sure."

"What kind of case is it?"

"It involves bubonic plague, and Oriental rat fleas, and a guy with a very long memory."

"I like it so far."

"Look—last week an old Chinese man came to see me. He told me a story you wouldn't believe—I'm not sure *I* believe it. It's either the biggest news of the century or the biggest whopper of all time, and we can't tell which. We have to know if the old man is crazy or not. That's why we need your help."

Macy stood up, closed her briefcase, and started for the door. "Tell them to count me in," she said. "'Crazy' is one of my specialties."

Donovan watched until the door shut behind her. "You're telling me," he said.

CHAPTER SIXTEEN

Tartus, Syria

KHALID STEPPED ON THE gas pedal, and the old Peugeot accelerated along the empty highway. The road to the port city of Tartus was almost new, a part of the recent network of highways and railroads connecting the inland cement factories and fertilizer plants with Syria's two major ports: the venerable old port of Latakia and its younger and more industrial brother, Tartus.

The drive was straight and level and required no thought at all. It allowed Khalid's mind to wander. His thoughts went back to Iraq, to the time almost fifteen years ago when he first met Dedushka in Baghdad at a briefing of battlefield commanders. It was December 1990, and the Americans were amassing their forces along the Saudi border in preparation for war. Everyone knew it was the final briefing before the American offensive would begin, and everyone waited on the edge of their seats for the high command to reveal the strategy for the Iraqi defense.

Khalid was dumbfounded when a tiny Oriental man was escorted to the podium—but when he was introduced as a Soviet biological weapons specialist, they all understood. Then the air became electric, supercharged with anticipation. Every officer in the Republican Guard knew about Iraq's biological arsenal; some of them had seen these weapons firsthand when they were tested on the Kurds just a few years before. All of them wondered if Iraq would have the courage to use them against the Americans. The talk was everywhere; the possibility hung over them like a gleaming scimitar.

The threat was directly implied when Saddam Hussein spoke of the "mother of all battles." No one believed Iraq's imported armor would last for long against the Americans' inexhaustible resources. The "mother of all battles" was an apocalyptic term, and Iraq's pitiful collection of jets, tanks, and aging Scud missiles would never bring about an apocalypse. The only thing powerful enough, the only thing *terrifying* enough to usher in the end of days would be an invisible onslaught of bacteria, viruses, and toxins. That, and only that, would be enough to defeat the Americans.

Khalid was elated when the old man began to speak. He outlined a plan for the battlefield deployment of biological weapons if the Americans attempted to approach Baghdad. The plan was simple and foolproof, but it would require great courage and sacrifice. As the Americans attacked, the Iraqis would fall back, allowing the enemy to advance. But, the old man said, a line of courageous volunteers must remain in their positions to seed the desert sands with a combination of anthrax spores and plague-infected fleas. Then they would bury their equipment before their positions were overrun, giving the Americans no indication of what had been done. As the Americans advanced, they would be infected; when they withdrew, they would take the deadly pestilence with them. Within weeks, disease would decimate the enemy's forces, perhaps even leaping across the ocean and devastating the American homeland as well.

For the volunteers, there could be no gas masks or protective clothing—nothing that might reveal the presence of biological agents. That would mean, of course, the death of every volunteer either by bullet or by disease. But that was the price to be paid, he said; that was the price to be a martyr. The old man spoke with such quiet confidence that it seemed like a price even a child should be willing to pay—a price he himself would gladly pay for the chance to punish the Americans.

And we were willing, Khalid remembered, *every last one of us. We stood and cheered. We were ready to volunteer to the man, gladly offering our lives to halt the American advance—but then our own commanders spoke, and we were horrified.*

The decision to use biological weapons, they said, would be made by each individual field commander. The authority belonged to us; the decision would be ours. We were mortified—it was clear to us what they were doing. The decision would be ours—and the responsibility too. Our commanders were cowards; they were unwilling to take responsibility for such a decision. They hoped we would have the courage they themselves lacked. We knew that if it went well, they would surely take credit for the success; but if it went badly, they would deny any knowledge of our actions. We would be martyrs, yes—martyrs who died to protect our commanders' careers.

There was an astonished silence in the room. I looked at the old man, and I saw that on his face was a look of horror equaled only by my own. And all at once I understood. I understood that we were somehow brothers—not brothers of blood, but brothers of will. We were the only two men in the room with the strength of will to strike back at the Americans, regardless of the cost.

That night, Khalid sought out the old man. Their conversation was quick and direct, almost in shorthand, as though the conversation had already taken place and they were only repeating the lines. They seemed to read each other's minds; they somehow knew each other's thoughts. They were not servants of Iraq, neither one of them; they were servants of a higher cause, and that cause would not be served by this weak-kneed and futile defense against the American forces.

When Dedushka spoke, it was almost a spiritual experience for Khalid. He spoke of his native country and what he called *bushido*—the warrior spirit his people once lived by. Raw courage, self-sacrifice, unstinting obedience, and utter contempt for death—this was the way of the warrior. He spoke with disgust of the dwindling will of modern nations. He said that the warrior spirit now must reside with individuals, those with the will to do what must be done. When Khalid mentioned his Syrian birth, the discussion seemed to accelerate. There are people in Syria, Khalid told him, people with connections and power. There are men who possess this warrior spirit—men who still live by *bushido.*

On a cold, clear night less than a month later, as American bombs rained down on Baghdad, Khalid and Dedushka calmly drove across western Iraq toward the Syrian border. In the backseat was a large steamer trunk.

Khalid's connections in Syria received Dedushka as a gift from Allah. The weapon he described to them was beyond anything they had imagined possible. He was provided with a house in Damascus, a generous stipend, and a laboratory at the Scientific Studies and Research Center. He was given whatever he requested without hesitation: equipment, supplies, even an isolated testing site in the Syrian Desert. To the Syrian government, Dedushka was simply a visiting research scientist; to a handful of wealthy Arab businessmen, he was their future and their hope.

And Khalid had served the old man ever since, acting as a mediator between Dedushka and his anonymous sponsors. For years they had accepted the old man's judgment as if it were the Koran itself; but lately, things had begun to change. They were becoming impatient, demanding, even critical. Perhaps too much time had passed, and their original excitement for the old man's plan was wearing thin. Or perhaps someone else now had their ear, turning their eyes and hearts in a different direction.

Khalid wondered: Why was he summoned to Tartus on such short notice? What was the purpose of this meeting? Khalid had communicated the old man's demands—his request for transport by ship and the specifications for the temporary lab. Was any of this objectionable? These people were said to own twenty ships—was this too much to ask? Perhaps it was the timing; perhaps they resented the old man's initiating his plan without their prior approval. But if it was only a question of timing, surely they would relent. After all, what choice did they have? The plan was already under way.

Khalid was in the heart of Tartus now, driving along the waterfront and watching the dry-bulk carriers and Ro-Ro vessels that lined the wharfs like cups on a shelf. Black-and-yellow forklifts darted back and forth across the docks, lifting pallets of fertilizer and phosphate, disappearing into yawning cargo holds and then suddenly reappearing. He turned away from the waterfront and drove three blocks, then parked his car at the address he had been given.

He entered the restaurant and glanced around at the lavish surroundings: soaring sandstone arches and draping date palms towering over an oasis of white linen, silver, and imported china. He was almost instantly aware of the shabbiness of his own clothing. He straightened himself and stepped into the main dining room.

He found the man seated along the far wall, dining alone at a table for four. His elegance and manner caused him to stand out even in these exclusive surroundings. He was tall and very thin, dressed in an immaculate Western business suit of olive green. His tie was golden silk, and on the third finger of his right hand he wore an enormous gold ring to match. His skin was a milky chocolate color and perfectly smooth. He was completely bald on top, but the raven hair on the sides of his head flowed back into well-oiled curls. He ate quickly and efficiently, and when he chewed, the sinews of his jaw flexed under his skin like a stallion's flank.

He glanced up at Khalid with eyes as black as ravens. He continued to eat and jabbed at the chair opposite with his silver fork. Khalid sat down across from the man and turned his missing ear slightly away.

"It is a pleasure to see you again, Khalid."

"And you."

"Will you join me? The *mezzeh* here is excellent. Try the aubergine or the stuffed vine leaves."

Khalid shook his head. "Why did you call me here?"

"You've just arrived. At least have a little wine to wash away the dust."

"You received Dedushka's instructions? Everything was clear?"

"Quite clear."

"Have arrangements been made for the ship? And the lab—have all specifications been followed?"

"Everything has been done according to specifications—*our* specifications. Let us not forget who serves whom, Khalid."

"Dedushka says he will allow no more outside interference."

There was a pause. "We understood the message, Khalid. To be frank, we found the old man's tone a bit demanding."

"He was very disappointed by your test."

"Yes, I'm sure he was. It was regrettable, but nonetheless necessary."

"He doesn't see it that way."

The man smiled as he continued his meal. "And how does your friend see it?"

"He says it was a mistake to ever vary from his plan."

"His plan was a foolish fantasy, filled with unnecessary risks."

"He says you must be willing to take risks. He says that without great risk, there is no great glory."

The man glanced up for the first time. "Are we averse to risk, Khalid? Does our goal seem timid to you? We are willing to risk everything in this great venture—but there is a difference between a calculated risk and a foolish risk. That is what your friend must learn."

"He has perfected this weapon for sixty years."

"And are we children? Does he have the only gray hair among us? For how many years have we been working and planning in pursuit of this goal? He is but one man, and we are many. Greater minds than his are at work on this."

"He says the earthen jars were a foolish mistake. He says this failure shows that the fleas cannot be delivered in that manner."

"Is that his interpretation? We think differently. We believe this failure reveals a fundamental flaw in his entire strategy. These insects are obviously too fragile to employ for this purpose."

"The fleas will work—but the old man must accompany them. He must wait until the very last moment to load the fleas into the shells."

"He must *accompany* them," the man repeated. "We accepted your friend's fundamental premise, and we attempted a test to determine if his premise was sound. The test failed. Now—what have we lost? The cost of four excellent forgeries, that is all. There was no trail left behind, no connection to our people. Now, suppose your friend had accompanied the fleas—suppose *he* had been captured. That is what I call a risk, Khalid—a most foolish risk."

The man spotted a waiter, snapped his fingers, and pointed to his empty wine glass. He waited silently while the glass was filled, then dismissed the server with a nod. He looked across the table again.

"You must be careful, Khalid. I know that you respect this man—perhaps admire him. But you must not allow your personal feelings to cloud your judgment. Why do you suppose your friend insists on accompanying these insects? Do you think his presence is truly necessary? I will tell you what I think—I think he is a bitter old man seeking revenge, and he wants to taste his revenge with his own eyes. That is understandable—but very dangerous."

"This is not some petty revenge," Khalid said. "Dedushka has pursued this goal for sixty years—this is his *mission.*"

"Does your friend think himself the only one with a mission? Are we here to serve an old man's wishes, or is he here to serve our cause? But perhaps this is too much to expect. Your friend is not really a friend at all, is he? He is not even one of us."

"The enemy of our enemy is a friend," Khalid said.

"No—the enemy of our enemy is a *tool.* An effective tool perhaps, even a faithful tool, but a tool must never be confused with a friend."

"Dedushka offers us an invincible weapon and the perfect delivery system."

"Dedushka offers us *one option*—one among many."

Khalid blinked. "You have other options?"

"Of course." Khalid watched as the man poked his fork into a deep-fried ball of falafel. "Your friend must learn to distinguish *means* from *ends,*" he said. "The end he seeks is the destruction of the Americans. Very well, let him join with us in our efforts to accomplish that goal. If the means we employ are his own, all the better for him; but if the means are ours, he should still be satisfied that the end he desires has been accomplished. We serve the *cause,* Khalid. Servants of the cause must be willing to put the cause before all personal considerations."

The man drained his glass again, then looked directly at Khalid. "I must ask you something, my friend—I must ask where *your* true allegiance lies. Tell me, Khalid: Do you serve this man, or do you serve the cause?"

"I serve the cause," Khalid said weakly.

"Good—because I must tell you, there has been a change of plans."

"A change? What sort of change?"

"We have reviewed the old man's strategy carefully. We think there are elements that remain useful. There are other elements, however, that we wish to abandon. We believe they would be unreliable, and we find them unsatisfying. We intend to implement our own strategy—one that maintains the sprit of the original plan while incorporating our improvements."

Khalid felt sick to his stomach. "But—Dedushka's plan is already under way."

"That is problematic," the man said. "Your friend acted irresponsibly and without authority. We have no choice now but to accept his timing—but the plan that proceeds will be ours, not his."

Khalid stared at the tablecloth. "How will I tell him this? I don't know what he will say—what he will do."

"That, too, is problematic. We are aware of Dedushka's passion—his commitment to not only ends but means. That is why you will tell him nothing."

"What?"

"You will inform your friend that all of his demands have been met. His ship will sail from Tartus on the agreed-upon date. His lab will be located in the lower cargo hold, outfitted according to his exact specifications. That is all you will tell him; that is all he needs to know."

"Nothing more?"

"Nothing more."

"You are asking me to deceive him."

"I am instructing you to say nothing. That is quite different."

"And me," Khalid said. "What part do I have in this new plan of yours?"

"A very great part," the man said. "You will be in command when the ship sets sail. You will carry out the new plan. You will continue to serve, Khalid—you will continue to serve the *cause*."

CHAPTER SEVENTEEN

THE AISLES OF THE Chinatown apothecary were impossibly crowded. Behind a long glass counter, a wooden cupboard held hundreds of small square drawers, each with a curling brass tongue and a tiny nameplate bearing a mysterious Chinese symbol. The drawers contained all the secrets of the Chinese pharmacopoeia. There were roots, and leaves, and bundles of dried grasses tied with straw; there was garlic and figroot, bupleurum and jujube dates, magnolia buds and dried chrysanthemums; there were warty, bulbous herbs and flat, thin slices of earthy-looking fungi.

Li studied the displays of deer legs and bear gallbladders like a child in a candy shop. Across the store, Donovan and Macy stood watching him.

"So what do you think?" Donovan asked.

"I loved the Triple Eight Palace," Macy said. "These people know how to eat."

"I'm talking about Li. What's your first impression?"

"He's a remarkable old man," Macy said. "You'd never believe he's over eighty. I've got graduate students who aren't as focused and alert."

"Maybe he takes this stuff," Donovan said, picking up one of the few products with an English label. "'*Qing Chun Bao*,'" he struggled to pronounce. "'The Green Vitality Treasure. Promotes blood circulation, benefits heart and kidneys, counters fatigue. Useful for poor memory, senility, fatigue, poor resistance to disease, and strengthening the heart.'"

"If he uses it, I'm buying some," Macy said.

"What about his story? What do you think?"

"It's incredible."

"'Incredible' as in *amazing*, or 'incredible' as in *no way*?"

"Have your people been able to verify any of it?"

"The historical background all checks out. There was a Unit 731 in Manchuria during the war, and they committed all the atrocities Li described—and then some. It was as big an operation as he said—it rivaled the Manhattan Project in size and scope. They recruited some of the best medical researchers in Japan. And he's right about another thing: They got away with it. The Russians hanged a few of them, but most of them went on to successful careers in the private sector."

"What about this Sato Matsushita?"

"There's only one mention of him, in a roster of past Unit 731 scientists; that's the entire extent of what we could find. Once the Japanese knew they'd lost the war, they apparently destroyed every record they had on Unit 731."

"Can't say I blame them."

"Most of what's known has been pieced together from eyewitness testimonies, testimonies that Li says he's been collecting for sixty years—testimonies from people who are dead now, stories we have no way to corroborate."

"You think he's making them up?"

"You're supposed to answer that one."

"It's possible," Macy said. "It may be that Li is using Matsushita as a personification of evil, the way some people do when they ascribe to Hitler every atrocity committed by Nazi Germany."

"You're saying Matsushita could be mostly fiction?"

"Maybe. If you've spent your life pursuing Nazis and there's only one left, that one Nazi could begin to take on mythical proportions."

"So how do we separate myth from reality?"

"We keep talking to Li," she said.

Donovan looked at her. "Hey, I really appreciate this."

Macy turned away. "I'm not doing it for you."

They crossed an aisle stocked with iodine-colored jars of astragalus and ligusticum powders, and another lined with clear plastic bins of dried, crumbling leaves. Li stood by the long glass counter, shaking his head in delight.

"Here's something you won't find in your local London chemist's shop," Li said. "Deer antler velvet. It increases stamina, strengthens the immune system, and even enhances athletic performance."

"Thinking of trying out for the Olympics?"

"You never know," he said. "Did you take note of the final medal count in Athens? China is rapidly gaining on the United States, you know—I could be just the one to push them over the top."

"Do you really use any of this stuff?" Donovan asked.

"Of course. For a cold I take *yin chiao*, just as my people have for more than a century. For headache: chrysanthemum flower tea. For occasional constipation—"

"Hold it—that's more than I need to know."

"We were wondering about the secret of your vitality," Macy said.

"Ah. Is that what you two were whispering about over in the corner?" He looked at each of them and smiled. "The secret is: clean Christian living."

"I figured you for a Buddhist," Donovan said.

"Buddhism, Taoism, and Confucianism are the three largest religious traditions in China," Li said. "Most people practice a combination of all three: a little ancestor worship, a little family piety, and a dash of the divine thrown in for good measure. Sort of a vague, eclectic hodgepodge—like most of the religion in your own country. I was educated through the London Missionary Society school in Nanking. It was my dream to one day become a missionary doctor. The war changed all that; the war ended the dreams of a lot of people."

Just then, a small, smiling woman stepped from behind the counter and approached. Her eyes were large and black and surrounded by a paper fan of wrinkles that seemed to flutter when she smiled. Her hair was pulled back in a simple bun, and her skin was as smooth and translucent as vellum. Her manner was quiet and dignified, almost noble; her peaceful face radiated compassion and sadness at the same time. She said a few words to Li; he nodded and turned to Donovan.

"She wants to know if you would like to be examined."

Donovan did a double take. "Me?"

"She referred to 'the big one.' I believe that would be you."

"Is she a doctor?" Macy asked.

"She is a practitioner of traditional Chinese medicine—an herbalist, perhaps an acupuncturist as well."

"Why me?" Donovan said.

"Practitioners of traditional Chinese medicine are quite intuitive. Perhaps she senses something wrong about you."

"What a gift," Macy said.

"Is this a joke? What am I supposed to do, step into the back room and drop my drawers for some quack?"

Li winced and looked at Macy. "Does he *try* to be offensive?"

"No, it comes naturally for him. That's *his* gift."

Li turned to Donovan again. "In the first place, she is not asking you to 'drop your drawers.' You're thinking in terms of Western medicine, which is much more invasive; you won't have to undress, and she promises not to cut you open with any surgical instruments. In the second place, this is not quackery. There is a growing regard for traditional Chinese medicine among Western doctors. Some of your largest American pharmaceutical companies are studying herbal remedies, searching for the active ingredients in some of our ancient cures."

"Go on, Nathan," Macy said. "Let's find out what's wrong with you."

"Shut up, Macy."

"Her examination room is in the back," Li said, "just through that curtain. It would only take a few short minutes."

"Tell her thanks anyway."

"Come on, don't be such a baby."

Li's eyes drifted away in boredom. "I was told that you federal agents are fearless—walking through fire, facing a hail of bullets, that sort of thing. Apparently the stories are a bit of an exaggeration."

"All *right*," Donovan grumbled. "If it's the only way to get you two off my back."

Li nodded politely and spoke a few words; the woman smiled and led the way through the curtain with the three of them following behind.

Li leaned close to Macy. "He's rather easy to goad, isn't he?"

She nodded. "It's a guy thing."

The back of the shop was partitioned into two separate examining rooms by simple white sheets. The woman motioned for Donovan to sit down; she took a chair across from him and began to look him over as if he were a prospective plow horse. She turned his head from side to side, felt his throat, and peered into his mouth. She motioned for him to exhale, then shook her head with a look of disgust.

"She's right about that," Macy whispered.

"This is humiliating," Donovan said.

The woman spoke a single word.

Li translated: "Quiet."

The woman took Donovan's left hand in hers and turned it palm-side up. She placed both thumbs on his wrist, closed her eyes, and began to gently rub.

"What's she doing?" Donovan asked.

"She's taking your pulse," Li said. "Your pulse will tell her about the condition of your internal organs."

Donovan rolled his eyes.

A few minutes later, she abruptly dropped Donovan's hand and nodded confidently. She turned to Li and began her summary report.

"She says that in the Chinese theory of medicine, diseases are divided into hot and cold types. Apparently, you are afflicted with the hot type. Your breath is foul and your eyes are bloodshot; these are indications of overheated blood, the result of overwork and stress. Also, a poor diet."

Donovan glared. "You threw that in."

"Think of me as a physician's assistant."

The woman rose from her chair now and, still speaking rapid-fire, exited through the curtain and into the store.

"Her prescription is a tea made of American ginseng," Li said. "This will cool your blood. Not Asian ginseng—that would have exactly the opposite effect. She will prepare a prescription for you now. This concludes your examination."

Donovan rose. "Do I get a little sucker with a shovel on the end?"

Li frowned at Macy. "What is he going on about?"

"Never mind. The heat affects his mind too."

In the shop, the woman placed a piece of paper on an old bronze balance and weighed out the proper amount, handing the concoction to Donovan in a small paper sack. He held it away like a doggy cleanup bag. "What do I do with this?"

"You make tea with it and you drink it, of course."

"Does it really do anything?"

"Traditional Chinese remedies are time-tested," Li said. "Five thousand years ago, the great emperor Shen Nung was the first to research and catalog herbal medicines. According to legend, he personally consumed 365 different medicinal plants over the course of his life to test their effects."

"What happened to him?"

"He turned green and died from a toxic overdose."

"Of which one?"

"No one knows. Fortunately, he discovered tea before he died. Are we finished here? Let's take a walk."

It was dark now, but the sidewalks were still as crowded as the apothecary shelves. Most of the street peddlers had closed up after a ten- or twelve-hour day, but the shops and markets remained open, casting their orange and yellow lights halfway across the street. The throng had thinned just enough to allow them to walk three abreast, but the going was slow. Li flowed through the mob effortlessly, like a bee through a busy hive, and Macy followed at his side. Donovan found progress a good deal slower; his broad shoulders were like a moving barricade, and irritated passersby seemed to constantly rebound off him like pinballs off a bumper.

"I'm pleased that you could join us for dinner," Li said to Macy. "Your choice of the shark fin soup was excellent; it relieves me to know that not all of your people are barbarians."

"I told Nathan, 'The Chinese know how to eat.'"

"It's a very important part of our culture. You know, Confucius divorced his wife because she couldn't cook." Li paused to allow a change of topic. "So tell me, what did you think of my story?"

"I think you're a master storyteller," she said.

Li smiled. "A polite evasion."

"Not at all. I was simply commenting on your delivery."

"And my content? As an expert in the psychology of terrorism, I assume you're here to help the authorities determine the possible veracity of my story."

"Something like that, yes."

"I assure you, the story is true in every detail."

"No one's questioning your honesty, Li. No one doubts what Matsushita did in the past. The question is what he's likely to do in the future—if he's still around. When did you last see Matsushita alive?"

"In 1942."

"And you haven't seen him since?"

"No—though not for want of trying."

"Then how can you be sure he's alive?

Li paused. "I'm afraid you won't like my answer."

"Try me."

"I know Sato Matsushita is alive the same way that practitioner knows Nathan has overheated blood."

"Li—that was just a guess."

"I assure you, it was more than that. I can't expect a Western scientist to appreciate this, but there is such a thing as *intuition.*"

"You're wrong," she said. "As a psychologist, I believe in intuition. But you're dealing with the FBI here, Li. They've got limited time and resources—and you're asking them to commit those resources just because of your *hunch.*"

"I've never liked that word," Li said with a frown. "All right—then let me suggest a more rational reason: Suppose a man is thought to be dead—but at the scene of a crime, his fingerprints are discovered. What would the authorities conclude?"

"That the man is still alive."

"Precisely—and this is what the FBI must understand: The Oriental rat fleas in TriBeCa were the fingerprints of Sato Matsushita—they could belong to no other. That reason alone should be enough to convince them that the man is still alive."

"And you're convinced that even after *six decades*, Matsushita still intends to use his plague weapon against the United States."

"If you knew the man the way I do, you would have no doubt either."

They stepped aside to let a street sweeper pass, collecting the fish heads, orange peels, and vegetable matter that choked the gutters from the day's commerce. Steam rose off the pavement as he passed, bringing with it a smell both sweet and foul.

Li glanced over at Macy. "You know, your presence here tonight gives me hope."

"Why is that?"

"The fact that they sent you tells me the FBI is at least concerned."

"They're definitely concerned—this kind of scenario is something we've been talking about for a long time. A lot of people today are worried about nuclear weapons; in my field, some of us are more concerned about biological attacks. Nuclear weapons aren't easy to make—not even the simple ones. It takes a lot of technical expertise, and the materials are extremely hard to come by. But any chemistry major with ten thousand dollars' worth of equipment and a lab the size of a bedroom can make herself a serious biological arsenal. That's what keeps me awake at night."

"Your fears are well founded," Li said. "A bomb or a chemical weapon destroys only what it comes in immediate contact with; a biological weapon spreads from one person to the next, vastly multiplying its effect."

"Several countries have developed biological weapons," Macy said, "but there are good reasons no one uses them. They're messy—no one can tell when the wind will shift and blow the pathogen back on you. They're uncontainable—if you start a real pandemic, how will you keep it from infecting your own people? And most of all, they're *taboo*—that's the biggest deterrent of all. There's an almost universal abhorrence of biological weapons, and nobody wants to be the first to use one."

"Yes—an *almost* universal abhorrence."

"But not in the case of Sato Matsushita."

"No."

Macy stopped and turned to him. "Help me understand that, Li—help me understand Matsushita the way you do. What's his motive? What's his driving force? What would make him willing to do the unthinkable?"

"It's really rather simple," Li said. "A man finds it easier to do the unthinkable once the unthinkable has been done to him."

CHAPTER EIGHTEEN

Japan, August 1945

IT WAS MORE THAN a mile by foot from the cottage to the University Hospital, but Sato didn't mind the daily walk. It gave him a chance to look at his new home. The seaside metropolis was now the eighth-largest city in all of Japan, home to a third of a million people, but it didn't look it. It was a peaceful, sprawling city, spread over six islands in the Ota River delta. Sato had arrived from Ping Fan by airplane less than a week before. From above, the islands of the city looked like the fingers of a crooked hand. The river bottom soil was rich black loam, where wheat and rice grew almost unattended. In the low, sheltering mountains that surrounded the city, fat yellow silkworms leisurely spun the fabric of the gods.

The mountains seemed to separate the city not only from the rest of Japan but from the rest of the world—from the fire, from the suffering, from the deprivation—from the war itself and the daily bombings that devastated so many of Japan's metropolitan areas. The city was like a Shangri-la, hidden away from all the plagues of civilization and all the ravages of war. Everyone had his or her own pet theory of why the city had been spared: Some said the city had no military significance, though in fact it was headquarters to the Second General Army and was an important port. Others believed it was because their citizens had so many relatives in the United States. Still others claimed that it was because of the city's great beauty; the Americans, they said, wished to preserve the city to use as a residential area after the war.

Sato didn't care. He was just grateful for this tiny oasis in the midst of so much horror—horror that he himself had been a part of until just a week ago. He thought of his three years of research at Unit 731. It never failed to bring a wave of—what was it? Shame? Guilt? But why should he feel this way? What had he done but his duty? He was recruited to serve his emperor, just as hundreds of thousands of his countrymen had been. And that's what he had done—serve his emperor. Unit 731 itself was established by royal decree; Ishii was a friend of the emperor himself. What more could any Japanese soldier do than serve the purposes of His Imperial Majesty?

It was not his place to question his superiors; it was not his place to challenge the overall strategy of the war. There were reasons for the things that took place, high and hidden reasons. It was war, and in war regrettable but necessary things took place. It was not as though he himself had done them—not his true self, anyway. In war, the soldier assumed the costume of war along with the duties of war. When war ended, the soldier discarded both and returned to his true nature again.

Besides, it wasn't as though they were human beings—they were Chinese. They were allies of the Americans, enemies of Japan. When Doolittle's bombers first dared to touch the skirts of Tokyo, it was the Chinese who received them with open arms. It was Chinese air bases that now launched American B-29s on their nightly raids, raining fire bombs and incendiaries on the wood-and-paper houses of Japan's cities.

It was war, and China was the enemy. And if China itself was the enemy, were not the individual Chinese? In war there were so many complexities, enough to drive a man mad; better for the simple soldier to focus on the duty at hand.

But Sato was sick to death of duty. He was secretly relieved when the Imperial Navy refused to release its I-400 submarines; he was relieved when he realized that Operation Cherry Blossoms at Night would not take place. For three years he had perfected his plague bomb, and it was a triumph of both biology and engineering—but to use it against a major city—against the Americans . . . No one knew what the full extent of the devastation would be. More important, no one knew what the Americans would do in response. An invasion of the Japanese homeland now seemed inevitable; farmers and peasants were now training at the seashore with pointed sticks as weapons, determined to resist to the last man—to the last child. How much worse would it be if the Americans came with a burning desire to wreak vengeance on Japan's own civilian population?

And when the Russians invaded Manchuria, Sato was relieved most of all. Then he knew that his duty was at an end; then he knew that Unit 731 would be destroyed, along with every trace of its research. He was relieved when Ishii granted his request for reassignment to the University Hospital here, where he could at last be reunited with his beloved Emiko. They now lived together in the heart of the city, in little more than a lean-to on a corner of his friend's property, but it was worth it. Here the war seemed already over. Here the healing had already begun, and Emiko would be a part of it. Her tender heart and gentle spirit were like a soothing balm for his soul.

He yawned. He had slept little the night before. There had been three air-raid sirens since midnight, but no one paid much attention. They were just a reminder that a war was still raging in some faraway land—but the mournful wail was still enough to interrupt sleep. Just an hour ago, a single American plane had been spotted high overhead, but it passed by without incident. Probably a weather plane, he thought. Perhaps taking reconnaissance photos.

He wondered about the time. He looked up at the university's clock tower, then remembered that the clock had ceased to work two weeks ago. He rounded a corner and started down a sidewalk, with a tall brick building on his left. A man passed on his right and stepped out into the street. Sato turned and called after him.

"Excuse me. Do you know the time?"

The man turned with a look of derision and pointed at the clock tower.

Sato shook his head. "It doesn't work. Hasn't for weeks now."

"That's Hiroshima for you," he said, pulling out his own pocket watch. "I've got 8:15."

Sato glanced at the tower. By the strangest coincidence, the clock on the tower was stopped at exactly 8:15.

At that precise moment, a blinding white light filled the street where the man was standing, followed by a blast of enormous heat. Sato's exposed skin stung and blistered; even behind the shelter of the brick wall, it was like opening the door of a furnace. The man in the street wore a white shirt and dark pants. The pants were instantly incinerated, but the shirt somehow remained. His thick black hair vanished, and his skin turned a crackled brown, like the mud when a pond evaporates. He opened his mouth, but no sound came out. For the first few seconds, everything was utterly silent—then a low, rumbling wall of noise hit, and with it a shock wave so powerful that everything in its path seemed to crumble away. The man himself was like a column of cigarette ash, standing one moment and then disappearing in a blast of wind.

The sky was an eerie yellow, and the air was filled with flying debris: stones, timbers, chunks of pavement, enormous sections of tiled roof and concrete wall, objects so huge that it seemed incomprehensible that they could be airborne for even an instant. Roofs were ripped off houses as if they were paper; telephone poles exploded like bombs.

Debris began to rain down on Sato now, pieces of brick and glass and wood from the wall beside him. He didn't know whether to run from the wall or hide behind it. There was no time to think anyway, and nothing to think about. Nothing like this had ever happened in Hiroshima before; nothing like this had ever happened in all the world.

He collapsed to his knees and covered his head with his arms. The rumbling grew in intensity until the sensation was shattering, until Sato was sure the universe itself would shake apart—but a moment later it subsided like an enormous passing train. When he looked up, the street was empty, and everything was preternaturally still. Then, from the opposite direction, the wind came back. Like a movie projector rewinding, the scene before him reversed itself; the city's debris came whirling back in winds of cyclonic force, bringing with it entire trees and pieces of houses from outlying areas.

It also brought fire. Flames leaped from building to building in blowtorch blasts, consuming every wooden thing in their path. The wind continued for what seemed like an eternity, and the sky above was a swirling maelstrom of smoke and dust in a haze of purple and red and brown. High above, a narrow column of smoke rose into the sky, swelling into a pinkish cloud at the top.

Sato staggered to his feet, wondering what to do first. He thought of his patients at the University Hospital—those who survived the blast would need his help now more than ever. There would be wounded and dying everywhere in the city, more than he could ever—

Emiko.

Sato imagined his sister in the tiny lean-to. There was no brick wall nearby for her, nothing to shelter her from the searing heat. He ran to the street and looked in the direction of the blast. He started back toward the city, into the heart of the devastation, his mind too frantic to even pray.

Blackened figures passed him everywhere, flooding out of the city. Some had no noses or ears; some had faces so swollen that they had no features at all, like mannequins in a clothing store. Some looked as though they had been dipped in blood; many were charred beyond recognition, and their flesh hung from their limbs in long curling strips. They held their arms in front of them and walked silently, without expression, without tears, like the dead returning to life—or the living on their way to the grave.

Sato knew what the blast was now; he knew what had happened—it was an atomic bomb. Japan's own scientists had spoken of the possibility for years now and had pursued it without success. Now America had perfected the weapon—and they had used it, without mercy and without hesitation. Sato knew that most of the people he saw would be dead by nightfall—and no scientist in the world knew for certain what the next few weeks would bring.

Surreally, it began to rain. The rising blast had taken with it half of the water from the Ota River, and great drops of water, black with dust and ash, fell like blobs of ink and pelted the half-naked and smoldering bodies, leaving long, gritty streaks on the skin that remained. The drops sizzled and hissed when they hit. Sato wondered if they were poisonous or contaminated. He wiped at his arms, and the flesh turned a grimy gray.

Sato stopped a man stumbling past. The outline of his nose was stenciled on his right cheek. "I'm looking for Emiko Matsushita," he said desperately. "Have you seen her?" The man looked at Sato as though he spoke a different language. He turned silently away and continued on his journey to nowhere.

At the Ota, Sato saw hundreds of burned and wounded people lining its banks, one by one leaping from the ledge and plunging through the wine-red scum that covered the remaining water. Few came up again; those who did slowly rose to the surface facedown. Each saw the fate of the one who jumped before him, but no one seemed to care. Anything was better than the burning.

The hypocenter of the blast was easy for Sato to trace. Near the university there were buildings still partially intact, with standing walls and portions of roofs still in place. Closer to the center, there was nothing but fragments of walls and blackened beams jutting up like the masts of a burned-out ship. Near the heart of the city, there was nothing left at all. The ground was perfectly level and covered in a thick layer of powder, as though a gigantic pestle had ground the city to dust. The periphery of the city was all in flames; at the center, there was no fire. There were no buildings, no statues, no trees, no bodies—no sign that life had ever existed there at all. It looked like the pit of an abandoned hell. From every crack in the ground, smoke and steam rose into the sky, turning the sun into a crimson ball.

He took his first bearings from whatever landmarks he could still recognize—the bend in the river, the Aioi Bridge—then he worked outward in circles, searching for the first recognizable outline of a street or structure. He found a main intersection and headed north, toward the mountains. He recognized a bank by its still-intact vault; he remembered its location and proceeded east. He continued in this way, working outward from the center, slowly picking his way through the smoldering rubble.

It took hours to find the cottage—or the place where it once stood. By nightfall he had located the property, which was nothing but a pile of smoldering refuse. In the corner of the lot lay a section of corrugated tin, now scorched and gunmetal blue. He scrambled across the pile of stone and timbers and pulled at the metal sheet; it crumbled in his hands like a rusted can. Underneath was a single figure, charred as black as coal. It was lying on its back with its knees drawn up in a sitting position. The two hands were raised to the face, covering both eyes.

Sato stared. It must be the wrong house, the wrong property. He could be mistaken; it was so hard to tell. Everything was in ruins; everything looked the same. He could be on the opposite side of town for all he knew. He was new to the city; how could he be certain? That was it—it was all a mistake. He would turn, and go, and search in another place.

It is not her. In the whole universe, it was the only thing Sato still knew. *It cannot be her.*

He reached down and took the figure by the wrists. He tugged; the limbs were rigid and hard. Then there was a cracking sound, and the cupped hands pulled away from the face. Underneath were two pale yellow circles surrounding half-open eyes. He looked into the eyes, and he knew.

He collapsed on the rubble and looked up into the sky. It was a strangely beautiful evening, without a cloud in the sky. He thought about weeping, but it was a faraway thought, like a man recalling a distant memory. Perhaps he should scream—but he had no anger, no rage, no feeling at all. He looked deeper into his soul; nothing was there. It was empty, abandoned. It was just a pile of smoldering timbers, a ruin of broken stones and twisted steel.

He looked down at Emiko. He wondered what sort of impotent god had allowed her a last split second to cover her eyes. What a useless gesture, what a laughable gift. But the gods themselves were laughable, weren't they, raining down fire from heaven while they sat idly by? Or were they idle? Perhaps they were just senile old men, straining to remember the names of long-forgotten mortals, eating the children's food but unable to give anything in return.

What kind of weapon could do this? He wondered about its size, its structure, its workings. Most of all, he wondered about the people who would use such a weapon. Did they know what it would do? Surely not. Surely it was the only one of its kind—or perhaps there had been no time to test the weapon in advance. Surely tomorrow, when the Americans examined photographs of the destruction, they would cover their own eyes in horror and shame.

Surely they knew that Hiroshima was a peaceful city, not an industrial center like Kobe or Osaka. Surely they knew that the population was largely civilian. It was a favored city, a protected city . . . Suddenly, Sato understood the nature of Hiroshima's "favored" status. The city was spared just as the fattest hen is spared for the feast. The city had been set aside for this specific fate. Emiko too—yes, Emiko too. She was scheduled long ago to die on this specific day, at precisely 8:15 in the morning—not by the will of the gods but by the will of the Americans.

He thought about the men who had dropped this weapon. Were they soldiers, conscripted into the army against their will, or were they eager volunteers? Were they scientists, just like him? Had they spent the last three years of their lives perfecting this device? And if the weapon had not been used, would they have been secretly relieved? Or did the weapon, once created, have a life of its own? Did the weapon demand to be used, simply because it existed?

In war there are so many complexities, he thought, *enough to drive a man mad.*

Quite mad.

He closed his eyes, collapsed on the rubble, and fell asleep.

CHAPTER NINETEEN

MACY FOUND HERSELF STANDING motionless on the busy sidewalk like a rock in the center of a stream. She wondered how long she had been standing there, lost in the details of Li's description.

"Li, how do you know all this?"

"That's what I keep asking," Donovan said.

"I mean, a lot has been written about the experiences of people in Hiroshima and Nagasaki—but how do you know all the personal details? How do you know about Matsushita's own experience?"

"From Matsushita himself," Li said. "After the war, Matsushita surrendered to the Soviets. In 1949 the Soviets held a war crimes trial in the city of Khabarovsk in eastern Siberia. Twelve former members of Unit 731 were prosecuted for crimes against the Russian people—Matsushita was one of the defendants. His presence was only for the sake of appearance, of course—the Russians understood that Matsushita was far too valuable an asset to hang over some petty offenses against the Chinese.

"The evidence presented at the Khabarovsk trial was based upon eighteen volumes of interrogations and depositions collected from the defendants over the previous four years. I was able to obtain those eighteen volumes; to my knowledge, they are the only copies in existence. In them,

Matsushita tells everything—about his plague research, about Hiroshima, about the loss of his beloved sister."

"What was the outcome of the trial?" Donovan asked.

"The defendants were given light sentences—two years of hard labor for most. Half of them returned to Japan within a decade. No one was executed."

"And Matsushita?"

"He went to work for the Soviet Union, as a pioneer in their budding biological warfare program. A trophy catch, wouldn't you say?"

Li looked at Macy. "So what is your opinion, Dr. Monroe—am I insane or not?"

"No one ever said you were—"

"Nonsense," he said, waving off her denial. "A crusty old man appears out of nowhere, with tales of ghosts from the distant past who have returned to wreak their vengeance . . . If the possibility of my insanity didn't occur to you, I would be disappointed."

"You're not insane," Macy said. "I wish you were."

Li smiled. "Why, Dr. Monroe, are you coming to faith?"

"The history of terrorism is divided into three phases," she said. "In the sixties and seventies, terrorist organizations like the IRA focused their attacks against a single enemy, against a single nation. In the seventies and eighties, terrorists began to operate internationally, but still under the sponsorship of a country—like Libya or Iran. But in the nineties, everything changed. Terrorist organizations began to operate independently, without any responsibility to anyone. Modern terrorists don't take hostages; they don't negotiate; they don't make demands. They just kill. It's not about what they hope to achieve; it's about what's going on inside of them."

"Then Sato Matsushita is a man ahead of his time."

She nodded. "Usually we're lucky. When a man goes off the deep end, he usually loses it completely—but every now and then, there's someone who loses all sense of empathy and compassion but still keeps his rational abilities. Those are the dangerous ones; those are the ones we have to watch out for."

Li turned to Donovan. "Your lovely companion is beginning to believe," he said. "What about you?"

"She believes the motive," Donovan said. "In a criminal investigation there are three things we look for: means, motive, and opportunity."

"So we have a motive," Li said. "And opportunities for a terrorist attack are everywhere, as I'm sure you know. That leaves only the question of means."

"A biological attack is no small undertaking," Donovan said. "A lot of people have tried it and failed. Even if Matsushita wanted to, are you sure he has the means to pull it off?"

"I'm quite certain."

"Well, I'm not."

"I know someone who might convince you."

"Who?"

"His name is Pasha Mirovik. I'm told he lives not far from here—I have no idea where. Your people will have to help with this; I believe it's something of a state secret."

"Okay—I'll check it out in the morning."

"Let's call it an evening," Macy said. "I'm teaching a summer session, and I have to give an exam in the morning."

Li smiled. "It would be a privilege to be a student of yours."

"I've enjoyed being one of yours. Thanks for the story."

"I'm full of stories. Next time I'll tell you another."

Macy shook his hand and started down the sidewalk.

"Wait up," Donovan said, catching up to her in two long strides. "I'll walk you to your car."

"I don't have my car. I took the subway."

"Then I'll walk you to the station."

"Are you looking out for me now, Nathan? Please don't." She wheeled and disappeared into the flood of oncoming pedestrians.

Donovan watched until the tip of her head was no longer visible, then turned back to Li. The old man had been watching them, observing. Donovan felt a flush of anger.

"Seen enough?" he asked.

"Oh, not nearly enough. How long were the two of you married?"

"Who said we were married?"

Li rolled his eyes. "Please."

Donovan paused. "Five years. How did you know?"

"There is a certain *tension* between you, the kind no two strangers can ever achieve. How does the old saying go? 'Heaven hath no rage like love to hatred turned.'"

"Confucius?"

"No, William Congreve—a fellow countryman. Perhaps you're more familiar with the second half of the quotation: "And hell hath no fury like the wrath of a woman scorned."

"I know that part," Donovan said. The two men turned and started slowly down the sidewalk again.

"Care to talk about it?" Li asked.

"No."

"That seems unfair. I've told you some of my very best stories, and yet you refuse to tell me one of yours."

"You asked me to listen to your stories," Donovan said.

"A minor point. You know, I like Dr. Monroe very much. Will she meet with us again?"

"For now."

"*Macy*—what a curious name. Like the large department store?"

Donovan smiled. "I'll have to remember that one."

"The hostility between you seems a bit one-sided."

"What?"

"Dr. Monroe—Macy—she seems to harbor more anger than you do. Not that you're short of anger, mind you; I'd say you're positively seething with it. But she seems like less of an angry person—her anger seems to be directed only at you. Would you say this is true?"

"I wouldn't say."

They passed an alley, and there was a flurry of movement in the shadows. "Let me show you something," Li said. "I think you'll find this interesting."

They walked several yards into the alley, to the point where the streetlights could no longer penetrate and visual details disappeared into silhouettes. The alley seemed old and narrow, with a cobblestone pavement that dipped in the center, allowing a rivulet of runoff from the street to trickle down the middle. The walls were lined with wooden crates and old appliances, the castoffs of a dozen former shops and businesses. Along the left wall, near a wooden doorway, was a row of black plastic garbage bags.

Li lifted one of the bags, and two plump rats scurried out into the center of the alley. They were big—a full eighteen inches from nose to tail. They were brown in color, with sooty white underbellies. They were shaped like elongated pears, with bulbous ends that tapered to a point at the snout. In the half-light of the alley, their eyes were black and glistening.

"*Rattus norvegicus*," Li announced, "commonly known as the Norwegian brown rat. There are fifty-one species of *Rattus*, but this is the only one you're likely to find in New York City—it has chased away all of the others. Watch this."

He stamped at the rats with his right foot. Instead of fleeing, they rose up on their hind legs and made a hissing sound. "Aggressive, aren't they? Rats are very territorial; they're letting us know who the boss is here."

"They could use a cat," Donovan said.

"It wouldn't last long. These rats would make a meal of an ordinary cat."

"They eat cats?"

"They've been known to eat dogs too—even pigs. A rat will eat virtually anything—they're omnivorous. They eat naturally occurring foods, of course—by some estimates, a third of the world's food supply is consumed by rats. They eat grains and fruits and vegetables, but they especially love garbage—our garbage. Some experts believe that rats develop 'local food dialects.' That means they develop a taste for the ethnic foods of the neighborhood in which they live. These are Chinatown rats—a particularly fortunate group."

Li replaced the garbage bag, and the rats darted behind it again. He wiped his hands on his trousers and turned to Donovan.

"Rats depend upon human beings for their survival," he said. "That means they're never far away. They live in our basements, our attics, our sewers—perhaps under the floorboards of your own house. They can fit most anywhere.

An adult rat can weigh up to two pounds, but it can fit through a hole less than an inch wide. Their skeletons are able to collapse, you see."

"I grew up on a farm," Donovan said. "As a boy I once helped my dad tear up the old threshing floor in the barn. When we lifted the boards, there were hundreds of them underneath."

"They breed prolifically. Some say there is a rat for every person in New York City."

They started back toward the street now. The streetlights, though dim, seemed blinding in contrast with the darkness of the alley. At the corner they turned left and continued down the sidewalk. It was getting late now, and only a few stragglers remained.

"Thanks for the nature lesson," Donovan said.

"Oh, it was much more than that. I wanted to make three important observations: Rats live near humans, rats can go anywhere, and in a city this size, there could be millions. The Norwegian brown rat, you see, was responsible for transporting the fleas that decimated medieval Europe. If Sato Matsushita were to disperse plague-infected fleas in New York, these rats would carry the disease to every corner of the city."

Li stopped in front of an old brick building. "This is it," he said.

"What?"

"This is where I live."

Donovan looked up. The building looked ancient, decrepit, like most of the buildings in Chinatown. "This isn't a hotel."

"New York hotels are a bit pricey, especially for an extended visit. I'm staying in a *gong si fong*."

"A what?"

"A kind of boardinghouse. Very cozy, very inexpensive. Would you like to come up?"

There was an open doorway that led to a tiny foyer, illumined only by the streetlights from outside. On the left wall was a long-abandoned doorbell system for the apartments above; nothing remained but a tarnished brass skeleton with holes where black buttons once protruded. The wooden stairway was steep and hollow sounding and awkwardly narrow.

Donovan's shoulders almost brushed both walls as he climbed from stair to stair. At the top was a brief landing, and then the corridor turned left. It was dark except for a single lightbulb at the opposite end; the glow from the bare bulb gave the hallway a haunting, tunnel-like effect.

Beneath the lightbulb was a door. Li used a key to unlock a small padlock, and they both stepped inside.

They were standing in the living room of a one-bedroom apartment. The living room was divided into four smaller sections by sheets of unpainted plywood.

"I love what you've done with the place," Donovan said.

"It isn't all mine. Let me show you my room."

Li slid aside a plywood panel and gestured for Donovan to enter. Donovan had to duck and turn sideways to fit through the opening. The space inside was smaller than some closets, no more than six by six. Most of the space was taken up by a bunk bed; there was no other furniture in the room.

"I'm fortunate to have a window," Li said.

Donovan looked. The outside of the glass had probably never been cleaned—it was like looking through waxed paper. Under the window was the only shelf in the room. It held a Bible and a coffee mug with a red toothbrush inside. Beside it was a dimpled black case, the kind that might carry a small musical instrument. Li silently took the case and slid it under the bed beside a canvas duffle.

"Which bunk is yours?" Donovan asked.

"I selected the bottom—then my roommate arrived and assigned me the top. I had a prior claim, but he was younger and larger. I thought it best not to press the point."

Donovan sat down on the bottom bunk. He could lean forward and touch the opposite wall. From the plywood panels, a series of twenty-penny nails projected, providing the only closet space in the room.

"How many people live here?"

"Eight—though I believe it holds ten."

Ten bodies packed into this dump? Donovan had seen these places before. Some greedy landlord bought a substandard apartment, then divvied it up into four or five bathroom stalls and rented each one for half the going rate. The landlord made a killing, and the renters didn't complain. They couldn't—half of them were illegal aliens.

"Li, this place is illegal."

"But affordable."

"I can't let you stay here. How would it look for a guest of the federal government to be staying in illegal housing?"

"What does the federal government suggest?"

"We'll put you up in a hotel. There are a couple not far from 26 Fed that the Bureau uses for visitors."

"What about the food?"

"You can eat in the hotel restaurant. Just sign it to your room."

"Yes, but what about the *food*?"

"Stop whining," Donovan said. "It's a step up from England."

"But it's a step down from Chinatown. Besides, I already know my way around here."

"I don't. I get lost every time I come down here."

"Well, I certainly don't want to put the whole burden on you. There must be some solution that would be equitable for both of us. Let's think for a moment." Li stood there, staring at Donovan.

Donovan considered the time he had already wasted picking his way through the crowded streets of Chinatown. He thought about his three-hour field trip to the Cloisters, seventy blocks past Columbia. He thought about Li's annoying habit of selecting meeting sites for their educational value instead of proximity, and he wondered what his next choice might be—Boston? Then he thought about the realities of depositing the old man at a hotel: picking him up, dropping him off, making sure he ate enough lousy American food . . . *Forget it,* Donovan thought. *The only way to reduce the hassle is to keep him close at hand.*

"Why don't you stay with me for a few days?" Donovan offered.

Li brightened. "What a splendid idea! It would be so convenient, and it would give us much more time to *talk.*"

Li was packed in an instant; everything fit into the canvas duffel. As

Donovan stepped into the doorway, a young Chinese man bumped into him. He was a head taller than Li, almost as tall as Donovan—but he had only half of Donovan's mass.

"Ah, my roommate," Li said. "Just in time to see me off."

Donovan and the young man squared off in the narrow doorway. Donovan locked eyes with him. "Do you speak English?"

The man nodded.

Donovan dropped the canvas duffel and stepped to the window. He shoved it open, then turned back to the lower bunk. He rolled up the mattress and bedding and stuffed it out the window; it disappeared silently into the alley below. He returned to the doorway and glared into the young man's astonished face.

"Now *you've* got the top bunk," he said.

CHAPTER TWENTY

DONOVAN PUSHED OPEN THE door and flipped on the light. Li stood in the doorway, peering inside. The central room was average in size and perfectly square. It was almost empty, except for a brownish-gold three-cushion sofa that slumped toward the center; one of the cushions was patched with crisscrossed pieces of gray duct tape. The sofa faced a small TV stand with spindly wooden legs that tapered to brass tips. On top of the stand was a nineteen-inch television with two chrome rabbit ears jutting out at the twelve and two o'clock positions; on the end of one was a crumpled piece of aluminum foil. From the center of the ceiling, a hanging lamp dangled from a length of tarnished chain. It was octagonal, like an Oriental lantern, but with panels of pebbled yellow glass framed in scrolling black metal. It was easily the ugliest fixture Li had ever seen.

"You consider this an improvement on the *gong si fong*?"

"There's no place like home," Donovan said. "Come on in."

Li took a step back and glanced from side to side. "There are prison bars on your windows," he said. "Is there something you're not telling me?"

"They're just for security."

Li glanced around the room. "If you don't mind my asking—what do you have to secure here?"

"Are you coming in or not?"

Li placed one toe on the matted carpet as if he were testing the thickness of ice.

"You can have your own room," Donovan said.

"Lucky me."

"Don't they have security windows in London?"

"Yes—in the bad sections."

"Well, the South Bronx is a tough neighborhood."

"I noticed that. There seem to be a number of dilapidated buildings."

"Just like Chinatown."

"Chinatown is simply old—a third of the buildings were built before 1900. Here the buildings just seem neglected."

"This part of the Bronx was practically abandoned thirty years ago. The whole borough was going under. Owners set fire to the buildings for the insurance money—there were twelve thousand fires a year here in the seventies. The city figured it would cost half as much to just gut the buildings and rebuild the insides as it would to knock them down and start over. The insides look pretty good; just the outsides look bad."

"Just the outsides," Li mumbled. "And this type of housing is legal?"

"Sure."

"Whereas the *gong si fong* was not?"

"Li—there were eight people living in a one-bedroom apartment."

"So the deciding factor is population density? If that's the case, New York City should be illegal."

"Will you stop complaining?"

"I'm not complaining. I'm just . . . readjusting."

"You should feel right at home here. In Chinatown you had what—Chinese, Koreans, Vietnamese?"

"Also Indonesians, Burmese, Malaysians, and Fujians."

"Well, here you've got Irish, Italians, Hispanics, and Russians. Take your pick."

"Who were the young men loitering on the street corners?"

"That depends on who owned the corner."

"And who owns *this* corner?"

"Me."

"Does everyone else know that?"

"I have to remind them from time to time. C'mon, I'll show you your room."

Through an opening in the far wall was a short hallway. On the immediate left was a closed door; straight ahead, a small bathroom; on the right, an open doorway. Donovan reached in and switched on the light. There was a flash of blue and white, and then the room went dark again.

"I'll get you a bulb," Donovan said.

"Please—take the one from that yellow lantern."

In the far corner was a single bed with a bare mattress; in the opposite corner was a particle-board dresser topped by a wooden frame but no mirror. They were the only two objects in the room. Between them, a closet with sliding doors stood open. One door was off its track, sloping down and resting one corner on the carpet. Inside the closet, a tangle of empty wire hangers was just visible.

Li sat down quietly on the edge of the mattress.

"I'll fix up the bed," Donovan said.

"The way you fixed my roommate's?"

Donovan smiled. "If I had a choice, I would have thrown your roommate out the window."

"You had a choice," Li said. "Why didn't you?"

"There's a little matter of the law."

"Ah, yes, the law. Is the law all that constrains you?"

"I don't like bullies," Donovan said. "I never have."

"Neither do I." Li looked up at him in the darkness. "I have fought against bullies all my life. A sad reality of life is that a time comes when a man must choose his battles. He must learn to fight in a different way—like a swordsman who loses his strong arm in battle. Do you understand what I'm saying?"

"I should have thrown him out the window with my left hand?"

"I'm saying that all men grow old. Young men fight with their bodies because their bodies are strong; old men fight with their minds because that's where true strength lies—in wisdom. The wise man puts away anger and violence before they betray him. He who lives by the sword dies by the sword."

"I'm not old yet," Donovan said.

"You're not wise yet either."

Donovan turned toward the door. "I'll get you some sheets."

"Nathan," Li said, "I want you to know that I appreciated that gesture very much. It was very decent of you—even noble. It's a difficult thing to grow old and to know that you can no longer defend yourself. Fifty years ago, I would have boxed his ears myself."

"Would that have been wise?"

"Touché." The old man smiled. "Can you sit for a moment?"

"Li—"

"Please." He patted the mattress beside him. Donovan let out a heavy sigh, then leaned against the dresser and folded his arms.

"May I ask you a question?" Li said.

"I figured you would."

"Do you always wear black?"

"What?"

"Black or navy blue—it's all I ever see you wear."

"It takes ten pounds off me. Macy taught me that."

"The Chinese prefer red—red symbolizes happiness, or wealth, or good fortune. Yellow is the color of nobility; green represents growth. To the Chinese, black is an unhappy color. Black is the color of servitude."

"Then I'm definitely switching to pastels."

"Nathan. Are you unhappy?"

Donovan groaned. "Li, you've spent your whole life worrying about Japanese war criminals and bubonic plague epidemics—are *you* happy?"

"You know, the Greek word for 'happiness' is *eudaimonia.* It means 'good spirit' or 'good soul.' To the ancients, happiness meant much more than some superficial feeling. It meant that everything was right with your soul."

"Is everything right with *your* soul?"

Li paused. "Not yet. But it will be."

"It's dark in here," Donovan said. "Let's go out to the family room."

"The 'family room'—that's rather euphemistic, isn't it? The *gong si fong* was more family-oriented than this place."

"What did you expect? It's a bachelor pad."

"But you were not always a bachelor."

"Let's not go there, okay?"

Li looked around the room again. "I'm a little surprised by your living conditions."

"It's *affordable.*"

"I had little choice in living arrangements; I would think you do. I assumed that federal agents were paid better than this. Do any of your associates live in this area?"

Donovan shook his head. "The commute's a little long."

"Yes, the commute. Tell me, do most FBI operatives enjoy approximately the same standard of living?"

"Look," Donovan said. "Most married agents live over in Jersey, in some nice little FBI neighborhood like Woodbridge, or maybe down in Monmouth County. Single agents live wherever they can find affordable housing."

"Like this?"

"How would I know? I haven't visited them all."

"And when you were married—where did you and Macy live?"

"We had a house—near the rest of them."

"I've heard divorce can be quite expensive."

"I'm not paying alimony, if that's what you're wondering. Macy makes more than I do."

"Child support?"

Donovan didn't reply.

Li looked at the dresser behind Donovan. Now that his eyes had adjusted to the darkness, he could see small shards of mirror still protruding from the wooden frame.

"I'd like to tell you a story," Li said.

"C'mon, Li, it's late. I'm off duty."

"You're off duty from gaining wisdom?"

"Is it a short one?"

"Is the path to enlightenment a short one?"

"Tonight it is. Give me the abbreviated version, okay?"

"If you insist—but it really hampers my style. Once there was a man—"

"Is this a Chinese story?"

"Of course. All great stories originated in China. The Greeks lifted a few, but the stories were originally Chinese. Now, where was I? Oh, yes. Once there was a man who possessed a magic ring, a ring that could make him invisible. But the ring was so precious to him, he feared losing it so very much that he took the ring and hid with it in the center of a mountain."

"Li—this is Lord of the Rings."

"You've heard it before? That rather spoils it."

"Everybody in America has heard it before."

"I never should have told it to Tolkien. Anyway, when the man emerged from the mountain and looked at his reflection in a stream, he realized that he had become a salamander."

"I don't remember that part."

"The story was later embellished to fill the pages of a book. Now, tell me, what is the lesson of the story—*my* version?"

"Men shouldn't wear jewelry."

"You're not trying."

"I give up."

"Don't you see? We are influenced by the things that surround us. Darkness begets darkness."

"I see darkness," Donovan said, "and I want to go to bed. I'll get you those sheets. You need anything else?"

"Just a few seconds to unpack. In the morning, what will our agenda be?"

"I need to track down that name you gave me."

"I suggest you check with your government's witness protection program. They might be able to help."

"Will you be okay here by yourself?"

"Just slip some food under the bars from time to time. Pleasant dreams, Nathan."

"You tell me a scary story and then you say, 'Pleasant dreams'? Some grandpa you are."

"Think about the story."

"I have—the elf woman was hot."

"Think about *my* story."

Donovan flipped off the light switch, but nothing happened. *Darkness begets darkness,* he thought.

CHAPTER TWENTY-ONE

"Don't lift until I tell you," Donovan's father said.

"Right." His father worked the pry bar along the edges of the long wooden planks. They creaked and groaned as they began to separate from the barn floor for the first time in years. A crack began to widen; Donovan squeezed his fingers in and felt for a solid grip. His father pried up one end just enough to force a two-by-four into the hole, then wedged a cinder block underneath it to use as a fulcrum.

"Okay," his father said simply, and they both began to lift.

The plank suddenly gave way, landing with a crash on the floor beside it. The gap left by the plank revealed a fist-deep space beneath it, and it seemed to be alive. It was swarming with a wriggling mass of brown and gray and white fur.

"Barn rats," his father said. "Lots of 'em."

Suddenly, the rats began to flow up and out from under the planks, like water bubbling up from a sewer. They kept coming, and coming, until there were thousands of them covering the remains of the threshing floor. There were too many, far too many, and it frightened Donovan. He stamped his foot at them and shouted, but the moment he did, he knew that was a mistake.

They turned and looked at him, and then they all began to rise up on their hind legs and hiss. It was a small sound at first, like a handful of garden snakes might make, but rat after rat joined in until the sound was like the growl of a jungle cat.

Then they all fell silent at once, and Donovan turned to run—but his father stood calmly, with his gloved hands resting on one end of the standing two-by-four. The rats swarmed up and over the man in an instant, covering every inch of his body.

Donovan raced to his father and grabbed two rats by their backs. They were thick and muscular, and they twisted in his hands like two sinewy eels. One turned and sank its curving yellow teeth into the base of his thumb. He felt no pain, but he threw the rats away from him and reached for two more, ripping them away from his father's face.

But it wasn't his father at all. Now it was a young boy, standing and crying softly.

"Make them stop," the boy sobbed.

Donovan felt a wave of panic. He began to pull the rats away faster and faster, but the instant he tore one away, another wriggled in to take its place.

"Help me," the boy pleaded, but he was invisible now, covered entirely in a roiling mass of squealing, scurrying fur.

And the pile began to grow smaller, and the voice grew fainter.

In desperation, Donovan grabbed for the two-by-four and swung at the center of the pile. The impact felt thick and rubbery. Rats flew everywhere, shrieking and hissing through the air. He swung again and again until the pile disappeared completely, but there was nothing inside.

"Daddy!"

DONOVAN JERKED UPRIGHT IN bed. He was breathing hard and fast, and his jaws were aching. *It's a wonder I have any molars left*, he thought. He didn't bother to look at the clock—he knew what time it would be.

No use trying to go back to sleep—there never was. By the time the adrenaline wore off, it was always time for work anyway. He got out of bed and stood directly in front of the window unit air conditioner. The old machine throbbed and groaned, and the plastic panel on the front made a buzzing sound. He jammed it with the butt of his hand, and it stopped—but several seconds later it returned again like an annoying mosquito.

He pulled on yesterday's crewneck and a pair of slacks and stepped into the hallway. Li's door was open just a crack. He tiptoed across the family room, turned the dead bolt on the front door, and closed it quietly behind him.

The night air had a slight coolness to it, and there was a gentle breeze that rose and fell like waves on a seashore. It was late June, still more spring than summer, when the New York air becomes thick and stagnant and the heat is impossible to escape.

At the street he stopped and looked both ways. *Which way tonight?* It didn't matter. He had no place to go anyway—he just had to *move.* Anything was better than lying in a bed in the dark with no chance of escape into the oblivion of sleep—and even when sleep came, it always brought the dreams. In the last year, Donovan had learned that there are different kinds of darkness. There's the darkness that fills the alleys of the South Bronx at night, the kind you can walk into and out of, and there's the darkness that comes from inside—the kind you can't fight or escape, the kind you can only lie there and feel, paralyzed and screaming, while it takes its own sweet time.

Just then the yellow streetlights to his right clicked off, recycling for a few moments, and he took it as a minor omen; he turned right and headed into the darkness. The streets were almost empty at four o'clock; they always were. *You learn a lot when you don't waste time sleeping,* Donovan thought, *things that other people never know.* You learn that every city has a cycle of life and death that repeats itself day after day. In the morning the city is an infant, full of hope and limitless possibilities. By afternoon it's already full grown, burdened with the endless responsibilities of life. The evening is the city's golden years, those pitifully few remaining hours that only a handful are allowed to enjoy. Then at midnight the clock silently strikes, and old age falls like a heavy curtain. The next two hours are a kind of death kick, when the feeble and dying frantically try to strengthen their grip on life. Two o'clock is a kind of funeral, when coffin doors are shut tight and lights are put out, and for the next three hours the city lies smoldering in its grave, awaiting its daily resurrection. Donovan looked at his watch. *Just my luck*, he thought, *to be alive when everyone else is dead and dead when everyone else is alive.*

He wandered for half an hour before starting for home again, keeping to the coolness of the shadows. He turned down alleyways, the narrower the better, and cut across vacant lots littered with the detritus of other people's lives. He emerged from one alley and heard voices; on a street corner he saw three men huddled together, some of the living dead who inhabit every city at night. As Donovan approached, the men looked up. He stopped directly in front of them. One mumbled a reluctant greeting, but Donovan said nothing in reply. He just glared at each of them, one by one, until they silently shuffled aside to let him pass. He pushed by them, bumping the shoulder of one, listening hard for any half-whispered curse or remark—anything to give him an excuse to turn back. He even hunched down a little as he passed, trying to look smaller than he was, but none of them were fooled. Maybe they had heard about him, the man in black who walked the streets at night. Maybe they were friends of the men who hadn't been as cautious—the one with the broken jaw, or the one whose forearm had snapped in two like an old broom handle.

Back at the house, Donovan quietly let himself in and bolted the door again. He walked to the kitchen and pulled the coffeemaker out on the counter. He opened the top and peered in at the filter; there were still some grounds left over from the day before. He sniffed. *Strong enough to squeeze out a little more caffeine*, he thought. *I'll just run it through twice.*

Then he heard a noise, and he froze. He was used to being alone in the house, and the only sounds he heard at night were inhuman: the pulsing of his air conditioner, a sudden crack from the walls as the old framing cooled and contracted—sometimes even the quick scurrying of feet in the rafters over his head. This sound was different—it was a high-pitched cry or groan, the kind a wounded animal might make.

Donovan thought about his Glock. He wasn't stupid enough to take it with him when he went out at night; it would be where it always was, on the nightstand to the right of his bed. He started down the hallway, then stopped. The sound was coming from Li's room. He put an ear to the crack and listened: The old man was crying—but it was unlike any human cry Donovan had ever heard. It was pure grief, raw and unadulterated. There was no anger or pettiness or self-pity in the voice. There was no shame or restraint either—the grief was simply there, and it flowed out of the old man like sap from a wounded tree.

The grief came in rolling waves. First there was a low groan, punctuated by woeful laments in broken Chinese; then his words began to quicken, and his voice rose until it crescendoed in a mournful wail and receded again in gentle sobbing. Donovan suddenly wondered if he himself had ever really cried in his entire life—when his mother passed, when he found his father hanging from the rafters in the barn, even when little Jeremy died. No, not even for Jeremy—not like this. Compared to Li's grief, he wondered if anyone else had ever cried at all.

Donovan thought about knocking—but it seemed somehow unholy to interrupt this moment with a sudden rap on a doorframe. Instead, he silently pushed the door open a few inches and peered inside. Li knelt on the floor in front of his bed; on the mattress was a faded black-and-white photograph of a young Chinese couple standing in front of a stone well. They were dressed ceremoniously, in long silken robes with dark-colored belts. They held hands, and they were grinning from ear to ear.

Each time Li's lament began to rise, he would take the faded photo from the bed and clutch it to his chest, rocking back and forth and weeping at the ceiling. When the weeping subsided, he would carefully return the photograph and study it again, waiting for the next wave to come rolling into shore.

Donovan felt suddenly ashamed. As an FBI agent, he was used to interrupting people at awkward moments. He had arrested men at dinner with their families, in bed with their wives—he once even dragged a man off a toilet in a public restroom. This was different. Those were embarrassments, those were inconveniences—this was something worse. He reached for the doorknob to pull the door shut again, but he moved too quickly and the doorknob made a slight rattling sound. Li turned and looked at him.

The two men stared into each other's eyes but said nothing. Donovan's mind raced, searching for some acceptable excuse, or even better, some glib remark that might reduce his offense from a blasphemy to a minor faux pas. But he could think of nothing to say; after a few seconds he simply lowered his eyes and quietly shut the door.

He stood in the hallway for a moment, then crossed back to his own bedroom and sat down on the edge of the bed, staring across the hall at Li's closed door.

What do you know? he thought. *I'm not the only one who can't sleep.*

CHAPTER TWENTY-TWO

Sato Matsushita knelt before a small Shinto shrine in his Damascus apartment. In the center of the shelf was a box made of Japanese cypress in the shape of a temple, with a door that opened on tiny brass hinges. In front of the box were three white bowls containing rice, water, and salt, and on either side were fresh cuttings from a Syrian olive tree.

Sato neatly scripted a wish on a small prayer paper, then opened the little door and placed the paper inside along with all the others—all bearing the same identical words. He bowed his head and closed his eyes for a moment; then he rose and stepped the few paces to his bed, the only other object in the room. He took one corner of the blanket and pulled it down diagonally across the bed, folding it as crisply as a piece of paper. He sat down on the edge of the bed and pulled his feet from his slippers, leaving them perfectly aligned on the floor beside him. He turned ninety degrees and tucked his feet under the blanket, pulling it neatly up over his body as he reclined with his head in the precise center of the pillow. He stared at the ceiling for a few moments, blinking; then he closed his eyes and willed a dream to return to him, a dream that he had carefully crafted one element at a time every night for sixty years.

By seven o'clock, tens of thousands already line the shores of the East River, setting up lawn chairs and spreading out blankets in anticipation of the event still two hours away. The FDR Drive is closed from Fourteenth to Forty-second Streets, providing thirty blocks of unimpeded view. In the center of the river, just below the tip of Roosevelt Island, three black barges sit silently in the water, each one honeycombed with hundreds of steel and fiberglass pipes. Across the river in Queens, hundreds of thousands more crowd rooftops, balconies, and parking lots. Soon every driveway and backyard patio within eyeshot will be filled, every spot that allows an unobstructed view of the western sky.

Just below the Brooklyn Bridge, two more barges lie deep in the water, midway between the boroughs of Brooklyn and Manhattan. The streets around the South Street Seaport and the Brooklyn Heights Promenade are already packed tight. In the final light of day, the towering skyscrapers of Manhattan cast their shadows clear across the river; in the deepening darkness, tiny figures scurry about like insects. Up the Hudson, two more barges are positioned across from the Village, and the piers along West Street and on the opposite Jersey shore are all crowded with people.

Farthest to the south, a single barge lies anchored in the Upper Bay, equidistant between the tip of Manhattan and the shore of Liberty Island. The view from this barge is spectacular, breathtaking, unparalleled in all the world. This is the master barge—this is where I will stand. From here I can see the entire skyline of Manhattan, its soaring spires glittering with dots of light against the darkening sky. From here I can see four of the city's five boroughs, containing 80 percent of the city's eight million inhabitants. From here I can see five of the eight rectangular barges, closing around the city like the teeth of a giant beast.

It is eight o'clock now. The sky is clear, and the air is perfectly still. The ground is still warm, but a cool blanket of air settles over it, creating an inversion that will keep the tiny fleas from being blown away by gusts of wind. Tonight the sun will set at exactly 8:30 p.m. At 9:03 civil twilight will end, when the sun dips precisely six degrees below the horizon and objects can no longer be clearly distinguished by the naked eye. The phase of the moon is a waning crescent with only 3 percent of its disk illumined, just a tiny silver sliver in the summer sky. At 9:04, when the first cannon shells are sounded, the sky will be almost completely black.

Young men recline on grassy medians and tune their radios to the musical simulcast. Mothers pass food around on paper plates and keep a watchful eye on wandering children. Fathers hold toddlers in their laps, pointing into the skies and building anticipation. Some take advantage of the darkness to embrace, while others scout for better locations, staking out new territories and waving for friends to join them. And still more people come, pouring out of the city and pushing toward the rivers, packing against the banks like drifting grains of sand.

Now it is nine o'clock, and I take a seat on the edge of the barge and allow my legs to hang down over the water. On the western horizon a line of light grows thinner and brighter, like the last light from a dying candle. As darkness settles, the night grows somehow quieter, as if the entire city is holding its breath before letting out its first astonished gasp. In a few moments the Americans will celebrate their day of independence, and I will celebrate with them—I will celebrate the independence of my soul.

And then it begins.

From all eight barges simultaneously comes a thundering cannonade that echoes off the sides of the buildings. Seconds later, the sky lights up in cascading showers of silver and gold. I can hear traces of the patriotic refrains that synchronize the barrage, and I can imagine the oohs and aahs and the scattered applause arising from the appreciative crowds. The detonations grow faster now, more than a hundred every minute from my barge alone, and I can feel the vibration of each explosion as it sends its shell rocketing into the sky.

I look out over the city. There are floral shells that cover the sky with multicolored blossoms. There are golden brocade crowns that drape down over the water like the branches of weeping willows. There are skyrockets that make spiraling silver columns as they rise, and there are spangled star mines that rise invisibly into the night before erupting in startling reds and greens. The sky explodes in time with the music, fortissimo and pianissimo, and everywhere faces light up in wide-eyed wonder.

It is a spectacular display, truly a work of art. It is a fitting closing ceremony for the world's most powerful city.

At last the finale approaches, and the sky is like a black fabric ripping apart so that the sun shines through from behind. Rockets, streamers, starbursts everywhere; the music rises to a fevered pitch, and then suddenly stops—one last detonation can be heard, lower and louder than any before it. The city holds its breath. Seconds later, eight brilliant cherry trees stand glistening in the nighttime sky—and then simultaneously vanish. In the silence that follows, I can hear the roaring cheers from the surrounding shores.

Now the sky is dark again, but it is not empty. The air is filled with clouds of smoke, and bits of ash and paper rain down everywhere. Some pick bits of wadding from their hair or clothing. Some brush away still-burning sparks or embers. Some absentmindedly scratch at the tiny, biting specks that dot their necks and arms. And in the gutters and alleys near the rivers, rats snap angrily at their haunches and then scurry into drainpipes and sewers.

Even before the applause dies away, people start back toward the city. Eyes turn away from the nighttime sky; blankets are gathered, belongings collected, children taken by the hand to begin the long walk home. Back to houses and apartments; back to childhood homes and hotel rooms held only for a night; back to Upper West Side lofts and tenement slums; back to New York City—and back to cities all over the eastern United States.

The first symptoms appear just two days later, first among the elderly and the immune-suppressed. The symptoms are minor—just a cough, or a chill, or a slight fever. They scold themselves for going out in the nighttime air, and they make a mental note to dress warmer next time. They take their favorite over-the-counter remedies and retreat to their beds.

But the next day they feel no better, and soon they are visited by friends, by loved ones, by little grandchildren bringing consolation and comfort. They sit together in the same little rooms, breathing the same air. There are coughs and sneezes; there are handshakes and kisses and hugs.

A cat plays with a dead rat in an empty lot. A child pets the cat. A mother embraces the child. The woman makes love with her husband. The husband shakes hands with a client. The client boards a jet for home. A woman greets the man at the airport. And so the Pestilence travels, with its own mass-transit system and port authority, taking in every sight in the city and visiting every corner of the nation.

The next to take ill are the children; because they breathe faster than adults, their lungs are more susceptible to inhalational agents. Soon even the healthy and strong begin to experience fever, headache, weakness, and shortness of breath. There are rumors of an influenza outbreak. Pharmacy shelves are stripped bare; physicians' waiting rooms and urgent-care centers are crowded to overflowing. Doctors make their first inaccurate diagnoses: pneumonia, bronchitis, flu. Broadband antibiotics are prescribed, hoping for a panacea. The first specimens of bloody sputum are sent to laboratories to grow cultures, a process that will take forty-eight precious hours to complete.

Within six days the Pestilence erupts all over the city—but in different forms, with different effects. In some victims the plague is bubonic. Agonizing purplish masses appear in groins and armpits and necks, pus-filled tumors the size of oranges. Fevers rise to brain-boiling temperatures, and everywhere they collapse in exhaustion and delirium.

In others, the plague goes directly to the bloodstream. The blood in their vessels begins to thicken and clot. Pustules open; purpuric lesions appear; the tips of their fingers and toes turn scarlet-black.

And in others, the plague is in the lungs. Pulses race; they pant like winded animals, stopping only to cough up bright red blood, ejecting particles of pestilence everywhere. There is no one to care for them; they lie untended on soiled sheets, their skin cold and dry from endless diarrhea.

A dozen genetically altered strains release invisible toxins into the blood. Each strain multiplies like a colony of tiny immigrants, claiming a portion of the city for its own. In Brooklyn, *myelin* toxin predominates. People lie paralyzed in hallways and on bedroom floors, staring helplessly up at the ceiling, choking to death on their own vomit.

Botulinum claims Staten Island. The toxin binds to nerve endings, blocking the signals that command muscles to contract, always beginning in the head and spreading downward. Eyelids droop, and speech slurs. They cough up blood but cannot swallow. Then the toxin reaches the lungs, and frantic victims struggle for final breaths of air.

Anatoxin A makes its home in the Bronx, where bodies drop to the ground in midstride. *Microcystin* prefers the suburban feel of Queens, causing liver enlargement, stupor, and shock. And Manhattan, the great melting pot, opens its doors to everyone. All over the city, toxins reveal their deadly surprises like exploding fireworks. There are starbursts of purple and red and black everywhere. Some sag slowly to the ground like brocade crowns; others drop like cannon shots. Some leave trails behind them like blazing skyrockets; others seem to appear out of nowhere, then vanish before your eyes. And the sounds are everywhere—the shrill cries, the booming shouts, the rocketing screams.

State and local health officials rush to the scene with neatly bound contingency plans tucked under their arms. But in their darkest dreams they never imagined something like this. They try every palliative in their pharmacopoeia: streptomycin, tetracycline, gentamicin, doxycycline. But nothing seems to work—nothing even helps.

There is no way to isolate the disease. Quarantine is impossible—the disease seems to have emerged everywhere at once. They desperately attempt to quarantine the city itself. They close airports and bus terminals; they barricade highways and shut down trains and subways. But it's far too late for that. Airplanes have already departed; trains have left the stations; ships have put to sea. Soon children of the plague will appear everywhere, like tiny blossoms sent out by a colossal floral shell.

And I will walk the streets of New York, just as I walked the streets of Hiroshima sixty years ago. But this time there will be no fiery sky, no choking clouds of dust. All the buildings will still be standing, all the parks still green and lush—but all the guilty will be dead or dying. And I will walk among them hand in hand with Emiko, and we will see the final blackness together—the blackened faces, the blackened limbs, the blackened bodies. We will see the blackness everywhere. Then at last there will be justice; then at last Emiko will have peace.

Truly a fitting end for the most powerful city in the world.

Truly a work of art.

CHAPTER TWENTY-THREE

Li stood in front of the open refrigerator and peered inside. It had the same desolate look as the rest of Donovan's house—just a handful of random items scattered across the shelves without any apparent logic. There were olives with plump red pimientos staring out from a half-empty jar of greenish brine. There was an oven-ready cheese pizza shrink-wrapped against a circle of cardboard, with furry patches of green and blue encroaching from the edges. There were plastic bottles of ketchup and mustard—though Li could not imagine what they would be used for. And there was a solitary silver can in the corner, sporting a plastic necklace with five empty holes where its companions once stood. The refrigerator was dark; Li put his hand inside to make sure it was cold.

"Help yourself," Li said aloud. "How very generous of him."

There was a knock at the front door. Li removed the chain, twisted the dead bolt, and opened it. He found himself staring up into the face of a thick-featured man with heavy, drooping eyelids and untamable gray hair.

"Hey," Poldie said. "You're that Chinese guy."

"A shrewd deduction," Li said. "And I recognize that voice—you must be Detective Satwyck; I spoke with you on the phone the other day."

Poldie stepped past Li and into the house. "Where's Donovan? We ride together on Thursdays."

"You've just missed him. I'm afraid that's my fault; I sent him on an unexpected errand, you see. Can you stay for a moment? Please, sit down. I'd try to avoid the duct tape if I were you—it will leave an adhesive residue on that lovely suit."

Poldie shrugged, turned, and hovered over the sofa before dropping onto it like an ox backing into a stall. The sofa made a squealing sound.

"Can I get you anything? Some beer and olives, perhaps?"

Poldie gave the offer serious consideration, then ran a hand across his sprawling midsection. "Better wait for lunch," he said. "So—what's this errand?"

"Nathan is attempting to locate Pasha Mirovik."

"Who?"

"Pasha Mirovik—a Soviet scientist who defected to your country a decade ago. He may be able to provide information on the whereabouts of Sato Matsushita."

"Oh, right." Poldie groaned. "The big conspiracy."

Li smiled. "Tell me, how is your investigation into the TriBeCa murder proceeding?"

"Uh-uh," Poldie said. "I already got my hand slapped once for talking to you."

"That's very unfair; they really should be thanking you."

"Huh?"

"Think about it: If you hadn't made the on-the-spot decision to mention those fleas to the *Times* reporter, I would not be here today. If by some chance I do make some small contribution to this investigation, *you* will be the one ultimately responsible."

Poldie blinked.

"I find it remarkable," Li said. "How does a police officer develop that kind of instinct? You could have mentioned anything to the reporter, I suppose, but you chose to mention the fleas. How do you know which bit of information to release to the press? You must have planned your strategy well in advance."

"It's a gut thing," Poldie said. "You got to think on your feet."

Li shook his head in admiration. "Tell me—how long have you been at this?"

"Thirty years now."

"Well, that accounts for your uncanny intuition. And how long has Nathan been your junior partner?"

"Donovan? Since just after 9/11."

"Then he's just a novice compared to you. You must be a very patient man."

"Huh?"

"I mean, for a seasoned veteran to be constantly surrounded by so much inexperience. Young men can be so reckless, so impulsive at times—don't you think?"

"Well, we all had a little more gunpowder back then."

"*Gunpowder*—yes, an excellent metaphor. It seems to me that Nathan has an abundance of 'gunpowder.'"

Poldie shrugged. "It helps in a business like this."

"Are you married, Detective Satwyck?"

"Me? Sure." Poldie reached into his back pocket and pulled out his wallet. He removed a small glossy photo and handed it to Li.

Li studied the photo. She was a broad-faced woman with hair almost as wild as her husband's—only hers had been corralled into tight gray curls that gave the top of her head the overall appearance of steel wool. She had an unusually narrow forehead, as though her hair were a hat pulled down low. Her eyes were very wide and had a penetrating quality—like two rifles holding the viewer in a cross fire. To her credit, she was smiling, though Li found her smile strangely unexpressive—something like the grin on a camel. She had an altogether Wagnerian quality, and Li could easily imagine her suited out in a Viking helmet and full battle gear.

"A lovely woman," Li said. "Tell me, Detective, isn't this business of yours rather hard on a marriage at times?"

"How do you mean?"

"The anger, for instance—the *gunpowder* as you called it—what happens when you bring it home with you at night?"

"Well, Truda doesn't take any guff."

"No, I can imagine."

"We got a saying in the NYPD: When you sign up you get a gun, a badge, and a sleeper sofa."

"Is that also true of the FBI?"

"Sure—only they get pajamas."

Li nodded, though he had no idea what that meant. "I understand that Nathan was married at one time."

"Yeah, Nathan and Macy. They were the FBI poster kids for a while—Ken marries Barbie."

"They changed their names?"

"What?"

Li paused—following this man was like chasing a chicken.

"You referred to them as 'poster kids.' I assume this means they had an exemplary relationship at first."

Poldie frowned. "You always talk like that?"

"Please forgive me; it's my fourth language. I understand that Nathan and Macy later divorced."

"Well, that was because of Jeremy."

"Jeremy?"

"Their boy."

"Nathan never mentioned a son."

"He never will."

"Why not?"

"'Cause Jeremy died when he was four."

"How very sad. How did it happen?"

"The boy started having headaches. They took him in for an MRI, found out he had a brain tumor—one of those 'astral' things."

"Astrocytoma."

"What?"

"I'm sorry; please continue."

"Well, they tried radiation, chemo, even experimental drugs, but nothing stopped it. The poor kid just wasted away to nothing."

"And you were Nathan's partner during this time?"

"Yeah."

"Tell me—how did Nathan seem to handle all this?"

Poldie shrugged. "He didn't."

"He didn't?"

"He was there at first—for all the tests and procedures, I mean—and let me tell you, they did some god-awful things to that kid. But after a while, I think Donovan just couldn't take it anymore. He just sort of backed off."

"Backed off? You mean he emotionally withdrew?"

"I mean he didn't show up anymore. He let Macy handle it."

"Until the end?"

"Until the end."

Li shook his head. "And did Nathan talk to you about all this?"

"He didn't talk to anybody—he just sucked it up. I mean, it's not like we had a lot of time to hold hands and talk; this was just after 9/11, you know, and we sort of had our hands full."

"And what about Macy? Did you ever speak with her?"

"She called; she asked me to try to talk to him. And I did try, but I didn't get anywhere. Then after Jeremy died I called her—but nobody was talking to anybody then. It was all downhill from there; nobody could stop it. They split up after that."

Li paused. "Why do you think Nathan withdrew from his son?"

"How should I know?"

"I'm not asking for an explanation, Detective; I'm asking for your *instinct.*"

Poldie thought for a moment. "Did you ever have to watch somebody die—somebody you care about? And you can't do anything about it; you just have to sit there and watch?"

"I have experienced that particular horror, yes."

"Well, then you know—what it takes out of you, I mean."

"Yes," Li said. "I know."

Poldie shook his head. "I don't know what I'd do if it was me."

"No one ever does." Li looked around the room again. "So that's why there are no photographs—no memories of any kind."

"That's why."

Poldie glanced at his watch now, then began to pry himself out of the sagging cushions.

"Must you go so soon?" Li asked. "This has been so informative."

"Some of us have jobs," Poldie said. He stretched, opened the door, and stepped out onto the tiny front porch.

Li rose and followed after him. "By the way, has Nathan been involved in any other relationships since the divorce?"

"I don't think so."

"And Dr. Monroe?"

"Haven't heard of any, but it wouldn't surprise me. Have you seen her? New York men aren't blind, you know."

They reached the car now. Poldie climbed in and lowered the window.

"I enjoyed our little visit," Li said. "Thank you for taking a moment from your busy schedule."

"No problemo. And keep working on that English—it takes time."

CHAPTER TWENTY-FOUR

Macy was in her favorite outfit: a loose-fitting, long-sleeved pullover, a pair of baggy gray sweatpants, and thick cotton socks. It was her lounging outfit, her comfort suit. Macy loved the fall and winter because they allowed her to bundle up like this, and it didn't seem fair that she should have to give up the joys of warmth and coziness just because the earth decided to rotate on its axis. In the summer, she just fired up her air-conditioning and bundled up anyway. For three months every summer her electric bill was astronomical, but she didn't care. There were very few pleasures in her life right now, and a pleasure that could be purchased was a pleasure worth paying for.

She had just settled down on the sofa when the doorbell rang. When she opened the door, she found Li standing there grinning with his arms folded behind his back.

"Well, hello!" he said cheerfully.

"Li."

"The very same."

"Well, what are you—why are you—"

Li held up his hand. "Perhaps I can anticipate your first few questions. What am I doing here? I came to pay you a visit. Is this visit personal or professional in nature? That depends largely on your frame of mind. How did I get here? In one of those infamous New York taxicabs. Does Nathan know I'm here? There are many things Nathan doesn't know, as I'm sure you will agree."

Macy just stood there, dumbfounded.

"This is such a lovely front porch," Li said. "One could almost remain here."

"Oh—I'm sorry. Won't you come in?"

Li stepped in and brought out a small paper sack from behind his back. "These are scones," he said, "true English scones, not the crude American facsimiles, which taste like sawdust with a binding of glue. I don't mind telling you, it was no mean feat to find them. It seems provisions were a bit short at Nathan's house."

"They sound wonderful."

"You'll find there are two of them."

"Then all we need is tea."

"What a lovely suggestion." He walked to the sofa, took a seat, and looked back at Macy with a warm smile. Macy still stood in the doorway holding the paper sack.

"You're wondering why I didn't call first," Li said. "In point of fact, I did. I remembered that last night you said you were giving an examination today, so I called your office at Columbia University. I was informed that it was a morning class and that you planned to return to your home afterward to grade the papers. I can't say I blame you—this is really a lovely setting."

"How did you get my home address?"

"I told the departmental secretary that I was your aged uncle from Great Britain, who just arrived from Heathrow to find himself stranded and forgotten at LaGuardia. It was my first time in the States, you see, and everything was so big and confusing. If only she would give me your home address, I could take a taxi and meet you there. The story had just enough pathos to do the trick."

"You lied?"

"I did *research*—a subtle but important distinction."

Macy smiled, shook her head, and headed for the kitchen.

Li looked around the living room. It was a sensual room, filled with deep colors and rich textures. Most of the furniture was upholstered, thick and soft and inviting. The walls were lined with glass-front bookcases, filled to overflowing. The coffee table and end tables were covered with glossy-jacketed books and knickknacks, and green plants draped over every available corner. The walls were covered with framed photographs and personal mementos, including several of a young boy. It was a warm room, a welcoming room, the kind that put its arm around your shoulder and helped you off with your coat.

"It's remarkable," Li called into the kitchen.

"What's that?"

"This room—it's the virtual opposite of its counterpart in Nathan's house."

"That's no surprise."

"This is truly a *living* room. His is more of a dying room, if you get my meaning."

"I do."

"I understand that you and Nathan were married for five years."

Macy poked her head around the corner. "He told you that?"

"Oh, yes. We discussed the situation at length."

"Really. What did he have to say?"

"He told me all about the lovely home the two of you shared—in Woodbridge, I believe. He went on and on about it. I could bore you with all the details, I suppose, but I'd really rather hear from you."

Macy brought out the scones on a tray with a china tea set. "Are you lying now, or just doing research?"

"I'm lying. The truth is, I couldn't get a thing out of him. I was hoping I could do better with you."

"So the scones are just a bribe?"

"I prefer to think of them as an *inducement.* Storytellers have always gathered around fireplaces and tables, you know. There's something about breaking bread together that brings out the storyteller in all of us. Personally, I think it's a response to boredom. You can sit and watch one another masticate for only so long before someone breaks the monotony with a story."

"You want me to tell you a story?"

"You see? And we haven't even taken a bite yet."

Macy smiled. "What story are you interested in?"

"You mean I have a choice? How very generous of you. Personally, I would like to hear the story of Macy Monroe and Nathan Donovan."

"That's a big story," Macy said.

"I have all day. Feel free to begin anywhere."

"It doesn't have a happy ending."

"The best stories never do. Americans have a bad habit of sanitizing their stories, but the original versions are always so much more rewarding. Remember the tale of Goldilocks? In the original version, the bears became enraged and impaled her on a church steeple. And in the story of Pinocchio—what was the name of that pesky insect?"

"Jiminy Cricket."

"Yes, that's right. In the original version, Pinocchio threw a boot at him and squashed him against a wall."

Macy let out a laugh. "That doesn't make a very good Disney movie."

"My point exactly. Americans want all their stories to be 'Disney movies,' so they clean up the endings and lose all sense of the darkness and complexity of life. Your story doesn't have to have a happy ending. I like to think it doesn't have an ending at all—not yet anyway."

"Trust me, Li, it has an ending."

"Then I would be satisfied just to hear the beginning."

"I grew up here in the city," she began. "I did my undergraduate work at George Washington University down in D.C.—they were starting a terrorism studies program just about the time I came through. I did my graduate work at the University of St. Andrews in Scotland."

"I had no idea," Li said. "We were practically neighbors."

"You did your studies at Oxford, didn't you?"

"Yes—but a half century or so before your arrival. I enrolled at Oxford in 1947. I took a first in biochemistry."

"Then on to medical school?"

"No."

"I thought your dream was to become a missionary doctor."

"It was—but as I said, the war changed all that. The end of one dream became the start of another. A different dream required different skills and training."

"So what did you do after Oxford?"

Li frowned. "It's an old trick, you know. Every student knows it."

"What is?"

"Sending the teacher off on a rabbit trail by getting him to talk about himself. I'm not as vain as all that, and I'm not so easily put off. You were beginning to tell *your* story; I believe we left you at the University of St. Andrews."

"Right. Well, I did an MLitt in Middle Eastern and central Asian security studies, and I did my PhD through their Centre for the Study of Terrorism and Political Violence."

"You're giving me your résumé," Li said with a roll of his eyes. "I was hoping for a *story*."

"My résumé is a part of my story."

"Yes, but only a part—and not the better part. Suppose I told the story of Goldilocks this way: 'There was once a girl; little is known about her background. About the age of ten, she began to take walks in the woods. She displayed a tendency toward criminal behavior, including breaking and entering—'"

"Okay, I get the point. I'm used to dealing with the bottom line, Li. Maybe you should just ask me some questions."

"An excellent idea." He thought for a moment. "Tell me, how did you and Nathan meet?"

"He was a new agent assigned to New York City; I was an associate professor at Columbia. I did a seminar for the FBI on terrorist threat assessment. Nathan was in the class."

"I see. And what attracted you to him in the beginning?"

Macy took a moment to fold her legs under her. The question felt a little awkward from a man old enough to be her grandfather. "He's tall, and he's very good looking," she said. "That was enough at first."

"He has very good hair."

"Yes, he has good hair."

"I find him rather complex."

"That's one way to put it."

Li paused. "Tell me about your courtship."

She shrugged. "We dated for a few months. We were married a few months later."

"You must have been very certain."

"I suppose I was—at first."

"And how did he propose marriage?"

Macy squirmed. "That's a little painful to remember."

"Do you remember the cause of your divorce?"

"Of course I do."

"Is that painful to remember?"

"Sure it is."

"But it's *easier* to remember, isn't it? It's odd, isn't it, how much easier it is to recall hurt than joy?"

"Li, are you asking questions or giving me therapy?"

"Both, I hope. Questions are the most effective form of therapy I know."

Macy suddenly realized that she was gripping the arm of the chair. She forced herself to relax a little.

"I noticed the lovely photographs on your walls," Li said. "Did Nathan take them?"

"No. Why?"

"He isn't in any of them."

"No, he's not."

Li looked around the room. "You know, Nathan's walls are completely bare, while yours are crowded with personal memories. It's as if he's trying very hard to forget something, while you're trying very hard to remember."

Macy said nothing.

"I see several photos of a small boy."

Macy stood up abruptly. "I think the tea is ready," she said and turned toward the kitchen. It was such an awkward evasion, such an obvious admission, and she despised herself for it. In the kitchen she took a few moments to compose herself before returning with the steaming teapot.

"I apologize if I've offended you," Li said gently.

"That part of the story is painful for me," she replied. "Would you be offended if I chose not to tell it?"

"Offended, no. Disappointed, yes." She poured the tea, and they sat in silence for a few minutes.

"Are you enjoying your scone?" he asked.

"It's excellent. I hate to eat without a story, though."

"Am I really that boring?"

"No, I love to watch you chew. It's just that you're such a great storyteller. I thought maybe you might have one to tell me."

Li smiled at her. "You're not really surprised to see me this morning, are you?"

"I was surprised to find you at my door—but I expected to hear from you, yes."

"You've spoken with Nathan, then."

"He called me early this morning. He told me about last night—about you, and the bedroom, and the photograph of the couple in front of the well."

"This photograph?" Li reached into his coat pocket and gently removed the ancient photo. "Please be careful," he said, handing it to her. "It's the most precious thing I own."

Macy held it in her cupped hands and studied it. The brittle paper was veined with tiny cracks, and the emulsion had worn off around the edges. The image was clear, but coarse and grainy; in some spots individual particles of silver could be seen.

Macy looked up at him. "Li, this is you."

"Give or take sixty years."

"You haven't changed a bit."

"Who's lying now?"

"The young woman beside you is very beautiful."

Li didn't reply.

She handed back the photograph and waited as he carefully returned it to his jacket pocket. "I would very much like to hear the story of that photograph," she said, "but I understand if you would prefer not to tell it."

"I would prefer not to," Li said. "At least, not for the purpose of some psychological evaluation."

"I'd like to hear it as a friend."

Li studied her face. "If you wish to take in a dog, you must have a leash and a bowl and a brush—you must have the things necessary to *receive* a dog. You're asking me to tell you a story that is closer to my heart than anything in this world—so I must ask you, Macy Monroe: Are you so used to dealing with the bottom line that you'll listen only for names and dates and places? Have you been hurt so badly that you are unwilling or unable to feel someone else's pain? Do you have the things necessary to *receive* my story?"

"I think so," Macy said.

Li leaned forward on the sofa. "Most important of all—can you still weep?"

Macy paused. "I sure hope so."

Li nodded. "Then pour me some tea," he said.

CHAPTER TWENTY-FIVE

Congshan, China, August 1942

LI KNOCKED HARDER THIS time. "Give me my bride!" he shouted. "Must I break down the door?" The young men in the wedding party crowded around the cottage, poking and jostling and carrying on. One of them set off a string of firecrackers reserved for the wedding procession, intended to drive away evil spirits.

"She doesn't hear you," one of them teased.

"She doesn't *want* you," another added, and the group erupted in laughter again.

"Quiet, quiet," Li said, putting his ear to the crack. Inside, the bridesmaids barred the door against this would-be intruder.

"First you must pass a test," said a voice through the door. "Only courage and wisdom can get you what you seek."

"If I did not have wisdom, I would never have chosen Jin—and if I did not have courage, I would not be standing here in front of all these fools." Howls and laughter from the audience.

"You must answer a question," said the voice. "What does this expression mean: 'Waiting by a tree stump for a rabbit'?"

There were groans and hisses from the wedding party, but Li hushed them and stood a little straighter. "There once was a farmer resting by a tree stump," he said in a loud voice, "when a rabbit, racing by at great speed, ran into the tree stump and died. The farmer took the rabbit to market and sold it for a good price, whereupon the farmer said to himself, 'I will never have to farm again—I will wait by the tree stump for rabbits to come to me.'"

"And what does this mean?" the voice asked.

"It means if I have to wait outside the bride's door much longer, I will never get married." The wedding party began to cheer and applaud, but Li raised one hand and silenced them. "It also means that if the bridesmaids don't open the door, they will never receive their wedding gifts."

That did the trick. The door slowly swung open, revealing a wall of grinning women with outstretched hands. Li handed each of them a small red packet containing a single coin. As each received her gift, she stepped aside, until Li stood face-to-face with his bride-to-be. She was dressed in a red silk robe elaborately embroidered in gold and white and blue. Her feet were covered with a pair of scarlet slippers. On her head she wore an ornate phoenix crown, the symbol of the bride, and a veil of beaded strings hung down over her face. Li's own gown was black, with a bright red sash and a big puff of knotted silk on his chest. He wore red shoes as well, and his head was covered in a cap of cypress leaves to declare his adulthood and his new family responsibility.

"You are more difficult to obtain than treasure," Li said to his bride.

"Some man might consider me a treasure."

"I am that man," he said. "What have you been doing in here?"

"The married women have been teaching me how to be a good wife."

"Have you learned well?"

She smiled. "You will soon know."

Now an older woman pushed her way through the crowd, clucking and shooing at the bridesmaids like a hen. She stepped to the doorway and looked back at Jin. "Your good-luck woman is ready," she said. Jin turned and bowed to her parents, then climbed up onto the older woman's back.

"Wait!" another woman said, opening a red parasol over their heads. "Now you are ready."

Just a few yards from the cottage, a decorated donkey awaited the bride. Hanging from the back of the donkey was a silver sieve to strain out evil, and a metallic mirror to deflect malevolent influences. The good-luck woman carried her passenger as though she were weightless—which she was, compared to the burdens the woman bore to and from the fields each day. She turned and neatly deposited the bride on the donkey's back. Then the wedding procession started on its journey, led by a handful of dancers and musicians with far more enthusiasm than skill. At the head of the procession was a young boy carrying the bridal box, symbolizing the couple's hopes for fecundity. The bridesmaids scattered grain and beans on the ground before them, adding their own amen.

The journey ended about a hundred yards later, at an even smaller cottage on the opposite side of the village. A red mat was placed on the ground at the donkey's side to prevent the bride's feet from touching the ground. The couple stepped hand in hand into their new home together, and the entire assembly crowded in behind them.

Li and Jin knelt briefly before a family altar, then turned and bowed to each other—and with that simple gesture, they were husband and wife.

Now they turned to their friends and neighbors. "My wife and I want to thank you all for your generosity and good wishes," Li said. "And now, if you will excuse us, we are very tired."

At this, the whole room erupted in laughter and closed in around the couple. The men seized the groom and the women the bride, half dragging and half carrying them into the bedroom and depositing them on the bed, which was scattered with candies, lotus seeds, peanuts, and fruits. Everyone drew back from the bed now, waiting in silence until Li patted the sheets and nodded—then all the children of the village scrambled onto the bed with them, devouring the sweets and adding their own blessings for fruitfulness.

The next morning, Li and Jin sat at their wooden table and shared their first breakfast together.

"You seem tired," Jin said.

"I am."

"Perhaps you didn't sleep enough."

"Very little, I'm afraid."

"I suppose it takes a while to get used to a new bed."

Li grinned.

"According to custom, this is the day we must return to visit my parents."

Li's expression changed. "According to custom, we have up to three days to pay our respects."

"Today is as good as any."

"Today is not as good as any."

"Our cottage is empty; we have none of our belongings yet. What else do we have to do?"

Li put his hand on hers. "We could get used to a new bed."

Two days later, Jin watched as Li assembled a bedroll and a small pack of food and clothing for his back. "Married only three days, and already you're abandoning me," she said with a pout. "Haven't I been a good wife?"

"You are the best wife I have ever had."

"I wish you wouldn't go. Nanking is not safe."

"No. But everything I need for my studies is there: my books, my microscope, my papers—"

"Things that can be replaced."

"Besides, I must talk to the people at the Missions School. They are the ones arranging for us to go to England. These things take time, and the war is slowing everything down."

"I remember the stories you told about the Japanese soldiers—about what they did to the people of Nanking."

Li said nothing but continued his packing.

"You said thousands and thousands of our people were slaughtered—mutilated, burned, beheaded."

"Those were rumors."

"You believe the rumors."

Li did believe. In December 1937, the imperial capital fell to the Japanese. For the next two months, the occupying forces engaged in an orgy of atrocity against soldier and civilian alike, unrestrained by their commanding officers. If it hadn't been for the Missions School, Li himself might not have survived. At the first indication the city would fall, a handful of Americans and Europeans formed the Nanking Safety Zone in an attempt to protect some portion of the city's inhabitants from slaughter. The Japanese high command reluctantly honored the Safety Zone, which encompassed Nanking University, a women's college, and various government buildings. Because it also contained the American embassy, the entire area was granted a tenuous diplomatic immunity. The Safety Zone became a city within a city, ostensibly to provide protection for foreign-born visitors, educators, and missionaries. In reality, the Safety Zone became a place of refuge for endangered Chinese, the first stop in an underground railroad that spirited away countless noncombatants to safety in rural areas. When the Japanese first attacked Nanking, half the city fled; of those who remained behind, half eventually sought sanctuary in the Safety Zone; of those who dared to resist the Japanese, almost all perished.

Li himself remained in the city for more than a year, continuing his studies until the danger became too great. Then the directors of the Missions School sent him to Congshan, his "visit" sponsored by Jin's family—a visit that had lasted four years now. Jin was only a girl when Li first arrived, and at first he found it relatively easy to focus on his studies in her presence. Perhaps it was her youthfulness, or perhaps it was his own blindness—but with time his eyesight greatly improved. With each passing year he found himself more and more distracted, until he seemed to do little more than stare at Jin as she went about her chores. Li came to Congshan with a single-minded purpose: to serve God by becoming a doctor. It wasn't long before his plans expanded to include a physician's assistant.

Li stopped and looked at his wife. "The war is going badly," he said. "I cannot complete my education here in China. If I remain here, I will end up serving the Japanese. The Missions School has arranged for me to finish my studies in England—but this opportunity is fleeting, and we must seize it while we can."

"We will come back English," Jin said with a frown.

"We will come back *educated*," Li replied, "and we will be much better prepared to serve God and our people. There will be a very great need for doctors after the war."

"You don't have to go in person," Jin said. "Write the school a letter, as you've done all along."

For four years Li had communicated with the Missions School only by letter, making carefully guarded references to any future plans for fear that the letters might fall into the hands of the Japanese. The letters were a risk both for Li and for the school. If the Japanese discovered that Li intended to travel to England, he would be executed as a traitor; if it was revealed that the Missions School encouraged such a journey, it could provide the excuse the Japanese were looking for to shut down the Safety Zone once and for all.

"I can no longer communicate by letter," Li said. "There are too many specifics to discuss, and I can't risk putting them on paper. It would put us at risk, and also many thousands of people in Nanking."

"How will you reach the Missions School?" Jin asked. "How will you avoid the soldiers?"

"The school will help. If they can smuggle me out, they can smuggle me in again. I should think 'in' would be much easier."

"I'm frightened, Li."

Li took his wife by the shoulders. "I will be back in three weeks. Please pack our things. I expect that we will leave for England soon after."

They walked together down a dirt road to a hilltop where a stark white pagoda marked the entrance to their village. They embraced, and Jin began to weep.

"Why are you crying?"

"Because I know that you'll never return."

"I will return," Li said, "and then you'll feel silly because you wasted all these tears."

"Tears are never wasted."

Li turned away before he started weeping too. He walked quickly down the path, resisting the temptation to stop and look back. Until he crossed the next hilltop, he could feel a pair of eyes on the back of his head.

CHAPTER TWENTY-SIX

THREE WEEKS LATER TO the day, Li returned. He walked in double time for most of the last day; when he reached the final hilltop, he broke into a run. He had fantasized that Jin might be waiting for him at the pagoda, but of course that was impossible. She had no way of knowing the day or the hour he would return. He began to envision how they would meet: He would creep quietly into the cottage and surprise her, or he would be sitting nonchalantly at the table when she returned from the fields.

In the center of the road he passed a dead rat. A bad omen, some would say, but by now Li had learned too much science to hold much regard for the traditional Chinese prophecies and portents. But twenty yards ahead he found another one.

He stopped and looked. Neither rat was crushed or flattened, as it would be if the wheels of a passing cart had caught it scurrying across the path. The rats had apparently died of some internal cause. And out in the open—a most unusual behavior for the reclusive rodents. Then Li looked farther down the road, and he saw a dead cow.

He threw off his pack and started running.

On the outskirts of the village he found a man lying facedown, drinking from a puddle of scum-covered water. "What are you doing?" Li shouted to him. "Don't drink from that—the water is bad!"

The man looked up at him in a stupor, then flopped over onto his back with his head still in the puddle, staring blindly into the sky. Li could see that he was delirious, consumed with fever, and under each armpit there was a purplish tumor the size of an orange.

Li left him and hurried across the village to his own home. Along the way he saw dead rats scattered everywhere, more than he thought the village could have ever contained. He passed the body of a woman he could recognize only by her clothing; her body was stiff and bloated, and her skin was almost black in color. He passed a friend sitting placidly in the middle of the dirt road, talking to the air like a village idiot. He heard screams and mournful wails from behind shuttered windows and bolted doors.

At his house, he threw open the door and rushed inside. "Jin! Jin! Where are you?" He checked the bedroom, he looked in the backyard, but there was no sign of his wife anywhere.

He ran to the closest cottage and pounded on the door.

"Go away!" said a voice from somewhere deep inside.

"It's Li! I'm looking for my wife! Have you seen Jin?"

"Do you have it?"

"What?"

"The pestilence—do you have it?" The voice was a little closer now.

"I've been away for three weeks. I just returned today. Please, tell me what's happened! Help me find my wife!"

The door opened just a crack, and a wary eye studied him from head to foot—then the door opened just enough for a timid-looking man to wedge himself into the gap.

"Don't come inside," he said.

"What happened here?"

"Don't you know? Two weeks ago a Japanese plane flew over the village. It came out of the west—from over there," he said, pointing. "It circled over the rice paddies. There was smoke pouring out of its end. We thought it was on fire; we thought it was going to crash. Everyone came out to watch. But the plane flew away, and the smoke began to settle. It wasn't smoke at all."

"What was it?"

"It was bits of cloth, and beans, and wheat—so much wheat that people swept it up to use for chicken feed. A week ago, all the rats began to die—then the chickens, then the cattle. A few days ago people began to get sick too. It's all over the village—it jumps from house to house like a fire. It brings fever and thirst and terrible swellings. It takes one family but leaves another; it kills a mother but spares her child. What kind of a curse is this?"

"Where is Jin?" Li demanded. "Where is my wife?"

"Jin was kind; Jin was good. She helped everyone; she cared for them. Then two days ago she took ill herself—but Jin is lucky."

"Why? Why is she lucky?"

"Because the Japanese have come to help us."

"The Japanese? Where?"

"They posted a sign at the temple—they will treat anyone who comes for help. Jin didn't want to go at first, but her suffering was too great. She went just an hour ago. She thought—"

But Li was already running toward the temple. He couldn't feel his feet pounding the ground; he wasn't even sure he was breathing. His terror was beyond feeling. His thoughts kept drifting to unthinkable possibilities, and he refused to let his mind come to rest on any of them.

Fifty yards to the right of the temple, he saw a small band of Japanese soldiers climbing aboard a personnel carrier; a few of them were dressed in white biological suits. Li started toward them but thought better of it. What might he say or do in his anger, and what would they do to him in return? *Jin first,* he said to himself. *Jin is the only thing that matters.* He turned to enter the temple but stopped in the doorway.

At the end of the short aisle, in front of the altar, a woman's naked body sat bound to a wooden chair. Her head was covered by a hood, and it hung back and to the right. Her torso had been opened with a Y-shaped incision, from both shoulders to the breastbone and then down the abdomen to the pelvis. The wound lay open and gaping, and most of her internal organs lay steaming on the ground around her.

Li squeezed his eyes tight, like a man trying not to swallow poison. He felt an overwhelming rush of nausea. He dropped to his knees and vomited, but not enough—not nearly enough to get all the poison out. It was too late—he had seen the unseeable and thought the unthinkable, and he could never get the poison out of his system again.

Jin! My beloved Jin!

Li turned and looked at the soldiers. The last few were climbing aboard the truck now, joking and lighting cigarettes. Only one remained in his biological suit, flipping through papers on a clipboard. Li struggled to his feet and staggered toward them.

Jin was the only thing that mattered, but Jin was dead—now nothing mattered. Li had no idea what he would do when he reached the soldiers. He had no plan; he had no thoughts. He was pure rage; that's all that was left, and rage has a mind of its own. Rage would know what to do when it got there. Maybe rage would kill them all; maybe rage would get him killed. No matter; it was all the same now.

Li approached unnoticed. The man in the biological suit was facing away from him. Li stopped directly behind him, trembling uncontrollably. Then he reached up and ripped off his cylindrical hood.

The man turned in astonishment and stared at Li, and Li looked into his face. An hour passed, or maybe only minutes—perhaps just a single second. It made no difference. In that span of time, however it would be measured chronologically, Li recorded every form, every nuance of feature, every blemish and pore, every line and crease. The face burned into his mind like the brand from a searing iron, and it could never be erased. It was part of him now, a part of the pain and the horror, and it would stay with him for the rest of his life.

Suddenly, a soldier shoved the man aside. He glared at Li with a look of anger and contempt and raised his rifle waist-high. Li looked back with no expression at all. Then the soldier barked something, lunged forward, and plunged his bayonet into Li's abdomen. Li felt something tugging at his shirt from behind.

Li's expression never changed. He looked down at the bayonet as if it were protruding from someone else. An instant later he saw the blade withdraw again, stained with someone's blood.

Now he knew that he would die, and he felt a sense of gratitude. He stood perfectly still, with his arms at his sides, waiting for the darkness to come. He felt no pain; he felt peaceful, and distant, and removed—like a marionette being removed from a stage.

He imagined Jin in heaven, standing by a white pagoda, with her arms open wide.

Then everything went black.

MACY DROPPED HER HEAD in her hands and began to weep—so did Li. He matched her tear for tear, rocking back and forth just as he had done the night before.

They wept together for several minutes. He stopped only when she did, and then they both sat in silence and wiped their faces.

"I can't stop crying," Macy said.

"Have you tried this?" Li suggested, demonstrating his rocking motion. "I find it helps. It's an Eastern technique—rather like squeezing the last bit of toothpaste from the tube."

"I'll have to try that," she said, drying her eyes. "The soldier in the biological suit—it was Sato Matsushita, wasn't it?"

"Yes. I didn't know his name until later, when I began my research."

"He killed your wife."

"He dissected her—alive, and without anesthetic."

"In God's name, why?"

"To study the progress of the disease on her internal organs. It was thought that anesthetic might interfere with their observations."

"Was it bubonic plague?"

"Yes—as indicated by the buboes and the skin discoloration. It's a shame I had not yet finished my bacteriology degree. I understood very little at the time. It wouldn't have mattered, I suppose; with my own wounds, I would have been of no help to anyone in the village. No one could have helped, really. One-third of Congshan perished in that attack."

Li lifted his shirt to reveal a pale, twisted line of flesh just beneath his left rib cage. "The Imperial soldiers in China were badly trained," he said. "But then, I suppose it doesn't take a lot of military expertise to deal with unarmed Chinese peasants. The proper technique is to insert the bayonet, then twist as you remove it—that creates a much larger wound. It seems the old boy forgot to twist. Had he done so, I would not be sitting here now."

"How long did it take you to recover?"

"Physically? The better part of a year. Mentally and emotionally, it took a bit longer. I'm hoping to recover anytime now."

"And this is why you've spent your life pursuing Sato Matsushita."

"When I recovered from my wounds, when I regained enough of my sanity to think clearly, I realized that God had given me a mission: I must find Sato Matsushita. I'm just like Simeon in the Gospel of Saint Luke, waiting in the temple for the Promised One—and I know that I will not be allowed to die before I find him."

"And when you do?"

"There's something I want to say to him."

"And that's all?"

Li paused. "No. There's something else."

Macy searched for a tissue. "I wish you weren't such a good storyteller."

"Why? So you wouldn't feel anguish, or anger, or hatred? Those are the very things I wanted you to feel. A story that never makes it past your head remains in your head until it is forgotten. A story that passes into your heart remains in your heart forever."

"I'll never forget it," Macy said.

"That is the greatest compliment you could pay me—and my wife."

"Have you been back to the village since?"

"There's little reason. Jin's body was burned for fear of contagion—so were her clothes and our cottage. The only remaining trace of her, the only proof that she ever existed at all, is this wedding photograph."

"I'm honored that you would show it to me."

"All our friends tried to discourage us from taking it, you know."

"Why?"

"The rural Chinese can be a very superstitious people. On wedding days especially, great care is taken not to incur any bad luck or invite the wrath of malevolent spirits. In those days, photography was looked upon with suspicion—and taking a snapshot on a wedding day was simply tempting fate. To make matters worse, we're posing in front of a well. On the wedding day, the bride is never supposed to look at a well."

"Why not?"

"Wells, and widows, and cats—they're all bad luck, you see. But we loved the well; we considered it the symbol of our relationship. In our early courtship, we used to sneak away and meet there. She would go out to draw water, and for some reason my studies made me very thirsty. Her parents must have thought I had a bladder problem."

Macy smiled. "Do you think they knew?"

Li winked. "Older people know more than you think."

He slid the photograph halfway out of his pocket and peeked at it again. "Her face was supposed to be covered by a veil. She wasn't supposed to remove it until after the ceremony. Thank God she did—can you imagine if my only memory of her was a veil of beads?"

He pulled out the photograph now, studied it carefully, then squeezed his eyes tight. "I look at it every day," he said. "I study it; I memorize her face. If I don't, when I think of my beautiful Jin, an unbearable image comes to mind, something that could take away my sanity. The photograph is a kind of antidote, you see. This is the way I want to remember her."

He put the photograph away again and glanced at his watch. "Look at the time," he said. "I'm afraid I've taken up your whole morning—and here you are with examinations to grade."

"My students will thank you," Macy said. "I'm in a much more compassionate mood now."

"May I use your telephone to call a taxi?"

"I feel bad that you have to take a taxi."

"Not at all—on the way up here, I had a chance to work on my Spanish."

"It won't help on the way home. You'll probably get Arabic."

She showed him to the telephone. Li started to lift the receiver, then stopped and looked at her.

"You know, in the East we have a custom. Whenever a gift is given, it requires that a gift be given in return—a gift of equal value. It's more than a custom, really; it's almost an obligation, and people take it quite seriously. If you give a lavish gift to a poor person, the gift may be viewed as a burden—because now they have to give something in return, something just as precious."

Macy wasn't sure where this was going.

Li smiled. "I've just given you a precious gift," he said. "Perhaps, when you are ready, you'll give me something in return."

Macy nodded but said nothing.

CHAPTER TWENTY-SEVEN

DONOVAN TOOK EAST RIVER Drive north to the Willis Avenue Bridge. The traffic was light, and he was making good time. He took particular delight in watching the southbound lanes, still choked with late-morning traffic creeping its way into the city. He didn't expect to be heading back home just a couple of hours after leaving—but then, he didn't expect his simple request for an address and phone number to set off bells and whistles all the way to Washington.

Pasha Mirovik—that was the name Li had given him. When he searched the Bureau's records, he found nothing at all; when he submitted the name to the Federal Witness Security Program at the U.S. Marshals Service, it was less than an hour before he found himself in Reuben Mayer's office, responding to the angry inquiries of no less than four different government agencies.

More than seventy-five hundred witnesses are sheltered by the Witness Security Program, but not all receive the same level of protection. Those who testify against only minor miscreants may find themselves rewarded with nothing more than a new Social Security card and cab fare to the airport. Those who are willing to defy organized crime bosses or drug cartels receive new identities, relocation for their families, housing, medical care, and even employment. Then there are a very few—maybe the favored ones, maybe the cursed—whom the U.S. government causes to virtually disappear from the face of the earth.

Apparently, Mirovik was one of those. Donovan had made a casual inquiry about a name that should no longer exist, and in the process inadvertently pushed a big red button on somebody's desk. Now a lot of angry people were demanding to know how he knew that name—and much to his embarrassment, he didn't have an answer. "I got it from this old guy" is not an answer that satisfies the State Department or the CIA. So the U.S. Marshals Service made it perfectly clear: Either Donovan would get further information from his source, or they would.

Donovan tried to call Li, but there was no answer at the house. The old man could have been sleeping—after all, he was up half the night. He could have been in the shower; hopefully he wasn't stupid enough to go wandering around the South Bronx alone. Donovan had no choice but to return home and talk to the old man in person.

He pulled up in front of the house, got out, and slammed the door of the Buick a little harder than he needed to. He was beginning to resent the old man's let's-go-fishing approach to information. Li could have warned him about Mirovik. He could have mentioned that this was no ordinary name. He could have told him that this was not a minor request; it was more like asking the Mafia about Jimmy Hoffa's body. He guessed it just didn't fit into the old man's story—not yet anyway.

The front door was locked, but the bolt wasn't fastened. Since Donovan had given him a key to only the doorknob, that meant the old man was out. He poked his head in and called out to make sure—no answer. He walked back down the sidewalk and looked up and down the street—no sign of him. He took out his cell phone and dialed Macy.

"Dr. Monroe."

"Macy, it's Nathan. I'm at home, but Li's not here. By any chance is he with you?"

"He just left. He dropped by unannounced this morning. I thought he might call, but I wasn't expecting a visit."

"Yeah, the old guy is full of surprises. Did he tell you about the photo?"

"He did. He told me a story that you've got to hear."

"I'm sick of stories right now. Can you give me the gist?"

It took less than five minutes for Donovan to get the summary. While he listened, he made his way back into Li's room. "Unbelievable," he said. "They cut her open, and he found her like that? No wonder he wants to get his hands on this guy." He got down on his knees and looked under Li's bed. He pulled out the canvas duffel bag and set it on the mattress. "I'm in his room," he said, "but I don't see the photo."

"He's got it with him. The woman in the picture is his wife—it was taken on their wedding day. They're standing in front of a well where they used to meet. Ask him about it, Nathan—get the details. This is important."

"Why?"

"This is Li's motive. You need to know who you're working with."

"Right. Look, I'll call you back—I want to take care of a few things before he gets back."

He sat down on the bed and opened the duffel. Along one side was the long black case he had seen in Chinatown. He slid it out and set it on the bed beside him. Also in the bag was a medium-sized Bible. Donovan removed it and flipped through the pages; he found a plastic bag containing a small stack of papers. He emptied it on the bed. There were his passport and visa, a document verifying his British citizenship, a list of Chinatown restaurants, and a few financial records. There were no unfamiliar names, addresses, or phone numbers. There were no notes or documents relating to the case at all. He looked through the duffel again. It seemed to contain nothing else but a stack of folded laundry. He reached down into the bag, feeling between each layer of clothing, all the way to the bottom—there was nothing more.

He set the bag aside and picked up the black case. It looked ancient. The edges and corners were nicked and dented. The color was flat black like a barbecue grill, but the surface had an orange-peel texture, and the tiny tip of each raised spot was worn smooth and glossy from sliding across countless surfaces. The hardware was tarnished brass. On the front, on each side of the leather handle, were sliding tabs that released two spring latches. He tried them; the case was locked.

"Please be careful with that. I consider it irreplaceable."

Donovan looked up. Li stood in the doorway, watching, with no expression on his face. "I didn't expect you back so soon," Donovan said.

"Obviously." Li stepped to the dresser, slipped the photograph from his coat pocket, and set it upright. "Is this what you were looking for, or is this a more general search?"

"I talked to Macy. She said you had the photo with you."

"The two of you seem to do a good deal of talking behind my back. Do all of your roommates enjoy this level of privacy? But then, I'm not really a roommate, am I? I'm not even an American citizen; perhaps I'm not entitled to the same legal rights."

"Come off it, Li—you're not just some British tourist vacationing in the U.S. You're cooperating with the federal government on a criminal investigation, and that changes the rules."

Li motioned to his belongings scattered on the bed. "Are these the new rules?" He walked over to Donovan, stopped, and held out his hand. Donovan hesitated, then handed the black case to him.

"Thank you," Li said. He slid the case back into the duffel, then picked up the Bible and plastic bag. "Are all my papers in order, then?"

Donovan ignored the jab. "Macy told me the story about your wife."

"Did she tell it well?"

"I got the basics."

"Then she didn't tell it well at all," Li said with a frown. "Or perhaps you didn't listen well."

"I'm sorry, Li. I can understand how you feel about Matsushita."

"Really? And how do I feel, Nathan?"

"If it had been my wife, I would have killed the man responsible with my bare hands."

"That opportunity was taken away from me. I believe I now understand why."

"I know why you want to find this man. I understand why you've been after him for sixty years. I would do the same thing—just to have a second chance to kill him."

Li looked at him. "Then you're really no different than he is, are you?"

"Look, I'm trying to be your friend here."

"Oh? Is this how you treat your friends?"

Donovan shook his head in exasperation. "What do you want from me?"

"What I would like from you, Nathan, is a little privacy, a little respect, a little *honesty*."

Donovan was losing his patience. "You want honesty? Okay, try this: I think you're hoping the FBI will help you find your wife's murderer so you can dispatch him yourself. You think we'll help you kill Matsushita because he's also a potential threat to the U.S.—but it's never going to happen, Li; *it's never going to happen.* The FBI doesn't want Matsushita dead—we want him *alive.* Counterterrorism isn't just knocking off everybody who might pose a threat to national security—if that's all it took, we'd just shoot everybody who thumbed his nose at us. We want Matsushita alive so we can learn from him. We want to know who he works with, who pays him, and who his suppliers are. We want to know what his methods are. We want to know if he's been able to penetrate our borders, and we want to know about any other vulnerabilities he's discovered. He's worth more to us alive than dead, Li, and that's the problem here. We want you to help us find him, yes—but once we find him, you'd better be satisfied to watch him rot in some federal prison—because once we find him, we won't let you within a mile of him. Do you understand me? We will *not* let you come face-to-face with Sato Matsushita."

There was silence between the men for a few minutes. Donovan reviewed his words; he had spoken in anger, but he regretted nothing. The old man asked for the truth, and that's exactly what he got.

"I appreciate your candor," Li said softly. "Now allow me to be candid with you. My life's mission is to come face-to-face with Sato Matsushita—not to have him found, not to have him killed, and not to simply contribute to his incarceration—to come face-to-face. I will assist your government just as long as it helps me to fulfill my mission. You are interested in Matsushita's entire network; I understand that. My business, however, is with one man. Please allow me to reiterate, Nathan: You will never locate and positively identify this man without my help. If I do not come face-to-face with Sato Matsushita, *neither will you.*"

Donovan glared at him. "You claim this man wants to launch a plague attack against the U.S. Are you saying that if we won't help with your personal vendetta, you're willing to allow hundreds of thousands of people to die?"

Li returned his glare. "Are you saying that your government is willing to risk the lives of hundreds of thousands of people simply to avoid a face-to-face meeting between two old men?"

Donovan took a deep breath and slowly exhaled. "I'm just telling you the way it is, Li. I don't make the rules."

"No—but you do play a significant role in enforcing them. I don't expect you to ignore the rules, Nathan; I'm just hoping for a liberal interpretation."

Donovan pointed to the duffel bag. "What's in the case?"

Li didn't reply.

"Okay," Donovan said. "A little respect, a little privacy."

He looked up at the old man. "I am trying to be your friend, you know. I like you, Li—I want you to know that. You can be an annoying old fart, but I think you mean well."

"Old fart," Li said thoughtfully. "It's not exactly the term of endearment I was hoping for, but it's a start."

"I do understand this mission of yours—and I want to help."

"I'm afraid you understand very little."

"Maybe not. But I want to be sure you understand something: The FBI is using you, Li. They'll accept your help right up until the moment your purposes run contrary to theirs—and then they'll cross you. Do you understand that?"

"Yes. And I want you to understand that I am using the FBI in much the same way."

Donovan nodded and rose from the bed. "I forgot to tell you," he said. "We're seeing your friend Mirovik tomorrow."

"You've found him?"

"He was never lost. The U.S. Marshals Service has been keeping him under wraps. They won't tell us where he is, but they'll take us to him—and only once. Better get some sleep—if you can."

Li followed Donovan to the door and closed it carefully behind him. He locked the door quietly, then pressed his ear against the door until he was satisfied that Donovan had moved away; he returned to the bed and slid the duffel bag out from underneath. He took out the black case and placed it on the bed in front of him.

He lifted a silver chain from around his neck; attached to it was an age-worn, F-shaped key. He fit the key into each of the locks and turned it to the right. The brass latches sprang open with a soft click.

The case opened like two halves of a casting mold. In the top were three cylindrical hollows spaced evenly apart and lined with red silk. In the bottom, three glass laboratory flasks rested in molded indentations. Each flask was topped with a black rubber stopper, and the stopper and neck were further secured by a thick ring of bright red sealing wax impressed with the signet of a Chinese symbol.

Li carefully worked one of the flasks out of the silk-lined case and held it up to the light. The flask was filled with a clear fluid, no more viscous than water, with flecks of some kind of contaminant stirred up by the removal. He turned the bottle carefully and searched for signs of damage or leakage.

There were none. He let out a sigh of relief.

He shook the bottle slightly and watched the sediment drift like tiny bits of ash.

CHAPTER TWENTY-EIGHT

"HOW MUCH FARTHER?" LI asked from the backseat.

"We'll get there when we get there," Donovan called over his shoulder. "You're worse than a kid."

"I'm just not used to driving such long distances. It makes me feel very American."

"We're only in New Jersey," Macy said. "You're not an American until you reach the Grand Canyon."

"How much farther is that?"

They had been headed south on the Garden State Parkway for what seemed like an eternity. It took most of an hour just to get out of the city and past the endless concrete jungle of Newark and Elizabeth. South of Perth Amboy, the industrial corridor gradually gave way to endless housing developments, which had slowly replaced the truck farms and orchards that once gave New Jersey its reputation as the Garden State. But they had left the fertile piedmont lowland half an hour ago; now they were in the outer coastal plain and still headed south, into a sparsely populated area known as the Pine Barrens.

Macy leaned over to Donovan. "Do you know where you're going?"

"No idea. I'm just following them."

Directly ahead, an unmarked Crown Victoria from the U.S. Marshals

Service slowed and turned right onto a smaller road. Donovan didn't bother to note the road number. The State Department made it very clear that they would be allowed to meet with Pasha Mirovik once and once only. Without the marshals guiding them, they would never find Mirovik—and they would never find their way back. There were parts of the Pine Barrens that had never been mapped. Donovan hoped the marshals remembered that; he sped up a little and closed the distance between them.

He glanced in the rearview mirror at Li. "I hope this is worth it," he said. "When I asked about Pasha Mirovik, all hell broke loose. The Marshals Service demanded to know what we already knew about him and *exactly* why we wanted to see him—and I didn't have any answers for them. Who is this guy, anyway?"

"I apologize," Li said. "I had no way of knowing how deeply protected Mirovik would be. To answer your question briefly, Pasha Mirovik was once a central figure in Biopreparat. Have you heard of it?"

"The Soviet Union's old bioweapons program," Macy said.

"Yes. When the Soviet Union began to crumble in the early nineties, Mirovik defected to the United States, and he told your authorities everything he knew—about the extent of the Soviet program, about advances in their research, about unheard-of new weapons. To put it mildly, it was a real eye-opener. Your government was scarcely aware the Soviet program even existed."

"No wonder he's in deep cover," Donovan said.

"When Mirovik first defected, his presence became briefly public. That's when I learned of his existence, and I attempted to contact him—but with the help of your authorities, he vanished shortly thereafter. This is one of the reasons I first sought your help; without the consent of your government, I cannot locate Mirovik."

"Why do we need to?" Donovan asked. "He must have already told our intelligence people everything he knows."

"I'm sure Mirovik answered every question he was asked—but there are questions your authorities never thought to ask."

The land was now paper-flat, dotted with scrub oaks and tall cedars.

Between them, stands of spindly pitch pines and junipers crowded together and poked up toward the sun. There were still blackened traces of a fire that swept the area a decade ago, and groups of bright green seedlings sprouted through the cinders. Around the stands of trees the thin crust of ash and pine straw gave way to wide, flowing rivers of white sugar sand.

The Crown Vic turned again—and again, and again, onto ever-smaller roads until they found themselves on an unmarked and unpaved path completely overshadowed by the towering pines. At a clearing a hundred yards ahead, the marshals pulled over and waved to Donovan to pull up alongside. Macy rolled down her window.

"Fifty yards ahead," the marshal said. "You can't miss it."

"Aren't you boys coming in?" Macy asked.

"We'll wait here, ma'am. One of us will stay with the car; one of us will patrol the perimeter on foot. If you need anything, honk your horn."

"Anything else?" Donovan asked.

"Yeah. Don't drink his vodka—he makes it himself."

The path in the clearing curved around to the right. Rounding the bend, they found an open, sandy area. On the right was a plain-looking farmhouse with white beveled siding and a gray corrugated roof. On the left was a small barn with open doors and a long row of chicken coops that ended at a short, tubular silo. A scattering of white, red, and brown chickens wandered across the sand, stopping abruptly to peck at invisible objects.

Donovan pulled up in front of the farmhouse. No sooner had he stopped the engine than the screen door burst open and a stocky, smiling man in a bloodstained apron came charging toward them. He reached Donovan first and eagerly shook his hand with both of his.

"I'm Special Agent Nathan Donovan," he said. "I'm with—"

"I know." He was already around the car, shaking Li's tiny hand in his ham-sized fist.

"Mr. Li."

Macy was just stepping out of the car; Mirovik reached in and took her daintily by the hand and elbow, cradling her arm as if it were a Fabergé egg.

"Lovely lady," he said, grinning from ear to ear. "Dr. Monroe from Columbia University, yes?"

His face had a distinctly Russian architecture, with high cheekbones and a broad, low forehead. His hair was mostly gray, but there were still streaks as red as bog iron. The hair was thick and stiff, and clumps of the stuff seemed to shoot in every direction. His skin was very fair, with a spray of titian freckles across his nose. He was of average height, but his stockiness made him seem somehow shorter. His build was thick and solid—maybe muscle, maybe only fat—but either way, there was little doubt that the man was not an object to be easily moved.

"I am Pasha Mirovik," he said with a thump on his chest. "You will stay for lunch, yes?" And with that, he started off across the open area toward the barn. Along the way, he made a quick dip and snatched a New Hampshire Red by the neck. At the barn, he reached inside the open door and took out a small ax, then started back toward them again.

"We have hen, and potatoes, and cabbage. After, we have blueberry pie. I grow them myself—New Jersey is good for blueberries."

He stopped at a tree stump, where two large nails protruded just an inch apart. He flopped the hen across the stump, positioning its neck between the nails. Then he jerked on the head and stretched the neck out like a feather boa. He stopped and looked up.

"Reds are okay for laying—much better for eating. Not a big bird, but a good breast."

The ax came around in a sudden arc and sank into the stump with a dull thud. There was a quick spurt of blood, and the chicken's body shot away like a punctured balloon. It ran for several seconds before slumping at the ground by Li's feet.

"I grow the potatoes too," Mirovik said. "Some for eating, the rest for—you know." He made a drinking motion, then realized he was still holding the chicken's head. He tossed it away and wiped his hand on the apron.

"We were warned about your vodka," Donovan said.

"Cowards." Mirovik grinned. "Come inside." He turned and headed into the house, letting the screen door bang behind him. A moment later he poked his head out again. "Bring the chicken," he said and disappeared.

The three of them stood staring at the feathered cadaver.

"I don't think he gets a lot of visitors," Macy said.

An hour later they were seated on the back porch around a simple wooden table. In the center was a roasted chicken surrounded by bowls of baked apples, boiled potatoes, and minced cabbage. Mirovik crossed himself, closed his eyes for an instant, then reached for the first bowl. He served himself a generous portion and then dug in, eating as if he were about to run out the door.

"The Bolsheviks came to power in 1917," he said between mouthfuls. "The glorious revolution—then war for four years, Red armies against White, from Siberia to the Crimea. Ten million Russians died, but not from bullets."

Mirovik glanced up. The others were just watching him, with nothing on their plates. He let out a snort. "What is the most dangerous animal in the zoo?" he asked.

Donovan looked at the others; no one had an answer.

"The arctic bear," Mirovik said. "Do you know why? Because the arctic bear never knows when he will eat next—so he kills whenever he has the opportunity, even when he is not hungry. I am from Siberia—we have arctic bear in our blood. I forget that Americans must be *invited* to eat. You would not last long in Siberia." He waved his hand vaguely over the table and returned to his own plate.

"Most died from typhus," he continued. "You are familiar?"

There was a pause from the group; it was Li who responded. "Typhus is a rickettsial disease, usually carried by lice," he said. "Seven to ten days after infection, the victim is stricken by headache and fever. There is a rash that covers the body, accompanied by gangrene on the fingertips, toes, and other extremities. Delirium follows, then death in about 40 percent of cases."

Mirovik nodded at his plate. "Soldiers are not 40 percent accurate with their rifles. Typhus taught us that there are better weapons than bullets. In

1928 the Revolutionary Military Council gave orders to turn typhus into a weapon."

"But the Soviet Union was a signatory to the Geneva Convention," Li said. "The convention banned the use of chemical and biological weapons."

"The *use*," Mirovik said, "not the development." He glanced up at Li and tilted his head. "You look Eastern; you sound Western. What is your country?"

"I am Chinese by birth, but I am a citizen of Great Britain."

"Great Britain signed too." Mirovik shrugged. "Your biological laboratory was at Porton Down. America's was at Fort Detrick in Maryland. Ours was the Leningrad Military Academy. We all agreed not to use these weapons—no one said we could not possess them.

"Our first experiments were all with typhus. We used rats; when the rats neared death, we crushed them in blenders and loaded the mush into small bombs. Crude, yes? But effective. We tested it at Solovetsky, at the gulag there."

"Did you test on human subjects?" Macy asked.

Mirovik looked at her. "You have read Solzhenitsyn? Everyone should read Solzhenitsyn.

"In ten years we had typhus in aerosol form, both powder and liquid. We thought we were geniuses—then came the Great War, and we learned better. In 1945 our soldiers entered Manchuria and captured a Japanese laboratory. Unit 731—you are familiar?"

"We are familiar," Li said quietly.

"We knew about them," Mirovik said. "They tested their weapons on some of our own people, on White Russians living in the North. We heard rumors, but we had no idea. Anthrax, dysentery, cholera, plague—they were years ahead of us. It was an entire industry—as big as the Soviet tank program.

"After the war all their documents were sent to Moscow, even the building blueprints. Stalin put the KGB in charge; within a year, we had our own laboratory at Sverdlovsk, built from Japanese plans."

"What about human testing?" Li asked. "Did that part of their research interest you?"

Mirovik paused. "We used rats, guinea pigs, rabbits—but monkeys are most like humans. A man breathes ten liters of air every minute—a monkey only four. If four particles of a virus kill a monkey, does it take ten to kill a man? That is the mathematical answer—but reality is always different. To know, you must test. But Russia, Britain, America—we are the civilized nations, yes? We were happy to benefit from the research of others, research we would not do ourselves. America was happy too—we all needed to know, you see."

The others had barely started their meals; Mirovik was already finished. He pushed away his plate and lit a cigarette. "In 1953 the structure of DNA was discovered. This changed everything—but not in Russia. We were not allowed to believe in DNA—insane, yes? It was not good Marxism, you see. In the next twenty years the whole world changed, but we did not. We knew nothing about gene splicing, about cloning—we had to smuggle in journals from the West. We could not travel to scientific conferences. We made no advances; we fell behind in everything.

"But our fears brought us to our senses; it was dangerous to fall behind the West in anything. So in 1973 Brezhnev founded Biopreparat. At first we worked in old army factories—at Sverdlovsk, and Kirov, and Zagorsk. Soon we had thirty thousand workers at forty facilities all over the Soviet Union. In Leningrad we made lab equipment and twenty-ton fermenters. At Omutninsk we studied bacteria; at Novosibirsk, viruses. At Chekhov we developed antibiotic-resistant disease strains; at Obolensk our focus was genetic engineering. That is where I worked—at Obolensk.

"Biopreparat took the brightest epidemiologists and biochemists in the country—I was one of them. I went to Obolensk in 1974, fresh from the university. By 1988 I was deputy director for all of Biopreparat. I left in 1992."

"When you defected," Donovan said.

Mirovik winced. "That word suggests betrayal—I betrayed no one. I am here because I wished to be loyal—to mankind and to myself. I was a physician, you see. I took an oath to do no harm—instead, I helped develop weapons of great power. Your people call them weapons of mass destruction; at Biopreparat we called them weapons of mass *casualty*, because they do not destroy buildings or bridges—only people.

"Biopreparat made advances no one thought possible," he said. "Pathogens are very fragile; we learned how to harden them, how to stabilize them. We learned how to protect them from ultraviolet light and changes in temperature. We perfected the aerosol—particles of virus or bacteria in a mist, particles just the right size to enter the lung. We weaponized seventy different pathogens: anthrax, tularemia, Q fever, Ebola, smallpox—"

"Smallpox?" Donovan said. "I thought smallpox was eradicated."

Li took the question. "From the world, yes—but not from laboratories. Smallpox is the most destructive disease in all of human history, Nathan. The last naturally occurring case was in 1977; three years later, the World Health Organization announced that smallpox had been eradicated from the planet. Only two laboratories were allowed to keep samples for future research: your own Centers for Disease Control in Atlanta and the Ivanovsky Institute of Virology in Moscow."

"We used ours for research," Mirovik said. "Weapons research. We kept a stockpile of twenty tons of smallpox weapons at Zagorsk."

"Did we know about this?" Donovan asked.

"America knew very little—until I told them."

Donovan let out a low whistle. "Thanks for coming."

Mirovik paused now and narrowed his eyes at the group. "The things I have told you today—all this I have said before. You did not need to visit me to ask these things. There is something else you wish to know—something I have not been asked before."

Donovan and Macy turned to Li now; they knew they were only spectators here. Li leaned forward and spoke to Mirovik as though they were the only ones there.

"I learned of your defection—your *visit*—to the United States shortly after your arrival, in 1992. Soon after, the American authorities concealed your whereabouts. There is a matter I have been hoping to discuss with you ever since."

"Yes?"

"At the end of World War II, when the Soviet Army captured Unit

731—documents and blueprints were not the only things brought back to Moscow. Scientists were brought back too."

"I have heard this, yes."

"I am searching for one of them—I believe he is still alive. His name is Sato Matsushita."

Mirovik thought for a moment. "I do not know this man."

"Are you certain?"

"You ask me about one man; in Biopreparat there were thirty thousand. Was he military or civilian?"

"He was an officer in the Kwantung Army—but I imagine he would have served the Soviet Union as a civilian."

"Biopreparat was military," Mirovik said. "There were thirty thousand *more* in civilian research."

"Please think carefully; this is very important to me. *Sato Matsushita*—he would have been about fifty years old when you first came to Biopreparat. He was Japanese, about my size and stature. He had two areas of specialty: bubonic plague—and human testing."

Mirovik's eyes widened. *"Dedushka!"*

CHAPTER TWENTY-NINE

I BEG YOUR PARDON?" Li said.

"Dedushka—that is what we called him. It means 'grandfather.' Back then we were all so young, and he was already old—so we called him Dedushka. I did not remember until you mentioned human testing."

"What can you tell me about him?"

Mirovik shrugged. "You must understand, the Soviet Union was very diverse. We had Slavs, Uzbeks, Kazakhs, Tartars, Tajiks—an Eastern man did not stand out as in your country."

"Anything you can remember would be a great help."

Mirovik slumped back and stared up at the ceiling; the back of his chair made a complaining groan beneath his heavy frame. "He was not at Obolensk," he began. "If he was, I would have known. I do not know where he was assigned. I do not know what ministry he belonged to. He was a kind of ghost. I saw him once each year—in April."

"Why April?"

"In April we tested our new weapons—at Rebirth Island, on the Aral Sea. You know this place? We called it *Tmu Tarakan*—it means 'Place of Darkness' or 'Kingdom of Cockroaches.' The sea is drying up, the water is polluted—no fish, no birds, nothing grows there. Desert all around, dust everywhere—a dead place. Just right for us, yes? Rebirth Island is a speck in the sea, shaped like a tear. A hundred of us met there every April—scientists, technicians, soldiers. That is when the ghost appeared."

"The man you called Dedushka?"

"Yes. We tested our weapons on monkeys, you see. But we did not expect to fight a war against monkeys—we needed to know how our weapons would work against Americans. That is the purpose Dedushka served."

"How?"

"He knew about humans. He helped us calculate the Q_{50} for each pathogen."

"The Q_{50}?"

"The amount of pathogen that must be used to infect 50 percent of humans within one square kilometer. It changes for each pathogen, you see. For anthrax, a man must take in ten thousand spores—but only three viral particles will give a man Marburg. You are familiar with Marburg?"

"I am familiar," Li said. "It is a filovirus—a hemorrhagic fever, like Ebola. It liquefies the organs."

"We gave Dedushka our monkey data; he gave us back human data. No one knew how—no one asked."

"He had personal experience in this area," Li said grimly.

"As far as I know, this was his only function at Biopreparat."

"Where was he the rest of the year?"

"I do not know. He was a strange man, a very quiet man. He did not drink; he did not smoke; he did not play cards with the other scientists on the island. He kept to himself. There were rumors; some said he had a small lab at Omutninsk where he did his own research. No one knew. No one cared, as long as he taught us what he knew."

"And what did you teach him?"

"Sorry?"

"He must have learned about the weapons you tested. He must have understood how they were developed, how they were improved from year to year."

"Of course."

"And he probably consulted with other research teams besides your own. It's conceivable that he would have been able to stay abreast of every advancement in Soviet bioweapons technology."

"That is possible, yes." Mirovik looked at Li more carefully now. "Why do you seek this man? What has he done?"

Li looked at Donovan for permission; Donovan nodded. "It isn't what he has done," Li said. "It's what he's planning to do. I believe your Dedushka is planning to launch an attack of bubonic plague against the United States."

Mirovik looked less astonished than any of them expected. Perhaps it was because he had imagined the unimaginable so many times that no new horror had the power to move him; perhaps it was because he had considered this possibility for so many years that the idea was too familiar to cause alarm. Whatever the reason, Mirovik sat in passive silence for a full minute before he spoke again.

"What makes you think this?" he asked.

Li recounted the story of Matsushita, the development of his plague weapon, the aborted Operation Cherry Blossoms at Night—and Hiroshima. Mirovik listened in silence but began to shake his head as the story reached its end.

"The idea is absurd," he said.

"Why is that?"

"This weapon you describe—it is the same one developed by the Japanese? It employs *fleas*?"

"Yes."

"Insect vectors were abandoned decades ago. Too unreliable, too fragile. Plague weapons are all aerosols now, released by cruise missiles—twenty-liter canisters that break apart in the air."

Macy interjected here. "There's reason to believe that Matsushita would keep the flea vector. It has tremendous psychological significance to him. It was his original weapon, the weapon he was never allowed to use. It would have an almost romantic appeal to him—like an old soldier who still wants to fight with his sword."

Mirovik looked annoyed. "Why fight with a sword when you have a rifle?"

"Wouldn't his weapon work?"

"It would have little effect."

"Why?" Donovan asked.

"The bubonic form of plague is not passed from person to person—the flea is the vector. The fleas could not be spread as broadly as an aerosol; the attack would be too localized. And the fleas would soon die—the disease they pass on kills them too. This kind of attack would be clumsy and primitive. After the initial infection, it would be easy to contain."

"Excuse me," Li said from across the table. "I think we must be very careful to separate the vector from the disease itself. First of all, Dr. Mirovik, would the flea vector work? Can fleas be used to spread plague?"

"Of course. Fleas are the natural vector of plague."

"And can fleas be purposely infected with plague for this purpose?"

"We ourselves have used this method—but not for many years."

"Then the weapon would indeed work; your objection is simply that it would not be your weapon of choice. And if the fleas could be distributed broadly, then the infection would not be localized, would it?"

"How would this be done?"

"I have no idea. I'm posing a speculative question."

"If the fleas were spread widely, the initial infection would be larger—but even then the disease would be easy to contain."

"That brings us to the second issue," Li said, "the disease itself. Dr. Mirovik, you said that this Dedushka might have been privy to every advancement in Soviet bioweapons technology. During your tenure at Biopreparat, were there any significant advances in plague research?"

"Wait a minute," Donovan said. "You told us Matsushita would want to use his *original* weapon."

"The handgun you carry," Li said. "Is it the only one you own?"

"No—I still have my Marine service sidearm."

"And when you fire it, do you use old ammunition or new? Your affection is for the weapon, Nathan, not the bullets it fires."

Donovan looked at Macy. "It's possible," she said. "Matsushita might want to retain the form of his original weapon but still enhance its effectiveness—sort of like putting a bigger engine in a classic car."

As they spoke, Mirovik lit another cigarette and rose from his chair. He walked slowly across the small porch and stood by the screen, pressing the ash of his cigarette against the small black gnats on the other side and watching them drop away.

"There were three advancements in plague research," he said quietly.

The group fell silent.

"The first advancement was in the disease itself. All plague is not the same; people do not understand this. Some strains are much more virulent than others. The worst come from the marmots of the Russian steppes. That is the strain we worked with—the one that almost destroyed Europe. It has a peculiar quality—it quickly becomes pneumonic."

Donovan frowned. "I thought all plague was *bubonic* plague."

"There is only one plague organism," Li replied, "*Yersinia pestis*—but plague takes one of three different forms, depending on the system it attacks. Plague is called *bubonic* when it attacks the lymph nodes—the buboes, if you will. Untreated, bubonic plague is fatal in about half of all cases. When plague moves to the bloodstream, it is called *septicemic*; septicemic plague is almost always fatal. When plague attacks the lungs, it is *pneumonic*. It, too, is almost always fatal—and it is the worst form of all."

"Why?"

"Because bubonic and septicemic plagues are rarely passed from person to person. As Dr. Mirovik said, the flea is the vector, and when the flea dies, the disease ceases to spread. But pneumonic plague is highly contagious—it can be passed with as little as a cough or a sneeze. The Black Death of the Middle Ages is something of a paradox: There are countless reports of the symptoms of bubonic plague, but the disease spread much too quickly and much too widely to be bubonic only. Experts believe that the Black Death was both bubonic and pneumonic in nature. It was the pneumonic form that spread the disease to millions—and it would do the same today."

"It was the same strain that Biopreparat used," Mirovik said. "After all, a biological weapon must be contagious to be useful."

No one said anything for a moment.

"Is there a vaccine against plague?" Donovan asked.

"Against pneumonic plague? No."

"Is there a cure?"

"Plague is treated with streptomycin. With rapid diagnosis and treatment, only half will die."

"*Only* half?"

"Yes—but that was before our second advancement. You see, we genetically engineered our plague to resist all major antibiotics."

"*All* of them?"

"All those currently used to treat plague."

"Then what would ever stop it?" Donovan asked.

"The same thing that stopped it in the fourteenth century," Li said.

"What's that?"

"No one knows. Our best guess is that the disease simply burns itself out—as it passes through body after body, it mutates into a less virulent form."

"How long would that take?"

"In weeks and months? No one can say. In human terms? Twenty-five million was the number in Europe, in cities far less densely populated than our own."

Another silence followed, even heavier than before.

Donovan turned to Mirovik again. "You said there were *three* advancements."

Mirovik nodded. "We also learned to splice toxin genes into the plague bacterium. The first was myelin toxin—a chemical that destroys the nerves. We tested it on rabbits; when the first symptoms of plague appeared, their hind legs were also paralyzed."

Donovan shook his head in disbelief. "Tell me something—exactly why is the State Department protecting you? If I had it my way, they'd do the same thing to you that you did to that chicken."

"Nathan," Macy said gently. "Dr. Mirovik is trying to help."

"He's trying to help kill a monster he helped create! You heard what he said—Matsushita's original weapon would be localized and ineffective. *He* made it effective—now it could kill millions instead of hundreds or thousands!"

Mirovik glared back at him. "What about your own country, Mr. Donovan? Do you know where Biopreparat obtained Bolivian hemorrhagic fever? We bought it from a U.S. laboratory! And when Iraq began its biological weapons program twenty years ago, where did they get their raw materials? They bought them from America! Thirty-six strains of ten different pathogens, all sent by mail in a nice little box—and Britain sold them growth medium so they could reproduce pathogens by the ton.

"And who developed nuclear technology—who released that demon on the world? Now every little country is trying to produce a bomb of its own. You must understand something: The Soviet Union turned to biological weapons because America had an atomic bomb and we did not. This monster belongs to the whole world, my friend. We all have blood on our hands."

"Gentlemen," Li interrupted. "We have only one chance to meet, and there is a much more important question to consider than who is to blame." He looked at Mirovik. "Sato Matsushita—Dedushka, as you called him—*where is he now*?"

Mirovik took his seat again. "When Biopreparat shut down, our scientists were without work—I know one who sold flowers on the streets of Moscow to feed his family. The terrible economic conditions have caused our people to seek work elsewhere."

"In other countries?"

"Wherever there is work. Our scientists could be very useful to any nation wanting to develop its own bioweapons program. The information they could provide, the experience—it could save them years of research. When the Soviet Union collapsed, many of our top scientists disappeared. Some went to Iran, some to North Korea, some to Europe—twenty-five came to America. Some of them, no one knows."

"And Dedushka?"

"This I know. Dedushka went to Iraq."

"How can you be certain?"

"In April of 1990—one of our last Aprils at Rebirth Island—Dedushka was not there. Everyone noticed—the ghost did not appear, you see. It was just before your war in the Persian Gulf. I was informed by the deputy director of Omutninsk that Dedushka had defected to Iraq."

"Was anything done?"

Mirovik shrugged. "Dedushka was a ghost. When a ghost vanishes, what is to be done?"

"Dr. Mirovik," Li said, "Iraq did not use biological weapons against the Coalition forces in the Persian Gulf."

"No."

"And Dedushka's presence in Iraq was never exposed. Had he remained in Iraq, it seems likely to me that sometime during the last fifteen years he would have been identified by Western intelligence—especially during the most recent conflict there. This suggests to me that he probably moved on to yet another country. Would you agree?"

"I would guess that Dedushka escaped to Syria. It would not surprise me if he took Iraq's entire program with him."

"What?" Donovan said.

Mirovik smiled. "What did you think—that the Iraqis destroyed their entire arsenal just to please the Americans? Tons of liquid anthrax? Nineteen thousand liters of botulinum toxin, plus aflatoxin and ricin? Nothing is easier to hide than a pathogen, my friends. A flask of liquid can fit into a pocket. A vial of freeze-dried powder can be as small as a pack of cigarettes. Dedushka did not need to drive a tanker truck across the Syrian border; all he needed was the *seed stock*—a small sample of each pathogen."

"And once in Syria, all he would need was the equipment to reproduce it," Li said. "Fermentation vessels, filtration equipment—it would all fit into a small laboratory."

"Why Syria?" Donovan asked.

"Syria shares a six-hundred-mile border with Iraq," Li said. "Across the border is Al Hamad—two hundred thousand square miles of Syrian desert. It would be a simple matter to slip across the border undetected and disappear—many parties did so at the beginning of hostilities. And

Syria has long been a haven to terrorists. I know about this—one of the last Nazi war criminals, Alois Brunner, is said to still live in Damascus. Syria denies this, of course, though Brunner would be easy enough to identify—he's missing an eye and several fingers, thanks to Israeli letter bombs. Syria has provided shelter for many terrorist groups—some say even funding and support."

"Try the university there," Mirovik said with a shrug. "They would have the necessary facilities."

After a pause, Macy leaned forward. "I have one last question, Dr. Mirovik. This scenario we've described—an attempt by one man to launch a biological attack against New York—could it really be done?"

Mirovik considered before answering. "One man alone—no. One man with the support of others—perhaps. No nation would be foolish enough to use biological weapons—even Iraq did not when facing destruction. No nation would dare—the world would tear out the throat of that nation like a Siberian tiger. But one man—one man who did not care about the cost or the repercussions . . ."

His voice trailed off, and he said nothing more.

Half an hour later they stood by the car, trading handshakes and final words. No one said, "I'll see you later," or "I'll give you a call." They all knew this was their one and only meeting and that they would never see one another again. Mirovik would finish his days on his tiny New Jersey gulag, raising chickens and picking wild blueberries from the Pine Barrens sand.

He shook Donovan's hand. "I want you to know something," he said, pointing to the tree stump with the ax still angling from its rings. "That is an option I have considered many times. Some of my friends chose that path; I chose instead to come to America, to tell what I know. I did a lot of very bad things. God will forgive me."

He turned to Li now. "Tell me—why do you seek this man?"

"I believe we explained that."

"No—why do *you* seek this man?"

Li paused. "For personal reasons."

Mirovik nodded. "Perhaps only one man can find one man, yes?"

"Perhaps only a ghost can find a ghost."

Mirovik turned to Macy last of all. "Lovely lady," he said again, "thank you for gracing me with your presence. Thank you for allowing me to look at you."

She glanced around the small farm. "Will you be okay here?"

"This is all I ever wanted—just a small chicken farm, like the one I grew up on in Russia. But life sometimes sends you down an unexpected path. Yes?"

She nodded. "Peace to you, Pasha Mirovik."

"Yes—peace."

HALFWAY BACK TO THE city, Donovan's cell phone rang.

"Nathan Donovan."

"Mr. Donovan, this is Elizabeth Mowery with the Art Theft Program. Are you still interested in funerary jars?"

"You bet. What have you got?"

"We've turned up another jar."

"Where?"

"Red Hook Container Terminal in Brooklyn."

"It came by ship?"

"That's right. When the first jar turned out to be a fake, we figured more of them would turn up eventually—so we sent out a heads-up to all the Customs agents and Port Authority officers at the docks and air terminals. We just got lucky; a Customs agent found the jar while he was doing a random search of a shipping container."

"Was the jar empty?"

"No fleas, if that's what you mean."

"What about the jar itself? Is there any way to know where it came from?"

"The ownership of the container is untraceable—but we know where the shipment originated. The ship sailed from the port of Tartus—in Syria."

CHAPTER THIRTY

"THE COMPANY FOUND YOUR report very interesting," the man in the navy suit said.

I guess so, Donovan thought. *The CIA isn't in the habit of sending over two of its analysts just to throw an office party.*

"This is very good. Which one of you wrote this?" the younger man asked, looking hopefully across the table at Macy.

"We both did," Donovan said. "I didn't catch your names."

"I'm Dave. I'm a science, technology, and weapons analyst for the agency."

"Hi, *Dave,*" Donovan said with a little too much enthusiasm.

"John Stassen," the other man said. "Clandestine service."

A geek and *a spook,* Donovan thought. *Not bad—we must have caught somebody's attention at Langley.*

"I just thought it was very well written," Dave said, eyeing Macy again.

"Thanks," Macy said, covering a smile. "I'm working on my writing skills."

"Your last report was forwarded to us," Stassen said. "We were asked to evaluate its feasibility and to write an estimate on the threat potential."

"And?"

"Let me see if I understand. This fellow Matsushita—we know his background, we know his motives, and we know his capabilities. The only thing we don't know is whether he really exists."

"That's where you guys come in," Donovan said. "The FBI's charter ends at the border; we need somebody who can do some digging overseas."

"We know that Matsushita was alive as late as January of '91," Macy said. "He was known to be in Iraq, possibly headed for Syria."

"That was a long time ago. He could easily be dead by now."

"Yes—but there's also the matter of the fleas in TriBeCa. They're consistent with Matsushita's modus, and so far nobody's offered any other explanation for their presence."

"Maybe somebody just used his calling card," Stassen said. "That doesn't mean it was Matsushita himself. It could have been a student of his, or a copycat—somebody who just read about his work. It's a pretty big leap to say it's the old man himself."

"It's a very big leap," Macy said, "but it's possible—and it's too important a possibility to overlook."

"We know somebody sent the fleas," Donovan said, "and we know that one of the ceramic jars was shipped from Tartus—in *Syria.* You think that's just a coincidence?"

"Hard to tell," Stassen said. "Syria is sort of a black hole for us—a lot of things disappear there: money, narcotics, terrorists. The current government keeps making overtures to us, but at the same time they look the other way for a lot of bad guys. They may even be funding some of them; we don't know for sure. Your boy just might be there. If he is, he'll be hard to find."

"What assets do you have in Syria?"

Stassen looked at him over the top of his glasses.

"Sorry," Donovan said. "I assume you've got a station there—I know we've got an embassy. Ask your people to do some looking, will you? Ask around—start in Tartus. See if you can find the source of those jars."

"I'll check with Mossad," Stassen said. "If anybody knows what's going on in Syria, Israeli intelligence does. They'll have more sources in place."

Stassen turned to his younger colleague. "Anything from you?"

"Well, the science is all there," Dave said. "The Japanese plague bomb, using fleas as a vector for *Yersinia pestis*, Soviet reengineering of the plague bacterium—it all checks out. It's definitely doable—but frankly, I find it very hard to believe."

"Wait a minute," Macy said. "The *science* says it's doable—*you* say it's hard to believe. Which one did you write in your threat assessment?"

"Well—both," he said sheepishly.

"That was sloppy," Macy said. "Tell me—*as a scientist*—why is this scenario so hard to believe?"

He hesitated. "Well—the technical resources it would take to pull it off."

"We were told this is a fairly primitive weapon—using fleas instead of an aerosol, for example."

"Yes, that's true."

"And I understand that it requires very little equipment to reproduce a biological pathogen—about what you would find in the average microbrewery."

"That's true too."

"Then it really requires very few resources to pull off."

"Well—it requires human resources too. He couldn't do this alone."

"But that's not a scientific objection now, is it?"

He didn't reply.

Macy slid a three-ring binder in front of her and opened it. "Let me explain to you gentlemen why this whole thing is not only doable but believable. This binder contains a document I printed off the Internet. It comes from a Web site hosted by Mr. Li, the Chinese gentleman you read about in our report. This document is an English translation of a book that was originally printed in Russia in 1949. It was part of an eighteen-volume series.

"The series contains the transcripts of the Khabarovsk war crimes trial the Russians held after World War II. This volume contains Sato Matsushita's testimony. If you read it, you'll find that he's barely lucid half the time; his grief almost drove him insane. He talks incessantly about his desire to seek justice for his dead sister. He expresses it in Shinto terminology: In Shinto belief, one of the greatest evils is to take the life of another person without showing gratitude and respect for that person's sacrifice. If you do, that person becomes an *aragami*—a powerful, evil spirit bent on revenge. That evil spirit will hold *urami*—a grudge—until justice is done.

"That's what Matsushita thinks—his sister was murdered without respect and without gratitude, and she will never be at peace until he makes things right. That's a very powerful psychological motive—durable enough to last sixty years and dogged enough to find its way around almost any technical hurdle."

She focused on Dave now. "Have you ever heard of the 'white lab coat syndrome,' Dave? It's what happens when people like you step outside their area of expertise. You're a scientist, so you have authority only when you speak *as* a scientist. But when you speak as a sociologist or a political psychologist, you have no more authority than anyone else.

"Now here's what I'd like you to do, Dave. I want you to go back to that threat assessment you wrote, and I want you to look for every personal-value judgment you made—I want you to look for every recommendation or evaluation you offered outside your area of expertise, and I want you to remove them all. I want you to rewrite that threat assessment, Dave, because you write these estimates for policy makers—for people who have the power to act and to allocate resources. This is an important one, Dave, and I don't want the National Security Council to ignore this because of some casual remark you made as a nonscientist. Okay?"

Dave blinked twice. "Okay."

"Fine. Are we done here? Thank you for your time, gentlemen." Macy closed the binder, rose, and headed for the door.

All three men watched until the door closed behind her. Donovan turned and smiled at Dave.

"Still want to go out with her?"

CHAPTER THIRTY-ONE

KHALID STARED DOWN FROM the long, narrow window of the ship's bridge. Thirty feet below, the deck stretched away from him the length of a soccer field. Three rectangular holes lined the center of the deck, hatchways to three of the ship's four cargo holds—three forward, one aft. Between the hatches, two tall gray king posts rose into the sky, each one capped by a crossbeam, forming the letter *T*. From the crossbeams, black cables draped down everywhere like threads, attached to the booms of the heavy-lift derricks. Aging motors groaned in complaint; cables tightened and went slack again. A long boom arm swung out over the docks, pausing just long enough for longshoremen to fasten straps and hooks to it. Then the cables drew taut again, and a long-ton pallet rose into the air as if weightless. Ten feet above the concrete, the derrick stopped; then a motor clicked and hummed, and the boom arm slowly turned, swinging the pallet up and over the gunnels, dangling the forty-bag pallet over a gaping hatch. Bare-chested men leaned out over the cargo hold to steady the swaying load—then there was a quick shout or whistle, and the pallet was slowly swallowed by the darkness.

The king posts and boom arms were flecked with peeling shards of paint. Motor housings and bollards were covered with rust. The deck's surface was blotched and blemished; rings of various colors marked locations where cable spools and grease drums once rested. The ship's gray hull was striped with long vertical stains of brownish orange, where runoff from the deck above had slowly corroded through the failing paint.

Khalid turned to the ship's master. "How old is this ship?"

The man let out a snort. "Young enough for this job," he said.

"Are you certain of that?" Khalid wondered if the rust was just a discoloration, or more like a cancer. He wondered if the entire hull might crumble apart at sea.

"If you don't like my ship, get off."

Khalid glared at him. "I am in command of this ship."

"You are in *control*—*I* am in command. You represent my superiors, so I will follow your instructions. But I decide how those orders will be carried out—unless you know more about ships than I think you do."

Khalid looked at his feet; the master nodded. "There can be only one master on a ship," he said. "If I fail to follow your instructions, you can relieve me. If you disobey my orders, I will have you thrown overboard. Do you understand?"

Khalid ignored the question. "How old?" he asked again.

"The *Divine Wind* was built in 1970, at the Austin & Pickersgill shipyards in England."

"An odd name for a British ship."

"She was christened the *Lancaster*. She's traded hands a number of times since then. When a ship gets to a certain age, she is no longer profitable. Her engines get older; she burns too much fuel; she's too expensive to repair and insure. Our friends picked her up fifteen years ago; they gave her the name *Divine Wind*. In case you wonder, most ships are ready for salvage after twenty-five years. The *Divine Wind* is living on borrowed time—but then, she doesn't have to live much longer, does she?"

Khalid shook his head.

"It's just as well," the master said. "I would rather have her end her life this way than have her bones picked clean on some godforsaken beach in Bangladesh."

"How long have you been the master of this ship?"

"As long as our friends have owned it—not that their ownership could ever be proved, of course. I'm sure the ship is registered to some nonexistent corporation."

Khalid looked out again at the patches of bare wood, the unprotected metal, the fungal splotches of orange and green and brown. "They should have bought a newer ship," he grumbled.

"Our friends know what they're doing. Newer vessels cost a fortune; a ship like this can be purchased for barely a million U.S.—an important feature for people who have to pay cash."

"I've heard they own twenty like this."

"We know they own at least two," the master said.

Khalid watched as yet another pallet disappeared into the darkness of the cargo hold. "How much cargo can she carry?"

"Nine thousand tons—plus crew, stores, and bunkers."

"Bunkers?"

"Heavy fuel oil. The *Divine Wind* has a sea speed of twelve knots. She can do fourteen, but she burns twenty-five tons a day to do it. She's got a tank for diesel fuel, too, the kind we're required to burn in port, but we won't need that; we're filling that tank with bunkers too." The master looked at Khalid's blank face. "You know nothing about ships, do you?"

"I'm a soldier."

"Well, you're a sailor now." He pointed out the bridge window. "That's the *bow*," he said. "Behind us is the *stern*. Toward the bow, that's *fore*; toward the stern, that's *aft*. We're standing in the wheelhouse, or bridge. Below us are three cabin decks, then the main deck—that's called the *weather deck*. The *Divine Wind* is a hundred and forty meters long, and she's twenty-one meters wide—that's her *beam*. When she's fully loaded, the weight will sink her eight meters into the water. That's her *draft*—that's what we need to know to keep from running her aground. Understood?"

Khalid nodded.

"The *Divine Wind* is one of two hundred ships that were built just like her; only fifty of them are still afloat. She's a general cargo ship—she loads and unloads herself through deck hatches, just like ships have done for thousands of years. But sixty years ago the entire shipping industry changed. Now everything is shipped in standardized containers. The ships are bigger, faster, and they load through the side of the hull or from dockside cranes. Ships like the *Divine Wind* can no longer compete. They're too slow; they take too long in port; they don't have the cargo capacity. Ships like this used to own the shipping lanes, but now they're just tramp freighters doing odd jobs all over the world. They keep to the smaller ports—ports like Tartus, where there aren't many inspections or regulations. Every year a few more disappear—sold for salvage or broken apart on some reef. No one misses them; as I said, our friends know what they're doing."

"How long to finish loading?" Khalid asked.

"A day or two—the plumbing and wiring will take a little longer."

"And the laboratory?"

"In the aft cargo hold, lower level. There is a bulkhead that separates it from the rest of the cargo hold. The compartment is isolated from the rest of the ship, as was instructed. It is accessible by a stairway from the weather deck."

Khalid studied his face. "You are aware of the purpose of this mission?"

The master smiled. "I would be a fool to begin a voyage without knowing how it would end, now, wouldn't I?"

"And you are willing?"

"I hate the Americans as much as you do," he said. "I serve the cause."

"Then your name will blaze in the heavens for a thousand years."

"I'm just a simple sailor," he said.

"Well, you're a soldier now."

There was a knock at the door. "Come," the master said.

The door opened, and two seamen entered. They were Filipino, very young and very slender. They were shabbily dressed, and their T-shirts were smeared with streaks of grease. They were part of the black gang, the unskilled oilers and wipers from the engine room who helped keep the ship's ancient five-cylinder diesel functioning.

"Your employer wants a word with you," the master said with a nod to Khalid.

They turned to him.

"We have no further need of your services," Khalid said. "When we put to sea in a few days, you will no longer be part of our crew."

They looked at each other. "Why? What have we done?"

"Your service has been exemplary. The decision has simply been made to replace this crew with another."

"Why?"

"That is not your concern."

"Do you have another ship for us?"

"Not at this time."

They were aghast. "You are dismissing us? You can't do that—we have contracts!"

"Forgive me for not expressing myself better," Khalid said. "We are not dismissing you—not at all. We are buying out your contracts." He reached into his pocket and took out a large roll of U.S. currency. He began to count out hundred-dollar bills into two stacks; the amount was three times the remainder of their contracts.

"Have you been ashore in Tartus yet?" he asked. "A port town offers many pleasures—for a man with money."

The two men stared at one another wide-eyed, then darted for the money.

"I want you off the ship within the hour," the master said. "Get your gear together and turn out your bunks. Understood?"

Thirty minutes later the two men bounded down the gangplank of the *Divine Wind,* the wad of dollars already burning a hole in their pockets. Halfway down the gangplank, they stepped aside to let an elderly Japanese man pass, slowly working his way up toward the ship.

"Did you see him?" one of them whispered. "He must have been a hundred!"

"No wonder they're replacing us," his friend replied. "They could pay him half as much."

CHAPTER THIRTY-TWO

DONOVAN WATCHED AS LI took a single french fry and placed it in his mouth. He held it by the very tip and put it all the way in until his fingers touched his lips, then pulled it out again. He repeated the process over and over until he had licked off the last trace of salt.

"This is obscene," Donovan said. "Didn't anyone ever teach you how to eat french fries?"

"Be my guest," Li said, gesturing to the red carton.

Donovan ripped open two ketchup packets and squeezed them out on a napkin. Then he took half a dozen french fries, folded them in half, wiped up a gob of ketchup, and stuffed the handful into his mouth.

Li turned to Macy. "How can he be a barbarian even when he eats french fries?"

"You should see him with soup," Macy said.

Donovan wiped his hands on his trousers. "I'd rather be a barbarian than a sissy," he said. "Who eats fries one at a time?"

"I do," Li said coolly. "I consider them a delicacy—one of the few accomplishments of American cuisine."

They watched while Li slowly savored several more.

"It's called *fast* food," Donovan grumbled.

"Fast food for obsessive people," Li replied. "Dining should be a break from the hurried pace of life. All other cultures seem to understand this; I'm not sure why you Americans are so slow to catch on. Dining should be a time to relax. Dining should be a time for *conversation.*"

Neither of them responded.

Li let out a sigh. "You know, you two can be quite dull. Must I always carry the conversation?"

"Okay," Donovan said with a shrug. "The CIA has agreed to check with its assets in Syria. They're going to try to find the source of those earthen jars, and they're going to ask around about Matsushita."

Li turned to Macy with a look of disgust. "That's the best he has to offer. Can you do any better?"

Macy looked at him sheepishly. "What do you want us to say?"

"I am surrounded by cowards. I mention conversation, and the two of you immediately turn to a professional topic—a *safe* topic. It's as though you have no personal lives at all."

"What did you expect?" Donovan said. "We're divorced—it takes time to build a new personal life."

"It takes time *and interest*—but I see no indication of interest. Neither of you is making an attempt to build a new personal life. Why is that? It's as though you're each leaving the space vacant that the other once occupied."

Li looked at each of them, but neither would make eye contact.

"I'm not 'leaving the space vacant,'" Macy said. "I'm just busy."

"You *stay* busy. There's anger between the two of you; that's obvious. What you fail to see is the love that still remains."

Donovan looked up. "What makes you say that?"

"I hear criticism but not contempt. I see conflict, but there is still restraint—as though there is something the two of you are still protecting. Truly hateful people can be quite brutal, you know."

"Maybe we're just being polite."

"To what end? No, there is still love between you. You said it yourself, Nathan."

"Me? When?"

"Just now. When I said, 'Love still remains,' you failed to deny it. Instead, you wanted to know the reason for my observation. That indicates *hope*, my young friend. Either you still love this woman, or you still hope to."

Donovan glared at Li now but still avoided eye contact with Macy. "Is this your idea of stimulating conversation?"

"Honest conversation, yes."

"Well, we could use a little less honesty."

"If you ask me, you both could use a lot more."

"No one asked you," Donovan said.

"I'm trying to be your friend here. Remember the old proverb: 'Faithful are the wounds of a friend.'"

"I was thinking of a different proverb: 'With friends like you, who needs enemies?' Butt out, Li. Macy and I will talk when we're good and ready."

"Will you? I wonder. I see too much pride and stubbornness in both of you."

"Maybe so," he grumbled. "What business is it of yours?"

Li returned his glare now. "I'd like to answer that question. I once loved a young woman very much—more than most people can possibly imagine. I lost her, Nathan, and when I did, my life became a series of endless regrets: things I could have said, things I could have done. It's quite amazing, the clarity of vision that death brings with it. But the mind is like that, isn't it? You never remember the thing you've forgotten until the door clicks shut behind you.

"So here you both are, with things left unsaid and things left undone. But it's not too late for you; the door is still open. So I'm here to plead with you both—talk with one another, say what needs to be said and do what needs to be done before it's too late. Please believe me—no matter how painful it may be, if you leave these things undone, your regrets will be far more painful later."

Li got up from his seat.

"Where are you going?" Donovan asked.

"I'm going home—to your home, that is."

"But I'm your ride."

"I've decided to take a taxi. I need to get my heart rate up after this heavy meal."

"Li—we can't just start talking."

"That's exactly what you can do—start talking. You don't have to finish, but you can at least start."

"It's not that easy," Macy said.

"Did I say it was easy? Forgive me; I meant to say it was *simple*. The two of you need to talk. It may not be easy, but it is that simple."

And with that, he turned and left the restaurant.

Macy and Donovan stared after him until it became painfully clear that he would not return. Then they slowly turned and looked at each other. When their eyes met, it was like crossing two live wires.

They looked away again.

LI WAS WAITING ON the sofa when Donovan opened the door.

"Well? How did it go?"

Donovan threw his keys on a side table and headed for the kitchen. "I don't know whether to thank you or punch you in the nose."

"I'm too old for punching," Li said.

"You're not too old to cause a lot of trouble." Donovan popped the top on his beer and sat down on the sofa beside him.

"What did she say?"

He took a long drink. "She asked me why I wasn't there—when Jeremy was dying."

"And what did you say?"

He paused. "I couldn't tell her."

"Why not?"

"Because I don't know."

"Then what did she say?"

"She said that if I couldn't answer that question, there was nothing else to talk about. We sat there for a few minutes, and then she left."

Li nodded. "This is good."

"This is *good*?"

"In folklore, the hero of the story always arrives at a place of ultimate darkness: a cave, or a pit, or even hell itself. There he must face a test, or answer a riddle, or slay a dragon. When he does, he returns with the golden key—the key to all his troubles."

"Li, this is not a story—this is real life."

"But life imitates stories, and stories imitate life. You've come to your place of darkness, don't you see? Macy knows it, and now you know it too. Why weren't you there when your son died, Nathan? That is the question you must answer; that is the dragon you must slay."

"And what's my prize when I do?"

"Forgiveness."

Donovan looked at him. "Funny thing," he said. "Macy's angry, and I'm angry—but you're the one who's been hunting down an enemy for the last sixty years. You're a strange one to talk about forgiveness."

Li nodded. "Stranger than you know."

CHAPTER THIRTY-THREE

THE *DIVINE WIND* PASSED the Strait of Gibraltar and the Moroccan port of Tangier on the morning of its eighth day at sea. The skeleton crew of fifteen men watched the landmasses of Europe and Africa open behind them like spreading hands. At twelve knots, it would be another three days before they reached the port of Ponta Delgada in the Azores, the last port on the last landmass before the endless expanse of the central Atlantic. They would not put in at the port, but they would pass close by. They needed no fuel or supplies; they needed nothing from Ponta Delgada at all. But Ponta Delgada needed to see the *Divine Wind* pass by.

Halfway to the Azores, the *Divine Wind* departed from the traditional shipping lanes and turned north. After ten miles she crossed the visual horizon, where no part of a funnel or mast would be visible to any passing ship. After twenty miles, she passed out of electronic range and disappeared from all ship and ground radar. At that point, the *Divine Wind* had effectively vanished from the face of the earth.

There the ship stopped.

On deck, crewmen threw ropes over the deck railings and lowered scaffolds loaded with drums of black paint. Atop the bridge, three men rigged blocks and tackles from the rim of the ship's tall stack. On the bow, the faded white letters that spelled out *Divine Wind* were already disappearing beneath strips of glossy black.

Khalid descended a long metal stairway from the main deck to the aft cargo hold. The cargo hold was divided into three separate compartments by floor-to-ceiling bulkheads running parallel to the ship. On an ordinary journey, all three compartments would be stacked from floor to ceiling with cargo or stores—but this was no ordinary journey. For this voyage, the starboard third had been converted into a temporary biosafety lab—Dedushka's lab, outfitted precisely according to his specifications.

Khalid ducked through a hatchway and into the long narrow lab. Ten feet ahead of him, a great sheet of milky polyethylene plastic draped from ceiling to floor, sealed tight around the edges with wide strips of tape. In the center of the sheet was a zippered doorway; beyond this doorway was the decontamination area. On the right Khalid saw a shower, a washbasin, and a cabinet for medical supplies. On the left was a simple wooden bench underscored by several pairs of rubber boots. Above the bench, a row of bulky white nuclear/biological/chemical suits hung from metal hooks like sleeping ghosts.

The decontamination area ended at a second plastic sheet with its own zippered doorway. Through this doorway was the final compartment, the laboratory proper, where Khalid could see the white-clad figure of Sato Matsushita bent over his worktable.

"Dedushka," Khalid called out. There was no response. "Dedushka!" He picked up a Stillson wrench from the floor and banged it against the metal bulkhead. Sato turned and stared at him through the translucent plastic. He raised one hand in greeting, then clumped to the plastic barrier and slowly pulled the zipper. He stepped through the doorway and carefully sealed the opening behind him again. In the decontamination area he stepped under the shower and pulled a long silver chain, rinsing off any clinging particles before removing his gas mask and hood.

The de-suiting process took several minutes; at last the old man pulled the zipper on the outer barrier and stepped out.

"How is the heat?" Khalid asked.

"Very bad," Sato said, mopping his forehead. "I must work in brief shifts to avoid dehydration. Is there nothing we can do?"

"It is a cargo hold," he said. "You are in the lowest part."

Sato nodded. "The fleas are not bothered by the heat—the fleas are all that matter."

"I came to tell you that the other ship has arrived."

"How long will we be stopped?"

"Only until the conversion is complete—perhaps a few more hours." Khalid looked at the old man. The temperatures in the lower cargo hold had caused more than one crewman to stagger to the top deck for air—and yet here he was, working hour after hour in a suffocating NBC suit. Perhaps it would be best if he died this way, slumping over from heat exhaustion in the middle of his work.

"You should get some rest," Khalid said. He turned and started up the stairs again. He could feel the heat lifting and the air lightening with every step.

At the top of the stairway, he turned left down a short corridor, then up three more flights of stairs to the bridge. As he entered, he nodded to the ship's master. Out the window, he could see the fourteen-thousand-ton *Southampton* sitting dead in the water a hundred yards ahead.

The *Southampton* was a virtual twin of the *Divine Wind*. It was the identical class of general cargo carrier, born in the same Sunderland shipyard in almost the same year. The two ships were identical in almost every detail: length, beam, draft, displacement. Their hull configurations were the same; they carried the same complement of heavy-lift derricks and hoists, the same rigging and masts and antenna mounts. Structurally, the two ships were identical; the only thing that distinguished them was their color—and that was about to change.

The *Southampton* flew the British flag and sailed from Cardiff in the Bristol Channel. Her hull was solid black, with her name across her bow in italic letters. Her superstructure was white, and her stack was solid red with a wide black stripe at the top.

The *Divine Wind* had a chalky gray hull, with a white stack topped by rings of gray and royal blue. Her name was in simple block letters, and she sailed under a flag of convenience—the flag of Saint Vincent and the Grenadines.

Crewmen hung from the sides of both ships, dangling from ropes and perching on scaffolds, stretching left and right with rollers and brushes. Within hours, the ships had traded colors. The *Southampton*'s hull was now a slate gray—but she looked too freshly painted to pass for her neglected sister, so buckets of acid were poured down her sides, stripping off some of the paint and exposing the naked steel beneath, followed by buckets of salt water to accelerate the rusting process. Her stack was now a boring white, the paint thinned slightly to lend the appearance of age. In a matter of hours, the pristine *Southampton* had aged twenty years.

Her hard-worn sister, on the other hand, had been rejuvenated. The *Divine Wind*'s hull was now a gleaming black, with a new name emblazoned in script across the bow. The fresh red paint rose up the sides of her stack like a climbing flame, with a crisp black smoke ring at the top. Finishing touches were added to the lettering, and flags were traded; and with those final details, the *Southampton* and *Divine Wind* had miraculously traded bodies—but not voices.

That, too, was about to change.

On the bridge, the ship's master sat in front of a laptop computer with Khalid standing behind him. Beside the computer, a small gray device with its own simple keyboard was mounted to the console.

"This is the Automatic Identification System," the master said. "Since last year, all ships over three hundred tons have been required to carry one. It is a transmitter and a receiver; it constantly sends out information about this ship, and it constantly receives information from others."

"What kind of information?"

"Information about the ship, its cargo, our destination, the number of passengers, our bearing and speed—all these things."

"Where does it get all this information?"

"Some of it we provide. When the unit is first installed, we enter the ship's name, our call sign, and a description of the ship. Length, beam, displacement—these things never change, so they are entered only once. Then there are things that change with each voyage. Our destination, our cargo, our draft—we must enter these each time we leave port. And there are some things that change at every moment. Our speed, our course, our precise position—these things the ship provides. Our speed and position come from the Global Positioning System; our heading comes from the gyrocompass.

"All this is transmitted every twenty seconds; every ship within twenty miles receives our signal. That is why we agreed to meet here, away from the shipping lanes and out of range of other vessels—except that one," he said, pointing to the *Southampton.*

"The information we provide," Khalid said. "What prevents us from changing it?"

"You are not as stupid as you look," the master said. "Watch the screen."

The master picked up the radio and contacted the bridge of the *Southampton.* Khalid saw several lines of text describing every detail of the *Southampton*'s structure, cargo, and destination. Every twenty seconds the image blinked momentarily and then refreshed again. After one blink, the name of the ship vanished; twenty seconds later, the name *Divine Wind* took its place.

"Welcome aboard the *Southampton,*" the master said, typing at the unit's keyboard. "We are now transporting nine thousand tons of steel, machinery, and newsprint from the West Midlands of England to the city of New York. I wish it was always this easy to load cargo."

He nodded out the window at the newly christened *Divine Wind.* "We'll give her a couple of hours' head start," he said. "When she passes Ponta Delgada, the vehicle tracking station there will pick up her signal—she will appear to be the *Divine Wind* out of Tartus, bound for La Guaira in Venezuela. When we pass a few hours later, we will appear to all observers to be the *Southampton.* And when we approach New York Harbor ten days from now, the authorities there will see just what they have been expecting to see—just a friendly little cargo ship flying a British flag."

The transformation was now complete.

CHAPTER THIRTY-FOUR

DONOVAN LEANED BACK IN his chair with his feet propped up on his desk. He'd gotten little done all morning, except to type up a report for Reuben Mayer on his meeting with the CIA analysts the week before. He couldn't seem to focus; when he thought about the meeting, he thought about Macy and the way she handled Dave the Science Guy. You had to admire that kind of ability—if you weren't on the receiving end of it, that is. What a formidable woman. *What made that wonk think he had a chance with a woman like Macy?* Every time he thought about it, he felt angry. But why was he angry? He kept thinking about something Li had said: 'The two of you are still *protecting* something.' Was that it? Was he still protecting Macy from other men? Or was he just protecting himself from imagining Macy with other men?

When he thought about Macy, he thought about Li. He wondered if bringing the old man to his house was a stupid thing to do. Now he had a roommate, and that was the last thing he wanted. Living with Li was like being back in ordnance removal—there was no way to know when he would go off; there was no way to tell what he would say or do next. He had to admit, though, there was something about the old man he liked. Maybe it was the same thing he liked about bombs—the honesty, the uncertainty, the risk.

And when he thought about Li, he wondered how this whole thing would end. The old man had his heart set on finding Sato Matsushita; Donovan wished he could make it happen. He wished he could find Matsushita and tie him to a chair, then leave the room and lock the door while Li did what he needed to do. But Donovan knew that would never happen. He wondered if, deep in his heart, Li knew it too. If he did, he wasn't letting on.

If the CIA found Matsushita in Syria, Donovan had no idea what would happen next. He knew that he himself would be finished with the case—it would be an international matter, under the jurisdiction of the CIA or the State Department. Li would demand to see Matsushita, but he would be refused in no uncertain terms. Matsushita would be extradited, interrogated, and then imprisoned or hidden away on some little chicken farm like Pasha Mirovik. Then what would happen to Li? What happens to an old man when he loses his only reason to live?

The phone rang. Donovan reached for it absentmindedly.

"Nathan Donovan."

"Mr. Donovan, this is John Stassen over at CIA. You got a minute?"

Donovan jerked his legs off the desk and sat up. "What's up, Mr. Stassen?"

"I thought you might like to know what's going on over here. This is purely a professional courtesy, you understand. Since you're the one who brought this to our attention, I thought I'd keep you in the loop."

"I appreciate that."

"We've heard from our people in Syria. We think we've located this Sato Matsushita character."

Donovan was focused now. "You're sure of that?"

"We think so. We took your advice and focused on the two main ports—Latakia and Tartus. Port towns are a great place to pick up information—sailors have a lot of time on their hands while their ships are loading. They tend to hang out in the waterfront bars. They drink a lot, and they talk a lot—about cargoes, and crewmates, and destinations. It's not too hard to listen in."

"What did you hear?"

"It was in Tartus, like you said. Two Filipino crewmen were making a lot of noise in one of the local establishments—flashing a lot of money, buying drinks for the house, that sort of thing. They claimed they got put off their ship. Not fired—bought out. Said the big boss called them in one day and bought out their contracts on the spot. Gave them three times what they had coming—in U.S. currency."

"That's pretty generous."

"No kidding—they pay these guys dirt."

"Sounds like somebody wanted happy campers."

"Somebody wanted them *gone*—off the ship pronto, no questions and no objections. We did some checking around town; we found three more crewmen who were put off the same ship. That makes five in Tartus alone—there may be more who already left town. We think there's a good chance they replaced the whole crew."

"Is that a red flag?"

"That's a big red flag. It takes time to train a crew, and you need veterans to train the new recruits. Nobody turns a crew over all at once—who would do the training?"

"Maybe you've just got a ship with a moron in charge of personnel. What does this have to do with Matsushita?"

"When the two Filipinos left the ship, they said they passed a new guy coming on board. They said he was a very old man—and he was Japanese."

"Did they get a name?"

"No."

"Is there any kind of crew manifest? Some way to get a positive ID?"

"Not that we can find."

"Where is this ship now?"

"In the middle of the Atlantic. It left port two weeks ago. Four days ago it passed the Azores; a VTS station there recorded its transponder signal. It's an old tramp freighter called the *Divine Wind.* The ownership is untraceable—but that's true for a lot of these old wrecks."

"Where's the ship headed?"

"It's headed for La Guaira, in Venezuela."

"Venezuela? Why Venezuela?"

"Beats me. Syria exports a lot of phosphates to South America. Maybe Matsushita is tagging along, looking for a back road into the U.S."

"If it's Matsushita."

"We think it's worth checking out. We know the *Divine Wind*'s exact location; a couple of tankers are passing her transponder signal on to us, and we've picked her up on one of our satellites. Right now there's a Navy missile cruiser on its way to intercept her."

"You're going to board her?"

"If necessary—whatever it takes to positively identify this old man."

"Tell your people to be careful," Donovan said. "If this guy really is Sato Matsushita, and if he's carrying this plague weapon of his, he just might use it. If you back him into a corner, what does he have to lose?"

"We're on top of it," Stassen said. "The cruiser is carrying a SEAL unit and a team from the Centers for Disease Control in Atlanta. They know how to handle these things; they're not going to walk into anything with their pants down."

"What if they won't let you board her? What then?"

"I can't comment on that."

"I understand. Look, do me a favor, will you? Let me know when you ID this old man. I've got somebody here who'd really like to know."

CHAPTER THIRTY-FIVE

THE SHIP'S MASTER TRAINED his binoculars on the horizon. There was no sign of the American missile cruiser itself, but a fast-run boat from the cruiser had appeared over the horizon and was approaching on the starboard side. He steadied the binoculars on the approaching craft, racing across the water toward him like a skipping stone. He estimated its speed at twenty knots; at that rate, they would arrive in minutes. He counted ten men on board—eight of them were armed, and all wore biological suits.

The missile cruiser identified herself as the USS *Leyte Gulf,* and her orders were simple and clear: Stop your engines and prepare to be boarded and searched. The ship's master complained that such a search was illegal, a violation of their rights on international waters. He demanded the reason for this intrusion. He offered to send them a complete passenger list and cargo manifest—but nothing deterred them. It was clear that the Americans were unwilling to believe anything except what they saw with their own eyes. They were intent on boarding the *Divine Wind*—and that could never be allowed.

He hurried down to the main deck and followed the starboard railing toward the bow. He raised his binoculars again; the boat was so close now that the binoculars were no longer necessary. He could see one of the men standing, holding a bullhorn and issuing demands. The voice was in Arabic. So the Americans knew who they were, and they knew where she was from—but what else did they know?

He turned and looked down into the open hatch of the number three cargo hold. The entire crew was huddled together on the lower deck, kneeling and bowing in as easterly a direction as was possible on a ship adrift at sea.

The master considered his options. He could not run; the cruiser would easily overtake them. His crew had enough weapons to repel this small boarding party, but there would only be another. It was a missile cruiser—it would fire on the ship; it would cripple her and then board her by force. And once on board, the Americans would quickly recognize that this was not the *Divine Wind* at all. It would only be a matter of time before the real *Divine Wind* was discovered—and then all would be lost.

It was a chance he could not take.

He turned to his crew again. "This is a great and glorious day," he called down into the cargo hold. "Today we will offer our perfect sacrifice; today we have been chosen to become *shahids* and to rejoice together in Paradise. Open the seacocks."

They opened two valves, and geysers of water gushed into the lower hull.

The master turned back to the railing again. The inflatable was almost alongside now.

"What is it you wish?" he called out to them.

"Stand down," the bullhorn blared back. "Prepare to be boarded. Instruct all crew members to report to the main deck immediately."

"This is a privately owned vessel, and we are in international waters. You have no right to board this ship."

The two closest men raised their weapons. "Step back from the railing. We are coming aboard."

"Americans," the master said, sneering. "There is no end to your arrogance." From behind his back he pulled a revolver from his belt. Before he could level the weapon, there was a burst of fire from the boat. The ship's master stumbled backward and over the edge of the open hatch; he was dead before his body hit the water in the bottom of the cargo hold.

A crewman stared down at the body, then turned his face to the blue rectangle of sky above him. "*Allahu Akbar*," he said.

Then he lifted the small box and grasped the protruding handle. He twisted it hard to the right.

The ocean erupted in a ball of fire.

CHAPTER THIRTY-SIX

LI WAS SITTING ON the sofa, staring at the television, when Donovan flung open the door and charged into the room. He reached the sofa in three steps and landed beside Li; the sudden counterweight caused Li's end of the sofa to rise three inches higher.

"Are you watching it?" Donovan asked.

"You certainly know how to make an entrance."

"The report on CNN—are you watching it?"

"I'm not certain what I'm supposed to be seeing," Li said. "They are reporting that a U.S. naval vessel intercepted a merchant ship in the middle of the Atlantic Ocean. The merchant ship unexpectedly exploded, killing several Navy personnel and apparently some civilians as well."

"Any other details?"

"Very few. What's this all about, Nathan?"

Donovan leaned forward and switched off the set, then turned and looked at Li. "Sato Matsushita was on that merchant ship," he said.

Li's eyes widened, but he said nothing.

"The ship was from Syria," Donovan explained. "It set sail two weeks ago, headed for Venezuela. Two former crewmen reported seeing an elderly man board the ship—an elderly *Japanese* man."

"Where did you learn this?" Li asked.

"From a contact at the CIA."

"*When* did you learn this?"

"Yesterday."

"Yesterday! Why didn't you tell me?"

Donovan hesitated. Li studied his eyes, then slowly nodded. "I see—you were hoping not to tell me at all."

"I didn't want to get your hopes up. We didn't know for sure it was Matsushita—that's why they sent the missile cruiser, to board the ship and get a positive ID on the old man."

"And did they make this identification?"

"The cruiser sent an inflatable with a SEAL squad and two scientists from the CDC to check out the ship—but when they pulled up alongside, the crew blew up the ship. The blast killed all ten men. The ship sank like a rock—there was nothing left of it."

"Then no one actually saw Sato Matsushita."

"Come on, Li, who else would it be? An elderly Japanese man boards a ship in Syria. We try to board the ship, but before we can, they blow it out of the water. Now, who rigs a ship to self-destruct? Somebody with something to *hide*, that's who. And let me tell you something—it takes a *lot* of explosive to tear a ship apart like that. Somebody wanted that ship to sink without a trace."

Li thought for a moment. "Can the ship be salvaged?"

"In the middle of the Atlantic? It could be three miles down—whatever's left of it."

"Could bodies be recovered?"

"Li—there's nothing left, okay? Nothing at all."

Li paused again. "Then we can't be certain it was Sato Matsushita."

Donovan rolled his eyes.

"You said the ship was bound for Venezuela. Why would Sato Matsushita want to go to Venezuela?"

"We never got a chance to ask him."

"That seems highly unlikely. And besides—"

"Li." Donovan put a hand on the old man's shoulder and spoke as softly as he could. "Sato Matsushita is *dead*. Do you hear what I'm saying?

Your old enemy is *dead.* There's no way around it; you have to face it. I'm sorry you didn't have the chance to kill him yourself—but at least you know he got what was coming to him. I've seen people die in explosions, Li. It's no pretty sight. He was probably torn apart, or—"

"Nathan," the old man said, "you understand so little."

Donovan leaned back. "Maybe so—but at least I understand this: Matsushita is dead, and you just have to get over it."

Li shook his head. "You have no idea what you're saying."

"I know it was your *mission,*" Donovan said, "but try to look at it this way: Without your help, we never would have found Matsushita at all. You told us about him; without you, we never would have tracked him to Syria—we never would have known he was on that ship. We only stopped the ship because you warned us about his plague weapon. He didn't die of old age, Li; he died because of *you.* In a way, you did fulfill your mission."

"My mission was not to cause his death," Li said. "My mission was to meet him face-to-face."

"I tried to tell you that would never happen."

"Yes—you did."

They sat in silence for a few moments. "So Sato Matsushita 'got what was coming to him,'" Li said. "But what about me, Nathan? Am I to remain imprisoned for the rest of my life?"

"You've got to let it go," Donovan said.

Li looked at him. "The way you've let Jeremy go?" He got up from the sofa, walked into his bedroom, and shut the door behind him.

THAT EVENING, DONOVAN SAT on the front step and pressed the cell phone tight against his ear. The Fourth of July was just three days away, and he could hear the occasional screech of a bottle rocket and the crackle of firecrackers in the distance. Fireworks were illegal in the city of New York, but the NYPD had better things to do than arrest every ten-year-old with a sparkler. After all, it was the Fourth of July, and New York was in a mood to celebrate.

"How did he take it?" Macy asked.

"Pretty hard, I think."

"What did he say?"

"He said his mission wasn't fulfilled—that he was still in prison."

"Where is he now?"

"In his room. He went to bed early."

"Check up on him, Nathan. Don't leave him alone."

"You think he might do something stupid?"

"I think he's a very old man who just lost his reason for living. What do you think?"

"I told him he had to get over it."

"Nathan—"

"I didn't mean right away—I just meant that eventually he has to find something else to live for."

"What did he say to that?"

Donovan paused. "Nothing."

"Stay with him, okay? Let me know how he's doing."

"Maybe we can all get together again. I think he'd like to see you."

"Okay. Call me."

"Hey," Donovan said. "It's nice talking to you again."

There was a click on the other end.

He got up and went into the house. Li's bedroom door was shut tight. Donovan turned the knob as quietly as possible and pushed the door open just enough to peer inside. The old man was lying on his back, staring up at the ceiling. His fingers were interlocked, holding the photograph of Jin against his chest.

"I'm not dead, if that's what you're thinking," Li said without moving his eyes.

Donovan stepped into the room. "Could have fooled me."

"I'm just having trouble sleeping."

"I have that problem too."

"Give it a few decades—you'll get used to it."

Donovan sat down on the end of the bed. "You okay?"

"In what sense? My body is quite well, thank you. My thoughts are extraordinarily clear."

"I mean about the news today."

"I haven't 'gotten over it' yet, if that's what you mean."

"I'm sorry," Donovan said. "I talked with Macy; she told me that was a little blunt."

"The two physicians conferring over their patient," Li said. "Dr. Monroe's specialty is the mind—what's your specialty, Nathan?"

"Survival."

"What a very narrow specialty. Life is more than survival, Nathan—life is about healing. The trick is to continue healing right up until the moment you die. The irony is, I'm more than eighty years old, but I'm healthier than you are."

"All I meant to say is you have to move on. It's all you can do, Li."

"Have you ever taken a holiday, Nathan? It's been my experience that there are two kinds of holidays. In the first kind, the destination is the thing—you cannot wait to get there; you have someplace to *be*. But in the second kind, the trip itself is the holiday. Imagine how dull a holiday would be if one could simply teleport oneself from place to place. Imagine how much you would miss. Life is a journey, Nathan, not a destination. You mustn't be in too much of a hurry to arrive. You really must stop along the way—even at the dark places. They're part of the journey too."

Li's voice trailed off now. He continued to stare at the ceiling, saying nothing, not even blinking. Donovan watched him, wondering how much of a journey the old man had left.

"May I tell you something?" Li said softly. "Something I've never told anyone before." He looked down at Donovan for the first time. "I knew my wife was dead before I approached the village."

"What?"

"Before I saw the first dead rodent. Before I even crossed the final hill-side, I already knew."

"How?"

"'The two shall become one flesh'—that's how the Scriptures put it.

When Jin's spirit left this world, I sensed her absence. It was as obvious to me as if we were two children playing on a seesaw, and she stepped off the other end. I knew, Nathan. It wasn't a premonition or a sense of foreboding—I *knew.*" He paused. "That's how I know that Sato Matsushita is still alive."

Donovan's shoulders slumped, and he let out a sigh. "Li—"

"I am joined to him, Nathan. If his spirit had left this world, I would know. I've been lying here thinking and praying all evening. God has reassured me that I will not die until I meet Sato Matsushita face-to-face. I will not die in bondage; I will have the chance to release my soul from prison."

"I hate to question God," Donovan said, "but what about the evidence? He was on that ship, Li, and that ship went down. There were no survivors."

"It was the wrong ship."

"What?"

"It was the wrong ship, or Sato was not on it. Perhaps he only boarded temporarily; perhaps he disembarked again before the ship set sail. I have no idea—I'm simply telling you that he is still alive. This is not my imagination, Nathan, or some desperate wish. I'm simply telling you what I *know.*"

"And I'm telling you what *I* know," Donovan said. He patted the old man's leg and rose from the bed. "Try to get some sleep," he said, "if you can."

Donovan closed the door behind him and went into his own bedroom. He stripped down to his boxer shorts and stood in front of the air conditioner, trying to shed the evening's heat before he attempted sleep. He parted the drapes and looked out; in the distance, he saw a trail of silver sparks slowly streak across the sky and then explode, dripping down in a shower of white and gold.

In bed, he found himself staring at his own ceiling and thinking about the old man next door. *Some holiday,* he thought. Li was wrong; some vacations were so bad that you'd gladly teleport from place to place—you'd skip the whole thing if you had the chance. But you don't get that chance—maybe that's what Li was saying. Maybe life is the vacation from hell, an endless road trip where you don't know where you're going but you're making really good time. And every town you stop at along the way is dull and disappointing, but you keep telling yourself that the next one will be better. You just keep driving; you never learn.

Li was wrong. Sato Matsushita was dead, and Li would have to get over it—it was a destination, not a journey, and the sooner he could get there, the better off he would be. Li was like some old poem—he sounded so wise, but the words never really made sense. Maybe Macy was wrong too; maybe Li was insane—or maybe he was the sanest man Donovan had ever met.

No—Li was wrong. But something the old man said kept bothering him, kept coming back to him. He couldn't ignore it; he couldn't put it out of his mind.

It was the wrong ship.

Donovan rolled over and reached for the phone.

CHAPTER THIRTY-SEVEN

MACY SAT UP IN bed and switched on the light. It was no use trying to sleep. Sometimes her thoughts were like a freight train, gathering momentum all day long. When she finally turned out the light and commanded her mind to rest, it was like hitting the brake. It took miles to come to a full stop—it took hours.

She dreaded the winding-down process. It was the loneliest part of her day, lying in the darkness and staring wide-eyed at nothing at all. There was nothing to listen to, nothing to touch or taste—no distractions at all. *That's the problem with darkness*, she thought. *It's a theater for the mind.* In the darkness of the bedroom, every thought became louder, every image more distinct. She tried sleeping on the sofa, with all the lights on and the television playing in the background, hoping to somehow pass directly from consciousness into perfect oblivion. It didn't work—nothing did.

"It's nice talking to you again," Nathan had said. It was a thoughtful sentiment, they were gracious words, but they made her furious. What did he think—that Jeremy was a topic they could just ignore, that they could just forget the whole thing and be pals again? Nathan was absent from his own son's death. Jeremy died alone, wondering why his father had abandoned him. That was over—that was history. But Nathan couldn't just show up again now, without apology and without excuse, and pretend that it never happened. It *did* happen, and it hurt worse than anything in Macy's whole life.

The more she thought about it, the angrier she became—angry at Nathan and angry at herself for letting her mind go there again. She could feel the adrenaline creeping into her system. *Terrific*, she thought, *there goes another hour. Maybe I can look through Jeremy's baby pictures again—that'll keep me up all night.* She turned to the nightstand and picked up the small book Li had given her at the restaurant. Might as well put the time to use. She slipped on a pair of reading glasses.

Just inside the cover was a note in Li's own immaculate handwriting. It read:

> *My dear Macy,*
>
> *The book you are holding is known as The Decameron. It was penned by Giovanni Boccaccio in 1353, while the Black Death was still ravaging Europe. It is the tale of ten young friends who fled to the countryside to escape the plague in the city of Florence. Each day, the group took turns entertaining one another with stories. The book is a collection of their stories. Some contain eyewitness accounts of the plague and its effects. I have earmarked one particular section for you; I think you will find it most interesting.*
>
> *With all respect and affection,*
> *Li*

Macy flipped through the pages. Near the center was a small sheet of rice paper marking the first page of a chapter. She set the paper aside and began to read.

> *I say, then, that the years of the beatific incarnation of the Son of God had reached the tale of one thousand three hundred and forty-eight when in the illustrious city of Florence, the fairest of all the cities of Italy, there made its appearance that deadly pestilence . . .*

In Florence, despite all that human wisdom and forethought could devise to avert it . . . towards the beginning of the spring of the said year the doleful effects of the pestilence began to be horribly apparent by symptoms that shewed as if miraculous . . .

In men and women alike it first betrayed itself by the emergence of certain tumours in the groin or the armpits, some of which grew as large as a common apple, others as an egg, some more, some less, which the common folk called gavoccioli. From the two said parts of the body this deadly gavocciolo soon began to propagate and spread itself in all directions indifferently; after which the form of the malady began to change, black spots or livid making their appearance in many cases on the arm or the thigh or elsewhere, now few and large, now minute and numerous . . . Almost all within three days from the appearance of the said symptoms, sooner or later, died . . .

They stayed in their quarters, in their houses, where they sickened by thousands a day, and, being without service or help of any kind, were, so to speak, irredeemably devoted to the death which overtook them. Many died daily or nightly in the public streets; of many others, who died at home, the departure was hardly observed by their neighbours, until the stench of their putrefying bodies carried the tidings; and what with their corpses and the corpses of others who died on every hand the whole place was a sepulchre . . .

It was the common practice of most of the neighbours, moved no less by fear of contamination by the putrefying bodies than by charity towards the deceased, to drag the corpses out of the houses with their own hands . . . and to lay them in front of the doors, where any one who made the round might have seen, especially in the morning, more of them than he could count . . . It was come to this, that a dead

> *man was then of no more account than a dead goat would be today . . .*
>
> *They dug, for each graveyard, as soon as it was full, a huge trench, in which they laid the corpses as they arrived by hundreds at a time, piling them up as merchandise is stowed in the hold of a ship, tier upon tier, each covered with a little earth, until the trench would hold no more . . .*
>
> *How many brave men, how many fair ladies, how many gallant youths, whom any physician . . . would have pronounced in the soundest of health, broke fast with their kinsfolk, comrades and friends in the morning, and when evening came, supped with their forefathers in the other world.*

Macy shuddered. She picked up the piece of paper to mark the place again, and only then realized that the paper bore Li's handwriting too. It contained two short excerpts from a book titled *In the Wake of the Plague*:

> *The level of mortality in the Black Death was so high and so sudden that—until germ warfare on a large scale occurs—to find a modern parallel we must look more toward a nuclear war than a pandemic . . .*
>
> *Nothing like this has happened before or since in the recorded history of mankind.*

Suddenly, she heard pounding at her front door. Someone was hammering it with his fist, shouting something through the door. Macy threw off the covers and scrambled into her robe. She stopped at her closet just long enough to grab the first shoe she could find—then she thought about her chances of fending off an attacker with a black Mary Jane, and she threw it back into the closet.

"Who is it?" she shouted through the door.

"It's Nathan and Li! Open up!"

Macy peered through the peephole and saw the fish-eyed images of the two men. She unlocked the dead bolt and knob. The door was only halfway open when Donovan pushed past her.

"Where have you been?" he demanded. "I've been trying to call."

"I took the phone off the hook—I was trying to sleep."

"That was a stupid thing to do. We wasted half an hour getting up here."

"What's the hurry? What's happened?"

"You've got five minutes to get dressed. They want us down at 26 Fed—*now.*"

CHAPTER THIRTY-EIGHT

THE CONFERENCE ROOM AT 26 Federal Plaza was crowded with people, high-ranking representatives of the thirty-odd organizations composing the Joint Terrorism Task Force. The conference table was littered with papers, maps, and open laptops with cellular uplinks to government offices, military bases, and the FBI's own Strategic Information and Operations Center in Washington. There were uniforms from three different services, though there were more civilians in number; there were men and women in formal business attire, and there were open collars with shirttails out. People hustled everywhere, making quick verbal exchanges and handing off papers to administrative assistants who darted in and out of the doors. On the far wall, a rear-projection screen displayed a satellite photograph of New York Harbor.

No one noticed Donovan, Macy, and Li when they entered. Donovan spotted Poldie and Reuben Mayer across the room; he motioned to Macy and headed for them. The room was in chaos—there was no podium, no microphone, no indication of who was in charge.

Donovan leaned over to Poldie. "Who's running this show?"

"It's opening night," Poldie said. "I think we got a few bugs to work out."

Donovan looked around the room, waiting for someone to take charge—but no one did. He put two fingers to his lips and produced a whistle that would stop any cab in New York.

The room fell silent. Donovan stood up.

"My name is Nathan Donovan," he said. "I'm with the FBI. I was in charge of this case; I'm not sure who's in charge of it now, but we need to figure that out fast. Let's start by finding out who's here. He's NYPD," he said, gesturing to Poldie. Then he nodded at Macy: "And she's Columbia University."

He began to point to people around the table. No personal names were given, only the names of represented agencies. There were intelligence experts, analysts, and state and local law enforcement. There was the CIA, the Department of Homeland Security, Customs and Border Protection, and the Transportation Security Administration. A Coast Guard Port Security Unit was present; so was a top official from the Centers for Disease Control in Atlanta. The Navy would ordinarily be represented by the Naval Criminal Investigative Service—but on this occasion a SEAL commander had replaced him, from the Naval Special Warfare Development Group out of Dam Neck, Virginia.

"Okay," Donovan said. "Time is short, so let's get right to it. CIA, we need a situation briefing—the short version, if you don't mind."

A man on the opposite side of the table rose from his chair. "By now you all know the basics," he said. "About twenty-six hours ago the USS *Leyte Gulf* intercepted a Syrian cargo ship called the *Divine Wind*. We now have reason to believe that the ship was not the *Divine Wind* after all.

"The vessel tracking station in the Azores picked up the *Divine Wind*'s transponder signal about four days ago. We worked backward from that date, tracing her course using satellite photographs. We found this," he said, pointing to the projection screen. He hit a button on his laptop, and the screen changed to show a satellite image of two ships so close together that they looked as if they were about to collide.

"About six days ago the real *Divine Wind* headed north, out of commercial shipping lanes. She stopped here, at this point; the other vessel you see in the photograph joined her a few hours later. We've traced that ship back to her point of origin—she's the *Southampton* out of Cardiff. She's exactly the same kind of cargo ship as the *Divine Wind*—and I mean exactly.

"Now watch," he said, changing the image again. "This was taken a few hours later. The top ship in the photo is departing first—that's the *Southampton.* But when she passed the Azores, her transponder signal identified her as the *Divine Wind.* We believe the two ships traded identities—flags, colors, transponder data, the works. We think it was a ruse to conceal the whereabouts of the real *Divine Wind.*"

"Where's the real one now?" the Coast Guard asked.

"About ten hours out of New York Harbor."

There was a second of complete silence—then the room erupted in noise.

"Let's hold it down!" Donovan shouted over the din. "Okay—that's the situation. You've all read the briefings on Sato Matsushita; you know about his possible plague weapon. We're proceeding under the assumption that Matsushita is on board this vessel and that he is carrying the weapon with him. Our job is to stop him. Options?"

Questions and comments began to be shouted from all around the table. Donovan held up both hands.

"How many of you represent the 'response and recovery' side of things? FEMA, first responders—all the disaster management agencies?"

Half of the hands in the room went up.

"Okay—for the next thirty minutes I want you people to keep your mouths shut. The rest of us represent the assets we have available to prevent this thing from happening. Now—how do we go about it?"

"The first priority is to stop the ship," the Navy said. "Deny her access to U.S. territorial waters—keep her out of range of the coast."

"How?" Donovan asked.

"We send out a CPB—a coastal patrol boat. It's small, it's fast, and it can carry a large weapons package and a full SEAL team. There are nine stationed at Little Creek, Virginia."

"Too far away," the Coast Guard said. "We can send one of ours directly out of New York."

"Hold it a minute," the CDC said. "This plague bacillus—what form is it in?"

"We don't know," Donovan replied.

"Well, is it weaponized? Is it a missile? Is it ready to be launched? What's its range?"

"Again, we don't know."

"Those are crucial questions," the CDC said. "We can't go sailing up to this ship in broad daylight—you saw what they did to their decoy. If they see a naval vessel approaching, they're likely to launch that weapon—if it's launchable, that is. What would they have to lose?"

"It's very unlikely it would have that kind of range," the Navy said.

"*Unlikely?* You've all seen the briefings; this strain of *Yersinia pestis* is reported to have been genetically altered. That means there's no vaccine and there's no cure. There are millions of people in New York. We can't afford to take a chance—we have to assume that the bacillus is weaponized and within range of the coast."

"Then our only option is to sink her," the Navy said. "A coordinated strike from a series of Tomahawk cruise missiles. They can travel just above the water at three-quarters the speed of sound—the terrorists would never see them coming."

"We'd better be sure about this," the State Department said. "We're talking about a military attack on a merchant vessel in international waters without any prior notice or warning. This is a political nightmare—are we sure about our intelligence here? We can't afford another 'We thought they had weapons of mass destruction' debacle."

"The intelligence is solid," the CIA said. "We can prove that the ship switched identities."

"That's circumstantial evidence. Can we prove that they definitely have this plague on board?"

"Sir—we don't *know* what she has on board. We're talking about a preemptive strike against a potential threat."

"We'd better decide how important this *proof* is," the Navy said. "If we hit her with a couple of Tomahawks, there won't be anything left."

There was a pause. "Well, I don't see any choice," the State Department said. "The potential threat to the U.S. is too great. We'll just have to take the heat later. I agree—we need to sink the ship."

Heads began to nod all around the room.

"Wait a minute," the CDC said, slowly rising from his chair. "There's something we're not considering here—something absolutely crucial. This strain of plague—it's unknown to us. If it's on this ship, then it's probably in a laboratory somewhere else too. That means even if we sink this ship, there could be another attempt to use this weapon against us later on. We need a sample of this plague. The CDC needs time to develop a vaccine. We can't afford to wait until the next attack—it'll be too late then."

"What are you suggesting?" the State Department asked.

"I'm saying we can't just sink this ship. We need to put somebody on board who can retrieve a specimen for us."

There were groans from all around the table.

"That's possible," the Navy said, "but not without some element of risk."

"Why?"

"Because it's almost dawn—the ship will be arriving in broad daylight. No matter how we try to approach, there's always a chance of being spotted."

"Can't you use divers?"

"That's our best option: Put a swimmer delivery-vehicle team on a passing merchant ship and drop them off a few miles away—approach from underwater. But they'll still have to scale the side of the ship—and then there's open deck to cross. There's always a chance they'll be spotted—we need to be clear about that up front."

"Any chance is too great a chance," the Coast Guard said. "These people aren't going to sail into New York Harbor with their hands in their pockets—they're going to be ready to act. And they're going to have lookouts all around the perimeter of the ship—if they've gotten this far, they're not idiots."

"We're losing sight of the priority here," the CIA said. "Maybe this plague is in some other laboratory; maybe it's not. Maybe there will be some future attack; maybe there won't. We can't prevent all possible future scenarios—we have to prevent *this* one. The priority is to sink this ship—*now.*"

"That's incredibly shortsighted," the CDC said. "Suppose they fire this weapon—suppose ten million people die from it. We all agree that would be unthinkable. Now suppose we sink the ship so there is no attack, but they still find a way to use the weapon next month, or next year, and we still have no protection against it—then ten million *still* die. Ten million now or ten million later—what's the difference?"

"There's a *big* difference," the CIA replied. "It's a real ten million now versus a theoretical ten million later."

"But maybe it's twenty million later—maybe a *hundred.* The minute we get our hands on this strain, we can get to work on a vaccine—and the minute we have a vaccine, this weapon is rendered useless at all times and in all places. If there's *any* chance to get a sample of this plague, it's worth taking."

"Is it worth ten million lives?"

"No, of course not—we have to reduce that risk."

"There's no guarantee that we can put a man on that ship unseen—it can't be done."

"We have to find a way."

"This is lunacy!"

Objections and opinions came from all around the table. The pace quickened, voices rose, and tempers flared. Donovan looked around the table. This was the problem with the JTTF: thirty organizations with very different perspectives and priorities and no clear lines of authority. The *Divine Wind* could sail up the Hudson to Albany while these guys were still arguing.

"Harbor pilots," said a voice across the table.

Donovan looked. The voice came from a very ordinary-looking man in civilian clothing. He sat quietly with his hands folded on the table in front of him. He had no computer, no cell phone, no administrative assistant. Up until now he had been just part of the wallpaper.

"Hold it down!" Donovan shouted over the group. He turned to the man. "I'm sorry—what did you say?"

The man looked a little embarrassed. "It just occurred to me that there's a way to put a man on that ship without anybody noticing. Come to think of it—make that three."

CHAPTER THIRTY-NINE

THE MAN HAD EVERYONE'S attention now.

"Stand up!" someone shouted. He slid back his chair and awkwardly rose to his feet.

"Who are you with?" Donovan asked.

"Sandy Hook Harbor Pilots."

"Okay, Sandy Hook, you've got the floor. We're all ears."

"See, it's this way," he said. "Any foreign ship entering U.S. coastal waters has to have a U.S. harbor pilot on board to guide her into port. It's the law."

"Why?"

"The ship's master knows his vessel, and he knows the open sea—somebody else has to know the harbor: the tides, the currents, the sandbars and shoals. A master can't be familiar with every port he calls on—and even if he could, conditions change. Some of these ships are the largest moving objects in the world. We can't have some fool running a thousand-foot bulk carrier aground and blocking the shipping channel just because he doesn't know the terrain. That's our job—we go out to meet the ships as they approach, and we pilot them in."

The man pointed to the projection screen. "Somebody had a shot of the harbor up there—can we get that back again?" A few seconds later the image reappeared. "Can you back it out a little? I need a wider view." The image refocused at a lower resolution, showing a broad overview of New York Harbor. At the top of the screen, the tip of Manhattan was just visible. Below it was a huge, hourglass-shaped body of water.

"Up top is Manhattan," he said, stepping up to the screen. "You can see Liberty Island and Ellis Island there and there—that's the Upper Bay. The bay narrows down here, where it passes between Brooklyn and Staten Island. See this little line? That's the Verrazano-Narrows Bridge—that's where our offices are, just above the bridge. Below the bridge, all this water down here, that's the Lower Bay—and you can see that the Lower Bay empties into the Atlantic over here.

"Now, you see this?" He pointed to a spot at the bottom of the screen where a narrow strip of land curled up and into the Lower Bay like a crab's claw. "That's Sandy Hook—there's a Coast Guard station there. And this," he said, tracing a line with his finger due east into the Atlantic, "is Ambrose Channel. It's the main shipping channel in and out of New York Harbor. This is the channel your cargo ship will follow to enter the harbor."

He put his finger on the eastern end of the channel. "Right about here is Ambrose Tower," he said, "a floating lighthouse that marks the entrance to the channel. Ambrose Tower is about twenty-five miles east of the Verrazano Bridge. Whenever a ship passes that tower, one of our pilots is there to meet it."

"How do they get out there?" Donovan asked.

"We keep a pilot boat floating in this area here—it's out there 24/7, twelve months a year, in good weather and bad. There are always pilots on board; we're like doctors—we're always on call. When a ship is about three hours out, she radios us to confirm her arrival. When she does, we put a pilot on a smaller, faster boat—we call it a launch. The launch ferries the pilot out to the ship."

"How does the pilot get on board?"

"The launch pulls up alongside, they throw a rope ladder down, and the pilot climbs up."

"You're kidding."

He shook his head. "I've climbed a couple and found nothing holding the ladder on but a couple of crewmen."

"And once the pilot's on board?"

"He's taken straight to the bridge, where he takes over for the ship's master."

"You do this for *every* ship?"

"Every domestic ship over sixty tons. And *every* foreign ship—no exceptions, no questions asked. See, that's the beauty of it: They're *expecting* a pilot to come on board—in fact, they'll get suspicious if he doesn't. And another thing—since 9/11, it's been common practice for a couple of Coast Guard guys to come along with the pilot, just to do a random inspection from time to time. They're called sea marshals—sort of like the air marshals on planes. Every ship's master knows about it; they all know they have to put up with it. The Coast Guard guys are always in uniform—and they're always armed.

"So I was thinking: When this ship passes Ambrose Tower, we send out a launch just like we always do—only this time, our pilot brings along two of your Special Forces guys dressed like sea marshals. They go straight to the bridge, where they take over the ship; then the pilot steers while the other two search the ship."

The group fell silent, and the man slowly returned to his chair.

"It's good," Donovan said, nodding, "but we don't need one of your pilots—we don't need to steer the ship; all we need to do is stop it. We don't want to put one of your men at risk—and if we're only putting three men on board, they all need to be professionals."

Donovan looked at the Navy SEAL commander. "Can you pick me two good men?"

"No problem. Who's the third?"

"Me. Somebody from the JTTF needs to be there—and this is still my case, if there are no objections."

He glanced quickly around the room. From the corner of his eye, he could see Macy slowly shaking her head.

"Done," Donovan said. He turned to the CIA. "How far is the *Divine Wind* from Ambrose Tower right now?"

He looked at his laptop. "Best estimate: less than six hours."

Conversations erupted all around the table again as all the details of logistics were considered. Suddenly, there was a sharp rapping sound from the far end of the table. Heads slowly turned. It was Li, rapping his knuckles on the hard wooden surface until the room grew quiet and every eye was on him.

"I have a question," he said. "How many old Japanese men are aboard this vessel?"

No one responded.

"It seems like a reasonable question," Li said. "After all, our goal isn't simply to board this ship—our goal is to locate and identify one individual *on* this ship."

"Li," Donovan said, "I think we can find one old Japanese man on the ship."

"That's very reassuring, considering the fact that until a few hours ago, you couldn't find the ship itself. It seems to me that these people went to extraordinary lengths to disguise this vessel—mightn't they attempt the same thing with the most important individual *on* the ship?"

"Sir, once we seize the ship, we have everyone on it," the Navy said.

"And while you're talking to the wrong Sato Matsushita, the real one launches a missile into the sky. Or perhaps he destroys the weapon rather than allow it to fall into your hands—and the plague along with it." He looked at the CDC. "It would be very simple to do, and then you would have no specimen."

"He's right," the CDC said. "We have to find this Matsushita as quickly as possible—that should be the number one priority."

"Is there a photo of this guy?" the Navy asked. "Is there some way to positively identify him?"

"Indeed there is," Li said. "I can identify him. I am the only one on earth who can."

"Sir," the Navy said, "with all due respect, there is no way—"

Li held up both hands. "I'm not suggesting that I replace one of your Special Forces men. That would be very foolish—though I must admit I find the idea exhilarating. I'm simply suggesting that I be close by in order to serve as a reference." He turned to the harbor pilot. "This 'launch' of yours—how big is it?"

"About fifty feet in length," he said.

"Sounds quite roomy. I assume this launch requires a pilot; in addition, it must carry Mr. Donovan and his two sea marshals. That makes four. By any chance, would there be room for me as well?"

"No problem."

Li smiled and looked at the group. "There you have it," he said. "I can tag along on the launch, safe and out of harm's way. When Mr. Donovan and his team secure the vessel, I will be available nearby to confirm the identification of Sato Matsushita. My services may never be required; perhaps Dr. Matsushita will be wearing one of those friendly name badges that says, 'Hello—my name is Sato.'" He glanced around the room. "Perhaps not."

Donovan looked at him; Li returned his gaze. The old man's dark eyes were perfectly still, unflinching. There was no apology in them, no evasion, and no shame. Donovan remembered Li's words: *I don't expect you to ignore the rules, Nathan; I'm just hoping for a liberal interpretation.* The old man knew it might come down to this. Donovan was in charge now, and if he stuck to the rules, he would end the old man's dream right now.

Li seemed to read his thoughts. *It is my mission,* his eyes said.

Donovan paused—then he nodded almost imperceptibly, and the old man blinked gratefully in reply.

"It's not a bad idea," Donovan said to the group. "We're only going to get one shot at this; we might as well have all the resources available that we can."

"Then you'll want me too."

It was Macy's voice. Donovan turned, but before he could say a word, Macy rose to her feet and began to address the table.

"I'm Dr. Macy Monroe. I'm a professor of political science and international relations at Columbia. I've been consulting for the FBI on this case, working in conjunction with Mr. Donovan and Mr. Li. I'm a specialist in terrorist psychology and hostage negotiation—I have regional expertise in both the Middle East and Japan. I speak both Arabic and Japanese." She looked around the table. "I know many of you personally. I've trained some of your people in hostage negotiation."

Donovan rolled his eyes. She was laying out her credentials one by one as if she were dealing cards.

"Mr. Li and Mr. Donovan are correct," she said. "We should have all the resources available that we can. Suppose Mr. Donovan and the sea marshals secure the ship, then immediately search for Sato Matsushita. It's possible they'll encounter no resistance, that they'll find Matsushita and take him completely by surprise. It's possible—but it's not likely. There could very well be some resistance, some exchange of hostilities, something to warn Matsushita that things have gone wrong. Suppose Mr. Li's scenario occurs; suppose Matsushita has enough time to consider using his weapon—or destroying it. Suppose he locks himself in his cabin or barricades himself in some corner of the ship. Who's going to talk him out?" She looked at Donovan. "How's your Japanese?"

Before he could respond, she continued. "I propose that I accompany Mr. Li and the others on the launch. I think we'd be foolish not to prepare for this contingency. If my services are needed, I'll be available. If not, like Mr. Li, I'll be out of harm's way. Are there any objections?"

She glanced around the table, turning to Donovan last of all. Her eyes were different from Li's—they were angry, defiant, challenging. Donovan paused, hoping that someone else would offer an objection. But no one did, and he knew he couldn't either. He had plenty of objections—but they all came from his heart and not his head.

As Macy took her seat again, Donovan slowly rose. "I think that completes our team," he said. "Let's cap it off here before this launch turns into a cruise ship."

Donovan, Macy, and Li were hustled down a corridor to an elevator, headed for the rooftop where a Coast Guard Dolphin recovery helicopter waited to ferry them directly to the Coast Guard station at Sandy Hook. On the elevator, Donovan turned to Macy.

"What are you doing?" he whispered.

"What are *you* doing?"

Li leaned forward and looked at both of them. "At least we all know what *I'm* doing."

On the rooftop, under the deafening *thup-thup-thup* of the beating blades, the Navy SEAL commander pulled Donovan aside.

"I don't buy the CDC's argument," he shouted over the roar. "Trying to grab this plague is insanity—it's just too big a risk."

"It's done, Commander," Donovan shouted back. "Anything else?"

The Navy nodded. "We need a contingency plan—a way to shut this thing down if it all goes bad. You understand what I'm saying?"

"What do you have in mind?"

"I'm going to instruct my two men to send out a radio signal from the bridge the minute the situation is under control—that will let us know that everything's going according to plan. I want to set a ten-minute time limit, Mr. Donovan—from the time you climb aboard until the time that signal is sent out."

"No good," Donovan said. "Equipment fails and signals get crossed—even for the SEALs. I'm not risking the lives of my people because a battery goes dead. Besides, the issue here isn't time; it's distance. The closer this ship gets to the harbor, the greater the danger."

"Okay, what do you suggest?"

"A distance limit, not a time limit. When we take control of the ship, we'll shut the engines down—we'll stop her dead in the water. We'll do our best to send that radio signal—but if you don't hear from us, keep an eye on the ship. If the ship stops, you'll know everything's okay."

"We need to agree on a limit," the Navy said.

Donovan considered. "The harbor pilot said it was twenty-five miles to the Verrazano Bridge. Give me ten miles—that should be enough to stop her, and that still puts us fifteen miles from shore."

"Fair enough, Mr. Donovan; we'll listen for the radio signal, *and* we'll keep an eye on the ship. But I'm requesting that a missile cruiser out of Naval Station Norfolk be kept on full alert; if we don't hear from you, and if the ship doesn't come to a full stop within ten miles, the cruiser will launch four missiles targeting the rudder, the engine room, the bridge, and the main deck. Are we clear?"

"Ten miles," Donovan said. "Let's hope it's enough."

"If I were you, I wouldn't do any sightseeing on the way to the bridge."

"Thanks for the advice." Donovan turned and ducked under the whirling blades.

They loaded into the helicopter and belted in. As it slowly lifted from the rooftop, Donovan looked down at the SEAL commander below, who held up the fingers of both hands.

"What's that all about?" Li asked.

"Ten minutes to Sandy Hook," Donovan said.

CHAPTER FORTY

THE HARBOR PILOT BOAT *New Jersey* bobbed like a cork in the rolling swells.

"Sorry about the weather," the boat pilot said. "Wish we could have arranged a better day for you."

"Is it always this rough?" Donovan asked.

The pilot shook his head. "This is what we call a 'summer southerly.' Just came out of nowhere this morning—looks like it might get worse. Too bad—this time of year the weather's usually good."

"Lucky me."

The *New Jersey* was no rowboat; at 145 feet in length, she had room to sleep twenty-four, complete with galley, lounge, and TV room. But to the waters of the Atlantic, the *New Jersey* was just another speck of floating debris. Donovan estimated the swells at ten feet, but in the wheelhouse high above the deck, the effect of the waves was amplified—it felt like twenty. The tall wheelhouse swayed from side to side like the top of a tree in a storm.

There were handrails on every wall and handgrips all across the ceiling, so harbor pilots never had to take a step without some way to steady themselves—but harbor pilots didn't need to steady themselves. Their trained legs were like shock absorbers, bending and flexing with the rolling water while their torsos remained stock-still. Donovan had lost his sea legs a long time ago; try as he might, he still found himself lurching with each unexpected wave.

Suddenly, Macy squeezed between them, swinging white-knuckled from handgrip to handgrip like a little girl on monkey bars. She had a look of panic on her face; she stared directly ahead, out the window at the horizon line. She inhaled and exhaled through her mouth, sucking and blowing as if she were in the final stages of labor.

"How much longer?" she asked, looking at neither of them.

"No way to tell," the pilot said. "A ship is supposed to radio us when she's three hours away, but sometimes they don't; sometimes they just show up. We call those 'ringers.' We don't like it, but there's not much we can do about it. All we can do is wait."

"Three *hours*?" she said.

"Maybe less."

Macy nodded fiercely, as if she had just been told, "We have to remove the leg." Then she turned and lurched away across the cabin.

The pilot looked over his shoulder at her. "Is she okay?"

"She gets seasick," Donovan said. "And I'm not talking about the garden-variety, green-around-the-gills type either—I'm talking about puke-your-guts-out comet vomit. I hope she hangs on; she was okay on the dispatch boat on the way out here."

"That's 'cause the dispatch boat is fast—it's when you slow down that the waves get to you. It's the rolling, you know?"

Donovan nodded. "We went on a cruise for our honeymoon—can you believe it? She lasted one day, then we had to airlift her back to Miami."

"What's she doing out here?"

"She volunteered."

"Did she know what she was getting into?"

"You mean the mission or the marriage?"

Donovan turned and looked at Macy. She was panting her way along the aft wall of the cabin now, following a long chrome handrail hand over hand from starboard to port.

"I'd better go talk to her," he said. "She's going to suck all the air out of the room."

He intercepted her in the corner of the cabin. "How're you feeling?" he asked.

"How do I look like I'm feeling?"

"You look like the Hulk—not the figure, just the color. Want to sit down?"

"No."

"Want to—"

"No!" She pushed past him and stared out the forward window. "Got to keep moving," she said. "If I look at you, I'll throw up."

"Well, that's normal anyway."

"Don't make jokes," she growled.

Donovan shook his head. "Macy, what are you doing out here? Why did you volunteer for this?"

"Don't you know?"

"I'm a guy, okay? I don't know anything I'm supposed to know."

"We've got unfinished business," she said.

"You think we'll get time to talk about it out here?"

"No," she said with a quick sideways glance. "I think you might die out here."

"I'm just doing my job, Macy."

"So am I."

Donovan looked at her. "I want you to promise me something," he said. "I want you to promise me that you'll keep your head down out here."

"Will you?"

"As much as I can."

"Me too."

"That's not good enough," he said. "I want you to promise me."

She glanced at him again. "Why should I?"

"You know why."

She shook her head. "I don't know anything unless you tell me,

Nathan. That's been our problem all along." She lurched forward again, continuing toward the front of the cabin. Donovan turned away.

In the center of the wheelhouse was a row of padded seats. In the far seat, Li sat peacefully with his hands folded in his lap, swaying like a pendulum with the motion of the waves. Like Macy, he was dressed in his civilian clothes. At his feet was a large backpack that was given to him by the Coast Guard at Sandy Hook. Each member of the team received one; each contained a white NBC suit and an integrated gas mask and hood.

But Donovan noticed an addition to Li's backpack: Protruding from under the flap was the corner of a small black case.

Donovan worked his way over and took a seat beside the old man. "I want you to listen to me," he said. "You've gotten this far only because of me. You were allowed to attend that meeting only because I got you clearance. All I had to do was say the word, and you'd be in a taxi right now headed for LaGuardia."

"I believe I'm being scolded," Li said. "Have I done something to offend you?"

Donovan pointed to the backpack. "You never told me what you've got in the case."

Li paused. "I've thought about telling you more than once—but all things considered, I think it's best that you don't know."

"C'mon, Li—I need to know."

"By this point in our relationship, I was hoping you might trust me."

Donovan glared at him. "Look, I stuck my neck out a long way just to get you here."

"Forgive me," Li said. "In all the excitement, perhaps I've failed to express my appreciation. To feel gratitude and fail to express it is like buying a lovely gift but never giving it away. Gratitude should be expressed liberally—*tangibly* whenever possible, don't you agree?"

"My point is that there's only so far I can go to help you."

"And *my* point is that gratitude should go both ways. You did not seek me out, Nathan—I sought you. As you said before, without my help you never would have found Sato Matsushita—you never would have known he existed. If it weren't for me, a disaster of unprecedented proportions might have taken your nation completely by surprise."

"Believe me, I appreciate that."

"How very kind—but as I said, gratitude should be expressed *tangibly* whenever possible. You'll forgive me, but at the present time your words mean very little; what I need right now is your assistance."

"I'll help you if I can," Donovan said, "but I need you to remember something: *I have a mission too.* If you force me to choose between your mission and mine—I'll choose mine."

"As you must," Li replied. "But I believe there is a way for both of our missions to be accomplished successfully."

"How?"

"I haven't the slightest." Li shrugged. "If I knew that, we wouldn't be having this—"

"There she is!" the pilot shouted back.

Donovan leaped from his seat and stumbled forward to the wheelhouse window.

"Where?"

"About ten o'clock, just coming over the horizon. See her? We're picking up her transponder signal now—the *Southampton* out of Cardiff. She's a ringer, all right—sailing right up to the front door without so much as a hello. She's still about three or four miles out; we'll meet her at two. Better get your team on the launch."

Donovan turned and looked once more at Li; he was working the black case deeper into his backpack.

Then he glanced at Macy. She stood perfectly still in the center of the cabin, staring at the approaching ship with no expression on her face.

"She looks a lot better," the pilot said.

"Yeah," Donovan replied. "Fear can do that."

CHAPTER FORTY-ONE

THE ALUMINUM HULL OF the launch plunged into the swells like a pelican diving for its dinner. The swells were almost twelve feet high now. The fifty-foot boat seemed to leap from peak to peak, and its engine raced audibly when the propeller broke free of the water.

Donovan and the two "sea marshals" stood beside the pilot in the wheelhouse. Li stood slightly behind them, bracing himself with a ceiling grip. The old man was surprisingly steady; his smaller mass was somehow less affected by the sudden shifts in speed and direction.

Just behind Li the wheelhouse ended, and three short steps descended to a main cabin where Macy sat quietly in a pilot's chair. Her condition was 100 percent improved, though the launch plunged in and out of swells at twenty-four knots. The pilot was right: Faster was better—anything was better than the rolling.

"How long?" Donovan asked the pilot.

"Seven, eight minutes tops. The ship will make a lee—that means she'll bear west a little, and we'll come up along her starboard side. The ship will block the wind, so the sea should be calmer on that side—but don't count on it."

Donovan turned to the two Special Forces operatives, who looked convincingly like a pair of Coast Guard petty officers, from their navy blue trousers, windbreakers, and shoulder-mount radios to their ball caps with gold brocade. There was one significant difference that only a professional would notice—the custom-made .45-caliber U.S. Special Operations Forces offensive handguns that hung from their belts. Donovan tapped his left ankle against the helm and felt the reassuring bulk of his own handgun tucked into its ankle holster.

He looked down at his clothing; he had been given a dark wool business suit with a flaming red tie. "Are you sure this is right?" he asked the pilot. "I look like George Bush."

"All our harbor pilots work in business suits," the pilot said. "It's tradition. Until just a few years ago, we wore fedoras too—sorry to see those go. Oh—one more thing," he said, handing Donovan a copy of the *New York Times*. "When you get to the bridge, the first thing you do is hand the ship's master a copy of today's newspaper. That's a tradition too—he'll be expecting it. You're supposed to be a harbor pilot; you should know that."

"What else do I need to know?"

"You expect me to teach you how to pilot a fourteen-thousand-ton freighter in seven minutes?"

"I don't need to know what I'm doing—I just need to talk a good game."

"Okay. What do you want to know?"

"For starters, tell me where we are."

"We're just outside the entrance to Ambrose Channel," the pilot said, "the main shipping channel into New York Harbor. The channel is two thousand feet wide and forty-five feet deep all the way to the piers."

"Forty-five feet? I figured the water would be a mile deep here."

"Uh-uh—they dredge it just deep enough for the biggest ships. A big container vessel might have a draft of forty feet; that means there's only five feet between her keel and the bottom."

"What if she steers a little wide?"

"Then she runs aground—an old wreck like that one might even break apart."

"So what does the pilot do, just steer down the center of the channel?"

"It's not that simple. It's about three or four hours from here to the piers, and there are thirty-five or forty course corrections you have to make along the way. One wrong turn and you're the *Exxon Valdez.*"

"How do you know where to turn?"

"The channel is marked by buoys, and the ship's GPS system tells you exactly where you are. You have to know where to turn—that's what they pay you for."

"All kinds of ships must come in here," Donovan said. "How can you know how to steer them all?"

"We don't have to," the pilot said. "Every bridge has a helmsman; all we do is tell him where to turn. Come left ten degrees; reduce to half speed; dead ahead slow. We give the orders; they do the steering."

"They all speak English?"

"By law, every ship in American waters is required to have someone on the bridge who speaks English."

"Do they?"

"Most of the time—no. We just use a kind of pidgin English. They figure it out." The pilot looked at him. "Anything else you want to know?"

"Like you said—not in seven minutes."

"More like four," the pilot said.

Donovan turned to the sea marshals. "Let's go over it one last time."

"I think we've got it, sir," the first man said. "We board the ship using the pilots' ladder—the two of us will go first, and you'll bring up the rear. At the top, we'll be escorted to the bridge. There we should encounter three crew members: the ship's master, a helmsman, and a mate. We will immediately neutralize the crew."

"Excuse me," Li said from behind them. "Does that mean you will kill them?"

"That will be up to them, sir," the man said, glancing over his shoulder. "As soon as we secure the bridge, we will immediately cut the engines and contact our people by radio."

"That's important," Donovan said. "Let's not forget that part."

"We will then work our way down through the crew cabins, repeating the process as necessary. When all topside crew members are secured, we will move below deck to the engine room, followed by the cargo holds."

"Good," Donovan said. "And the target?"

"Dr. Sato Matsushita. Japanese, about eighty years of age, small stature." He nodded at Li. "Are we sure that's not him?"

"We're quite sure," Li said in annoyance.

"Sir," the second man said to Donovan. "If you don't mind my asking, how long has it been since you've pulled this kind of duty?"

Donovan looked at the two men. "Is either of you a Marine?"

"We're Navy, sir."

He nodded. "Try to keep up with me, then."

Donovan looked out the window again. The *Divine Wind* was approaching fast now, bearing almost directly toward them. The launch began to make a wide arc to the left, preparing to circle around behind her and come up along the starboard side. To Donovan the ship looked enormous, maybe ten times longer than the launch, but it didn't fare much better than they had in the rising swells. The mammoth ship rocked and swayed like a sea buoy.

As they swung wide to the left, Donovan could see the pilots' ladder dangling over the railing and down the starboard side. It drifted in the wind like a ribbon, swinging out over the water one minute and crashing back against the metal hull the next. *This has got to be a joke*, Donovan thought. Scaling that ladder would be like holding on to a loose fire hose.

"Please tell me that's not the ladder," Donovan said.

"Relax," the pilot said. "Here's how it works: When we come up alongside, the ship will reduce her speed to a slow bell—maybe seven knots. The ship will be *pitching*—that means rocking from bow to stern. It will also be *rolling*—swaying from side to side. And it'll be rising and sinking with the swells too. That means the ship will be moving in three directions at once—up and down, back and forth, and side to side. Now, our boat will be doing the same thing—only worse, and not at the same time. If our boat goes down when the ship goes up, you may find yourself looking up at the bottom of the ladder. If they pitch forward when we pitch back, the ladder will swing past you like a grapevine. Got the idea?"

"Tell me the truth," Donovan said. "How hard is this?"

"It's kind of an art."

"It takes time to learn an art."

"Yeah," he said, "it does."

"Have you ever tried this in swells this big?"

"I've done it in swells twice this size."

"Does anybody ever get killed this way?"

The pilot glanced at him. "You don't want to hear about that now, do you?"

"It's not so bad," one of the SEALs said with a grin. "But then, you're not Navy, are you?"

The pilot pointed out the window at the deck of the launch. "When we come up alongside, your team will move out to the foredeck."

Donovan looked. The foredeck was rising and dropping like the end of a diving board, and he wondered if it would have the same effect. "We go out *there*?"

"There are railings all along the way, see? You always have something to hold on to. You work your way out to that break in the railing—that's where I'll line up with the ladder. Then all you do is wait for the right moment and jump."

"And if I pick the wrong moment?"

"Then watch the propellers."

Donovan turned to Macy; she had been staring at the back of his head. He started toward her and motioned for Li to join them. They sat down together in the row of pilots' chairs.

"I want you both to stay back here, out of view," Donovan said. "We're going to secure the bridge and locate Matsushita—if we need either one of you, we'll send for you. Otherwise, you are *not* to approach the ship. Is that clear?"

They both nodded.

Donovan started to get up, but Macy grabbed his arm. "There's something I want to tell you," she said. "You're a stubborn, pigheaded fool."

"Thanks," Donovan said. "I'll treasure that always."

"I wasn't finished—I was about to say, 'but you're a good man.' I still believe that, Nathan. This is a good thing you're doing, and you're a good man."

Donovan wrapped his arms around her and pulled her in tight. He felt grateful; it was almost worth all this just to have the chance to hold her one more time.

"I want to finish that business," he whispered into her ear.

She nodded against his chest. "You know where to find me."

Donovan released her and stood up; so did Li.

"Nothing for an old fart?" the old man said.

Donovan hesitated, then extended his hand. Li looked at it, smiled, and took it.

"When I find Matsushita," Donovan said, "I will *not* bring him back to this boat. Do you understand? This is as close as you'll get, Li. Are you okay with that?"

"Of course not. I still believe that God will allow us to meet face-to-face. But if, as you say, this is as close as I get—then thank you, Nathan. I do not wish to be thought ungrateful. Thank you for helping an old man with his dream."

Donovan nodded, then turned and climbed the three short steps to the wheelhouse. They were coming up close on the starboard side now; through the window, the ship's black hull loomed over them like a wall of coal.

"This is it!" the pilot called back.

Donovan glanced over his shoulder one last time. Li smiled and nodded, but Macy looked away.

CHAPTER FORTY-TWO

THE LEAP FROM THE launch to the ship's ladder looked impossible. Both vessels pitched, and rolled, and rose and fell with the swells—but the huge ship rocked slowly, like the pendulum of an old grandfather clock, while the little launch bobbed like a bar of soap in a tub. One minute the ship's hull loomed so close that Donovan could almost stretch out and touch it; the next minute it tipped so far away that he couldn't reach the ladder with a running start.

Neither of the SEALs looked concerned. Why should they? They did this kind of thing every day. They were trained to throw grappling hooks up and over stern railings and climb ropes hand over hand. *Sure, they can do it,* Donovan thought. *They can do it because they're ten years younger and thirty pounds lighter.* Donovan felt old, and he felt angry—and he felt grateful that he had two men to watch before it was his turn to try.

The first SEAL crouched down on the edge of the foredeck, steadying himself with the railings on both sides. His eyes were glued to the ladder. It swung left and right before him, first tantalizingly close, then impossibly out of reach. Donovan watched, too, second-guessing him. Seconds went by; then the great ship dipped low in the water while the launch rose, and the ship tipped toward them while their own boat remained level.

"Now!" Donovan shouted—but the SEAL didn't flinch. An instant later, the ship pitched forward and the ladder swung away toward the bow.

The SEAL turned and glared at Donovan.

"Sorry," Donovan said. "Your call."

A few seconds later the SEAL sprang from the deck like a panther, catching the ladder perfectly by both ropes. Then the two vessels rocked away from each other and the SEAL seemed to rocket into the sky. For a moment he hung on only by his hands; then he fitted his feet against the wooden rungs and began to climb.

Now the second SEAL stepped up to the edge of the deck. His wait was a little longer; he was a little less decisive. But Donovan knew he would make it—after all, he had a larger margin of error than Donovan did. It helps to have legs like a thoroughbred and a body made of nothing but sinew and bone. Donovan wondered what would happen when his own 220 pounds left the deck. He wondered how far he could still jump; he wondered if the aging ladder would support his weight.

The second SEAL caught the ladder and began his ascent. Now Donovan gripped the railing and eased his way up to the edge.

He tensed and waited, studying the movement of the ships—but there was no repetition, no cadence to count or pattern to predict. Now he realized that the decision was a lot easier to make when someone else was doing the jumping, the same way strikes and balls are easier to call when someone else is standing at the plate. He could see now that it had to be a split-second judgment—and there was no room for error.

Suddenly, the launch swerved left just as the ship rolled right, and the two vessels crashed together. The thick black bumper that surrounded the launch made a dull, rubbery sound as it bounced against the ship. The hull and ladder slammed into Donovan, knocking his hands from the railing. As he fell to the deck, he grabbed the rope ladder with his left hand.

An instant later the two vessels veered apart again, and Donovan was catapulted off the deck and into the air. He still held the rope in his left hand; as he rotated clockwise in the air, he could see the launch lunging along below him. Then it suddenly swerved to starboard, and there was nothing under him but churning water.

Now the ladder swung back hard toward the ship, and Donovan's back and shoulder slammed against the hull. The impact rippled through his body like a bomb blast, and he felt his grip loosen. It was sheer luck that he was looking down when he hit—if his head had struck the iron hull, he would be sinking unconscious into the sea. He swung wildly to his left and grasped for the ladder with his right hand. He found it. He repositioned his hands and tried to strengthen his hold, but his legs still swung free. His hands slipped down a little on the ropes, and he felt a pop in his right shoulder.

The launch slowly eased under him again, offering whatever assistance it could. When the ship rolled right again, Donovan found himself dangling directly over the boat's foredeck. For an instant he thought about releasing his grip and dropping to the deck below, but he no longer trusted his timing or his judgment. He knew that by the time he reached the deck, the boat could be gone again. The only thing to do was hold on.

When the ship rolled left again, the ladder started its long swing back toward the hull, and Donovan braced for impact. His body snapped against the hull like a whip—first his hands and arms, then his torso, then his legs and feet. He felt the Glock in his ankle holster slip out and drop away.

The impact knocked his wind out; he knew he couldn't survive another one like it. He had to climb; he had to shorten the radius of the ropes. He drew his aching legs up under him and felt for the rungs. He found one, and he started up toward the railing. He climbed slowly, checking each rung for reliability and testing each new handgrip before releasing the last.

A minute later he felt two powerful pairs of hands grab him by the shoulders and drag him onto the deck. He took a second to catch his breath, then rolled to his feet and began to stand.

"Thanks," he said, "I really—"

The bodies of the two SEALs lay on the deck before him, each shot through the forehead as he stepped over the side of the ship. Three crewmen stood in front of Donovan; two of them shouldered Russian-made AK-47s, both trained on his own forehead. The third man pulled a handgun from a leather holster and stepped forward. He spoke in broken English. "You are the pilot?"

CHAPTER FORTY-THREE

DONOVAN WATCHED AS THE crewmen stripped the bodies of their shoulder radios. He felt numb. He looked down at the two Navy SEALs, still alive only minutes ago. He thought of their youthfulness, their training, their physical prowess—all gone in a flash of muzzle fire, vanished before they even had a chance to draw their weapons. This was more than murder; it was disgrace—disgrace that men so utterly inferior should be able to take their lives.

"You—this way." The man with the handgun motioned for Donovan to follow.

Donovan looked down at the bodies one last time as he stepped across them. He remembered a part of the SEALs' cherished creed, never to leave a fallen comrade behind, and he felt as if he were betraying them. But he also recalled another part of the SEALs' creed: *I will always place the mission first; I will never accept defeat; I will never quit.* He stared at each of the crewmen as he passed, and he made a silent promise.

They entered the superstructure on the starboard side—Donovan first and the gunman behind. They passed down a short corridor, then turned right and started up three flights of metal stairs. Donovan walked slowly, his mind racing. *How much do they know?* Did they somehow know about the plan? Did they know the men were Special Forces? No, they couldn't—

if they did, they would have known that he was FBI and they would have killed him too. No, they believed the men were Coast Guard sea marshals—they killed them just to avoid inspection. That meant they still believed Donovan was a harbor pilot—and as long as they believed that, he still had a chance.

But what would happen if they stopped believing?

He kicked himself when he remembered his words on the launch: "I don't need to know what I'm doing," he'd told the pilot. "I just need to talk a good game." Well, he needed more than talk now. These people expected him to steer this ship all the way into the harbor. Forty course corrections along the way, and the first one he missed would give him away. "You have to know where to turn," the pilot said. "That's what they pay you for." Why didn't he listen more closely? Why didn't he ask more questions? He tried to remember every word the pilot had spoken to him, piecing the memories together like the fragments of an old manuscript.

They reached the top of the stairs now, and there was a wooden door directly ahead.

"Inside!" the man behind him barked.

Donovan opened the door and stepped onto the ship's bridge—the first bridge of any commercial ship Donovan had ever seen in his life. The room was not deep, but it was very wide. Along the far wall was a long instrument console filled with glass-covered gauges, illuminated indicators, and chrome-handled levers. There was an open laptop computer in the center, and a gray metal box beside it with a small keyboard of its own.

Above the console was a row of rectangular windows that stretched from wall to wall, looking out on the ship's long deck and forward cargo holds. Donovan was astonished at the sense of height and the expanse of the forward deck. It seemed impossible that an object so large could be controlled from such a tiny room, and by only one man—especially if that man was him.

There was a voice inside his head that told him to blurt out, "Wow! Look at this!" It was a voice he recognized, a voice soldiers hear when their lives are on the line. "Stand up and wave your arms," it says, or "Lie down here and fall asleep." Donovan remembered the voice from his days in ordnance removal. "Cut all the wires at once," it told him. "Just grab a handful and rip them out." It was a child's voice, the voice that told you to scream before your hiding place was discovered. Every soldier knows it; it's a siren's voice, and if you listen, it will get you killed.

The man behind him closed the door and stepped around to Donovan's right, still leveling the gun at his chest. Donovan took his first good look at the man. He was Arab—thirty-five, maybe forty years of age. He was dressed like a soldier, though he wore no insignia or rank. He had a thick salt-and-pepper mustache and black hair. And when the man turned to face the console, Donovan saw that his left ear was just a stump.

The man said something in Arabic. At the console, a helmsman stood facing the window and made no reply. Instead, a captain's chair to the left of the helmsman swiveled around, revealing a taller man, leaner and with darker skin. He was dressed in civilian clothes, but he wore a weathered captain's hat. This was undoubtedly the ship's master. He nodded to the gunman and spoke a single word in reply—then he turned to face Donovan.

"Good morning," he said in perfect English.

Donovan winced—so much for the language barrier. He had hoped that the pilot was right—that no one on the bridge would speak English. Then no one could ask him questions, and his ignorance might be concealed.

"What's the meaning of this?" Donovan demanded. "You've murdered two Coast Guard sea marshals. Why?"

"I'm not at liberty to explain," the ship's master said. "Let me simply point out that they are dead, while you are still alive. You will remain alive as long as you are needed to pilot this ship."

"And if I refuse?"

The ship's master smiled. "Personally, I consider you nothing but a convenience. We had to allow your people aboard, or your port authorities would have been contacted immediately. But I have called on the port of New York before, and I believe I am capable of navigating the harbor myself."

"You think so?" Donovan said. "Take a look at the weather out there—those are twelve-foot swells. We've had some sandbars shifting lately—do you know where they are?"

The man paused. "All right," he said. "Perhaps you are more than a convenience—for now."

"What's this all about?" Donovan asked. "What's this ship carrying, anyway?"

"Again, I'm not at liberty to say."

"You've already killed two men. Even if I take you into the harbor, you'll kill me anyway."

"Perhaps—perhaps not. One thing is certain: If you refuse to pilot this ship, you will be of no value whatsoever—you will die immediately. You have two choices, my friend: certain death or possible survival. The choice seems clear to me."

Donovan's mind was spinning. His only way to stay alive was by piloting the ship. But if he did pilot the ship, if he somehow managed to guide it successfully more than ten miles ahead, he would die anyway—they all would, in one colossal ball of fire caused by four Tomahawk missiles. He had no idea what to do—but he remembered something he'd learned years ago when a mission went bad: Sometimes the only thing to do is to do the next thing.

"Okay," he said. "You've got a pilot—for now."

"Then let's get started," the ship's master said. "We do have a schedule to keep."

Donovan slipped off his backpack and opened it carefully so that no one caught a glimpse of the NBC suit inside. He pulled out the copy of the *New York Times* and handed it to the ship's master. "I wish it was next week's," he said. "It would have your obituary."

"Perhaps beside your own," the man replied. "Where is your computer?"

Strike one, Donovan thought. "In this weather? Are you kidding? We'll use yours."

"But mine has no charts of the channel."

Donovan rolled his eyes. "I know where to turn—that's what they pay me for." Now he paused, carefully considering the wording of his first instruction. He made a split-second inventory of every nautical term he knew. "Take her into the channel," he said—that seemed vague enough.

The ship's master repeated the instruction to the helmsman in Arabic; then he turned back to Donovan. "At what speed?"

What speed? How fast does a ship like this go? He thought about the launch: *It did twenty-four knots, the pilot said—but it was a tenth the size of this behemoth. He did the math. That couldn't be right—a ship couldn't cross an entire ocean at two or three knots—it would take forever. It must go faster—maybe half as fast?*

"Twelve knots," he said with authority.

"Twelve knots? We proceed into the channel at sea speed?"

Strike two. "We're only in the entrance to the channel," he said. "We'll slow her down in a minute." *Terrific,* he thought. *I just gave the order to proceed at full speed. How long will it take us to cover ten miles at this rate?*

Donovan stepped up to the helm now and glanced over at the helmsman. "Where you from?"

"He speaks no English," the ship's master said.

"Yours is good," Donovan replied. "Where did you learn it?"

"I was educated here. America educates most of her enemies—I find that delightfully ironic."

Donovan nodded to the gunman. "How about your boy there? Looks like somebody talked his ear off."

The ship's master smiled. "His name is Khalid, and he is not my 'boy.' He is my employer—that means he is your employer too. Fortunately for you, Khalid speaks only a few words of English. If I repeated your comment to him in Arabic, he would kill you."

Three men on the bridge—only one speaks English; only one is armed. If only I had my gun, Donovan thought. *If only it hadn't fallen into the water. Three men and only one armed—that's workable. All I'd need is a distraction, something to give me time to draw the Glock from my ankle holster.* He shook his head. *Might as well wish for a bazooka while I'm at it.*

He stared ahead out the window now. There was no sign of land on the horizon yet—but there would be soon enough.

CHAPTER FORTY-FOUR

THE LAUNCH HUNG BACK slightly, giving the pilot a view of the ship's entire starboard side. He kept a beam's width away, trying to avoid another unexpected collision. He leaned forward over the helm, staring up at the ship's railing.

"She's increased her speed to twelve knots," he called back to Macy and Li.

"Is something wrong?" Macy asked.

"I'm not sure. We should have heard from them by now—they were supposed to stop the ship the minute they got the bridge under control. But they've increased their speed like they're going ahead into the channel."

"What should we do?"

"My instructions are to get out of here as fast as I can if the ship doesn't stop."

"That's excellent advice," Li said quickly, "and we should obey those instructions—*if* the ship doesn't stop. But all we know is that the ship hasn't stopped so far. She may stop at any moment now."

The pilot shook his head. "I'm not sure how long to hang around here."

"Dr. Monroe and I are vital elements of this operation," Li said. "It's crucial that we remain here as long as possible. If Mr. Donovan sends for us and we are unavailable, this entire operation could be put in jeopardy."

"Okay," the pilot said. "We'll wait and see what happens."

CHAPTER FORTY-FIVE

IN THE AFT CARGO hold, Sato Matsushita selected another rat from its cage. The hairless rats were perfect for the procedure. *If only we'd had them at Ping Fan,* he thought, *how much more efficient we would have been.* Hairless rats offered two distinct advantages: They had no thymus, which crippled their immune system, making them especially susceptible to the plague; and they had no hair, which rendered their entire bodies accessible to the ravenous fleas.

Sato worked in his NBC suit. The late-morning heat was already unbearable; he blinked constantly to keep the sweat from dripping into his eyes. He stared into the cages—there were hundreds of rats, pink and silky smooth. The rats wandered about slowly, lethargically. Some stumbled haltingly around the cage; others lay on their sides, prematurely stricken by the bacteria ravaging their internal organs. Below the cages, the shriveled bodies of hundreds of dead rats rested in hermetically sealed containers.

Sato lifted the Plexiglas cover from a tray and gently placed the rat inside. He had to be careful; if the rat turned on him and managed to penetrate his glove with its teeth, then he would be infected. That would happen soon enough, but it must not happen prematurely—not before he had the chance to see the blackness with his own eyes.

The sides of the tray were made of simple wood. The bottom was covered with coarse screen wire, with openings more than large enough to allow a flea's narrow body to pass through. There were a dozen rats in the shallow tray, all approaching the final agonies of death—but all still full of blood, warm blood, blood now dominated by a strain of *Yersinia pestis* for which there was no known cure.

Sato carried the tray to the opposite wall, where dozens of other trays rested on an elaborate shelf. But these trays were different—they were slightly larger and made of white porcelain. He lifted the lid from one of them and looked inside. The bottom of the tray was covered by an inch of water—and the water was covered by a speckled gray crust consisting of thousands and thousands of Oriental rat fleas.

The fleas remained motionless; the water prevented them from jumping. Sato took the tray of rats and lowered it into the porcelain tray until it rested just a few inches above the water. Then he opened a valve, and the water slowly drained away.

As the last of the water disappeared, the fleas began to ricochet off the porcelain like microscopic bullets. A handful of tiny dots began to appear on the rats' naked skin—then more, and more, until no pink at all remained. Each rat looked as if it wore a tiny wool suit, with only its glistening eyes, its tail, and the nonvascular tips of its toes still visible.

Now Sato opened another valve, and a thin layer of water returned to the bottom of the tray. He must wait now. The fleas would feed until they were engorged, and then they would drop off onto the water one by one, where they could be skimmed off and loaded into the shells.

The ceramic shells rested on a table along the aft bulkhead, nested in a layer of thick, high-density foam. Each shell was about four feet long and eight inches wide. The bottom two-thirds of each contained the cherry tree firework effect, the product of hundreds of thousands of dollars and years of research. The top third of each shell held five kilograms of infected fleas, an oxygen supply, and a canister of dried blood for sustenance. When the shell detonated at precisely eight hundred meters, the explosion would send the top third hurtling even higher, safely above the heat of the firework display. Then, as the cherry tree vanished from the sky, the fleas would gently rain down all around in search of their next meal.

Sato looked at the shells proudly. They were works of art—not like the primitive, hand-thrown pottery shells they used at Ping Fan. They were bullet-shaped, like large artillery shells, but they were as smooth as glass and gleaming white in color. And each shell was embellished with a brilliant hand-painted image of a cherry tree in the classic style of the Edo period.

Four of the shells were already loaded and rested on the tabletop. Four more waited on the floor under the table, ready to receive their tiny passengers.

Sato started back for another tray of rats—but as he turned, his bulky sleeve caught a flask of acid and sent it crashing to the floor. He looked down at the puddle spreading slowly across the floor toward the plastic barrier. He had to clean it up—he couldn't take a chance on the acid dissolving the seal and allowing the dressing area to become contaminated.

He looked around the laboratory; there was nothing suitable. He needed a mop and a bucket—surely he could find those things somewhere in the cargo hold. He unzipped the doorway into the dressing area, then sealed it carefully again behind him. He stepped under the disinfectant shower and pulled the chain; then he pulled off his hood and mask, grateful for the chance to release the pent-up heat.

He considered removing his NBC suit entirely, but he decided against it. Why bother? The process took several minutes, and he would need to return to his work as soon as possible. He looked around the dressing area—no mops, no sponges, no rags. He unzipped the second doorway and stepped into the outer compartment. Again he found nothing.

He looked at the hatchway and thought of making the long climb to the main deck—but he was already exhausted from the heat; he didn't need additional exertion. He looked around the outer compartment again and spotted a sealed hatch in the metal bulkhead that separated his laboratory from the rest of the aft cargo hold.

He had been sternly warned never to open this hatch. Khalid reminded him that they were guests on an ordinary merchant vessel, and they must not interfere with the vessel's cargo or schedule in any way. In return, Sato's own facilities would be strictly off-limits to the crew. To open the hatch was to risk revealing everything, and that was the last thing Sato wanted to do.

But this was an emergency—surely this was an exception.

He turned the handle on the metal hatch. Two bolts withdrew from the top and bottom frame, and the door swung outward. Sato poked his head through and looked. There was no sign of anyone—but there was a utility sink, and beside it was a mop and a metal pail.

He stepped through and pulled the hatch shut behind him. He quickly picked up the mop and bucket and turned back toward the lab. But as he did, he glanced around the cargo hold—and he was astonished at what he saw.

The cargo hold was stacked from floor to ceiling with wooden pallets, each bearing forty bags of unmarked paper sacks. Each stack of sacks was wrapped in layer upon layer of transparent plastic, forming a kind of huge cocoon. Near the top of each pallet, a small plastic pipe punctured the cocoon, and the hole was tightly sealed off with gray duct tape.

And protruding from each hole was an electrical wire.

Sato let out a gasp. He dropped the mop and bucket and hurried back to his laboratory. He unzipped the first doorway, not even bothering to seal it behind him again. In the dressing area he opened the medical cabinet and removed a scalpel and a rubber glove.

Back in the cargo hold he cut through one of the plastic cocoons and into the side of a paper sack. White granulated powder poured out. He scooped up some of it and poured it into the rubber glove; then he took the glove to the utility sink and added water. He twisted off the open end of the glove and shook the mixture. He pulled off one of his own thick gloves and felt the rubber with his bare hand.

It was cold.

Sato charged through the hatchway and up the stairs toward the bridge.

CHAPTER FORTY-SIX

DONOVAN HAD NO IDEA how long they'd been traveling at twelve knots—five minutes? Ten? It seemed like an hour. The ship was plunging straight down the center of the channel. How long could it be before one of those forty course corrections would be required? One thing was for sure: He was in no hurry to cover the next ten miles. He needed time to think. He had to slow it down.

"Reduce speed to five knots," he said confidently.

The ship's master stepped closer. "That's a bit cautious."

A series of responses ran through Donovan's mind, but none of them sounded convincing. He turned to the ship's master with a look of disdain.

"This is the way I learned it," he said. "If you know better, be my guest."

The ship's master turned to the helmsman and repeated the order. "You wouldn't be trying to slow us down, would you?" he said to Donovan.

"The sooner we get this over with, the better," Donovan replied.

"How long have you been a harbor pilot?"

"Seven years," he said without missing a beat. He started to add, "Before that, I was an apprentice for three," but he stopped short. *Play it safe,* he reminded himself. *Don't volunteer information—that's an amateur's mistake.*

"I assume you were once a ship's master yourself."

"Sure." Donovan had to stop this line of questions. The only way to do it was by asking his own. "What's the draft on this vessel?"

"You don't know?"

He paused. "I thought I did—but this ship isn't exactly what she seems to be, now, is she?"

"Her draft is twenty-nine feet."

"Is she fully loaded?"

"She is."

"With what?"

He smiled. "I'd rather talk about your ship. When you were a ship's master, what type of vessel did you command?"

He was thinking fast now. "She was called the *South Bronx.* How old is this ship, anyway?"

"Thirty-five years. You sailed from New York Harbor, then?"

"Yeah. You said you've called here before—how many times?"

"What class of vessel was she? What was her displacement?"

Strike three, Donovan thought. *I'm out.*

Just then the door opened with a crash. The ship's master spun around, and so did the helmsman—it gave Donovan an excuse to turn and look too. In the doorway was a small man, dressed in a bulky white biological suit, but with no hood. He was an old man, and he looked very angry—and he was Japanese.

Donovan took his first look at Sato Matsushita.

The old man charged up to the gunman and thrust out his right hand. He was holding something—it looked like an inflated rubber glove. The bloated fingers dangled down like a cow's teats. The old man shouted something in Arabic; the gunman's shoulders rounded, and he shuffled backward a step or two. *Khalid may be the employer,* Donovan thought, *but Sato looks like the boss.*

The conversation that followed was all in Arabic. Donovan didn't understand a word of it—but he watched carefully, picking up anything he could.

"Feel it!" Sato shouted, holding out the glove.

Khalid hesitated. Sato took another step forward and thrust the glove in Khalid's face. "I said *feel it*!"

Khalid slowly reached out and touched the glove. "So?"

"I know what this is, Khalid! I am not a fool! Ammonium nitrate is endothermic—it becomes cold when water is added!" He threw the glove to the floor; it landed with a squashing sound, sending water flecked with white granules everywhere.

"Where did you get that?" Khalid demanded.

"Where do you think? The cargo hold is stacked from floor to ceiling with it!"

"You were instructed never to go in there!"

"And now I know why! This ship is designed to be a bomb, isn't it?"

A pause. "Yes."

"Why did you not tell me?"

"I was instructed not to. The plan was—changed."

"Changed! Don't these people understand? Did you not tell them that I will allow no further interference, no variation from my plan? These people are fools, Khalid! They almost destroyed my strategy once—are they trying to do so again? What is this change you speak of? All I required was transportation and a simple laboratory—was that so difficult?"

"I told you," Khalid mumbled. "It is their money."

"Idiots!" Sato shouted. "My plan is perfect—it requires no additions and no alterations! There is no need for a secondary attack! There is no—"

Sato fell silent. His mouth dropped open, and he stood staring at Khalid, blinking hard. Khalid looked away.

"This change you speak of—what is it?"

Khalid stared at the floor.

"Please, Khalid—tell me."

Khalid looked over at the ship's master.

"Tell him," the ship's master said with a shrug. "I would want to know. What harm can it do now?"

Khalid stared back at the floor and began to speak. "The ship is a bomb," he said quietly. "It carries nine thousand tons of nitrate fertilizer. Each pallet is wrapped like a sack; the sacks are joined by pipes to the main fuel tank, and each one is wired with a detonator. When the command is given, the oil from the fuel tanks will be pumped into the sacks."

"An understandable precaution," Sato said hopefully. "But if there is no interference, if my strategy goes according to plan, then there will be no need for this alternative. Is that correct?"

He didn't reply.

"It is only a precaution, is it not? Khalid?"

Khalid closed his eyes. "When the ship enters the Upper Bay, the command will be given and the fuel oil will mix with the fertilizer. When the ship reaches a point halfway between Liberty Island and Manhattan, the bomb will be detonated—about two hours from now."

Sato gripped his head in his hands and let out a cry like a little child.

"Think of it," Khalid implored. "It will have the force of a small nuclear bomb. It will destroy far more than a simple pair of towers—it will collapse buildings all along the shores, it will destroy ships and piers, and it will ignite fires everywhere. And think of this, Dedushka: It will destroy the statue too."

Sato looked at him in horror. "Are you so simpleminded, Khalid? Is that the extent of your vision—to knock down a *statue*? I thought you were different from the rest of them. Your people are ignorant and primitive, barely out of the Stone Age. They're like children with firecrackers, running around the streets, making big sounds but accomplishing nothing at all. I offered them something more—something great, something inspired, something to be spoken of for generations to come. But your people know nothing of these things, do they? Arabs and their bombs," he said in disgust. "All they want is to make a little noise, a little puff of smoke, and then they are satisfied."

Khalid still made no reply.

Now the old man looked at him with sorrow in his eyes. "I should have expected this from these people," he said. "But not from you, Khalid, not from you. You have betrayed me."

Khalid slowly looked up from the floor and glared at the old man. "I have *not* betrayed you," he said. "I do not serve you; I serve the cause. You are wrong, Dedushka; *you* are the one who acts like a child—a spoiled child, a child who receives many gifts but still pouts because he doesn't get the very one he wanted."

"This is my *mission*," he said. "Can you not understand that?"

"Your mission is to strike at the Americans."

"Not in some clumsy, brutish way! Not without poetry, or beauty, or grace!"

"I could have left you behind to rot in Damascus," Khalid said, "dreaming of your precious *mission* that would never take place. Instead, you have been given the honor of participating in this great cause."

"By perishing in some mindless explosion? By being acted upon rather than acting? This is not an honor, Khalid; this is a death sentence! Your people feared what I would do if they rejected my plan. *That* is why I am here!"

"They were wise to fear you," Khalid said. "Perhaps I should fear you too." He raised the gun and pointed it at the old man's chest. Sato looked down at it, then back at Khalid.

"Is this to be my end?" he said quietly.

"That is your choice, Dedushka."

Sato paused. "If I have but two hours to live, I wish to prepare myself. Will you allow me?"

"Go."

Sato turned and exited the bridge. Khalid stared after him.

The ship's master spoke up. "The old man could still make trouble," he said. "I'd follow him if I were you."

Khalid handed the gun to the ship's master and followed.

Donovan listened to every word but understood nothing. Something was seriously wrong—but he had no idea what.

CHAPTER FORTY-SEVEN

KHALID TOOK THE THREE flights of stairs down to the main deck. He turned left at the bottom, down the narrow corridor toward the starboard side of the ship. Dedushka had a few seconds' head start on him, and he had no idea where he went. Where does an old man go to spend the last two hours of his life? *Where would* I *go*? Khalid asked himself. *To a stinking laboratory in the bowels of a ship? No—I would go out into the fresh air, out to feel the sun on my face one last time.*

He opened the hatch and stepped out onto the deck. The wind was strong, and the swells were still high. The rolling of the ship felt even more pronounced in sight of the heaving waves. He glanced to his right; to his surprise, the pilot boat still followed astern, just off the starboard side. But why would the boat still be following them? Perhaps they were waiting for some kind of signal, something that told them all was well and they could return to port. But what if the signal was never received? What if, by killing the sea marshals and seizing the pilot, they had prevented the signal from being sent? The pilot boat had a radio; it could contact the authorities—and if they did, there was still time for the authorities to intercept the ship.

Khalid raced back up the stairs to the bridge. He burst through the door, breathing hard.

"The pilot boat is still following!" Khalid shouted to the ship's master. "Ask the pilot why—ask him what we need to do to send it away!"

The ship's master repeated the question for Donovan. He listened, then calmly replied.

"He says it is the sea marshals," the ship's master explained. "The boat is still waiting for a signal from them. He says if they fail to receive the signal, they will contact the authorities. He asks permission to contact the boat by radio."

"No radio," Khalid said. "I will take care of it myself."

Back on deck, Khalid approached the bodies of the two SEALs. He grabbed one of the dead men by the shoulder and dragged him over onto his back. He removed the belt, then began to unbutton the shirt. A few minutes later he was dressed in the sea marshal's navy blue uniform. He removed the safety from his handgun and slid it into the empty holster. He donned the cap last of all, pulling the bill down low over his face.

He backed over the railing of the ship and began to descend the ladder. He let go of the rope with his right hand; keeping his face to the hull, he waved to the pilot boat to come up alongside.

"One of the SEALs is coming back," the pilot called to Macy and Li.

"Why would he do that?" Macy asked.

"No idea—but it's a good sign. If something was wrong, they sure wouldn't let him come back."

"Why didn't he just radio?"

"Perhaps they require our services," Li said. "Perhaps the young man is returning to assist us in boarding the ship."

"Could be," the pilot said. "We'll know in a minute."

The pilot pushed forward on the throttle, and the launch accelerated. He turned the wheel slowly, bringing the boat closer to the hull of the ship. The SEAL descended the ladder a few more rungs; he was level with the boat's bridge now, but still several feet above the foredeck. He waved again for the boat to draw up alongside.

The ladder was even with the foredeck now, and the pilot waited for the SEAL to descend the last few rungs and drop onto the deck—but he didn't. Instead, he waved for the pilot to pull up even farther.

"What's he doing?" Macy asked.

"I don't know. Maybe he just wants to give us a message—maybe their radios aren't working."

The pilot steered away from the ship slightly; if the SEAL wasn't coming aboard, there was no sense risking contact with the ship's hull. He nudged the throttle and eased the boat forward until the SEAL was even with the port bridge window. The man still clung to the ladder, facing the side of the ship.

As the pilot turned his head to the port window, Khalid released the ladder with his right hand and drew his gun. He spun around wildly, firing a spray of bullets into the bridge. The window's safety glass shattered into a thousand tiny pieces. The first three bullets struck the helm; a fourth caught the pilot in the left shoulder, and the final shot found the side of his head. He died instantly, slumping forward on the controls. Khalid turned back to the ladder, holstered his weapon, and looked up toward the ship's deck.

Inside the boat, Macy and Li sat frozen. Against the sound of the engines and the crashing waves, the gunshots sounded tiny and faraway—not like gunshots at all, but like the cracking of a stick. Even when the window shattered, it was unclear what had occurred. Maybe something had struck the window; maybe something had come loose. But when Macy saw splinters of wood and plastic fly off the helm, she thought something must be wrong—and when she saw the pilot slump forward, she knew.

She lunged forward and grabbed the pilot with both hands, thinking to pull him out of the line of fire. But as the body slid off the helm and onto the floor, it pulled the wheel sharply to the left, and the boat veered hard to port—directly toward the side of the ship.

Just as the launch began to turn, the ship pitched down into a deep trough. Now Khalid was no longer above the boat's deck—he was even with it. The boat's black bumper crashed against the iron hull with a shuddering thump, catching Khalid across the back of the legs, pinning him against the hull. He screamed in agony. Now the ship slowly started to rise again. Flesh ripped open, tendons tore, and bones splintered like dry wood. His legs hung limp and lifeless; his grip loosened, and he slid down the ladder a full rung.

The impact of the collision sent the launch rebounding away, but its rudder was still turned to port. The boat veered back again, this time crushing Khalid's pelvis with an audible crack. The next collision caught the center of his back—then his shoulders—then his skull. His arms fell limply to his sides, but he didn't fall. He just jerked slowly downward like a sheet of paper disappearing into a shredder, ground to dust between a giant's fingers, until he silently dropped away into the rolling water.

CHAPTER FORTY-EIGHT

THE SHIP'S MASTER STARED anxiously at the bridge door.

"Problem?" Donovan asked.

"Pilot the ship!" the master shouted, waving the gun wildly in the air.

Donovan watched the way he handled the sidearm. He was obviously not a soldier, like the rest of them. He looked awkward and self-conscious with the handgun; he carried it like a lit stick of dynamite. Donovan had no doubt that the ship's master would use the weapon. But his aim might be off, and he just might hesitate for an extra second or two—and that could be all Donovan needed.

The ship's master charged toward the bridge door—but he stopped abruptly and looked back at Donovan, seeming to reconsider his decision. He walked slowly back toward the helm again.

"If you interfere with the progress of this ship in any way, I will kill you," he said.

Donovan did his best to look disinterested. "If you want to go check on your employer, go ahead. I'll be here when you get back."

The ship's master stood motionless, considering.

Go, Donovan thought. *Get out of here. Leave me alone with this helmsman. I can break this guy in half; I can kill the engines and use the ship's own radio to send the signal. I can contact the launch—I can tell the pilot to get*

Macy and Li out of here; then I can bar the door and buy myself some time. He knew this was his chance; he searched for something additional to say, something that might sway the man, but he said nothing more. This was no time to overplay his hand. Donovan just stared ahead out the bridge window, willing the man to leave.

The ship's master barked something at the helmsman, who nodded and glanced quickly over at Donovan. Then the master slowly turned away and walked to the bridge door.

But just as he reached for the doorknob, the door opened. It was Matsushita again, still dressed in his NBC suit—but this time he was wearing his hood. He stepped forward, directly toward the ship's master, until they were only a few feet apart.

The old man raised his left arm and motioned for the ship's master to come closer. The man hesitated, then took a step forward and leaned down. As he did, Matsushita brought his right arm up; in his hand he held what looked like a small spray bottle. There was a quick hiss and a mist of clear liquid—and the ship's master crumpled to the floor like a puppet dropping on a stage.

It all happened in a single second. There was no gasping for breath, no clutching at the throat, not even a look of shocked realization. It was a sudden and instantaneous death. *It must be VX,* Donovan thought, *or maybe some other nerve agent the old man cooked up himself.* He'd heard about these chemicals in Bureau briefings—toxins that were absorbed through the skin, nerve agents so potent that a single drop caused instant death. Donovan never would have believed anything could kill that fast—but it was hard to argue with results.

Now Matsushita started toward the helm, holding the spray bottle in front of him as he walked. The helmsman stumbled backward into Donovan, who shoved him aside. Matsushita shouted an order in Arabic; the terrified helmsman nodded, then crept back to his position at the controls and pulled back on a series of levers. Donovan felt his weight shift forward as the ship slowed to a stop.

The old man barked a second command, waving the bottle menacingly in the air. The helmsman scrambled away from the console again, staying well out of Matsushita's reach. Donovan had no idea what was said, so he stood motionless and waited. Matsushita looked at him and paused; then he said in English, "Please step away from the controls."

Donovan moved to the back wall. He watched as the old man turned back to the helm and began to spray every lever, every switch, and every knob with the clear fluid. He sprayed the keys of the laptop computer; he sprayed the radio; and he sprayed the throttles most of all. One thing was for sure—the old man didn't want this ship to budge.

As soon as Matsushita turned his back, the helmsman used the opportunity to scramble through the doorway and off the bridge. But Donovan waited, considering his options. He could run too—but where was he supposed to go? This was Sato Matsushita; this was the man he had come for. He measured the distance to the hooded figure. There was no way; he could never reach him before the old man had a chance to turn and raise that spray bottle of his. And this was not like the ship's master; this was not some gunman spraying 9mm chunks of lead. The old man didn't have to aim for the heart or the head, and Donovan wouldn't be able to take a hurried shot in the shoulder or leg and keep charging forward. All it took was a single drop, and it would be lights-out.

The ship's master. Donovan turned and looked; the body lay facedown with the right arm bent underneath—on top of the gun. Would he have time to reach the body, turn it over, and grab the gun before the old man could get to him? And even if he did reach the gun first—was anything on it?

One drop was all it took.

Before Donovan could move, before he even had a chance to speak, the old man wheeled around and charged out of the room, leaving Donovan on the bridge all alone with no idea what to do next.

CHAPTER FORTY-NINE

FBI Headquarters, 26 Federal Plaza

"THE SHIP IS DEAD in the water," a young technical assistant announced, watching the radar image on his laptop screen. There were expressions of relief and enthusiasm all around the table.

Over the last few hours, the Joint Terrorism Task Force had changed. It had evolved into something larger, something far more powerful. The National Security Council had been briefed on the situation in an emergency session, which included the secretary of defense and the chairman of the Joint Chiefs of Staff. The decision was quickly made to keep the Incident Command Center where it had originated, at FBI headquarters, rather than take the time to transfer all the task force members to a new location—but the members themselves had each been slowly replaced. One of the four deputy directors of the CIA was now in attendance; so was a more senior State Department official. The military representatives had all been superseded by officers of higher rank, including the Navy SEAL commander, who had been replaced by a vice admiral—a man with the authority to push much larger buttons.

Additional technicians and support personnel had also crowded into the room, providing access to every possible asset and source of information. There were open lines to government offices all over Capitol Hill; even the president and vice president were updated at regular intervals. It was a truly national task force now, like a giant neuron with axons stretching all over the eastern seaboard. But at this moment in time, the nerve center was still at 26 Federal Plaza in New York.

"Let's hold it down," the CIA director shouted over the din. "Have we received the radio signal yet?"

"Not yet, sir."

"That's more than an oversight—the radio signal should have been the first priority. Something's gone wrong."

"What's the exact position of the ship?" the Navy said to a technician.

"Just under nineteen miles out, sir."

"That's cutting it awfully close. They were given ten miles to bring the ship to a stop—they did it in just over six."

"If everything was on task, we would have received the radio signal by now," the CIA said. "We're blind here—we have to assume the worst."

"But they did manage to stop the ship."

"Somebody did—but we don't know why, and we don't know for how long. For all we know, they could be setting up this plague weapon right now. I think we should launch the missiles; it's our only safe bet."

"I've got two men on that ship," the Navy said.

"We've got eight million here," said a woman from the mayor's office.

The CDC representative was still the same individual, though his status in the group had decreased significantly. The sudden loss of seniority had made him a little more supplicating and a lot less demanding. "Maybe there's another option," the man said. "These cruise missiles of yours—how accurate are they?"

"Within one meter," the Navy replied.

"Well—do we have to destroy the ship? How deep is the channel here? Does anybody know?"

Half a dozen support personnel clicked away at their keyboards. Just a few seconds passed before someone said, "Less than fifty feet."

"Okay then," the CDC said. "Suppose we just sink her—quickly, I mean, so that no one on board has a chance to respond. Can that be done?"

"We can strike just above the waterline," the Navy replied. "We can target the fore and aft cargo holds. We can use tactical warheads designed to open the hull but not tear the ship apart. What's your point?"

"We need that plague specimen," the CDC said. "The safest way to get it is to board the ship and carry it off. But if that option has failed, then there might be another way: We can sink the ship and send in divers to retrieve it. The bacillus has to be contained in some way—it should be protected from the seawater. And at that depth there's not much pressure—even a glass container might survive."

"If it survives the blast."

"That's a chance we have to take. Speaking on behalf of the Centers for Disease Control, we need that plague specimen. But the mayor's office is right: We've got eight million people to think about—maybe more."

The Navy considered. "We can do a tactical strike with two missiles," he said, "then launch two more with conventional warheads a minute later. If anything goes wrong with the tactical strike, we can guide the second two in and destroy the ship completely—but if everything goes the way we want, we can abort the second two missiles and drop them in the water."

Heads began to nod all around the room.

"Excuse me," a low voice said from across the room. Reuben Mayer slowly rose from his chair and smoothed his tie. Mayer was no longer the senior FBI agent present; the assistant director in charge was in attendance as well. But Reuben Mayer was the only man in the room who knew Nathan Donovan.

"I have a man on this ship too," Mayer said. "Some of you met him earlier—his name is Nathan Donovan. He's a CT agent for the Bureau, and he's an ex-Marine. I've been with the Bureau longer than some of you have been alive, and in all that time there's one thing I've learned: You always back your people. The CIA director said something that I think is important here: *We're blind.* We don't know what's going on. We tell our men to send out a radio signal—no signal. We give them ten miles to stop the ship—the ship stops. So why are we assuming the worst? Sounds to me like the job is half-finished—and for that we send in missiles and take them all out? I don't think so. That's not how you do business. That's not how you back your people. We put three good men on board this ship, and we gave them a job to do—I say give them a chance to do it."

There were objections and comments everywhere, but Mayer just raised his voice. "All I'm saying is, we set that ten-mile limit for a reason. This ship is no greater a threat to us now than it was six miles back. As long as it stays where it is, we can afford to give our people time. We told them ten miles; I say we give them ten miles."

"The men might survive the tactical strike."

"What if they're below deck? What if they're searching a cargo hold? Your 'tactical strike' will send the ship to the bottom with everyone on it."

"And what do we do if the ship starts forward again?"

Mayer paused. "If we have no radio signal *and* the ship starts forward again, then I agree—we have no choice. *Then* we launch. But let's wait until then." He looked slowly around the table, then sat down again.

"This man of yours," the State Department asked. "How good is he?"

Mayer shrugged. "He's FBI. What else do you need to know?"

There was silence around the table.

"Maybe he's right," the Navy said. "These men are our only assets in place; our best chance of taking that plague specimen intact is to give them a shot at it. The ship's not going anywhere—we don't have to pull the trigger just yet."

No one said anything for a minute.

"I'm willing to give the men more time," the CIA director said, "but I want to add a stipulation: If that ship moves a single foot closer to our coastline, I say we consider the mission scrubbed and we launch the missiles—no conditions; no questions asked. I see no reason to wait until she crosses the ten-mile mark; the missiles will take a few minutes to get there anyway."

The Navy looked around the table. "If there are no further objections, let's get on the phones and get the necessary approvals—and fast. We'll convene again in ten minutes."

As the group scattered, the CIA director worked his way across the room to Reuben Mayer. "I have a question for you," he said. "If this man of yours is so good, why do you think we haven't heard from him? What's your theory?"

"How many men are on this vessel?" Mayer asked.

"We have no way to know. They falsified all their documents."

"You suppose they're armed?"

"I would think so, yes."

Mayer nodded. "He could be a little busy."

CHAPTER FIFTY

THE LAUNCH CONTINUED TO pound against the side of the ship's hull. Macy grabbed the wheel and jerked it to the right, steering the boat away. At the same time she grabbed the throttle lever and pulled it back hard, and the boat lurched to a stop. She looked out the bridge window, expecting to see the ship pull away from her and continue on down the channel—but it didn't. For some reason, the ship had also come to a stop. Now the two vessels floated side by side like a great black swan and her tiny cygnet, slowly drifting closer again with each rolling swell.

"He's dead," Macy said.

"Yes," Li replied, struggling to drag the pilot's body away from the helm and into the main cabin. "May God rest his soul."

"No—Nathan's dead."

Li looked up at her. She stood motionless at the helm, her hands still gripping the steering wheel, staring straight ahead out the window. Li put his arm around her shoulders and gently turned her away, leading her down the three short steps to the row of pilots' seats. They sat down together, and Li took her hands in his.

"We don't know that," he said gently.

"That man was wearing one of the SEALs' uniforms—how do you think he got it? Something went wrong, Li. The SEALs are dead—and so is Nathan."

"We must not jump to conclusions. Apparently, the SEALs were unable to take control of the ship—that's all we know for certain."

"He was wearing his *clothes.*"

"One does not have to be dead to surrender his clothing. Perhaps the men were only taken captive."

"They murdered the pilot of this boat. Do you think they treated Nathan any better? He's dead—I can feel it."

"Nonsense," Li said sharply. "We must not give up hope—and we must remain focused. We are now in command of this vessel, and we must decide what to do next."

Macy tried to clear her thoughts. "We should radio for help," she said. "Let the others know what's going on."

"We don't know what's going on. What would we tell them?"

"That the mission has failed."

"Has it? Are we certain of that? We must be very careful here. If we announce to your superiors that this mission has failed, what do you suppose their next alternative will be?"

Macy considered. "They'll destroy the ship."

"Of course they will. Why do you suppose the pilot said that if anything went wrong, we were to 'get out of here fast'? If we declare this mission a failure, we will ensure the deaths of everyone on that ship—*everyone.* Are you willing to take that risk, Macy? Are you *that* certain that Nathan is dead?"

They felt the boat shudder, and they heard a sound like a tire swing rubbing against a tree. The waves had carried the two vessels together again. They looked out the port window and saw nothing but black.

"And another thing," Li said. "If we use the radio, the crew of the ship might overhear our message—and they may be unaware of our presence here. Even if that gunman caught a glimpse of us when he fired at the pilot, he's dead now—as far as the crew of the ship knows, there's no one left on this launch. That's a very great advantage, Macy—it means no one will be looking when we board the ship."

Macy's jaw dropped open. "What?"

"That's why we came here, isn't it?"

"Li—you saw what happened to that gunman."

"Yes—that was rather unpleasant, wasn't it?"

"You could be crushed—or you could fall into the water and drown."

"What a shame," Li said. "I was hoping to die in perfect health."

"You saw what happened when Nathan tried it."

"That wasn't particularly graceful, was it? I think we can do better."

"But—I can't drive this boat. Can you?"

They felt the hulls bump together again. "I don't think we'll have to—if we act quickly, that is."

"Li—this is crazy."

The old man smiled. "I didn't come along just for the ride, Macy—and neither did you. It's been my intention all along to board this vessel. And if I'm not mistaken, you came along to assist your husband."

"My ex-husband."

"Really," Li said. "Do you also repair past houses and work at past jobs? No, my dear, no one goes to this much trouble for an *ex*-husband."

"That's a different matter."

"That's the *heart* of the matter," he said. "Everything else is peripheral. You need to forgive him, you know."

"I'm not sure I can."

"I know—but you want to, and that's what's important. That's why you're here."

"You think I came all the way out here to forgive Nathan?"

"May I tell you something? Something that Nathan does not yet understand. Your mission and my mission—they are the same. Do you understand what I'm saying?"

"No."

"You think we came out here because of a plague—and we did, in a sense, but the plague is not on that ship. *We* have the plague, Macy, you and I. We both came out here in pursuit of a cure."

"It's too late now," she said.

"No, it isn't. Nathan is still alive."

"How do you know?"

"Because *I* feel it—and I have more experience with these things than you do. Of course, we'll never know for certain until we board that ship."

Another dull thump from the two colliding hulls. Macy looked out the broken window at the rope ladder still dangling over the ship's starboard side. The ladder dipped low and then hesitated for a moment, as if inviting her to climb aboard—then it suddenly jerked up and away until the last rung of the ladder was above her head. It was like dangling a string in front of a cat's face, waiting until its paw reached out before snatching the string away.

"We'll never make it," Macy said.

Li patted her hand. "God has brought me this far; I don't believe He will abandon me now. Who knows? Perhaps He'll assist you with your mission too."

Li pulled on his backpack and stepped out onto the deck. He worked his way down the railing and stepped into the opening. He stood perfectly erect, like a plastic figurine on the dashboard of a car. He stared directly ahead at some fixed point. He raised both hands until he looked like a bear that was about to attack—and then he waited. Seconds passed—then a minute.

Macy held her breath. She wondered if he was frozen, if fear had paralyzed him. She started to call out to him—then the ladder dipped low and close again. When it did, Li simply extended his arms, gripped the ropes, and stepped onto one of the rungs. A moment later he was whisked away into the sky.

Macy shook her head in amazement. The old man knew what he was doing. The younger men threw themselves at the ladder, but Li let the ladder come to him. *Maybe that's what you have to do when you grow old,* she thought. *Or maybe that's what you learn to do when you grow wise.*

Macy worked her way out on the deck now. She looked up; Li was already at the top of the ladder, pulling himself over the side of the ship. She hoped he was right—she hoped no one knew they were coming. She stood in the opening now, waiting just as Li did for her golden opportunity.

Then the ships began to drift apart.

At first she thought it was just a momentary separation, and she waited for the waves to bring her in closer again. Then she realized to her horror that the hulls were slowly separating. This was as close as she would get—and she was getting farther away all the time.

She began to panic. She measured the distance to the ladder. She thought about jumping out and trying to land on the ladder on all fours. But it was too far away for that now; she would miss the ladder entirely and disappear into the waves. And then a terrifying thought occurred to her, worse than anything she had contemplated yet: Maybe it was too late. Maybe she had missed her chance—maybe she had no choice now but to stand on the deck and watch helplessly as Nathan drifted away.

I'm sick of separations, she thought, *and I hate being helpless.*

She crouched down low, swung both arms out, and dived for the ladder.

CHAPTER FIFTY-ONE

SHE SEEMED TO HANG in the air for an eternity. When her feet first left the edge of the boat, her fingertips were pointed at the middle of the ladder—but in midair the ship began to rise again, and she watched in dismay as the rungs flashed past her one by one. She couldn't bear to look down. She kept her eyes straight ahead, fixed on each rung until it disappeared from her sight, praying that there was at least one more to follow.

Her hands caught the final rung, and for a split second she looked like an arrow shot into the side of the ship—then her body swung down hard. She managed to bend her legs slightly and turn her side into the impact. It was still a gut-wrenching blow, but she kept her grip. Now she hung there, staring up at the ladder, knowing she didn't have the strength to pull herself up hand over hand.

And she wondered if the boat was drifting closer behind her.

Then the ship rolled to starboard again, and Macy found herself dipping into the ocean like a tea bag. She was up to her neck now, and the ladder kept going down. She released her hands and used the water's buoyancy to lift her, taking a new grip several rungs higher—and this time placing her feet on one of the rungs below. When the ship rolled back again, she was out of the water and on the ladder—and she was starting to climb.

A minute later she pulled herself over the gunnels. She saw Li, standing motionless and staring down at the bodies of the two SEALs. One of them was dressed only in his underclothes; both had gaping bullet wounds in their foreheads.

"Oh, no," she said with a moan.

"Come on," Li said. "We can't stay here—we have to get out of sight."

He took her by the arm and led her to the hatchway in the starboard side of the superstructure. He peered around the corner—there was no one in the corridor. They both stepped inside. At the first door they came to, Li quietly knocked. There was no answer; they entered and shut the door behind them. It was an empty cabin.

Li immediately sat down on the edge of a bunk and opened his backpack. He pulled out the NBC suit and began to unfold it.

"What are you doing?" Macy asked.

"I'm going to find Sato Matsushita, of course. Help me with this, will you?"

The suit was a single unit from head to foot. A long zipper ran from the crotch to just below the hood. He pushed his legs down into the lower half and worked his feet into the boots; then he stood up, and Macy held the suit while he slid his arms into the sleeves. He pulled the hood over last of all, positioning the gas mask over his mouth and nose and the lens in front of his eyes. Then he slowly drew the long zipper, closing the seal.

"How do I look?"

"Li—how are you going to find Matsushita?"

"I'm going to ask someone. Unlike most men, I'm not ashamed to ask for directions."

"Be serious."

"I'm quite serious." He looked in his backpack again. It was empty now, except for a small black case with tarnished brass hardware. He fastened the flap on the backpack and pulled it over his shoulders.

"I need a box of some sort," he said, "something heavy. Look around, will you?"

Under the bunk they found a corrugated box containing medical supplies. Li lifted it, testing its weight.

"This will do nicely," he said and started for the door.

"What are you going to do?"

"Wait for me here. When I find Matsushita, I will come back for you."

She stepped in front of him. "Li, you can't just walk around the ship. You don't exactly look like an Arab."

Li looked up at her through the lens of his hood. "No—but I just might pass for Japanese."

CHAPTER FIFTY-TWO

LI STEPPED OUT ONTO the main deck and looked to both sides—there was no one in sight. He turned to his right and headed toward the rear of the ship. Over the railing, to his left, he could still see the launch floating in the water below.

At the corner he turned right and started across the back of the superstructure toward the opposite side of the ship. On the port side of the deck, he spotted a crewman coiling a steel cable around a capstan. Li lumbered toward him, waiting for the crewman to glance up; then he set the box down heavily, straightened, and slowly rolled his shoulders in his best imitation of exhaustion. The crewman shouted something across the deck in Arabic; Li responded in Chinese.

The crewman approached. Li pointed down at the box, jabbed his finger impatiently at the crewman, then planted his hands on his hips and glared at him.

The crewman shook his head, muttered a colorful Arab expression, and hoisted the box. He started back across the deck in the direction from which Li had come. Li turned and followed.

Li trailed the crewman through a hatchway and down a long flight of metal stairs. At the bottom of the stairway, there was a second hatch. When Li stepped through, he found himself standing before a huge sheet of white translucent plastic draped from ceiling to floor. Li tapped the crewman on the shoulder and pointed to the floor. The crewman deposited the box without comment and disappeared through the hatchway again.

Li peered through the first sheet of plastic; beyond it was some kind of locker area, and then a second plastic barrier with a sealed doorway of its own. Beyond that barrier he could just make out the dreamlike image of a biological laboratory. He recognized the screen-wire fronts of the animal cages; he saw shelves full of porcelain basins draped with surgical tubing—and on the far wall, he saw something that looked like a series of tall white cylinders. No, wait—they tapered at the ends, like bullets.

He carefully unzipped each flap and stepped through.

Li found the laboratory horrifyingly familiar. He examined the cages; there were hundreds and hundreds of rats, like the ones the rat-catchers combed the alleys of Singapore for sixty years ago—like the ones the Indian and Malay boys were forced to pick fleas from with pincers. But these rats were different—they were hairless; no one would have to shave their bellies as they did at Ping Fan.

He stared into the porcelain basins and saw the speckled crust of fleas, exactly like the ones they had raised in oil cans at Ping Fan. He saw the hardwood trays with their mesh bottoms, and he shook his head in astonishment. Every piece of equipment in the lab was of the latest design, precision-engineered to the highest modern standards—but it was exactly the same as the process developed by Unit 731 scientists more than six decades ago.

Li stopped for a moment and drew a few deep breaths. The heat and humidity in the lower cargo hold were oppressive, and in the heavy NBC suit, there was no relief at all.

He turned to the aft wall now and examined the items on the long worktable. In the center, standing in a transit case lined with thick protective foam, were the four bullet-shaped cylinders. He pried one of the cylinders from the foam; it was extremely heavy. It took all of his strength just to ease it onto the worktable and slide it forward to the edge. He worked slowly, pacing himself; this would be a most unfortunate time to faint from heat exhaustion.

He turned the cylinder and ran his glove over the surface. It was certainly a thing of beauty, a flawless ceramic piece fire-glazed to a glassy finish. He studied the intricate painting now. It was a tree, the unmistakable image of a Nanking Cherry—but there was one significant difference. In the place of each puffy pinkish-white blossom was something that looked like a spiny thistle. The spines of some pointed straight out, while others draped down slightly like the ribs of an umbrella. What were they? What did they symbolize? Li stepped back from the cylinder to take a wider view—and then, suddenly, everything came into focus.

They weren't thistles—they were showers of sparks.

They weren't cylinders—they were mortar shells.

They were fireworks, and today was the third of July.

Li looked for a place to sit down.

CHAPTER FIFTY-THREE

Macy peered down the corridor from behind the cracked door, watching for Li to return. She had been able to see him until he stepped through the hatchway and onto the deck—but once he turned to his right, he vanished, and she had seen no sign of him since. She looked down at her watch. How long was she supposed to wait here? How long would it take Li to find Matsushita and return for her? And what if he never came back—what if he was discovered first; what if he suffered the same fate as the two Navy SEALs?

And if he did, how would she ever know?

It was too much to think about now. Macy knew from experience that imaginary roads are the darkest to travel, and the mental side trip only makes you more afraid to face the genuine item when it comes along. She shook it off and tried to focus on what she would say to Matsushita when they met—if they ever did.

Suddenly, she heard footsteps in the corridor. Someone was approaching from the opposite direction, moving fast. She pressed the door tighter until only a slit remained, and she waited with her heart pounding in her throat. She thought that at any moment the door would burst open, crashing into her and sending her flying across the cabin—but the figure hurried past, racing toward the same hatchway that Li had used just a few minutes before. The form that passed by was only a silhouette in the darkness of the corridor; all she could tell was that he was a big man, broad-shouldered, wearing something across his back. But in the light flooding through the hatchway, she could see him in every detail.

Nathan!

She threw open the door and shouted his name. It was a stupid thing to do, announcing their presence to everyone within earshot—but she didn't care. She imagined Nathan stepping out onto the deck and vanishing just as Li did, and the thought was more than she could bear. There was a basic human instinct that Macy was compelled to obey, foolish or not—it was the voice inside her that said, *I don't want to die alone.*

Donovan spun around and looked at her. For an instant he stood paralyzed, incredulous—then he charged toward her and into the cabin, swinging the door shut behind him. He wrapped her in his arms and held her—then he took her by the shoulders and pushed her away.

"What are you doing here? I told you to stay away from the ship!"

"The launch pilot is dead," Macy said.

"What?"

"Somebody from the ship put on one of the SEALs' uniforms. He climbed down the ladder—we thought it was one of the SEALs coming back for us. When we pulled up alongside, he shot the pilot in the head."

"Why didn't you get out of here?"

"And just leave you here?"

"I can take care of myself."

"Just like the SEALs?"

"Macy—now I have to look out for you too."

"I don't need a babysitter," she said. "I came here to help."

"Did you try the radio? Did you tell them what was going on here?"

"I didn't *know* what was going on—I still don't!"

"Still no radio contact," Donovan said. "We could have a problem here."

"What's wrong?"

"The Navy gave me an ultimatum. They said if they didn't hear from me, I needed to stop the ship within ten miles—or else."

"But the ship did stop."

"Yeah—but I have no idea how close we are to the line, or which way the tide is carrying us. I don't know how long we've got."

"Then we can't afford to wait. We have to go after Li."

"Li! Isn't he still on the launch?"

"No—he's here, Nathan; he went to look for Matsushita."

"You let him go after Matsushita—by *himself*?" Donovan sank down on the end of the bunk and put his head in his hands.

"What else could I do? I can't go walking around the ship. Li put on his NBC suit—he can pass for Matsushita; he can look around without being recognized. He's coming back for me as soon as he finds him."

"He's not coming back for you, Macy."

"Why not?"

"Did he take anything with him?"

"He was wearing his backpack—that's all."

Donovan groaned.

"What's wrong?"

"I don't have time to explain—and we don't have time to waste. How much of a head start does he have on us?"

"Maybe ten minutes."

"Then we have to hurry. Wait here a minute—I'll be right back."

Donovan ducked out the doorway and down the corridor to the hatch. He poked his head out and looked left toward the bow; the bodies of the two SEALs were still lying faceup on the deck. Donovan searched up and down the deck—there was no one in sight. He crept quickly down the deck to the still-clothed body and drew the sidearm from its holster. Then he hurried back to the cabin, hopefully unobserved.

"We've got to find Matsushita before Li does," Donovan said, tucking the weapon into his belt.

"How do we find him?"

"We'll just have to search the ship. I checked the other cabins on the way down from the bridge. There's nobody up here—they must all be below deck."

"There don't seem to be many people on this ship."

"I thought the same thing. When I boarded the ship, there were two with automatic weapons; there was a third with just a handgun. On the bridge there were two more—but one of them is dead."

"How?"

"I'll explain later. Have you seen anybody else?"

"Just the crewman who shot the pilot. But he's dead too—he got caught between the ships."

"That leaves only three—that we've seen, anyway." He looked at her. "He got caught between the ships?"

"It was terrible."

"Sorry I missed that," he said. "How did you get up here, anyway?"

"I climbed the ladder, just like you did."

"*Just* like I did?"

"Well—I like to think I looked a little better."

"So do I. Come on, let's get out of here."

"Where are we going?"

"Which way did Li go? If we can't find Matsushita, we can at least find Li."

"He turned right, toward the rear of the ship. That's all I could see."

"Then that's where we'll start—with the aft cargo hold."

He waited by the door as she pulled on her backpack with her NBC suit inside.

"Nathan—why do we have to find Matsushita before Li does?"

"Because Li is going to kill him," Donovan said, "and I don't think it's going to be pretty when he does."

CHAPTER FIFTY-FOUR

IDIOTS, SATO THOUGHT, *INCOMPETENT morons and fools! I offer them the chance to stand on the shoulders of giants, but no—they prefer to grovel like rodents in their little desert burrows, gnawing at the soles of the Americans when they could be striking a death blow to the head!*

He charged down the stairway and through the hatch, blind with his own rage.

I give them the benefit of sixty years of my own research—and before that, the work of hundreds more at Ping Fan! I grant them access to the astonishing discoveries of all of Biopreparat—I offer them the collective genius of the greatest scientific minds of the last century, and when it comes time to strike, what weapon do they prefer? A bomb*—a clumsy, barbaric device that a Chinese peasant could devise!*

He stepped through the first plastic barrier and into the dressing area. He returned the plastic spray bottle to the medical cabinet, then pulled down the long zipper on his NBC suit and ducked his head out from under the hood.

A boat filled with explosives! A floating tin of gunpowder! And the only detonator their feeble minds can devise is a handful of their own people—one to push the button, no doubt, and the others to bolster his courage. Truly a ship of fools! If only we could load all of these people onto a single ship—then perhaps we would have a bomb worth detonating!

He wrestled the suit down off his shoulders and pulled his arms from the sleeves. He squatted down on the wooden bench and bunched the leggings down around his shins, then worked his feet up and out of the boots. He hung the suit up on the wall, then turned to the second plastic barrier and opened the zipper.

And what glorious purpose will this brilliant weapon fulfill? It will destroy a statue*! What idiocy is this? Why strike at the giant's shadow and hope for the giant to fall? This bomb will destroy a single row of waterfront buildings, and the first row will shield the second row from harm. What genius! Why strike at useless buildings instead of at the lives they contain? It is not the buildings that will strike back—it is the enemy within, the enemy left alive because of their ignorance and shortsightedness!*

He stepped into the laboratory now and sealed the flap behind him. He turned immediately to the cages on his left. He absentmindedly ran his fingernail down the screen wire of one, half observing the dull response of the dying rats.

I will not allow this to happen. I will not allow my weapon and my mission to be destroyed in a clumsy puff of smoke. This ship will not proceed until I say so. Khalid will reconsider—Khalid will recognize his foolishness, and he will come to me, and we will talk. I will make him understand that here, on the other side of the ocean, we are under no obligation to obey the foolish commands of his so-called superiors. We are the ones who must decide, we are—

He stopped and drew a sharp breath.

In the center of the worktable he saw his foam-lined transit case—but one of his beautiful shells was missing. He jerked his head to the right—there it was, standing upright on the far corner of the table. Standing beside it was an elderly Chinese man, smiling and resting one hand on the tip of the shell. Beside the old man, on the floor, was an NBC suit and an empty backpack.

And on the table beside the shell, a small black case lay open, with three glass vials inside.

CHAPTER FIFTY-FIVE

DONOVAN STEPPED THROUGH THE cargo hatch with Macy right behind him. He held the .45 at eye level, with the butt of the gun resting in his cupped left hand. He swept the room as he entered. He kept his right finger outside the trigger guard, knowing that the Special Forces handgun would have a very light pull. He only had a single clip, and he didn't want to waste a bullet on the first sudden noise that made him flinch.

"I still don't see anybody," Macy said.

"Me neither."

"How many people does it take to run a ship?"

"Beats me—I sure figured more than this."

"Where do you think they all are?"

"Maybe in the engine room—but I don't think Matsushita would be with the rest of the crew. I think he'd have his own space; I'm betting they set him up in one of the cargo holds."

"Is this a cargo hold?"

"I think so. Let me find the lights."

A moment later there was the click of a circuit breaker, and rows of yellow incandescents went on high above. Macy let out a gasp. The room around them was cavernous. It was at least forty feet wide, and it was impossible to tell how deep. It was stacked floor to ceiling with palletized sacks, forming a wall so high that it seemed to curl over them like a breaking wave.

There were less than two feet of clearance between the bulkhead and the first row of pallets, creating a narrow aisle just wide enough to squeeze through sideways. They peered down the aisle in both directions. To the right, the aisle ended at the outer hull of the ship; to the left, it ended at a second metal hatch.

"That way," Donovan said. "That must lead to the next cargo hold."

"Wait," Macy said, breathing hard. "I need a second." She bent over and rested her hands on her knees.

"You okay?"

"It's this heat," she said. "It must be a hundred and twenty down here. I felt bad enough already—this isn't helping."

"Let's take it slower," he said, "but we've got to keep moving."

They sidestepped down the aisle with their backs against the bulkhead. As they passed column after column of stacked pallets, Donovan stared down the long narrow spaces between them. As his eyes adjusted to the dim light, he began to make out strange shapes in the shadows between the columns. There seemed to be something attached to the top of each plastic-wrapped pallet, something long and straight like a board. And there was something around it or beside it, something that wound and curled like surgical tubing.

He stopped to take a better look, but the spaces between the pallets were too deep in shadow to reveal any more details.

"Back up," he said to Macy.

They worked their way back to a space where the incandescents hung directly above, casting their yellow light deep into the narrow gap—and then Donovan saw it.

They weren't boards; they were pipes—and it wasn't surgical tubing; it was electrical wire.

He studied the layout of the pipes; the side of the column of pallets looked like a family tree. Pipes from the lowest pallets joined with larger pipes above, merging as they rose into ever-larger diameters until they all joined together near the ceiling into a single six-inch conduit that traveled back through a hole cut through the bulkhead.

The wires from each level of pallets gathered with others at a metal junction box. A single wire emerged from the top of the junction box, joining with others above it and traveling in undulating bundles through the same hole as the pipe.

Donovan looked at the pallet directly in front of his face. Through the thick plastic wrapping, he saw layer upon layer of hundred-pound sacks bearing no apparent label or identification. He grabbed at the plastic and tried to tear it open, but it was too thick. He pressed the distorting plastic tighter against the brown paper and searched more closely for some distinguishing mark that might identify its contents. On the end of one sack, in tiny dot-matrix letters, he found the phrase *ENGRAIS CHIMIQUE.*

"What does this say?" Donovan asked Macy.

She squinted at the tiny line. "Chemical fertilizer."

Donovan leaned back against the bulkhead and slid down to the floor.

"What's wrong?"

Donovan just stared straight ahead.

Macy sat down on the floor beside him. "Nathan, what is it?"

"The ship is a bomb," he said. "The sacks—they're filled with ammonium nitrate. This whole ship is rigged to explode."

"What?"

"Sixty years ago, in Texas City, they were loading a ship like this one with ammonium nitrate. They had about two thousand tons of it on board when the ship caught fire. A couple of hours later the ship blew up—and it destroyed half the city. Pieces of the ship came down a mile away. The blast knocked two planes out of the sky—they say you could hear it a hundred and fifty miles away." He pointed around the room. "Look at the pallets," he said. "Each one is wrapped in plastic, like a bag, and each bag has a pipe attached to it—see there? Those pipes carry fuel oil from the ship's tanks."

"Why?"

"Because ammonium nitrate is a low-grade explosive—until it's mixed with a hydrocarbon like oil. Then it's known as ANFO: ammonium nitrate/fuel oil. Remember the Oklahoma City bombing? That's what they used there—ammonium nitrate mixed with nitromethane, a kind of racing fuel. In Oklahoma City they only used about two tons—a thousand times less than in Texas—but it still took off half the Federal Building. The difference was the fuel oil, plus a sophisticated triggering sequence." He pointed up at the ceiling. "See the wires? I'll bet the triggering sequence is computerized."

Macy looked around again at the cargo hold. There were pallets everywhere, as far as the eye could see.

"How much do you think is here?"

"I have no idea. This is just one cargo hold—if they plan to blow up the ship, they probably loaded them all. There could be five times more ammonium nitrate here than there was on the ship in Texas City—but it's rigged for maximum effect, like the bomb in Oklahoma City. If this thing goes off anywhere near the harbor . . ." His voice trailed away. "Well—at least we know why there's nobody on the ship. Talk about a skeleton crew."

"I don't get it," Macy said. "They already have Matsushita and his plague weapon. Why the bomb?"

"I have no idea. But there's some kind of conflict going on here. They're fighting among themselves—maybe not everybody is on the same page. I was on the bridge when Matsushita came in."

"You saw him?"

"Yeah—and he was *ticked.* He was in an NBC suit, and he had a spray bottle with him—some kind of nerve agent. He killed the ship's master, and he ordered the helmsman to stop the ship—then he sprayed all the controls so no one could touch them. Apparently Matsushita doesn't want this ship to move."

"Why not?"

"We'll have to ask him," he said, climbing to his feet. "Come on—we've got to hurry."

"Nathan, wait. This ammonium nitrate—is there any other way to set it off?"

"Like what?"

"Say, for example—a missile?"

CHAPTER FIFTY-SIX

WHO ARE YOU?" MATSUSHITA demanded.

"My name is not important," Li replied.

"How did you get on this ship?"

"Again, a trivial detail. We have very little time together, Dr. Matsushita, and we must focus on more important matters."

Matsushita's eyes began to dart around the laboratory.

"Nothing is missing, if that's what you're thinking. Nothing has been tampered with, and nothing has been taken—except this," he said, patting the white shell beside him.

Matsushita started toward him.

"I would not do that," Li said, tipping the shell precariously over the edge of the table.

Matsushita froze. He raised both hands in an entreating gesture and backed slowly away.

Li rocked the shell back again. "It would be rather embarrassing for two eighty-year-old men to end up in a wrestling match," he said. "I think discussion is more appropriate to men of our station in life, don't you?"

"What do you want?"

"I want to tell you a story. I know you'll enjoy this story, because it involves you—and I imagine that by this point your twisted soul is interested in nothing else."

"I do not have time for this."

"You took sixty years of my time," Li said. "The least you could do is give a few minutes in return. Now then—where shall I begin? There are so many possible starting points, and the beginning of a story is the most important part. How about this: Once upon a time there was an ambitious young man who wished nothing more than to become an excellent doctor. But it was not to be. Instead, he was conscripted into the Imperial Japanese Army, where he was assigned to a biological warfare facility in Manchuria known as Unit 731."

"How do you know this?" Matsushita demanded.

"Please—you're interrupting my story. At first, the young man found the practices of Unit 731 abhorrent. But then, like many men in times of war, his heart grew hard and unfeeling. But war does not make men demons—it simply releases the demons within them. And within his own heart there were demons, though he was too young to know them yet—things like arrogant nationalism, and intellectual snobbery, and racial bigotry. Soon these demons had taken over his heart, and he became an eager and willing accomplice of Unit 731. The dissections, the bloodletting, the human testing—they were all just daily activities to him. And the Chinese peasants who begged for mercy while he cut them open to study their living remains—they were just like laboratory animals squealing in their cages."

Li paused. "Are you enjoying my story?"

"No."

"Then perhaps I should begin somewhere else," he said. "I know: Once upon a time there was a young Chinese man. He, too, wanted only to be a doctor one day—but along the way he discovered that he wanted something else: He wanted to be a *husband.* He was quite surprised to discover this; he had never thought of being a husband before. But one day he met a young Chinese woman, a simple peasant girl—but she was as beautiful as the Yangtze at sunset and as gentle as a woodland fawn. The young man was captured by this vision; he was enraptured with love for her—and to his great and undeserving delight, she loved him in return.

And from that day forward, in all the world there was only one thing he really longed to be: her husband. But it was not to be.

"One day, an airplane flew over her village and ejected something from its tail that looked like smoke. The people of the village thought little of it, but a few days later they were stricken with a strange disease. My wife was among them. She was in agony, Dr. Matsushita. She was told that medical help was available if only she would report to the village temple. She did so—and when she got there, do you know what happened? She was tied to a chair and vivisected."

Li's voice was trembling now. "Is this story familiar to you, Dr. Matsushita?"

"No."

"The village was called Congshan. Does that help?"

"I cannot remember."

"When you finished with my wife's internal organs and discarded them on the floor, you returned to your truck. Do you remember? A young man approached you from behind. He put a hand on your shoulder and turned you around. He looked at your face; he stared into your eyes. He memorized every contour and pore. He charted the blood vessels in your eyes. Do you recall this? You looked back at him, Dr. Matsushita. Do you remember his face? Would you recognize him if you saw him again?"

Li took a step closer but stayed within arm's length of the shell. "One of the soldiers—he pushed you aside. The soldier stepped forward and plunged his bayonet into the young man's belly." Li slowly lifted his shirt, revealing the jagged scar below his ribs.

"Do you remember me, Dr. Matsushita?"

The old man shook his head.

"But why should you?" Li said. "It was only a bayonet wound, barely two inches in length. Now, a vivisection—that's something different; that's something to *remember*."

Li's voice began to break; he paused for a moment to compose himself.

"I really don't mind if you don't remember me," he said. "But I must know if you remember my wife. Her name was Jin Li. Did you hear me? *Jin Li.* Please, Dr. Matsushita—tell me that you hated her, or tell me that her memory has haunted you every day since. Tell me that you're glad you butchered her, that her death has been a source of constant satisfaction to you. Tell me that you selected her for a reason—tell me there was something different about her, something that to this very day makes her stand out in your mind. But please, in the name of all that is holy, don't tell me that you can't *remember.*"

"I cannot be expected to recall a single person," he said.

"You mean you cannot remember one murder among thousands? How very odd the human heart is. If I commit a single murder, it weighs on my soul like a mountain of fire. If I commit a second murder, my burden is increased—but not doubled. And when I commit a thousand murders, my burden is somehow relieved. How fortunate for your conscience that you were a mass murderer and not some petty assassin."

"It was a time of war," he said.

"Yes—that's what the Americans said when they dropped the bomb on Hiroshima and incinerated your precious sister. Did that justification satisfy *you*, Dr. Matsushita? That it was a time of war, and ordinary morality had to be set aside for the sake of ultimate victory? Is that what you tell yourself even now?"

Matsushita's face flushed. "How dare you speak of my sister!"

"I do dare—I dare to speak her name: *Emiko Matsushita.* I speak her name that she might be remembered. Have you ever spoken my wife's name, Dr. Matsushita? Of course not—you never knew her name, did you? I'm curious: How was my wife distinguished from all your other human experiments? Was she assigned a case number? Was she simply described as 'Congshan female'? Or was she not interesting enough for that—perhaps her organs were too ordinary to merit any notation at all."

"It was *war*," he said again. "All nations had to sacrifice."

"Nations don't make sacrifices—people do. Strange, isn't it? Nations win victories, but individuals make sacrifices. Take me, for example: My nation was among the victors, and yet I lost everything I held dear in the world. I am a victor, yet I suffer among the vanquished. Do you know why? Because there is no victory great enough to compensate me for the loss of my beloved Jin."

"What is it you seek from me—an apology?"

"In your current spiritual condition, that would be far too much to expect."

"I will not apologize! When my helpless sister was scorched to death in atomic fire, who offered an apology to me? And now her soul is in agony!"

"I assure you, it is not Emiko's soul that is in agony."

"Tell me what it is you want!"

"I want you to listen. I want you to try to allow some tiny shaft of light into that blackened soul of yours. You think that the taking of a million lives will somehow compensate you for the loss of your sister—but it never will. You *loved* your sister, and when you truly love something, you assign it a value above everything else in the world. Nothing can repay the loss of your sister—*nothing.* Not a single life; not a million. You think the destruction of the Americans will somehow satisfy you, but their deaths will mean nothing to you. You felt nothing after the thousandth death—why should you be satisfied with more? But if you do this wicked thing in the name of Emiko Matsushita—if this is how you allow her to be remembered—then I assure you, your poor sister's soul *will* be in agony."

"You have no right to say these things to me!"

"I have *every* right. Do you know why? Because you are the victim of the Americans, but I am the victim of *you.* You have pursued the Americans for sixty years, and I have pursued you. The hatred you harbor for them is the hatred I have harbored for you. The debt that is owed you is the debt you owe me. Look closer, Dr. Matsushita—do you still not recognize me? Do you still not know who I am? I am your cell mate—I am your fellow prisoner."

"You wish to prevent my mission!"

"No—I wish to fulfill mine."

Li turned to the black case. His hands were shaking so badly that he could barely remove one of the vials. He twisted the top, and the old wax seal cracked and crumbled into pieces.

"I brought something for you," Li said. "Something I brought with me from China; something I have saved for a very long time."

Matsushita took a step back. "What is it you want from me?"

"Right now, I want you to stand still."

Just then, there was a heavy metallic sound from beyond the two plastic barriers. Li turned. He saw the shadowy figures of a man and a woman stepping through the hatch.

CHAPTER FIFTY-SEVEN

DONOVAN SAW THE HUGE sheet of plastic with the zippered doorway in the center. Beyond it was another; they hung like flat curtains from the ceiling, dividing the cargo hold into three airtight compartments. He stared through the plastic and saw the blurred images of two men at the opposite end of the room. They were about equal in stature and build—and neither of them wore biological suits.

"Li!" he shouted. "Is that you in there?"

"Hello, Nathan. Your timing is always extraordinary."

"We're coming in!" He pulled the first zipper.

"You must not come in yet," Li said. "The doctor and I have unfinished business to attend to."

"Who are these people?" Matsushita demanded.

"Friends of mine," Li said. "I believe they have business with you too."

Donovan and Macy were through the first barrier now. With just a single sheet of plastic remaining between them, Donovan could make out more details. Li and Matsushita were standing face-to-face at opposite ends of a table. Li's right arm was extended—his hand was resting on something that looked like a white artillery shell. His left hand was holding something, too, something smaller—something made of glass.

Then he saw the open black case.

"Li—we're coming in there!"

"As usual, Nathan, you're not listening. I said you must not come in just yet."

"Stay back!" Matsushita shouted through the plastic. "You must not enter my laboratory!"

"You see?" Li said. "The doctor and I are in agreement."

When Donovan reached for the second zipper, Matsushita lunged forward and grabbed the shell from Li's hands. He pulled hard on the ceramic tip, rocking it off the table and onto the floor. It landed nose-first, shattering into a dozen gleaming white shards, and a mound of pepper-gray powder poured out from inside.

Donovan and Macy stood frozen outside the plastic, staring at the floor.

"Li," Donovan gasped. "What is that thing?"

"Well, now," Li said, staring at the pile around their feet, "I really didn't anticipate this."

"Are those the fleas?"

"I'm afraid so. These bullet-shaped capsules you see are fireworks—some type of skyrocket or aerial display, no doubt intended for New York's Fourth of July celebration tomorrow. The good doctor here has loaded his plague-infected fleas into the tops of these shells. Just imagine all the people lining the waterfront on the Fourth of July—I must say, you have to appreciate his ingenuity, twisted though it is."

"Li!" Macy said. "You've got to get out of there!"

"I'm afraid it's a little late for me—for both of us, in fact. The doctor and I can no longer leave this ship; the risk to others would be too great. Oh well, I suppose it seems appropriate that our missions would end here, together—a poetic justice, one might say. And now if you two will excuse me, I have one more matter to attend to."

"Li—don't do it! I still need to talk to him!"

"Now, Nathan," Li said, "by now you must know that I'm really quite intent on this—and now I have all the more reason. Perhaps you'll have time to speak with him when I am finished."

"Li, I have a job to do!"

"And I have a mission to fulfill. Which comes first, the mission or the job? You were assigned yours just a few weeks ago. I was assigned mine six decades ago—and by a much higher authority."

Nathan pulled the gun from his belt and leveled it at Li.

"Nathan!" Macy shouted. "What are you doing?"

"My job," he said.

"You and Dr. Matsushita are kindred spirits," Li said. "He once did his job too."

"I mean it, Li. Step away from Matsushita."

The old man looked back at him sadly. "Could you kill me, Nathan? Please don't imagine you could merely wound me—to stop me you would have to kill me. Could you do that?"

"Don't make me find out."

"I must do what I came to do," Li said, "and you must do what you must." He took two steps toward Matsushita.

Donovan clicked the safety off and slid his finger inside the guard.

"Nathan, don't!" Macy shouted.

Li turned and looked at him. "I'm confident you will do the right thing," he said, "but perhaps I should take this opportunity to point out that if you shoot me, you will also poke a hole through this plastic barrier—and the two of you are hardly dressed for the occasion."

Donovan lowered the gun and looked at the plastic. It was all that stood between them and a disease for which there was no cure.

"You old fool!" he shouted. "Come on," he said to Macy, "we've got to suit up—fast!" They both wrestled off their backpacks and dropped to the floor.

Li turned back to Matsushita, who continued to stare down at the remains of his broken shell, watching the mound of fleas slowly dissipate as tiny specks collected on his trouser legs and shoes.

"Now where was I?" Li said. "Oh, yes—my story. I've attempted two different starting points, Dr. Matsushita, and you've failed to appreciate either of them. Perhaps I should try one more."

Donovan and Macy were dressing as fast as they could. Donovan shoved his left foot into the boot so fast that he almost ripped through the butyl coated nylon. Macy had both legs inserted into her suit, and she lay back on the floor for a moment, panting. The heat was draining the last bit of energy from her body, and her head was starting to swim.

"There once was a young man who loved someone very much—more than anything else in the world. But that person was taken from him most cruelly, and then he was terribly alone. At first he thought he would go insane with grief—in fact, he wished for it, preferring madness to the inescapable horrors of his rational mind. Some say he did go insane; others simply say that he was never quite the same again."

Donovan and Macy were on their feet now, helping one another pull the bulky suits up over their shoulders. Donovan's business suit rode up his back, bunching up in a ball between his shoulders. He took an extra few seconds to rip it off and throw it aside.

"Over time his grief became anger; then his anger turned to bitterness; then his bitterness cooled and hardened like magma until his heart was as hard as stone. His soul collapsed like a dying star, folding in on itself in hatred and loathing and rage.

"Some said the man was a tragic victim, imprisoned by the injustice of others. It was something he desperately wanted to believe, something he told himself over and over again, because it justified all the darkness in his heart. But it was a lie. He was a victim, yes—but he lived in a prison of his own making, a prison without locks or bars or even walls. He sentenced himself to a life in solitary confinement, where he could wallow in sorrow and self-pity—where he could nurture his longing for revenge."

Li stared at Matsushita. "Do you recognize the man in this story?"

Matsushita said nothing.

He shook his head sadly. "Of course you don't—how could I expect you to? You see, the man in the story is *me.* Sixty years ago, you took my beautiful wife away from me—and I have lived in a prison of anger and hatred ever since. But you and I are different, Dr. Matsushita. Unlike you, I am not willing to die in prison. For sixty years I have been on a journey to free my soul—and today my journey ends here, face-to-face with you."

Donovan and Macy were almost suited up now. Macy's skin was dry and clammy; when she pulled the hood and mask down over her face, she felt as if all the air had left the room and the walls were beginning to close in on her. She only had the zipper halfway up when Donovan grabbed her by the arm.

"Come on!" he shouted, opening the plastic barrier.

Li stood directly in front of Matsushita now. He raised the glass vial to eye level and spoke slowly and solemnly. "Sato Matsushita," he said. "Freely I have received; freely I give. In the name of the Father, and the Son, and the Holy Ghost—*I forgive you.*"

He brought the vial down quickly in a diagonal, slashing motion, and the clear fluid splashed across Matsushita's face and chest. The old man staggered back, sputtering.

Macy and Donovan stood frozen, waiting—but nothing happened.

"It didn't work!" Donovan said.

"What ever do you mean?" Li said indignantly. "It worked perfectly."

"Maybe it lost its potency."

"How does water lose its potency?"

"It was *water*?"

"I suppose holy water does have a certain potency, but I'm unaware of any expiration date."

"*Holy* water?"

"Yes—from a certain well near the village of Congshan."

Just then, Macy's eyes drooped shut, and she slowly sank to her knees at Matsushita's feet. The old man looked down at her and saw the half-open zipper. He leaped forward and grabbed her by the hood, ripping it back and off her head, exposing her face and neck.

"No!" Donovan shouted. He lunged in front of her, butting Matsushita out of the way with his shoulder. He grabbed Macy by both arms and jerked her kneeling body up from the floor like a limp doll. Then he charged forward with her, directly into the first plastic barrier, ripping it from the walls and ceiling. The thick plastic wrapped around them like a clinging shroud, but Donovan kept plowing forward, through the second barrier and toward the hatch at the opposite end of the room.

The cargo hold was in chaos. The collapsing barriers dragged everything along with them: benches, cabinets, biological suits—even a row of rat cages crashed to the floor and sprang open, and half-dead hairless rodents wandered out onto the floor.

Donovan kicked and tore the plastic away from him, shoving Macy through the hatch and onto the metal stairs. "Can you walk?" he shouted in her face.

She stared at him through half-open eyes.

He shook her by the shoulders. "Macy! Can you walk?"

"I think so."

"Then get away from here! Get up to the top deck and get out of this suit!" He spun her around and shoved her up the first few stairs; she stumbled, but she kept moving upward.

Donovan turned back to the room—it was a ruin. The floor was covered with mounds of crumpled plastic, and various objects hung suspended in the folds like flecks of debris in foam. On the far side of the room, he saw Li still standing by the table.

But Matsushita was nowhere in sight.

CHAPTER FIFTY-EIGHT

DONOVAN WADED BACK THROUGH the sea of crumpled plastic toward Li. He saw the old man wrestle a second of the four loaded shells onto the table and then send it crashing to the floor beside the first.

"What are you doing?"

"I think it's best to destroy them all," Li said, prying a third shell from its padded case. "That old devil is really quite shrewd, you know. He thought that by sacrificing one of his shells, he would make us all flee—leaving him with seven shells still intact."

"But he killed himself in the process."

"I suspect Dr. Matsushita only planned to live a few days longer anyway—just long enough to witness his revenge. With this attempt he lost only a single day of life and potentially saved his mission in the process. An excellent wager, all in all."

"Where is he? Where did he go?"

"There are only two exits to this room," Li said. "You and Macy occupied one of them; I imagine he left through the other. I didn't really see—things were rather busy. I must say, you really have a flair for entrances and exits."

"Li, do you think Macy was infected?"

The old man stared sadly at the floor. "I pray not," he said. "She was exposed for only an instant—but she was on her knees, so close to the floor. You snatched her away so quickly. But her face, her bare neck . . . I pray not," he said again.

Donovan looked the old man over. "How do you feel?"

"Free," he said. "It's a wonderful feeling—you should try it."

"I mean physically."

"Oh, that. I feel like a dog in need of a flea bath. These things are really quite irritating." He pulled the third shell onto the floor—it shattered beside the others.

"I've got an idea," Donovan said. "If these suits can keep bacteria out, then they can keep bacteria in. We'll suit you up—then we can find a way to get you off the ship."

"For what purpose? There is no cure for this disease, Nathan. I am covered with these annoying creatures, and I am undoubtedly infected. Removing me from this ship will not add a single day to my life. And besides, I can't just walk out of here like a sackful of pestilence—the risk to others would be too great."

"I can't just leave you here."

"I'm afraid you have no choice."

Donovan stared at him. "I can't leave you."

The old man smiled and patted his sleeve. "You called me an 'old fool,'" he said. "That's much better than 'old fart.' Is this what you call a growing relationship?"

"He's killed you, Li. He murdered your wife, and now he's killed you too."

"He's only sped up the process. One thing an old man learns is not to be too greedy. Life mustn't be measured only in days, you know—you're looking at a man who lived to fulfill his mission."

"Your *mission*," Donovan said. "You told me you wanted to kill him!"

"I never said any such thing."

"You led me to believe that!"

"I led you only where you wished to go."

"Why, you old fox."

"That's even better than 'old fool.' We're moving right along."

"Li—why didn't you tell me?"

"Now, Nathan. Suppose I told you from the beginning, 'Please let me come along—I wish to forgive him.' What would you have said?"

"I would have said, 'Stay *home* and forgive him. You don't need to come along for that.'"

"Precisely. The only reason you allowed me to come along is because you thought I wished to kill him—because you thought I needed to get my hands physically around his throat."

"But, Li—why *did* you need to come along? If all you wanted to do was forgive him, why didn't you just let it go? Why all this trouble? Why all the risk?"

"Forgiveness is serious business, Nathan—forgiveness is the business of life. There is enormous power in forgiveness—but for that power to be experienced, forgiveness must be *expressed*. Forgiveness is a transfer of title; it's a canceling of debt—it's infinitely more than a simple change of heart."

"He didn't deserve to be forgiven."

"It was never about him, Nathan; don't you see that? I was the one imprisoned; I was the one who wished to be released. So I sought out my tormentor, and I handed him the title to my hatred and my bitterness—and then I was free."

"But your forgiveness meant nothing to him."

"That's an entirely different matter. There is enormous power in forgiveness—but for Dr. Matsushita to experience it, he must choose to *receive* it. I choose to believe that somewhere deep inside he wants to be forgiven—because that is what every human heart longs for, to be released from a debt it can never repay."

Donovan shook his head. "You waited sixty years and traveled halfway around the world just to forgive this guy? You must be a saint."

"You mustn't think that," Li said. "We label others 'saints' to avoid our own responsibilities—yours, for example."

"I know my responsibility," Donovan said. "I'm going after Matsushita."

"You'll do nothing of the kind."

"I still need to talk to him, Li. I need to find out who his backers were, where his lab was, if anybody else has this plague of his."

"Be reasonable, Nathan—you're talking about a bitter old man whose dreams have been shattered, who now has only days to live. What will you do, *interrogate* him? He'll tell you nothing, and you'll waste precious time finding whatever rock he's slithered under."

"I should find him just to kill him."

"Do you think I forgave this man just so you could destroy him? Don't be a fool—and don't make a mockery of my life. You're still thinking about your job, Nathan. Your job is finished—now you have a mission."

"What mission?"

"Nathan—*the business of life is forgiveness.* Up on deck is a woman who has pursued *you* halfway around the world—halfway across the city, anyway, because she desperately wants to forgive you."

"You'd never know it."

"You've hardly made it easy for her, now, have you? You must not expect Macy to be like me, Nathan; you must not expect her to do all the work of forgiveness herself. And *you* must not be like Sato Matsushita—you must not harden your heart against her; you must not let your anger and pride keep you apart. I hate to have to say this, Nathan, but Macy and I may leave this world together. You have no more time for stubbornness; you have no more time for delay. You never did—but you were too foolish to know."

"What do I say to her?"

"Tell her why you ran away when your son was dying of cancer."

"I *didn't* run away—"

"You did run away, because you were afraid."

"I've never been afraid of anything in my—"

"*Please,*" Li said. "We have very little time here, and I don't intend to waste it listening to your empty clichés. Of course you've been afraid, Nathan. All men are afraid—only a fool fears nothing. You and I have something in common, you know: We were both forced to watch someone we love suffer while we stood helplessly by. Did you ever wish that you could switch places with your son? Did you ever wish that you could suffer *for* him?"

"Every day."

"And you would have done it, gladly, if only you were given the chance. But you weren't given that chance, Nathan; there was nothing you could *do*. Let me tell you something: The worst form of suffering is not to suffer yourself, but to watch someone you love suffer and not be able to stop it. That's what it means to be *powerless*—and that's something all men loathe and fear.

"And so you ran away. And ever since, you have been walking through fire and throwing yourself in front of bullets to prove to yourself that you are not a coward. You are not a coward, Nathan—you simply could not stand to see your child in pain. I was luckier than you; I saw the results of my wife's suffering, but I didn't have to bear it day after day. I'm not sure I would have had the courage either."

"Macy did."

"Yes, she did."

"What do I say to her, Li—'I'm sorry for being weak'?"

"I think that covers it nicely."

"She could never forgive me."

"Give her a chance, Nathan. Perhaps all she needs is something to forgive."

Donovan looked into the old man's eyes. "Li," he said, "I want you to know something. It's been an honor—it's been my privilege—"

"I know," Li said with a smile. "I've become quite fond of you too."

Donovan wrapped his arms around him and pulled him in tight. Li was right—if he could somehow draw the plague from the old man's bloodstream and put it in his own, he would do it gladly.

"Enough now," Li said, pushing himself away and swatting the gray specks from Donovan's NBC suit. "You have a mission to fulfill, and I'm not one to interfere with a man on a mission. Go now."

"Wait," Donovan said. "I've got to get a specimen of that plague. It's what we came here for."

"I've taken care of that," Li said. He handed him his own black case, sealed tight again. "What you want is in here," he said. "This is what you came here for."

Donovan tucked the case under his arm. "What are you going to do now?"

"I'm going to look for Sato Matsushita."

"Why?"

"I think he could use some company."

"You never give up, do you?"

"No—and I hope you don't either."

"Li, you need to know something. The Navy, they told me—"

"I know." He nodded. "That's why we both must hurry. Good-bye, Nathan. Thank you for helping an old man fulfill his dream."

Donovan turned and hurried toward the hatch. Halfway across the room, he turned back. He tried to speak, but nothing came out.

Li smiled. "Give your wife my love, won't you?"

CHAPTER FIFTY-NINE

On the bridge, the helmsman crept slowly up to the controls. He held his arms upright, like a doctor preparing for surgery. On his hands he wore an oversized pair of yellow rubber gloves.

He hesitated over the controls. He touched the throttle with a single finger and backed away again, waiting. Nothing happened.

He stepped forward now and grabbed the throttle in his fist. Still nothing.

He pushed slowly forward on the throttle, and the ship began to move.

"Sir!" the technician shouted across the table. "The ship is moving again, and it's headed for the harbor!"

Quick glances were exchanged all around the table. The State Department said, "If anybody has any second thoughts, he'd better speak now."

There were none.

"Okay," the Navy said. "I'm giving the order to fire."

On an Aegis-class missile cruiser somewhere in the North Atlantic, two hatch doors opened, and a pair of cruise missiles lifted off on plumes of white smoke.

CHAPTER SIXTY

MACY LEANED OVER THE railing, still trying to regain her strength. She shed the remains of her NBC suit as soon as she got to the deck, and she felt instant relief—even the glaring midday sun was an improvement over the sweltering cargo hold. The sea had calmed considerably; the giant swells were only rolling hills now. Her legs were still rubbery, and her head ached terribly, but overall she felt considerably better.

She wondered how long she would feel that way.

Suddenly, she noticed something: The launch was no longer beside the ship. It was a hundred yards behind them now and slowly drifting away.

Behind her, Nathan burst through the hatchway and onto the deck. He stopped for an instant and looked at her, then ripped his own NBC suit off and threw it aside. He started toward her.

"Stay away!" Macy said, backing away from him.

"We're getting off this ship," he said.

"Not me—I can't, Nathan; I've been exposed. I'm just like Li—I can't leave this ship; the risk would be too great."

Donovan kept walking toward her.

"Stay back! Don't touch me!"

But he threw his arms around her and pulled her close to him. She struggled in his arms, twisting like a wild animal—but he wouldn't release his grip.

"Get away from me! There could be fleas in my hair!"

"You need to bathe more," he said. "You've really let yourself go." He began to stroke her long brown hair again and again. "You were only exposed for a second, you know."

"That could be all it takes."

"Then I guess I've got it too—I've been stroking your hair longer than that."

He released her now, and she pushed away and looked at him.

"Why did you do that? You could have left."

"I didn't want to leave—not without you."

"Nathan, there's no cure for this strain of plague. Now we *both* have to stay."

"No, we don't," he said. "We'll swim to the launch—we'll quarantine ourselves there and wait. We'll just—" He looked over the railing; there was nothing but empty sea. "Hey! Where's the boat?"

She pointed. "Back there."

Nathan looked—the boat was now two hundred yards away and diminishing fast. Then he spotted the churning wake behind the ship.

"The ship's moving again," he said. "Come on—we're out of time!"

"Nathan—I don't think I can swim that far."

"You'll make it," he said. "I'll help you."

She looked down at the water below. "It's too far to jump."

"Macy, we don't have time to argue. Either you climb over that railing and jump, or I'll throw you in myself."

She glared at him. "I hate bullies!"

"And I hate whiners!"

She sat on the railing and swung her legs over. "I have *never* whined," she said, "without good reason." She pushed off from the railing and hurtled silently toward the waiting water.

Donovan put one hand on the railing, swung his legs up and over, and plunged into the ocean beside her.

It seemed to take forever to reach the launch. They were able to swim only as fast as Macy's exhausted body could manage. Donovan hooked his arm around her chest and tried carrying her like a drowning victim, but the pace was even slower. All he could do was swim along beside her, encouraging, cajoling, and threatening. There was a moment when she almost panicked—when she was still a hundred yards from the launch, and she glanced back at the ship and saw it receding away—but Donovan took her by the arm and pulled her along, half gliding and half swimming toward the boat.

They reached it at last and dragged themselves onto the deck. They made their way onto the bridge; the pilot's lifeless body still lay facedown in the cabin behind it. Donovan tried the engine and prayed—it started the first time. He shoved forward on the throttle, and the boat tipped back and accelerated.

"Where are we going?" Macy asked.

"Away from the ship—that's all that matters right now. Get on the radio—tell them everything. See if we can call off those missiles."

"What if they've already fired them?"

"They can still call them off—but we don't have much time."

Macy reached down for the microphone. She picked up the cord—but there was nothing on the end but a shattered chunk of plastic and a few tangled wires. She held it up and showed it to Donovan. "A bullet must have hit it," she said.

"Then we've got a problem—there's no way to call off the attack."

"What happens if those missiles hit all that ammonium nitrate?"

He quickly did the math. "At twenty-four knots, we couldn't get far enough away in an hour—and I don't think we have an hour."

Donovan scanned the horizon; to his left, he saw an enormous container ship approaching in the channel, heading out to sea. It would be even with the *Divine Wind* in just a few minutes, passing on her starboard side about a thousand yards across the channel. Donovan estimated the distance to the container ship—then he turned the wheel and steered directly for it.

"What are you doing?"

"If we're in open water when those missiles hit, we won't have a prayer. Our only chance is to duck behind something—and out here, there's just not much to duck behind."

"Can we make it in time?"

"You want the honest answer or the hopeful answer?"

"The hopeful answer."

Donovan looked at her. "I doubt it."

CHAPTER SIXTY-ONE

DONOVAN SHOVED HARDER ON the throttle, but the launch could go no faster. At first it felt as if they were flying across the water, but now, in the open expanse of the channel, they seemed to be almost standing still. The gap between them and the *Divine Wind* widened with agonizing slowness because they were fleeing at a diagonal, in the same direction the ship itself was moving. But that was the path they had to take—that was the shortest route to the oncoming container ship.

From a distance, the container ship looked no larger than the *Divine Wind*—but as it grew closer, its enormity became apparent. It was more than twice the size of the old cargo ship, at least a thousand feet in length. Its weather deck was forty feet above the water, and the deck was stacked another forty feet higher with row upon row of multicolored shipping containers. It was the perfect shelter, a virtual floating fortress—that is, if they could reach it in time.

Donovan glanced over at Macy. She stood beside him on the bridge, with one hand gripping the edge of the helm and the other clinging to an overhead grip. He thought about telling her to go back to the main cabin, to lie facedown and find something to cover her head—but what was the point? It wouldn't make any difference—and besides, he was glad for her company.

She looked over at him, and their eyes met.

"I want you to know I'm sorry," Donovan said.

"I don't want to hear it," she said, turning back to the window. "We'll have plenty of time to talk later."

"Well, just in case we don't—"

"Later."

"Isn't that what you call 'denial'?"

"No, that's what you call 'focus.' I know you, Nathan—whenever you start talking, you take your foot off the gas. Just drive."

"Yes ma'am."

They heard the first deep bellow of the huge container ship's horn. Someone on her bridge had apparently spotted them and must have recognized their collision course. Not that the big ship had anything to worry about; the launch's aluminum hull would smash against the great ship's iron side without even leaving a dent. But then there would be wreckage to recover and survivors to fish out, and that would involve a costly break in schedule—and so the bellow of the horn came in repeating blasts, warning the smaller boat away.

Donovan aimed for a point just ahead of the ship's bow. There were only a hundred yards left between them, and the two vessels were closing fast. He suddenly realized that he had misjudged the ship's speed—the container ship was approaching faster than he'd estimated. If he failed to reach the ship before it crossed his path, he'd have to veer left and travel four hundred yards down her starboard side, and that was a chance he didn't want to take. If the *Divine Wind* did go off, it would be bad enough to be caught in open sea—but trapped against the container ship's iron hull, they would be smashed like a bug on a windshield. He steered farther to the right, trying to increase the clearance—and now they really were on a collision course.

And now the ship's horn was a constant thundering roar.

"We're not going to make it!" Macy shouted.

"We'll make it."

"Turn left!"

"Too late."

The ship was on top of them now. Her massive prow sliced down on them like the blade of a guillotine. The bow of the launch just managed to squeeze past.

The rest of the boat did not.

CHAPTER SIXTY-TWO

LI FOUND MATSUSHITA IN the far corner of the cargo hold, squatting in the darkness by the ship's hull, staring up forlornly at the tall stacks of pallets. A stream of white granules slowly trickled from the side of the pallet directly in front of him, forming a cone-shaped mound on the floor. There was a vertical gash through the plastic wrapping, and the side of each brown sack had been ripped apart. At the old man's feet was something that looked like a crowbar.

"There you are," Li said. "I've been looking for you."

Matsushita made no reply.

Li turned and squatted beside him. He stared up at the endless towering stacks, then down at the single vandalized pallet. "You have a ways to go," he said.

Matsushita stared directly ahead. "What do you want?"

"Have you ever read the book of Job? It's one of the oldest books in the world. Job was in anguish over the loss of everything he held dear, and three of his friends came to comfort him. They sat down on the ground with him for seven days and seven nights, and no one spoke a word to him, for they saw that his pain was very great. Later, they started offering advice and got into all sorts of trouble—but I think their original intention was quite admirable."

"What do you want?" he asked again.

"I offered you my forgiveness," Li said. "I suppose I wanted to know if that meant anything to you at all."

"Go away," he said. "I owe you no apology."

"You know, when you tipped that shell over and released those fleas of yours, you sentenced me to a rather gruesome death."

"I will die too."

"Is that supposed to be a consolation?"

"You interfered with my mission."

"And I suppose this is the price I pay for fulfilling mine. Fair enough, then—my life for your mission. But what about my wife? What about Jin?"

Matsushita sneered. "She was Chinese."

"I find it hard to believe that a man of your intelligence could so quickly descend to ethnic bigotry. But I suppose I shouldn't be surprised; even a demon can be well educated."

"She was one woman," Matsushita said. "Thousands died for a greater cause."

"Your sister died for someone's greater cause. Is that satisfying to you? I know you find this hard to accept, but your purebred sister and my mongrel wife were sisters of a sort: Either they both deserved to die, or they both deserved to live. You can't have it both ways."

"Go away!" he said. "Leave me to die in peace."

"That's exactly what I'm hoping to do," Li said. "You know, I've had only two dreams in my life: One was to become a doctor, and the other was to become a missionary to my people. I wanted to help heal bodies and save souls—nothing more. You took the first dream away from me—I never became a doctor. I thought you ended my second dream as well—but it's just now occurred to me that I did become a missionary of sorts. I am a missionary to a single man—*you.* I now understand that the Lord has sent me halfway around the world in pursuit of your soul—so great is His love even for you."

Li reached around behind his back and pulled Donovan's handgun from his belt. "I must say, I feel rather dashing carrying this. My friend left it behind, you see, and I've appropriated it." He turned the gun in his hands, examining it. "Now let's see. I've never been very good with these things." He pulled back on the slide a little and found a bullet ready in the chamber. He turned the gun over; he pushed a small lever on the bottom of the handle, and the clip ejected. He rose and stepped up to the pallets; he tossed the clip into a space between two of them, and it disappeared into the darkness. Then he turned and extended the gun to Matsushita.

"This is for you," he said. "Please, take it."

Matsushita slowly stood up, glaring at him. "What is this?"

"This is your salvation—or your damnation. The choice is up to you."

He placed the gun in Matsushita's hand.

"You stand before me an angry, bitter, resentful man," Li said. "Your mission is unfulfilled, and your sister is unavenged. You will not get your chance to repay the Americans. Your soul is still in agony, still searching for someone to lash out at for all your misery and pain. Well—here I am. I am not personally responsible for the failure of your mission, Dr. Matsushita—I wish I could claim that honor, but I cannot. I believe the powers of heaven itself have opposed you, but I represent those powers—I as much as anyone.

"And now the Lord asks you a question, the same hard question He put to me many years ago: Who is to blame for your suffering? Who is responsible for all the torture and misery of your life? I offer you one last chance to understand. Think, my friend. *Think.*"

Matsushita stared down at the gun in his hand. He began to tremble from head to foot. When he finally raised his eyes, they were still as hard as flint, seething with hatred and rage. He slowly raised the gun and leveled it at Li.

Li looked back at him with sadness. "I am so sorry for you," he said. "Sato Matsushita, may the God of all grace have mercy on your soul."

CHAPTER SIXTY-THREE

THE CONTAINER SHIP STRUCK the launch astern, splintering the deck and caving in the port-side hull like an old beer can. The big ship never flinched; it swatted the tiny boat aside like an annoying insect and continued on its way. The launch rocked hard to port and the stern pitched down; the impact of the collision threw Donovan and Macy against the wall and then to the floor. For a moment it seemed as if the ship might plow the boat right under—then the stern bobbed up again, and the boat was pushed clear of the ship's prow.

Donovan scrambled to his feet and tried the throttle. It was useless—the engines were dead. But at least they made it past the great ship's bow; at least they were behind her now.

At that instant two Tomahawk cruise missiles hissed past just ahead of the container ship, skimming six feet above the water's surface. At five hundred miles per hour, it took the missiles less than four seconds to travel the final thousand yards across the channel. They carried limited warheads, designed only to penetrate the ship's hull—but just behind that hull lay nine thousand tons of ammonium nitrate fertilizer.

They struck just above the waterline, one fore and one aft.

And then came the blast.

There was a blinding flash of light from behind the container ship. A pulverizing shock wave instantly filled the air around them, and Donovan collapsed to the floor again. It reminded him of the flash-and-bang stun grenades they used in the Marines, the kind that could turn your legs to rubber—only amplified a million times. He felt as if his bones would turn to powder and his muscles liquefy, reducing his body to a blob of quivering jelly. He thought for sure the boat would shake apart into all its component pieces and drop into the water like a bucket full of rocks.

And lying on his back on the floor, staring up through the shattered windows, he saw the container ship come crashing down.

The ship rocked so abruptly and so far to port that its hull looked like a giant black flyswatter arcing down. The hull slammed down on the boat's roof and crushed it in, jamming the boat to the side and shoving it down into the ocean until water poured over the deck and halfway up the bridge door. And Donovan wondered if the ship would continue to roll, pressing them under the water and holding them there, maybe even taking them with her to the bottom of the sea.

But an instant later the crushing stopped. There was a moment of stillness, and then the ship began to lift up and right itself again. Donovan struggled to his knees and peered through the remains of the bridge window—and right before his eyes a twenty-foot-long metal shipping container dropped out of the sky.

It caught the starboard edge of the boat, smashing down the railings and tearing the black bumper from the side. The impact pitched the bow forward, and the boat rocked like a seesaw, launching Donovan off the floor and smashing his head into the crushed-in roof. Now a second container landed in the water beside them, sending up a geyser of water like the blast of a depth charge. A hundred yards ahead, a massive chunk of the ship's white superstructure tore away and dropped into the water like a bomb, sending a five-foot wave surging in all directions. Another shipping container landed to the right—then another, and another, and then a hailstorm of metal began to rain down and dot the water for a mile all around.

Donovan spun and threw himself to the floor, crawling up and over Macy's unconscious form, uselessly shielding her body with his own.

CHAPTER SIXTY-FOUR

THE DISPATCH FLOATED SILENTLY on the now-glassy ocean. Her crumpled hull and cabin rested in exactly the same spot where her engines had ceased to function almost three days before, moving only with the drifting tides. There was nothing around her but open sea—but on the horizon, a virtual armada of naval vessels surrounded her, cutting her off from all contact with the outside world. No ship of any size or nature was allowed within that protective perimeter. Any unfortunate vessel wandering into the quarantined area would be warned once and then summarily destroyed—no questions asked; no apologies accepted.

The *Divine Wind* vanished without a trace, scattering pieces of her hull like shrapnel over a ten-mile area. In homes and businesses facing the ocean, plate-glass windows shattered over a thirty-mile stretch of the Long Island and Jersey shore. The blast was registered by university and Department of Defense seismographs all over the eastern seaboard. The greatest monetary damage was caused by the resulting wall of water that destroyed boats and piers and flooded low-lying areas up and down the coast.

Apart from the handful of passengers on the *Divine Wind*, the only loss of life was on the bridge of the ill-timed container ship, which was towed away for salvage the following day.

The genetically altered strain of bubonic plague was incinerated by the blast. The only remaining specimen lay in a small black case on the tiny broken launch—and possibly in the bloodstreams of its two passengers.

Half an hour after the blast, the first Coast Guard patrol boat approached—but Donovan waved them off. He fastened a yellow life raft to a gaff and hoisted it aloft, the age-old signal for a quarantined vessel. The authorities heeded the warning, clearing the area and forming a floating wall of iron around her. A few hours later, the patrol boat broke from the perimeter and approached again. A hundred yards away she stopped and fired a line across the launch's bow. Donovan reeled it in; attached to the opposite end was an inflatable raft loaded with provisions, supplies, and a portable radio. They made themselves as comfortable as possible. Their instructions were simple: Sit and wait.

Macy's symptoms began on the morning of the second day.

It began with a cold sweat that left her feeling feverish and weak. Her skin grew pale and tender, and she couldn't bear the slightest touch. Then came the nausea and the hours of gut-twisting vomiting and dry-retching that left her in utter exhaustion, longing only for death.

"Give me your gun," she groaned to Donovan. "I'm begging you."

"Sorry—I left it on the ship. Besides, in your current state of mind, you'd probably shoot me first."

"You've never been seasick—you don't know what it's like."

"Let me guess: not a lot of fun, right?" Donovan started to peel the plastic off an egg-salad sandwich.

She struggled to a sitting position. "If you open that in front of me, I swear I'll tear your arms off."

He handed her a bottle of water. "Better keep your fluids up," he said. "They want us to do one last blood draw in an hour."

"I thought they said we were all clear."

"They're doctors. They probably want to bill us for another appointment."

Macy looked over at the small black case resting on the floor in the corner. "I wish they'd get that thing out of here. I don't like having it around."

"They say they don't want to risk sending it over on the raft—too much chance of something going wrong. They want to wait until we're in the clear, then get the CDC to take it off the boat themselves."

He set the case on the floor in front of him and started to open it.

"What are you doing?"

"Just taking a peek."

"Nathan, leave it alone! What if you break it?"

"I jumped off the ship with it," Donovan said. "If it hasn't broken by now, it isn't going to."

Macy shook her head. "Men."

He swung open the lid and rested it on the floor. Inside the case were two glass vials filled with a clear fluid; beside them was a third, empty indentation.

"Wait a minute," he said. "These are the same two bottles that were in here before. Look—they're still sealed with wax. He lied to me—there's no sample of plague in here."

"You're sure he said there was?"

"Of course I'm sure. I said, 'I need to get a specimen of that plague,' and he said—"

He stopped.

"What?"

"He said, 'This is what you came here for.'"

Donovan stared down at the bottles for a long time. When he finally looked up at Macy again, he said quietly, "I was afraid."

"What?"

"That's why I wasn't there when Jeremy died—I was afraid."

She waited for him to continue.

"I wanted to be there," he said. "I know you don't believe me, but it's true."

"Then why weren't you?"

"I just couldn't bear it. I couldn't stand to watch him suffer and not be able to help."

"I couldn't bear it either," she said, "but I didn't have much choice."

"I know—and I'm sorry—and I'll be ashamed of that for the rest of my life."

"Where were you, Nathan? Where did you go?"

"I was working double shifts. I was responding to every late-night call; I was volunteering for every high-risk activity I could find. I was crazy—I was out of my mind. I was picking fights, I was taking stupid risks. I think I was trying to experience all the pain I could—I was trying to absorb it, to draw it all away from *him.* Does that sound nuts?"

"Yes—but very human."

He shook his head. "I've never been afraid of anything in my life—but that's because there was always something I could *do.* This time, there was nothing—and I was afraid that I just wouldn't have the strength to stand there and watch him die."

He pried each of the bottles from the foam packing and slid the case aside.

"Li said this is what I came here for—he said this is what I needed. He was right, Macy. Is it possible—do you think—could you ever find a way to forgive me?"

She took the two jars from his hands. "What exactly is this?"

"Holy water—from the well in China where Li used to meet with his wife. I thought it was some kind of biological agent—something that would rot the flesh right off you."

"We could use some powerful stuff," she said. She handed one of the jars back to Donovan.

"What's this for?"

"That one's for you," she said. "I think you need to use it on yourself."

"What about the other one?"

"I'm going to hang on to it. I need a little time to think."

He nodded. "Well, like you said—we've got plenty of time."

"Yes, Nathan—we've got plenty of time."

THE LAZARUS TRAP

DAVIS BUNN

THOMAS NELSON
Since 1798

NASHVILLE DALLAS MEXICO CITY RIO DE JANEIRO BEIJING

For Isabella

With all my love

"*A wife of noble character,*
who can find?"

Published in Nashville, Tennessee by Thomas Nelson. Thomas Nelson is a trademark of Thomas Nelson, Inc.

Thomas Nelson, Inc. titles may be purchased in bulk for educational, business, fund-raising, or sales promotional use. For information, please e-mail SpecialMarkets@ThomasNelson.com.

Publisher's Note: This novel is a work of fiction. Names, characters, places, and incidents are either products of the author's imagination or used fictitiously. All characters are fictional, and any similarity to people living or dead is purely coincidental.

Library of Congress Cataloging-in-Publication Data

Bunn, T. Davis, 1952–
The Lazarus trap / Davis Bunn.
p. cm.
ISBN 0-8499-4485-6 (trade pbk.)
1. Attempted murder—Fiction. 2. Embezzlement—Fiction.
3. Amnesia—Fiction. I. Title.
PS3552.U4718L39 2005
813'.54—dc22 2004021238

Printed in the United States of America

07 08 09 10 11 QW 5 4 3 2 1

HE DID NOT KNOW WHERE HE WAS, ONLY THAT HE WAS RETURNING from a far, dark place. The smell was the only thing he was sure of. He used it like a rope, pulling himself hand over mental hand back from the pit. There was a sharp familiarity to the smell. He knew he had been in a place before that had worn this appalling odor like a badge. In this addled moment, that knowledge was all he had.

He arrived back to a point where he could open his eyes.

He lay on a concrete floor under a cold fluorescent sun. Pain attacked with the return of sight. His head thundered. Every inch of his body cried out. His mouth felt gummed shut.

A bellowing thirst drove him to move. Testing each motion before committing, he managed to roll over. Next to him sprawled a snoring mountain of beard and leather and stink. He crawled around the other man and searched for water.

"Well, lookee here. The dead is commencing to rise."

The words were meaningless. But he knew the tone. It fitted into the blank puzzle of his brain. It connected to the smell. He spotted a sink in the corner. He used a bench that was bolted to the floor to push himself to his feet. Only when he started shuffling across the yawning distance did he realize he had no shoes.

Bending over the sink almost dislodged his skull. The faucet creaked open. He stuffed his mouth under the flow and groaned as he drank. He doused his head, then used his one remaining jacket sleeve to dry his face. The other sleeve appeared to have been torn off. Colored threads dangled over his shirt like military braid. If only he could remember the battle!

He blinked through the sheen of moisture. Two sides of the chamber were the same grey-painted concrete as the floor. The other two were floor-to-ceiling metal bars. He shared the lockup with perhaps a dozen other men. More than half were still sleeping. Two youths in shiny athletic gear argued in words that he could not piece together. Only one man, perhaps the largest in the cage, met his eye. His weather-beaten features and flat, dark gaze had once probably sparked with intelligence, but now were merely aware.

The stranger waved him over. "You come on over here and sit yourself down."

He hesitated.

"You heard me. Get yourself on over here."

He shuffled over. The stranger waited until he was seated, then turned to the youths and said, "Give the man back his shoes."

One youth responded with a curse.

"You want to get on the wrong side of me? That really what you want?"

"What are you, his mama?"

The other youth said, "No, man, it's just fresh meat. The dude's looking after his own self. Wants to get the meat all close and cozy. Ain't that right, meat?"

The man said, "I'm not asking you again."

The youth took off the soft black loafers and threw them. Hard. "Wait till your honey drifts off, meat. I'll be watching."

"Don't you listen to him. Put your shoes on."

"I'll be watching," the youth repeated. "Got me a blade with your name on it."

The man eased forward a trifle. The youth was suddenly blocked from view. "The difference between y'all and me is, I know what I'm in for. I made a mistake. Again." The giant spoke with a steady monotone. As if he'd been over this terrain a billion times. "I fell. Again."

"Like I care."

"When I fall, these days what I do is I drink. After that, I got a problem with my anger management. So you two best hush up while you still can. Otherwise I'll have to spend time on my knees for smashing you like a couple of shiny bugs."

The mountain let the silence hold a moment before turning around. "Do you know your head is bleeding?"

He reached up and touched the spot that thundered the loudest. His fingers came back red. But when he spoke, it was about what worried him the most. "I don't know who I am."

"Me, I go by Reuben." Nothing seemed to surprise this man. "I heard the cops talking about you. You were at a bar they had under surveillance. The bartender and his ladies, they had a scam going. They was slipping something in the johns' drinks and rolling them. What you want to be going in a place like that for?"

"I don't remember a thing."

"They brought you in on account of you duking it out with one of their own. Sounds like you might need some of that same anger management yourself."

"I hit a cop?"

"You tried. That's what counts. Looks like they're the ones that connected. Turn around and let me have a look at your head."

When he did not move fast enough, the man swiveled him easy as a doll. Fingers probed the wound. "They gave you a couple of good licks, that's for sure." Reuben held up fingers. "How many you see?"

"Three."

"Follow my hand. No, don't move your head. Just your eyes." The fingers went back and forth, then up and down. "I used to be an ER nurse. Which is where I got hooked the first time. That place is full of the most awesome drugs. Okay, cross your legs."

Reuben poked beneath the kneecap, making his leg bounce. Then Reuben gripped his chin and the base of his neck and swiveled the skull, still probing. "You getting dizzy?"

"No. But everything hurts."

"It ought to, after what you put your body through." Reuben dropped his hands. "Probably shoulda had a couple of stitches. But you don't seem concussed."

"But I can't remember."

"Weren't you listening? You got drugged, you took a couple of hits with the stick. You're gonna need a while to wake up."

A steel door clapped open as a guard stepped from the bulletproof viewing station across the hall. "Adams!"

"That you?"

"I told you, I don't know—"

The cop pointed straight at him. "Jeffrey Adams! Front and center!"

The black man helped him rise to his feet. "Ain't everybody gets called back from the pit, man. Question is, what are you gonna do when you find out who you are?"

WHEN THE OFFICE STAFF STARTED HUSTLING IN AT A FEW MINUTES after eight, Terrance d'Arcy was at his desk as usual. Just another Tuesday morning in downtown Orlando. Except, of course, for the seeds of mayhem he expected to watch sprout. Any minute now.

When his secretary knocked on his door and asked if he wanted anything, Terrance did not acknowledge her. She gave him ten seconds of her patented mask, then left. Terrance remained as he was, his wireless keyboard in his lap and his back to his office. The credenza behind his immaculate rosewood desk held three flat screens. One showed quotes from the European markets and early currency dealings. The second was tuned to Bloomberg News with the sound cut off. The third scrolled through his daily cascade of e-mails. Terrance saw none of it. His fingers remained locked in stillness. Waiting.

Then the middle monitor burst into sound. An hour earlier he had keyed in several words to unlock the volume. Though he had been hoping for it, still the voice hit his shock button.

"—explosion," the newscaster intoned. "Reports are sketchy at this point. But it appears that several floors of the Rockefeller Center have been destroyed. Police are refusing to rule out terrorist—"

Terrance slapped the keys to kill all three screens and bolted from his chair. He did not run down the hall. That would appear unseemly. He walked at a pace just slightly slower than a trot. He skipped the elevators and took the stairs. Only when the steel door slammed shut behind him did he bound up the three floors to the penthouse.

When Terrance entered the chairman's office, he was greeted with Jack Budrow's customary glare. The CEO detested Terrance d'Arcy. When time had come for the board to approve Terrance for the senior vice-presidency he now held, Jack had voted against him and for Terrance's corporate enemy, Val Haines. Jack suspected that Terrance had counterfeited documents and effectively stolen the promotion, as Val maintained. Terrance's admittance to Jack's inner sanctum was a constant irritant. There had been times when Terrance wished he could wind back the clock and dislodge himself from the whole affair. But today, this minute, he was delighted to be here. Positively thrilled.

Terrance d'Arcy considered himself to carry a true Englishman's heart. This despite the fact that he was only half British by blood, had lived most of his life in the U.S., and could not disengage his American twang no matter how many elocution coaches he hired. But one did what one could. Terrance's suits were staid Saville Row. His shirts were Turnbull and Asser and starched to perfection. His cufflinks were twenty-two-carat-gold Dunhills. His only other splashes of color were his reddish-gold locks, a sprinkling of freckles that women considered boyishly attractive, and a four-hundred-dollar I Zingari tie. Terrance had a polite word for everyone. Combined with his freckles and his crystal blue eyes, this was enough to charm those who did not know him well.

Jack Budrow's office encompassed almost a third of the former Dupont Building's top floor. Dupont had erected the structure in the early eighties as an investment property, back during the first faint glimmerings that Orlando might become a regional powerhouse. Dupont had been right, but too early. The rents were too high for back then, the lobby too ornate, the building too New York flash for the gentrified South. But times changed. In the ensuing quarter century, Orlando's dismal downtown had experienced an extreme makeover. Money and power and strict zoning enforcement had removed most of the dives, spruced up the remaining smaller structures, bricked the streets, and added art deco streetlamps with hanging floral arrangements. Newer high-rise centers shouted big money. Now the Dupont's atrium was too squat, the marble too dull, the chandeliers not flashy enough. The metallic pinnacles fronting the building's stepping-stone roofline were now faded by the fierce Florida sun. Insignia, Jack Budrow's company, had obtained the long-term lease for a song.

The wall opposite Jack's desk held a shoji screen of antique hand-painted silk. Behind this resided an eighty-two-inch plasma screen, the largest made. Jack used it for teleconferences and showing guests what was supposed to be an introduction to Insignia International. Terrance thought of it as a five-minute stroll down Jack Budrow's personal hall of fame. Today, however, the screen showed three talking heads on *Good Morning Orlando*. Which, for Jack Budrow, was about par for the course. *Good Morning Orlando* newsbreaks ran an ice age behind the national wire services.

Terrance walked to the desk, picked up the television's controls, and switched to Bloomberg News.

The CEO barked, "Do you mind?"

"Ease up, Jack." This from the third man in the room, Don Winslow.

"Last I checked, this was still my office. Change back the channel!"

"Ease up, I said." Don came out of his customary slouch. "You got something?"

"Listen."

"—We can now confirm that the top two floors of the Rockefeller Center building fronting Forty-Eighth Street were completely destroyed early this morning by what appears to have been a massive explosion. No report of casualties has yet come through. According to preliminary police reports, the early hour spared New York from what otherwise would have been a massive death toll, as debris rained down on sidewalks that two hours later would be jammed.

"The floors were home to Syntec Bank, an international merchant bank based on the island of Jersey. Police refuse to comment on the possibility of a terrorist attack. Adjacent buildings have been evacuated while a full search is underway . . ." The announcer touched his earpiece, then added, "We now take you live to our reporter at Rockefeller Plaza."

The rap on the door startled them all. Terrance killed the television. Budrow's secretary, a stone-faced woman of indeterminate years, opened the door. "There's a caller on line one."

Jack's voice sounded raspy from the sudden strain. "I said no interruptions."

"This one is for Mr. Winslow. The caller knew he would be in this office and insists it is urgent."

Don asked, "He give a name?"

"It is a woman, sir. All she would tell me is that you are expecting the call." The secretary was clearly displeased with having her authority breached. "She was most adamant."

Don said to Jack, "I guess I better take it."

"Put it through, Consuela. And no more interruptions."

When the door shut, Don said, "This must be Wally."

Her name was Suzanne Walton, and she was a former cop. She had been working narcotics in Baltimore and got greedy. Don had insisted they hire her as their outside security consultant. When Terrance had asked what for, Don had merely replied, *In case we ever need ourselves a hammer.*

The phone rang, and Don hit the speaker button. "Winslow."

"I been trying to reach you for an hour."

"My cell phone's doing a fritz."

The woman asked, "You heard?"

"We were just listening to Bloomberg. They're talking terrorists."

"They do that with everything these days." The woman's voice rattled like a deluge of glass shards. "It'll pass."

Terrance watched Don smile approval of her attitude. "So what now?"

"You get confirmation. I get payment."

"We'll be waiting." Don glanced at Terrance, then added, "You need anything more, you go through Terrance d'Arcy."

"Who?"

"The man who signs your paycheck." Don gave her Terrance's

cell phone number. "My dance card's about to get extremely full. When you talk to Terrance, you talk to me."

"I don't like change."

Don's tone hardened. "Deal with it."

They waited through a long moment, then the line went dead. Click and gone. Terrance shivered once more. He really had to meet that woman. See if reality lived up to the mental image and the one photo he had obtained through his sources. Wally was a tall brunette who would have been truly striking, had it not been for the scar running from her hairline to her left eyebrow. That and her dead-eyed cop's gaze. Well, former cop, actually.

Don stretched his arms over his head until his joints popped. Don Winslow was executive vice president of Insignia, a company whose revenue topped two billion dollars a year. He was a graduate of Columbia Law School and earned a high six-figure income. But the man looked like a tramp. He could take a top-line suit straight off the rack, wear it five minutes, and look like he had fed it to his three Dobermans. The only hairbrush Don owned was the fingers of his right hand. He was a tennis fanatic, a long-distance runner, a fitness freak. He possessed no waistline to speak of, boundless energy, and a total absence of moral convictions. Terrance admired him immensely.

Don asked no one in particular, "Can you *believe* this?"

Jack responded as only Jack could. "With our luck, they'd already finished their appointment and left the bank."

"No, Terrance checked that out carefully." Don wagged his fingers. "Remind the man."

"I downloaded their latest schedules at midnight. They both showed at the Syntec meeting beginning at six-thirty this morning."

"Which is a little odd, if you think about it," Don said. "Our Val does love the New York nightlife."

"They obviously wanted to get in and get out before the bank woke up."

"Astonishing," Jack Budrow mused, perhaps for the thousandth time. "I still can't believe that Val Haines was a thief."

Don gave Terrance a sideways look. "Right, Jack."

"Well, really. The man's been a trusted employee for almost seven years. Of anyone on my payroll, Val would be the last person I would ever imagine to do such a thing. It's positively astonishing."

"Astonishing," Don repeated, still watching Terrance. "Absolutely."

"And he was at it for almost three months," Terrance added. The pleasure of watching his corporate nemesis crash and burn was exquisite.

Jack Budrow shook his head. "Being so wrong about someone is unsettling."

"Tell you what I think, Jack." Don pointed with his chin at the television screen. The top of the New York building was a smoldering ruin. "Looks to me like you won't need to worry about him anymore."

A TRIO APPROACHED WITH FLAT COP EXPRESSIONS. ONE WORE A rumpled suit. The other two, a man and a woman, had gold detective badges clipped to their belts. "Jeffrey Adams, that right?" The male detective slid into the seat behind the desk. He was burly and pockmarked with eyes the color of congealed molasses. "You recognize me?"

His cop escort had led him into a bull pen of an office and manacled his wrist to a metal plate clamped to a desk's corner. His wooden chair struck his bruised body like a paddle. Across the room a phone rang and rang. "No, sorry."

"Wish I could say the same." The detective swiveled far enough around to ask the woman, "You got a Kleenex or something? The guy is leaking."

"Thank you." He accepted the tissue and applied it to his oozing temple. Mentally, he repeated his own name. Jeffrey Adams. The words meant nothing.

His one free hand lay limp in his lap. His suit pants were filthy and one knee was torn. The ringing phone sounded like a panic alarm. The absence of any knowledge was like a vacuum inside his brain. The mental void threatened to collapse his head like an empty paper bag.

"I'm Lieutenant Dangelo. This is Detective Suarez. The suit over there is Peters from the DA's office. You got any recollection of taking a swing at me? I'm asking on account of the state you were in at the time. When I restrained you, you tried to lay me out with a roundhouse. Which is why you got clipped."

"No," his partner corrected. "First you tore his jacket trying to restrain him. When he wouldn't calm down, then you clipped him."

"Mind telling me why you were in the Barron's Club last night, Mr. Adams?"

"I have no idea."

"Do you realize you could be facing felony charges for striking an officer?"

He made a procedure of inspecting the stained tissue. "It looks like I'm the one who's bleeding."

The prosecutor leaned on a desk across the narrow aisle. He wore a heavy brown suit and an expression to match the cops'. "How long have you lived in Des Moines, Mr. Adams?"

Des Moines. The name echoed through his pounding skull. "I don't remember."

"You don't know how long you have resided in your own hometown?"

"I told you. Everything is very muddled. Was I drugged?"

The prosecutor exchanged glances with the cops. "Have you been through this booking process before, Mr. Adams?"

"I assume you've pulled up my records."

"There are no outstanding charges or convictions," the woman detective said.

"Barron's is an odd place for a tourist to visit, Mr. Adams. Where did you learn about the place?" When he did not respond fast enough, the prosecutor barked, "What exactly do you recall about last night?"

Their gazes formed a pressure that shoved him with rude force. He deflected it as best he could by turning away. Midway across the bull pen, a woman wept and wrenched a handkerchief as an officer filled in a form. At another desk, a narrow-faced black man responded to a cop's questions with the flat drone of someone already claimed by a fate he loathed.

He was surrounded by other people's tragedies. The air was tainted by jaded indifference and a trace of the chemical odor from upstairs. But he was terrified of examining the space where his memory should have resided. The internal nothingness bore the metallic taste of death.

"I asked you a question, Mr. Adams."

"Look. I honestly don't remember anything about last night." He looked from one face to the other. "Or anything else."

The two detectives looked at the suit. The prosecutor shrugged. "What have we got?"

"He solicited an undercover cop," the male detective said.

"In other words, we got nothing. You know the drill. What exactly did he say? Was money mentioned?"

"He flashed a roll."

"I take that as a negative." The suit shook his head. "Unless I'm mistaken, stupidity is not a crime in this city."

"How do we know that's all it was?" The male cop upended a manila envelope on the desk. A driver's license and a gold watch tumbled out. These were followed by two bundles of cash. One was rolled up tightly and held by a rubber band. The other was in a gold money clip. "Mr. Adams, were you in Barron's to buy drugs?"

He reached over and picked up his driver's license. He had not seen a mirror. He could not even identify the photograph as belonging to his own face.

"Are you a user, Mr. Adams? Like a little snort from time to time? Somebody told you Barron's was the place to score a few rocks?"

"If I am not going to be charged, could you please release the handcuffs?"

The trio exchanged a glance. The woman leaned over and opened the manacle. An odor rose from her, a smoky, metallic scent that hinted at the night where she operated. She set the manacles on the desk and moved back. He could see it in her flat, hard gaze, the nearness of something more awful than losing his memory.

He rubbed his wrist. "Can you tell me what drug they used on me?"

"Tit for tat, Mr. Adams. Would you be willing to testify in court that you were drugged and rolled while visiting the Barron's Club on West Hundred and Eleventh?"

"If I can remember any of it."

"You don't recall being dragged outside?" The woman sounded doubtful. "I heard you protesting. You want us to believe it's all gone blank?"

Their hostile disbelief and his own empty panic were a terrible mix. His words sounded a lie in his own ears. "I don't remember a thing."

The woman snorted. "You believe this guy?"

"This is going nowhere," the suit agreed.

The male detective said, "Mr. Adams, we probably saved your life last night. All we're asking in return is help in prosecuting your attackers." The detective's chair creaked as he turned to the prosecutor. "I still say we should press charges."

The suit replied, "You got none to press. One look at that guy's head, and his attorney would be screaming foul all the way to settlement."

The male detective said, "I didn't see any wrongdoing on the part of any police officer. Did you?"

The female detective smirked. "I don't remember."

The prosecutor asked, "Mr. Adams, how much longer do you plan to remain in New York?"

"I'm not sure. A few days." Until he remembered where he lived. And what he would be going back to.

"Where are you staying? Or do you not remember that either?"

When he did not reply, the suit rose from the desk. "I'm out of here."

The woman leaned forward and said, "Mr. Adams, a word to the wise. If you want company, have your concierge arrange it. The Barron's neighborhood might like to claim it's stylin' these days. But the area between Morningside Heights and Harlem is still high risk." She pointed at the two wads of cash. "We have a name for people who carry this much money and a Cartier tank watch into the Upper West Side at one in the morning. We call them dead."

"Would you tell me what drug they used—"

"You come back when you feel like providing information we can use to prosecute your attackers, Mr. Adams, and we'll be happy to help."

"But I'm telling—"

"The door's behind you, Mr. Adams. Have a nice day."

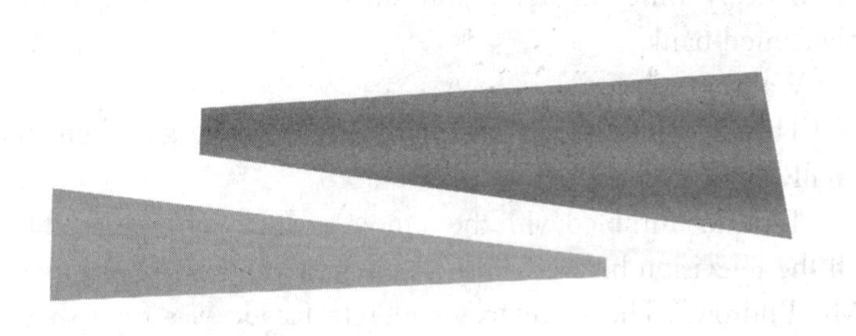

THEY REMAINED LOCKED INSIDE THE CHAIRMAN'S OFFICE. TERRANCE stationed himself on the suede sofa with the silver-plated arms, using the remote to switch back and forth among the wire channels' televised broadcasts. He kept the sound turned down to a low murmur. There was no need for outsiders to know what occupied every shred of their concentration. Jack Budrow made no further objection to Terrance's holding on to the control. The CEO slipped into a glowering silence so complete he did not seem to notice Terrance at all. Which was not altogether a bad thing. Don remained where he was, pretzeled into a visitor's swivel chair.

Waiting.

The morning stretched out over several eons. None of them made any move to return to their offices. They had no interest in showing themselves and being drawn into the normal office routine. The chance of getting real work done was nil.

Waiting.

If Terrance had scripted the moment in advance, he would have seen himself pacing. All his computers would be busy with search missions. Don would have gone out for a ten-mile run. Jack would be wounding some hapless office prey with his acidic bluster. But none of that happened. They hunkered down. They did not speak. They scarcely acknowledged one another's presence. The deal had already been talked to death. They were tied together now. The implications of what they had set in motion buffeted them every time the television showed another glimpse of the blackened bank.

Waiting.

They were lunching on salads and sandwiches when notice finally arrived.

Terrance fumbled with the remote and scarcely managed to cut off the television before Consuela opened the door. "I'm very sorry, Mr. Budrow." The secretary's concrete facade was fully shattered now. "I know you said you weren't to be disturbed again. But there is something, well . . ."

"It's all right, Consuela. Come in." Jack did his part well, Terrance had to hand it to the man. He showed the proper distracted concern watching the office's stone lady come totally undone. "What on earth is the matter?"

"I'm really not . . ." Consuela gave a frantic little hand-wave. The young woman behind Consuela took that as her cue. Terrance recognized the newcomer as Val Haines's PA. She looked even more distraught than Consuela.

"Tell me what it is," Jack ordered.

"Sir, there's been an explosion," the young woman said.

Jack was instantly on his feet. As was Don. "In which factory?"

"No, sir. It's not . . ." The woman began leaking tears.

"My dear young lady." Jack moved around his desk, all fatherly concern now. "What on earth has happened? Is it your family?"

"It's Val."

"Who?"

Consuela took over. "Val Haines, sir."

"What about him?"

"He and Marjorie Copeland. They're in New York."

"I know that." He helped Val's secretary into the suede chair across from where Terrance still sat. His sandwich dangled from his right hand, napkin tucked into his shirt collar. Just another busy exec watching his world shift out of normal rotation. Jack said, "Consuela, get this young lady a glass of water."

"I'll do it." Don moved for the executive bathroom.

Jack waited until the woman had taken a sip and almost choked in the process. “Now try and give it to me straight.”

“Val and Marjorie had an early morning meeting at Syntec,” she said.

Terrance made his first contribution. “Our bank for international funds transfers.”

“Yes, sir.” Normally Val’s PA did her best to pretend Terrance was invisible. An ethereal vampire who did not register on her screen. Today she was too distraught to notice who spoke. “Syntec’s been hit by terrorists.”

“What?”

“I saw it on the news,” Consuela confirmed. “There’s been some huge explosion. Two floors of the Rockefeller Center were totally demolished early this morning.”

Now both women were crying. “I checked his calendar. Val had a meeting set up for six-thirty. Right before the bomb went off.”

“That isn’t possible.” Jack pointed a shaky finger at his desk and ordered nobody in particular, “Get on the phone. Call their hotel—”

“I’ve already done that,” Consuela replied. “Nobody answered. His cell either. Or Marjorie’s.”

Don now. “This can’t be happening.”

“It’s almost one. Val hasn’t shown up for any of his other morning appointments. The lunch they had scheduled has called twice.” She cast frantic glances at them all, pleading with them to tell her it was a dreadful mistake. “I don’t know what else to do.”

Terrance had a sudden chilling sensation of standing just beyond the gathering’s visual range. A conductor’s white baton was in his hand. He counted off the beats. One, two, three silent seconds. Okay, now. On the downbeat. Hit it.

As though on cue, Jack turned to Don Winslow and said, “What would you suggest?”

Terrance’s baton continued to count off the cadence of shock and sorrow. Don followed the silent script to perfection. His hand even shook as he raised the telephone receiver and dialed information. “I need a number for New York police. What? Oh. Right. Manhattan.”

He hesitated then, staring at Terrance as though making sure he held to the proper beat. "Missing persons, I guess . . . No." Another hesitation. Then he dropped his voice a full octave. "No. Scratch that. I think I might need to speak with Homicide."

Both women began weeping full out.

"MR. ADAMS? I'M DR. MARTINEZ. WHAT SEEMS TO BE THE PROBLEM?" The doctor was a slight lady with tired eyes, a soft voice, and a fleeting smile. "Other than the fact that your temple is bleeding."

He had spotted the walk-in clinic's address on a street sign just down from the police station entrance. The clinic was connected to an inner-city church housed in a renovated warehouse. The exteriors of both the church and the clinic were painted an orange that hurt his eyes. The clinic's waiting room held a dozen plastic chairs, a cross on one wall, and health posters on the others. The waiting room was crowded with faces that gave his wounds only a cursory inspection. He had discarded his jacket outside the police station. Other than the tear on his left knee, his remaining clothes were stained but intact. He had dozed through a two-hour wait, then awakened to the sound of someone calling a name he was still having trouble claiming as his own.

He told the doctor, "I can't remember anything."

"A lot of people would pay money to trade places with you." The examination rooms were curtained alcoves in a long, open chamber. The floor was faded linoleum. The air was stained with the odor of a strong disinfectant. From behind other curtains came soft voices. Somewhere a woman moaned.

"Have a seat on the chair there." The doctor swept the curtain around the ceiling corner and enclosed them in an off-white realm. "I don't suppose it would be proper to ask if this has happened before."

He liked that enough to smile, the first in a very bleak day. "Cute."

"I was always a sucker for puns." She slipped on gloves. "Can I have a look at your head?" Her touch was as soft as her voice.

"I wish I knew what happened," he said.

"I imagine you do." She unscrewed a bottle and dabbed a cloth. "This may sting a little."

In the distance a baby wailed. The doctor paid it no mind. She had an unshakable calm similar to the cops', but with a compassion that showed in her eyes as he related what the cops had told him. He asked, "Does that sound like any drug you know?"

"What I know, Mr. Adams, is that you have suffered multiple traumas to your system. Just a cursory examination of your head shows another spot where you have been struck hard. How old are you?"

"I have no idea."

"I'd put your age at thirty, maybe thirty-one. Young enough to heal fast." She taped a bandage over his temple, then touched a place at the back of his skull. "Does this hurt?"

"Ow. Yes."

"It's going to hurt even more, because I want to clean off this clotted blood. No, don't touch. Hold still, please." She had to tug to dislodge the blood from his hair. "You really should have a scan. But we don't have the equipment here." She probed the base of his skull, then began the same twisting, turning routine Reuben had. "Do you feel disoriented? Dizzy? Nauseous?"

"No. I was put through the same routine earlier."

"The cops let you see a doctor? Why didn't they clean you up?"

"An ER nurse was in the lockup with me. He did the finger thing and the head twist and said I didn't appear concussed."

She came around to reveal another quick smile. "Did he charge?"

"He should have." He looked down at his feet. "He saved my shoes. And maybe my life."

"What was he in for?"

"He says he got drunk."

"If we canned everybody in this place who fell off the wagon, you'd see tumbleweeds blowing down the center aisle. Have him stop by when he gets out. We're always on the lookout for good nurses." She shone a light into his eyes. "Follow the light. Good. Okay, how many fingers?"

"Three."

"Close your eyes and bring your left forefinger up and touch your nose. Now do the same with your other hand. Good. Well, I agree with your nurse's opinion. But I'd still like you to stop by the hospital and have a scan. As for the drug they slipped you, there are several options." She began making notes on a metal-backed clipboard. "My guess is GBH. That's the street name, which stands for Grievous Bodily Harm. It's a tablet derived from an anesthetic known as GHB. The user remains vaguely conscious, but loses muscle control. Behavior can often become extremely erratic, sometimes illogically violent. Which mirrors what the cops said."

"But I don't—"

"Remember. Right. Not a total surprise. I assume you were drinking alcohol?"

"The cops said I was tanked."

"Had you done any other drugs?"

"I don't . . ."

"The bar where you say this all took place has quite a reputation. You went there for some reason. There are a lot of other bars you could have gone to for a drink, Mr. Adams. Safer places closer to your hotel. I assume you're staying somewhere midtown?"

"I wish I knew."

"So what we have is a night of heavy drinking, with possibly some recreational drug use added for good measure. Then you were slipped something that brought you to the verge of unconsciousness. After which you were struck repeatedly on the head." Another swift smile. "I'm surprised you made it this far on your own steam, Mr. Adams."

"Everything hurts."

"You'll get over it. I don't want to give you anything for the pain unless you're in desperate agony. It might only slow the process of your brain ridding itself of whatever toxic mix it's struggling through already. Can you manage?"

"Maybe."

"Come back if you can't. I'll leave a note in your file saying whoever is on duty should give you a prescription for Percodan."

"Can you suggest someplace for me to stay?"

The doctor halted in the process of reopening the curtains. "Excuse me?"

"I don't know where I was booked. I need someplace to sleep."

"Wouldn't you prefer someplace south of the park?"

He found himself unable to confess just how desperate he was not to lose connection to the one face that seemed concerned about him. "I'd rather stay around here."

She drew the curtains aside in a slow sweep. "The Everest is around the corner on Lenox. It's clean and safe. Or as safe as you can get in this area."

"Thanks."

"Trauma such as you've experienced can result in a sense of severe disorientation. More than likely your memory will begin to return in a series of flashes. It could be very disconcerting. Remember what I'm saying, Mr. Adams. This is a normal part of the process. But if you have not seen any improvement within the next forty-eight hours, I want you to stop by and see me again." A final smile. "Now go get some rest."

He stopped at a men's store midway down the same block as the Everest Hotel, desperate to get out of clothes that felt glued to his frame. He dared not move enough to try anything on. He pulled items from the shelves and carried them to a Hispanic shopkeeper who watched impassively as he peeled the cash off his roll.

The shopping bag formed his only luggage as he entered the hotel. The Everest was a postwar brownstone conversion with an ancient mosaic on the lobby floor and an authentic brass railing around the check-in counter.

The desk manager was a light-heavyweight who showed no curiosity whatsoever over his battered state. "How do you want to pay for this?"

"Is cash okay?"

"Cash is always okay by me. Long as you don't mind leaving me a two-night deposit. You got some kind of ID?"

"Yes."

"The authorities, they're very big on us keeping records. Me, I'm not so worried." The clerk could have easily tossed his new guest across the room. His neck was too thick for the shirt collar to be buttoned. His shoulders formed lumpy ridges beneath his jacket collar. "Long as my guests are willing to pay for the service."

"How much extra?"

"Call it another twenty a night."

Remaining anonymous until his head straightened out sounded like a very good idea. He set another forty dollars on the counter.

The desk clerk made the bills disappear. "Enjoy your stay, Mr. Smith."

Soon as he entered the room, the bedside clock caught his eye. He stood on the frayed carpet and stared at the red numbers counting out time that was not his to claim. Somewhere there was a life ticking away without him.

He picked up the phone. The receiver felt sticky with old sweat. He pulled out his shirttail and wiped it down. He dialed the operator.

"Desk."

"How do I get an outside line?"

There was a click and a dial tone. Val dialed information, then pulled out his driver's license. He gave the state and city and name in response to the automatic prompts, wishing he did not feel like he lied with every word.

An operator came on the line. "That listing is for Des Moines?"

"Yes."

"I have several J. Adamses but no Jeffrey. Do you have a street address?"

He read off his license, "One eighteen Hawthorne Boulevard."

"One moment. I'm sorry. We have no listing for that address."

"What about under a different first name for Adams?"

"Sorry. No Adams on Hawthorne."

"There has to be. Could you please check again?"

The operator muted the line. Then, "No Adams on Hawthorne, no Jeffrey Adams at any Des Moines address."

He stared at the face on the license.

"Can I help you with another listing? Sir?"

When he remained silent, the operator hung up.

Slowly he set down the phone and slipped the license back into his pocket. His head throbbed with the compounded pressure of needing desperately to know, yet being increasingly afraid of the answers.

He took a blisteringly hot shower, then opened the door, rubbed down the glass, and spent half an hour in front of the bathroom mirror. There was a larger mirror on the wall opposite the bed. But the lightbulb in the hotel room's only lamp was yellow and weak. When he had been with Dr. Martinez in the clinic, he had absorbed a trace of her weary confidence. Now the tight coil of unease twisted and writhed in his gut.

Even with the bruises and the smudge stains beneath his eyes, he studied a strikingly handsome face. The lines were strong and clearly drawn, which made the swelling around the cut on his temple even more noticeable. His hair was a dark blond with a hint of a wave. His chin had a slight cleft and his lips were a trace overfull. His irises started as dark green around the outer edges and lightened toward the pupils. But their color was not so important. Nor did his looks hold his attention for long. The hollow void at the center of his gaze dominated everything.

This stranger's face stared back at him, blank and wounded. He put a dry bandage over his right temple. Over and over he watched his mouth form the words "Jeffrey Adams." Try as he might, he could not force himself to claim his own name.

The bed was soft as a sponge. He lay down and was instantly enveloped in cheap sheets and the odor of someone else's ashes. He rolled back and forth, trying to find a position where he was not being poked by the springs. Finally he rose and stripped the bed. He folded the bedcover and stretched it out on the floor. On that went the mattress cover, then a sheet. He lay down and covered himself with the second sheet and the blanket. An instant later he rose again, crossed the room, and turned on the bathroom light. He lay back down on his pallet. He fell asleep to the sound of television gunfire from the next room.

The dream came in stages. Before he saw anything, he smelled the odors. The air was rich with the fragrance of burgers on the grill and overripe oranges. Gradually the world came into focus. He stared up into a deep blue sky. Dappled fruit pulled ancient tree limbs down to where they almost touched a manicured lawn. To his right the sun descended behind the roof of a sprawling ranch-style house. *His* house. The dusk was intensely vivid, as though each image he examined was cut with crystal blades and set upon a backdrop of endless blue. Even the laughter he heard behind him was etched in perfect clarity. He knew he should have been able to name the people laughing and talking. Especially the woman who was laughing loudest of all.

The woman stepped into view. She was slender and taut. She wore shorts almost hidden by one of his old short-sleeve shirts starched until it hung on her like pin-striped armor. She had hair that he knew smelled of honeysuckle. And a smile that caught every fragment of the day's remaining light.

She called out. One word. She said, "Valentine!"

The next thing he knew, he was standing in the center of the drab hotel room. His chest was heaving. His legs trembled so hard he had to lean against the wall to make it to the bathroom. He washed his face, taking care to avoid the fresh bandage on his temple. Then he leaned on the bathroom sink and waited for his heart to calm down.

It had been such a happy scene. He could still hear the laughter. The woman with her lovely brown legs stood before him still, smiling at him with a special sense of ownership.

So why was his chest crimped by a tight and ancient sorrow?

He left the bathroom light on and the door fully open. He returned to bed, chased by the worst question of all.

This time, sleep was not swift in coming. The pallet was so thin he could feel the frayed carpet threads beneath his shoulder blades. The room smelled of age and dust and a multitude of worn-down visitors. His gaze measured the hard-edged shadows formed by the bathroom light. How many other hotels had he stayed in? How many other places had he thought he would never forget? What multitude of memories had he possessed, events he was certain would remain branded upon the fabric of his life?

Yet now the hunger to remember was tainted by the dream. Fading sorrow flavored his night like the prison's lingering scent. He rolled over. With his ear pressed against the pillow, he could hear a couple shouting from the floor below.

Exhaustion and pain finally carried him into a half-sleep where he argued with himself. He stood before another mirror and shouted at an indistinct face.

His sleep deepened; the dream sharpened. He looked into a mirror cracked with age, as though scarred by all the faces that had studied its depths. His awareness expanded until he saw an antechamber with a floor of broad Mexican tiles. The ceiling was ribbed with hand-painted beams. To his right, a trio of peaked wooden doors were open to a lazy summer breeze. In the mirror he saw rows of tall candles, rising like flaming steps. He knew then where he was, and what it meant.

He was in a church. He was instantly certain church had once been important. Back then, he had searched out structures like this one, where the faith of cultures and centuries was on display. He had liked the sense of standing united against the rush of uncaring time.

He knew he was dreaming, yet knew as well that this visit had actually taken place. He had come with another person. A woman. He dreaded seeing her again, even in an image he knew was just a dream. She had brought him here. She had found this church, one of the oldest in Florida, dating back to the earliest Spanish conquistadors. They had come because she had insisted on it.

The candles were placed in three metal stands that formed a U.

Seven pews rested in the center space shaped by the flickering barriers. He watched as the image in the mirror deepened and extended until the woman came into view. It was a different woman from the first dream. The sight of her crystallized the moment with the intensity of an animal's howl.

He had a sudden ability to touch every memory connected to this moment. Audrey. That was her name. Audrey d'Arcy. She had loved him with depth and passion. She had brought him to this church because she yearned to see him reconnected to a life he had given up as utterly and hopelessly lost.

Audrey sat alone in the middle pew. She was an intensely striking woman, with determined features and an intelligent strength. He knew she was also tall, such that if she rose to her feet she would stand only a few inches shorter than him. And she loved him. So much it tore her face into fragments. She had suspected from the beginning that he would refuse her love. And yet she had loved him still.

The candles burnished her copper hair, forming a halo or a crown—he could not tell which. He watched helplessly as, in the dream, he turned away, following the same course he had taken in real life. His heart keened a dirge of loss and yearning, for that had been the last time he had ever seen her.

In his dream she called to him, a one-word litany that mirrored his own remorse. She cried, "Valentine."

The shock woke him up a second time. His heart thundered and his chest heaved. The veil had been pierced with the precise agony of regret.

He rose from the pallet and stalked about the room. He pumped the stale air in and out of his chest. He strove as best he could to halt the sudden torrent of images. He was no longer asleep. But the nightmare stalked him. The memories clamored like wolves.

He beat at his temples, and one fist came away red. Still the memories tore at him. His name was not Jeffrey Adams. He felt assaulted by a storm of mystery. Why he carried an ID with someone else's name, he could not say.

He clenched his eyes shut. But the image only intensified. He stopped pacing. He no longer leaned against the wall of a dismal hotel room. Instead, he stood in an office corridor. He looked at the closed door to a corner office, and knew it should have been his. He also knew he hated the man inside so fiercely that just seeing the closed door filled him with acidic rage. He turned away, consumed by a desire for vengeance and destruction.

He opened his eyes, but the image did not go away. He saw himself moving further down the corridor. He entered another office and stared down at the desk. He looked at the name on the document awaiting his signature.

The image vanished. He stood once more in the threadbare hotel room and stared at his reflection. He could finally put a name to this face. He also knew that he wanted to know nothing more. But he was certain he had no choice.

He spoke to his reflection, greeting himself and all the mysteries yet to be revealed.

"My name is Val Haines."

BY THAT AFTERNOON, WORD HAD SPREAD ABOUT THE EXPLOSION and the missing personnel. Solemn workers clustered about the office's open-planned center. Terrance knew they were talking about Val and Marjorie. Mostly Val. Marjorie Copeland was a colorless woman with a severely disabled child. She did her work, served her time, and left. She was in it for the medical and the security. Val was something else entirely. Terrance had once heard a trio of secretaries refer to Val as Häagen-Dazs in a suit. When Val's wife had left him two years earlier, the office women had declared her legally insane. When Val's ex revealed in court that she had been having an affair with Terrance and was carrying his child, Terrance had become the office leper. The fact that Val had never fully recovered from the loss had only added to his mystery and appeal.

Terrance's secretary knocked on the door and announced, "Don Winslow called to say the guests have arrived and you should stop by his office."

"Tell him I'm on my way up." Through the interior glass wall he spied Val's secretary weeping on a young man's shoulder. Val had a lot of friends. The young guy, a newcomer doing his stint in petty accounts, looked close to tears himself.

He opened his briefcase and extracted the folders from his office safe. They felt radioactive in his hands. He took a deep breath. He had slept only three and a half hours last night, but he felt as energized as if he had just returned from a month's holiday.

"I'll be in the boardroom if anyone needs me." Terrance noticed his secretary's red eyes. "Any word about Val?"

"Nothing."

"This really is terrible. Be sure and interrupt us the instant anything further is discovered."

Terrance headed for the elevator. When the doors closed around him, he sighed with genuine pleasure, loving the tight adrenaline gleam in his eyes.

Terrance said, "Let the show begin."

Four days earlier, Terrance's entire world had been permanently canted within the space of a few minutes.

Two, to be precise.

Friday evening, he and Don Winslow had been seated in Terrance's office. Terrance had the inside drapes open, a rarity. The floor's central arena was quiet. A couple of gofers hustled through last-minute duties. Otherwise the weekend wind-down was complete. He and Don were running through a possible timeline. As in, when they might head out into the sunset, and how. There was a nice low-key tone to their discussion. They had been through this several times before, basically just kicking ideas around. Terrance didn't mind the repetition. Talking about this stage of the game made his blood fizz.

Then Terrance's private line rang. The one that didn't go through either the main switchboard or his secretary's desk.

As soon as the voice came on the line, their evening grew far less frivolous. He knew instantly that this caller was not the sort who would take time out for idle chatter. Whatever this man had to say, it would be bad.

The caller confirmed it with his first words. "I've got some serious juice."

"Hold on." Terrance hit the mute button and looked over at Don shuffling paper like a coach going over his early-season playbook. "You know about the chap who is counsel for the SEC?"

Don glanced up. "I know we're paying a retainer to some joker who hasn't done diddly for us."

"He's about to earn his keep," Terrance said, and hit the speaker button. "Go ahead."

"What, we're into public performances here? I don't think so."

"Nonsense. I'm totally alone." Terrance hushed Don's paper rattling with a look. "I merely want to jot down some notes as we talk."

"Long as you don't jot down my name."

"Certainly not. You mentioned something about bad news?"

"Bad as it gets. Unless, of course, you're squeaky clean."

Terrance watched Don as he spoke. "Well, of course we are."

His contact announced, "The Securities and Exchange Commission is growing concerned about possible irregularities in your company's books."

Since Insignia was traded on the New York Stock Exchange, any possible illegality that implicated the senior management required a direct intervention and public inspection of their accounts.

Don huffed like a guy taking a blow to the solar plexus. This shook Terrance harder than any news the Wall Street guy might deliver.

"You say something?"

"Just clearing my throat." Terrance couldn't quite erase the tremor from his voice. "Can you perhaps give me further details?"

"What, you're saying this isn't enough? Give me a break here."

"We are indeed grateful. But details might prove crucial."

"All I know is, they're planning to make a public announcement before they pounce."

Terrance watched Don grow paler still. Making a statement at the outset of an investigation, rather than once the teams arrived and began digging, meant they were confident of finding something. "You're certain of this?"

"The confab ended an hour ago. They brought in Legal. Meaning me. From what I heard, they've got everything but the smoking gun."

Don grabbed his notebook and wrote out a single word. His papers spilled unnoticed to the floor as he jammed the page in front of Terrance's face. *When?*

Terrance struggled to keep his tone light. "I'd certainly appreciate hearing your best guesstimate as to when they'll arrive."

"Sooner rather than later. I'd say you've got until the end of this week. Four days max."

Terrance and Don silently tried to come to terms with the news. The caller finished, "You don't call, I don't answer."

"Understood," Terrance said.

But the line was already dead.

Terrance punched the button and said to his superior, "This is not good."

"Tell me about it." Don tried to rub the blood back into his features. "But at least we know more than we did five minutes ago."

Terrance pointed at Don's papers sprawled all over the carpet. "We need a minimum of four more weeks to put these plans into motion."

"There's no time for that. We've got to act now. Tonight."

"But the timing is not up to us."

"Isn't it?" Don stared at him. "You heard what your contact just said. Our train's about to hit the wall."

"We still haven't answered the most crucial question. Unless the pair we want to pin this on chooses to disappear now, they can always deny involvement."

Don Winslow had a wolf's face. Everything drew back from a fleshy predator's nose. Big bony growths encircled eyes that glowed almost golden, holding a fierce life and no compunctions whatsoever. Don Winslow was as close to a true psychopath as Terrance had ever known. Terrance envied Don's utter lack of remorse and coolness under the strain of wrongdoing. Like now.

Don replied, "That's the first dumb comment I've ever heard you make."

"But—"

"Pay attention, hoss. Either we clean up our tracks and get ready to show the world three pairs of lily-white hands, or we're toast."

Terrance knew Don wanted him to say the words for them both. The chasm yawned there before him. He remained mute.

Finally Don said it. "They've had their chance to disappear. Now we'll just have to make it happen."

Terrance found it odd, how it seemed as though they had always been headed in this direction. From the very beginning. "How?"

"You find out their movements for the next few days. We need them together and away from here." Don stooped and gathered his papers. "Don't we have the auditors and outside counsel coming in?"

"In four days. It's their periodic review."

"Well, at least that's in our favor."

"What do you have in mind?"

"You just be ready. We're going to war. That's all you need to know."

Upstairs, Don appeared his normal rumpled self. It was hard to tell whether the man's frenetic force was new and genuine, or just an uncovering of his constant interior state. Don said, "Quarter past three, and this day already feels two years old." He pointed at the ceiling. "Our man Jack has needed some major help staying sold on the idea."

"Tad late to be altering course."

"He knows that. Which only makes his grousing worse."

The phone buzzed. Don hit the speaker. His secretary announced, "Your guests are in the boardroom."

"Tell Jack five minutes." Don cut the connection and went on, "Been on the horn twice more with New York's finest."

"What did they want?"

"About what you'd expect. Have we heard from either of the missing employees, what were they doing so early at the bank." Don held out his hand. "One of those files for me?"

"Yes."

He leafed through the pages. "We have any unfinished business?"

"No. None."

"Ready to face the hired guns?"

"Anytime."

He smiled at Terrance with all but his eyes. "As of this morning, how much do we look to clear on this?"

Terrance held the door for his boss. "Why don't we go upstairs and share that bit of news with our guests?"

The boardroom had the powder-keg scent of coming tempests. Whatever lighthearted chatter the five men and two women might have brought in with them, Jack Budrow had successfully choked off. His pallid features and clenched jaw shrieked calamity. The company chairman gripped the arms of his chair so hard that his knuckles looked carved from chalk. "You're late."

"Sorry, Jack." Don nodded his greeting to the room and slid into his customary slouch in the nearest open chair. He waved his hand at Terrance. "You know our in-house numbers whizzo."

Terrance grimaced with all the skill of an actor entering the role of a lifetime. "Good afternoon, all."

The two external board members watched Terrance with worried gazes. Insignia's outside counsel and external auditors greeted him with subdued murmurs. Terrance could almost see the antennas searching the air for danger. And who they were going to blame.

Jack said, "You know I detest being kept waiting."

"Just going through the wreckage one last time," Don replied.

The senior attorney cleared his throat. "That, ah, does not sound good, Don."

"It isn't. Believe me. I assume you all have heard about our missing employees."

"I was just filling them in," Jack said.

"Right. We would have preferred to postpone this meeting until we know more. The day has already held enough trauma. But this can't wait." Don waved at Terrance. "Might as well go ahead and destroy their day."

"Enough histrionics. Just get on with it," Jack groused.

Terrance remained where he was, staring down the table's length to the company's chairman. Jack Budrow's grandfather had started the family business from the front porch of the family home. Back then it had been known simply as Budrow's Dairy. Jack's father had made the name change, realizing that Budrow's was too cracker to fit a company he intended to grow into an empire.

The dairies had been expanded to include beef cattle ranches. A total of fifty thousand Florida acres. Then came the orange groves and fruit-packing plants. Another twenty-seven thousand acres total. All bought at near Depression prices.

Nineteen years later, the builders started stopping by the farm.

Palm Beach was expanding west. Lake Worth was about to move from sleepy cow town into the big league. Budrow owned or controlled under long-term lease almost every available acre. Jack's dad led the builders through a merry waltz around his cow stalls. He pretended to have no interest whatsoever in selling. Finally one came up with the idea of not buying the property outright, but rather taking Budrow on as minority partner. Which was what Budrow had been after all along.

One development led to another. On and on, each one richer than the next. The state tried to condemn other parcels for building the Florida Turnpike and the Bee-Line Expressway. Budrow hired an army of lawyers and held out for a minor fortune.

Then the mouse kingdom came calling. Overnight, Budrow's fortune was multiplied tenfold.

The old man remained in feisty control right into his nineties. Finally a massive heart attack felled Jack's father one midsummer dawn as he stooped over his cane, supervising the milking operations on his family homestead. A man with a personal fortune of almost half a billion dollars, coming to rest in a pile of dirty hay. The local press had a field day.

At the age of sixty-three, a bitter and impatient Jack Budrow had finally inherited full control. Despite Jack's best efforts, however, he could not fill his old man's shoes. He tried. Time and again he tried. But the massive South American ranches he invested in never panned out. The Patagonians might herd good beef, but they proved even better at milking empty promises. Whenever Jack or one of his minions flew down, they were handled like royalty, flown about on a company chopper while the locals painted visions of vast holdings and untold wealth. Just a little more time and money, they repeatedly promised, and the half-million acre spread would finally start turning a profit. But Insignia's gold just kept sliding into a bottomless pit. When the board finally revolted and forced a sale of the interlinked ranches, Insignia retrieved one and two-thirds cents on the dollar.

In concept, Jack Budrow's other business projects made sense. But his move from minority investor into full-on owner of Florida hotels could not have been worse timed. The terrorist strike and subsequent slide in Florida tourism hit hard.

But bad business decisions were only part of the problem. Jack Budrow remained in his father's shadow long after the old man rested in his grave. He was nervous and defensive. He hated to be told he was wrong. He found slight everywhere.

He also loved to spend.

Jack Budrow's first act as CEO was to turn half of Insignia's top floor into his own private fiefdom. The renovations cost Insignia almost nine million dollars. Insignia now had two private jets, an executive dining room that was staffed eighteen hours a day, a box at TD Waterhouse stadium, a box at Daytona, and another for the Buccaneers' home games. The outside shareholders might be screaming in protest, but Jack Budrow personally controlled over half the company's voting stock. Those who were close to Jack came to believe that the CEO took little pleasure in his lavish lifestyle. Jack Budrow spent to show the world who was king.

A couple more bad judgment calls, a few more real-estate deals that went south, and suddenly Jack Budrow was gasping for financial breath. Without his power cushion, life was proving a terribly rough ride.

It was Terrance who had discovered that Jack was using company accounts as his private source of funds. Some people might think a man earning a seven-figure salary and sitting on several hundred thousand shares would not require additional funds. But Jack could outspend the Pentagon.

Terrance had shown the good sense to come to Don Winslow. Already he and Don had been building a rapport of shared avarice.

Don had instantly agreed with Terrance that this was the venom they needed. Two days later, Don Winslow had walked into Jack's office and gently sunk in his fangs.

Don had gone to Jack with not an ultimatum but an offer. Look at these minor misdeeds, see the danger you're putting yourself into? The feds would love to nail you for things that five years ago would have cost you a slap on the hand. You know as well as I do how the atmosphere's changed. They'll nail your hide to the wall. We're talking twenty years, Jack. Which at your age is tantamount to life. Is that what you want?

Don accepted Jack's sweaty panic as all the answer he needed. Then he laid out the plan he and Terrance had cooked up. A way for Jack to gain so much money that not even Jack could run through it easily. Or so Don had claimed.

Which had led them to the day's events.

Terrance walked around the room, setting down his files with the solemnity of a mortician.

Don and Terrance played tag-team, laying it out. The seven visitors grew increasingly ashen. Jack Budrow did not speak at all.

Two and a half hours later, the company's outside counsel placed the call over the speaker phone. He was put straight through to the chief of the SEC's investigatory arm, an old golfing buddy. The SEC chief greeted him with, "I'm on my way out the door. I'm due at a reception the governor is hosting for—"

"You're going to be late," the attorney ordered.

Don and Terrance listened as the attorney put the news in perfect legalese, how an in-house investigation had revealed that two executives, Val Haines and an associate in the pension funds division, had embezzled funds. How the company's pension funds both in the U.S. and Great Britain had been systematically stripped bare. How yesterday evening Don and Terrance had finally uncovered both hard evidence of the theft, and the scheme's outside partner.

"You got a name?"

"The New York corporate account manager at Syntec Bank."

The intake of breath was audible. "You can't be serious."

"Our two employees were apparently lost in the bomb blast. Since their disappearance this morning, we have been searching the pair's private files and confirmed they were indeed the perpetrators."

"You're telling me the two guys you lost—"

"Actually, it was one man and one woman, a Ms. Marjorie Copeland."

"Whatever. These two and a bank exec got themselves blown up so totally they can't even identify how many other bodies might be in there, and these are your culprits?"

"That is correct."

"Have you notified the authorities?"

"As I said, we are just now working through the ramifications of what we have discovered. You are the first person outside this room who is privy to the discovery."

"So it wasn't terrorists. Who planted the bomb, I mean."

"That's our reading as well."

"If the bank exec was culpable, as you say, he might have been scamming other corporate clients."

"That's a distinct possibility."

There was another pause. Terrance could almost hear the mental gears grinding in the Wall Street office. After all, this call was from a company they were preparing to investigate. The SEC man's tone grew harder. "There will be a formal complaint lodged about your attempt to keep this from the authorities."

"On the contrary." Their counsel was subdued, but equally firm. "No such attempt has been made. We are the ones bringing this matter to the SEC's attention."

"Only after the perpetrators have vanished."

"Only after they have been *identified*," the counsel corrected. "We could not discuss it prior to being certain who they were for risk of having the real perpetrators take notice and flee."

The SEC chief mulled that over. "All right," he sighed. "Let me have the bad news. How much are we talking about?"

It was the counsel's turn to take a very shaky breath. "It appears that there were two schemes, one relatively small and another that is, well, somewhat larger. We are uncertain that we have uncovered everything. We think so, but—"

"Ballpark figure."

The counsel shuffled through the file's papers, dragging out the moment.

"I'm waiting."

"Somewhere in the vicinity of $422 million."

The SEC guy groaned. "How much can you recover?"

The counsel looked at Jack Budrow. Terrance also risked a glance. The CEO was greyer than the counsel. Jack was apparently realizing just what this would mean, having such funds stolen under his watch. The board would search out a sacrificial lamb. Why not the founder's son, the exec most of them had come to loathe?

"I'm waiting," the SEC guys said. "How much is traceable?"

The counsel cleared his throat. But the obstruction was not dislodged. "None of it."

"What?"

"As I stated, all of the funds were channeled through the Syntec Investment Bank."

"And?"

"The bank is *gone*. Their entire records department was shredded by the explosion."

The SEC chief was shouting now. "What about backup!"

"That too. We have spoken at length with the Jersey head office. This was a quasi-independent arm." The counsel was visibly sweating. "Syntec operated like many small banks. Their home office maintained no detailed duplication—"

"A full investigatory team will be arriving on your doorstep tomorrow morning!" His rage had a scalding effect. "Heads are going to roll!"

Terrance stood in the boardroom doorway, watching Consuela usher out their guests. The auditors and outside counsel clustered like an anxious flock by the elevators. Their faces wore uniform expressions of sickly dread. They knew the score. A hit this big would strike their careers with the effect of wrecking balls.

"Shut the door, will you?" Don's attention was focused on Jack Budrow. The CEO had his head in his hands.

When the three of them were alone, Don walked to the front of the boardroom table and bent over. "Think, Jack."

"It's all I can do."

Don held his fingers a fraction apart and said, "We are *this* close to being rich for the rest of our lives. And we are *this* close to losing everything. Including our freedom."

Jack straightened. "Yes. All right. I see."

"You sure, Jack?"

"Yes. Yes, I understand."

"Good." Don straightened slowly, watching the CEO very carefully. "You've got to pull your weight from now on. Terrance and I are looking at dance cards that are full to the brim."

Jack nodded once, his pallor easing. "So what should I do?"

"You have contacts at the *Wall Street Journal*, right?"

"Of course. I partnered with the vice-chairman at last year's Bermuda golf tournament."

"Swell. Call the guy. Give it to him just like we've done with the SEC." Don's gaze was jury-taut. "Can you remember your lines, Jack?"

"Certainly."

"He'll most likely hear you out, then have a reporter join him and tape a second round. They'll listen to that tape about a hundred thousand times. If you leave a thread dangling, they'll pull it and they'll unravel it and they'll hang us with it." Don inspected their chairman. "Maybe we better let Terrance make the call."

"No." Jack Budrow rose to his feet. "I'll do it."

"Do it right, then."

Jack was at the door leading from the boardroom to the trophy hall and his office when he quietly observed, "I see the torch has already passed from my hands."

VAL HAINES ATE AT A NEARBY DINER. THE SUNSET WAS SHROUDED by city shadows and the diner's grimy front window. He sat on a stool at the counter, one of a dozen faces staring at nothing. He kept his gaze aimed at the *Times* laid out on the counter beside his plate. He forked the food into his mouth and tasted nothing. His actions were a calm lie. His mind remained as frenetic as the traffic racing beyond the diner's window.

Another memory had assaulted him just as his meal had arrived. In this one, he held a sleeping infant. The most beautiful baby girl in all the universe rested on his shoulder. Her breath came in tiny puffs he could feel on the nape of his neck. One hand grasped his finger. Val pulled out the hand far enough to look at the perfectly formed little fingers and even tinier nails. Her beauty was so complete he wanted to weep. Like all the other memory pulses, this one arrived with a ton of baggage.

It was the only time Val had ever held his child.

"You need anything else there, hon?"

"What?" Val jerked up. The waitress stood with one hand cocked upon her hip, the other holding a smoldering pot. "Oh. No, thank you. Just the check."

"Sure, hon." She set down her pot and scribbled on her pad. "Everything all right?"

Val pushed away the paper he had not really seen. The waitress observed him with the dull concern of one not able to offer anything to anybody. He dropped bills he could not see onto the counter and said, “Memories are a terrible thing.”

The soft edges of another dusk gradually vanished, joining all the other pasts lost to him. He walked a street of New York nighttime energy. People hurried past and refused to meet his eye. Traffic shoved and blared. Vendors shouted back. Val turned away from his hotel, not headed anywhere in particular. Just walking. Caught up in the pressure of other people’s lives.

Val was no longer certain how much he wanted to know. Uncertainty over what might strike next made his past feel very distant. He stopped before a shopfront window and stared at the stranger captured by the night. Maybe this was why he had gone into that bar in the first place. Just looking for a little distance.

Then he realized what he was looking at.

Val pushed through the door and entered the cyber café. It was empty save for the woman behind the counter. The woman had pink hair, two nose rings, and a wary gaze. The two side walls were segmented into semiprivate spaces, with scarred desks holding keyboards and flat-screen monitors. Hip-hop blared. Val approached her. “Can I use a terminal?”

“Why we’re here. You want anything to drink?”

“Coffee. Black.”

“I need a deposit. You got some plastic?”

“No. I left it . . .” He waved away the lie. “How about a twenty?”

“Works for me.” She rang it up and pointed him midway up the left-hand wall. “Take number three.”

The chair wobbled. The keyboard was filmed with other people’s stress. But that was not why Val sat and stared at the monitor. He knew the computer was part of his former life. He based that on no specific memory, just an awareness that here before him was something vital. The question was, how much more did he want to discover? How much more could he take?

The woman called over, “That thing not working again?”

"No. No, it's fine." He sat and sipped his coffee. Passing headlights etched his silhouette into the monitor's surface.

The woman said loud enough to be heard over the hip-hop, "I got to charge you long as you're tying up the computer, whether you're using it or not."

Val waved without looking over. He sipped his coffee. He set down his cup and pulled out the two wads of cash, one from either pocket. Using the desk as cover, he counted it out. The money clip held eight hundred and sixty dollars. The roll bound by rubber bands was tight as a fist and held another fifty-four hundred-dollar bills. Six thousand two hundred and eighty dollars. What kind of person carried that much cash around with him for a night on the town?

He slipped the money back into his pockets. Everything he knew about himself suggested that he was not happy. A happy man did not go into the sort of bar where he would be drugged and arrested. A happy man did not rely on a false ID to mask whatever it was Val had been doing two nights back. So far his returning memories had been hazardous as grenades.

The young woman left her security behind the bar and walked over. "More coffee?"

He looked up. If he could ignore hair the color of cotton candy and the nose jewelry, she was actually very attractive, in a knowing New York sort of way. "No thanks. I'm good."

She stared at the blank screen. "Everything okay here?"

"Yes." He could tell she was making herself available. The smile was there in her eyes, just waiting for an excuse to break out. Was this part of what he didn't remember, a way with strange ladies? "I'm just trying to work up the nerve."

She wanted to ask more, but something in his face kept her silent. She picked up his cup and retreated.

Val pulled the keyboard closer. He had to know. He drew up the Google search engine and typed in two words: Valentine Haines. He put his name in quotes, so the engine would treat it as a single concept and not flood him with offers for romantic getaways. Then he hit Search.

The retrieval didn't take long.

Recovery from the shock, however, did.

Val realized the young woman had returned and spoken to him. He stared up at her. "Excuse me?"

"I was just wondering . . ." She seemed uncertain whether to stay or flee. "You went all white there."

He turned back to the screen. The blue headline across the top of the screen screamed so loudly at him he could no longer even hear the music.

"Right. Sure. Whatever." She went back to the counter.

Val clenched and unclenched his hand. He gripped the mouse and slid the pointer over to rest upon the first blue line. The arrow became stuck on the headline's last word.

Dead.

TERRANCE HAD PURPOSEFULLY KEPT THE AFTERNOON AND evening clear, a rarity. He normally liked to surround himself with chattering faces. He found wry pleasure in observing the human zoo at feeding time. Terrance considered himself a species apart. All proper Brits did, in his opinion, whether they admitted it or not. Attitude and power went hand in glove. The British Empire had not been lost to armies but rather to a generation lacking the will to rule. His own father was the perfect example of modern British spinelessness.

Though the sky was fiery with a patented Florida sunset, Terrance kept the top up. He wanted neither to see nor be seen. His Lexus sportster bored a hole through the violet dusk like a polished bullet, seeking only the target ahead.

His home was a palace of creamy brick set on the ninth tee at Isleworth. It had originally been built for an Orlando Magic star forward, who had been traded to Los Angeles just as the contractor was polishing the granite master bath. The property was actually two houses connected by an ornate indoor-outdoor pool. Apparently the Magic player had wanted his entourage close at hand, but not actually sharing his home. Terrance parked the Lexus beside his weekend toy, a classic Mercedes gull wing he had bought at auction after winning his latest promotion. He entered his house and listened to his footsteps echo off the atrium's forty-foot ceiling. Daily maid service left the place gleaming with a sterile air.

He lived alone, yet today he felt as though he were being observed by a thousand eyes. Terrance stripped off his jacket and tie, then opened the sliding doors leading to the pool. Steel girders supported a screened cathedral over the poolside veranda. A covered atrium contained an outdoor kitchen with built-in gas range and party-sized refrigerator. Ten imperial palms in giant wooden tubs marched down the pool's other side. A waterfall timed to come on at sunset poured musically into the Jacuzzi. Beyond the pool and the screen and his border of oleanders, a final trio of golfers raced the twilight.

As hoped, Terrance spotted lights gleaming in the guesthouse parlor. He crossed the mock Venetian bridge and knocked on the door. He heard a voice call from within and entered. "Mother?"

"Hello, darling. You're just in time." She appeared in a sweeping flow of silk and jewelry. "The hook on this bracelet is just impossible."

"Let me."

"You're a dear. How was your day?"

He pushed the catch into place. "Actually, it was rather horrid."

"Do I want to hear?"

"I'm not sure."

She turned and walked back to the second bedroom, now serving as her dressing room. "I suppose you'd best tell me."

Eleanor d'Arcy was a woman born to reign. She deserved castles and private jets and servants offering the bended knee. She should have hosted monarchs for tea. She seated herself at the Louis XIV dressing table and used the silver-backed brush to bring her hair to perfection. Terrance said, "You look lovely."

"Don't vacillate, dear. The news won't improve with age."

"No, perhaps not. You remember Val Haines?"

"That dreadful man. I had hoped never to hear his name again."

"He's dead."

"What?" She stared at him in the mirror. "How?"

"Rather odd, that. It appears he was blown up."

"Don't joke."

"That is the farthest thing from my mind, I assure you." Swiftly he related the day's events.

"Do you mean to tell me he was in the bank when the terrorists attacked?"

"They don't know that it was terrorists. And his location has not yet been confirmed. All we can say with any certainty is that neither he nor his colleague have been heard from since."

She mulled that over. "I can't say I'll be sorry to see the back of that man. No doubt you feel the same."

Terrance was too aware of the thousand eyes to respond.

"Your sister was sweet on him, I suppose you know that."

"Yes." Which added a very special flavor to the moment.

She misunderstood the gleam to his eyes. "I would prefer that you maintain proper civility with your sister."

"Of course."

But she was not fooled. "Why do you despise her so?"

"I suppose there is too much of Father in her for my taste."

His mother started to respond, then let it slide. "I am hosting a charity dinner tonight at the club."

He accepted his dismissal and turned to go. His mother had been in Orlando for only seven years. Yet already she ruled the upper tiers of what passed for the social hierarchy. She was lithe and very fit and professionally slender. Her face and neck were miracles of modern surgery. Some people took pride in aging well. Eleanor d'Arcy had no intention of giving time's passage an inch.

Returning across the bridge, Terrance was halted by a sudden realization. He had mentioned his father. He never did that. Terrance could not remember the last time he had spoken about his father. Years. To bring him up now was a serious breach. To not even notice it at the time was far worse.

Despite the evening's closeness, a chill sweat pressed from his forehead. He could afford no such slipups. He must control everything. Right down to the smallest detail. Eyes would soon be holding them under constant scrutiny.

He entered the house via the kitchen and began warming up the meal prepared by his maid. He was not the least bit hungry. He had felt no craving for food since this critical phase of their plan had begun. He ate his meal standing at the granite-topped center console. He turned the pages of the *Journal* as he forked the food into his mouth. Nothing registered, neither the food nor the news. The television in the recessed alcove above the oven was tuned to MSNBC. Twice while he ate, the bank's charred image flashed on screen. The first time he used the remote to turn up the volume. The other time he left the image silent. The television was merely background activity for the theater he was shaping. The newscasters had nothing new to report.

He finished his meal and moved to the apartment he had fashioned from the house's far end. The first room opened both to the house and the apartment's private rooms. Terrance did not turn on any lights. The rooms were horribly bare. In the dim light that followed him from the living room, Terrance was able to reshape the rooms in his mind.

Terrance had always been alone. Even as a child, Terrance had known he inhabited a solitary universe. The tight core of seclusion never altered. Nothing could reach him. Terrance could stand in the middle of a dense pack of people and remain trapped within his interior void. Only one person had ever managed to pierce his shields and enter the hidden spaces. This room had been meant for her daughter. The next was a studio apartment for the nanny. After Terrance had secretly torn her former husband apart bit by mangled bit, Val's wife had finally agreed to enter Terrance's world. Then, at the last moment and without warning, she had fled to Miami. Terrance had gone wild with rage, smashing the handcrafted nursery furniture with a ball-peen hammer.

That night, after the fury had subsided, Terrance had confessed to his mother. How the core of his being was filled with a void. How he felt born to solitude.

Eleanor had patted his cheek, a rare show of affection. "My dear darling boy," she said. "Has it taken you this long to realize?"

"Realize what?"

"Kings are not merely born to rule," his mother told him gently. "They are born to eternal isolation. It is their destiny."

Terrance made himself a drink, switched on the digital radio to a random channel, and pretended to read a book. Everything was merely theatrical moves for the hidden audience. Two hours later, his mother returned from the club. Eleanor tapped on the glass and waved him a goodnight. She did not ask if he was going to bed. Terrance had never needed much sleep.

When the guesthouse went dark, he turned off the downstairs lights and proceeded up the central stairs. He padded down the hall to his study. Across from his desk was a narrow cupboard for storing his personal tax records. The rear of the bottom shelf now contained a set of all-black running gear. He dressed in the dark. He hefted a waist kit containing a black knit cap, a penlight, a screwdriver, two keys in a manila envelope, and three sets of surgical gloves still in their sterile packs. Silently he went back downstairs and let himself out the back.

He left the house by the kitchen door. He stood by the property boundary and searched the night. When he was certain he was alone, he jogged across the golf course.

He exited the gated community by way of the golf course's maintenance entrance, which he knew from earlier reconnaissance was locked and empty after nine. The workmen's gate was easily scaled.

Don Winslow's Escalade was parked just down the highway. Don greeted him with, "Look at this traffic. You sit here long enough, the whole world goes by." Don wore a black sweatshirt with the sleeves cut off, black track pants, and black high-tops. A black headband held the graying hair out of his face. He looked like a killer ready for the night's rampage. As soon as Terrance shut his door, Don slapped the Escalade into gear. "Where are we headed?"

"Val's." Terrance did not need to think that one through. "We hit Val's first."

VAL LEFT THE INTERNET CAFÉ AND RETURNED TO THE HOTEL because he had nowhere else to go. He needed to retreat and work things out. But as he pushed through the outer doors and entered the lobby, memories buzzed about him like vultures over carrion. Retreating to his lonely room would only give them the chance to pick his bones.

The lobby was empty save for the dark-suited desk clerk. "If it ain't Mr. Smith. How we doing today?"

The lobby's only sofa was a brown as toneless as the clerk's gaze. The clock behind the clerk's head read a few minutes after midnight. Val could find no sense to the numbers. The hotel and the night had been divorced from life's natural cadence. Val took a seat and replied, "Not so good."

"Yeah? Sorry to hear that."

Val studied the ancient tiles at his feet. The hotel's name was inscribed in a mottled design almost lost to the years. The air smelled of cleanser and time distilled to a futile blend. Val sighed his way deeper into the sofa's lumpy embrace. What he needed was a way to shoot the mental vultures out of the sky before they could attack him again.

He realized the clerk was watching him and asked, "You mind if I sit here?"

"Do I mind?" The clerk showed genuine humor. "I been working this job, what, five years now. That's the first time a guest ever asked me permission."

"You're the boss here."

The clerk's reply was cut off by the ringing phone. He answered and began speaking in a low voice. But his gaze remained steady upon Val.

The Internet search had taken Val from the blue-flagged headline to an article in that morning's *Orlando Sentinel.* As soon as Val had seen the newspaper banner, he had known he was looking at his hometown. Not Des Moines. He lived in Orlando. The new memory and the newspaper article formed a heat pungent as steam rising from a lava bed. Val watched the clerk talk quietly into the phone and felt pummeled by the words he had read. According to the report, Valentine Haines and Marjorie Copeland, executives of a company called Insignia, had apparently been killed by a massive bomb blast. Terrorists were not believed to have been involved.

The blast had demolished the top two floors of a building within the Rockefeller Center complex. The floors were home to the Syntec Investment Bank. The only reason there had not been a bloodbath was that the blast had occurred at six forty-five in the morning. The bank's premises, however, had been completely destroyed.

The clerk set down the phone. His eyes remained upon Val's face, inspecting, gauging. "Looks like it's my turn to ask permission, Mr. Smith."

"What for?"

"See, there's some guys, they want to do a little business. Maybe you'd be better off heading upstairs."

The prospect of entering his solitary cell held no pleasure whatsoever. "Do I have to?"

The clerk's name tag read *Vince*. His eyes flickered through an instant's change, something that might have been humor. "There you go, asking me what I never heard before. Do you have to? That ain't the question. The question is, are you trouble?"

"Not for you. Definitely not." Val waved in the direction of the stairs. "I just don't . . ."

A pair of young men pushed through the outer doors. They crowded the lobby with uptown swagger and noise. The atmosphere palpably condensed. One of the men was rail-thin, dressed in a vest and no shirt, with a thick gold chain bouncing on his chest as he walked. "Man, this is some place, right, Jamie?"

"Sure." His partner was thicker in every possible dimension. He wore an off-white sweater and cotton boat pants. But his swagger was the same, as were the wraparound shades. "It's something, all right."

The thin man stalked to the counter. "Hey, Vince, my man."

"Long time, Arnold."

The desk clerk's tone stopped the slender man just as he was reaching out to shake hands. Arnold kept his hand moving up and swept off his sunglasses. "Jamie, meet Vince. As in, the man you need to know."

"Vince."

The desk clerk nodded once. Val felt as if he had aged into one of the old men normally dressing up the lobby. Pretending that by watching somebody else live the moment he could lay claim to a life himself.

Arnold went on, "I was just telling my buddy how midtown is moving into Harlem. The prices they're asking up here these days, it's unreal." He did a nervous feint in front of the counter. "A guy wants to do business, uptown is the place to come. Give you a for instance. How much you got out these days, Vince?"

The desk clerk scowled. "What kind of question is that?"

"Hey, we're all friends here."

"Correction. You I know." Vince turned to face the stockier man. "You can't be too careful these days. You got undercover cops dressed seriously street, looking to do business."

"I'm telling you, Jamie's a friend."

"That's not the issue here. Are you telling me you vouch for this guy?"

The dance grew more nervous still. "'Course I do. Why else would I bring him in here?"

"Stop this two-step you're doing and look me in the eye. I asked you a simple question. Do you or do you not vouch for this man I don't know?"

Arnold grew utterly still. Even time seemed trapped in the amber force of Vince's gaze. "Yeah, sure. I vouch for him."

"All right, then." Vince offered his hand. "Jamie, good to meet you."

"Likewise."

"Do me a favor. Lose the shades. I'm talking business, I like to look a guy in the eyes."

"No problem." Jamie used his sunglasses to point toward Val. "Who's the stiff?"

Vince's gaze shifted and drilled Val where he sat. A measuring instant, then gone. "Nobody. He's cool."

Val resisted the urge to probe his chest, see if Vince's gaze had punctured a lung.

Arnold asked again, much more subdued this time. "So how much you got out, Vince?"

"Not a lot." Vince looked back at Val again, communicating something Val could not understand. "Couple hundred, round there."

"Two hundred large, you call that not much?"

"It's nothing, compared to some guys I know. Keeps me under the radar screen of the big guys."

"You hear that, Jamie? Vince don't pay nobody but Vince."

"I go much bigger, I got to sit down with the man. He'd slap me around a little for working somebody else's territory. They'd shake me down, tell me they got to get a piece of everything I do."

"They slap *you* around?" Jamie tried an ingratiating grin. "Man, they must be some kind of tough."

"They're pros is what they are. I get any bigger, I got to sit down with them. These guys, a smack in the face is cheaper than a cup of coffee, and it wakes you up a lot faster."

Arnold was grinning now too. Eager to be part of whatever was going down. "Nothing personal, right?"

"Just making sure they got my attention. Just doing business. Speaking of which." Vince made a point of looking at the wall clock. "That about does it for the chit-chat, fellows."

The two on Val's side of the counter exchanged a look. "Jamie's looking to do some business, Vince."

"Yeah?" He showed no interest whatsoever. "You two want to rent a room?"

"No, man. Not like that. Tell him, Jamie." When his friend hesitated, Arnold hurriedly added, "He's good for it, Vince. He's an expert down at the phone company. What he does, I can't even explain it. But he's making good money, I know that."

"Wait a second here. You bring in somebody I don't know, tell me he's got a straight job, but somehow he's blown everything he makes, and I'm supposed to be impressed?"

Jamie cleared his throat. "I got this problem, see. My old lady—"

Vince sliced the air with his open hand. "You can stop right there. I don't know what kind of line you spent the trip over working up, thinking you're gonna walk in here and lay it out. So let me tell you up front. Your problem, it don't mean nothing to me."

"This is for real, what I'm saying."

"Maybe it is, maybe it isn't. I don't care either way. You could be the worst gambler to ever hit Atlantic City for all I know. That's your problem. All I want to know is, can you pay what you owe?"

"I'm good, man." He was visibly sweating now.

"Yeah, Vince, he's a straight-up guy."

"Straight, curved, crooked, looped like the Jersey Turnpike, it's all the same to me." He took aim with his forefinger. But he might as well have leveled a pistol at Arnold, the way the guy flinched. "You know what you're doing, vouching for this guy?"

"He's good, I tell you."

"For your sake, he better be. You hear what I'm saying?"

"Yeah, Vince. I hear you."

"Okay, then." Vince turned to the stockier guy. "How much you need?"

Jamie sniffed and backhanded his nose. "Twenty large."

"You want to get into me for twenty thousand dollars?"

"Yeah, see—"

"No. I told you. Whatever your business is, you left it outside." Vince tapped the counter once, twice. "Okay, here's how it's gonna play. I'll give you the twenty."

"Thanks, man. You won't—"

"Just shut your mouth and pay attention. You work the phone company, so your payday's Friday, right? Don't talk, just nod your head. Okay. So every Friday for the next seven weeks you're gonna be down here with forty-three hundred cash."

Both men gaped. Jamie recovered first. "You're charging me fifty percent for seven weeks?"

"That's the rate."

"You can't be serious."

"Oh really. Let me tell you why you're here in my place of business. You know other guys on the street, they'll give you the twenty large. But then they own you. They'll keep you paying for the rest of your life, which with a lot of these guys won't be that long. They'll get all you got, then take you out. After that they'll put your old lady on the street. Tell me I'm lying."

The two men were now very pale and utterly still.

"So you come to me. And I give it to you straight. Just like you heard before you got here. The twenty will cost you ten." Vince pointed with his chin. "You don't like it, there's the door."

Jamie's voice was down to a hoarse murmur. "No, no, it's good."

"Right." Vince reached under the counter, came out with a cracked leather pouch. He unzipped it and began unpacking banded notes. "Check it out."

Arnold tried for weak levity. "Hey, Vince, if you say it's good—"

"I'm telling you to count the bills."

Jamie ruffled the notes, but from his expression it was unlikely anything really registered.

"It all there?"

Jamie nodded.

"When am I gonna see you?"

"Friday."

"Right. Good doing business with you." Vince pointed at the door. "Stop by anytime."

After the pair left, the desk clerk refused to meet Val's eye. Which meant Val could openly study the man. He was fairly certain what would happen if he told Vince about the bar and the bomb and the attacking memories. "Deal with it," the guy would say, and shrug away the trauma.

He rose to his feet, driven by a restless urge to get on with doing just that. Vince gave him a single measuring look, then went back to his records. Val crossed the lobby and pushed through the outer doors. If only he could adopt a bearing so severe and cold nothing could touch him. A Kevlar vest to shield him from the next rain of mental bullets.

Val entered the night. He was filled with a bitter envy for the clerk and his world chopped down to emotionless little squares. A life spent running under the radar. Val understood him with unique clarity.

TERRANCE AND DON DROVE TWICE AROUND VAL'S NEIGHBORHOOD, an old development overlooking the Rio Pinar golf course. The night was utterly still. Live oaks formed a canopy over the road. Most homes were sprawling ranch-style, built when property was measured by the half-acre rather than the square meter. They parked a block away, just one more SUV in a world of minivans and tricycles. Don breathed heavily as they trotted down the empty street. This was the part Terrance hated the most, being out in the open and risking it all on a sleepless neighbor. But they needed to do this themselves.

While Don scoped the night, Terrance drew the manila envelope from his pack. Forging copies of the house keys had been easy enough. Like many commercial road warriors, both Val and Marjorie had kept extra sets of house and car keys with their secretaries. The lock turned easily. They entered, shut the door, and waited. Terrance had searched Val's desk and his secretary's and come up with no alarm code. As hoped, the old place was not wired. Terrance slid on a pair of surgical gloves and pulled the flashlight from his pocket. It was just like Val to hide in some old-fashioned neighborhood and pretend he was shielded from time. Sit behind his plate-glass armor and hope the world's changes afflicted everybody but him.

Terrance did a slow sweep of the front rooms. This was the first time he had entered the enemy's lair. Val's home had the impersonal nature of a hotel. There was nothing on the walls save bare shadows where pictures had once hung. The mantel and the window recesses and the side tables were empty. The living room carpet still had deep imprints where large pieces had once stood.

Don moved up beside him and studied where the flashlight's illumination fell. "Looks like the wife pretty much cleaned him out."

Terrance shook his head. "Stefanie only took what she brought with her."

Don aimed his flashlight into Terrance's face. "So how come you two aren't an item?"

"The clock is ticking, Don."

"This is not a difficult question." Don's tight grin was illuminated by the pair of flashlights. "You won the round hands down. Knocked the other guy out of the ring. So how come you and she aren't doing the happy couple thing?"

"She needed time alone." Terrance gave the room another sweep. "Stefanie was too good for Val."

"Yeah, looks like she'd agree with you on that one."

Terrance pushed Don's light out of his eyes. "Let's get to work."

They moved into their planned routines. Don hunted for hard evidence. Terrance attacked Val's home computer. He did not have Val's personal ID code. So he wiped clean all files dating from the past six months. Terrance did not need to know what Val had. He simply had to be certain nothing except the evidence he had planted would show up when the official investigation opened. Evidence that showed how Val Haines and Marjorie Copeland had stolen more than four hundred million dollars from Insignia's coffers.

Midway through his work, Don appeared in the doorway. "I think I found something."

Terrance followed Don back through the house. A narrow hallway opened at the rear of the kitchen, led them past the laundry room and into the double garage. One half was empty, Val's car no doubt still in the airport parking lot. The other half was a mess of woodworking equipment. Terrance steadied his flashlight on a half-finished cabinet. The work was good.

"Over here."

Don had shifted a long trestle table doing duty as a workbench.

Thumbtacked to the wall was a world map. Terrance's flashlight picked up a number of underlined locales—Tahiti, Kuala Lumpur, Costa Rica, Java, New Zealand, Cape Town. With the table out of the way, a set of floor-to-ceiling doors to a recessed cabinet came into view. The doors were padlocked shut.

"Help me move this map." When that was done, Don gripped a set of heavy-duty shears and took a bite on the padlock. He grunted with effort and squeezed the handles shut. The padlock finally gave and rattled against the concrete floor.

Don twisted the handle, then gave a shout of alarm and jumped back. Books and boxes tumbled out, so tightly packed in the tall cupboard they might as well have been spring-loaded.

The two flashlights played over the pile. Don shoved an album of wedding photos with his shoe and said to no one in particular, "Do you believe this?"

Upended boxes revealed mementoes of a lost life. Dozens of music CDs spilled over a cedar chest of wedding silver. Dusty frames held the frozen lies of once happy faces. Terrance stared down at Stefanie laughing beside his enemy. His gut churned at the sight of her happy with the wrong man. "We can't leave it like this."

"It'd take us days to cram it all back inside." Don began cramming stuffed toys into the nearest box. "Stack the books that fit on that empty shelf."

The books were a mixture of marriage counseling, Bibles, and crisis resolution. By the time they were finished and the map repinned to the wall and the table moved back into place, both men were breathing hard.

Don stepped back, surveyed the blank space, and asked, "What happened to this guy?"

Terrance went back to Val's office.

When he was finished with the computer, Terrance opened the rear French doors in the living room. He stood listening to the night. The overcast sky was illuminated an orangish yellow by the city's false dawn. A rising wind blew in from the south. The palms rattled like angry observers, irritated by his calm. Terrance wondered if this was how triumph was supposed to feel. Like a barrier had been erected between himself and all of life. Perhaps this was why warriors of old paraded through the streets and danced around mammoth fires. They sought to create externally what they should have felt inside.

"Val doesn't even have a safe." Don came in with a trash bag full of papers. "All the interesting stuff was in a shoe box on the closet's top shelf. Have a look at this."

Terrance turned his flashlight onto the paper in Don's hands. "A false birth certificate?"

"Unless he's done a name change and forgot to tell us." Don shook his head. "He'd use the birth certificate to apply for a passport, right? Looks like our guy was getting ready to fly."

Terrance read the name on the birth certificate. "Jeffrey Adams."

Don shone his flashlight down on the photograph dangling from Terrance's hand. The picture was of a laughing infant, held by an adult excluded from the frame. "That Val's kid?"

Terrance stared out at the night and declared, "Mine. The child is mine."

Saying it often enough almost made it so.

THE NIGHT ACTED AS AN AMPLIFIER TO THE STREET'S ENERGY. Everything outside Val's hotel was louder, faster, harsher. He walked back the three blocks to the cyber café. Cars cruised the avenue, their salsa rock and hip-hop punching the air with pneumatic fists. Val was just another solitary guy walking the concrete in search of his fix. Just another mark.

Val reentered the café. A spiky-haired youth with spiderwebs tattooed on both forearms had replaced the young woman. The guy accepted Val's deposit and directed him to a computer without seeing him at all.

Val went to the Yahoo.com Web site. The screen address had come back to him while he had been seated in the hotel lobby. Just another shard of memory, another fleck of another guy's past. Val punched the button for e-mail retrieval, then typed in his screen name and password.

A long sweep of e-mails filled the screen. Val went through them carefully. The names and the messages formed imperfect mental fragments. Some e-mails asked him to get in touch with them if he was able. Most held the formal air of concerned business colleagues. After reading each one, Val hit the "keep as new" tab, so there would be no record of his having stopped by for a read. What he found there revealed no reason to go back.

Then a screen name leapt out at him. She used her own name, of course. Audrey d'Arcy. A very direct woman, surrounded in Val's mind by candlelight and sorrow of his own making.

Val hit the key to open her e-mail.

My beloved Valentine,

I can't believe this time you've left me for good. Now I'm alone and sinking inside the void where a heart used to be. Asking questions to a night that threatens to swallow me whole. I prayed for nothing more than to connect with you. Why was I doomed to fail with the one man I ever truly loved . . .

Val masked the letter and glanced around. No one paid him any attention. He stared at the front window and the night beyond, seared by her words.

He rose to his feet and went back to the counter. "Can I print something out?"

The guy still refused to glance his way. "Dollar a page."

"Fine."

The server keyed his register. "Just hit print. The pages come out back here."

Val returned to his keyboard and clicked on the print button without looking directly at the letter. He wanted to read the rest of what Audrey had to say. He had to. But not now.

Val stood by the register, keeping himself close enough to ensure the clerk would not take time to read. But the guy showed no more interest in the pages than he had in Val. Val paid and returned to the computer and began the process of shutting down.

The screen showed an instant-message e-board. The message struck him with five furious bullets.

You vile, despicable, evil worm.

The return address was the same as the letter stowed in his pocket. Before he could gather himself to respond, Audrey shot another assault.

Here, let me help. You stole Val's password in one of your noc-

turnal forays. And now you're checking things out. Making sure there's nothing to tie you to your appalling deeds. But I know. I know.

Val felt the yawning gap of all he wanted to leave behind. The prospect of becoming reconnected kept him unable to respond.

The screen blasted through one more blow.

Murderer.

Val took a sharp intake of breath. His hands moved from his heart's volition. He typed in, *It's me, Audrey.*

He sat and waited. He could see her now, the strong features and piercing ice-blue gaze. The hair of burnished copper, which she hated because of its impossible waves. The direct manner of speech, the overlarge mouth, the features that were sparked to animation by the slightest hint of emotion.

Like the anguish he had caused her any number of times.

The screen remained blank. So he typed in, *Really. It's me. Val.*

Another long pause, then, *You're not dead?*

The world thinks so. I intend to keep it that way.

The screen slapped him again.

Oh, Val, Val, you terrible beast of a man, I have wept for twenty solid hours. Couldn't you possibly have let me know? Is that so very much to ask?

Audrey, I've had an accident. I—

She broke through with yet another question. *Where are you?*

New York.

You can't possibly.

Yes.

Val, listen to me. Hide yourself.

You are the only person who knows I'm alive.

You have to get out of there. Out of the country, if possible. Come here, if you can, but don't travel under your own name. Can you do that?

Why?

The answer was slow in coming.

Because my brother thinks he has killed you. And if he learns you're alive, he will try again.

AS THEY DROVE AWAY FROM VAL'S, TERRANCE TURNED HIS CELL phone back on. The message signal began flashing almost instantly. Terrance scrolled through a number of calls from financial players. He said, "Two o'clock in the morning and I'm still fielding calls from Wall Street."

"Bound to happen. People wired into breaking news want to check our pulse before the markets open." Passing headlights reflected off Don's face as if his features were sprayed with oil. "I'm thinking we should head back to the office, camp out there."

Terrance gave a mental shrug. He would not sleep much wherever he lay down. He continued to scroll through his messages, then stopped. He recognized the former policewoman's voice with the very first word. "I got something with explosive potential. Call me."

He pressed the phone to his chest. How should he play this? He had seen Don at work. But he was not Don.

"What's up?"

"Wally wants a word." He pushed the redial button.

She answered on the first ring. "Don?"

"No. Terrance here."

"A change like this," the woman declared, "is a very bad idea."

Suzanne Walton had been a highflier in the Baltimore police force until Internal Affairs caught her taking a bribe from a local vice czar. The woman loved to gamble beyond her means. The woman also lost. The money had to come from somewhere. Because she was one of the first women to earn a detective's shield, the force had let her quietly resign.

"We don't have any choice," Terrance replied.

"Explain that one to me."

There had been nothing the press could pin a story on. Which of course was what the Baltimore police had wanted. But they let word slip out quietly. When Don had come up with the idea of hiring Wally Walton, it had taken Terrance's sniffer hounds less than a day to come up with the goods. Walton was dirty. The Baltimore authorities had spread the quiet word far and wide. Walton was bad news.

Terrance replied, "Things are in motion now. The exec who actually pulls the corporate strings has to be the key player."

"Meaning Don Winslow."

Don stopped at a traffic light and stared at him. Terrance said to the phone, "That is correct."

"So he won't have time for me."

"Precisely. Plus, one of us must stand watch over Jack Budrow. I can't. He despises me."

"Why?"

"I've never quite been able to figure that one out."

"This way you're talking," Wally said. "Does this mean you're going to play it straight with me?"

"I can't think of any other way to work this through."

She mulled that over, then decided, "I guess I can live with that."

"So what do you have?"

"Maybe nothing. You haven't heard anything from Haines, have you?"

Terrance's chest was clutched by a titanium vise. "What?"

"Val Haines," she repeated. "Any word from the guy?"

"You have got to be joking."

Don was watching Terrance now more than the road. "What's going on?"

Terrance waved him to silence as the woman continued. "Like I said, it's probably nothing. But he didn't spend the night in the hotel."

Terrance turned his face to the side window, concentrating fully. "Are you sure?"

"I got a couple of friends on the force up here. You'll be hearing from somebody later today. The official word is, the guy is history. But they went into the hotel yesterday afternoon and found that the guy's bed wasn't touched."

The car turned into the office building's parking garage and halted in the executive space. Don cut off the motor. And waited.

Terrance was unable to move. "This is confusing."

"Maybe not. You told me the guy was a night creature."

"Yes." Terrance laid his forehead upon the cold glass. "Particularly when he's up there."

"Right. So maybe he got lucky. Found himself a more pleasant place to sleep."

His thoughts emerged in congealed lumps. All the documents had been structured to point at Val as the thief. Outside counsel and the auditors had been brought in. The files were now in the hands of the authorities. The scheme was in public play. Terrance forced himself to straighten. There was a damp spot where his forehead had rested on the glass. "We have to be certain."

"NYPD is setting up a citywide alert."

"They can't find him."

"Yeah, well, like I said. Most likely he's not anywhere to be found."

"No. You don't understand." Terrance's breath was so constricted he could only find air for one word at a time. "The authorities *cannot* find Val Haines."

WHEN VAL REENTERED THE HOTEL, THE CLERK WATCHED HIS approach with an impersonal gaze. Vince's hair was cropped as close to his head as his graying goatee. The bones of his temple, jawline, and cheeks were as pronounced as his steely muscles. His skin was pocked from beneath his left eye to his ear, like he had been whipped with a chain or scarred by buckshot. He wore a dark-gray suit and a white shirt, with a tie as matte-black as his eyes. The muscles of his thick neck formed a slanted decline to massive shoulders.

"Mr. Smith." Vince showed him nothing. Not in the gaze, nor the greeting. "What's going on?"

Val forced himself to meet the man's eye. The walk through the New York night back to the hotel had solidified his thoughts into a single focused objective. Val asked, "Did you mind me listening to what went on earlier?"

"That depends. You a cop?"

"Definitely not."

"No, I don't think so. You come in here all beat up, your clothes a mess. Only thing you're carrying is a shopping bag full of new clothes. And you're wearing those now."

"You're observant."

"Comes with the territory. Actually, you know what you look like to me? You look like a sucker."

Behind Val, the old man now camped out on the sofa wheezed

a chuckle. Vince leaned to one side so as to look around Val. "Hey, why don't you take a hike upstairs."

"I ain't bothering nobody."

"That so? Well, I'm telling you it's time to hit the sack." Vince waited until the old man shuffled into the elevator and disappeared. Then he returned his attention to Val. "You were watching what went down with those guys."

"Yes."

"Tell me what you saw."

"You're a loan shark."

"Don't call it that. I'm a service provider. I've helped out a lot of people. They come to me when nobody else is gonna do a thing for them, except maybe break their legs."

"What happens if they don't pay you back?"

Vince did something with his eyes. The voice maintained its flat calm. But the eyes opened into bottomless pits. "Oh, they always pay me. Always."

"I believe you."

"Personally, I got a soft spot for suckers. I know what it means to be down and out."

"I'm glad to hear it."

"What I need to know is, are you trouble?"

"I told you, I'm not a cop."

"That's nice to hear and all. But I got to *know*. Somebody comes into my place of business, all beat up, pays cash, no plastic, no nothing, now he comes up to me like he's wanting to do business. I got to know what's going on with this guy."

"It's like you said, I got beat up and arrested."

"You got any ID?"

"All I've got is a driver's license. And it's fake." Val fished it out. "It says Iowa. But I'm from Florida."

Vince inspected it carefully. "Nice work." He handed it back. Vince moved like a boxer, his motions smooth and economical. Balanced constantly on his toes. His fingers rested lightly on the countertop. But he put no weight there. He leaned on nothing. "An honest out-of-town sucker. You get rolled?"

"Almost. I was in the process when the cops arrived."

"So why'd they arrest you?"

"They say I attacked them. I don't remember."

"You hit a cop? In this town? Man, you're lucky to be alive."

Val touched the bandage on his temple. "They gave me this."

"That ain't nothing. That's a love tap. Where I was brought up, that'd be a cop's way of saying hello." He cocked his head. "You know what I see? I see a clean-cut kinda guy, never been in trouble, never done time. No tattoos, am I right?"

"No."

"Show me your arms."

"What?"

"Roll back your sleeves. Yeah, like I thought. No tracks. Okay, you can roll 'em back down. People say they want some ID, what they're telling you is, show me you're street. You understand what I'm saying?"

"I'm not sure."

"Guys doing heavy drugs, they hear that every time they hit on a new source. Show me your ID. What they want to see are needle tracks. Undercover cops won't have tracks. They do, they're one step from turning."

"I told you—"

"I know, I know. You're not a cop. You're just a guy in trouble."

"Right."

"You're not street. You don't have idea one. And you're being straight with what you're saying."

"As much as I know how."

"See, normally to do business with me, you got to have an introduction. This ain't about, what you call it, a résumé. Somebody brings you in, tells me you're good for what you want to borrow, say you're after twenty thou like that guy. You don't pay, you skip town or get hit by a bus or whatever, this guy brought you in here? He's got to be good for the loan and the vig."

"That's hard."

"Welcome to life uptown." Vince turned away to deal with the phone. Back again. All business. As impersonal as a robot. "So what are you after, anyway? Money? Blow? Something special in the meat department?"

"A passport."

"You want paper. That's tough. Tough and expensive. Since the terrorist thing they been cracking down on the paper handlers."

"Can you help?"

"Maybe. Yeah, I might. Like I said, I got a thing for suckers." A flick of a smile. There and gone. "You got money to pay for the work?"

"Can you give me some idea how much it'll cost?"

"You want a new name too?"

"No."

"So this Jeffrey Adams you just showed me on the ID, it ain't real."

"No."

"For a passport, good work, I'd call it four, maybe five thou."

"I've got that much."

"Then yeah, maybe I can help you out. But I got to know up front, what's in it for me?"

Val wiped his hands up and down his trouser legs. What choice did he have? Vince simply stood and waited. Facing a sweat-stained man at the moment of decision was nothing to this guy.

Val unstrapped the watch from his wrist. "I can give you this."

Vince held the watch up to the light. Squinted and inspected carefully. "Cartier tank. Twenty-carat frame. With the alligator band. Nice. This hot?"

"Not to my knowledge."

"What, it was a gift? Got some sentimental value?"

"Not anymore."

"I like that. Cutting all ties. Neat and tidy." Vince made the watch disappear. "Okay, Jeffrey or whatever your name is. Let me make a few calls. I'll get back to you."

He stared at the pocket now holding his watch. "Can I wait?"

"Not a chance. I don't like the sound of heavy breathing when I'm working. Go do like the old man, use the bed you're paying for." Vince reached for the phone. "I'll let you know when it's time for round two."

TERRANCE WAS SO DEEP IN A MIDNIGHT COMA HE COULDN'T even tell if the pinging sound was a nightmare.

He rolled over and landed on his office floor. His eyes were open now. He crawled to the ringing cell phone perched on the corner of his desk. "What?"

"It's Wally."

"Wait one."

Terrance forced himself to his feet. He crossed the hall to the bathroom and washed his face. He had never slept in the office before. He had laid down thinking he could at least remain prone for the two hours until dawn.

Terrance returned to his office. His watch lay on the coffee table. He did not need to check it. He picked up the phone and said, "All right."

"What I've got, it's not the best news."

Terrance went from stupor to as awake as he had ever been in his life. Liftoff in three seconds flat. NASA should take lessons.

Terrance raced out of his office and down the side corridor in his T-shirt, pants, and socks. No belt. His front was still damp from splashing himself.

"Are you there?"

"Yes." He hit the stairwell door with his shoulder. The steel handle struck the wall like an angry gong. "What do you have?"

"Like I told you earlier, I've still got some buddies up here in the force. I had them keep an eye out for me. Which has been expensive. You hear what I'm saying?"

"Spend what you need." He took the steps three at a time. Ripped the door open.

"I'm spending. Believe me. Spending isn't the question here. It's getting paid."

He sped down the hall. "We'll take care of you."

"You better."

"Haven't we always?" Terrance burst into Don's office. The man was dead to the world. Terrance kicked the sofa. Again. Don lifted his head but didn't open his eyes.

Terrance said to the phone, "You're telling me Val Haines is definitely alive?"

Don did a human catapult off the sofa. He crouched before Terrance, his face a rictus snarl.

"Not definite. Nothing definite about this case. But the evidence is definitely not in our favor."

"Tell me what you have."

"It occurred to me that if we couldn't get information on who got toasted in the explosion, we could at least find out who was still walking around. You with me?"

"Go on."

"I did a run through the local precincts. Just to be sure, you know, since your guy has a rep for going wild when he's up in the big city. I thought, okay, maybe he wasn't at the dance because he was held up somewhere else."

"You found something."

"A possible only. The precinct station in question is very far from the trail you'd expect a highflier to take. In the borderlands between Morningside Heights and Harlem."

Terrance huffed out each word separately. "Do. They. Have. A. Name."

"Jeffrey Adams."

Terrance staggered across the room and clutched the wall.

"I've never met Val Haines face-to-face. I been working from a company mug shot. And I couldn't be sure. But I thought, you know, it was worth checking."

"You were right."

"This guy Adams was comatose when they brought him in. Apparently he was in a bar that caters to the hard core. Carrying a wad of cash and a driver's license. No plastic. You with me?"

Terrance's senses were in hyperdrive, the same power he saw there in Don's gaze. "Using a fake ID to stay anonymous."

"Exactly. Some cops were there undercover. Apparently they saved this mark from a bad end. Only Adams took a swing at an undercover cop. So they brought him in. I'm not clear on why he wasn't charged. But they let him go. They've got a mug shot, the name I gave you, and a Des Moines address."

"Do you have a scanner?"

"Up and rolling."

"E-mail it through." Terrance watched as Don scrambled for pen and paper. "Use this address. And stay by your phone." He hung up.

Don powered up the flatscreen on the wall opposite his desk. He keyed in net access, watched the screen a moment, then said, "Here it comes."

They stood side by side. The download seemed to take eons. Finally front and side mugshots illuminated the office.

Don moved in close and intently studied the image. "I can't tell."

"It's him." Terrance pressed his fist to his gut, pushing against the nausea.

"You can't be positive. His own mother couldn't make a definite ID from this."

"I'm telling you. This is Val Haines. And his mother is dead."

Don slumped onto the sofa. "Tell me what you know about this guy."

"We've been through this before."

"It'll help me think."

Terrance walked behind Don's desk. The first time ever. He slid into the high-backed leather chair. Propped up his feet. Twisted the chair slightly so he was aimed at Don and not his nemesis. "Valentine Joseph Haines. Mother died when he was twelve. Father and he were very close. No other siblings. One aunt. They are not close. Father died, let's see, nineteen months ago. Val took it very hard."

"Get your feet off my desk."

Terrance remained as he was. "About a week after the funeral, his wife of four years filed for divorce. It becomes very messy here."

"Nineteen months, that's about the time you beat Val out of the promotion, am I right?"

"As I said. Messy. The divorce turned into a battle over a child that Val apparently did not know his wife was carrying."

"Your child."

"In court it was revealed she had been having an affair for some time. Val's lawyer demanded a DNA test to determine parentage. Which was when everything came into the open. Things became quite vicious."

Don's gaze could pierce Kevlar. "She was having an affair with you, and Val found out when the DNA test came back?"

"Val took this very hard."

"I can imagine."

"No, actually, you can't. In court that day, Val became unglued. We're talking totally insane. He accused me of everything except murder." Terrance's voice remained steady. But inside he felt the old acid biting deep. "He was yelling so loud guards showed up from three courtrooms away. He actually accused me of stealing his child as well as his wife by tampering with the DNA test results."

"Did you?"

"Don't be absurd. When they finally silenced Val, the judge handed down a restraining order."

"So Val loses his father. His wife files for divorce. He discovers she's carrying his child—"

"I told you. The child is mine."

"Far as Val's concerned, it's his. Am I right?" Don picked up the coffee mug from his desk and pointed with it at Terrance. "To top things off, he loses his place on the corporate ladder because he got stabbed in the back."

"That promotion was mine as well."

"What we're talking about is what Val thinks." Don smiled grim approval. "No wonder the guy went bad."

There was nothing to be gained from holding back. Not now. "I never expected Val Haines to steal. He was always one for the straight and narrow."

"That's simple enough. You pushed him over the edge."

"The plan had always been to snare Marjorie Copeland. Marjorie was a desperate woman who basically endured the corporate life only to get her pension. I left just enough of a trail for her to realize the pension funds had effectively been drained. If she went public, the company would be pushed to the brink. Whether it actually folded or not, Marjorie's pension was history. You know all this. We'd planned for her to steal what she could and disappear. Then we'd blow the story, only increase the amount she stole from a few million to half a billion."

"Then Val discovered what she was up to and went along as well," Don said.

"Which is the only item that has not gone according to plan."

"You mean, other than our Val missing out on the bomb." Don drained the remainder of his coffee like medicine. He said to his empty mug, "Remind me what your personal take is from this operation."

Terrance repeated the words, anchoring the moment, giving a solid sense of reason to what was about to go down. Which of course was what Don was after. "Eighty-three million, two hundred thousand dollars."

Don motioned to the image on the far wall. "There's no chance you could be mistaken about that being our Val?"

"None."

Don tapped the mug's rim on the desk. Slowly. Deliberately. In time to his words. "Do I need to tell you what has to be done here?"

In response, Terrance picked up his cell phone and punched in the number. When Wally came on the line, Terrance said, "We need to talk. I'm coming up to New York. In the meantime, see if you can quietly locate this Jeffrey Adams."

"I need something more to go on."

"He has to be sleeping somewhere."

"And if he's moved on?"

Terrance thought hard. "My guess is, he'll try to reach England."

"The precinct ID'd this Adams guy on his driver's license,"

Wally mused aloud. "It was the only form of identification he was carrying. If he's headed to Europe, he'll need a passport."

"You know where he would go to get fake papers?"

"Sure." Wally paused, then added, "My contacts at the precinct want to know if this is our man."

"I think it's safe to tell them," Terrance replied, his eyes steady on his partner, "that Val Haines is dead."

VAL LAY ON HIS HARD PALLET ON THE HOTEL ROOM FLOOR. HE HELD Audrey's letter flattened against his chest. Growing daylight filtered through slatted blinds. He stared not at the ceiling, but at the images circling him from all sides. Audrey's letter had released a hurricane of fragmented memories.

Before his life had fallen apart, Val and his wife had attended Orlando's Thirty-third Street Baptist Church, which had moved to a new larger structure out by Isleworth. It was a good place. Good people, nice social life, growing fast as the city itself. His wife, Stefanie, was involved with this and that. He had played in the church basketball league. Their friends all went there. Which made the gradual revelation that their marriage was falling apart that much more public and harder to endure.

His father's death, the divorce, the revelation that his wife had been having an affair with the same man who then stole a promotion Val should have received—one blow followed another with merciless consistency. Val's days held to the same empty pattern, just going through the motions, waiting for the next strike of life's wrecking ball.

Fourteen months after the divorce, a church friend concerned about his lonely state introduced him to a visitor from England. She was over to see her mother and brother. A wonderful lady. The friend failed to mention she was also sister to Val's arch nemesis, Terrance d'Arcy. If he had not been trapped by agony, Val would have laughed himself sick at life's awful irony.

The desire to use Terrance's sister as a means of revenge for her brother's actions had been strong as lust. But Val couldn't bring himself to do it. Audrey d'Arcy had been the one good thing in a dismal and storm-swept era.

Audrey was what in Britain was called a Christian counselor. She had both a private practice and a government contract to work with prisoners coming up for remand. She extended her stay in Orlando four times, not masking her growing love for Val. Audrey had accepted his tale of woe with the tragic recognition of her brother at work. Val had feasted upon a woman who wanted only to care and comfort and succor.

So why had he forced her to leave? Val searched and found nothing save a clearer recollection of their last day together. Outside the church, Audrey had held him for what had seemed like the lifetime he refused to share with her. The way she had touched his face, the taste of her final kiss, the soft sound of her broken farewell, all drifted now in the hotel room's dusty air. Val rose from his pallet and stared in the mirror as he dressed. Silently he condemned the man before him for ever sending her away.

Vince was not on duty when he arrived downstairs. Val left the hotel just as the sky overhead began going dark. The thunderheads rolled and boomed their way down, ready to devour the higher buildings.

Val entered the diner and took a booth from which he watched the first drops strike the glass by his side, big as bullets. They dimpled the glass and chased the pedestrians to an even faster pace. Further memories rained down, a jagged-edged deluge. Val could no more halt the torrent than he could the thunderstorm outdoors. He ordered the first thing that caught his eye on the menu and remembered how, four months earlier, he had caught one of his most trusted employees with her hand in the honey jar.

Marjorie Copeland was a single mom, abandoned by her former husband soon after she had given birth to a severely handicapped boy. The child was now ten. The day nurse cost almost half her salary. Marjorie clung to her job with desperate fervor because she needed the medical. Since his divorce, the two of them had shared a silent bond over life's raw injustice. That morning four months back, Marjorie had looked more rumpled and exhausted than usual. Val laid out what he had discovered, hoping against hope she could show how he had gotten everything wrong.

Instead, Marjorie had shut and locked his door, drawn the blinds over his inside window, and asked him to cancel his appointments and hold all calls. Then she laid it out for him. How someone had been dipping into the company's pension fund. Gradually siphoning off the employees' retirement money into a series of false accounts and dummy investments.

Soon as the shock had eased, Val had supplied the name behind the scheme. "Terrance d'Arcy. He did this."

Marjorie had nodded slowly. "You're probably right."

"No probably about it. I can smell his hand all over this." The certainty opened like a poisonous bloom. "I have to stop him."

"If you go public," Marjorie said, "I'll kill myself."

"Don't talk insane."

"Take that pension away from me, and I have nothing to live for." She had the fathomless gaze of one already dead. "I've checked carefully. The money is gone, Val. And there's nothing definite to pin it on anyone."

"That's still no reason to talk about suicide."

"Isn't it? I have *got* to keep my pension. Otherwise my boy is going to be imprisoned in some concrete cage for the rest of his life." Her eyes were so drained of hope their color was a lie in physical form. "I want to take what's mine. That's all. Not one cent more. Just let me get out and then you can do whatever you please."

"I can't believe you're planning to steal from our company."

"It's not stealing and it's not my company." Emotional exhaustion had pounded her voice to a toneless drone. "They *owe* me."

"How much are we talking about?"

"I've worked this out. If I live to the median age, my pension payment would be a million three. Down in Costa Rica that would take my son through a long, full life."

Then she waited. Not saying it. Just letting him taste the unspoken for himself.

Val tried to push the thought away. "I'll find a way to pin it on them."

"I don't think so. I'm good at my job. You know that. I've *checked.* All we've got is a drained pension fund and false trails that lead nowhere. So you get some minor evidence, so what? There will be a lot of suspicion and maybe some talk. They'll have four hundred million and change to hire the best lawyers. Sooner or later they'll skate." She let him mull that over, then added, "There is another alternative."

He glanced at his watch. Twenty-three minutes past nine on a Tuesday morning. Marking the time when he went from dedicated employee to criminal. "I'm listening."

"You caught me because I can't do this cleanly on my own. You sign off on all the transfers. You have connections with all our banks."

He nodded, but not to her words. The fact was simple and unavoidable. Terrance would walk. He knew this with the utter certainty of someone who had fought the man and failed. Terrance d'Arcy was a master of the dark arts. The only way to capture the man was to obtain all the answers. Which meant following his trail. Doing exactly the same. Then laying it out for the authorities. The bloom of vengeance sprang so easily from this putrid seed.

The second thought followed naturally on the first. What if he failed? What then?

The answer to this came just as easily.

Val refocused on the woman seated opposite him. "You've done the same calculations for me?"

"Yes."

"Assuming the same median age thing, what's my take?"

"Two million, two hundred and eighteen thousand dollars."

"You can get this out?"

"With care."

"You've tracked how they did it?"

"All the dummy fronts run through one guy at Syntec Bank in New York."

"We can follow the same pattern," Val said, thinking aloud.

The two of them realized together what he had just said. *We.* Marjorie's features crumpled. Val let her sob quietly for a time, then said, "How were you planning to disappear?"

"I found out how to obtain a false birth certificate on the Web." She took a handkerchief from her purse and repaired some of the damage. "I'm using a Des Moines temp office for an address and applying for a driver's license. After that, getting a passport is a breeze."

"Can you do the same for me?"

"Of course." Her mascara had run, leaving her face painted with the grief of ancients. "I never dreamed you'd go for this. I mean, I'm glad and all. But I just don't understand."

Val rose from his chair. "You don't need to."

When Val returned to the hotel from breakfast, Vince was behind the counter. The lobby was empty. Vince watched him approach the counter. There was a change to the atmosphere, a charged compression that signaled business about to be done.

Val walked straight up to the goateed weightlifter and demanded, "Where's my watch?"

"The watch is being checked out." Vince handled the question with his standard calm. "Forget the watch. Far as you're concerned, the watch is history."

"So you've found a guy who'll do me a passport?"

Vince did a thing with his shoulders. "Maybe yes, maybe no. Things are tough in this town. You hear what I'm saying?"

"I hear the words but they're not connecting."

"Especially since the Rico Act. I introduce you to somebody and you get caught, I go down with you."

"So how much will the passport cost me?"

"You need to focus here. We're not talking about the passport yet. We're not even close to that point. First you got to take care of me."

"You're telling me an eight-thousand-dollar watch isn't enough?"

"Forget the eight. Your watch is maybe gonna bring two-five on the street. So yeah, the watch makes for a nice down payment." He studied Val. "You don't get it, do you?"

"Obviously not."

He moved forward. It was a fractional shift, just a slight inching forward onto his toes. But the man's menace reached across the counter and gripped him hard. "Where'd you hide your stash, Jeffrey?"

"My money?" Val's voice sounded strangled to his own ears. "You know I can't tell you that."

"Tell me, don't tell me. It makes no difference." He did that thing with his eyes again. Opening them into a blank void. One large enough to swallow Val whole. "If I want it, it's mine."

"I thought—"

"You're in the city now. This means you got to learn a different way of thinking." Vince's words punched at Val with silken fists. "It cost you money to get into this town, right? It's gonna cost you a lot more to get out. You got no place to run, no place to hide. You're an easy mark."

"What are you saying?"

"You been straight with me. An honest sucker. So I'm gonna lay it out. I look at you, I know you're sitting on serious money."

"All I've got—"

"No, wait. Just hear me out. I'm not talking about what you're carrying in your pocket or got hidden away upstairs. Most guys in my situation, that's all they'd be interested in. How much are you carrying and how are they gonna take it from you? Gun, knife, alley, lobby, it's all the same."

"But you're different."

"We're standing here talking, aren't we?"

Val fought the words around the steel band constricting his chest. "So you're looking for a reason not to fleece me."

"See, I knew you were smart."

Val struggled to think beyond the world of trouble inside that guy's gaze. Things he had no interest in ever coming closer to than the other side of this counter. "Let's say you're right. Let's say we agree the watch is, what you said."

"Down payment."

"Right. And I accept what you're telling me. That I've got to pay you twice. Now I owe you for two services. Not one. First, I pay you for making the call. And second, I pay for you to keep me safe from everything bad out there I don't want to know about."

"Now you're talking." Vince eased back. The threat slipped a notch. "Now you're thinking street."

"Okay."

"Okay, what?"

"You get me the passport and you keep me safe. When I get where I'm going, I promise to wire you another ten thousand dollars."

"I'm thinking more like twenty."

There was no arguing with that face. "Twenty it is."

"You're asking me to take a serious risk here."

"Is that a yes?"

"You're asking me to make an investment in your future. Do I take you now, or do I take this chance you're an honorable man? I've done this before. Guys nobody else would've given a dime, I've loaned them a ton of money. Every week, I don't have to go looking for them. I don't have to call them on the phone. They show up. They appreciate what I've done for them."

Vince's gaze peeled away skin, bone, pulse. But Val did not look away. "I'll do what I say."

Vince must have found what he was looking for. He reached for the phone. "Don't you let me down, man. That's all I got to say to you. You better not let me down."

THE COMPLEX OF NARROW TOWNHOUSES OVERLOOKED THE Intracoastal Waterway and one of Miami's millionaire islands. Terrance rang the doorbell and stared over the concrete balustrade at wealth on display. A twenty-five-foot Donzi powered past, the motor's rumble thudding in his chest. Across the waterway he could see gardeners working on an island palace's lawn. The island contained perhaps three dozen homes and two high-rise condos. The cheapest apartment went for two and a half mil. Terrance smiled into the sunlight and turned as he heard footsteps dance across the tiles inside. Stefanie deserved just such a place. And he was just the sort of person to give it to her. But not Miami. This town held too much baggage for them now. Bermuda, perhaps. Yes, that was just the ticket.

She opened the door, the shadow staining her face. As always. "Hello, Terrance."

"Good morning, my dear. How nice to see you." He kissed the proffered cheek. "Thank you so much for allowing me to stop by."

"Come in. You look exhausted."

"Yes, well, as I said, things are threatening to unravel at work."

A queen. That was how she had looked the first time Terrance had seen her. And a queen she remained. Even dressed as she was in linen shorts, sneakers, and a white shirt knotted about her tanned midriff. Even bearing the shadow of another man. "Would you care for coffee?"

"That would be splendid, thank you." He climbed the stairs behind her and entered the living room. Terrance pretended to take great interest in a sailboat beating upwind. But his gaze remained upon the island mansions. A year should be enough time for public attention to swing away from Insignia and focus upon whatever commercial disaster came up next. Then he would quietly slip in his resignation and depart. A waterfront palace in Bermuda and an elegant city estate on Eaton Square.

"Why are you smiling?"

He turned away from the future he was determined to give her. "Happy to see you. As always."

Her gaze flitted away, resting nowhere for very long. "Melissa is still asleep, I'm afraid."

"Ah, well, never mind." He accepted the bone china cup and sipped. Freshly brewed, a dash of milk, half a sugar. Perfect. "Excellent coffee, my dear."

Her eye caught sight of the Town Car parked across the street. A uniformed chauffeur leaned against the gleaming hood, staring out over the water. "Is that yours?"

"Yes. As I said on the phone, this is just a swift in-and-out."

"You didn't drive down?"

"No time for that, I'm afraid. I came by plane. It's rather an around-the-elbow sort of journey. I'm actually on my way to New York."

"You flew from Orlando to Miami to connect to New York?"

"I've rented a jet. Rather, the company did. Swifter, don't you know?"

"I suppose I could wake Melissa—"

"Don't be silly. I'll be quite happy to step in and have a glance."

He followed her down the hallway toward the bedrooms. "You look lovely, Stef."

She gave no indication she had heard him. Which was why he said it when he had, in motion, her back to him. He knew she was listening, taking in every word. He saw her steps falter slightly, then speed up. He was nothing if not observant.

And patient.

He had wanted her from the first moment he had set eyes upon her. A reception at the new art gallery. A gathering of Orlando's elite. Someone had pointed her out to him. Her father was an orthopedic surgeon who taught at the University of Miami and held a residency at the new Celebration hospital south of Orlando. Stefanie was an art historian and professional evaluator. She also consulted on rare porcelains to a dozen or so museums around the country.

But Val Haines had met her four months earlier. The night before she and Terrance had met, Val had proposed. And Stefanie had accepted.

By then, Terrance and Val were already corporate enemies. Val had beaten Terrance out of a major promotion, the first time anyone had ever managed such a victory at his expense. By the night he met Stefanie, Terrance had been smiling around bitter vows of vengeance for over a year.

Terrance had tried to break them up. Stefanie had been enormously attracted to Terrance as well. They had met several times at art events and charity functions, the sorts of affairs Val loathed. Terrance had tracked her movements and inserted himself where he knew Val would not show up. They had even met once for lunch, his mother in attendance for good measure, there to discuss an item that had been in Terrance's family for three generations. A Meissen vase. His mother had approved of this sloe-eyed beauty with the hair that was both brown and gold. Which was in itself a revelation. His mother approved of almost nothing and no one.

But Terrance had not managed to interrupt her marriage to Val Haines. So he waited. He was always there, never pressing. Just close enough to snag her attention from time to time, always there with a laugh, a friendly observation, a warm hello. Waiting.

When the fractures in her relationship with Val had started, Terrance was the first to know, because she had told him. How Val was so desperate to start a family. How he adored his parents and his growing-up years, and yearned for such a relationship with a child of his own. But Stefanie felt none of this. She felt like she had been put on a highly public and extremely traumatic treadmill, racing from doctor to doctor in a constant desperate search for what was wrong.

By then, of course, Terrance's corporate battles with Val Haines were public knowledge, at least among those who followed such goings-on. Which had actually worked in his favor. For as the fissures grew worse between Stefanie and Val, who better should she approach for comfort than her old friend, the man Val hated most in the world? It really was too sweet.

Then came their affair, followed by the very messy divorce. All according to plan. The fact that she had become pregnant was the perfect crowning element.

Only at this point, something went very badly awry.

Rather than move in with him, Stefanie had retreated to Miami and a rental property owned by her father. She needed time to sort things out, was the only explanation she had given him. They had had their only argument at this point. But thankfully Terrance had retreated before tearing everything apart. He had played the hurt but loyal friend. Who wanted to be more than friends, of course. Particularly because of Melissa. Or so he claimed.

Stefanie arrived at the end of the hall and opened the door leading to her daughter's bedroom. Together they padded across the carpeted expanse and stood staring down at the crib. Melissa had emerged from her babyhood and was growing into quite an adorable little girl. Particularly when she was asleep. Terrance had no way with children. He found them odd little things, really. Particularly when they reverted to squalling bundles who could not properly communicate their needs. This was the time when it was good to have a nanny on constant call. Someone to take care of the nasty bits and return the child when it was freshly scented and smiling. But there were moments like now, when the little thing was bundled up in her flannel nightie, the hair soft as frost across her unblemished brow, and a pink tiger tucked snugly beneath her chin, when Terrance could imagine nothing finer than taking on the role of proud father.

He slipped his hand into Stefanie's, and counted it a minor triumph when she did not pull away. He had made no insistence upon seeing her. Instead, he had merely requested visitation rights to the child. Stefanie was far too much the lady ever to refuse him that.

As usual in such moments, Terrance inspected the little face for any sign of Val. The light was too meager, however, and his experience in such things utterly nil.

One hundred and fifty thousand dollars. That was how much it had cost him to bribe the technician. It was not merely the matter of changing a name on a document. The young woman had needed to depart these reaches forever. Terrance stared down at the daughter legally declared his own, holding the hand of the woman who would soon bear the same title, and counted it the best investment he had ever made.

He sighed with contentment and turned away.

To his satisfaction, Stefanie kept hold of his hand back down the hall and into the living room. He pointed to an earthen vase occupying a place of prominence on a fairy-legged side table. "That's new."

"Ming. I discovered it at an estate sale. Quite a find, actually. I've already been offered twice what I paid by a local curator."

Of course his mother had approved of Stefanie. They were so much alike. With one crucial difference, of course. Terrance's mother was unapproachable on any terms but her own. Stefanie, however, would soon be his to possess.

She seated herself on the curve of the sectional sofa, so that she could both be beside him and look at him. She never let go of his hand. "You didn't come just to see Melissa."

"No, Stef. Of course not." The walls were decorated with the oils taken from Val's home. There were seven of them. Four here, one in the third bedroom she had turned into a private space, two in her own bedroom. The oils were all late Renaissance and worth more than the townhouse. They had been left to her by her grandfather, also a surgeon and a Beacon Hill Brahman. Which is from where Stefanie received her bearing and her poise. Her looks and the soft Southern lilt to her vowels came from her mother, an Atlanta socialite. Terrance knew all these things because he had made it his business to know. He knew a great deal about this woman and her life. Information was a vital part of tracking any quarry.

"No, Stef," he repeated. "I came to see you as well."

"I know that."

"I look forward so much to these visits."

"I know you do." She stared at him. "You are the most patient man I have ever known."

"I have great reason to be."

"I wish . . ."

He let it sit there between them. The air was charged with all the silent desires. "What do you wish?"

"Nothing."

"If you don't tell me, Stef, I can't give it to you."

She smiled at that. "You would, wouldn't you? Give me what I ask?"

"Anything and everything," he replied.

"Why do you put up with me and my mess?"

"You know the answer to that."

"It's not just Melissa."

"It never was."

"No. I know that also. I keep thinking if I just sit here long enough and take care of my daughter and get on with my work, I'll heal. Life is such a dreadful mess." She paused, then added more quietly still, "And lonely."

"Only because you insist upon it being so."

"I'm not seeing anyone. I tried. But it didn't work. So I stopped."

He knew that too. She had gone out twice, once with the curator of a local museum and once with a University of Miami professor. Terrance continued to receive regular reports.

"I keep hoping one day I'll just wake up and things will be back to normal and I can start making a new life." She looked at him. Not saying the words out loud. But the message was clear in her eyes. *A new life with you.*

Terrance wanted to force her to speak the words. The desire was so fierce it must have blazed in his eyes, because Stefanie released his hand and rose from the sofa. She walked to the porch's sliding glass doors and stood there, her back to him and the room, hugging herself. "He was here."

The shock was a fist straight to his heart. "Val?"

"Last week. I came out of my front door and there he was. Standing across the road by the water. He looked awful."

Terrance did not recognize his own voice. "What did he want?"

Stefanie remained turned from him, hugging herself, silent.

Terrance clenched his entire body in the effort to keep himself from exploding. "You didn't. Stefanie, please tell me you—"

"He begged to hold her. Just for a moment. It caught me completely off guard."

He could not speak. To utter a single word would have been to unleash the beast. He envisioned a rage that left the entire room in shambles.

"Val wanted children so bad. You should have seen his face. He slipped Melissa from my arms before I could think of anything to say. The look he gave me, it was like he was being tortured." She stared out over the water, her back trembling as though sensing the emotion Terrance refused to let loose. "I took her back. He didn't object. He just walked away. I've never seen anybody look so totally destroyed."

The antique mantel clock struck the half hour. Terrance took a dozen slow breaths, forcing himself back to calm control. The so-called investigators he was paying a small fortune would reap the whirlwind. "Stef, please come over and sit down."

She relinquished her position very slowly. "What is it?"

"I have some rather dreadful news. And nothing's confirmed. I've spent two sleepless nights wondering whether it would be best to be the one—"

"What on earth are you talking about?"

"Sit down. Please." He snagged both her hands. "I fear Val is dead."

"What?"

"Nothing is confirmed. But it has been so long now, and the police . . ." He paused, released a hand, took a slug of cold coffee. "I can only tell you what I know. It appears that Val has been stealing from the company."

"That's impossible!"

"I know, it goes against the grain. But the evidence is rather compelling. A large amount of money has gone missing. The SEC has been called in. There is going to be a huge scandal."

Her mouth worked. "Val?"

"He, another Insignia employee, and a senior New York banker were apparently involved in perpetuating a massive fraud. The authorities think the bank might have bilked several major customers. Insignia among them. The bank was destroyed by a bomb. Val has not been heard from since."

There were tears, of course. Terrance held her and repeated the details, fleshing out the story. Being the bearer of bad tidings, the martyr. As he stroked her hair, he observed. He knew she retained some connection to Val, a few stubborn tendrils of affection. How exquisite it was to personally demolish them. Finally making room for her new future. Her destiny.

She gathered herself and asked the question he had known would come. "Why are you telling me this?"

"News about Val being lost in the bomb blast broke this morning in the local Orlando papers. Tomorrow word is bound to get out about the scandal. At that point it will be national news. This may not be as big as Enron, but it is by far the largest scandal to hit a Florida company."

"That's why you came?"

"In part. I didn't want this to catch you totally unaware. I had to do it in person. And it's like I said on the phone. I won't be available for a week or so. Perhaps longer."

"That's why you're going to New York?"

"Damage control." He glanced at his watch. "Speaking of which, my dear, I really must fly."

She rose with him. "I can't believe this. Val."

"Of all people. I agree."

"He hated you."

"I am well aware of that."

"You must be pleased." Her words crumbled wetly.

Terrance dropped his voice an octave. "I do not deserve that."

"I suppose not." But she was unconvinced.

"In all the time we have been together, I have never spoken a word against Val Haines. Not once." He made as to turn for the door. "I shall not start now."

"No, wait. That's not—"

"I know you're deeply upset. You have every right to be. I knew also I took the risk of being painted as a culprit by bringing you this news. But I had to prepare you, Stefanie. Even if it meant wounding myself. I had no choice."

"Don't go like this. I didn't . . ."

"You see, I love you more than I have ever loved anyone. That is why I came. And why I must now go." He bent over and kissed her tear-stained cheek. "Adieu, my dear."

He shut the door firmly behind him and hurried over to where the chauffeur was opening the door. He seated himself and kept his face pointed straight ahead. But out of the corner of his eye he saw Stefanie open the sliding glass door and call down to him. He gave no sign of having noticed. The car pulled away. He could hear her call faintly through the closed window.

He smiled. That really had gone rather well.

WHERE THE TAXI LEFT VAL OFF, THE SKYSCRAPERS FORMED A steel-and-concrete noose. He was the only pedestrian who bothered to look upwards, searching out a glimpse of the dull grey sky. Val crossed the street and entered Grand Central Station. From where he stood on the upper veranda, the space looked larger than the outdoors that he had just left behind. The four-faced brass clock rising from the central information booth said he was five minutes late. He crossed beneath the distant ceiling's mythical star chart and asked directions from the hostess at the Michael Jordan Steakhouse above track thirty. He took the side passage to the western balcony and spotted the entrance to the Campbell Apartment. There he stopped.

"See, that's why I like this place for the meet-and-greet." A voice by his elbow said, "The first-timers, they come in here and do their gawk, and you know them straight off. You tell me you look like this or that, it doesn't matter. You need directions to this place, you know the fellow is going to come in here and freeze."

The man's hair was dyed a ridiculous orange. He had a crooner's voice. Everything else about him was mummified. He scarcely reached Val's shoulder. "You have also kept me waiting."

"Sorry."

"It's going to cost you." He pointed Val to a table opposite the bar. "The drinks in here are horrendously expensive."

The room belonged in a European palace, not a New York train station. The galleried hall was perhaps seventy feet long with a gothic fireplace dominating the far wall. The ceiling was thirty feet high and ribbed by hand-painted beams.

"Campbell was a man with power and an ego to match. He took this space because it was the city's largest ground-floor office. When he moved in, it was a barracks. He copied the salon of a thirteenth-century Florentine manor. He installed a pipe organ, a piano, and over a million dollars in antiques. That was back in the twenties, when a million dollars meant something." He held out his hand. "Let's have your ID."

"Excuse me?"

He gave a mirthless smile. "My, but we are new to this game, aren't we. The only ID that matters. Guess what that might be."

Val glanced around the room. No one seemed to be watching.

"Don't worry about them. This is New York, remember? Land of the professionally blind." He snapped his fingers. "The clock is ticking."

Val dipped into his pocket and pulled out his roll.

"Fan the pages just enough to show me this isn't a pack of ones I'm seeing. Okay." The man drained his glass. "You're after what, social security card, plastic, birth certificate, total makeover?"

"Just a passport."

"Expensive. What about the name you aim on using. Is it clean?"

"Yes."

"It better be. On account of the authorities, these days they do a computer search every time you pass through the border."

"It's clean."

"Sorry, I need a little more assurance than just your say-so." The scars where his face had been cut and surgically stretched ran from above his ears to his turtleneck. "See, if you're lying to me, they'll ask you where you bought your paper. They'll ask you very hard."

"I was arrested two nights ago. The police ran me through the national system. The name came up clean."

"Vince will vouch for that too?"

"Call him and see."

He tapped his finger on the glass, studying Val hard. "Nah. Like the man said, you got an honest face. So where did you buy your new tag?"

"My . . . I don't remember."

The surgical scars refused to move when he smiled. They formed two flat creases down each side of his face. Which was perhaps why his smiles came and went so swiftly. "Look there, you're learning. Okay, let's see what you got."

Val passed over his driver's license.

The guy pulled a set of reading glasses from a pewter case and lifted the card up to where it reflected the neighboring lamp's light. "This is good work. Almost as good as mine." He slipped off the spectacles. "Five thousand."

Val snagged the driver's license and stuffed it back in his pocket. "Four."

The man flashed his false smile. "Aren't we cute. Look, this is not bargain basement land. You want, you pay."

"All right. Five."

"My studio is just around the corner. Not nearly as nice as here, I'm afraid. The lighting's too strong and it smells like a lab. But you'll be in and out in no time. Me, I'm still looking for my ticket to paradise." The man rose to his feet. "Where did you say you were headed?"

"I didn't."

"No, silly me. Of course not." He pointed Val toward the bartender. "I should have said, five plus tip. Pay the man and let's do business."

TERRANCE MET THE EX-COP, SUZANNE WALTON, IN A MANHATTAN diner made for the blues. They sat in the corner booth. Beyond his grimy window, the street was a concrete canyon filled with grinding traffic and sullen faces and smoking vents. To his other side, the chef leaned against the kitchen windowsill and yelled at the lone waitress in some gutteral tongue. Terrance asked, "Why are we here?"

"You mean, so far from the parts of the city we all know and love?" She had a cop's voice and ate like a feral beast, watching him over her sandwich. "You sure you don't want anything?"

"I'll wait." His suite had been reserved at the Plaza. Their wine list was legendary.

"Number one, because up here we're faceless. Number two, I wanted you to see this terrain for yourself. My guess is, your man came in here and disappeared."

The woman's blunt manner helped enormously. Her attitude suggested that any problem could be handled and disposed of. "Which means he knows we're after him."

"Maybe yes, maybe no. I talked to a buddy at the precinct. This Jeffrey Adams character claimed to have lost his memory."

"What?"

"I'm just telling you what I heard. Jeffrey Adams was so drunk or drugged or both he took a swing at a cop trying to save him from getting rolled. The cop promptly clocked him. The next day Adams checked out of the holding cell claiming amnesia."

Wally Walton was not an unattractive woman. For someone fascinated by life's seamier side, she would even be classed as alluring. Terrance guessed her age at early to midthirties. She wore a jacket and skirt of midnight blue. A matching silk T-shirt did nothing to hide her feminine curves. She had mannish hands and strong wrists, but her nails were buffed and polished. Her dark hair framed a face of uncompromising angles. Her eyes were her worst feature, large and brown and utterly without bottom.

Terrance asked, "He doesn't remember? Not anything?"

"He didn't then. No telling about now." She used the grimy napkin to clean the sauce from her hands and mouth. She balled it up, dropped it in her plate, and pushed the plate aside. "I checked the neighborhood. They've pegged me for a cop. Probably vice, since I'm not showing them a badge. Which means I don't get much help. But he did check in at a local street clinic. That cost me a hundred, by the way. Head banged up, complaining of amnesia, everything checks out with what the cops said."

"They don't know where he went after that?"

"Either they don't know or they aren't saying. I've gone by all the hotels and boarding houses in the area. But these places, it's not like downtown. They play loose with the records around here, Terry."

"Don't call me that."

She caught the edge to his voice and smirked. "If you're right, what you said about him wanting to leave the country, he needs a passport. The precinct shows him as only holding a driver's license. That won't get him far. Not these days. He's going to have to get hold of false papers."

"Can't you get flight records?"

"Not a chance. Since 9/11 you got to go through Homeland Security. My guys would face FBI scrutiny for even asking. Our best bet is to locate his source for false papers. There aren't so many of those around. I'm working on that as we speak."

A fist formed from the diner's grimy smoke gripped his gut. "So he might already be gone."

"Put that aside for a second and focus on what we know. The guy is alive, right?"

"Yes." Terrance swallowed against the bile being forced up his gullet. "Which is why we still need you."

"Let's take a look at that. You don't just want this guy dead."

"No."

"We're way beyond that now."

"Yes."

"You've gone public. Which means you need this guy to vanish. You need him to disappear so completely it's like he never came back from the dead in the first place."

"And fast."

"What do I call you? And don't give me d'Arcy. I can't say that with a straight face."

"Terrance."

"Okay, Terrance. This is going to cost you. This is going to cost you big."

"You're only being asked to do what you should have—"

"Stop right there." She planted an elbow on the table and jabbed the air between them with her forefinger. Dried sauce from her sandwich collected around her fingernail like unnoticed blood. "I did the hit exactly as ordered. The bank is gone. Not just your guys. I was ordered to destroy the bank's records, computers, files, the works. Which I did, correct?"

"Yes." They had needed to destroy all banking records. The only ones that survived were held by the parent company on Jersey. The island was beyond U.S. reach. Jersey banks answered only to Jersey law. Jersey banking records were open to no one. The only records available now to the SEC investigators were those in Insignia's hands. Which contained some of Terrance's best work. "Why couldn't you at least be sure they'd actually entered the bank?"

"Come on, Terrance. Stay with me here. First off, the place is a warren. Rockefeller Center has, what, nineteen street entrances spread over two city blocks. Second, I had to set the charges after the cleaning crew had been through. Me. Working alone. Don was very clear on this. I asked for a team and he said this was to be a one-woman job. So you gave me the where and the when. And I followed orders, right?"

There was no way Terrance could hedge the facts. Not and meet this woman's gaze. "You did exactly what we asked of you."

She relaxed a trace. "So you're still playing it straight with me."

"We need you."

"I know that. But it's good to hear you know it too."

"I assume you've checked on Marjorie Copeland?"

"First thing I did after hearing about your guy. Night before the blast she stayed in and did room service. Hotel clerk noticed her leaving on account of the time, six in the morning sharp, and because she hung around the lobby for a while like she was looking for somebody. Used the hotel phone twice, paced awhile, then left on her own."

"Which brings us back to Val Haines."

"Right." She leaned forward. With him now. "The problem, Terrance, is your guy has probably left the country. Which means bringing in outside help."

"You can do that?"

"I know people. But it's going to be expensive."

"It already is."

"What you've paid so far, that's nothing. That's chump change. We're talking serious money now."

"This is your windup?"

"This is fact. There's nobody else you can turn to but me. So listen very carefully to what I'm telling you. First we've got to find the guy. Then we've got to make him disappear so there'll never be a trace he even surfaced in the first place. This means a lot of legwork. Especially if he knows we're after him. Does he?"

"Let's assume the worst."

"Which means we don't need a guy with a gun. We need an organization. Let's break this down. First you're going to have the upfront. Call it the conversation charge. Then there's the fee for finding this guy. And finally the vanishing act."

"You're forgetting your portion for all this extra work."

The first glint of humor he had ever seen entered Wally's eyes. "I haven't forgotten anything, Terrance. You have a clean picture of this guy?"

"In the car. You're sure you can get in touch with the right people for this work?"

"I already did. I figured if your guy was on the move, the faster we hit, the better. Right?"

"Yes. Definitely."

"So I contacted some people I know in England. I've done business with them before. They're tops. And connected. They're watching the airports. This guy shows up, they're on him. Any idea where he'll be headed?"

"Jersey."

"Where?"

"It's an island in the English Channel."

"But first he's got to go to England like you told me on the phone, right?"

"Yes. Or France. But he's been once before and went through London."

"Okay. So we'll stay with England for the moment, and if he doesn't show then we'll move to this island. It's really called Jersey?"

"Yes."

"You bring cash with you?"

"Yes."

"How much?"

"Enough."

"I doubt that, Terrance. I doubt that very much."

Here it comes, Terrance thought. He willed himself not to move a muscle.

She spoke the words almost lovingly. "A million dollars."

"What?"

"I'm not done. A million now. A million the day this guy disappears from the face of the earth. In return, I bring you in contact with people who can do this job. I make sure they take their money and vanish too. While all this is going down, I make sure the cops don't pinch you." She breathed the words in a soft murmur, her face inches from his. "Then I make like smoke and evaporate too."

He leaned back. Crossed his arms. She remained where she was, but there was a constricting about her. The muscles drew in tight around her eyes, her mouth, her shoulders. Her fingers looked ready to claw hunks from the table. Prepared for battle. Terrance said, "Here's my counteroffer. I'll give you two hundred and fifty thousand dollars in cash now. To spend as you see fit. A million dollars will be wire transferred wherever you tell me by the close of business today. From that you will pay the new hired help whatever you see fit."

"That's not—"

He raised his hand. "Allow me to finish. A million and a half more will be paid to you the day Val vanishes for good. Again, you pay your cohorts whatever is correct. They deal only with you. I am simply along as an observer."

Terrance leaned back over the table. "And another two million at the end of two years. Just to make sure you stay our very own silent lady."

The tensile power eased from her shoulders and neck and face. "I'm not a lady, Terrance."

"No. But the situation hardly requires one, does it?"

"This deal you've got going down." They might as well have been lovers sharing secrets across the scarred linoleum, they were that close. "It's very big, isn't it?"

Terrance just smiled.

"How—" She was interrupted by the pinging of her phone. She leaned back, checked the number on the screen, then flipped it open and said, "You got something?"

She listened intently, showing him the mask. "Give me a name." She made notes on her napkin, then slapped the phone shut and said, "I need to get moving here."

"Who was that?"

"Maybe a lead. Maybe nothing. But I got to check it out."

"I'm coming too."

"You sure?" She didn't quite smirk this time. Just a slight tightening to the edges of her mouth and eyes. "This is a long way from the Plaza, where we're headed."

"I'm ready," Terrance said. And he was.

Outside on the street she told him, "I need some cash."

"How much?"

"Ten grand should cover it."

Terrance stopped, ready to play the money guy and beat her down. It was his nature. He was good at this game. But again he caught the taut battle fire in her features. He gave a mental shrug. Why bother? He might as well get used to a little outgo. "My valise is in the car."

She slid into the back seat beside him. While the driver shut her door and went around to the front, Terrance flipped the locks on his briefcase and handed her two banded sets of hundred dollar bills. He gained a little satisfaction from her being disconcerted again by his ready agreement. Not ten thousand dollars' worth, mind. But some.

She stowed the money away before the driver slipped behind the wheel. She said quietly, "Five is for the information. The other five is to ease our way inside."

"You don't have to explain."

"That's right. I don't."

"But you do need to tell our fellow where we're headed."

She turned to the driver and said, "Find a place on South Park down by Murray Hill where you can pull over and wait." When the car pulled into traffic, Wally gave him that cop's smile. "You're okay, Terrance."

"From this point on, whatever you spend comes from your share." Terrance leaned back in his seat. He did so love the hunt.

THE CLOUDS WERE TOO LAZY TO HANG IN THE SKY ON THEIR OWN. Instead, they leaned upon the highest towers, compressing the upper elevations and packing the city even more densely. There was no open space in any direction. No horizon upon which he could focus and find respite.

Val emerged from the subway and headed south from Douglas Circle. He turned left and walked to Morningside Avenue. The clinic was three blocks further north. In the distance the road dipped where the subway emerged from underground. The rail network rose to an overhead station, supported on painted steel beams. The sense of entering a man-made cavern was almost overwhelming.

The clinic's waiting room was empty save for a few mothers holding preschoolers and one ancient black man seated at the reception desk. He fiddled with his cane and watched Val's approach with rheumy eyes.

The receptionist asked, "Can I help you?"

"I was wondering if Dr. Martinez is working today."

The woman was the color of oiled ebony and very large. She spoke words that had clearly been said a million times before. "The clinic's doctors operate strictly on a rotating basis."

"Right. I understand that. But I saw her a couple of days ago—"

"Your name?"

"Adams."

She tapped into the computer. "First name Jeffrey?"

"Yes."

"She left you a prescription for Percodan. Is that what you wanted?"

"No. Thank you, but I really need to ask her something."

The receptionist breathed disapproval. "Then you'll just have to wait. Dr. Martinez is out on break."

"When will she be back?"

She glanced at the wall clock. "Half an hour. But you'll still have to wait for her turn in rotation."

"Sure. That's fine. Thank you."

Val left the clinic and stood for a time on the street corner. The city's clamor held a New York air of uncaring hostility. He spotted someone entering the orange street-front church's doors and decided to follow.

Inside, however, Val was met by crowding thoughts, dangerous as any mugger. Val sighed his way into a pew at the back. Such places had once been a haven. But now he felt nothing. To pray for anything, even a return of what he could remember, would be a lie.

Here in this quiet space, Audrey's words haunted him like the hounds of heaven. Val drew the letter from his pocket. Holding it raised a paradox of comfort and silent keening. He ached for this woman. Yet he had sent her away.

Val unfolded the letter and read,

You are gone and still I cannot stop this empty dialogue. How often have I argued with the empty space where you should be standing? How many letters have I written and burned in the past six months? But this letter will be sent. I shall lie to myself the best I know how, and say this medium reaches even beyond the grave. I have so much experience at tear-drenched lies. After all, I almost convinced myself that one day you would return and grant us that most joyful of titles, a couple.

Life's wounds have never pierced me as they do this night. This dreadful, endless night, when I am reduced to writing to a past that no longer exists, a future that is now myth. Were it not forbidden me, I would use the dagger, I would drink the poison, I would join you. Wherever you are. Were it not forbidden.

Val folded up the letter and rose from the pew. The only answer that made sense lay with this half-remembered woman. That realization gave focus to his otherwise empty state. He looked inward now and took subtle comfort from the void. He had no interest in remembering anything more. Why bother with a man recently deceased?

He would go to England and rescue her. He had broken it off, no doubt for reasons that had made sense at the time. But that no longer mattered. He would get his money and steal her away. But not as Val Haines. That life was over. The world already thought he was gone. Why not make the vanishing act complete?

May the poor man rest in peace.

When the receptionist finally sent him back, Val found Dr. Martinez seated at a metal desk writing busily into a file. "Have a seat, Mr. Adams. I'll be with you in just a second."

"Thanks for seeing me."

"Any of the other doctors could have given you what you needed."

"Maybe."

She gave him a momentary inspection, then went back to her notes. "You clean up good, Mr. Adams."

"That's not my name."

This time she set down her pen and swiveled her chair around. "Say again."

"I was carrying a false ID."

"So your memory is coming back. Good." The doctor's air of unflappable weariness remained intact. The chair's metal rollers scraped across the scarred linoleum floor. "How do you feel otherwise?"

"I'm moving easier and I don't hurt so much." Val leaned over so she could pull off the bandage over his temple.

"You're certainly keeping your wounds clean. Let's have a look at the back of your head." Gently she swiveled his head around. "Things are looking good. So what can I do for you?"

"I want something to keep me from remembering."

She moved back around to where she could see his face. "Give me that one again."

"Is there a drug or something that can keep my memory from returning?"

She pushed herself back further. "Look . . . What should I call you?"

"Do I have to tell you?"

"You don't want to tell me your real name?"

"Jeffrey Adams has worked well enough so far."

"Right. Okay. So you've started recalling certain portions of your past, and they have not been pleasant. Remember what I told you when you were first in here? The experience will be somewhat jarring."

"It's more than that."

She crossed her arms. "Correct me if I'm wrong here. But running away is what got you into this mess."

The air was thick with lemony disinfectant and the traces of all the reasons people like him came through those doors. "I asked you a simple question."

"And I'm giving you a simple answer. Are there drugs that can erase memory? Certainly. Most have a temporary effect. But just keep in mind, after your last bout you wound up in here with your head bleeding."

He was intensely aware of the gauzy curtain's inability to keep this a private conversation. "Could you lower your voice a little?"

"Listen, Jeffrey or whatever your name is. You're asking the wrong question. You don't want to erase your memories. You want to escape your pain."

His chest pumped as if he had entered the race of his life. "Whatever."

"Don't dismiss me here." A crucial intensity burned through her weary veil. "Knowing which question to ask is vital to finding the right answer. Think what would happen if a doctor inspected you for a cold when you had an intestinal problem. To achieve the proper solution, first you have to know what it is you're really hunting. Which in your case is a way to leave your pain behind. Not forget. Never forget. What you want to know is, how can you turn what you've been running from into something you can properly use?"

He was acutely aware of how quiet the chamber had become out beyond the wraparound curtains. "Can we get back to my original question?"

"No problem at all. Here's what you do." The doctor rose, swept back the curtains, and pointed to the exit. "Head out that door. Go fifty feet in any direction. Find the nearest bar and fill your own prescription. Take up where you left off." She stepped away from him. "See you on your way back down, Jeffrey."

THEY LEFT THE CAR AT SOUTH PARK AND EAST THIRTY-SIXTH. THE area was mixed, like a lot of Manhattan. Two blocks further east, the air was concussed by traffic pouring in and out of the Queens Midtown Tunnel. Their destination was a decrepit brownstone poised above the tunnel's maw. The fumes were worse than the din. The building's front door was locked, but Wally pulled a switchblade from her pocket and easily flipped the latch.

"A woman of many talents."

"Stay close."

Through partially open elevator doors emerged a stench from garbage dumped down the shaft. Wally took the stairs to the fifth floor. A chemical odor worse than the garbage filled the corridor as they reached the top landing. Terrance was about to complain when he caught sight of Wally's smile. "What's that foul smell?"

"A good sign." She knocked on the door at the corridor's far end. "You mind if I run the show?"

"By all means."

The smiles came more easily now. "You married, Terrance?"

"For all intents and purposes, I suppose I am."

"Shame." She knocked harder.

"I never mix business with pleasure."

"Yeah? Well, I do it all the time, baby." She pounded the door. "All the time."

A querulous voice said through the door, "Go away!"

She stowed the smile away and called back, "Horace, this door is coming down one of two ways. One, you turn the key. Two, I bust it down."

"Who are you?"

"We're people standing out here with your money burning a hole in our pocket."

A pause, then, "Who sent you?"

"Ben Franklin, Horace. Fifty of them. Five large. Now open the door."

Three bolts crashed back. The door opened the length of the final chain. "Show-and-tell time."

Wally fanned the bills, then pulled back when he reached through the crack. "You need my boot to help you with the chain, Horace?"

He studied the both of them for a moment, then shut and unlatched and reopened the door. "What do you want?"

"Five thousand buys us a minute inside, Horace."

A clown. That was Terrance's first impression upon entering the apartment and seeing the man clearly. A short, little clown with orange hair and a potbelly. A caricature who could only exist in a place like New York City.

"Shut the door." When Terrance had done so, the little man said nervously, "You're inside. So what is it you want?"

"A name, Horace."

"I don't divulge—"

"No. We give you a name. You give us either a yes or a no. If it's the right answer and you can back it up, we give you the five grand."

"What are you, a cop?"

"Come on, Horace. Does this guy here look street to you?"

"DA, then."

"We're not trouble, Horace. Not unless you want us to be."

"What I want is for you to get out of my life."

She did that thing with her face. From crudely feminine to wickedly severe without moving an inch. Her feral rage forced Horace back. He tripped over a lighting tripod and almost went down. Wally said softly, "I made the connection, Horace. I'm here.

I'm offering cash. I could just as easily offer you something else. It's your choice. But you're going to tell me in the end." She lifted her hand. Horace flinched. "Which is it going to be, Horace? Rough or smooth? Your call."

The man quavered, "What do you want to know?"

"You're selling paper, right?"

His swallow was audible where Terrance stood by the door. "Yes."

"Passports?"

"Sometimes."

"See, we're making progress." She crossed her arms and leaned back a fraction. The room's fissured stress eased slightly. "Over the past day or so, have you done a passport for a guy?"

"Couple."

"One of them about the age of my guy here, name of Adams?"

His trembles formed a nod.

"First name?"

"I don't . . . Wait, no, I remember. Jeffrey. He was a mistake, right? I knew it the instant I laid eyes on him. I told myself he was trouble. But hey, a guy's got to make a living."

"Describe him for me."

Terrance had not moved. But Horace had somehow sensed his eagerness. Horace said, "For another thousand, I'll go one better and give you a photograph."

"Don't look at him, Horace. He's nobody. I'm the one standing here with your fate in my hands."

"An extra thousand's not too—"

"Thirty seconds, Horace. Then I'll assume you need a demonstration to understand we mean business."

Horace scuttled away. Or started to.

Wally was on him like a striking snake.

Terrance gasped. He had never seen anybody move that fast.

Wally's hand gripped Horace's wrist as he reached inside a drawer. "What you got in there?"

"Nothing!"

"You going for a gun, Horace?"

"Ow, you're hurting me! It's just a picture!"

"So open the drawer. Nice and slow. Okay. Good." She backed off. "What is this, your personal rogue's gallery? You do a little blackmail on the side, Horace?"

"What do you care?" The man's sullen tone was contradicted by a serious case of the shakes. He flipped through the pictures. "Here. This is the guy."

Wally took the photograph. She gave it a cursory examination. She flipped it onto the counter and said to Terrance, "It's not him."

Horace grabbed it back, studied it intently. "That's Adams! That's the man!"

"Sorry, Horace. Not our guy." She turned away. "Unless you got something else to show me, we're all done here."

He wailed, "What about my money?"

"What can I say? You didn't come up with the goods." But Wally stopped in the process of reaching for the door. She gave Terrance a look, then turned back. "You good at keeping secrets, Horace?"

"Like the grave."

She reached into her pocket, came up with the cash, and set it down on the camera. "We were never here."

Terrance waited until they were back on the street to say, "The picture you saw."

"Hmmm."

"It was our guy, wasn't it?"

"Yes."

"Val Haines. You're absolutely certain?"

"Positive ID, Terrance. Five by five." She reached for her phone.

"Alerting your friends?"

"Yes." Wally punched in the number, then gave him the eye. "The money better be there, Terry."

"I told you not to call me that."

"These guys, they may talk funny. But you don't want to mess them around."

"Soon as we return to the hotel, I'll arrange the transfer." He waited until she had finished her call, then walked with her back toward the car. "If they're anything like you, I don't need further convincing."

She gave him that smile of hers, the one that was equal measures feminine appeal and molten shrapnel. "You sure what you told me, about being tied up?"

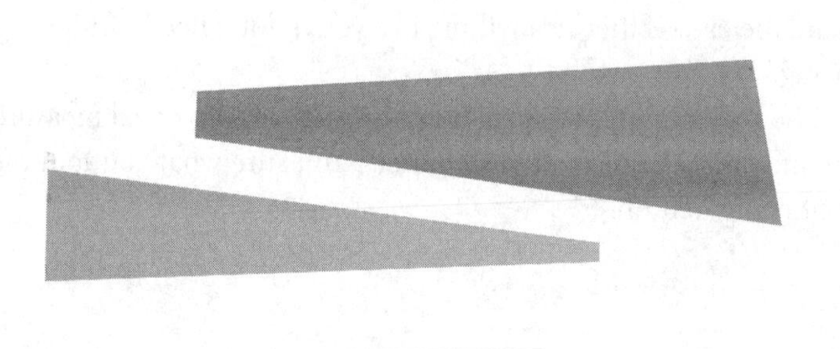

THE TRAVEL OFFICE WAS LIKE MUCH OF THIS PART OF THE CITY, threadbare and grim and utterly lacking in frill. The agent was Asian and proud of his ability to find Val the absolute lowest price on a one-way flight to England. He pushed Val to take a return ticket. The second leg was only $119 more, plus taxes and fees. But Val was not listening.

Val returned to the Internet café and was directed to the pay phone. He called the number in England that Audrey had given him. But the phone just rang and rang. He returned to the counter and paid his deposit to yet another metal-studded attendant. This time Val was on and off the Internet in a flash. It was not because of Audrey's warning that her brother might be watching that he hurried. Val had no interest in triggering further memory flashes. That life was all but buried. He wrote Audrey a quick note that he was coming and would call. Then he retrieved his deposit and fled the café as he would a morgue.

He walked back to the police station and mounted the precinct stairs. He pushed through the scarred swinging doors and entered the front room's bedlam. He took a number and seated himself on the hard wooden bench running down the wall opposite the reception counter. To his left, a transvestite cuffed to the bench's arm rubbed toes blistered by too-tight high heels. Val leaned his head against the wall and fingered the airline ticket in his pocket. Another set of unwanted memories began taking shape, these starring his nemesis, Terrance d'Arcy. Val fought them down and wondered why he had not disappeared long before.

"Number seventy-three."

"Here." Val approached the counter.

"Name?"

"Jeffrey Adams."

"ID?" The policeman reached over without looking up from his metal-backed pad. He copied down the false details, then handed it back and said, "Okay, what can I do for you?"

"I was arrested the night before last. There was a man in lock-up with me. Reuben somebody. An African American."

"You were locked up here?"

"Two nights ago."

"Charges?"

"Dropped." He found himself adopting the cop's terseness.

"And?"

"I want to know if he's still here."

"The reason being?"

"I want to bail him out. If I can afford it."

"Say again?"

"The guy probably saved my life."

"Probably?"

"Look. I don't know for certain what would've happened if he hadn't been there. All I know is, I owe him."

The cop turned to one of his own. "You believe this?"

The other policeman shook his head and returned to his paperwork.

The cop said to Val, "What's this guy's last name?"

"I have no idea. He just introduced himself as Reuben. He's probably six-seven and three hundred pounds. Heavier."

"Reuben James," said the guy working the files. "Yeah, he's still in the lockup. Couldn't make bail."

The cop gave Val a long look, then went back to a desk and tapped into the computer. "James is in on D&D. Drunk and disorderly. Bail is set at $900."

Val counted out the bills. His roll was thinned down to $470. It would have to be enough. He waited while the cop wrote him out a receipt, then moved back outside.

He stood on the precinct's front stoop, ignored by passing officers and offenders alike. An old woman made hard going of the six concrete steps, but fended away his offer of help with an upraised hand. Val retreated to his corner position and breathed the diesel-infected city air. Perhaps it didn't matter whether his memories fully returned or not. Maybe their imprint remained wrapped around his body tight as cellophane tape. There for all save himself to see.

Both precinct doors squeaked open and a hard, dark mountain came into view. Reuben James stood beside Val, blinking up at the sky. "Tell me that sight ain't sweet as heaven's glory."

Val gave the leaden clouds a cursory glance. He found nothing of interest.

The black man turned slowly. "I remember you. How's the head?"

"No concussion. Just like you said. Here, take this."

When he realized what Val held out to him, he showed two pale palms. "Man, that's your receipt. You don't want to be giving me that."

"It's yours."

"That's a ticket for nine hundred dollars, you'll get it back when I show up at court. Which I will. I'm good for what I owe you."

"You don't owe me a thing. I'm headed out. Take it."

"You're talking crazy."

"Look. You kept me safe in there. I just want to thank you."

"You bailed me out, that's all the thanks I need."

"I'm leaving the country tonight. I don't know when or even if I'm coming back. They may or may not mail me the money if I left an address, which I'm not." He pushed the paper into Reuben's hand. "So I want you to have this."

Reuben formed a massive fist around the receipt. "Why you doing this, man?"

"One more thing. There's a clinic three blocks away. Morningside."

"Like the street. Sure, I know it. Down by the church."

"They're looking for a nurse." Val turned away. "Ask for Dr. Martinez."

"Hang on a second. Ain't no place far enough away, you can run and leave the bad behind." He reached for Val, but missed. "Listen to me, man. I know what I'm talking about."

Val started down the steps. "I just want to do the right thing. That's all."

At the end of the block, Val glanced back to make sure Reuben wasn't on his trail. And collided with Vince's car.

Vince shouted at him through the open window, "What are you, drunk?"

"I haven't had a drop since that night."

"Like I care." He waved a hand like he wanted to punch a hole in the air. "Get in the car!"

Val opened the door and dropped into the seat. Vince hit the gas so hard the door slammed shut of its own accord. To his right a horn sounded ready to climb inside the car with them. "What are you doing?"

"Protecting my investment. What do you think?"

The car did a four-wheel skid around the corner and ran a red light. "Take it easy."

"I'll give you easy." Vince hit an air pocket and slid between a delivery truck and a cab. His feat earned him another horn blast. "I just left some old geezer who ain't got a brain sitting duty behind the desk. Promised him a week's free stay, I get back and the place is still standing."

"I don't get it."

He shot Val a look. "You owe me. That's all you got to understand."

"I know that already."

"This is new. This is add-on. I'm thinking another ten grand."

"For what?" Then he noticed the clothes piled in the back seat. "My flight doesn't leave for another three and a half hours."

"That's not the point. Unless they already got the airport covered, this way you're safe."

"Who's got it covered?"

"Now you're listening. That's good. You're hearing me when I say I'm earning this extra ten grand by keeping you alive." He squinted at signs zipping by overhead. "Which airport?"

"Kennedy."

"So it's Triborough to Central." He zinged around a limo, barely avoiding three pedestrians clustered on the corner, and zoomed away from the horns and the screams. "There I am, sitting behind my little counter, reading the *Post*, minding my own business. In comes this lady. Only she ain't no lady. She's trouble of the feminine variety. And she's looking for you."

"What?"

"Yeah. Imagine my surprise." He spared Val one quick look. "She knows your name, Jeffrey. And she's showing your picture around town."

"Is she behind us now?"

"For both our sakes, I hope not."

"Then slow down, will you?"

"Yeah, I guess I could do that." Vince eased his foot off the gas. "Look at me. Getting this worked up over a dame."

"Who was she?"

"The way she was asking her questions, I'd say a cop."

"You mean, from the precinct?"

"Nah, I know all of them. And she didn't flash no badge. So I'm thinking a bad cop." This time the look lingered. "Who you got after you, they'd go and hire themselves a rogue ex-cop?"

There was only one name. "Terrance d'Arcy."

"Who?"

"You don't know him."

"No, I don't. And seeing the company he keeps, I don't want to either."

"What did you tell her?"

"What do you think? That I never heard of you."

"Did she see you leave?"

"Nah. I waited 'til she got back in her limo and pulled off."

"She was riding in a limo?"

"Her ride isn't the problem here, Jeffrey." Vince pulled up in front of the terminal and stopped. "A limo is just wheels with a suit thrown in for good measure. Worry about how you're gonna stay alive long enough to send me my money."

Val stared out his side window. Passengers disembarked all around them, hugging friends and relatives, shaking hands, waving farewell. Val sat in a late-model sedan with a loan shark for company. Yet he made no move to leave. Vince did not press him. He seemed to be waiting as well.

Val turned around. "Who do you think my enemy is here?"

"You know this guy, not me."

"I'm not talking about the guy. I'm talking about the woman who's hunting me. You talked with her. Tell me what you think."

Vince gave his single nod, clearly approving of the question. He settled a fraction back into the seat. Probably it was as close to relaxed as this man ever came. He tapped his fingers on the steering wheel as he did on the hotel's countertop. Once. Twice. Even this simple gesture revealed Vince's quiet menace.

"A bad cop, like I said. I'm guessing early thirties. Dark hair. Everything about her very tight, you know what I mean? The lady stays in shape. Definitely somebody who'll never run from a fight."

"A bad cop," Val repeated, searching for a handle.

"Lot of them out there, believe me. Probably on the job awhile. Got greedy. Might have a drug habit, but I doubt it. She don't have the look for that either. Most of your bad cops are heavy on the juice. But she didn't have the look. Probably got into a lotta trouble over something. Gambling, maybe. Or a scam that went wrong. End result, she tumbled."

"Sorry, I don't follow you."

"What, that she tumbled? Means she started off taking one wrong step, now she's dragged down so far she'll do anything, say anything, just to stay alive. You know what I'm saying?"

"I hear the words, but that's all."

Vince slowed down, giving it to him with patience. "We're talking street here. She slipped up. Maybe she thought she could get into the man for a taste. Needed some extra cash, liked the thrill, was angry with the boss over something, whatever. You remember what I told those guys wanting to do business? Most people on the street, you get into them, they *own* you. My guess is, she got into the wrong guy in a big way. This guy, he's keeping her on a tight leash, and it's killing her breath by breath. She's desperate and looking for a way out."

"What does this mean as far as I'm concerned?"

"Yeah, that's what you got to be thinking on." Vince gave him the gunslinger's grin, there and gone so fast it might never have happened. "If I'm right here, one thing you can say for certain about the lady. She thinks you're her meal ticket, you better watch out. This dame won't leave you breathing."

"You're about to get me very scared here."

"The people you got after you, fear's a good thing to have on your side. Help you grow eyes in the back of your head. Which you're gonna need." Vince took aim with his pistol of a forefinger. Cocked his thumb. "You see them coming at you, run."

Val bought a nylon duffel bag at an airport newsstand, then returned to Vince's car and packed up all his belongings. Vince drove away without a backward glance. Val checked in and went straight through security. He seated himself two stations down from his departure gate and watched the hustling flow. Val spotted no familiar face, nor anyone who paid him more than passing notice. After a while the faces became part of a half-seen collage.

A young woman took the chair opposite his. She held a young girl, scarcely more than an infant. The daughter fretted and kicked. Finally the woman let her child down onto the floor. The girl used her mother's finger as a support and rose unsteadily to her feet. Then she sang a child's laughter. Most of the surrounding travelers turned to smile with her.

Val should have walked away. There was no need to remain and be tortured by a fragmented past he was determined to leave behind.

But walking away would make no difference. He ached for what had been denied him. He did not need a perfect set of memories to know he had never seen his daughter laugh. Nor that this life sentence was the work of one man.

Val had never known hatred before. He had never thought it was possible to want to murder another man. But Terrance d'Arcy had created in Val a rage of the lethal variety. The divorce, the revelation about Terrance's affair with his wife, the child, the stolen promotion—the body-blows had almost destroyed him. One thing had kept Val intact. One thing had given a framework for his otherwise negated life.

Val knew his current rage was a mere shadow of what he had lived with for almost a year and a half. Which was as it should be. He was, after all, a different man.

A half hour before his flight was scheduled to depart, Val walked to the men's room and washed his face. He stared at himself in the mirror long enough for others using the facilities to glance nervously in his direction. Val paid them no mind. He was too busy searching for a future.

He was as free as any man could ever be. He did not even possess a decent set of memories. All he had to do was arrive safely in England, make it to Jersey, pick up his two million and change, gather up Audrey, and disappear before Terrance could destroy anything more. Simple.

Yet all he could find in his gaze was the same empty core.

When his flight was finally called, Val was first in line. But the questions barked at his heels. The bored New York attendant took forever to stop tapping into his computer and process Val's boarding card. Val scouted the hall a final time, seeing nothing because there was nothing to be seen. He found no comfort in that, however. The faceless crowd only amplified his own solitude. When the attendant wished him a good journey, Val breathed a silent farewell to all he hoped would chase him no longer.

The race was on.

THE SUN WAS AN INCH AWAY FROM MELTING INTO ORLANDO'S western buildings. Don Winslow and Jack Budrow ordered an early dinner and ate seated at the corporate boardroom, which was connected to Jack's office by the Insignia trophy hall. Don had little appetite. Nor was he all that keen to spend more time in the chairman's company. But the day had been too full for them to speak privately. Outsiders swarmed all over the company. Reporters crammed the lobby and streets surrounding the building. Even their homes were marked. Don pushed food around his plate and watched a pair of thunderclouds mar the sunset. The coming tropical storm was a fitting end to a torrential day.

Jack Budrow did not look well. Which was not altogether bad, since his face was the public image for Insignia's gaping wound. Don might have worried about the man's long-term prospects, if he could have spared a thought. Which he couldn't. Not then. "Looks like we might have a handle on Val Haines."

"You're absolutely certain this Haines is still alive?"

Don stared at his boss. The man shoveled prime rib into his mouth like a demented robot. "We've covered this, what, a billion times already. Yes, Jack. Val is above ground. But not for long."

"Where is he headed?"

"Terrance found the guy who supplied Val with a fake passport. So we assume Val's headed for Jersey and his stash. Our security lady put Terrance in contact with people over there. She claims we can trust them with this job."

"This job," Jack muttered around his next bite. "This *job*."

Don decided to let that one slide. "Right now Terrance is meeting New York's finest, giving them the lay of the land. Soon as we hear from the people over there, he'll wing his way across the Atlantic."

Jack dropped his knife and fork with a clatter. "I'm still concerned about trusting d'Arcy with this."

Don had played long enough with food his stomach didn't want. He pushed his plate aside. "Terrance is perfect as far as we're concerned. Those two guys have been enemies for years. Terrance and Val joined the company about six months apart. Val was dating a sweet young thing from Palm Beach. Terrance fell hard for her too, but Val won that round. Soon after he and the lady were married, Val beat Terrance out of a vice-presidency. Terrance doesn't take losing well, Jack. He just smiled and pretended everything was fine. And he waited. Then Val and his lady started having trouble on the children front. They went through all the doctors and clinics, apparently because Val was the one hot for a kid. He was desperate to be a dad. Don't ask me why."

"Terrance stole the man's wife?"

"About the same time he stole Val's promotion. Sweet, wouldn't you say?"

Jack hid his reaction by swivelling his chair around. "Which drove Val to steal from the company, something I never thought would happen."

"Two million and change. I've seen the records."

A bit of the acid emerged. "You're certain Terrance didn't doctor those books as well?"

"Ease up on your partner, Jack. We're not after a choirboy here." Don knew the real reason behind Jack's ire was that Terrance had caught Jack with his own hand in the till. But there was nothing to be gained from mentioning that. "You know who Terrance's father is, right?"

"Some employee of mine, you've already—"

"Arthur d'Arcy is a divisional manager. An engineer by training. Came up through production. Runs the facility we acquired a while back over in Hastings, England. Young Terrance, now, he and the old man don't get along. Not at all. We're talking about some serious friction."

Jack turned back around and gave Don his full attention. "You know why, don't you?"

"Makes for a fascinating tale. Terrance's grandfather was the real deal. A duke. Made a fortune in shipping. Some of it very shadowy, from what I hear. When Terrance was nine, his grandfather divorced Terrance's grandmother. Two days after the divorce was final, the old man married a twenty-four-year-old blond dumpling, then adopted her two-year-old son. Later blood tests proved the kid was his. The grandfather was apparently a real piece of work. The day Terrance turned eleven, the old man kicked the bucket. Problem was, the old man left everything to this young kid and the blond dumpling. Titles, lands, country estate, shipping company, London townhouse, money, the works. Not a cent to Terrance's father, or to Terrance. Who, by the way, was formerly listed as the old man's heir apparent."

"Is that legal?"

"Terrance's mother didn't think so. Her name's Eleanor, by the way. Lives here in Orlando now. Her house is connected to Terrance's."

"Eleanor d'Arcy. Of course. I've met her several times. Quite an impressive lady. But she's not British."

"Born and raised in Philadelphia. Old family. As close to aristocracy as America can claim. She pressed her husband, Terrance's father, to take the old man's estate to court. Arthur d'Arcy refused. Claimed it was a matter of principle."

Jack stared out over the dimming twilight, no doubt imagining the same happening to him. He said, "Eleanor did not take this well."

"To say the least. Divorced her husband, scooped up their son, and left. Bang and gone. Terrance did his studies here in the U.S. and joined us straight out of school. Never mentioned who his father was. Worked his way up through our ranks. Finally Terrance won promotion to VP and in-house auditor. Through some real shenanigans. Like I said, he basically stole the position from Val Haines, who's been his chief rival for years. He planted some incriminating evidence suggesting Val had botched a serious project and tried to hide it. Terrance was given the top slot and Val was sidelined in the pensions department. Left there to rot, basically."

"How do you know all this?"

"Because Terrance told me. I suspected. I asked. He makes no bones about it. Not between us. We're almost family now, right, Jack?"

The CEO stared out the window at the gathering night.

"Pay attention, Jack. It's important you understand how Terrance is earning his keep here. He hasn't just laid blame for this fiasco on our dear departed Val. He's also slipped in a hidden kicker. When the authorities start their investigation, they'll discover that Val managed to keep this from us because he had a secret partner in crime. One far enough away to hide his work from the U.S. authorities."

Jack was back to watching him intently. "Not Terrance's own father?"

"The very same. A careful investigation will show that Arthur d'Arcy was siphoning off funds from his own division's pension fund. Draining it dry, in fact."

Jack's face registered sudden shock. "Hastings. Now I remember. That's the plant—"

"We're scheduling for closure. Still very hush-hush."

"This was Terrance's idea as well?"

"It makes sense as a cost-cutting measure. But, yeah, he managed the study."

"So with the British pension fund raided . . ."

"The laid-off workers won't get a dime. And it'll all be Arthur d'Arcy's fault. He'll spend the rest of his days in prison. A guest of Her Majesty's government, is what they call it. With his good name in tatters." Don let that sink in a moment. "Whatever it takes, Jack. That's what we can expect for our boy to do out there in the field. Whatever it takes."

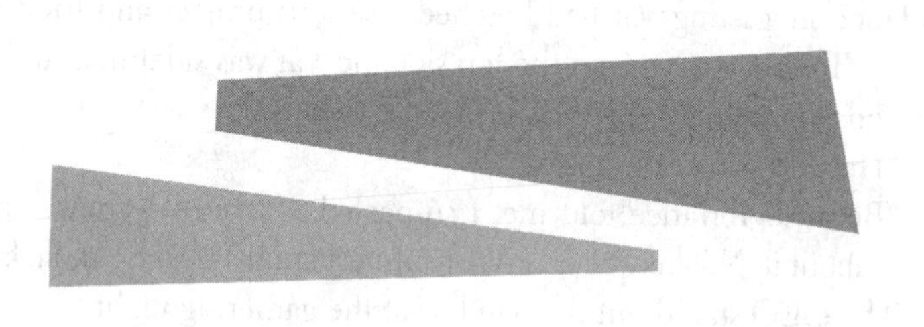

WALLY RODE WITH TERRANCE TO THE ROCKEFELLER CENTER BUT declined to accompany him further. Her presence at a meeting with the police would accomplish nothing. She slipped into the crowd and vanished with a professional's ease. Terrance told the driver to find someplace to wait, smoothed his jacket, and entered the fray.

The combined pressure of events coming together worked to Terrance's advantage. He was clearly exhausted, harried, and needing to be elsewhere. Which was what everyone would have expected. And they were watching. He could already feel the spotlight swiveling his way. He had played many roles up to now. But none so critically scrutinized as this one.

Terrance slipped through the army of reporters and photographers and gawkers bound behind the yellow tape. Rockefeller Center was a series of nine buildings covering two city blocks. The blast was high enough for Terrance to spy the gaping hole in the easternmost pinnacle. He heard footsteps approaching, but remained as he was, reviewing the role ahead. He was the executive in to make a cursory visit, do his best for his company, and worried sick over what was happening.

"Mr. d'Arcy?"

"That's right."

"I'm Detective Harris, homicide." He gestured to the grey-suited man hanging two steps back. "This is Agent Frost, FBI. We're expecting an investigator from the SEC, but she's hung up in traffic. She's bringing one of the bank execs with her."

"Fine. Can we go on up?"

"Are you looking for anything in particular?"

"I want to know about our people." Terrance was already moving.

The detective hastened to keep up. "We've talked to your security chief about this. What was her name?"

"Suzanne Walton."

"Right. Like I told her, there's nothing to go on."

"I want to see."

"Okay. Sure." They followed him toward the entrance. "Your security chief, she's ex-cop?"

"I believe that's correct."

"I made a couple of calls. Walton left Baltimore under something of a cloud."

Terrance pushed through the doors. "If you know all this, why are you asking?"

Harris flashed his badge at the security guard. "We have three people missing and presumed murdered, Mr. d'Arcy. It's my business to ask. So this Walton, how did you manage to find her?"

"You'd have to ask our executive vice president, Don Winslow."

The elevator pinged and they stepped inside. The FBI agent tracked Terrance's movements like a grey wraith. Harris asked, "Where is he?"

"Keeping his finger in the dike down in Orlando. Don is also chief in-house counsel."

"We have to get off two floors below and walk up the rest of the way. We're lucky the bank occupied the top-most floors. The rest of the building appears intact. The blast was directed up and out." Harris punched the button for the fifty-second floor. "So there's nothing you can tell me about Walton?"

"That's not what you asked me, Detective. You asked how she was hired. If you want information about her current status, you need to inquire more specifically." Terrance rubbed his forehead, pleased to see his hand shook. His senses were on hyperdrive. Every second was sliced into microscopic bits, so fine he could be utterly involved in the moment and yet able to expend his awareness out in a thousand different directions. He wondered if this was how it felt to be on stage. "Two years ago, Insignia acquired six hotels that were going under. In my first inspection of the books, I uncovered evidence that the hotels were being ripped off in a highly organized fashion."

"You hired an ex-cop to hunt down some missing towels?"

Terrance cut him a single look. "I said organized, Detective. Initial estimates put the losses at a quarter of a million dollars annually. Per hotel."

The FBI agent spoke up for the first time. "That's a lot of little soaps."

"We found evidence of rooms being rented and showing no revenue."

"How'd you do that?"

"I measured the outflow of laundry, bed linen, food, everything. I compared it with other hotels in similar categories. We were using between a quarter and a third more resources than the billable rooms and restaurant takings required."

The doors opened. Terrance followed the detective into the lobby of an empty law firm. A chandelier had fallen from the ceiling, leaving a hole now covered by cardboard. Two recessed fluorescents had shattered and not yet been replaced. One part of the ceiling and the Persian carpet below it were both badly stained. The left-hand wall of glass bricks bore a sizable crack.

The detective led him to a steel door flagged with yellow police tape. The stairwell smelled of water and oily smoke. There was noise from below. Nothing came from above them except a thickening of the air with each step. Terrance went on, "I discussed the hotel problem with Don, my boss. I needed someone who could identify the thieves without alerting the guests or the press. This needed to go away quietly. Suzanne Walton did an excellent job. Within three months of her hiring, the problem vanished."

There was no door. Terrance halted on the landing because there was nowhere further to go. The blast had wrecked the steel and concrete structure overhead. He stared out across a blackened expanse. Plastic sheeting replaced the former floor-to-ceiling windows. They billowed slightly in the evening breeze.

Harris pointed at the plastic sheeting. "The engineers tell us that's why the building didn't suffer any real structural damage."

"The blast focused upwards, like you said."

"Right. But it pretty much destroyed everything on these two floors, as you can see. We figure it for eight charges, all timed for just after half-past six. Which suggests they aimed to take out your people, Mr. d'Arcy."

"Or the banker they were here meeting," Terrance said.

"What do you know about the banker?"

"Nothing except the name. Which we lifted from Val Haines's calendar."

"How well did you know the victims?"

"Val Haines I thought I knew well. Marjorie Copeland less so. She was an employee of long standing in our pensions department." Terrance shook his head, apparently distracted by the chaos. "What a calamity."

"And Val? That's his real name?"

"Valentine Richard Haines. He was previously in my own department."

"So you've known him for how long?"

"Five years, almost six."

"And you guys were friends. He never mentioned any anger at the company, any desire to—"

"You misunderstand me, Detective. Val and I were not friends. Far from it. You're going to find out sooner or later. Val Haines hated me."

"Why is that?"

"First because I won a promotion he thought was his." Terrance grimaced. "Then he and his wife divorced. I was named in the suit as his wife's lover."

"Yeah, I'd say he had probable cause. What about you?"

Terrance turned from the ruin. "Me?"

"I'd say you had reason to hate this guy. Want to see him destroyed."

"Most certainly," Terrance replied. "Only there's one thing missing from the equation, Detective. With Val and Marjorie gone, we have no chance now of recouping our losses. Or, for that matter, bringing them to justice."

"What about . . ." The detective halted at sounds rising through the stairwell.

They were joined by a wiry accountant-inspector from the SEC and the U.S. director of Syntec Bank. The bank director looked as if he had been hollowed by the incomprehensible. His corporate world stretched out before him, utterly destroyed.

Terrance suffered through a second series of questions, many of which returned to the same ground all over again. He answered with the same weary strain he saw in the banker's features.

Terrance had spent his entire life assigned a part that was not his. Forced into a role meant for someone else, stuffed into a cheaper set of costumes because his father had refused to do his duty. His own father, the man he should have always been able to rely on, had shown all the backbone of a jellyfish. That was how his mother had described Arthur d'Arcy on the day she had told her son the news. There had been a great deal for a nine-year-old boy to take in. How his own grandfather had willed everything to a floozy and her illegitimate offspring—his mother's words again. How Terrance's father, her husband, had refused to fight the decision. How they had been left with nothing. How Eleanor was divorcing her husband. How Terrance was never to mention his father's name again. Eleanor had cried as she had told him, the only time Terrance had ever seen his mother weep. He had promised her in as manly a voice as he could manage that he would take care of her. She had smiled through her tears and called him her little king. But Terrance had known even then that the title did not fit. From that moment, as he danced his multiple roles upon stages on the wrong side of the Atlantic, he had known that someday he would return and claim what was rightfully his.

All his life he had been preparing for the big role. Life was, after all, just theater. Nothing more. Most people thought actors were remarkably adept at impersonations. This was ludicrous. The champions of stage and screen were people who had learned one simple truth.

All life was false. There was nothing at the core of existence save death and despair and an endless unfillable void. Most people spent their entire lives running from this inescapable reality. Actors were unique in that they had *embraced* this. They utilized the fear and pain by *confronting* the void. By *mastering* the power of their sorrow and anguish. Just as Terrance had.

Either people got the big roles or they didn't. Terrance was born to be a star. Anyone who stood in his way became dust and fond memories. As his wretched father soon would discover.

But Val Haines was more than just another unfortunate. Terrance had savored taking Val down in stages. When Terrance was ensconced in his Bermuda palace or his Belgravia townhouse, sated from a lovely meal, watching his daughter play with his lovely wife by his side, he would look back on Val's demise as one of life's sweetest triumphs.

Terrance decided to dine in his suite. He loved the Plaza's dining room, with its palatial surroundings and impeccable service. But he felt drained, as exhausted as he had ever been in his life. The previous day's work, the travel, the visit with Stefanie, meeting Wally, confronting the counterfeiter, the cops, the shattered bank. He needed time alone to unwind.

And the news about Insignia was breaking. Terrance dined on rack of lamb au jus with a rosemary and Dijon mustard topping. He had the waiter set up the table where he could eat and watch the television. MSNBC was giving Insignia the lead position. Between the on-site reporter and Insignia's building, Terrance counted eleven other television vans. And these were only the ones he could see.

He waited until he had poured his second cup of coffee to call Don. "How was your day?"

"Brutal. Where are you?"

"Plaza. Dining in my suite, watching the bomb go off."

"Bomb is right. Any word on our guy?"

"He's left the country."

"You're sure?"

"Fairly. Wally says we can handle it."

"If Wally tells you that, you can take it to the bank."

"That's my impression also."

"What's next at your end?"

"I've got the plane on standby. Soon as he's found, we move."

"You want to be there for the kill, is that it?"

"We have to be sure this time, Don."

"Yeah, I guess we do."

"I'll go by the Jersey bank afterwards, make an appearance, ask for our money back. Hire a lawyer, that sort of thing."

A burst of noise poured through Terrance's cell phone from Don's end, loud as static. Don's voice turned edgier still. "Got to go. Stay in touch."

Terrance disconnected, rose from the table, and headed for the bedroom. He doubted he could sleep. The internal circuits were jammed on high. But he needed to stretch out, try and get his taut muscles to unlock. He pulled off the covers and sprawled on the bed. His joints felt connected to a power source, jerking in tight spasms. He shut his eyes.

The next thing he knew, his cell phone was ringing. Terrance lay as he had fallen, his legs dangling over the edge of the bed. He fumbled in his pocket. "What time is it?"

"Late. You awake?"

"Barely." Terrance rolled over. "Where are you?"

"Idlewild. Planeside. Waiting for you." Wally's voice carried the taut eagerness of a pack leader on the scent of prey. "I just heard from England."

Another day began with an adrenaline jolt. "And?"

"Your man has been spotted."

"I'M VERY SORRY, MR. ADAMS. BUT THERE'S NO WAY WE CAN FLY you to Jersey until late tomorrow." The Gatwick check-in attendant tapped on her keyboard. "No, I lie. All those flights are fully booked. You'll have to wait until the day after."

Val's hearing was impaired by jet lag and the disorientation of arriving in a new country with nothing to claim, not even an identity. "Why so long?"

"This fog is not expected to lift until tomorrow midday, if then. Flights to Jersey do not have the instrumentation required to land in such conditions." The British lilt added a courteous smile to her voice that was not reflected in her features. "The first flights out are already fully booked."

"I've just come in from America. I really need to get over there."

"You could take a ferry. There's a new high-speed service." She pointed him to the concourse's other side. "Take the escalator down to the railway terminal. Trains for Portsmouth depart from track four."

The one known as Matt made the call. "I've got the mark."

"You sure it's this bloke Haines?"

Matt caught sight of his reflection in the vending machine and stopped to preen. Black lace-up boots met skin-tight black jeans that joined to a black silk T-shirt. Matt liked to think of himself as a human stiletto. The other blokes who worked for Boss Loupe, the ones who fitted into their Cerutti suits like muscular sausages, called him a weasel. But not loudly. Matt was too good at his work.

"You there?"

"The face fits the photo you gave me. I've tracked him out of customs. Bang on time from the New York flight."

"Where's your mate?"

"Jocko's tailing the guy."

"So what is Haines up to now?"

"Made a beeline for the Jersey flights. Isn't having no luck there, though."

"Why's that?"

"Weather. It's a right mess."

"So what's his option, then?"

"Wait the night or take the boat, far as I can see. Can't drive to Jersey, that's for certain."

Matt's wit was lost on the other end. No surprise there. "Stay close. Find out where he's headed."

"And then?"

"Do him like I told you. Nice and clean."

"No worries."

"The boss is watching this one."

"Yeah?" Matt tried to keep his voice light. "That translate into a little extra dosh for us?"

"Just do your job. Keep it simple. The boss wants this one put away where nobody will ever find him. Clear?"

Val used a pay phone by the checkout counter and called Audrey's number. This time a man answered. Val held the phone an inch or so from his ear, caught utterly off guard. The man had a gentle sounding tone, even when speaking to dead air. Val hung up.

Val replaced the receiver, hefted his nylon duffel, started for the escalator, then was snagged by the smell of fresh coffee. He stopped so abruptly the man behind stumbled into him. "Sorry, mate."

"No problem." Val would not have noticed the contact except that the guy was so solid. It had felt like backing into a brick wall. Val stepped into the newsstand and bought an *International Herald Tribune*, then joined the coffee line. He shoved his satchel forward with his foot, idly scanning headlines.

Then he froze.

"Sir? Did you want to place your order?"

Val looked up at the cashier. Neither the place nor the words registered.

"Can I get you something?"

Wordlessly, Val hefted his case and stepped away from the counter.

In the terminal Val returned to the paper, futilely hoping the words would have rearranged themselves on the page.

Insignia, his former company, was front-page news.

Val turned to where the report continued on the first business page, then returned to the front page and started over. The words did not sink in until the third read.

He refolded the paper and scanned the terminal. No one appeared to be paying him any great attention. But there was no way he could be certain. There were too many faces. Too many strangers. The threat could be anywhere.

Val hefted his satchel and ran.

THE TWO-HOUR TRAIN JOURNEY TO PORTSMOUTH COMPACTED VAL'S thoughts into lines of determined panic. Everything had finally come together with lethal force. The ease with which he and Marjorie had extracted what they claimed as their due, the bank explosion back in New York, Audrey's warning, his returning memories—everything meshed together now.

Portsmouth station was the next stop, and the train's remaining passengers were already collecting their belongings. Val glanced out the window. A dreary grey landscape came and went as the fog drifted and condensed. Val spotted a few buildings, cars racing by on a neighboring highway, a world washed of all color. He returned his attention to a newspaper article he knew now by heart.

He had been set up from the beginning.

Knowing Terrance, the man had probably left clues in clear enough fashion for Marjorie to have realized the pension fund was being stripped to the bone. Terrance had used Marjorie as he had used everyone else. People were nothing to Terrance unless he wanted them for some purpose. Then they became fodder for his plans. Nothing more.

Unless they got in his way.

The train pulled into the station and halted. Val rose and joined the other passengers flowing through the doors. He stepped onto the concrete and tasted air far too metallic for late April. He spotted the ferry-port sign and joined the throng. Val stumbled over the curb as he tried to read and walk at the same time. The newspaper article feasted upon the lurid details of the corporate thieves being killed in a bomb blast. Syntec Bank U.S. was also under investigation for its hand in draining Insignia's pension funds.

A theft of $422 million.

Val stuffed the paper into the satchel's side pocket and hurried. The walkway was crowded with other passengers whose flights had been cancelled. By the time Val arrived at the ferry terminal, the grayness had condensed into something too thick to be called fog and too fine to be rain. It felt like he was breathing cold diesel tea. The waiting room was a linoleum-lined warehouse with industrial lighting, filled with echoes. Val headed for the bank of phones lining one wall. He dialed Audrey's number. The same man answered. Val hung up and stood with his hand poised on the receiver. Had she found someone else since he had sent her away? If so, why had she written as she had, then urged him to come? Val turned away. His next step remained perfectly clear. Go to Jersey and grab the money. He would call her again from the bank. If the man answered again, Val would forge ahead regardless.

Val purchased his ticket, tried to make himself comfortable in a molded plastic chair, and hid behind his paper. He reread the story and added what the paper could not supply. Terrance had let him get away with the theft because Terrance had always been in control. Terrance had needed a fall guy. In order to make a clean sweep of the larger theft, Terrance had let Val and Marjorie and their tame Syntec banker get away with pocket change. Two million dollars had seemed like the world to Val. But to a guy planning the theft of four hundred million, it was nothing. Val started to wonder who else at Insignia had been in with Terrance on the grand scheme. Don Winslow, for starters. He was the man who had cast the deciding vote against Val and for Terrance in their latest bout. Val wondered if Jack Budrow, the spineless son of a great and good man, could have stooped so low. Then he decided it didn't really matter. Whoever thought they were controlling this particular dance, Val knew Terrance d'Arcy was the one really calling the tune.

Matt made the second call while standing in line to buy ice cream. Two young children at the front of the queue couldn't make up their minds. The ferry's waiting room was large as an airplane hangar and all hard surfaces. Outside, the fog had condensed into drifting rain. Six kids ran in tight little circles around the chairs and played like fighter planes. A mother screeched at them to give it a rest. Matt could have discussed the crime of the century and nobody would have noticed.

Matt's contact at head office demanded, "Give me the good news."

"Don't have none, do I. There's been no chance so far to do it clean like you said. Haines has stayed in crowds every step of the way."

"So what's the bloke doing, then?"

"He's going for the boat."

"You're certain of that?"

"I'm standing in the Portsmouth terminal with him now."

"Follow him."

"I never been one for water. Not even in a glass."

"I didn't ask that, now, did I? Matter of fact, I don't give a toss. You do what you're told."

Matt swallowed against a nervy stomach. He could handle most things. But watching a ship go up and down on the telly was enough to have him shutting his eyes and humming a little tune. He glanced over to where his mate stood in line at the ticket counter. "You want this bloke clean away, not seen away."

"That's the ticket."

"Like an accident at sea, maybe."

"Nobody's meant to notice a thing. Do him quiet and do him fast. You got that?"

"I heard you the first time." Matt swallowed against the dread of his first journey ever on a boat. "Bad weather, no sky, he'll never be missed."

"Where's our lad now?"

The loudspeaker blared overhead, announcing that the ship was boarding. Matt stepped from the line. "He's headed for the gate."

"Hang on, the boss wants a word."

If Matt had not already been green, this would have done the trick. In all the years he'd been on the old man's ticket, Matt had only spoken to Boss Loupe twice. Even so, he instantly recognized the old man's voice. "Matthew, is that you, lad?"

"Yes, Mr. Loupe. Sorry about the din."

"Never you mind. Listen carefully, my boy. Word is, the gentleman you're tailing is headed for the Syntec Bank on Jersey." The old man spelled out the name. "Above all else, your job is to make sure he doesn't arrive."

"I'll do him on the boat, just like you said."

"Nice and quiet, mind. Not a soul's to notice. Leave it for the island if you must. So long as he doesn't enter that bank."

"He'll be gone like smoke, sir. You can count on me."

"I am, my boy. We all are."

Matt shut the phone and swallowed hard a second time. Messing up a job the boss was watching didn't bear thinking about.

If only it wasn't going down on a poxy boat.

VAL COULD'NT BE SURE. BETWEEN THE JET LAG AND THE NEWSpaper article, his senses were jammed on overload. Not to mention the disorientation brought on by this featureless grey day. His world had been jarred too far off its axis. Nothing was registering with clarity.

But he was fairly certain he was being followed.

The two men back in the terminal had been noticeable by their size. One rose almost to Val's height but was cadaver thin. He wore skin-tight clothes that only accented his narrow frame. The other was a bullish giant with a shaved head and a tattoo on his neck. Both had been watching him as he went through the boarding process.

What was more, Val feared he had seen that same tattoo on the guy who had bumped him in the airport. But he could not be certain.

The departures terminal was connected to the boat by a covered walkway. This led to a sloping ramp rising to the middle-deck entry. Val's heart drummed in time to rain striking the walkway's canvas cover. At the gangplank Val slipped the duffel bag to his other hand, gripped the rail, and turned as if to give England a final glance.

The beefy guy was just slipping past security. His narrow-faced mate was nowhere to be seen.

The vessel's entry hall was crammed with excited passengers and squalling kids. Val slipped around a bustling tour group, crouched, and scurried down the main hall. He entered a largish chamber done up as a ship's salon from a bygone era. A café stood at one end and a bar at the other, with circular brass-rimmed tables and wire-backed chairs and Tiffany lamps and polished wood flooring. Val stepped into the bookstore by the opposite wall and slipped behind a revolving magazine stand. He crouched almost to his knees.

A massive pair of Doc Martens boots hustled by, stopped, and turned back. A few moments later they were joined by a set of black lace-up boots with pointed toes. The two stood there together for what seemed like eons. Then they split up.

A young woman with an olive complexion approached Val and asked hesitantly, "Are you all right, sir?"

He made a very feeble pretense of searching the bottom rack. "Do you carry *The New Republic?*"

"Is that a journal?"

"No, never mind." He raised himself up in stages, checking carefully. The pair were nowhere to be seen. "Thanks anyway."

He had to find someplace to hide.

MATT AND JOCKO HAD WORKED TOGETHER ANY NUMBER OF TIMES. There was little chatter, or need for it. Jocko joined the queue of foot passengers jostling good-naturedly toward the gate and the gangplank beyond. Their mark was about fifty feet ahead.

The metal detectors and security inspectors were trouble. Matt always preferred to carry a full set of tools on him. Today he'd just have to rely on Jocko. He slipped back to the gents' and pulled his knife from the special sheath tucked in the small of his back. The handle was a lovely set of brass dusters made special to fit his undersized hand. He wrapped the knife in paper towels, climbed onto a loo, and stored the bundle up top of a cistern. He dropped down and surveyed his handiwork. He would so miss that knife. It was like parting with his best mate.

When he came back into the terminal, Jocko was already through customs. Matt rejoined the queue, passed through the metal detectors, handed his false ID to the coppers, then headed for the boat. It was raining harder now, really coming down in buckets.

The high-speed craft was one of those new jobs, lifting up on an angled V like something off the telly. There was limited car space. The entire ship could have fitted into a larger ferry's main hold. Which made their job all the easier. Matt slipped around the crush of families milling about the entry, telling himself there was no need for the way he already felt. Not while they were still tied up at the dock.

Jocko waved him over. The big man was looking none too pleased. "I've lost him."

"You can't have."

"He's not here, I tell you."

The boat's turbines chose that moment to rumble awake. Matt leaned against the side wall. "You're sure he came on board?"

"I walked the plank right behind him. I'm telling you, he's done a Houdini."

"He must've made us."

"That's what I reckon as well." Jocko looked more closely. "What's the matter with you?"

"I don't like boats."

"So what's the plan?"

"We find him, is what." Queasy or not, Matt had no choice in the matter. "Where do you think he's gone?"

"He don't have all that much space to maneuver. This boat's tiny. There's the level below us for cars; it's locked tight as a drum. There's these four great rooms and whatever they got up top, and that's the lot."

"So you have a gander around this level." Matt kept one hand clamped to his gut. "I'll go search up top. Keep your eyes peeled."

"And if I catch him, what then?"

"We got to do this one clean. That's the word. Don't do him if there's anybody about." The motors rumbled and the boat slipped away from its mooring. Matt swallowed hard. "The boss spoke to me personal."

"When was this?"

"Back in the terminal. We don't do this job right, we never go home. That's as plain as it gets."

Overhead the loudspeakers started up their cheery hello. "You're not having me on, the boss gave you the word?"

"Mr. Loupe himself." Matt forced himself off the side wall. The boat was already pitching. "We find this bloke, and we do him."

The boat was claustrophobic. And fast. The rain was a solid sheet of water upon the forward facing windows. To either side, spumes flew up high as the third floor where Val now stood. Below him was the boat's only car deck, now locked. He knew because he had tried both doors. Below that, he assumed, was the engine room. Above him was the observation deck where people huddled in protected alcoves and enjoyed the sea air.

Val took a chair in the central salon between the two passenger compartments that ran the entire length of the ship. His table was by the wall, which gave him a view of both entrances. But he was totally exposed.

The ship's motors sounded a single deep note, thrumming in his body. Val needed to rest. Despite his adrenaline-stoked fear, he could feel the jet lag and the missing night's sleep deep in his bones. Val leaned his head against the rear wall. The soothing vibrations carried through his temple. He blinked slowly. Then he forced himself to his feet. If he stayed there, sooner or later he would doze off.

The problem was, the boat was constructed to do away with all blind corners. Val stationed himself at the opening to the crammed luggage rack and searched the forward compartment. The boat was all noisy crowds and rain-swept glass and open spaces.

Val retreated into the bathrooms, one after the other. But the places were crawling and the stall doors were symbolic at best. Every new face threatened to become the mammoth bruiser with the tattoo.

He hesitated in the doorway leading back into the hallway. As a trio of beery louts shouldered past, he spotted a door marked "Staff Only." Val watched as two officers passed through. They remained deep in discussion. The younger of the pair used a key connected to his belt by a silver chain to open the door.

Before the door could lock shut, Val slipped across the hall and caught it with his heel. He waited through a pair of breaths. Then he pushed the door open a fraction and glanced inside. The doorway opened into a short hall, which then descended down a series of steps. Val heard the sailors' voices disappearing into the distance. He saw no one. What he could see of the hall was narrow, windowless, and empty.

He stepped inside.

Jocko knew full well what the world thought of him. He was the silent muscle, not meant to have even half a brain. Nobody expected him to speak. Which suited Jocko just fine. He had no time for idle chatter. He wanted a bloke's attention, he clapped him one. That always worked.

Problem was, Matt was always telling Jocko what to do. Even when Jocko had his job down cold. Like now. It was simple enough, really. Clean was clean.

Yammer, yammer, that was Matt in a nutshell. But Jocko was the one seeing to what needed doing. When time came to shut the gob and act, Matt played like smoke. Just like now.

This guy was such an easy target. That was Jocko's first thought when the bloke popped back into view. Haines was already injured, his head patched. Jocko slipped back a notch, to where the coffee bar met the side wall. One little tap and Haines would be laid out clean as you please.

Haines hovered in the doorway leading to the gents'. His eyes were doing the dance, seeing danger everywhere. Jocko snorted quietly. Matt thought he was the brains? So what would he be doing this minute? Telling old Jocko to sort this bloke out, that's what. Give the word and take a giant step back.

Jocko was watching this Haines. Oh yeah. Watching him make all the mistakes.

And he had just made a big one.

Val spied the rushing hulk a split second before impact. The simple fact that Val's senses were on hyperalert granted him just enough time to step back from the door. Or try to.

The attacker's strength was shocking. Clearly he had intended to pin Val between the steel door and the bulkhead, breaking Val's ribs and halting him in his tracks. Instead, the door's glancing blow blasted Val back three paces. The door struck the side wall with the force of a cannonade.

Val could have caught himself on the top stair with the railing for a brake. But he let himself fall. In fact, he used the railing as a slide, stumbling backwards down the nine steps. He hit the bottom landing and sprawled. But the guy was already thundering down from overhead. Val did a crabwise backwards crawl down the corridor.

His foe leapt down the final three steps. The narrow passage made his bulk even more monstrous.

A side door opened. A woman in uniform peered out. She gaped at Val's panic-stricken crawl, then spotted the massive intruder. She started to scream.

The attacker heaved her back with an open-palmed punch to her chest. His strength was such that he catapulted her across the chamber and slammed her against the far wall.

The attacker peered in the open door, a single instant to ensure she wasn't able to give him trouble. Val took this as his only hope for escape. He clawed his way to his feet and raced down the hall.

The thunder behind him added wings to his flight.

The door at the hall's end opened. The young officer stepped into view. Val ducked down and slipped past the man and through the doorway.

On the other side was open space and noise. The landing was metal and about four feet square. A spiral staircase headed downwards. Val ignored the shout behind him, gripped the rails with both hands, and hit every fifth step.

Above him, the officer's second shout cut off abruptly. Val leapt over the railing and dropped the final ten steps. He landed upon a catwalk that ran the entire length of the ship. To either side roared a giant pair of turbine engines painted a monochrome green. They bellowed a constant note.

The metal catwalk bounced like a trampoline beneath Val's feet when the attacker landed. Val did not risk a glance backwards. He knew the man was closing. Val pounded down the metal road.

Up ahead, a mechanic in greasy overalls talked to the senior officer Val had seen by the upstairs doorway. They peered at some valve or meter. The mechanic looked up, spied Val racing toward them, and shouted a warning.

These men were far more experienced than the younger officer. They spread out in a flanking pattern, barring his progress.

Val leapt up and over the metal railing. He hit the lip of the motor, a narrow ledge running down the entire side with bolts protruding like painted traps. The machine's vibrations almost knocked him off his feet. Val could not maneuver on that tight strip. He did the only thing that came to mind, which was to climb the motor's rounded hump to the top.

The motor's tremors traveled up through his hands and legs. They rattled his vision. The two crewmen yelled at him and at the bruiser who was scrambling across the catwalk railing.

The mechanic raced forward and grabbed the attacker's leg. The bigger man kicked him, a casual motion as if he were shaking off a pest. The mechanic went down hard.

The senior officer turned away from both Val and the bruiser and raced down the catwalk. Val kept going in the same direction, hoping for a diversion. The vibrating motor felt like a galloping metal horse. He was threatened with falling into an abyss of pumping iron and oily darkness.

Behind him, the bruiser hesitated in the act of climbing onto the motor's ledge. The ship's officer was headed for a red alarm box. The attacker shouted an oath and clambered off the barrier. He raced after the officer.

Val turned and did a monkey scramble in the opposite direction. He slid off the motor, leapt over the railing, and raced back down the catwalk toward the stairs.

The oil on his hands and feet and knees turned the curving stairs into a nightmarish assault on a slippery metal mountain. Val clawed his way up. The young officer sprawled on the upper landing, moaning and moving slowly. Val leapt through the doorway, left an oily stain on the opposite wall, and plunged down the hall. The young woman in the office-cabin called weakly for help. Val scrambled up the final stairs and reentered the ship's public space. The antechamber was full of passengers astonished by his sudden appearance.

Only then did Val realize that his head was bleeding again.

Val took the most likely avenue of escape, which was up. The stairs ended in a small antechamber with a door to either side. He flung one open and entered the rainswept maelstrom.

The rain was turned into blinding pellets by the wind and the vessel's speed. To his left, a few passengers huddled within an open-ended chamber and shouted against the din. Ahead, the grey hulk of Jersey emerged from the storm.

Val could not risk becoming trapped in the passengers' steel-sided alcove. He gripped the wet rail and started around the back of the central smokestack.

Val turned the corner and came face-to-face with the second man.

The attacker gripped the railing with one hand and his gut with the other. He gaped in utter shock at Val's appearance, then reached below his jacket and shouted a name, or started to.

Val did not think. He roared his anger and his fear and raced forward until he slammed into the thin man.

The attacker slid backwards until he rammed the opposite rail. Val continued pushing, trying to fling the man into the flying spray and the slate-grey water. To his left, the passengers huddled within the second metal-walled alcove gaped in shock at their struggle.

The man was smaller than Val, but he was streetwise and vicious. He was also fighting for his life. The first punch connected with Val's leaking temple and almost blinded him with the pain. Val hung on and struggled with all his might to shove the attacker over the railing. Below them, the vessel's wake was a constant roaring wave.

Voices shouted and moved toward them. But Val did not loosen his grip until the hands forced him. Countless hands. Too many for him to fight against. The pain in his temple was a great booming force, stronger than the thrumming motors. His vision leaked with the spattering rain.

Val shouted against the wind and other voices, "Who sent you?"

The man struggled against other hands gripping him. He stared at Val with a manic gaze and said nothing.

"Who sent you?"

The boat slowed as it passed through the Jersey harbor entrance. Somewhere overhead a horn blasted.

The door behind Val blew open. The bruiser from downstairs shoved his way forward. He reached over the knot of people surrounding Val and grabbed for him.

"Jocko!"

The bruiser hesitated.

"Move it!"

The brute flung aside the other passengers and freed his mate. The two of them raced toward the stern. Val watched the pair slip down a ladder, then another, until they stood on the lowest open deck. They stripped off rain-washed jackets, then waited as the boat slowed further. The smaller of the pair turned and looked back up at Val. He leveled a finger and took aim. Then the bruiser gripped his arm.

Together the pair dove over the side.

"SIR, THE PORT AUTHORITIES WOULD VERY MUCH LIKE TO HAVE A word with you."

"Fine. I'll talk to anybody you want." Now that the battle was over, he had to fight the words out around chattering teeth. "But they've got to come here."

"I'm afraid that's not possible. This boat keeps to a very tight schedule."

"I have no problem with that." He nodded his thanks to the orderly who brought him a cup of strong black tea. Val needed both hands to bring it to his mouth. He blew, sipped, said, "Let's take off. Now works fine for me."

The officer wore short-sleeved whites. They were seated in a room across from where the woman now lay being tended by the ship's first-aid officer. Val's temple throbbed beneath his new white bandage. His duffel had been located, and he wore a dry tracksuit. A blanket was draped over his shoulders. His tremors rocked the cup he held. He did not feel cold now so much as utterly drained. His voice sounded raw and empty to his own ears.

The officer had the no-nonsense air of former navy. He was seated upon the fold-down desk opposite the bunk where Val sat. "You're saying you do not wish to disembark on Jersey?"

"You kidding? Those brutes are out there waiting for me."

"I presume you mean the pair of men who reportedly attacked you over football."

"Crazy, isn't it? I had no idea they were that drunk." Every word needed to be pried from a brain that felt gummed solid with fatigue. He named the only British team that came to mind. "Or Manchester United winning some cup was all that big a deal."

The officer crossed his arms. "Indeed."

A young sailor knocked on the open door. "Customs says his documents are in order, sir."

He reached over and accepted Val's passport. His eyes never left Val's face. "Thank you."

Val hid his relief at having his passport back within grabbing distance by sipping from his cup.

"My officers confirm that you were the victim and the large man the attacker." The officer tapped Val's passport on his thigh. "What I fail to understand, Mr. . . ."

"Adams."

"Is why you felt it necessary to go after the man on the deck."

"I saw he was going to attack me," Val said, still examining the dregs of his teacup. "I didn't want to give him a chance."

"And yet the passengers claim the man had spent the entire voyage being extremely ill."

"Like I said, none of this makes any sense to me."

A young woman tapped on the door frame. "Master's compliments, sir. We're ready to begin boarding."

"Carry on."

"Sir." She departed.

"I agree, Mr. Adams. None of this makes sense." The officer pushed himself off the desk. "But I have no reason to deny you passage home, much as I might like. I can, however, insist that you spend the journey isolated in this compartment."

"Could you have someone bring me a sandwich?" He tried futilely to dredge up a smile. "I missed lunch."

Val woke to the drumming of the engines and the motion of a ship at sea. The vessel did not rock so much as slice the waves. It buffeted, but not harshly, like an ax cleaving the sea's surface. Val struggled to sit upright. He glanced at his watch. But he could not recall what time it had been when the ship's officer had finally left and he had lain down.

A tray had been brought in and left while he was asleep. He reached across the narrow cubicle and pulled out the stool hidden beneath the desk. Val seated himself and ate with ravenous appetite. Val's temple throbbed and his body ached. His shoulder throbbed from being struck by the door, his hands from abrasions as he flew down the stairs, his knees and ankles from scrambling along the motor.

A mirror was embedded in the alcove wall. He finished eating and stared into his reflection. The face looked flaccid with exhaustion, the eyes cavernous. Val examined his features, seeking a simple answer. What was he to do? And once he knew, would he have the strength to do it?

He lay back down. In an instant he was asleep once more.

The boat's altered motions woke him. This time he felt far more alert. He glanced at his watch. He had been asleep for almost two hours. The motors were rumbling at a lower pitch now. Val rose and entered the cramped washroom. Whoever had brought him lunch had also left a disposable razor and a small bottle of mouthwash. The motions helped loosen the muscles still cramped and sore from the attack. His mind was sluggish, however. There was still a sense of being disconnected. Whether this was from jet lag or the attack, he could not say.

The young male officer who had returned Val's passport unlocked the cabin door. "Ship's docking, sir."

"Thank you." Val stuffed his wet belongings into the duffel bag and headed out. The officer refused to meet Val's eye. "Just up the stairs ahead of you."

"I know the way."

"Certainly, sir." There was a toneless etiquette to the young officer's voice. Like a prison officer on public view. He dogged Val's steps, hanging just far enough back to keep from tripping over Val's feet. At the top of the stairs he said, "To your left, sir."

The entry salon was empty save for three cleaning staff. They did not look up at Val's passage. He had the sense of being officially declared a leper. To look was to risk infection. Unclean, their silence shouted. Unclean.

The officer halted at the gangplank. No farewell word. Nothing. A pair of customs officers awaited him at street level. They had clearly been forewarned. Their search of his bag, his passport, and his body was extremely thorough. Val maintained his story, and kept his tone mild. A day trip to an island he had read about but never visited had been disrupted by two drunken louts. He was terribly sorry for all the trouble he had caused, and extremely glad to be back in England. He gave as his address the West End hotel where he had stayed the last time over. The customs officers had no reason to keep him, and finally let him go.

Val crossed the ferry port's vast parking area, taking great draughts of free air. The evening smelled of sea and salt and rain. Trucks passed in a slow convoy, headed for the continent. He was soon drenched. He did not mind in the slightest, though he had no more dry clothes. The rain helped wash away the mental fog. He left the port area and headed down the main road. There was bound to be a nearby bed-and-breakfast catering to the trucking crowd and accustomed to admitting bedraggled men.

Mental gears meshed begrudgingly as he walked. Clearly his attackers were still on the island. The bank was definitely going to be watched. Which meant he could not access his funds. He and Marjorie had arranged the numbered accounts so that their money could be withdrawn only in person.

Which meant Val was now extremely stuck.

He had less than three hundred dollars to his false name. He was as incognito as he could have asked. A nameless man, unloved by all, seeking freedom from a stranger's past.

TERRANCE AND WALLY JOURNEYED ACROSS THE ATLANTIC IN A Gulfstream IV outfitted like an elegant hotel suite. Wally tried hard to pretend it was all part of the game. But the private steward and the crystal decanters and the kid-leather seats and the walnut burl table and the filet mignon with fresh truffle sauce left her gaping. When they finished dinner, the steward turned the seats into two beds with Sea Island cotton sheets behind hand-painted privacy screens. Five hours later, they were awakened by coffee served on a silver tray and fresh-baked croissants.

The bathroom was cramped but contained a miniature shower. Wally came out toweling her hair and announced, "I'm busy making a list of everything I didn't know I needed until right now."

They landed in a fog so thick they saw nothing until touchdown. Terrance peered through the soup. Waiting upon the tarmac was an elderly gentleman standing beside a vintage Bentley.

The old man stepped forward as the steward released the stairs. Only then could they get a clear look at his face. Wally halted Terrance with a hand to his arm. "That isn't my guy."

Terrance waved the steward away. "What are you telling me?"

"The suit. He's not who I called." Wally took another worried glance beyond Terrance. "My guess is, we're looking at our guy's boss."

"So? This is good, isn't it?"

"I don't know what it is. I don't like changes in plan. Especially not this one." Wally had the tight look of taking aim. "This deal is my ticket out. The score that is going to get me out of the hole once and for all."

The gentleman halted at the base of the plane's stairs and called up, "I'm looking for a Mr. Terrance d'Arcy."

Terrance asked her, "Aren't we overreacting a little here?"

"Maybe." Wally squinted through the grim day. "But where's my guy, that's what I want to know."

The gentleman called, "I say—"

Terrance ducked under the doorway. "I'm d'Arcy."

"And right on time. How splendid." The man's smile was far brighter than the overcast day. "Josef Loupe, at your service."

The air was heavy with a chill foretaste of rain. Terrance met the outstretched hand as he stepped off the bottom stair. The skin was papery with age, but the muscles underneath were firm. "How do you do."

"Such an honor, Mr. d'Arcy. I have so looked forward to this encounter." He bowed slightly over Terrance's hand, in the manner of bygone courtiers, then indicated a uniformed gentleman waiting two steps back. "If I might trouble you for your passports, we can make your arrival official."

As the customs officer leafed through their passports, Terrance inspected their contact. Josef Loupe wore a camel-hair overcoat draped across what once had been very powerful shoulders. Now he had a scarecrow's frame and a face to match. Up close, the smile revealed capped teeth so white they appeared painted. The man's age was impossible to tell. Somewhere between sixty and eighty, with a calculated tan and eyes dead as cold tar. He chatted lightly through the process. "Such is the pleasure of private aircraft these days. No queues, no intrusive inspections. One lands far from the tourist hordes and is treated with proper respect. You cannot put a price on such items. Either you can afford it, or you cannot."

The officer demanded, "What is the purpose of your visit to England?"

"Just a quick stopover before continuing on to Jersey."

"How long do you intend to remain in the United Kingdom?"

"Not long. A day."

Loupe cleared his throat. "Regrettably, events might require you to remain here a bit longer."

Behind Terrance, Wally huffed as though taking a blow to the gut. Terrance glanced over. Wally refused to meet his eye.

"I should think three days would be more than adequate," Loupe went on.

The officer stamped both passports, then nodded at the cases that the steward had set on the tarmac. "Anything to declare?"

"Nothing."

He handed Terrance both passports. "Enjoy your stay."

Terrance waited until the officer was well away to say, "We were expecting to be met by someone else."

"Your contact is seeing to matters in Portsmouth."

"Matters?"

"A temporary setback, nothing more." Loupe indicated the waiting limo. "I shall endeavor to explain everything once we are underway."

The car was a vintage Bentley with a front end long as a polished blue locomotive. Terrance let the elderly man settle him into a seat soft as rarefied butter. Loupe slipped the overcoat from his shoulders and handed it to his aide. The attendant was neither tall nor big, but carried himself with a pent-up menace. His face was professionally blank, his motions as tightly silent as a panther. Wally watched while Loupe's man loaded their bags, then climbed into the front seat. She never looked directly at Loupe. The old man did not seem to register her on his radar. Terrance heard Wally sigh as she shut her door. Her disengaged attitude was more irritating than worrisome.

The Bentley's rear compartment was so spacious Terrance could stretch out his legs and still not touch the front seat. Terrance faced a triple set of television screens set in sterling silver frames, with clocks to either side. A bar extended to form a tongue of walnut burl. On it rested a coffee service and a silver tray holding magazines and the day's *Financial Times*. Loupe indicated the coffee service. "May I offer you something?"

"It's not necessary."

"No, please. I insist." The faintest tremor touched his hands as he filled the delicate porcelain cup.

The Bentley pulled through the airport's security gates and powered away so smoothly the coffee did not even sway in the cup. "Where are you from?"

"Ah. The accent. Over fifty years in this country, and still I talk like an immigrant."

Terrance leaned back and took a sip. Perfect. "On the contrary, your English is better than mine."

"You are too kind. I came to England in 1947. Before that time, I carried the same name as the town where I was born. Josef Lubavitch. You have heard of it?"

"No. Sorry."

"No matter. It was a place of mud and misery. Stalin should have destroyed it. He started to, then stopped. Don't ask me why." He gave an old man's smile this time, a thinning of his lips. Perhaps the first genuine gesture Terrance had seen from him. "When I was fourteen I began fighting in Stalin's army. Just another child soldier meant to feed war's ravenous maw. We all were given different names, part of building camaraderie in the face of coming defeat. I was known as Loupe, French for *wolf*."

Loupe opened the door beneath the coffee service and offered Terrance a linen napkin. There was an elegant servitude to his gestures, a subtle layer of messages. He unpacked sandwiches and set two on a bone china plate. The bread was white and cut very thin and the crusts had been trimmed away. Terrance was not hungry. But he did not refuse. The old man's actions were not about food.

"My battalion commandant was a rarity, a nobleman who had survived Stalin's purges by being the most fervent Communist alive. As a youth he had spent his summers taking the waters at Cannes. He returned to fight alongside his Russian brothers. As I said, a genuine fanatic. He liked to sprinkle his addresses with French. He said it added a certain dignity to our cause."

Loupe placed a pair of sandwiches on a second plate and settled back into his seat. He did not touch the food either. "He was an absurd figure, no doubt. Standing in a wilderness of mud and death, draped in a tattered uniform and waving a bayonet because his saber had been broken on a helmet or a rifle or a tank. We were all dressed in rags. Our boots we had stolen off the bodies of fallen comrades. We were starving, of course. That is what I remember most about my war years. The hunger. That and the smell. The odor of a battlefield is so fierce it leaves you unable to taste anything fully ever again. I was always famished. When I arrived in London I weighed one hundred and nine pounds. I was twenty-three years old."

Terrance leaned forward far enough to set the plate down on the newspaper. Wally stared straight ahead, apparently blind and deaf to all that surrounded her. In a flash of insight, Terrance understood her disconnectedness. This was no run-down tenement in a city she knew. They were surrounded by an alien level of luxury, hosted by a gentleman of the old school. The woman was utterly out of her element. Which, truth be told, suited Terrance just fine. He was the master performer when it came to power and privilege. This was his realm.

"Newly arrived in England," Loupe continued, "I assumed I was invincible. After all, I had survived the Nazis and the Reds. But Stalin was not my worst enemy, Mr. d'Arcy. Time is such a subtle foe. You think you have mastered everything. But in the end, time always wins. Look at me. Seventy-four, no sons, no one I can trust with my business. So a mistake has been made, and I must personally travel out to meet you, and apologize."

Terrance set his coffee cup down. "Tell me what happened."

"I assure you, Mr. d'Arcy, we took your request most seriously. I sent two good men to cover this job. I had formerly considered them to be some of my most reliable people."

Loupe's accent was such a subtle shading it was almost lost behind his careful diction. Clearly the man had spent a fortune on elocution. "They failed?"

"An utter shambles." No amount of plastic surgery could fully hide the creases of concern. "Your man is alive and back in England."

Rain began falling heavily. The only sounds inside the Bentley were the gentle thunking of the wipers and Loupe's recounting of the foiled attack. The two people occupying the front seats remained motionless. Wally might as well have been turned to dark-haired stone.

"The only bit of good news is that your man has not come close to the Jersey bank. My men are now stationed there twenty-four hours of the day." Loupe mused to the side window. "I am thinking that perhaps I might leave them there on permanent assignment as punishment for having failed us."

The Bentley pulled through an arched stone gate and entered the grounds of a palatial hotel. "Where is our man now?" Terrance asked.

"We are doing our utmost to determine that, Mr. d'Arcy. And I can assure you that there will be no second failure. I intend to personally ensure that everything is done according to our agreement. And done swiftly." Loupe nodded as the bellhop opened his door and bid them welcome. "We'll give you a night to recover from your journey, and tomorrow we shall go on the attack."

VAL PLACED THE CALL FROM THE CHEERLESS FRONT ROOM OF A rundown guesthouse, just another weary brick rowhouse in a street by the port. The front room had a small television set by the windows overlooking the street. The program was something about gardening. A trio of truckers snored beerily from the sofa, the grime and fatigue of constant travel a stain as deep as their tattoos. The wall clock claimed it was only nine, but the night felt eons old. Val sat in an alcove formed by removing the door from a rear closet. The walls were carpeted and smelled of ten thousand cigarettes. The telephone was brown plastic and had a counter that counted down the seconds remaining before he had to feed in more coins. Val unfurled the rumpled page with Audrey's number and dialed.

"Hello?"

"It's me, Audrey. I'm sorry to be calling so late."

Her tone instantly went frigid. "Did you do it?"

"Not the four hundred million like they're saying."

"That's not what I asked. Did you or did you not steal money from the company?"

"This is not the sort of greeting I was expecting."

"I take that as a yes."

Her voice was so arctic Val felt it necessary to beg. "Don't hang up. Please."

"You of all people. Never in a million years would I have thought you capable of such a thing. Why ever did you do it?"

"I don't remember."

"Hardly the most brilliant of excuses."

"I was sort of hoping for a different reception. You know. After your letter."

"Forget the letter, Val. That was before."

"Before what?"

"Just put the letter down as the ramblings of a distraught woman. Pay it no mind."

Val's pay telephone beeped a warning signal. The slot where he fed in coins was stubborn, as though even the apparatus was trying to tell him it was a mistake to have called. "How did you know? About my taking the money, I mean."

"Don't be daft. Terrance is my brother, remember? His forte is finding another's weakness and going on the attack." She paused, then asked, "Where are you?"

"Portsmouth. The Seaside Bed and Breakfast on Wyckham Lane." Val felt her uncertain silence compress and squeeze. Leaving him no way out. "I really need your help, Audrey."

"You're stubborn enough to think you're doing the right thing when you're only causing further harm. Which is precisely why I have to see you, I suppose. To ensure you don't make matters worse than they already are."

She hung up on him then. A new first. As far as he could remember.

The street held the night in a narrow embrace made slick by rain. A car coughed apologetically as it passed, the tires slicing dark rivulets along the asphalt. Val could have remained inside. But the guest-house stank of the landlady's constant cigarettes and the guests' bleak weariness. Val had no idea whether Audrey would show up. He decided to wait for a time before letting the bed claim him. He extracted Audrey's letter from his pocket, his movements slow. It was not that he wished for more of her instruction. He simply found comfort in unfolding the well-creased pages. The words revealed a woman who thought well of him. The knowledge of love, even one now past, warmed his bones.

Val raised his gaze to find Audrey leaning against a car. She observed him with crossed arms and a hostile expression. The truth was, whatever she wanted to hit him with, he probably deserved it. He showed her the pages and said, "Your letter has meant an awful lot."

Audrey bit off the words very carefully. "I suppose it's my nature to reach out. Even when the cause is utterly lost."

Val was determined not to offer her a reason to rage. He stowed the letter away and rose to his feet. "I just want you to know how grateful I am."

She stabbed the air between them with a blade of a hand. "I want one thing understood right here at the outset. You are not to try and draw me back in again."

Val remained mute, while his heart keened at her closeness and the distance between them.

Audrey opened her door and slipped behind the wheel. "I suppose you'd better come along."

"Where are we going?"

"Home."

"Are you sure that's—"

She started the engine and jammed down on the gas pedal, drowning out his protest. "Just get in the car."

Her automobile was a vintage Rover, a boxy vehicle turned an indeterminate grey by the night and age. Val felt as though he knew the car, which was impossible, for he had never seen Audrey in England before. Of that he was certain, and little else. "Why did you come for me?"

"You'd prefer I leave you for my brother to devour?" The car had an oversized steering wheel of hard plastic, which Audrey constantly kneaded. When Val did not respond, she finally said, "The police came by."

"Why would they want to talk with you?"

"Not me. My father. This could not have come at a worse time for him."

Val took this for the male voice on the phone, and breathed easier. "Is he sick?"

"Dying, actually." The words caught in a throat clenched taut. For the first time her stern facade cracked slightly. "The cancer has spread to his lymph nodes."

"I'm so sorry, Audrey."

"Everything that is good in me I owe to him." She spoke with determined matter-of-factness, and patted the steering wheel. "Even this old dear of a car."

"You went back to care for him?"

Her tone hardened instantly. "I left because you ordered me to go."

Passing headlights painted her in brief flashes. She looked so strong, so vibrant. Val could see so much of Terrance in her, the same determined set to her features, the same brilliant luster to the hair. But in Terrance everything was tainted. Never was Terrance's twisted state more evident than now. "Tell me about the police."

"They came with some dreadful man in grey from the American embassy. He had some official title, I don't recall what." Audrey's gaze reminded him of a lifetime seafarer. Her eyes appeared focused upon some infinite horizon. Even when she was looking at him. Like now. "They claim Pop was behind the theft."

"Why would Terrance take aim at his own father?"

"You've forgotten all our discussions?"

"I don't remember a lot of things."

"In this case it's perhaps for the better. My family's history no longer concerns you. You're here because we have to stop him before he does further damage to a fine, dear man."

Hastings preserved its medieval village charm even at night. Gas lamps lined the thoroughfares rising from the rocky beach. Tudor houses marched in complacent camaraderie up the steep slope. Beyond the market square and the ancient church tower glistened a holiday port. The sea had the radiant quality of oiled silk. The rain had stopped. Audrey waited until she parked in front of a thatched-roof house with walls of wattle and blackened beams to ask, "Did Terrance do that to your head?"

"Not directly, no." He did not hurt in any particular place so much as throb in general. Residual jet lag mixed with the day's battering to form a potent mixture. "Where are we?"

"My father's house."

"This is a terrible idea, Audrey. Terrance's hired goons attacked me on the boat to Jersey. They're probably still on the island hunting for me. But there could be others."

She said in a tightly compressed voice, "You were just going to sail away, weren't you?"

"I was hoping you'd . . ." The closed door behind her eyes stopped him in midflow. He changed direction to, "Terrance has muscle on my trail. I don't know how they tracked me to the boat, but they did. This wasn't just some random attack. They wanted to kill me."

"I should have known. This is what you were planning all along, wasn't it? This was why you stole." Her face took on the pinched quality of having received the worst possible news. "Val, there is only one way to die to the past and all its burdens and mistakes. Stealing money and running away is not it."

"Please, Audrey, listen to what I'm saying. Terrance knows about us. Sooner or later they'll come here looking for me."

"Oh, why on earth do I bother? You wouldn't listen to me then. Change was your worst enemy. Why should now be any different?" She rose from the car and slammed the door. Her shoes clicked an angry pace up the stone walk. She unlocked the door and entered without a backward glance.

Casting worried glances behind him, Val followed her inside. The home's interior was as charming as outside. Beams thicker than his chest laced overhead. The floor was polished tongue-and-groove planking two hands broad. Val guessed the wood was oak, but centuries of polish had masked the grain. Antique brass candelabra had been refashioned to hold lightbulbs. The windows were squared with lead, the panes hand-blown and so old they had run like clear honey. Lamplight danced a soft tune upon antique furniture and a stone fireplace large enough to contain a bench and cooking station. The rooms smelled of beeswax and a roast.

She was already busy in the kitchen. Audrey said through the framed partition separating her from the living room, "Do you think you might possibly delay running away by a few days?"

"First I need to find someplace where you won't be endangered."

She waved at him with the carving knife. "Let's move beyond that, shall we? Are you or are you not going to help us stop Terrance?"

"Who is we?"

She finished slicing a lamb roast into thick slabs and began slapping hot English mustard on fresh bread. "Answer my question."

Val felt something ugly and unwelcome crawl around in his gut. Terrance had outmaneuvered him very badly. The attackers on the boat had terrified him. His entire focus had been on one single tactic. Cut and run.

Audrey's attitude became clear to him now. His conception of this woman and her state were entirely wrong. She was not pining away for him. Nor was she planning to help him escape. She had brought him here with the exact opposite in mind. And she was worried he would let her down.

Again.

The kettle whistled behind her. She moved with the efficient motions of an experienced chef, drawing out plates and saucers and cups, fixing a pot of tea, slicing fresh lemon, squeezing it into one cup, stirring in two heaping spoonfuls of sugar. Reaching through the partition and setting it on the counter for him. Val stared at the steaming mug. He was far less sure what he wanted than Audrey was.

"Go tell Father his tea is ready. No doubt you'll find him in the garden."

Nighttime had been banished from the rear of the house. Spotlights were fastened to the back wall, and others embedded in the garden soil. A postage stamp of a lawn was rimmed by flowers that sparkled from the recent storm. The perimeter wall was fifteen feet high and made from brick so old it was crumbling. The garden was on fire with color.

Arthur d'Arcy puttered by the back wall and hummed a single

faltering note, a soft message that his entire universe was bordered by these brick walls. Val stood in the doorway, breathing in the scent of tilled earth and an evening stolen from some softer season. Overhead he spotted a first star.

"Mr. d'Arcy?"

"Eh? Yes?" The old man slowly rose from his stoop. "Ah. You're Audrey's young man."

Val watched him ease up in very gradual stages. The hand holding the trowel was slightly curved, like a bird's claw, and pressed tightly against the base of his ribcage. "Audrey says your tea is ready."

"Splendid." He set the trowel down by the flowers he was planting and stripped off his gloves. "The weather has been positively atrocious, wouldn't you agree?"

Val pointed to where roses the size of pink dinner plates climbed the rear wall. "Those are some amazing flowers."

"Yes, my high walls trap the spring heat. That is, when there is any sun at all." His walk was not quite a limp, but he carefully favored his left side. "But those roses have very little to do with me, I'm afraid. I trim them back each November and till in a bit of bonemeal every spring. The rest is up to God and nature. Have a look at the stems where they emerge from the earth. Thick around as your thigh, they are. I wouldn't care to hazard a guess how long they've been standing sentry there by my wall, doing their proper duty each and every spring."

D'Arcy smiled at Val as he took the back steps one at a time. "Pity not all of life follows such a proper course, wouldn't you agree?"

Val matched his pace to the older man's and followed him back inside. The home's ease relaxed him so thoroughly that, in his already weakened state, he had trouble lifting his feet over the top step.

Arthur d'Arcy washed his hands in the kitchen sink and asked his daughter, "What has he determined?"

Audrey kept her gaze on her work. "Val hasn't said."

The two of them stood by the back window, eating their sandwiches and sipping tea in the companionable silence of people who had long since left behind the need for empty chatter. Val's provisions were stationed on the kitchen's other side, a silent message that he was relegated to the fringe.

Arthur reported to his daughter, "Gerald phoned you."

"What did he say?"

"That he was back and he had your message." Arthur held his cup out for refilling. "He said if you were absolutely certain, he would go along."

Audrey cut Val with a glance, but said nothing.

Val stared through the partition to the empty living room. An ancient anger barely managed to flicker up through the blanket of fatigue. But he knew it was there, banked up and hidden behind the same walls that kept out most of his memories.

Val turned around. He could hear weariness gum up his words, but could do nothing about it. "What exactly is it you want?"

Arthur smiled slightly, then buried it in his cup.

His daughter replied. "Terrance drained the British company's pension fund. He has blamed it on my father. Now we learn that the plant is due for closure."

"Spun off, I believe is the word they're using." Arthur shrugged. "The employees will be left penniless. This simply cannot be permitted."

"They're going to blame it on Dad. They've said he might be brought up on charges."

"Hardly a major concern," Arthur replied. "Given my current state."

"I won't let that happen."

Val stared down at his hands. He knew what the next step should be. Not even the weight bearing down on his eyelids could keep that out. He told them, "I need access to a computer wired into the company system."

"Listen to you," Audrey said. "You're asleep on your feet."

Arthur drained his cup. "Gerald should be able to arrange that."

"Who's Gerald?"

"A chief engineer at the company," Arthur explained. "Splendid chap. My former protégé."

"You'll be staying at his place." Audrey slipped her keys off the counter. "Safer for us all."

Arthur went on, "I won't have this turned into a vendetta against my son."

"Pop, please."

"This is about saving the livelihoods of hundreds of good men and women. People I have worked and lived with for years. People who trust me. I can't let them down. But I will not be party to a lynching of my firstborn."

Audrey slipped by Val without actually looking his way. "We've been all through this."

Arthur waved that away. "Mind what I say. This can't be about attacking Terrance. No matter what he's done. Two wrongs have never been known to make a right."

THE NEXT MORNING'S HIGHWAY WAS A SWIFT-RUNNING TRENCH six lanes wide. The weather made no difference to British driving patterns. The Bentley kept to the middle lane and drilled through the dismal day at a steady eighty-five kilometers per hour. The spray formed sheets higher than the car. The car behind them was less than five feet back. The Bentley was even closer to the one ahead. Trucks hemmed them to the left, a Porsche hammered past on their right. Inside the Bentley, it was so quiet Terrance could hear the clock ticking in the distant front dash, the chunking sound of the wipers, the quiet hum of the bar's refrigerator.

Terrance knew he should be highly worried about this turn of events. But he could not get beyond his sense that he was seated by a true professional. Loupe's features were mottled with age spots, but he handled himself like a prince. His voice was as solicitous as it had been the previous day. Loupe inquired if Terrance was hungry, if there was anything further that might be done for his comfort. Terrance knew he was on the receiving end of a charm offensive. And did not mind in the least. Wally remained stonelike in the front seat. Terrance did not mind this either. He was in control now. Let her play the dutiful servant until her skills were required.

Portsmouth struck Terrance as the epitome of all that was wrong with England's towns. The highway clogged as it fed into a frenetic ring road. The rain was blowing in hard off the sea now, dissolving colors and turning the town a shade of industrial grey. The driver's phone chirped as he maneuvered through a traffic-snarled roundabout. He raised his voice to announce, "They might have found something, Boss."

"Ah, a welcome gift for our arrival. Don't you agree?" He flashed the chalky teeth. "Take us there."

The street was a weary Victorian hedge against the tides of upward mobility. The houses marched down either side of a narrow lane, each with a front garden the size of a welcome mat. The houses were all brick, all leaning tightly against one another, with cars crammed down the road almost as firmly as the homes. A pair of hardfaced professionals left their sentry duty by the front door of a bed-and-breakfast. They stepped forward and did homage to Joe Loupe, giving little bows and deferential murmurs. Wally rose from her car seat but did not move forward with the others. She stared at nothing, was recognized by no one. Just a hard-faced woman standing at the edge of the action.

An older woman appeared in the bed-and-breakfast's doorway. She greeted all this commotion with a raspy cough and fished in her sweater for a cigarette. "Any you gents spare a light?"

The driver flicked open a gold lighter and held it for her. She thanked him with another cough. Ashes formed intricate grey swirls on the front of her cardigan, surrounding a multitude of burn holes. The woman was greasy and unkempt. Up close, Terrance could see the pink bald skin beneath hair of woven glass. "Like I told the gents, your honor, I didn't see a thing."

"But surely you must recognize one of your own guests."

"The blokes that come here, they ain't after being recognized. They want a stroll to the bar, a quiet kip, a slap-up breakfast, and they're off." She dragged in about a third of her cigarette. "The less I ask, the more they'll come back. That's the way it is these days, your honor."

"Of course, my dear lady. You do what you must."

"The only reason I noticed him at all is on account of how he's taken a room and dusted off already. Didn't take no breakfast."

The muscle confirmed, "His room's empty."

Loupe lifted one hand. Instantly the muscle passed over a photograph. "Just have one more look at this, would you please?"

She reluctantly glanced over. "Like I told your blokes, they come, they go. It mighta been him."

"I find a bit of cash can do marvels for the memory. A veritable wonder drug, don't you agree?" He pressed the photo closer still. "Say, a hundred pounds?"

The woman had clearly been waiting for this. "Said his name was Adams. The bloke sounded American."

"Did he, now? How very splendid." He motioned to his driver. "Pay the dear lady. Now then, you see? We have established a line of communication. Might there be anything else you could share with us?"

"For another hundred knicker?"

"I pay for what I receive, dear lady. You bear witness to that."

"He made a call."

"From your own line?"

"Separate. Got it set up in the front parlor for my guests."

"A pay phone, is it? And you receive a list of all calls made, don't you?"

She pretended a casual shrug. "I suppose I could print you out a page."

"How very splendid. Michael?"

When the money was handed over, she extracted a well-creased page from a pocket big as a pouch. She pointed with a yellow-stained finger. "That's the one. Down there at the bottom. Last call but one going out."

Terrance craned forward, though he already knew what he would find. One glance was enough. "That's our man." He turned and stamped away. A dozen paces beyond the Bentley, he pulled out his cell phone and dialed.

Don came instantly on the line. "What?"

"It's me."

"And?"

"Val is still on the loose."

Don huffed quietly. Again. Then, "This cannot be happening."

"He took the boat to Jersey. They had two hit men stalking him. Val got away. He hid on the boat, didn't get off at all, and returned to England."

Don's voice kept to a light musicality. Despite the late hour, Don must have already been on public display. "Let me get this straight. We're down here spreading out all our evidence, which they are all taking as solid gospel, let me tell you. We're claiming Val Haines has managed to slip away with $422 million. Boom. He's gone. They are raking through this with electron microscopes and SEC sniffer hounds, looking for some way to tie us in and drop us in the pit."

"The inspectors are with you now?"

"Inspectors, auditors, external counsel, we have an army of suits in here. The entire office building is smelling blood. Their own. So my job is to walk around pretending that everything is just fine. Which they know is absolute fabrication." His breaths were tight little wisps. But his words kept coming out light as air. Terrance could imagine the rictus grin he was wearing. "We're spinning our tales and they're swallowing our bait. I'm singing and I'm dancing and I'm lying with every breath. And everything depends on this one thing going down. Everything. Our lives, our futures, our money. And you're telling me this guy is *on the loose?*"

"I know where he is."

"So tell."

"Hastings."

"You mean, he's headed for our plant in Hastings?"

"That would be my guess."

"What for?"

"He'll try to access the company system. Break into our own files. See what's up."

"Can he do that?"

"Maybe."

"This is not the answer I need to hear."

"He oversaw installation of the system related to the pension department. People have always liked Val, you know that as well as I do. It's possible our in-house nerds told him about a backdoor."

"A what?"

"Software engineers often insert hidden entries into their systems. They're called backdoors. Supposedly they can be used for ongoing repairs. Often it's just to show how smart they are. If Val was told about one, he could use it to access our data no matter what firewalls I insert around the standard entry-points."

"That *cannot* happen."

"You need to have our IT people cut Hastings off entirely. The computer system needs to be completely disengaged. No interoffice traffic in any guise."

Don's pause was microseconds long. "Done. Now what are you going to do about the crisis?"

"I'm on it."

"Hastings is a town, right? There's a lot of places where he can hide in a town."

Terrance pushed a fist into his gut, trying to still the churning nausea. "I know where he's headed."

"You're sure?"

"He's had a thing with my sister."

"If we weren't talking about our collective futures, I'd be laughing out loud." Don paused a long moment, then, "What I need to know right here, right now, is this. Can you handle what needs handling?"

"And I'm telling you I am on top of this."

"What if he gets to the bank? Can he access the funds?"

"His, yes. But not ours."

"You're sure of that? Absolutely certain? I'm asking, you know, on account of my neck is on the chopping block here."

"You have a set of access codes. I have the other. Yours are in your bank's safety deposit box. Mine are in the microcomputer in my briefcase. Those are the only sets. Nobody else has any connection whatsoever. So that is not the problem here. That is not what we have to be focusing on."

"Val."

"If he shows up at the bank, Syntec will inform New York, New York will go ballistic, and we are *dead*. Josef has two men stationed permanently on the island to see that doesn't happen."

"Who?"

"Our ally over here. Never mind."

"This the same ally who didn't get him like he was supposed to when he arrived? This is a reason to trust him?"

Terrance cut the connection and stalked back to the car. The rain was so light as to drift in the air, settling on nothing, drenching everything. Josef stood smiling slightly and smoking a cigar. He waved it in Terrance's direction. "Would you care for a panatela?"

"No. Thanks." He panted from the strain. Don's frantic state had seeped through the phone like a viscous acid. Terrance hated this day. This place. This seedy district of weary houses and rain too disdainful to even fall correctly. People with worn-down faces. Air that smelled of sea and industry and dense hopelessness. Terrance wiped the moisture from his face. "You just better not fail again."

Wally was leaning on the Bentley's front end. She rolled her eyes at Terrance, shook her head, and slid into the seat. Taking up the position again, eyes front, seeing nothing.

The boss casually rolled his cigar's glowing end around his fingernail. Terrance saw how the repeated act had charred a slender half-moon, staining it like a blooded talon. Josef asked, "Shouldn't there be an 'or else' after that little statement?"

"I need this job done."

"Of course you do. But it seems a bit odd, a gentleman like yourself taking such a tone with the only man in England who's able to offer a helping hand." Loupe gave Terrance a look, his eyes holding nothing at all. Just dead air.

Terrance sensed something behind him, like an unseen furnace door had opened. He knew without turning that the driver had stalked up with a predator's silence, moving in tight. He resisted the urge to glance back. "I need this man to vanish immediately."

"That's why we're all here together, now, isn't it? To make sure I live up to my part of the bargain." The man dropped his half-finished cigar to the road, where it sizzled and died, and reached for Terrance's arm. "Shall we continue with our little journey?"

Terrance let Josef steer him around. To his astonishment, the driver was by the car, holding open the door, giving him that same blank mask. Only now there was a different face to the day, as though he could peel away the soft, rich facade and hear a faint scream. At least it was Val's pain he was hearing. He was fairly certain of that.

AN HOUR AFTER RISING WITH THE DAWN, VAL KNEW HIS PLAN WAS futile. Even so, he remained where he was, isolated in his host's home office, listening to the house come alive around him. Gerald was a production engineer working the line at Insignia. Like most engineers, his home computer was hardwired into the company system. Even so, Val did not have a chance to even try his backdoors. The UK computer system had effectively been frozen out.

Sunlight pierced the house with an unfamiliar tone. Val took his empty mug back to the kitchen. Three men sat at the table, their morning chatter silenced by his appearance. The atmosphere was stale as the overcooked coffee. Val poured himself a mug and retreated to the office.

He stood by the side window and sipped at coffee stewed to its bitter dregs. He watched as Audrey's dilapidated Rover pulled up to the curb. Val found himself unable to walk out and greet her. Instead, he touched Audrey's letter through the fabric of his shirt, as he would a talisman.

When the doorbell rang, a burly middle-aged man emerged from the kitchen. He opened the front door and greeted her with, "All right, love?"

"Hello, Bert." Audrey's voice held to a comfortable burr. "Everyone behaving themselves?"

The big man liked that in the manner of old friends. "Looks like we should be asking you that one."

Gerald walked down the hall from the kitchen. He gave Val a single glance through the open office doorway, then bussed Audrey on the cheek. Gerald was lean and taut in build, with hair one shade off blond. He had pianist's hands, long and supple and very strong looking. He wore a button-down Oxford shirt of pale blue and had three pens in his breast pocket. Everything about him shouted engineer.

Audrey said quietly, "Thank you, Gerald."

"Glad to help," he said, but he cut Val another look that suggested something else.

"Have you discussed things yet?"

"We decided it was best to wait for you."

"All right." Audrey finally acknowledged Val, but showed him nothing. "Did you sleep well?"

"Fine, thanks."

"Perhaps we should get started."

Val felt Gerald's gaze steady and hard on him as he followed the others into the front parlor. A third man entered through the kitchen. Dillon was younger than the others but bore the same scarred rigidity as Bert. Val stationed himself by the doorway, giving himself an out in case the natives turned hostile.

Gerald's home was a bachelor's sort of place—monochrome carpet, bare walls, functional furniture. A pair of mismatched sofas were permanently reshaped by the bodies lodged there. Pastel drapes framed windows pleading dustily for a good cleaning. Val saw a lot of his own dwelling space in how Gerald lived.

Gerald selected a hard-backed chair by the empty fireplace and asked, "Is it true what they say, that they're closing us down?"

Audrey replied, "I don't have anything definite. But the rumors seem pretty conclusive."

"What about our pensions?" Evidently Gerald was their appointed spokesman. "Is that true?"

"Yes. I'm afraid it is."

"Someone has stolen from them?"

Audrey gave Val the resigned expression of one knowing it had to come out. Val said, "Not someone. Terrance d'Arcy."

Gerald asked Audrey, "Your brother has tapped into our pension fund?"

She nodded at Val, who replied for her, "Not tapped. Drained. Terrance has effectively stolen it all. Or enough so that everything else will go to the company's creditors."

"What about us?"

"There are always other liens and priority claims on a pension fund. Legally, pension holders are the last in line. They have no secured interest. It's wrong, but that's the way it is."

"You're telling me that Insignia is going to shut us down and we won't have any pension to tide us over?"

"That pretty much sums it up."

Audrey nodded at him once more. Val took a very hard breath and added, "I stole from the fund as well."

Gerald looked at Audrey again. His voice was perplexed. "You've been keeping the torch for a thief?"

"Val isn't a thief."

"Excuse me, love, but you heard him the same as I."

"I know what he said." Audrey met Val with an unwavering gaze. "But Val Haines is not a thief."

Gerald crossed his arms across his chest. Holding himself back bunched his shoulders and corded the muscles in his neck.

The large man seated on the sofa asked Val, "What'd you do that for, mate?"

"I don't remember."

Gerald snorted. A quiet puff of sound, there and gone. Like a coiled spring wound tight for far too long.

"I had an accident. I suffer from amnesia. I remember parts now. But not everything. I know I stole from the fund. Maybe it was just to get away. I remember telling someone that. But it doesn't fit. I can't figure out why I'd go against everything just to . . ."

The gazes around the room and the struggle to remember felt like fists squeezing his head. Val knew the reason was there. He could almost fit the pieces together. He pushed at his temples with the palms of both hands, adding to the external force. He lifted his gaze. It wasn't coming. He said, "I'm sorry."

Gerald snorted again. He jerked his chin at Val. "This is the best we've got?"

"He's our only hope," Audrey replied.

Gerald kicked at the wall behind him with one heel. Softly. Just releasing a bit of the excess steam.

Bert said from his place on the sofa, "Well, all right, then."

Gerald wasn't ready to let it go just yet. "What chance do we have of getting back what's owed us?"

"Slim to none." Val was not going to lie. Not anymore. "But I think we should try."

"Oh, and it's 'we' now, is it?"

"Gerald," Audrey said quietly.

The taut man looked down at his floor and went back to kicking the wall.

Audrey rose and gave Val a fraction of a head motion. The two hard-faced men watched him depart with blank stares. She exited the house by the front door and started down the street. As Val fell into step beside her, Audrey took an intense aim at something on the far horizon. She cupped her elbows with her palms and walked stiffly. Their footsteps formed the only discordant note to a lovely sunlit lane.

The previous evening, Audrey had driven him up the steep lane leading away from the medieval town and the sea. She had driven west about twenty minutes, to where a housing estate sprawled around an aging industrial park. Gerald's unassuming house was made spectacular by its setting. Two dozen modest homes fronted a narrow lane marking the industrial township's outer boundary. Behind the houses stretched an expanse of English myth, a great bowl of highland pasture shining in pristine splendor. Rising in the far distance was a steep-sided hill with veins white as old bones.

"Where are we?"

"The border to the downs." But Audrey paid no attention to her surroundings. "Your plan failed, didn't it? I can see it in your face."

Val explained what he had tried to do. "I should have known Terrance would have shut down the company's systems."

"What can we do?"

"I'm working on that." He gestured behind him. "They don't want me here."

"What do you expect? A stranger from head office declares they're about to lose their jobs and that he's stolen from a pension fund that won't pay them a farthing?" She took hold of the fence. "Those are good men, Val."

"The two guys look like they've had a hard life."

"Bert and Dillon have both done time, yes. I met them through my work. They're friends now." She leaned heavily upon the words. "Good men, the both of them."

"Gerald thinks a lot of you."

"It seems like the entire town is busy making sure I am fully aware of that. We met in an Alpha course I'm teaching at the church. You've heard of Alpha?"

"I don't—"

"Remember. Of course. How convenient."

"It's the truth."

More than the morning light tightened her gaze as she inspected him. "Did you truly believe you could actually leave it all behind?"

The pressure mounted again, her words squeezing at him, working to dislodge what he could not quite grasp. "I thought . . ."

"Yes?"

"That you might come with me."

The message was clear in her gaze long before she spoke. "What tore us apart before is still there between us now."

There were a hundred things he could say. But he remained trapped in the moment, staring at someone who had once cared for him deeply. Despite all the worries and unanswered questions, he felt his life constrict to this lane, the rusted old fence fronting the downs, the birdsong, the sunlight that turned the pastures into a green mirror, these words, this love. How could he have ever left her? "Audrey—"

Whatever she saw in his gaze was enough to make her grateful when someone called from the house. Audrey stepped away. "We'd best go see what's got them stirred up."

The men said nothing to Val as he entered. But the way they watched him was clear as an oath. Bert said, "Something's happening inside the town, love. Something bad."

"Is it Terrance?"

Bert motioned to his younger mate in the doorway. "Tell her."

Dillon carried himself with the hardness of streetwise life. "A mate's just come off the hotel's early shift. These men show up, not your basic run-of-the-mill toughs."

"What do you mean?"

"He means trouble, love." Bert was a hard man with the grime of years ingrained in his gaze and his voice. "Trouble that don't bear thinking about."

"One of them was an older guy with a funny sort of accent." The young man looked pained by his news. "Another was a Yank."

"Terrance?"

"My mate says he looks a lot like you."

Gerald added, "Word's come down from the works. There's been visitors in and out, talking to the dodgy blokes on the shop floor."

"I heard the same." Bert aimed his thumb at Val but kept his gaze on Audrey. "They been asking for the bloke here."

"Did they name him?"

"Not in so many words. But it's him they're after, all right."

Gerald directed his words to Audrey, not Val. "What about the plan you told us he had?"

Val replied, "I can't access headquarters. They've locked the system down tight."

Audrey said, "We'll just have to think of something else."

The room's silence gradually condensed around Val.

Bert was the one who spoke aloud what the men were all thinking. "Say we was to let them have the bloke."

"No," Audrey replied. "Val is our friend."

"He's a thief, Audrey." This from Gerald. "He said it himself."

"No."

"What if . . ." Bert looked at the others, drawing support from two stone-hard faces. "What if they was to offer to give us our due and return the pension money? What then?"

"You don't know Terrance. He'll promise you whatever it is you want to hear. But he'll give you nothing. He'll take what he wants and disappear."

"But if we was to get a guarantee, like."

"Val knows the system. Val is our only hope of making things right." Audrey gathered up her purse and keys. "I have to go see to Father."

"Audrey . . ."

"I'm telling you that we need Val."

The others parted to let her through, but Gerald remained where he was, blocking the hall. "*We* need him, or *you* do?"

"Val has told us nothing but the truth since he arrived. He came up with one possible option. He'll come up with another." She turned to look at him. The others followed her lead. "Won't you?"

Val confirmed, "If Terrance is in town, there is definitely something we can try."

"There, you see?" Audrey started to force her way past, then caught herself. "Terrance is here, Gerald. Father is by himself. I must go."

"Perhaps I should come with you."

"Stay and work out the next step. I won't be long."

Val felt the eyes rake him as he moved down the hall behind her. He waited until they were outside to ask, "You're leaving me here?"

"I told you before, Val. These are good men."

"They'd like to feed me to the wolves." When she continued her march to the car, he asked, "Don't you want to hear what I'm thinking?"

"I'm not the one who needs convincing, Val." She slid behind the wheel. "Go in there and talk with them. I'll be back as soon as I can."

Audrey did something then, a gesture that pained him like a hook through his heart. He realized he had seen her do it many times before. She lifted her chin with a determined jerk and shook her hair back. It tumbled over her shoulders in a burnished cascade. The lines of her face and the cast of her eyes were caught clearly by the sunlight flooding through her open door. Her lips were a translucent wash of palest rose. A determined woman, bearing the weight of so many different things that were both out of her control and not of her liking. Val knew that he looked upon someone far stronger than he would ever be, and far better. The reasons he had insisted upon leaving her were lost. Even worse, they were meaningless. He loved her. He had lost her. The knowledge rocked him forward just as she restarted the motor and shut her door.

He called through her open window, "Audrey . . ."

But she was gone.

WITHIN AN HOUR OF THEIR ARRIVAL IN HASTINGS, THE BAND OF people surrounding the boss had swelled to eleven.

Hastings's finest hotel rose like a grey Victorian wedding cake where the old town met the port. Foppish towers and curlicues adorned the roofline. Flags made a colorful row beneath the second floor window. A doorman in maroon uniform with gold braid stood sentry outside the grand entrance. Josef Loupe had taken the two-bedroom penthouse suite as well as rooms to either side. Sunlight flooded the suite's parlor like a persistent intruder. Terrance stood by the bowed portside windows and observed families at play on the rocky beach. The children raced through the sunshine, chasing seagulls and each other to the water's edge. Many adults still wore streetclothes, their pants legs rolled up and their pale heads covered by handkerchiefs with corners tightened like four white pigtails. A pair of merry-go-rounds with diesel-driven calliopes stood at either end of the beach. Gaily colored stands sold Italian ices and grilled spicy sausages and draft beer. The benches lining the streetside sidewalk were jammed with old people. Families carrying buckets walked along the southern rock wall, searching among the seaweed for cockles. Terrance felt he had entered a time warp where there was no place for him or his ambition.

He turned away. Let the peons have their day in the sun. He was hunting bigger game.

The area around Arthur d'Arcy's home had been staked out, as had the two entrances to the Insignia factory. Insignia employees who pilfered components or sold drugs on the factory floor or shook down the unions had all been contacted. Bribes had been offered. People came in and out of the hotel suite in a fairly constant stream. A house a quarter-mile from the hotel had been rented for Loupe's men. It stood on a cul-de-sac, well removed from its nearest neighbors.

The boss sat in the center of his parlor suite like a cashmere-draped tarantula. He smoked his cigar, talked on the phone, and greeted each of the shadowy newcomers as brethren. Terrance felt encased in an exquisite tension. He observed Loupe's face as through a magnifying glass, seeing every pore, all the avarice hidden beneath that genteel calm. He glanced at Wally, sitting in the far corner by the door leading to the bedroom, smoking a chain of cigarettes and staring at nothing. Terrance found himself pitying her in a mild way.

Loupe turned to him. "Are you sure I can't offer you anything, Mr. d'Arcy? A fresh pot of coffee, perhaps?"

Terrance knew the old man shared his enjoyment of the mounting tension. "I think we should hit the house."

Loupe nodded thoughtfully, as though considering this for the first time. "There are problems. It is a busy street. Your father's home is connected on the south side to its neighbor. Any disturbance is bound to draw the wrong sort of attention. You said yourself we must act with discretion. I assume that has not changed?"

"There is a way." He could feel the words linger on the tongue. Each held a distinct flavor.

Terrance found himself recalling a meal he had once had. A New York waiter had brought a fresh white Italian truffle big as two fists. Using a silver cheese serrator he had sliced off paper-thin wedges. The truffle had filled the entire restaurant with its perfume. The flavor had been unlike anything Terrance had tasted before. A superb nuttiness, almost musky in texture. An essence as strong as now.

Loupe watched him with eyes of wet agate. "Yes?"

Terrance realized that the man had known all along, and had been waiting for Terrance to make the move. Commit himself. He was, after all, the key. "No one would suspect a son coming to visit his own father."

"You would do this thing?"

"I'll need help."

Loupe smiled benevolently. "You are a man after my own heart, Mr. d'Arcy."

Terrance was almost sorry to draw the moment to a close. "We had better get moving."

The air in the town held the same condensed ambiance as the hotel suite. The early wind had completely died. Every sound carried for miles. The sun pounded with uncommon strength upon Terrance's head as he stood on the sidewalk before his father's house. He had never been here before.

The place was exactly as Terrance had envisioned. A proper little slice of England, a miniature castle for a man who had never dared think big. The home was bordered by a front garden the size of a throw-rug. Rose petals, the color of dried blood, were scattered across the flagstone path. Terrance turned the polished brass handle. His father had never locked the door to any house they had ever lived in. It was one of the many things that had driven Terrance's mother insane. And rightly so.

Instantly the scents threw him back to the impossible years when he had been young and helpless. Back when his father had elected to destroy Terrance's life. He heard a scraping sound in the kitchen. His nerves began to crawl under his skin like angry electric worms.

His father shuffled into view. He was far older now, yet unchanged. The core of this man was exactly the same. A man who had never known the exquisite thrill of going for a kill. A stranger to his own son.

"I should have known you would come." His father shuffled forward. He favored his right side, as though winded by a long run. "Perhaps I did, and tried to hide it even from myself."

"Where is he?"

His father made no pretense of hiding his knowledge. "Not here."

"That's not what I asked."

"You won't find him."

Terrance glanced at Loupe's driver, standing by the open front door. Wally had elected to stay out front on guard duty. The driver wore his dark hair in a bowl cut plastered tightly to his skull, such that Terrance could see a shallow indentation at its center. The well-cut suit did nothing save accent his wiry strength. "Shut the door."

The man slipped to one side and closed the portal. When Terrance turned back to his father, he saw fear in the old man's gaze. The worms beneath Terrance's skin thrashed about more wildly, feeding upon a lifetime of futile rage. "You think you can save him, is that it?"

In response, his father pulled out a dining room chair and slowly sank down. His gaze went to the floor by his feet and remained there.

Terrance's movements were jerky as he crossed the front room. He could feel his muscles hungering for motion, a driving force to tear and rip and flay. "My entire life has been shaped by your spinelessness. Your futile yearning to avoid conflict of any kind is despicable. You cared so much for your rigid peace, you would sacrifice anything to keep it. Even me. Isn't that true? Isn't it?"

His father said to the floor by his feet. "They tell me you're a thief."

"Who says that—Audrey? Your dear self-righteous freak of a daughter? Why should I care what she says?" Terrance laughed, and to his own ears it sounded like the baying of wolves. It was beyond delicious, this ability to finally release a tiny shard of the loathing for this man he had carried for a lifetime. "What if I am? Who do you think brought me to this point?"

"No one is responsible for your actions but yourself."

"What an utterly typical response. You let your own son languish in poverty rather than stand up for what was my rightful inheritance. You let *my* titles and *my* estate go to the offspring of the *real* thief. And you did it without raising a finger! Why? Because nothing mattered to you except maintaining this figment of your own imagination, this ridiculous sham of an existence."

"That's not true."

"What nonsense." Terrance's panting breaths seared his throat. "Of course I steal! What choice did I ever have? I steal because I've been stolen from! Not by my grandfather and his floozy. By you! You wanted peace at all costs. You wanted calm. You wanted a myth of an English country life. Even if it meant sacrificing your own son!"

Arthur sighed and slumped further still. He might have said something. He might even have mentioned Terrance's mother by name.

"This whole rotten mess comes down to your failure to be a father!" Terrance felt himself standing outside the situation, as if the years and his success and his power all had been stripped away in a single instant, by this man who was incapable of any response. Terrance was both the raging banshee and the invisible observer. "You are going to tell me what I need to know."

The front door crashed back. "You!"

Terrance whirled about. And smiled. "Hello, sister."

She was taller than Terrance recalled, or perhaps it was merely her ire that added stature. She vaulted into the room, screaming as she raced for him. "You get *away* from him!"

Loupe's driver moved like a cat. He came up behind her and pressed something to her neck. There was a soft zapping sound. Audrey jerked into a full-length spasm, then sighed quietly and came crashing to the floor by her father's feet.

"No, please." The words carried no strength, as though Arthur knew they were futile even before he uttered them.

The moment was just too delicious. Terrance touched his father's shin with the toe of his shoe. "Look at me, Father."

Arthur locked gazes with his son. Terrance opened the hidden door, the one he had revealed to no one before this moment. And showed his father the full extent of his rage-driven ferocity. Arthur flinched and looked away. "I don't know where he is. They took him away somewhere. I can't tell you anything."

"Ah, but for your dear daughter's sake, you must. You cannot possibly imagine what they will do to her if you don't." Terrance signaled to the silent man. The driver lifted Audrey as easily as he would an empty set of clothes. Terrance drew out pen and pad and wrote down his cell phone number. He dropped it into his father's lap, between the unmoving hands. "Just give me Val."

Terrance crossed to the front door. "I sincerely hope you find a way to help me. For once."

THE HOME'S ATMOSPHERE WAS POISONOUS. DILLON GLARED AT him from the hallway, Gerald did sentry at the kitchen doorway. Bert stood by the sink and measured him for a coffin. Val forced himself to reenter the kitchen and sit at the table.

"I have an idea," Val said. And waited.

Bert finally said, "Let's be hearing it, then."

Val did not respond. He remained as he was, crouched over the table, staring at his hands.

Finally Bert sighed and dragged out another chair and seated himself. Val kept to the same position. Waiting.

Dillon slipped past Gerald and joined Bert at the table. Bert said, "All right, mate. Let's hear what you've got."

Gerald remained leaning against the kitchen door frame, arms crossed over chest, gaze heated. Val turned his attention to the men seated at the table. Given the circumstances, two out of three wasn't bad.

"Terrance will be carrying the codes with him," Val began.

"Codes," Bert repeated.

"To access the bank funds," Val explained.

"This is the money he stole we're talking about," Bert said. "Our pension money."

"Right. The newspapers are onto this theft. Which means the SEC has been called in."

"Official government investigators," Gerald supplied from his position, speaking for the first time since Audrey departed.

"Right. Terrance wouldn't dare go hunting for me without keeping tabs on his money. He would never trust his partners. And he's definitely not in this alone."

"How can you be sure of that, mate?"

"Because if he was, he wouldn't be free to come over here now. He's needed back in the States to handle the inquiry into the disappearance of the funds. There's someone else on the inside, someone high up enough to cover for Terrance." Val rocked back in his seat. "Don Winslow."

Bert asked, "That name's supposed to mean something?"

"Executive vice president," Gerald said. "I've seen his name on documents."

Val explained, "Don backed Terrance's hand when he stole a promotion from me."

Gerald said, "I thought you had amnesia."

"My memory was a total loss right after the accident." Val forced himself to meet the man's gaze. "Things are coming back. But it's patchy. And most of what I remember are things I'd just as soon forget."

Gerald snorted quietly. But he subsided.

Bert refocused the discussion with, "So you've got a history with Audrey's brother."

"Six years."

"Bit of bad blood there, I take it."

"About a year and a half ago," Val replied, "Terrance seduced my wife. Then he stole a promotion that should have been mine by falsifying documents, pinning a series of losses on my watch. That I know for certain. He bribed a lab or a doctor to alter a DNA test so he could steal my child as well."

"You got proof?"

"No. No proof. But I'm sure it happened."

Bert looked at Gerald, who said, "You have quite a way with the ladies."

To that Val had no response.

Bert continued playing the moderator. "So Terrance is going to be carrying the codes with him."

"These days, access to a numbered account can be as simple or as difficult as you want to make it," Val said.

"Know this from personal experience, do you?" Gerald said.

Val lifted his gaze. "That's right. I do."

Gerald shook his head. Pushed off the doorjamb. Walked over to the window. Gave his attention to the green vista out back.

Val waited until the others' gazes had returned to him. "Knowing Terrance, there will be a series of very complicated maneuvers required to access those funds. Something that has to be done in strict order. He'll have part of it in his head. The other part will be in a computer. Terrance has always loved his toys."

"You're thinking he's carrying this computer with him," Bert said.

"That or something else."

"Something we can lift."

"Right."

"Something we can use to renegotiate our position with."

"That's my thinking."

The youngest of the trio spoke up. "They've taken the grandest suite in the hotel where I work. I could get in and out, no problem."

"Not you," Val said. "Me. There's no need to get anybody else in trouble. And I'd have a better idea what to look for."

"Just whose position would you be after saving here?" Gerald asked the window. "Yours or our pensions?"

Val decided he'd had enough. He rose from the table and walked outdoors. Clouds were piling in from the north. The afternoon sky contained a riot of tainted moods. The narrow strip of shadow between cloud and hill was shot with silver where sunlight struck the falling rain. Val futilely searched the horizon for a single shred of the confidence he had exhibited inside.

His mind returned to the same unanswered dilemma. Why had he forced Audrey away? The incident in New York might have scrambled his memory, but something far earlier had tainted his heart. How could he have felt something this powerful and still made her leave? Val pounded the post marking the boundary between city and verdant fields, convicted anew by all he could not remember. There was no escape. It was not the exterior that trapped him. It was everything inside. All the things he could never let go.

A siren sounded far in the distance, so faint it should have been possible to let it flow into all the other city noises and disappear. Yet this one rose and fell with the strident force of an alarm meant exclusively for him.

Then he heard the shouts rising from inside the house. One word was cried in anguish. A woman's name.

Dillon said nothing as they walked down the alley leading to the hotel's rear entrance. The lane held a sickly sweet odor of rubbish bins and coming rain. Dillon ducked inside the metal "Employees Only" entrance, then swiftly reappeared. "Ready?"

"You can wait out here if you want."

"If I'd wanted to wait I'd still be in the van with the others." Dillon led Val down a concrete hall painted a grim yellow. He pushed open the door to the gents'. "Stay put till I come for you."

The room was cramped and lined with rusting metal lockers. A shower dripped. Machinery clanked overhead. Val moved to the sinks and pretended to wash his hands. The mirror revealed the same helpless fury that knotted his gut. It was no longer the past only that held a blank void. Audrey had been kidnapped by Terrance. That Terrance had gutted Val's future once more was irony at its most vile.

After Arthur d'Arcy's panic-stricken phone call, Bert and Gerald had gone into town and fetched Audrey's father. The man had been so distraught his words had emerged only half formed. They had learned what they could, then tucked him into the bed last used by Val. Afterwards they had regathered in the kitchen and grimly run through Val's strategy. Doing nothing was not an option.

Bert had toyed with the salt shaker, the glass pyramid tiny in his hands. "I know what the dear would be telling us just now."

Val asked, "How do you know Audrey?"

"The lady managed to drag me and Dillon here out of one truly dark pit. You know she works as a prison counselor?"

"We don't need to be going there. Audrey was there when our trouble was at its worst. That's all you should be telling the bloke." Dillon rounded on Val. "This plan of yours. Is it going to work?"

"You can use me as a trade if you think that has a better chance of success."

"That's not what I was asking, mate."

"Yes it was."

"All right, then," Bert said. "Straight up. Tell us why that's a non-starter."

"If you give me up, we're empty handed. They have all they want. They have no reason to give Audrey up."

The men studied him intently. "Know what I think, mate? There's more to your plan than just stealing the bloke's phone."

"Computer."

"Whatever. You're after more, aren't you?"

"I'm just thinking ahead."

Bert's gaze was hard as his tone. "You're out to shut him down."

"If I can."

"And restore our pension fund?"

"I'd like to."

Gerald remained against the doorway, arms crossed, voice an iron rod. "What about the bit where you stole some for yourself?"

Val had nothing for them but the truth. "I don't understand why I did it. Money's never been all that important to me. Before, I was working for a wife and the children I hoped we'd have. Now I don't have either."

Bert looked at the others. "I say let's do the job."

Dillon returned in uniform, bearing a second maroon-and-yellow outfit in a plastic cover. He was nervous but bearing up well. Clearly he had been in tight spaces before. The only real sign of his fear was the way his eyes tightened and his cheekbones pinched white against his skin. "I can tell you already this is too small. But it's the only one I spotted."

The uniform was scarcely better than a clown's outfit on Val. The trousers were a full four inches too short, the waist impossible to fasten. The jacket's wrists and shoulders were scarcely better. He did all of the jacket's gold buttons up the front except the one at his collar, which would have fitted him like a noose.

Dillon set a matching maroon-and-gold pillbox hat on Val's head and grimaced. "All you need is a tin cup, mate. You'd be ready for the monkey's dance down the boardwalk."

"If I bunched my shoulders I bet I could split this thing from top to toe."

"We'll move fast, hope nobody gets too good a look. Ready?"

They took the service lift up to the top floor. Over the clanking lift motor Val could hear the same sibilant noise he had been catching ever since news had arrived of Audrey's abduction. The sound was somewhere between a drill and a very shrill scream. The fact that the sound had traveled with him left Val in no doubt of its origin. The day was being ground down to a raw and fiery edge.

They came out of the elevator and started down an empty corridor. Val was consumed by how little chance they had of succeeding. He should never have sent Audrey away. Val no longer cared what his justification might have been at the time. It was insignificant now. He followed Dillon into the pantry. His body was a shell encasing nothing more than a void. A fragmented past and no future. And it was all his fault.

Dillon piled his arms high with terrycloth robes and fresh towels. When he was done, Val was masked from his waist to his chin. Dillon looked down at Val's exposed ankles and shook his head. "Nothing to be done about that."

"Except move fast," Val said. Forward motion of any kind gave him at least a shred of hope.

Dillon's gaze tightened further, as close to a smile as the guy could manage just then. "You're all right, mate."

Val replied, "Let's do it."

THEY FINALLY LEFT AUDREY AT THE HOUSE RENTED FOR JOSEF'S thugs because Terrance grew tired of wasting his time. Audrey might know where Val was, but they could roast her over live coals, plug her with arrows, and she would give them nothing. Audrey would relish playing the martyr. Terrance ordered them to cuff her to the radiator in the smallest of the upstairs rooms. Her mouth was taped, but nothing could be done about the daggers in her gaze. As usual, his darling sister refused to let him have the last word. Even when she couldn't speak.

The driver had already returned to the hotel, and Loupe's men did not want to leave without word from the boss. Which was fine by Terrance. He felt enclosed within a cage the size of this proper little English town.

Wally spoke to him for the first time since their arrival. "I need to walk, get a little air."

"My thoughts exactly."

The muscle protested, "We can't raise the boss."

"Stay here," Terrance replied, already moving for the door.

"The boss—"

"Your boss," Terrance corrected.

The senior man said to one of his men, "Make sure they make it okay."

"It can't be more than ten blocks." Terrance protested. "Hastings hardly looks like a dangerous place."

Loupe's man said nothing, merely walked a few paces behind them. Wally remained the silent wraith throughout. The sky was split so definitely in two they might have been witnessing a schism of the universe. To the west and south was an aching empty blue. To the north a storm approached, strong as night. Thunder rolled across the vacant reaches, bringing expressions of real fear to the scurrying tourists. Only Wally seemed unfazed by the squall. By the squall, by the day, and by the fact that they were walking down Hastings' main street, six thousand miles from where they needed to be, and still minus Val Haines.

Terrance pulled out his cell phone and checked for messages. Nothing. The action had become reflexive, something he did every few minutes. He had tried Don repeatedly for hours with no results. Not even on what Don called his red line, the number only a few people knew and one that Don had promised would lift him from the grave. Terrance had left five messages there and still had not heard back. Being this far from his home turf and not being able to contact his chief ally left Terrance extremely unsettled.

He could sense Audrey's helpless fury like smoke rising from a branding iron. He should be feeling some sense of vindication, having trapped her and isolated her and finally left her helpless and silent. But the day was not working out as it should. Terrance snapped his phone shut as the hotel doorman greeted them and held open the portal. They had to find Val. Find him and finish him. Fast.

When they entered the hotel lobby, Terrance realized that Wally was watching him. "What?"

"I didn't say anything."

Terrance turned to their shadow. "Go on up to the suite."

The muscle glanced uncertainly around the reception area. Clearly there was nothing of danger. Still, he hesitated.

Terrance put as much weight as he could on the words. "I need a minute alone here. We'll meet you upstairs."

When Loupe's man entered the elevator, Terrance turned back to Wally and hissed, "As a matter of fact, you haven't said or done a thing."

"You got a beef?"

"Of course not. What do I have to complain about? After all, you've contributed so very much to all that's happened since our arrival. Offering suggestions and advice and wisdom at every turn, that's our Wally."

She gave a cop's laugh, a quick huff of sound without humor. "You don't get it, do you?"

"Obviously not."

Wally shook her head. "You've lost it."

"On the contrary, I have everything under control."

Wally huffed another laugh, a verbal pistol with a silencer attached.

"I asked you a question."

She stepped over to where a pillar and a potted palm hid her from both the elevator and the reception desk. Having to follow Wally's lead made Terrance even hotter. Which, given the other frustrations of this rather fractious day, was not altogether a bad thing. At least he could let off some steam. "Would it be too much to ask for you to try and help me out here?"

"You're hopeless."

The words and their flat tone stung. "I am paying you good money—"

"You're paying me what I've already earned ten times over."

"Since our arrival you have done absolutely *nothing*."

Wally punched him in the chest with a finger of flesh-covered stone. "You think you're going to collar your guy, pay this Loupe his change, and just waltz off to never-never land. Is that it?"

"Not collar."

"Whatever."

"And you're the one paying Loupe, remember? It comes out of your share."

"You just don't get it."

"You've said that before."

Her every breath blasted him with heat and ashes. "Listen to me. The boss is not here because his guys goofed."

"That's what he said when—"

"Forget what he told you. This guy wouldn't know the truth if it arrived on the business end of a thirty-eight hollow point. He's here because he wants it *all*."

A snake of fear found the weak spot just north of his navel. "All what?"

"What do you think? *Everything*."

"He can't have it."

"Oh, is that so? And just who is going to stop him—you?"

"That's your job."

Her final huff carried very little force. "I may be good, Terry. But I'm just one gal."

Terrance stared around the lobby, as though searching for a way out. A bellhop stared through the front window, watching the sky with a worried frown. "I told you not to call me that."

Wally closed in on Terrance with her lips drawn back from her teeth. A feral beast smelling of cigarettes and fear. "Listen to what I'm telling you. You want to have one single shred of anything left, you get out."

The snake just kept burrowing deeper, lodging itself with venomous ferocity, coiling around Terrance's spine. "You mean leave? I can't do that."

She bit off each word in even little gasps. "You have *got* to. *Now*."

"You're running out on me, is that it?"

"Are you deaf? Do you not hear a word I'm saying?"

"All I hear is the woman who's here to protect me saying she's ready to run out on me."

"Not me, Terry. *Us*. We leave, we live to play with what you've got."

"But Val Haines is still out there!" The snake began dislodging oily drops of sweat that dribbled down his back. "One word from him and—"

She gripped his lapel and shook him. Punching his chest with the fist that held his jacket, while the snake fed on his guts. "Forget Val! You stay here and the man upstairs is going to take us down!"

"If I run now, Val will destroy us." Terrance was jabbering now. He knew it but couldn't stop. "Everything I've done to keep us safe will go up in flames."

"Safe? You call this safe?" Her eyes held a manic gaze. "I'm sitting up there just waiting for Loupe to tell one of his men to take us out back and smoke us."

"If they do that, they lose the money you promised to pay them."

"He's not after what we agreed on, Terry. This has gone way beyond that. We're talking *everything*. Including your *life*."

"Loupe doesn't know what I've got. Unless you told him."

"Do I sound like a rat? You think somebody working both sides would be telling you to run?"

"No." Terrance breathed. Or tried to. "No."

"Loupe will get what he wants out of you. It's only a question of how hard he's got to ask before you talk." Her gaze had gone blank on him. Just two empty glass voids, windows to nothing. "If Loupe starts asking, you tell him whatever it is he wants to know. Tell him fast."

"This can't be happening."

"Exactly. So we run. Now." Wally stood so close they might have been lovers. She whispered with the coarse burr of shared terror. "So Haines is still out there. So what? Last I heard, Barbados doesn't extradite."

"How can you be so sure about this? Loupe hasn't said a thing."

"I know these guys. Okay? Not Loupe. His kind. The boss. I'm into one of them for a lot of money. More than that. He *owns* me. This deal, it's my only hope of getting free. So it's in my own best interest to keep you alive and get you out while we still got legs to carry us."

"I have to contact Don. He's got to go along with this."

"Call him from thirty thousand feet. We run now, we just might live to . . ." She caught sight of something behind them and straightened. "Heads up."

"What now?"

"We got company." The hard mask was back in place. Wally stepped away. "You just be ready for my signal."

THEY CAME OUT OF THE PANTRY AND STARTED DOWN THE HALL. VAL just managed to see above the pile of bathrobes and fresh towels in his arms. They came around a corner to find two dark-suited bruisers standing outside a suite entrance. Dillon tensed but played his part well. "Can I help you gentlemen?"

The pair eyed Dillon and Val like they would a free lunch.

"Right, sirs. Anything you need, just ring room service, I'll be up in a jiffy." Dillon guided Val to a halt at the neighboring doorway. "Six eighteen, this is where the lass said to do the drop." Dillon knocked, then asked the bruisers, "You know if anybody's around?"

"He's out."

"Makes our job tons easier, that." He knocked again just to be certain, then used his passkey. He let Val enter first, then said to the pair, "Trainee." And sniffed.

Dillon flipped on the light and called, "Housekeeping."

The room was empty. There was a closed door to Val's left, no doubt leading to the suite's parlor. Val could hear the soft murmur of voices.

Dillon shut the door and released a shaky breath. "Dump that lot in the bathroom."

When Val came back Dillon was doing a professional job on the bed, straightening the cover and plumping out the pillows. "Do what you got to do, mate. I can only keep this up for so long."

Val moved to the desk. The file opened on top was useless, all travel documents. The drawers were empty. He moved to the closet. Terrance's shoes were lined up like polished soldiers on parade. The two suits hanging overhead smelled slightly of their occupant.

The briefcase was set behind the shoes. Val slipped it onto the bed and knelt. The catches refused to give.

"Move aside, mate." Dillon flipped open a switchblade and jimmied the lock. "You didn't see me do that. And if you did, you won't tell Audrey."

The briefcase was new and almost empty. A series of files contained official documents related to the missing funds. Passport. More travel documents. Backup credit cards. Notepad. Silver Dupont pen. Val felt around the edges. "Is there a false bottom?"

"I'll have a go." But the switchblade did nothing save slit the threads connecting the leather base to the backing. "This isn't looking good, is it?"

In response, voices rose in the adjoining room. Both Val and Dillon looked up, frozen in the headlights of very real fear. A voice barked once, like a verbal gunshot. Beside him, Dillon jerked like he took the hit himself. "We can't stay here much longer."

The suite's door banged open and shut. They crouched and listened to footsteps thunder down the hallway outside their room. Then nothing.

Val shut the briefcase, stored it back in the closet, and cast frantically about the room. Then he found it.

The safe was tucked inside what formerly must have held a miniature fridge. "Can you open it?"

Dillon flipped open his wallet, pulled out a metallic blade like a shiny credit card. "Last time I did this, it earned me eleven months inside." He slid the card through a narrow slot running underneath the numeric keypad. Then he hit six numbers.

The safe pinged and the locks slid back. "I can't redo his code," Dillon warned. "Soon as he tries to enter, he's going to know."

"We'll worry about that later." Val flipped back the door. "Bingo."

Inside was a wafer-thin mini-laptop. As Val scooped it out, voices rose once more from inside the parlor. Someone shouted angrily.

Val slammed the safe door shut and punched in random numbers and hit the lock button. He handed Dillon the computer. The young man hid it under his jacket, catching it in place with this belt. He moved to the bath where he bunched up towels to make them look soiled and crammed them into Val's arms.

Dillon stepped to the outer door, opened it, and said loudly, "You got to speed things up, you want to keep this job."

They entered the hallway.

Dillon continued scolding as they hustled down the hall. "I'm telling you, mate, you got thirty rooms to turn down, you can't be crawling around like you're in some tortoise-and-hare race."

They were almost free. Two more steps and they would have turned the corner and been in front of the service lift. Punch the button and step inside and away.

"You two! Hold it right there!"

Val hissed, "Fire escape."

Dillon needed no second urging. He rammed open the stairwell door. Just as Val moved to follow, however, the elevator doors opened down at the hall's far end.

The day's discordant screech rose to a fever pitch. Val had no choice but to yell in reply.

Wally didn't like the way the pair hustled them toward the elevator. "Let go of my arm."

"The boss wants to see you."

Wally was not particularly large. But when she planted her heels in the lobby's carpet she put enough force into the act that the guy gripping her elbow jerked around. "I'm not asking you again."

"Look, the boss—"

"He's not the guy doing the grab here. You are. You want your fingers to stay intact, you let go of the merchandise."

The guy looked pained. His mate said softly, "There's people watching."

"That's right, boyo." Wally's face was stone, her eyes blank glass. "Listen to your pal. We don't want to make a scene, do we?"

The guy dropped his hand.

"Right. Now once more from the top. My friend and I are standing down here having a nice little chat, when you front us."

"The boss wants a word."

"So let's go." Wally gave him a meaningless smile. "See how easy things are when you play nice?"

Terrance tried to match Wally's easy tone and blank wall of a face. But he was certain his thundering heart showed. He could feel the muscles beneath his right eye begin to pull down in tight little jerks. Like the strain of not screaming had to come out somewhere.

He walked alongside Wally to the elevators. One of Loupe's guys moved a half-step ahead, the other a half-step behind. In tight, but not touching. Close enough for Terrance to feel the heat and the threatening force. Whatever the boss wanted. No question. Those guys would do it and not blink.

The doors slid open. They stepped inside. The guy who had released Wally's arm hit the button. He glanced at the woman. "The boss didn't like knowing you two were down here alone." Almost apologetic now.

Wally shrugged. Like it was nothing. "Nice to know he's so concerned about our well-being."

The guy turned back and faced the doors. Overhead the elevator's speaker droned a tinny version of *The Girl from Ipanema.* Terrance glanced at Wally. Her warning had bruised his psyche. He wanted to convince himself that it was nothing. She had to be wrong. It was his money, his job, his work. They would finish this bit, take Val Haines out of the equation, and leave.

Then he saw it.

A tiny bead of sweat pressed out by her temple, penetrating Wally's stonelike mask. It trickled down the side of her face. Wally either did not notice or did not want to draw attention to it. Terrance could not take his eyes off the moisture until it disappeared into her collar. Wally glanced his way. Her eyes looked glazed with all the other sweat she was trying hard not to release.

Terrance turned to face the doors, as scared as he had ever been in his life.

The doors pinged open. Loupe's two men stepped out.

There was a shout from somewhere along the hall. Wally still had enough of the cop in her to want to be in open space if there was trouble. But the only person visible was a bellhop just this side of where the hall jinked around a corner.

Terrance was the last to exit the elevator. He had a sudden urge to take Wally at her word. Use this chance to slip away. Hit the lobby button and flee as fast as he could for the airport and the waiting plane and Jamaica.

But no. She was wrong. She had to be.

Terrance stepped out.

The doors pinged and began to close.

But before the doors could slide shut, a crazed bellhop raced forward. He tossed his pile of towels into Wally's face.

One of the bruisers started in with, "What the—"

The bellhop slammed into Terrance. And drove him through the closing elevator doors.

Then the fist smashed into Terrance's jaw. And suddenly he was fighting for his life.

VAL WAS SLIGHTLY OFF WITH HIS FIRST BLOW. HE KNEW BEFORE IT connected that his aim was worse than his timing. He was still running when the rear wall of the elevator stopped Terrance up short and bounced him back into Val's incoming fist.

Even so, Terrance's eyes fluttered slightly as his brain went through the scramble brought on by taking one on the chin. Terrance flapped one arm up to protect his face. The other wrapped around Val's neck.

Val got one quick jab into Terrance's gut. The guy grunted, but again Val was off. Terrance gripped Val's neck harder and shortened the distance to nothing. Val tried to swing his fist around to the side, shoot off a kidney punch. But Terrance sensed it coming, or perhaps he was just thrown off balance. Whatever the reason, he caromed them over to the side wall. The elevator boomed from the impact of two bodies locked in strangle holds. A bell went off somewhere. The light flickered. The idiotic music faltered, then started back up with the elevator's downward motion.

Terrance clawed at Val's face with his fingernails for talons. The fingers felt like iron rods, jamming hard for Val's eyes. Val ducked down onto Terrance's shoulder, still going for the kidney shot. Terrance rammed him against the doors and the elevator bonged again. The alarm bell came on and stayed on.

"Where is Audrey?"

Terrance had no chance of answering. He flayed at Val with all limbs now. Their bodies were locked into a parody of dance, a vicious waltz to the music of rage. Val kneed Terrance hard enough to break the man's hold on his neck. He shoved Terrance against the side wall, bonging the cage so hard the brakes came on. The alarm bell was constant and shrill.

Val hooked Terrance on the ear. But his intent to slaughter his opponent left his own face open. The next thing he knew, an unseen hammer smashed into his wounded temple.

The sudden pain stunned him, and he fell forward into Terrance, who tried to shove him away. Val clenched harder, shaking his head. Terrance hissed in his ear, a shrill sound one note lower than a scream. Terrance pounded him in the ribs and got in two solid knees before Val's vision cleared. Partially, that is. Blood flowed anew from his wound, drenching his right eye. Val flipped it clear, spraying the wall and Terrance both.

The elevator started moving again. Terrance dislodged Val's grip enough to shove them slightly apart. But this time Val was ready. He jammed his arm between their bodies and got off two solid punches to Terrance's chin. The eyelids fluttered once more.

"*What did you do with Audrey!*"

In response, Terrance yelled with a fury to match his own and shoved.

Only the doors had opened, and there was nothing behind Val to halt his motion.

They careened out of the elevator and into a crowd of people drawn to the elevators by the alarm and their shouts and banging. Val's fall was softened by landing on a hotel manager and two bellhops. Terrance remained intent on locking his hands around Val's throat, his voice reduced to a constant beastly screech.

Val could feel his strength drain along with the blood flowing from his head wound. Thankfully, the blood kept Terrance from gaining a solid grip. Val got off one more hammer, putting everything he had into one solid right to Terrance's ear. When he felt his enemy's grip slacken, Val broke Terrance's hold and rolled away. He shoved his way free of the milling bodies scrambling with them on the lobby's carpet. He crawled to his feet and kicked hard at the hand gripping his ankle. Once free, Val lunged for the revolving glass doors.

Only then did he hear the tumult. The entire lobby was an arena of waving arms and shouting voices and running feet. Someone behind the desk was shouting for the police.

A hand gripped him from behind, one strong enough to wheel him about. Val half turned and faced one of the well-dressed killers.

Val clawed for something, anything. He caught hold of a brass ashtray standing by the nearest pillar. Val gripped the supporting rod with his free hand and whirled about.

The heavy was reaching for something under his jacket. Val reacted instinctively. He lowered his swing and batted the man's shoulder.

The man grunted in pain. His fingers flopped uselessly.

Val wrenched himself free and swung again, two-handed this time. He connected with the elbow that came up to protect the man's forehead, driving him back a step.

He was armed now, and his prey was still crawling out of the morass on the carpet. Val took a step toward Terrance and took aim.

But before he could unleash the blow, a woman slammed out of the stairwell beside the elevators. Her lips were drawn back from small animal teeth. She charged.

Val reaimed and caught her square on the shoulder, driving her to one side. She collided with another heavy, and they went down in a tangle of scrambling limbs.

People shouted and pointed and raced in every direction, just so long as it was away.

Two of the bruisers were rising to their feet, watching with deadly expressions. Val dropped the ashtray and sprinted with the others for the exit.

He shoved aside the bellhop who tried to halt him. He banged through the revolving doors. His head scarred the glass surface with red trails. Then he was through and lurching down the street.

His legs refused to obey his commands. They merely stumbled when he wanted to run.

Then Bert's van roared up alongside, climbing over the curb.

Val could not make himself stop. He rammed into the side and stayed there as the door flew open and hands gathered him up and bundled him inside.

Dillon pulled Val into the seat beside him and stared aghast at Val's bloody face. Bert wrestled them off the curb and roared away. Only when they were three streets out from the center did Bert risk a glance and a grin in Val's direction. "My guess is you won't be offered a second chance at that job, mate."

Val remained silent. He bent over his legs, the aftershocks sending weak tremors through his frame. He was still being assaulted. Only now it was by memories.

Dillon stripped off his own bellhop jacket and handed it over. "Stick that on your face before you bleed to death."

Val pressed the jacket to his temple. The pressure did nothing to stem the flood. He remembered.

Bert demanded, "What's the matter, mate?"

Val straightened in stages. "Do either of you have friends servicing the rentals around here?"

"What, you mean cottages to let?" Dillon looked askance at Bert. "I might do. Why?"

When Val explained what he wanted, Bert laughed out loud. "I'm ruddy glad we didn't meet up back before I took the straight and narrow, mate. You're a right one with the planning, you are."

"You just watch the road," Dillon said.

Bert paid him no mind whatsoever. "Our Val is covered in it, and all he wants to know is, can we help him with what comes next."

Dillon asked, "What do we do now?"

"That's simple enough," Bert replied for him. "We're off to save the lady. Isn't that right, mate?"

Val only pressed harder at his temple. But the mental torrent would not abate.

He remembered everything.

THE STORM HAD NOT YET ARRIVED WHEN VAL LEFT GERALD'S STUDY. He walked through the kitchen, easing his shoulders and wincing at the bite of new bruises. Dillon and Bert were busy at the stove making a late supper nobody much wanted. They must have seen the frustration in his face because they did not speak. The pressure of time and unspoken terrors weighed heavily upon them all. A pot of coffee had been sitting on the eye long enough to almost congeal. Val poured himself a mug and stepped out back.

The greatest source of anxiety was that no one had called. No threats had been made. No ultimatums. Nothing.

The hillside was a dark silhouette cut from sunset and the impending storm. The horizon was a solid wall of black cloud. The air smelled of coming rain, heavy and sweet. Thunder rumbled low and menacing. The chalk veins glowed faintly, as if the heat Val felt fulminating inside his heart lay exposed and gleaming.

He yearned for love. No incoming barrage of memories could change that. He yearned for the touch of a good woman. A lady who cared enough to see in him what only love could illuminate. What he had denied himself for far too long.

Gerald let himself out the back door and came to stand beside Val. Gerald had dumped the contents of Terrance's laptop into his own computer, then he and Val had worked in tandem for three frantic hours. Now his voice carried the grainy tension of a quest unfulfilled. "Further north they refer to such hills as fells. It's a good

Gaelic-sounding word, that. The fells. Brings to mind all sorts of dark and craggy depths. Places where evil might thrive unobserved."

Bert and Dillon let themselves out the kitchen door and padded over to stand beside them at the fence. Bert said, "You might as well go ahead and say it."

Gerald said, "All we have to show for our efforts is a long string of numbers belonging to a file named after this bloke here."

"That's something, right?" Bert searched both faces with frantic concern. "One of you tell me we're closer to getting the lady back."

When Gerald merely rubbed his tired eyes, Val explained, "It's something. But not as much as we hoped. My guess is, Terrance set up the accounts in my name so the U.S. authorities can track how the money flowed, maybe even get a figure on what's sitting over there. But that's it. Jersey banking laws make Switzerland's system look like fishnet."

"You guess," Gerald quietly scoffed.

But Val was seeing anew how the file with the numbers had been set up. It was marked simply as *Haines*. "Terrance can claim they found the account numbers in searching me out. That's why he can carry them like this, to show the authorities. But they'll have some prearranged electronic signal for moving the money on. That's what we didn't find. I should have figured Terrance would set up firewalls."

Bert complained, "You lost me back there around the first word."

"Maybe they set up a secure Web site somewhere. One way in, one out. He brought the computer because there's a signal embedded in here that opens the electronic door. We have no idea where to look on the Web. He could have this thing hidden anywhere. A server for the phone company in Tasmania, an insurance group in Shanghai, anywhere at all."

"Without the codes and the address, we're lost," Gerald said. "I say it's time we called in the police."

"Absolutely," Val said.

Dillon pointed out, "If we do, mate, they're bound to discover your role in all this."

"If you're hesitating on my account, forget it," Val said.

Gerald said, "So maybe we should arrange a trade. You for her. The one thief within reach for Audrey."

"I'm ready," Val said. Meaning it.

"No, mate," Bert decided, shaking his entire upper body. "We can't do that."

"Why not?" Gerald's voice was flat as a cop's.

"They'll murder the bloke. You know that same as me."

"So what do you think they're doing to Audrey?"

Bert sneered. "You're telling me it'd be right to feed the bloke to the lions?"

"If it saves Audrey, absolutely."

Val backed away from the three men. "I'm the one who brought this down on you people. I'm the reason the bad guys have Audrey. I've made a total mess of everything."

"What about your plan?" Bert said.

"Will you just listen to the man!" Gerald snapped. "We can't access the computer codes!"

"Your plan," Bert insisted to Val. "The one you were thinking of back before we hit the hotel."

"It could still work. Maybe. I'm not sure of anything anymore except that first you need to decide whether it'd be better just to offer me up for her."

A silhouette appeared in the kitchen doorway. Arthur d'Arcy held himself canted slightly to one side. He pushed futilely at the back door and then turned away. Val started back for the house.

Gerald shouted, "We're not finished here!"

Val kept going. A gale-force wind blasted out of nowhere. Thunder tore shreds from the feeble sunset. When Val let himself in through the door, Arthur d'Arcy was seated at the kitchen table. Arthur looked once in Val's direction, then planted his elbows on the table and placed his face in his hands. The motions of a defeated man.

Val understood perfectly how he felt.

The kitchen held a sulphurous odor. Far more than coffee had burned down to sullen residue. Val poured a second mug. The coffee was black as pitch and smelled charred. He doubted very much that Arthur would notice. Val set the mug down by the old man's elbow and took the chair on the table's opposite side.

Val tasted his own mug. "Apparently the fight with Terrance jostled my brain. Things are coming back to me now."

There was no sign from Arthur that he had heard at all.

"I remember everything. Well, not everything. But enough. I remember why I sent Audrey away. Right now, that's pretty much all that matters."

"I long to forget." Arthur did not raise his face from his hands. The words came out malformed, shards of trauma and regret. "My entire life has been quilted together from horrific errors. I should never have married Eleanor. But I was convinced my love was great enough for the two of us. I should have fought my father's decision. I should have . . ."

Val sipped his coffee and waited the man out. The voices out back had gone silent. The only sounds were the tick of the kitchen clock and distant thunder.

Arthur went on, "Everything Terrance accused me of was true."

"Partly," Val corrected.

Arthur lifted his head. He blinked slowly, having difficulty placing the man across from him.

"Partly true," Val repeated. "Finding his enemy's weakness and attacking hard are Terrance's trademarks."

"His enemy," Arthur croaked. "What a dreadful legacy I've created."

"What about Audrey?"

"They have her."

"That's not your fault. If you want someone to blame for that particular calamity, you're looking straight at him."

But Arthur was too lost in self-remorse to accuse anyone else. "I thought giving my family peace and harmony and stability was doing right by them. But that was what I wanted. Not them. They wanted . . ." He dropped his face back into his hands. He might have finished with the word "everything." But Val could not be certain.

The clock on the wall above the stove sounded like a pick working at the wound on Val's temple. Chipping away at his composure, exposing the bubbling fear that threatened to erupt at any time.

They had Audrey. He had looked into the faces of four of them, Terrance and the woman and the two bruisers, and he knew them for killers. Val wanted to grab the clock and fling it onto the stone floor and stomp it to bits.

"Fourteen months after my wife left me for Terrance, I met Audrey," Val went on, his voice steady. "She showed me the same talent as her brother, only in reverse. Terrance hunts out weakness to attack. Audrey seeks only to help. She is the most giving person I've ever met. The most loving. I saw it even then. But I couldn't accept it. Back then I woke up every night drenched in rage. I couldn't see further than wanting to tear a man apart with my own bare hands."

Val looked down at his hands. He was amazed to find that they were not trembling. He could remember now what it was like, walking into the bathroom at one or two in the morning, knowing he would not return to sleep. Living on three or four hours of sleep a night because that was all he could have. All he would ever have. His bathroom was like the rest of the house, empty of life. Even when he was there. Two o'clock in the morning was a terrible time to face the fact that he had lost everything. All because of one man. His hands had trembled then. He would wash his face and clench his fists and press them to his forehead, trying to cram the rage and the hatred all back inside where it lay hidden during the day.

"Audrey arrived in Florida a week after I learned Terrance was stripping the pension funds. I had not slept in seven nights. I never knew a man could live without sleep. All I could think of was, how was I going to catch Terrance red-handed? If I blew the whistle too early, the fund would collapse and pull the company down with it. And Terrance would escape free and clear. And I wasn't going to let that happen. I was going to bring him down. I was going to crush him."

Val was lost in a morass of remembrances. The kitchen's sulfurous odor was identifiable now. It came from himself and the rage he had refused to let go. "Audrey caught me at my weakest. All she wanted was to give me hope in the future. I see that now. But at the time, I thought she was asking the impossible. She wanted me to forgive Terrance." The words were almost too large to fit inside his mouth. "She gave me an ultimatum. Give up the hatred, or her."

He could hear Audrey's voice so clearly she might as well have been seated there beside him. He felt anew her intense longing to reach him. To *turn* him. "She told me the only way forward was to release my desire for vengeance. Otherwise I would serve a life sentence, trapped in a prison of my own making."

Val saw her face again, the flame he had extinguished burning so strongly it illuminated his own heart. "But I wouldn't let go. I couldn't see beyond my hatred for Terrance. I knew it was consuming me, and I didn't care."

Val raised his gaze. Arthur had lifted his head free of his hands. Bert and Dillon were stationed by the rear door. The three men watched him with knowing eyes. Val swallowed against the hurt and the helplessness. "I'd made my choice. I wasn't going to be one of the good guys anymore. Audrey accused me of allowing Terrance to remake me into himself. She was right."

From behind him Gerald said, "So you sent her away."

Val nodded to the accusation in Gerald's tone. "Audrey never told me to stop going after him. But she wanted me to do it for the right reasons. To save the pension. To protect the company and the employees. But that wasn't enough for me. I wanted . . ."

"Vengeance," Arthur murmured.

"Everything," Val said, shamed by his confession. "I wanted it all."

"You wanted back what the man had stolen." This from Bert. "Audrey knew you couldn't have it. She offered you something else. You turned her down."

"Guilty," Val said.

Gerald came around to look Val in the eye. "Explain to me why you didn't go to the authorities as soon as you knew the money was missing."

"If I couldn't pin the loss on Terrance, from inside the company and knowing the books as I did, no outside examiner would find enough to put him away, much less recoup the losses. I couldn't blow the whistle until I had both hard evidence on Terrance and knowledge of where the funds had been hidden. But the more I looked, the more I realized . . ."

Gerald gave him a tight moment, then pressed, "What?"

"I realized the only way to track him was to put myself in his shoes."

"You mean steal funds yourself."

"That's right."

"Sounds very convenient to me."

"Gerald, mate, give it a rest."

"No, it's okay. He's right." Val stared at Gerald but saw only the past. "It wasn't Terrance that I first discovered at all. There was a woman in my department, Marjorie Copeland was her name. She had a severely disabled son and no life whatsoever. The last person you'd expect to be caught dipping. She revealed that she had found out someone else was taking huge sums. She was three years from retirement, and her son could not survive without her pension. I started looking and discovered she was not only right, but it was far worse than she had thought. Enough had been stolen to bring down the entire company. I knew it was Terrance. But I couldn't prove it."

Bert was growing impatient. "So you went after him by following his tracks. Sounds simple enough."

But Val kept his gaze on Gerald, his judge and jury. "It started off that way. But I knew the life Terrance had stolen from me was gone. Demolished. So I decided to take my own share of the pension, expose Terrance, and disappear."

Gerald repeated, more softly this time, "So you sent Audrey away."

"My life was over. I wanted to leave and never come back. I wanted to start over and do right all the things that had come out so wrong the first time."

He stopped then. And sat listening to his past and the ticking of the clock.

Gerald still challenged, but the heat was absent. "You said you have a plan."

Val took a breath, and stared into his dimly lit future. "That's right. I do."

TERRANCE D'ARCY PACED A DARKENED BEDROOM. THE ROOM'S only illumination came from a cheap bedside clock radio and light slipping beneath the closed door. He heard soft voices somewhere in the distance. His two suitcases lay open beside the bed with his clothes heaped on top. Such disorder would normally have sent him into a tailspin. Right now, however, he had more pressing issues on his mind.

When they had returned upstairs after the attack, Loupe had explained in his mildest voice that their struggle had attracted the wrong sort of attention. He asked if Terrance would temporarily relocate to their rented cottage. The silken voice had left no room for complaint. The police would be coming around, asking questions. Bound to happen, what with five of them involved in a dust-up in the hotel lobby and Terrance brawling in the lift.

His jaw throbbed where Val had struck. His body felt stiff with hints of pain yet to come. The bedside clock taunted him with red eyes that blinked out the minutes. He turned on the overhead light. Still the darkness would not go away. He was desperate for answers and had no one with whom he could talk. Wally had remained at the hotel. Don was still not answering his phone. But Terrance's mind was such a muddle he needed someone to help him strategize.

Terrance stopped his pacing and stared at the side wall. To even consider such a move revealed just how frantic he had become.

Terrance stripped off the clothes trashed by his battle with Val. From the pile on the floor he selected a freshly starched shirt. A navy suit of finest gabardine with a slight hint of charcoal pinstripe. Baume et Mercier watch. Gold stud cufflinks. Donning the only armor he possessed.

He exited the room. Two of Loupe's men were seated at the kitchen table. They greeted his appearance with vacant gazes. "Everything all right, Mr. d'Arcy?"

"I just wanted to speak with my sister."

"Mr. Loupe didn't say nothing about that." The two men exchanged glances. "Think maybe we should call it in?"

"Look here. I was the one who ordered her brought in. She's my sister. If she is going to tell anyone where Haines is, it will be me."

The men looked doubtful but did not stop him as Terrance walked to the other bedroom and opened the door.

Audrey was handcuffed to a bedpost. She had risen to a seated position at the sound of his voice. She greeted him with, "I wouldn't dream of telling you anything."

Terrance gently shut the door. He picked up the room's one chair and carried it to her side of the bed. Audrey drew her legs up under her at his approach, as though fearful of contamination. "There is nothing I could possibly say of any help to you," she said.

Terrance opened the window wide. The mist floated in, and the room's air chilled. But it was his only hope of not being overheard. Audrey watched his movements but made no protest.

He lowered himself into the chair. He steepled his fingers. He spoke the words, "I am trapped."

Audrey remained motionless, her gaze guarded.

"I have only just realized how serious the situation has become. I don't know what to do."

"And you're asking me? For advice?"

"Help me strategize, and I will see that you are immediately freed." It was a lie, of course. But it was all he had. "I will set you and Father up in luxury and comfort for the rest of your days."

"You must be in far deeper than I thought." Audrey untangled her legs, and slid over. The handcuff rattled against the bedstead. "Brother, look at me." She waited through the long moment it took for Terrance to lift his gaze. "You have been trapped all your life."

"You don't understand."

"On the contrary. I understand all too well."

"Could we please dispense with the self-righteous claptrap for a moment? I am in very serious trouble here."

"Of that I have no doubt."

"You have remained persistently determined to misunderstand everything I am and do." Terrance felt the exasperation of centuries. "Why I came in here is utterly beyond me now."

"Because you're desperate. Because you have nowhere else to turn."

"You needn't sound so pleased."

"As a prisoner counselor, I deal with people in your situation day in and day out. The only difference is, they are wearing the cuffs. And their jailers are not normally in suits. But I have seen this situation more often than you can imagine. So I shall make things easy for you. You are completely trapped. You have nowhere to go. All your normal maneuverings have brought you nowhere but down into a pit of your own making."

He felt the old anger surge. "You and I are more alike than you ever imagined. You take precise aim for the jugular. Perhaps it's a family trait, one that passed over our dear father's generation."

"Don't you dare speak of him. Don't you dare." She stopped, pushed herself back. "Terrance, I have only one hope to offer you. One answer. One way out of the misery you have created for yourself and for everyone around you." She wiped a hand across her face. Plum-colored caverns had been excavated below her eyes. "Why did you come in here?"

A puff of wind blew night mist over them both. "You're right, of course. I shouldn't have bothered."

"No, no, that's not what I meant. You came in here looking for answers, isn't that so?"

"Clearly none of those you have to offer."

Terrance heard the phone ring in the distance. A moment later, one of the guards opened the door and announced, "The boss wants a word. In person."

"But it's four in the morning."

The guard shrugged. "The boss never was much for sleep."

Terrance rose and turned his face to the open window and the squall. The night was such a terrible foe. But he had triumphed over worse enemies. There had to be a way.

Audrey reached over and gripped his arm. "Listen to what I'm saying, will you please?"

Terrance looked down at her hand. He could not remember the last time they had touched. "I was wrong to come here."

The guard warned, "Best not to keep the boss waiting."

"Terrance—"

He pulled his arm free. "Farewell, Audrey."

THE RAIN CAME WITH THE NIGHT. BY THE TIME DAWN SPREAD A COLD, grey blanket over the world, they had worked through Val's plan. Arthur held in there gamely, offering little besides his presence, refusing their repeated request for him to go upstairs and lie down. The five of them sat in grim determination, staring at the many problems for which they had no answers. Audrey's absence was a gaping wound Val saw in all their faces. Sharing this woe was a unifying force, the only answer he could find to whether he had the ability to pull this off.

Finally Gerald nodded once. A very small nod. "This is good."

Every tick of the clock was a hammer aimed at Val's temple, banging down on the need for speed. But he waited. There was nothing else he could do. To work this plan he needed them all. In truth, he needed an army. But these three men would have to do.

Arthur cleared his throat. "I would ask that you gentlemen do something for me."

"Anything." Bert's response was visceral. "Whatever you need, mate. Consider it done."

"When we got out of the joint," Dillon explained to Val, "Arthur here landed us both jobs."

"First honest wage I'd ever earned," Bert agreed. "You just name it, mate."

Arthur spoke for ten minutes. When he finished, the room remained locked in stunned silence.

Arthur slid his chair back and used both hands to push himself erect. “And now I fear I really must rest.”

“We’ll do it,” Bert said, but weaker.

Dillon’s voice was as strained as his features. “Are you certain—”

“Yes,” Arthur replied. “I am. As certain as I’ve ever been in all my life.”

“We can make this happen,” Val admitted, though saying the words left him nauseous. “But we’ll need your help.”

“I thought as much.”

Val followed Arthur down the hall and up the stairs, resisting the urge to help when the older man faltered. Only when Arthur entered the guestroom and sighed his way down onto the bed did Val say, “I’m not doing this for you, and I’m sure not doing it for Terrance. If I’d been the one holding the trigger and Terrance had been upstairs in that bank, I would not have hesitated one instant.”

Arthur did not seem particularly surprised by his words. “And now?”

“I’m doing this for Audrey.”

From the foot of the stairs, Bert called up, “Val, mate, it’s time to roll.”

Arthur’s pale hands held out the keys to his battered old Rover. “I can only hope her love works on your magnificent stone of a heart.”

Val accepted the keys. “I don’t know if I’ll ever be able to free myself like she wants—to let go of the hate and the pain. But I want to try. She deserves that much. Even if she won’t give me another chance, still she deserves . . .”

Arthur watched him swallow against the tragedy of all he had lost, all he had done wrong, all he had failed to achieve. Arthur said at last, “This is the first good feeling I’ve had since the police stopped by.”

Val set the portable phone on the bedside table and headed for the door. “I wish I could say the same.”

Tension resided like an expanding bubble at the base of Val’s ribcage. He swallowed twice as he descended the stairs, and three more times as he followed the trio out to Bert's van. The other men's grim silence only pushed more air into the bubble. The one sound in the van was the swish of the wipers. Val wondered if he showed the same lie in his own features. He had heard the way the breath caught in their throats whenever they mentioned Audrey's name. The only comfort Val found in that taut and colorless dawn was that they cared for her almost as much as he did.

They dropped Dillon off at the top of the road leading to Arthur d'Arcy's home. The young man solemnly shook hands with each of them before heading down the slope. They sat in tense silence until he unlocked Audrey's Rover and pulled away. There was no sign of unwanted interest. No sign of life along the wet and sleepy street. The remaining three men took a single unified breath of relief and headed out.

They skirted the industrial park and headed along the narrow high road toward Brighton. The early morning traffic was limited to trucks, delivery vans, and a few farm vehicles. Wet sheep huddled against stone troughs and sheltering groves. Cattle stared blankly at the passing cars, unaware of the day's momentous hold.

The airfield was a pair of whitewashed hangars, a stubby concrete tower, and one runway. The windsock was pulled to nervous attention by the gusting wind. They left the van and hustled into a steamy-windowed café that formed the tower's base. Bert took a satisfied breath of the grease-stained air and declared, "Believe I'll have me a fry up."

Gerald grimaced in disgust. "You best be ready soon as I say."

"Don't you fret, mate. You give us the word, and Bob's your uncle." Bert watched Gerald depart with something like fondness. "Just like Dillon, that one. Lad never did have much of an appetite before a job. Mind you, after it was over he could eat a horse and have room left over for the saddle."

Val followed him over to the corner booth. There was nothing to see outside but traces of rain patterned against the steamed-over glass. "You and Dillon have been together long?"

"Been years now. I claim to have raised him, just to see him do his nut."

The day was such that Val could ask easily, "You were both thieves?"

"We had our hands in a bit of this and that." Bert smiled at the waitress. "Hello, love. I'll have the lot. Beans, fried bread, four eggs, chips, rasher of bacon, sausages, what have I forgotten? Oh my yes, and mushrooms. And tea. Oh, and toast. Got to have something to wipe up the grease."

The waitress turned to Val. "What about you, love?"

"Just tea, thanks."

Bert smiled his thanks when the waitress returned with their teas. "What were we talking about?"

"You and Dillon."

Bert took a noisy sip. "Lad's the best second-story man I ever knew."

"And you?"

"Smash and grab, driving, fence, whatever paid, mate."

"Where did you meet Audrey?"

"Little place by the name of Wormwood Scrubs."

"A prison?"

"Worst there ever was." Bert watched the waitress deposit his plate, his good humor vanished. "Been there for donkey's years. Ghosts rattle around the place at night, ready to suck the breath straight out of your body." Bert used the scrunchy fried bread as a ladle for his eggs and talked around his food. "Audrey was counseling a mate of mine getting ready for parole. I went on account of any excuse being a fine one if it gave me visiting time with a lady. Took about six months before I realized she was drilling holes in this thick skull of mine. By then it was too late."

"Wish I'd had your sense."

Bert used his toast to sop up the grease. "Noticed you take something out and read it from time to time."

"Audrey wrote me a letter."

The knife and fork clattered down and he glanced at Val. A quick there-and-gone, nothing behind it. "Not my business to ask."

Val opened the letter. The creases had worn into soft patterns now. Val scanned the sheet, the biting affection known by heart. "She was just trying to reach me."

"Audrey has a way of talking," Bert agreed. "Brings to mind a sentiment I don't deserve."

Val refolded the pages. "Made me wish I was a better man."

"I remember once, she was talking to me on death. Death of hope, death of dreams. Watching life take the wrong turn that can't never be made right again." Bert turned and stared at the window, seeing something neither the rainswept day nor the misted glass could bar from vision. "What we do then is, we hide in our dark little cave and seal it up tight with a boulder of our own making. Before we can ever get out, we have to name the stone for what it is."

Rage, pain, hatred. Val found the words there waiting for him. All he said was, "I know exactly what you mean."

Bert said to his window, "Takes me back, that does. First time I heard her say the words, felt like she was tearing a hole in my chest."

The café's door opened. Gerald called through, "We're ready."

Val could not have come up with a better scenario to forget how bruised and bone-weary he was. He flew in the copilot's seat of a small single-engine plane. Below him was unmarked blackness. Above him was nothing at all. The windscreen was lashed by rain. The plane was buffeted by roller-coaster winds.

Val shouted above the roars, "Does it rain all the time here?"

"Don't be daft. It was lovely yesterday." Gerald pointed at the instrument panel with his chin. His complexion was green from the panel's illumination. At least, Val hoped it was the panel lights. "You just keep a sharp eye on the NAVS."

Bert filled both rear seats to overflow and groaned softly.

Val could not help but notice Gerald's death grip on the stick. "What's the matter with you?"

Gerald confessed, "I've never done this before."

"Done what, flown over water? Flown in a storm?"

"Take your pick."

Bert groaned louder. "Great time you picked to be letting us in on your little secret, mate."

"You can just ease up." Gerald never took his eye off the controls. "You heard him same as me. Val needed to get to Jersey without risking contact with the police. The authorities might be watching for him now that the news has broken."

"The important thing is getting there in one piece," Bert pointed out.

"Which I'm doing, if a certain somebody would tone it down with the distractions."

An hour later, Jersey appeared off to their right, a rainswept apparition rimmed by jagged white teeth. Gerald went through the landing protocol with an unseen tower. The voice coming back to them over the plane's loudspeaker spoke absolute gibberish as far as Val could tell. But Gerald altered his direction slightly and began a hard-fought descent. The wind struck them with invisible fists, jamming them about so hard the engine screamed to keep them on track.

They passed over a cliffside manor-hotel and a neighboring golf course. Two men working the first green halted their work, shielded their eyes against the tempest, and watched the plane's unsteady approach. The airfield appeared from the wet gloom. The landing strip looked about two inches wide.

Gerald took aim for the strip only to have a gust shove them brutally toward a neighboring grove of trees. He pulled back on the stick so hard his teeth were bared. The squall caught them full-force and sent them rocketing out and over the cliff. From where Val sat, it appeared they took aim straight for a grey and angry sea. Gerald continued hauling back and finally managed to straighten them out.

He regained altitude, dipped one wing, and circled back over the hotel. "Let's try that one again, shall we?"

"Just land the ruddy thing this time, all right, Gerald?"

Gerald straightened his shoulders, leaned in close to the windshield, and went for the strip. The wind mashed the surrounding grass into a shivering tabletop. The windsock by the tower looked ironed flat.

They hit hard. Bounced. The plane rose and almost touched

one wing to the tarmac. They landed again. Gerald slapped the controls. The motor powered back. They stayed down.

When they stopped before the lone hangar, they crawled from the plane like cross-tied marionettes. Val glanced around the rainswept vista. The workers by the first green had not budged.

TERRANCE SAT IN THE CORNER OF THE SUITE'S PARLOR. HE HELD a plastic hotel laundry bag full of ice to his jaw. The swelling was coming in thick and purple. When the skin stopped burning and turned numb, he switched the bag to his eye.

A newspaper lay beside the silver coffee thermos. The front page was folded back so that one word of the headline stood front and center. It shouted across the room at him. *Insignia*.

Loupe sat at a room-service table set up by the empty fireplace. The two heavies who had accompanied Terrance in the elevator stood before him. The men quaked in terror. Loupe did not raise his voice. Nor did he threaten. "Explain it to me again. I'm trying hard to understand, you see. Describe how it was that two such great hulking brutes could let the very man we've been tracking for two days get by them."

"Boss, it's like this." The man swallowed loud enough for the sound to carry across the room. "The bloke was wearing a bellhop's uniform."

"A uniform."

"With a hat, boss. We didn't get a clean look at his face, see."

Loupe turned his attention to his driver. The man stood sentry by the parlor's main doors. "What do you have to say for yourself?"

"I was right here. You called the house and ordered me back. I came."

Loupe pushed his breakfast plate aside and pulled out a cigar. He made a production of trimming the end and flicking open a heavy gold lighter. He sat back and puffed hard on the cigar, then inspected its glowing end. "A hat," the boss repeated. "This is the best excuse you can come up with? My so-called finest men?"

"All we saw was this hotel staff bloke carrying a wad of towels, coming down the hall. He wasn't nothing to us but the uniform."

Wally sat in the parlor's opposite corner, as far from Terrance as she could get. She watched Loupe with a cop's absence of emotion. Terrance wanted to shriek at her to give the signal. But Wally did not even glance his way.

Loupe asked, "What was it, the shiny brass buttons?"

"We just didn't recognize him, is all. Nobody knew who he was."

Terrance shifted the ice bag back to his eye. This was not supposed to be happening. He was the one in control. It was his forte. He *managed* things. He *manipulated*. All his problems came down to one man. Terrance whispered, "Val."

Loupe nodded vigorously in agreement. "Exactly. Val Haines is still out there. Who knows what mischief he might be cooking up?"

But a niggling concern had taken root in Terrance's mind. As though he needed another. He rose and headed for the parlor's side door, the one leading to what had formerly been his room.

Loupe tracked Terrance with his gaze, but said nothing.

As Terrance entered the room, he heard the guard pleading openly now. "He came at us so fast, boss. Running down the hall, whacking our guy, then gone."

Terrance set the ice pack down on the tray holding the glasses and ice bucket. Val had been here. Terrance could sense the man's lingering presence.

Terrance crossed to the cabinet and opened the front. Dropping to his knees, he punched in the code to open the safe. Nothing. He repeated it, going more slowly this time, making sure the numbers were correct.

The safe's display replied that his numbers were invalid.

He walked back to the parlor entrance just as Loupe said thoughtfully, "Maybe I should show you both what a real whacking is."

"Boss—"

Loupe glanced over and noticed Terrance's expression. He waved the guards to silence. "What is it?"

"I know why Val was here."

"That's obvious enough. He came here looking for the girl. He failed. He went after you."

"That's not all. It probably wasn't even in the original plan." Terrance leaned against the doorjamb. "He's stolen my computer. I had it in my room safe. Now the safe won't open. Val broke the code, stole the computer, then shut the safe and recoded it to make it look like he hadn't been here."

There was a pounding at the door. Loupe motioned with his cigar. The sentry opened it.

Don Winslow burst inside.

Don was red-eyed and instantly raging. His gaze swiveled about the room like a sniper seeking prey. He fastened upon Terrance and shouted, "What are you *doing* here?"

Terrance could only shake his head. "You shouldn't have come."

"That's your idea of a news flash?" He sighted Wally and his scowl deepened. "So how come you're not out doing what we're paying you to do?"

Wally gave him an empty stare in reply.

Loupe demanded softly, "Who is this man?"

Don stalked over to where Terrance sat. "Do you have any idea the storm I left behind at headquarters? I've got SEC guys crawling all over the place with electron microscopes. So I fly over here, expecting to hear you're wrapping things up. What do I find?" Don flailed the air with his fist. "You guys sitting around having a tea party!"

"I asked you a question," Loupe said.

Don stared at the seated old man like he would a bug in the road. "I'm the top guy, is who I am. And the top guy is wondering why I'm talking to you at all."

Loupe paused long enough to puff on his cigar. He replied with the smoke, "I'm your new friend and partner."

Don laughed out loud. "In your dreams, pal."

The boss settled his cigar into the ashtray. "I fear that is the incorrect response."

"Like I care." Don wheeled back to Terrance. "Who danced on your face?"

"Val."

"Where is he?"

Terrance watched as Loupe set his cigar down in the ashtray. Terrance had never felt more helpless. Not even the day his father had betrayed him. Never. "We don't know."

Don's face reddened. "You're sitting here while the man we need dead and disappeared is out strolling around the town?"

Loupe bent over and picked up one of the sofa pillows. "We were discussing strategy."

Don wheeled about. "I wasn't talking to you."

"Again, the wrong answer."

"What, you're making the rules now?"

Loupe slipped his hand beneath the jacket of his nearest man. He came out holding a pistol. Terrance was trapped in the amber of helpless foreknowledge.

Loupe brought up the pistol, cushioning the muzzle with the pillow.

And shot Don Winslow in the chest.

The bang was a sharp punch to the air, no louder than a single bass drumbeat. Everybody save Loupe jerked, knowing the next shot could just as easily be aimed at them.

Terrance watched his own life fall to the carpet with his former partner.

Loupe stood over Don and replied, "That is correct. I now make all the rules."

The boss nudged the body with the toe of his shoe. Then he handed back the gun, returned to the table, and reached for his cigar. He puffed long enough to get the cigar drawing fully, then said with the smoke, "Get rid of this filth."

The two men who had been awaiting judgment leapt to obey. Loupe watched them roll the body into a pair of blankets and toss it over one man's shoulder. "Don't either of you for a minute think I'm done yet."

A tremor went through both their frames. The driver opened the door, scouted the hallway, then pointed them toward the service elevator.

When the door shut behind them, the boss turned to Wally and said, "You know a gentleman by the name of Gennaro, I believe."

Wally might have nodded. But Terrance thought more than likely it was merely a shudder.

"Of course you do. He owns you, doesn't he?" Loupe tapped off the ash. "He and I had a little chat last night. I think it's time you went back and reported in, don't you?"

Wally struggled to her feet. She did not glance in Terrance's direction as she headed for the door.

As she opened it, Loupe added, "I don't need to say a thing to you, do I? About all that must remain between us and such as that."

Wally stared down at the hand holding the doorknob. She shook her head and murmured, "No. You don't."

"The first time I set eyes on you, I knew you for a smart lady. Be sure and give Gennaro my best, now, will you?"

Loupe waited until the door shut behind her to say, "I do so hope these new arrangements meet with your approval."

Terrance did not respond. Of course, he was not expected to.

Loupe dragged a chair over to Terrance's corner and seated himself. He patted Terrance on the knee with the hand holding the cigar. The smoke clogged Terrance's every pore.

The boss said in his mild tone, "Now perhaps you'll be so good as to tell your new partner just exactly what the stakes are in this little game."

AS FAR AS JOCKO WAS CONCERNED, THE ISLAND OF JERSEY WAS A wee tight place. Especially for two men who'd shared a berth in Wormwood Scrubs, as cramped a set of quarters as ever there were. The walls here might be liquid, the food a ruddy sight better than inside the grey-bar hotel. But the sentence Jocko served out was the same. Forever and a day.

They were set up in a hotel across the street from the bank's only entrance. The room Jocko shared with Matt was almost as small as their cell. The hotel was a glorified boarding house, not even deserving its single star. But it was the only one they could find with a clear view of the place. When Matt had complained, Loupe had offered to fit them out with something smaller. A barrel, perhaps.

So there they sat, day in and day out, one or the other of them staring at the ruddy entrance until their eyes were ready to fall out of their heads. They even did it all night long, which was the stupidest thing going, according to Matt. The bank had these great steel doors that wheeled out at five every afternoon, locking the place up like a streetside vault. They made no sense, as orders went. Jocko's mate, the brains of the pair, was given to complaining more with every passing hour. Jocko, though, he found the alternative a ruddy sight less appealing. He had been around long enough to hear the tales of what Loupe did to those who disappointed him. Jocko had no interest in finding out if the tales were true. No, mate. Not him. He'd sit by the ruddy window until he fused with the chair, he would.

Which had almost happened. Jocko had been at it for five poxy hours. Sitting by the window, watching the grey light strengthen and the rain fall and smoking his head off. The noisy bedside clock taunted him all night with how slowly time moved. Finally he couldn't take it anymore.

Jocko walked over and kicked the bed. Again. A third time, and finally his mate was up and complaining again. The rain, the day, the stink from Jocko's cigarettes even with the window wide open. Matt's voice was persistent as a drill. But at least Jocko heard some other noise now besides the drip-drip-drip of this rain.

Soon as Matt was dressed and moaning by the window about another day lost to nothing, Jocko left. The hotel manager was already at his desk. The old geezer didn't think much of two men sharing one of his cramped front rooms. Jocko left the hotel and walked through the cold rain and wondered why anybody would ever want to live in such a place. Stone the crows, but this was a miserable excuse for a town. Cramped rooms and tiny streets and small-minded people, surrounded by miles and miles of empty water and rain. Jocko stopped by the newsagents' and bought a *Sun*. He rounded the corner and entered the steamy café. He took his regular place in the booth by the window and ordered his regular breakfast. He opened his paper and almost moaned over that first sip of tea. Breakfast was the one thing this place had not managed to ruin.

Jocko was about midway through the morning feast when something caught his eye.

At first he wasn't sure what it was he'd seen, what with the window so misted over and the rain falling in sheets. Jocko rubbed the pane clean. Yes. Stepping away from a shop connected to a church. Walking there on the main road. Headed for the bank. A man who looked a lot like . . .

Jocko sprang from the booth and barged out the door. He raced around the corner in time to watch the bloke walk up the front steps and enter the bank. It might have been their man. Only Jocko was looking at this bloke from the rear. And it had been a while. And the wind was rising and blowing this pelting rain straight into his eyes. Jocko swiped angrily at his face and started forward.

Then he stopped. Because there were two men stationed at the front of the bank. One of them was a bloke big as himself. Definitely someone who knew how to handle himself.

Jocko took another step. This one took him over by the corner of the hotel. He squinted against the driving rain.

He'd seen that man before.

Jocko turned up his collar and sauntered along the lane. He took the hotel stairs easy as you please. Once through the hotel entrance, though, Jocko hurtled across the lobby and thundered up the stairs.

Jocko flung open the door to their room, only to discover his mate seated by the window, his head in his arms, dead asleep.

Jocko kicked the chair out from under him.

Matt fell to the floor, picked himself up, and cuffed Jocko. The blow was about as potent as a fleabite. Cross and sour, Matt picked up the chair, slammed it back down, and started complaining about how Jocko didn't even bother to bring him a cup of tea and something hot—

"He's here."

Matt paled. "The boss? Here?"

"No. Our target."

Matt almost fell out the window in his panic. "Where?"

"The bank. Maybe."

"What's that supposed to mean, maybe? Either he's in the bank or he's not."

"Only saw the bloke from behind, didn't I. And look there. See the muscle? They showed up with him."

His mate was seriously alarmed. "Are they ours?"

"Have a look at the bloke on the right. I've seen him before."

"With Loupe?"

"No. Inside. He was in another section. Somebody pointed him out. Savage. Yeah, that's the bloke's name. Bert Savage."

"The boss didn't say anything about heavies."

Jocko squinted out the window, wanting to tighten down his gaze and pierce the stone wall. "Maybe it wasn't him."

"But what if it is?"

"Think we should call it in?"

"Have you gone totally round the bend? What if you're wrong? You want to give Loupe another reason to bring us in for a little chat?"

Jocko did not need to answer that one. "What do we do, then?"

"I'm going over."

"Wait, the boss, he said we weren't supposed to show our faces."

"We've got to know, right? You heard the boss same as me. The second that bloke shows up, we're to phone it in. Not thirty seconds later. Not even two." Matt grabbed his jacket. "Wait here."

VAL, BERT, AND GERALD SHARED A TAXI INTO ST. HELIER, THE CAPITAL of both Jersey and the Channel Islands. The town was fairy-tale clean and laced with sea salt and safe mysteries. Not even the pelting rain could wash away the island's romantic feel. Early morning tourists clambered about the cobblestone lanes, so enchanted they accepted the windswept chill as part of the magic. The wealth on display was very discreet, like a lady's subtle hint of silk.

The taxi let them off by a church tea shop down the block from the Syntec Bank of Jersey. By the time they'd settled at a table with their tea and scones, a numbness had invaded Val's bones. He felt enveloped within an altered state somewhere between exhaustion and an electric high. Val was no longer angry. The day held no space for such mundane elements as personal feelings. The three of them shared a rapidly cooling pot of tea and waited for the clock to crawl once around the dial.

At nine sharp they watched through the tea shop's front window as two uniformed guards rolled back the curved steel gates sealing the bank's entrance. Silently, Val and the others left by the shop's side exit.

When they arrived at the bank, Bert took up station under the front awning. "You get yourself in there and save the day, lad. We'll camp out here and wait your word."

"You both know what to do?"

"We've been over it a dozen times, mate. More."

Gerald almost smiled. Not quite, but almost. "I don't suppose it would help to say the fate of the world rests in your arms."

"No. It wouldn't." Val entered the bank alone.

Syntec bank's public chamber was a long, narrow hall with brass-caged teller's windows down the right-hand wall. Brass footrails ringed the oval marble writing stand. Brass chandeliers hung from the high ceiling. The floor was marble, the front windows high and arched. The back of the room was given over to executive stalls with waist-level mahogany partitions. The woodwork gleamed. The entire chamber smelled of centuries of money and polish and the subtle terrors Val carried in with him.

Val took off the raincoat and shook it. His clothes were borrowed from Gerald. They consisted of a grey flannel suit, Oxford shirt, and a silk tie printed with the emblem from Gerald's college. He felt only marginally better dressed than when he wore the bellhop's uniform. Then again, it probably was not the clothes that constricted his gut and made it hard to draw a decent breath.

A guard approached. "Can I help you?"

"I'm here to see Mr. Francis Richards."

"Is *Sir* Francis expecting you?" The guard gave gentle emphasis to the title.

"I called earlier this morning and left a message on the bank's answering machine."

"Certainly, sir. May I have your name?"

"Jeffrey Adams."

"Very good, sir. If you'll just come this way." The sentry guided Val to the rear of the chamber, where a receptionist was already on her feet. "A Mr. Jeffrey Adams to see Sir Francis."

"Do you have an appointment, Mr. Adams?"

"My visit came up at the last moment. I called before you were open and asked for this meeting."

"Are you a client of Sir Francis?"

"In a manner of speaking. But we've never met."

"Might I trouble you for some form of ID?" When Val handed over his fake passport, she said, "If you'll just wait here a moment, I will see if Sir Francis is available."

When the receptionist cupped the phone to her ear and turned slightly away, Val asked the guard, "What is Sir Francis's position?"

"Senior account executive, sir."

The receptionist swiftly returned. "If you'll just come this way, sir."

Val was ushered upstairs and into an antechamber of rosewood paneling. Cigar smoke hung vaguely in the air, like a lingering fragrance of the previous day's millions. Val found the odor faintly nauseous and breathed through his mouth. His heart sounded loud as gunfire.

A slender man approached with outstretched hand. "Mr. Adams?"

"That's right."

"Francis Richards. What a delight. Received your message first thing this morning. Shame about the weather, don't you agree? Tragic spring we're having. Lashes of rain and cold and no end in sight. Won't you come this way?"

Richards wore a double-breasted navy jacket with gold-embossed buttons. A scarf matching his overloud tie dangled slightly from his breast pocket. An ornate family crest was woven into this same pocket. His hair was long and foppishly styled. His teeth were huge as he smiled Val into his office. "I believe you'll find that chair quite comfortable."

The office was rather cramped and narrow. But a royal crest matching the one on Richards's jacket hung from the wall behind his desk. Val took the seat before the desk as directed and looked carefully about. The room's only window overlooked the rainwashed street. A photograph of a grand estate hung from the right-hand wall. The manor looked enormous. But the photograph was in black and white, and the man standing upon the front steps was dressed in a bygone style.

Richards crossed behind his desk. "I checked our records after hearing your message, Mr. Adams. I failed to find any record of your being a client of our bank. Not that you're not welcome, of course. It's just we do rather like to keep tabs of whose money we're holding."

Val would normally have disliked the man and his upper-crust bray on sight. Today, however, he considered him ideal. No man, dressed like a titled duke and bearing his overarched accent, would be doing duty as a bank staffer unless he possessed more title than cash. He pointed to the photograph. "That's some spread."

"Ah. Yes. It is rather nice. Or was, I suppose I should say. Lost in the Depression, along with far too much else. I really should dispose of the wretched photo."

Val nodded slowly. He could well understand why Terrance had chosen to do business with this man.

Richards steepled his fingers. "Is there something I might do for you today, Mr. Adams? We are rather pressed for time, you see, and—"

"My name is not Adams."

Richards froze. "Pardon me?"

"It is Valentine Haines."

"Haines, Haines. Now that is a name I do recognize." He slid his chair over and tapped into his computer terminal. "Of course. Mr. Haines." Then a light dawned. "Did I not hear something of your recent demise?"

"All false, I'm afraid."

"And how frightfully glad I am to hear it. I don't suppose you happen to have any form of identification on you."

"No. But you have my photograph in your records." Stored in advance, to ensure personal security and access to their funds. "Along with my fingerprints."

"Indeed we do." Richards turned to his credenza and came up with an electronic pad. "If I might ask you to be so kind?"

Val pressed his hand onto the glass screen. And waited.

It did not take long. "Verified and confirmed." Richards was now all smooth professional. "What might we do for you today, Mr. Haines? Or should we remain with Adams?"

"I'm here to make a withdrawal."

"Certainly, sir. How much would you be after?"

"Two million, two hundred and eighteen thousand dollars."

The banker tabbed the keyboard. "But that's—"

"All of it," Val confirmed. "Plus any interest I've earned. And I want it in cash."

Matt did the innocent's walk across the street to the bank entrance. Ambling along, collar up against the wet, not looking at anything really. Just minding his own business and headed inside. Going up the stairs, he slowed enough to give both the blokes a careful look. Up close the muscle to his left didn't look any more familiar than from the window. Which didn't mean Jocko was wrong. The two men gave Matt an inspection of their own, using the cold eye of blokes who know their way around a tight corner.

For a moment Matt hesitated. He did the pocket-pat, like he belonged there at the bank if only he could find his papers. Thinking maybe he should go back for Jocko. But if they were there guarding the man Matt was after, leaving and coming back would only alert them. And what good would it do? Matt's orders were to call in soon as they spotted the bloke. Nothing more. Having a dust-up on a dank street in the middle of this poxy town was not on the list.

No, best just play the hand and act like he owned the place.

Which might've worked, only one of the heavies decided to follow Matt into the bank.

Inside, the bloke just stood there by the entrance. Hovering. Ready.

Matt gave the place a quick look-round. The bank was almost empty. Three customers up front, all women. One old geezer in the back, talking soft like he'd spent years learning how to handle coin. Definitely not their man. Which meant either their bloke was upstairs somewhere, or Jocko was wrong.

What to do?

Matt sighted the guard sauntering over. Taking it slow. Not wanting a fuss.

Matt turned and left. The muscle followed him out.

Matt scampered down the stairs and across the street and into the hotel and up the stairs and into the room.

Jocko was all over him in a flash. "What'd you see?"

Matt collapsed into the chair. "Go bring me a tea and two fried-egg sandwiches."

"Was it our guy?"

"He wasn't there, was he?"

"So he's upstairs somewhere?"

"If it was him."

"What do we do?"

"We wait." Matt snapped his fingers. "Large tea. Extra milk. Hot mustard and white toast, and the eggs better be fried up hard enough I can nail them to the wall."

"What if it's him?"

"We call it in. Say he's just arriving." Matt didn't take his eyes off the bank's only entrance. "Now hop to it. I need you back here and ready."

THE BANKER PUT UP A RATHER HIGHBROWED PROTEST AT VAL'S demand for over two million dollars in cash. But obviously Val was not the first person to come in seeking that sort of withdrawal. The papers were eventually filled out and passed over for Val's signature.

The conversation drifted over inconsequential matters as the money was gathered. Suddenly Val spied a face in a window across the narrow street. He leaned forward, searching his memory. But he couldn't be certain. Then he spotted a second man, a larger one whom Val had seen much closer and for far longer than the narrow-faced man. Suddenly he was back on the ferry.

Val stood and turned his chair around. When he reseated himself, he realized the banker was observing him with mild alarm.

"The light," Val said. "It bothers me."

The banker stared out his window. "But it's raining cats and dogs."

"Exactly," Val said.

The banker's secretary returned with a polished rosewood tray. On it resided a very substantial block of cash. Richards could not completely hide his avarice as he surveyed the money. "Perhaps you might like to count it," he suggested brightly. "Then you can be on your—"

"We're not done yet," Val said. He turned to the secretary and asked, "Would you mind leaving us alone?"

Richards gave her a befuddled nod. "Give us another moment, would you, Fiona?"

"Certainly, sir."

When the door closed again, Val reached into his jacket pocket and brought out several sheets of paper. He handed over the first page, which held the six strings of numbers they had found on Terrance's computer. "Have a look at these, please."

The banker's eyes rounded as he read the data. He swung his chair around and tapped into his computer. His eyebrows crawled up into his hairline.

It was the response Val had been seeking. The one they desperately needed for this to work. Val interpreted for him. "Your bank holds deposits totaling four hundred and eighteen million dollars. These accounts are in the names of Val Haines and Marjorie Copeland. As you have heard, Mrs. Copeland died in the explosion that destroyed your New York offices. This leaves me the sole holder of these funds."

Richards continued to study his screen. It was all the confirmation Val needed. "I am countermanding whatever standing orders you have controlling access to these accounts."

Richards read off the computer screen, "I require detailed codes to unlock them."

"They were destroyed in the explosion." Val handed over a second sheet. "I want all these funds transferred to this account."

Richards worked his mouth a few times before managing, "But this is . . ."

"That's right," Val agreed. "It is."

The banker looked from the page to Val and back again. "Without the codes, I fear—"

"But wait, there's more. In a couple of minutes, your phone is going to ring." Val offered the banker a third sheet. "This man will be calling you. He is going to ask if the funds are still in the account here in this bank. Tell him yes. He will then probably give you transfer instructions. He will have the codes. Tell him you'll do as he orders, but only once you have confirmation that this person is released. Confirmation must come from the father, Arthur d'Arcy. Who must come on the phone and speak with you."

Richards sputtered, "I couldn't possibly even consider—"

"Do these two things," Val said, "and all the money piled here on the desk is yours."

The banker went pale.

Val carefully repeated the instructions. "There will never be anything in writing about this conversation. No record whatsoever of this ever having happened." Val pushed the tray slightly closer. "One transfer. One phone call. And it's yours."

The instant Val slipped through the front entrance, Bert gripped his arm and spun him about. "Face the wall, that's a good lad."

Gerald explained, "Bert thinks we've got some unwanted attention from the hotel across the way."

"I spotted them from the banker's office," Val said.

Bert shielded him from the street with his bulk. The bank had a circular awning of colored stone, from which the rain dripped in a steady translucent curtain. Gerald asked, "What's the word?"

"He went for it."

The two men sighed in unison. Gerald announced quietly, "Dillon rang. His contact came through."

"We have to be certain."

"You can count on the lad." Bert looked from one face to the other. "Then we're good to go, are we?"

Val forced himself to say, "Let's make the call."

Bert took his phone from one pocket and a slip of paper from the other. He dialed the hotel's number, listened, and handed Val the phone. "Good luck, mate."

The phone spoke to him. "Good morning, Hastings Palace Hotel. How may I help you?"

"Suite eight-eighteen, please."

"One moment."

The phone rang twice before a male voice answered with, "We're still waiting on a fresh pot of coffee up here."

Val swallowed hard. "I'd like to speak with Terrance d'Arcy."

"Who's this?"

"Just tell him there's four hundred and eighteen million good reasons for him to get on the phone."

TERRANCE LAY IN THE SUITE'S SECOND BEDROOM AND WATCHED daylight stain the walls. It had stopped raining during the previous hour. A steady drip-drip pattered upon the windowsill beside his head. Every now and then one of the sentries glanced through the parlor's open door. Terrance lay in his clothes except his jacket, which was cast over the back of a nearby chair. His tie was down a notch. He rubbed his chin. He needed to shave. He could not recall the last time he had been so bedraggled. Or a time when it had mattered less than now. He stared up at the ceiling where the window drapes formed a guillotine's shadow.

One of the sentries stepped into the doorway. "The boss wants a word."

Terrance knew there was nothing to be gained by arguing. Besides which, he had no interest in lying there any longer. He donned his jacket, tightened his tie, slicked back his hair, going through the motions as though they mattered.

"Pour our guest a cup of coffee," Loupe ordered.

Terrance did not want any, but he accepted it and held it. Loupe slurped happily from his own cup. "We were discussing the safety measures you kept in your machine. What did you call them?"

"Firewalls. We've gone through this before."

"Indulge me. Firewalls. Yes. A fascinating concept. Are these firewalls secure?"

Old cigar smoke clogged the parlor. "Anything can be broken into, given enough time and expertise."

"So nothing has changed. We enter a new electronic age, and yet the old rules still apply." Loupe seemed to find a bizarre satisfaction in that pronouncement. "And there is no way for you to access your accounts except with your machine?"

"My laptop, my home computer, Don Winslow's computer. But only with them." The codes had to be entered in a precise fashion. All electronic banking was done in this manner, but Terrance had introduced new restrictions such that the bank's computer would only communicate with another computer that reconfirmed as it worked, an ingenious means of ensuring that no outsider could access their accounts. It required both the codes and a knowledge of which bank they accessed.

Which Val Haines possessed.

"Which means we must not grant our opponents sufficient time to move." Loupe toyed with his cup. "Remind me once again the sum we are discussing here."

"Four hundred and eighteen million."

"Dollars."

Terrance wanted to raise his fists and scream. "Dollars. Yes. Dollars."

Loupe finished his coffee and sighed contentedly. He asked the sentry, "Still nothing at the old man's house?"

"Not a peep, boss."

He asked Terrance, "You are certain there is no other number where we might . . ."

His words were cut off by a pinging from the hotel phone. The nearest muscle answered and said they were still waiting for the coffee. Then he held the phone out to Loupe.

The man on the other end did not bother to cover the phone as he spoke to someone else. "There's a bloke on the phone asking for d'Arcy. Sounds like a Yank. He knows about the money."

A longish pause, then a slightly accented voice asked, "Who am I addressing, please?"

"Val Haines."

"Mr. Haines. How wonderful. I have been so looking forward to having a little chat."

"Who is this?"

"Let's be frank, Mr. Haines. There's only one name that matters here, wouldn't you agree? And it's certainly not mine."

The two men supported Val with their steady gazes. "Audrey."

"It's so good to deal with someone who can move directly to the matter at hand, don't you agree?"

"I asked to speak with Terrance."

A faint steel edge crept into the voice. "You're dealing with me now."

Val fought hard to keep his quivering stomach muscles from affecting his voice. "Long as I get what I want."

"My thoughts exactly, Mr. Haines. You have something of ours, I believe."

"That's right."

"So how would you wish to play this out?"

"A straight swap. The hotel lobby."

"I would prefer somewhere a bit less public."

"I know you would. But this is how it's going to be. I want Terrance and Audrey in exchange for the computer."

"I do not care for your tone, Mr. Haines. Perhaps I should have one of my men help your dear young lady to sing for you."

"I'll be there in three hours. The two of them for the computer. Your call." Val punched off the phone. Clenched it to his chest with one hand and reached for the metal pillar supporting the veranda's roof. Pumped his lungs hard. "I'm going to be sick."

Gerald looked as nauseous as Val felt. But Bert replied, "No time for that, lad. You said it yourself. Timing's everything now. Straighten up, big easy breaths, that's the ticket."

"Time for the second call," Val said weakly, and handed Bert the phone.

"No, mate." Bert coded in another number and handed it back. "You're the captain of this ship."

The phone rang once, then Arthur d'Arcy said, "Yes?"

"We're on."

"Bless you, son." The old man sounded positively joyful. "A thousand times over. Bless you."

"You be careful."

"Don't worry about me." Arthur almost sang the words. "God is on our side."

Val cut the connection and handed back the phone. "You won't believe what he just told me."

Bert pointed over his shoulder at the hotel across the way. "I might've recognized one of the blokes. From inside."

The sick feeling started to press up into his chest again. Val damped it down as best he could. "Nothing we can do about that now."

"No, suppose not," Bert said, and followed Val back inside.

"Is it him?"

"For the tenth time, I can't say." Matt pounded the windowsill and hissed across the street, "Turn around!"

"I'll go over there and sort this out proper."

"Stay where you are."

"But—"

"The boss didn't say anything about getting ourselves made, did he?" Matt clawed the sill. "What're they doing standing around in this weather, that's what I'd like to know."

"We can't sit here doing nothing."

"Hang on. He's going back inside." Matt groaned. "And the muscle is going with him. Of all the ruddy luck."

"What do we do?"

Matt slumped back into the chair. "What we been doing since we started this life sentence. We wait."

WHEN THEY ARRIVED UPSTAIRS, THE BANKER'S SECRETARY WAS waiting to show Val back into the banker's office. Her eyes widened at the sight of Bert. Most likely she did not often see bruisers with arms larger than her waist come waltzing in, wanting to talk about two million dollars in cash. Val said simply, "He's with me."

"Of course, sir." She scurried to stay well ahead of them. "Right this way."

When they arrived back in Richards's office, the cash was still there on the desk. Richards's gaze rounded at their entry. But less so than the secretary's. He was too busy with his mental games, playing out what he could do with over two million dollars.

Val said, "This is my associate. I have to leave. He will remain here through the telephone conversation, then depart. He knows what you need to say."

Richards rocked back in his seat. "And if I don't?"

Bert warned, "A deal's a deal, mate."

Whatever Richards saw in Bert's face was enough to drain his own features of blood.

"No, none of that," Val said sharply. "You agreed. But if you decide to change your mind, we'll just take the cash and leave."

"A little late for that." Bert punched the air between them, causing the banker to flinch. "We've already set things in motion because of him."

"Bert." Val waited until the big man stopped glaring at the banker and turned around to say, "Audrey wouldn't go for that."

Bert's shoulders slumped. "What a thing to be telling me now."

Richards cleared his throat. "Audrey?"

Val kept his eyes on Bert. "We do this right, or we don't do it at all."

"The right thing for the wrong reason is just adding to the problem," Bert mumbled to his feet.

"Is that from Audrey?"

"Sure didn't come from me, mate." Bert nodded once. "Okay, then."

"You're sure?"

"Yeah, I'm right as rain."

Val turned to the banker, who was watching with wide-eyed confusion. "It would help us to know now what you're going to do. A woman's life may hang in the balance."

Bert covered his eyes.

Richards's gaze went from one man to the other. "Something's happened?"

"The man who is about to call you is holding her against her will. We don't think he will hold to his side of the bargain and let her go. You're part of our insurance policy."

"I-I'm not quite sure I understand."

"You don't need to," Val replied, and waited.

Richards touched the knot of his tie, rubbed his jaw, patted his foppish hair. "Well, naturally, if we're intending to help a damsel in distress, who am I to refuse?"

"Then you'll do it?"

"Certainly. For a good cause, and all that."

"And two million two in cash, free and clear."

"Well, yes." His gaze swiveled back to the money. "There most certainly is that."

Val pulled the final sheet of paper from his pocket, inspected it carefully, and said, "There's just one small thing more."

Richards blanched. "I beg your pardon?"

"Nothing complicated. Just a straight transfer, for which I do have clearance." Val handed over the page. "Can you handle that while you're waiting for the call?"

Richards had difficulty bringing his computer records into focus. "Oh. Yes. Of course. I see no problem here."

"Great." Val rose from his chair. "Is there a back door? If I can, I'd like to slip out unobserved."

"There's the employees' entrance at the rear." Richards saw nothing beyond the cash on his desk. "I'll have my assistant show you the way."

"Ask her to bring my associate in from your front porch before she does. His name is Gerald." Val patted Bert on the shoulder. "We'll call as soon as we've got something to report."

Bert did not look up. "You just make ruddy sure things go to plan, mate."

"I'll try."

"And when you see her, tell the lass Bert says hello."

Matt leapt from the chair. "I don't believe this!"

"What is it now?"

"They've all disappeared!"

Jocko pressed in beside him. "They can't have."

"They did, I'm telling you. One comes out, two go in, now a lady shows up and the third does like smoke."

"You think they made us?"

"How am I supposed to know that?"

Jocko leaned out the window and was drenched by the rain. "It's like they never were there."

"The boss hears about this and we're good as dead." Matt pounded the windowsill. "What do we do now?"

Jocko ducked inside and wiped his face. "You want me to go have a look?"

Matt let his hand drop to his side. "What good would that do?"

"You're asking me?"

"Wait, let me think." Matt's face glistened with the same fear churning through Jocko's gut. "Okay. Here's the deal. You go have a quiet look around the outside. I'll keep watch. First sign it's really our man, we call like we just spotted him, right?"

Jocko swiped his own face clear of the fear-sweat. "But what if they don't show, Matt? What if we sit here all ruddy day and the bank closes and we still don't get another look? The guy's scarpered, we've let him go, what then?"

Matt's features were green. "Then *we* scarper."

"What?"

"Morocco. Or the Philippines, maybe. Someplace far away."

"Leave England?"

"We've already left England, you dolt."

"This is different."

"Too right it is. This time we're never coming back."

GERALD PHONED THE AIRFIELD FROM THE TAXI AND PROMISED A huge tip if the plane was fueled and ready to go. When they arrived, the mechanic was there to unhook the wings.

The mechanic slipped Gerald's cash into his coveralls and asked, "Where are you headed in such a rush?"

"England."

"In this?" Rain dripped off the hood of his jacket, causing him to squint. "Better you than me, mate."

Gerald powered up the engines before Val had his seatbelt fastened. The wind mocked them with its force, rocking the plane before they were even moving. Now that he was once more behind the controls, Gerald's features adopted the same grim cast as before.

He taxied them out to the runway, rogered his take-off to the tower, then glanced at Val. "You ready?"

"Just remember," Val replied. "If we crash and burn, this whole thing goes to pot."

The roller coaster started as soon as their wheels left the ground. The plane yawed furiously, swept up by a sudden gust, tilted sharply, and the engine howled in protest. Val took white-knuckle grips on the edge of his seat and the roof. The cliffs swept by beneath them, to be replaced by raging whitecaps stretching out to where everything became lost in the rain and wind.

An hour and a bit into the flight, however, everything changed. One moment they were flying through grey skyborne froth, surrounded by a dismal noonday twilight. The next, they entered a vastly different realm.

The storm peeled away as though ripped from the earth. The wind calmed.

They entered a placid universe, so different Val doubted his own senses. Even the motor was comforted into a softer purr.

Val looked at Gerald. "What is this, the Twilight Zone?"

Gerald released his death's grip on the stick. "Just your basic schizophrenic English spring."

The sky stretched blue-black ahead of them, washed sparkling clear. Below and to Val's right, two freighters carved white streamers from a jewellike English Channel. Up ahead he could just glimpse the white coastal teeth and the emerald fields beyond.

Gerald asked, "Do you think we might take this as a sign?"

Val refused to answer.

The phone chimed just as Gerald began his initial approach to the Brighton airfield. "Get that, will you? Right jacket pocket."

Val pulled it out. "Haines."

It was Dillon. "Can you believe this ruddy weather?"

"I understand why you talk about it all the time. It never ceases to amaze."

"Where's Gerald?"

"Landing us."

"I'm sitting at the entrance to Alders Way. Ask him does he know where that is."

Gerald replied, "Tell him yes."

"You lads get over here right sharp. I found the house they're using."

"You're sure?"

"Pretty much."

"We can't be wrong on this."

"Just don't hang about. We'll see what we see when you get here."

Fifty-five minutes later, Val and Gerald pulled into the entrance of a cul-de-sac jammed hard against the base of a steep hill. The mound grew out of nowhere, punching up into the impossibly blue sky like a grass-covered block. A pair of trails crawled up the side, probably where kids climbed and played over the flat top. The houses ringing the base were nondescript clones, ten in all. White stone bases rose to red mock-Victorian fronts, three linked together, then a tight space, then three more. Only the middle house stood alone. Opposite the cul-de-sac's entrance, the sea sparkled between rooftops and Hastings's narrow lanes. A few sailboats were already leaving port and putting tentatively to sea. The morning's storm was merely a fading memory.

Dillon rose from Audrey's grey Rover at their approach. He had his phone plastered to his ear. He wore an open-neck shirt and jeans wrinkled below the knees by the rain. He waved them around the corner. Gerald halted his van behind a house, blocking them from view. Dillon walked over and nodded a tight welcome. "Everything go right in Jersey?"

"Far as we know. Where's Audrey?"

"Hang on a sec." He tapped one hand nervously on the van's roof. "The house is in the middle, the only one standing all by itself. Inside that little wall there, see it? Number eight. Three toughs came tearing out of there and jammed into a car. Black beemer."

"When was that?"

"An hour back."

Which meant they were gathering forces before Arthur's arrival at the hotel.

"I ducked down as they came roaring past, but not before I got a good look," Dillon went on. "Audrey wasn't with them. So I phoned for some backup. Here she comes now."

The woman could have been forty or sixty. She turned the corner and approached the van with a balanced limp, as though both feet hurt her equally. She wore a buttoned cardigan and a flowered dress and reading glasses draped around her neck. She carried a rolled umbrella in one hand and a metal clipboard in the other. She bussed Dillon on the cheek. "All right, love?"

"Yeah, not bad." Dillon slid open the van's rear door. "Lads, this is Doris. Doris, these are the mates I told you about."

"Help me in, that's a dear." Her features held the dignified sternness of someone who bore much in silence. Her hair was a chemically induced shade of copper. When Dillon slipped in beside her and shut the door, she asked, "Staying out of trouble, love?"

"Up to this morning." Dillon explained to the others, "Doris is mum to a young lady I'm seeing."

"Only so long as you keep your nose clean."

"I'm trying, aren't I?"

"Trying isn't good enough."

"Yeah, so you keep going on about." Dillon said to the men up front, "Doris runs the largest holiday rental agency in Hastings. Yesterday one of her cleaners was telling her about a cottage where all the men wear suits. And we're not talking about your basic business geeks, are we, Doris?"

"I manage eighty-three cottages. The things you see don't bear thinking about." She shook her head in disgust. "Do I want to know what's happening here?"

"Probably not, love. No."

Val turned fully around in his seat. "Dillon is not going to get involved in anything, ma'am."

Doris inspected him carefully. "You're going to see to that, are you?"

"Yes ma'am. I am."

She studied him a bit longer, then nodded her head. Satisfied. "I've had a word with Susie, like you asked."

"Susie being the cleaning lady," Dillon explained. To Doris, "You trust her, do you?"

"She's a good lass in her own simple way. We're not after rocket scientists here. We're after honest, hardworking folk who won't pocket what's not theirs."

"She saw something, your Susie."

"Four men, just like you said. All in dark suits. Expensive cut. Drive ever so nice a motor. Foreign, she thought. Dark like the suits."

"Not your normal sort of tourists."

"What's normal in this day and age, I ask you? So when you phoned back I decided to go have a look for myself. Delivering fresh towels, carrying my clipboard, just going about for a normal inspection. The bloke in there tried to give me some lip."

"Just one man?" Val asked.

"That's all I saw."

"You gave him some lip right back, didn't you, love?" Dillon said.

"They rent from us, we've got certain rights and obligations, I tell him. It's our way of keeping up with the houses in our care. So he lets me in, but he doesn't half keep an eye out. Stalking me, he was. And he wouldn't let me near the back bedroom. Claimed there's a mate of his in there, not feeling well. I can't complain about that, long as he lets me into the lounge and the kitchen and the loo. Which he does."

Val asked, "Tell me what you thought of the guy."

"Big hulking brute," she said crossly. "A thug in a suit is still just a thug. Made my skin crawl, just being inside with the likes of him."

"Thanks, Doris." Dillon slid open the door. "You've been ever so helpful."

"We run a proper service here for proper people." She started for the door, then paused. "Straight up, now. You're not back on the game, are you, son?"

"Not me, love. No. Not ever."

"That's right, he's not," Val confirmed. "We're just trying to help a friend."

"I'll be off, then." She stepped from the van. "You lads play nice."

WERE IT NOT FOR THE PIPED-IN MUSIC, THE ELEVATOR MIGHT AS well have been a coffin fitted for six. They rode downstairs in silence. Terrance was hemmed in on all sides. Loupe had hardly spoken to him since getting off the phone with Val. Something about the conversation had unsettled the man. It was not a pleasant sight, the boss being unnerved. All his men were brought to the edge of barely contained violence, just waiting for Loupe to tell them which way to explode.

They entered the hotel lobby in a phalanx of muscle and gabardine and crossed to the opposite end from the front desk. Men were stationed at either side of the empty corner, their expressions telling anyone who approached that this entire area was off-limits. Terrance spotted more of Loupe's men around the lobby and still others outside on the street. The old man sighed his way into the sofa, and pointed Terrance into a chair by his left.

Dust motes danced in the air. A stringed quartet played Debussy over the ceiling speakers. Elegant people passed wearing springtime pastels. The lobby held an atmosphere of moneyed calm. To Terrance's left, sunlight splashed upon high rain-speckled windows.

The sight of his father limping into the hotel struck Terrance with such pain he actually gripped his chest.

Loupe observed Terrance carefully. "Who is that?"

"My father." Terrance carted his stricken gaze back and forth between the two men as his father approached. "What is he doing here?"

But Loupe had dismissed Terrance now. The boss rose to his feet and demanded, "Where is Haines?"

Arthur d'Arcy glanced once at Josef Loupe, then returned his gaze to Terrance. "How are you, son?"

"Your boy is fine," Loupe said. Their highly public surroundings kept his snarl very soft. "For the moment."

Arthur's gaze remained gentle upon his boy. "You look tired."

Terrance was kept mute by the rising dread of this day. Just when he'd been certain it could grow no worse, another blow arrived. A constant rain of hellish force. His father, of all people, here to witness his failure.

Loupe was not accustomed to being ignored. He snapped, "I was addressing you, sir."

Arthur d'Arcy displayed a remarkable strength of will for so frail a figure. "You do not control this moment. You only think you do."

"Where is Haines?"

"Where is my daughter?"

"So." Loupe drew out the word until it stretched his features with a tight smile. "It appears we must deal with the emissary at hand. Sir, I believe you have something I want."

"I asked you a question."

Loupe gave a dignified smile and resumed his seat. "I do so hope we shall be able to avoid any unpleasantness."

"Where is my daughter?"

"She is safe." Loupe snapped his fingers. Instantly an aide brought out his phone, keyed the pad, and handed it over. Loupe said, "Put her on."

Very real pain coursed through Arthur's features as he took the phone and murmured, "Hello, darling. Are you all right?"

A boulder was lodged where Terrance's heart should have resided. Every word his father spoke caused the stone to tremble. The motions bruised his chest. He reached up and massaged the spot over his ribs. The agony was fearsome.

"Enough." Loupe gestured with one finger. Instantly the aide reached forward and slipped the phone from Arthur's hand.

Arthur said, "You promised Val my daughter would be here."

"It appears we have both been somewhat inconvenienced."

"You don't want Val. He means nothing to you."

"True." Loupe extracted a cigar from a leather case, then pulled a tiny gold guillotine from his inner pocket. As he trimmed the cigar's tip, he went on. "Your daughter will rejoin you soon enough."

Arthur glanced around the room, taking in the men stationed like soldiers in Cerutti uniforms. "I must call Val."

"By all means." Loupe lit his cigar and nodded to the aide. "Allow me to explain to him how things stand."

THEY SAT IN THE VAN AND WAITED. THERE WAS NOTHING MORE TO be said. Every now and then one of them walked to the end of the block and back, just checking on the cul-de-sac and the middle house. In and out of sight in a matter of seconds. Everything was placid, calm, just another lovely day by the seaside.

The call came right on time. Arthur sounded faintly breathless, but steady. "It's me."

"And?"

"Audrey isn't here. He says he won't release her until the money is in his hands."

"Put him on."

The afternoon's glory was tainted by the voice on the other end. "I was so very sorry not to have the pleasure of meeting you, Mr. Haines. You're not living up to your part of the bargain."

"That's something, coming from you. Maybe I should tell Arthur to walk away."

"Very dangerous, that. People who get in my way tend to regret it as long as they live. Which is not as long as they might like. Do I make myself clear?"

"Yes."

"So I advise you to instruct d'Arcy senior here to hand over what is mine." There was a protest from the other end, to which the man said, "Do be quiet, that's a good lad."

"Was that Terrance?"

"What d'Arcy junior wants or does not want at this point is immaterial."

"Call the Jersey bank. The man in charge is a Mr. Richards." Val's words were punctured by his thundering heart. Short verbal bursts proved easier to hold steady. "Terrance will access the codes for you. Richards will only release the funds when Arthur confirms that he, Terrance, and Audrey are safe."

"I can well understand your desire for personal vengeance on young d'Arcy here." The words were softly spoken. Merely a quick breath of smoke. But the dragon's flames licked the side of Val's face. "But do you think you are any more capable of wreaking havoc than I?"

Val pressed a fist tight against his gut. "That's the deal."

"I fear you do not hold all the cards, Mr. Haines. Do I need to send you a taped message from the young lady to prove my point?"

The cramp wracked his gut so tight that Val doubled over, drenching his knees with the sweat from his face. "No."

"Now here is how things are going to play out. You will tell d'Arcy senior to hand over the computer which you stole. I will walk through the transfer process with d'Arcy junior. The two gentlemen will depart. When I am satisfied that everything has gone smoothly, and no pesky authority figures come around asking difficult questions, I shall release your young lady." He might have been smoking a cigar. Or perhaps it was merely that the flames had finally escaped and were eating away at the phone. "Do we have a bargain?"

"Put Arthur on the line."

"A wise choice."

There was a moment's pause, then, "Yes?"

Val swallowed hard against the gorge. "You heard?"

"I did."

"We have no choice."

"No."

"Good luck."

"Ah. That is not required."

Val shut off the phone. The effort of dragging in another breath left him unable to lift his head. He felt a heavy hand pat his back. He heard Dillon ask, "All right there, mate?"

"No."

"Ease up, now. That's it. Can't go to pieces on us now."

Gerald asked, the dismay and nausea there in his voice, "What did he say?"

Val let his hands guide him upright. There was a dark stain of dread on his knees where his face had rested. "They're not going to let her go."

Dillon's voice carried the pained ease of one used to life's impossibles. "We knew that going in, mate."

But now was different. Now it was no longer a plan spoken in the safety of a night-draped kitchen. Val heard anew the anguish in the old man's voice and swallowed hard. The two men waited him out.

Finally he managed to unclench his grip and hand Gerald the phone. "It's time."

LOUPE REFUSED TO EVEN GLANCE TERRANCE'S WAY AS ARTHUR rose from his seat. Terrance watched his father cross the lobby in that odd tilted gait of his. Loupe sat and smoked his cigar, examining the glowing tip between puffs, until Arthur limped back inside the hotel. Terrance's computer was at his side. He reseated himself and placed the laptop in Terrance's hands.

When Terrance did not move, Arthur said gently, "Son, this man intends to kill you."

"Nonsense." Loupe spoke the words to his cigar tip. "What an absurd concept. Young d'Arcy is a valued ally."

Arthur ignored him entirely. "His kind does not share. You know this far better than I."

"My kind." Loupe seemed mildly amused by the exchange. "My kind."

Arthur reached over and opened the laptop. "Give the man what he wants."

Terrance watched his own hands betray him. They turned on the laptop, coded in the ID, made the wireless online connection, and entered the secret Web site. He swiveled the computer around, pointed to a line of numbers across the top of the screen, and fell back into his seat. "That's it? That's the lot?" Loupe snapped his fingers. The driver handed him a cell phone. Loupe asked directory assistance for the Syntec Bank's main number in Jersey. Terrance listened as Loupe asked for Mr. Richards. But all

Terrance truly heard was the shards of ambition and of his plans falling about his feet.

Loupe read off the numbers, then demanded, "What is the total in those accounts?"

Terrance watched as the boss flushed at what he heard on the phone. Dust. All was dust and ashes.

Beads of sweat appeared on Loupe's forehead. "I want you to transfer the entire amount to my account in Luxembourg." He gave the bank details from memory.

The banker replied with something that caused Loupe's eyes to shift from father to son and back again.

Loupe said, "I was given to understand that these computer codes granted me full access without any such conditions." He waited a fraction. "I see. Very well. You will please remain on the line."

The hand holding the phone out to Arthur trembled slightly.

Arthur replied, "Not until my son and I are seated in a taxi."

Loupe was already rising to his feet. "Mark my words. Any hint of mischief and your daughter—"

Arthur raised his voice for the first time. "Threaten me or my family in any way, and I will call for the authorities."

"Just so long as we understand one another."

In response, Arthur pushed himself from the sofa, then motioned for Terrance to rise. When he did not move fast enough, Terrance felt himself lifted by one of Loupe's men. Arthur gripped his son's arm and turned him toward the door. "Not long now."

Loupe said into the phone, "Are you still there? Excellent. We will only be a moment longer."

As they exited the hotel and entered the blinding sunlight, Arthur said, "Do you know, this is the first time in six months I am not in pain."

Had he been able to speak, Terrance would have replied that he felt sufficient agony for them both.

VAL FORCED HIMSELF TO STEADY UP. "GO AHEAD."

Gerald darted nervous glances first at Val and then Dillon. The younger man agreed, "Do it."

Gerald asked, "What was this neighbor's name again?"

"Smathers. Lives at number nine Alders Way. For the twentieth time."

Gerald puffed like he was finishing a marathon, and gave it a high-pitched breathless note. "Yes, good morning. It's Smathers here, down Alders Way. I've been hearing the most horrid noise from next door. Yes, Smathers. What kind of noise? Oh, a horrible racket. Just the worst possible sort of din. Like a woman screeching. Yes, that's right. Like she was being hurt something fierce. Oh, oh, there it goes again. Can you hear it?"

Gerald listened a moment. "Number nine, Alders Way. Down at the bottom. What is the number . . . Oh, you mean next door. That would be number eight, wouldn't it? There's some strange lot renting over there, I saw them move in yesterday. Six or seven men, great hulking brutes and all wearing dark suits. What sort of holiday rental is that, I ask you? Carrying on at all hours of the day and night."

Dillon stuck a fist to his mouth and turned to look out the side window.

Gerald went on, "I've been after those agents before, you know. Here we sit, down here for a bit of peace and quiet. Oh, there they go again. That poor woman, I know they must be up to something beastly in there. It's the agency, you mark my words. They'll rent to anybody with ten quid in their pocket, never mind us who have to live with this horror. We're left waiting for blood to run down the front steps. Yes. All right. Good-bye."

Dillon took a moment to turn back around. "That was inspired, that was."

"Long as we're in time." Gerald looked at Val. "Perhaps I should stay."

"Can't neither of us pilot the plane, mate," Dillon replied.

"Go collect Arthur and Terrance." Val opened his door. "Take them to the plane. Be ready to move the instant we arrive."

"If I'd been planning a job, one look at this place would've earned it an instant pass," Dillon told him. "One way in, one out. A recipe for disaster, that is. And ruddy little to show for the effort besides. Basic two-up, two-down fifties council house, not worth a second glance save for the location. That's what people who don't know better pay for. Take a nothing sort of place like this, give it a garden the size of a throw-rug, set it in tight like sardines on toast, throw in a bit of the sea, and people think they're somewhere exotic."

They were seated in the Rover. Val was behind the wheel. The old car smelled of dust and oil and age, with a vague sense of Audrey's perfume thrown in for good measure. Dillon had grown talkative with the wait. Val did not mind the noise. The quiet was unnerving. Nothing moved on the cul-de-sac.

"Before you two showed up this morning, I was busy recollecting my first talk with Audrey. Not my first meeting, mind. That came four months before the other and doesn't bear thinking about. When I got out I tried a couple of times to apologize for the things I said back then. But Audrey always claimed not to remember. It being Audrey and all, I almost believed her."

Val nodded slowly. "I know just what you mean."

At the sound of a car, Dillon turned and then slid below the dash. "Crouch down, mate. It's the old bill."

"The police?"

"What I just said." Dillon eased himself up a fraction as the police car passed them. "Quite a difference from the early days, me being glad to see the likes of them show up. Back then, one glance of the men in blue was good for heart failure."

Val glanced up, but lowered himself at a hiss from Dillon. Dillon kept popping up for the occasional glimmer. "Leave the looking to an expert at not being seen, why don't you."

"Tell me what's happening."

"Two blue bottles are approaching the house. A third is hanging well back, hand on his radio. It's taking a while for somebody to answer their ring. Hang on, here he comes. Hello, what's this?"

Val risked a look. The man who answered the door looked straight out of a tourist brochure. Pleated shorts and polo shirt and a watch that glittered down the length of the lane. No socks. Deck shoes. Legs springtime pale but well muscled.

"Took time to lose the suit, didn't he? Smart move, that. Look at the smile he gives the johnnies, will you. A real charmer. Chatting up the coppers like he's paid for the duty. Which he is, in a manner of speaking."

Val watched his hopes fade. The cops wanted to go inside, but the guy wasn't having any of it. Why should he, since they had no warrant and him standing there with a valid rental contract. "This is bad."

"He's got the coppers off-balance, no question." Dillon chewed his lip. "They're turning this way; get down."

Val slid back below the level of the console. Dillon waited a moment, then risked another look. "That tears it."

"What's happening?"

"The copper who was hanging back, he's headed round to the house next door. Going to question this Smathers bloke who called it in."

"Who won't be there."

"Too right. We got us a sweet old dear in fuzzy slippers answering the door. Waving a hello to her neighbor." Dillon slapped the dashboard. "The coppers are apologizing to the bloke and calling in their report. Bang and done and on their way. What do we do now?"

"Get out of the car. Stay low." Val fiddled with the gearshift and controls, trying to orient himself to everything being on the wrong side. "If something goes down, I'm going to use a false ID that claims my name is Jeffrey Adams."

Dillon must have seen something in Val's expression. "Not on your life. I've never run out on a mate, and I'm not starting now."

"You're not running. You're being sent." When Dillon looked ready to argue, Val added, "You just heard me promise Doris."

Reluctantly Dillon opened his door. "What are you going to do?"

"Whatever it takes." Val started the car. "You just hang back and be ready."

Val rammed the car into first as the cops slipped back into their car. The Rover's gears meshed improperly, as though the old car was well aware of the fate in store.

Dillon stepped away. He might have said something more, but the roaring engine cut him off. Val had a little trouble on takeoff, as he'd never driven a car with steering on the right. Pity his first lesson would be so brief.

"In for a penny," Val said. It was another of Audrey's sayings. He recalled how she had carried a photo of Arthur standing beside this old car in her billfold. Two hundred and seventy-seven thousand miles on the clock, and it still managed a full-throated roar as Val jammed the accelerator right down on the floor.

Arthur had bought the car soon after the sky had fallen. Disinherited, divorced, and a son who refused to even speak his name. Arthur could not afford anything else at the time. After a while he wanted nothing more. A contented man, was how Audrey had described him, touching the photograph where the old man stood beside the car. Audrey claimed to have kept the car as a symbol of all the good that could come from bad. If only one learned the secret formula to a happy life. Another of her wise little sayings.

Val smiled as he took aim down the empty road. Memories were such a grand thing.

The old car was a bit sluggish on takeoff. But by midway down the lane it had built up a full head of steam. Val slid into second, liking the way the motor bellowed up through the revs.

The cops caught sight of him about then. Which Val decided was not all bad. After all, if he was about to do an Evel Knievel of his own, it would be nice to have an appreciative audience.

His last thought before striking the curb was that it'd be just his luck to discover Audrey had been shipped off to Yalta.

The curb had a bit of lip to it, enough to lift the car like a launcher and send him straight for the bowed front windows. Val thought he might have glimpsed an astonished face staring out at him. But it might have been just wishful thinking.

Val took out all three windows and a fair-sized portion of restraining wall before coming to rest in a hail of plaster, brick, and shattered glass. The curtains lay over the fractured front windshield like a shroud to all the miseries of his now-distant past.

The floating dust had the cops coughing so hard they couldn't place him under arrest as they dragged him from the wreckage. Val, too, found it hard to form the words, and at first nobody paid any attention to what he had to say. But as they dragged him back into the brilliant sunlit afternoon, he managed to form a very hoarse shout, "My fiancée's chained up in there!"

This, following Gerald's phone call, got the police's attention. "Say again?"

"They kidnapped my fiancée! She's being held in the back room!"

"Get him out of here." The senior cop pointed at the policeman not holding Val. "You. Come with me."

The thug in the pleated shorts decided not to hang about. He burst out the back door, leapt the side fence, and started for the hill.

"We've got a runner!"

"You there! Police! Halt!"

Val's view of the proceedings was cut off by the third cop hustling him back to the car. He was planted on the side, legs spread, hands in plain view. All the neighbors were outside by now, gaping at the proceedings. Dillon arrived then, his head turned to the sunlight and smiling broadly. Val grinned in reply. It felt as though his face was trying to recall something from the very distant past.

"Something funny, sir?"

"Just glad you're here, officer."

"We'll see about that."

Then there was a shout from the house, echoed on the policeman's radio. The cop thumbed his radio and barked, "Say again?"

Val caught enough of the repeated words to know they had found someone. He set his forehead down on the roof and shut his eyes tight. Just giving thanks. Just getting ready. Because here she came, clearly the worse for wear but walking out on her own two legs. Dillon and the officer helped her clamber through the opening, like Val had carved the way just for her. Which, in a sense, he had.

"Oh, Val." She rushed up to him and gave him a fierce embrace. "What on earth have you done?"

"Remain as you are, sir."

Val kept his hands in plain view as she hugged him. "Are you all right?"

"I am now."

"Madam, I must ask you to step away."

"Adams," Val told her softly as the policeman pried her arms from his neck. "The ID in my pocket says I am Jeffrey Adams."

"Please, madam, you are only making matters worse."

Val could not stop grinning. Not even as the policeman wheeled him about and ringed his wrists with cold steel.

"Stop that! What on earth do you think you're doing?"

"We have to follow procedure, madam."

"But this man just saved my life!" When the policeman continued undeterred, she demanded, "Where are you taking him?"

"Eastbourne, ma'am. He'll be booked and processed there."

As Val was guided into the police car's backseat, he heard other sirens whooping in the background. Val told her, "Dillon's going to stay with you—"

The door was slammed in his face. Audrey shouted her protest and tried to reopen the door. But the policeman remained adamant and gently but firmly moved her away.

Val smiled out at Audrey. As the car pulled away, he cast a final glance at his handiwork.

Shame about the car.

AS FAR AS ELLEN LAINEY WAS CONCERNED, THESE DAYS INSIGNIA'S head office held all the warmth and congeniality of an open coffin.

The only reason she stuck around at all was, she had inherited Val Haines's position. The suits upstairs called it a promotion. But Ellen had made it this far by staring facts and figures straight in the eye and calling them as they stood. Her predecessor had been toasted in a bomb blast that had the investigators crawling around the office like roaches in Gucci. The office to her left was home now to a half-dozen pinheads with badges and bad attitudes. The future looked decidedly grim.

Rumors continued to fly. New ones popped up every morning. This morning the coffee cluster had it on best authority that Don Winslow was missing. Which meant nothing, really. At seven the previous evening she had heard the same group talking about alien abduction.

A young accountant knocked on Ellen's open door. The guy had been on the job for six weeks. Ellen knew what he thought of her. A hard-timer, just punching her ticket and working the corporate treadmill, hiking her way toward an Ocala retirement community with a pink poodle for company. He assumed her flat-panned expression was the product of a thousand fifty-five-hour weeks. What he did not know, what Ellen was keeping all to herself, was how the SEC goons had locked up the pension funds tight as a Wall Street safe. All her fund-related systems were shut down. She could not access anything.

Her questions had been answered with blowtorch glares and silence. Ellen was not asleep at the wheel. She knew something was seriously wrong. She also knew her job description included an unwritten order not to fuel the rumor fire. She could play the poker-faced lady and keep what she suspected locked up tight. For the moment.

The new accountant was named Jerry. He was both very smart and very shy. He also had a tendency to stutter slightly when he was nervous. Which he almost always was when he was in the presence of his boss. Any conversation with him could stretch over eons.

Ellen greeted him with, "I do *not* have time for you today."

Normally this would have been enough to send Jerry scurrying for his cubicle. But not this morning.

He stepped further inside her office. "We have to talk."

Ellen started to scream at him. She had not slept at all the previous three nights. When she lay down, she tended to watch the corporate figures dance across her darkened ceiling. What they added up to made for a waking nightmare she could not banish with thoughts of her new title.

But were Ellen to vent the worry-steam in Jerry's direction, the guy would probably do an implosion right there in her doorway. Which would mean getting buried by more paperwork. Ellen sighed, went back to her file shuffling, and said, "So talk already."

"I've been doing my weekly check of all the office petty cash accounts, like you ordered."

Unbelievable. Here she was, imagining a corporate meltdown the papers would call Florida's very own Enron, and the guy wants to point the finger at somebody overspending on stamps. Ellen did a solid drumbeat on her desk with the stack of folders. "Jerry, this can definitely wait."

Jerry slipped fully inside her office. And shut the door.

This was enough to halt her next outburst.

Jerry flitted up close to her desk. "I've found it."

"Found *what?*"

"The money. All of it."

Something inside the guy's expression had her heart pounding. Which of course made no sense at all. "*What* money?"

"At least, I think it's all. I never saw any figures. Did you?"

Ellen worked at making words. But nothing actually fit the moment. So she shut her face and waited.

"All I'm going on are the rumors." He cleared his throat. "But I think it's all there. It's got to be. As much as it is, it's the only thing I can figure out."

She was not aware that she had risen to her feet. "Just how much are we talking about here?"

Jerry revealed a true accountant's heart in how he reverentially said the numbers. "Four hundred and eighteen million dollars."

"You're telling me you found four hundred million dollars *in our petty cash account?*"

"I called the bank. They confirmed that the transfer came in last night." His eyes had gone round from the revelation. "It's just sitting there. Waiting for us."

THE ISLAND OFFERED THEM A GLORIOUS WELCOME THE DAY THEY laid Arthur d'Arcy to rest. Val stood by the entrance to the stone church on the outskirts of St. Helier and hoped his remaining strength did not let him down. He was drawn as finely as he had ever been, stretched by days and nights of planning and work and worry. Audrey had done little since their arrival save sit the death watch with her father. Bert and Dillon and Gerald had done what they could. But most of the critical issues not related to Arthur's passage had rested on Val's shoulders alone.

A comforting breeze drifted down the little lane, flavored by wildflowers and the sea. The village was lost beyond two sharp bends and a hillside blanketed in spring finery. Overhead the sun played games with scuttling clouds. Undulating meadows shivered and sheened with the paintings of light and shadow. In the distance the waves wrote their own frothy script of farewell.

Val heard voices before the crowd rounded the corner and came into view. Bert and Dillon had volunteered to go down and meet those arriving with the afternoon ferry. Val pushed off the ancient stone and went to greet them. There were perhaps four dozen mourners, a motley assortment of polished gentry and rough trade, united now in grey cloth and grief.

Dillon pulled him to one side and said, "Gerald says you're needed back at the cottage."

"Terrance?"

"The bloke's just sitting and staring at all the yesterdays he's wasted. Needs a swift kick, if you ask me."

"Not today."

"No, suppose not. How is it you're the only one who knows how to wind his motor?"

Val started down the lane without replying.

A copse of trees separated the hamlet from the parish church. Val arrived at the cottage's front walk just as Gerald came out with Audrey, and resented the sight of another man standing where he wished to be.

Audrey made even grief look alluring. "Terrance says he won't come."

"He'll be there."

"He wouldn't even look at me. I begged and he wouldn't even meet my gaze."

"Leave your brother to me. You've got enough to worry about already today."

"He's right, you know," Gerald said. A truce had settled between Val and Gerald. Whatever else, they had been through enough to know the other's measure. Their unspoken agreement was loud and clear. Audrey would have to decide between them. "If Terrance will mind anybody, it's the lad here."

Audrey's hair caught the sunlight in a brilliant weave. "Perhaps I should just let him be."

Val started for the door. "We'll meet you at the church."

The stone cottage was so old the lichen decorating the slate roof grew in layers. They had rented the place because it was within walking distance of the St. Helier hospice. The three downstairs rooms were more charm than comfort. The four upstairs bedrooms were closets with windows. Val found Terrance just as Dillon had said, seated on his bed and staring at an empty side wall. Val had accepted Audrey's request to try and reform her brother, rather than send him to jail. Val had even suggested the method. And he did his best to do away with his burden of hate. Even when Terrance had confessed to doctoring the lab reports and stealing the child Val had always known was his. Even then.

During Arthur's steady decline, Val had done what he could to ensure their future safety and Terrance's ongoing obedience. Nights already turned sleepless by tending to Arthur had been extended even further. He had carefully quizzed Terrance and then prepared a script. In the backroom of a local photographic studio, Terrance had sat beside Val and read the script in the buzzing drone of a crypt dweller.

They had express mailed a copy of the DVD to an attorney in London, who had hand-delivered the package to the address the same attorney had located for Loupe. They had included no message. No warning. Nothing.

The fact that they were all still alive was the only evidence Val needed that the message had been received, loud and clear.

Arthur had held to his considerate nature right to the end, slipping away quietly six days after their arrival. Audrey was asleep by her father's bed at the time, awakening to a glorious spring dawn and birdsong and a man who looked so very pleased to journey home.

Terrance gave no indication that he was even aware of Val's presence. Terrance had not shaved since performing for the camera. Nor did it appear that he had slept. His eyes had retreated back into plum-shaded caves. Nowadays Val addressed Terrance in a prison warden's manner, unemotional direct commands.

Val told him, "We leave for the church in ten minutes."

Slowly Terrance's head lifted. "What did you do with the money?"

"We've been through this a dozen times."

"Tell me the truth."

"I already have. I wired it back to Insignia's accounts."

"You couldn't have."

"Terrance . . ." Val had a sudden sense of staring into a mystic mirror, one that revealed how close he had come to living solely for vengeance.

"What?"

"Do this thing for Audrey," Val said, still captured by the image of his journey to the brink. "I won't make you come with me when I visit Stefanie."

Terrance's head sank back to his hands.

Val retreated from the room. "You've got ten minutes to shave and dress."

The church's interior was unpainted stone. The slate floor was washed by the tide of centuries. The windows were tall and narrow and set deep in slanted recesses. The priest's robes were from another era, as was his chant as he lit candles at the coffin's head and feet. Audrey sat between Val and Gerald. Terrance sat further along the same pew, sandwiched between Bert and Dillon. Incense wafted from two burners set to either side of the altar. The painted medieval frieze behind the priest's lectern came alive in the smoke. In Val's exhausted state, the ceremony's measured cadence carried him back through time, joining him with centuries of worshippers long gone, yet with them still. Then he felt Audrey's hand reach over and take his own. He wrapped her hand in both of his, and wondered if perhaps she recalled another time, when she had brought him to such a place and sought to give him only the best of what she had. And what she had, he needed as strongly as breath.

The priest invited those who wished to come forward and say a few words. Audrey rose and walked over to stand above the coffin. Val tried hard to hear what she said. But his heart spoke too loudly just then. Strange how such a time and place could generate such an overwhelming sense of gratitude.

As she returned to her seat, she glanced at Terrance. But he gave no sign he saw her. Dillon nudged the man. Still Terrance did not respond. Audrey sighed and shook her head, a single tight gesture.

Val rose to his feet, slipped from the pew, and stood at the coffin's head. He said, "Arthur's daughter told me recently that everything good in her came from this man. I can only say that he must have been a very fine man indeed. One I wish I had known better."

He looked at her then. And said, "One whose example I can only hope to follow."

VAL ARRANGED THE MEETING FOR SIX FORTY-FIVE IN THE MORNING, precisely the time he had been scheduled to be blown up. The sense of living irony helped steady his nerves as he stepped out of the elevator and walked through the penthouse foyer. The Insignia chairman's office was empty, but he heard sounds emanating from the adjoining boardroom.

Jack Budrow was tucked into a sumptuous breakfast and surrounded by a lovely spring sunrise as Val stepped into view. The chairman's expression was almost comical, his fork frozen in midair as he searched for an appropriate response. All he could think to say, however, was, "I can have security up here in thirty seconds."

"Don't bother."

"You're that man. What's his name."

"Val Haines."

"I . . . I don't understand. The call came from . . ."

"Terrance. He decided to remain downstairs."

The mental tumblers flipped and spun. But nothing of worth came to mind. Jack Budrow pushed his plate aside. "I can't tell you how glad I am to see—"

"Save it." Val walked to the front of the room and slid aside the shoji screen hiding the television, then slipped the DVD into the slot. "I want you to see this."

It took him a moment to work out the remote's unfamiliar controls. By the time the television and sound came to life, Terrance was already into his spiel. He heard Jack Budrow choke on the sight of Terrance seated there beside Val.

"—Arranged with my two partners, Jack Budrow and Don Winslow, to defraud Insignia Corporation's pension funds of four hundred and eighteen million dollars. We arranged to pin the theft on Marjorie Copeland and Valentine Haines."

Terrance looked like a talking corpse as he read from the prepared script. His hands trembled slightly in time to his voice's tremor. "Using the services of Suzanne Walters, we arranged to blow up the New York offices of Syntec Bank, destroying both the people we were framing, the banker through whom we had worked, and all records not held in-house and doctored by myself."

"Turn that off!" Budrow sputtered. "I didn't know anything about this!"

"But Val Haines did not die as expected in the New York blast," Terrance droned. "With full support from Winslow and Budrow— "

"That is a lie!"

"—I flew to England with Suzanne Walters. We accepted the services of a local mobster, Josef Loupe." In a cryptlike monotone, Terrance detailed their work, Loupe's scheme to steal all the money for himself, and finally, "I personally witnessed Josef Loupe murdering Don Winslow with one shot from an automatic pistol to his chest."

Jack Budrow stumbled around the boardroom table. He pawed the other chairs out of his way, leaving wreckage in his wake. He grabbed the remote from Val and hammered it with tight bursts of breath, as though throwing punches. When the television finally cut off, he threw the remote to the ground. "I knew nothing about any of that. Winslow and d'Arcy were acting completely without my knowledge— "

"Here's how it's going to play out," Val said. He slipped the DVD from the machine, placed it back inside the jewel box, and slid it down the table. It sparkled in the growing sunlight as it spun and slid and finally came to rest beside Jack Budrow's unfinished breakfast. "Today you are going to resign all your positions with Insignia."

"You can't possibly think I would even consider—"

"You will relinquish all retirement benefits. You will refuse any consulting position. You will turn over your stock options and all your shares in the company to the Insignia pension fund. It is a benevolent final gesture to repair the damages made to the hopes and futures of all your loyal employees."

Jack Budrow's face had drained of blood. One hand gripped his chest. The other used the doorjamb for support. "You're insane."

"If that announcement is not made public by tomorrow, copies of this DVD will be delivered to the chairman of the SEC. Others will go to the *Wall Street Journal*, the local papers, the television, and everywhere else I can think of."

Budrow whimpered a protest that died before it was fully formed.

"One day," Val repeated. "And one day more to make good on the promises. Otherwise I go public."

Val slipped past the chairman and started for the exit. He turned back and repeated, "One day."

When Val arrived back at the car, Terrance gave no sign that he was aware Val had departed, much less returned. His gaze carried the bleak emptiness of a man staring a life sentence in the face. Which, in a sense, he was.

From the rear seat, Audrey observed Val with cautious reserve. "How did it go?"

"Fine." He started the car. At least she had decided to accompany them to America. Nor had she bothered to claim it was to keep an eye on her brother. Val started the car and said, "Everything is just fine."

Forty minutes later, they pulled up in front of a mammoth steel-and-glass building, headquarters of the long-distance and cell-phone company that ran its international operations from this campus north of Winter Park. Outside, brilliant Florida sunlight splashed against the stream of corporate employees racing the morning clock. In the rearview mirror, Val saw that Audrey was still watching him. He hoped his sense that something was melting inside her was not just his imagination. Until he was certain, however, he was determined to wait it out. He wanted to give her whatever space she needed. This time he wanted to get it right.

Terrance touched the knot of his tie and murmured, "I suppose I should be reporting for work."

Audrey leaned forward and said to her brother, "You're doing the right thing, Brother."

Terrance opened his door, grabbed his briefcase, and walked into the sunlight.

Audrey sighed and leaned back. Shook her head. Closed her eyes.

Val turned around in his seat. "Give it time."

"He's had a lifetime. That isn't long enough?"

"You've reached hard cases before," he replied.

She opened her eyes. "Have I?"

"Absolutely."

After a long moment, Audrey opened the rear door, rose from the car, and slipped into the seat vacated by Terrance. She asked, "When do you leave?"

He started to say, when he could be sure she would be there when he got back. But that sort of statement was too far a reach into a tomorrow she had not yet offered him. "A few days. As soon as Terrance delivers the first batch of goods, and I can be certain he'll be okay on his own for a while."

She spoke the words with slow caution, as if needing to assess the texture of each individually. "Do you want me to do anything while you're gone?"

"Does this mean you're going to stay?" He swallowed, then added the words, "With me?"

"Let's just take this one step at a time, all right?"

In reply, Val put the car into gear. Wondering if perhaps the faint stirrings he felt at heart level meant there really might be a future he could call his own.

VAL HAD THE CAB WAIT FOR HIM OUTSIDE THE HOTEL EVEREST. Vince watched him push through the doors. "If it isn't Mr. Smith. How we doing today?"

"So far so good."

"Glad to hear it." Vince gave him a careful once-over. "I don't see any open wounds. You meet any trouble?"

"Some."

"There ain't no partial when it comes to trouble. Either you did or you didn't."

"Yes."

"And you came out on top?"

"Sort of."

Vince gave that flicker of a smile, like he tasted something alien. "You come walking in here without a limp, I say you did okay."

"So would I."

"Way to go." He glanced at the wall clock. "You got my money?"

Val took out the zippered pouch supplied by the bank and set it on the counter between them.

The final transfer request Val had given to the Jersey banker had been in regard to Marjorie Copeland's funds. It had been her idea for Val to have signatory rights over her account as well. Just in case, Marjorie had said, asking only that Val make sure her child was taken care of. Just in case. The majority of the funds, after this sum for Vince and their expenses on Jersey, was now safely resting in a trust established in her son's name.

Vince opened the pouch, peered inside, zipped it closed, and made it disappear. "What do you know. Looks like I was right to trust you, Mr. Smith."

"The name is Val. Valentine Haines."

"This trouble you were in. It's officially over?"

"Getting there."

"Which means you won't need to be staying uptown again. You're moving back to the other side of the park, right?"

"I'd still like to drop in from time to time, if that's all right."

Vince gave a fractional head-shake. "You don't want to hang with me. I'm street. It might rub off."

"Not a bad thing. Especially where I'm headed."

"Yeah? Where's that?"

"Looking for trouble."

Vince liked that enough to offer his hand. "Feel free. You hear what I'm saying?"

The man's touch was surprisingly light, as though Vince did not want to connect too heavily even through a handshake. "Thanks. For everything."

"You're not a bad guy, for a sucker. You need something, you say the word."

Val sat in the outer office, surrounded by New York bustle. He might as well have been invisible. Which he did not mind. A moment to rest in the eye of the storm was fine by him. He leaned his head against the wall and closed his eyes. The image was there again, the same one he had carried since traveling to New York by way of a certain Miami waterfront condo.

Val had stood by the living room window and stared out at the waterfront palaces and the floating wealth as Stefanie had cried her way through Terrance's on-camera performance. Val had remained mute and motionless while she regained control. There were a number of things that would have to be said. A multitude of legal matters to be rewritten, a myriad of issues to be resolved anew. But not this time. Val did not want to mar this moment with anything other than the reason for his coming. Which was not revenge. Nor to tell her that he had been right all along. None of that mattered. He could see just enough of his reflection in the sliding-glass door to know that this was not merely fatigue or momentary ruminations. He stared into eyes that seemed full of the day's sunlight, a translucent image so powerful he could almost blank out the sound of his ex-wife sobbing behind him.

When he was certain the tears were over and her composure restored, Val turned around.

He said, "I'd like to see my daughter now."

The aide ushered Val into the office. The SEC's chief investigator eyed him with open curiosity. "You're Haines?"

"Yes."

"Valentine Richard Haines?"

"That's right."

"You got some ID?"

Val handed over his recently recovered passport. The man inspected it carefully. "You want coffee?"

"No. I'm good."

He tossed Val's passport onto his desk. "Now this is real interesting. First off, funds you supposedly stole suddenly wind up in Insignia's petty cash account. Then, if that's not good enough, a guy who's supposed to be fully dead calls me up and says he wants to stop by, talk to me about a job."

"That's right."

"With me."

"Right again."

The chief slung one arm over the back of his swivel chair. "So talk."

Val opened his leather portfolio and extracted a set of documents. "You're concerned about possible financial improprieties at a major Florida-based telephone company. But you don't have the required evidence to go in with a full investigation."

The chief unslung his arm. "Who says?"

Val offered the papers. "These might help you move forward."

The chief studied them intently. From behind the man's desk, a silver-plated clock ticked precise New York minutes. That and the flipping of pages, a ringing phone, and the sounds of Wall Street traffic rising from far below were the only sounds.

"Where did you get these?"

"I've got eleven in the business," Val replied. "I know all the tricks. I can help you."

The chief picked up his phone and punched in a number. He said, "Get in here. I don't care. Come here *now*."

A harried young woman entered without knocking. "You of course realize we are due in the mayor's office in three hours, and I am two weeks from ready."

The chief handed over Val's documents. "Tell me if we're looking at the real deal here."

The woman went through them with rising delight. "Where did you get this?"

"Is it real?"

"Looks that way to me."

"Is it enough?"

"It's a ton more than what we've got now, I can tell you that much. The rest will have to wait."

"Call the mayor's office and cancel. Have the team in here and ready. One hour."

"You know the mayor. He won't like this."

"Move."

The chief waited until they were alone again to say, "You've got an inside source."

"One that will move from project to project," Val agrees. "One that answers only to me."

Val and the chief talked through the entire hour. Only when the woman returned to get the chief for the meeting did the man say, "When can you start?"

"It looks like I already have."

The chief nodded acceptance. He shook Val's hand, ushered him from the office, and finally said, "One thing I don't get. What's the motive here?"

Val did not turn back to reply, "Penance."

ABOUT THE AUTHORS

TED DEKKER is known for novels that combine adrenaline-laced stories packed with unexpected plot twists, unforgettable characters, and incredible confrontations between good and evil. The son of missionaries whose incredible story of life among headhunters in Indonesia has been told in several books, Ted Dekker learned at a very early age the difference between authentic Christianity and so-called religion. Surrounded by the vivid colors of the jungle and a myriad of cultures, each steeped in their own interpretation of life and religion, Dekker received a first-class education on human nature and behavior. This, he believes, is the foundation of his writing. He lives in the mountains of Colorado with his wife LeeAnn and their four children. Visit his website at teddekker.com.

TIM DOWNS has received high acclaim for his recent thrillers *Head Game* and *Plague Maker*, and his quirky "bug-man" novels *Chop Shop* and *Shoo Fly Pie.* After graduating college, he created a comic strip, *Downstown*, which was syndicated by Universal Press Syndicate until 1986. His cartooning has appeared in more than a hundred major newspapers worldwide. Tim lives in North Carolina with his wife and three children. Visit his website at timdowns.net.

DAVIS BUNN is an internationally-acclaimed author who has sold more than four million books in fifteen languages. He has been honored with three Christy Awards for excellence in historical and suspense fiction and is a sought-after lecturer in the art of writing. Bunn was named Novelist in Residence at Regent's Park College, Oxford University. Some of his best-known works include *The Book of Hours, The Quilt,* and *Heartland.* He and his wife make their home in England. Visit his website at davisbunn.com.